ADMIRAL HORNBLOWER

C. S. FORESTER

Admiral Hornblower

*

Comprising

FLYING COLOURS
THE COMMODORE
LORD HORNBLOWER
HORNBLOWER IN THE WEST INDIES

LONDON
MICHAEL JOSEPH

This edition
first published in Great Britain by
MICHAEL JOSEPH LTD.
52 *Bedford Square*
*London, W.C.*1
NOVEMBER 1966
SECOND IMPRESSION JULY 1972

7181 0019 0

Printed in Great Britain by
Biddles Ltd., Guildford
Bound by James Burn, Esher

Flying Colours

I

Captain Hornblower was walking up and down along the sector of the ramparts of Rosas, delimited by two sentries with loaded muskets, which the commandant had granted him for exercise. Overhead shone the bright autumn sun of the Mediterranean, hanging in a blue Mediterranean sky and shining on the Mediterranean blue of Rosas Bay – the blue water fringed with white where the little waves broke against the shore of golden sand and grey-green cliff. Black against the sun above his head there flapped the tricolour flag of France, proclaiming to the world that Rosas was in the hands of the French, that Captain Hornblower was a prisoner. Not half a mile from where he walked lay the dismasted wreck of his ship the *Sutherland*, beached to prevent her from sinking, and in line beyond her there swung at their anchors the four ships of the line which had fought her. Hornblower, narrowing his eyes and with a twinge of regret for his lost telescope, could see even at that distance that they were not ready for sea again, nor were likely to be. Even the two-decker which had emerged from the fight with all her masts intact still had her pumps at work every two hours to keep her afloat, and the other three had not yet succeeded in setting up masts to replace the ones lost in the battle. The French were a lubberly lot of no-seamen, as might be expected after seventeen years of defeat at sea and six of continuous blockade.

They had been all honey to him, in their French fashion praising him for his 'glorious defence' after his 'bold initiative' in dashing in with his ship to interpose between their four and their refuge at Rosas. They had expressed the liveliest pleasure at discovering that he had miraculously emerged unhurt from a battle which had left two-thirds of his men killed and wounded. But they had plundered in the fashion which had made the armed forces of the Empire hated throughout Europe. They had searched the pockets even of the wounded who had cumbered the *Sutherland*'s decks in moaning heaps. Their admiral, on his first encounter with Hornblower, had expressed surprise that the latter was not wearing the sword which the admiral had sent back to him in recognition of his gallantry, and on Hornblower's denial that he had ever seen the weapon again after giving it up had instituted a search which discovered the sword cast aside somewhere in his flagship, the glorious inscription still engraved upon the blade, but with the gold stripped from hilt and guard and scabbard. And the admiral had merely laughed at that and had not dreamed of instituting a search for the thief; the Patriotic Fund's gift still hung at Hornblower's side, the tang of the blade protruding nakedly from the scabbard without the gold and ivory and seed pearls which had adorned it.

The French soldiers and sailors which had swarmed over the captured ship had torn away even the brasswork in the same fashion; they had gorged upon the unappetising provisions in a way which proved how miserable were the rations provided for the men who fought for the Empire – but it was only a few who had swilled themselves into insensibility from the rum casks. In face of similar temptation (to which no British officer would have exposed his men) British seamen would have drunk until nine-tenths of them were incapable or fighting mad. The French officers had made the usual appeal to their prisoners to join the French ranks, making the usual tempting offers of good treatment and regular pay to anyone who cared to enlist either in the army or the navy. Hornblower was proud that no single man had succumbed to the temptation.

As a consequence the few sound men now languished in strict confinement in one of the empty storerooms of the fortress, deprived of the tobacco and rum and fresh air which for most of them represented the difference between heaven and hell. The wounded – the hundred and forty-five wounded – were rotting in a dank casemate where gangrene and fever would soon make an end of them. To the logical French mind the poverty-stricken Army of Catalonia, which could do little even for its own wounded, would be mad to expend any of its resources on attention to wounded who would be intolerable nuisances should they survive.

A little moan escaped Hornblower's lips as he paced the ramparts. He had a room of his own, a servant to wait on him, fresh air and sunshine, while the poor devils he had commanded were suffering all the miseries of confinement – even the three or four other unwounded officers were lodged in the town gaol. True, he suspected that he was being reserved for another fate. During those glorious days when, in command of the *Sutherland*, he had won for himself, unknowing, the nickname of 'the Terror of the Mediterranean', he had managed to storm the battery at Llanza by bringing his ship up close to it flying the tricolour flag. That had been a legitimate *ruse de guerre* for which historical precedents without number could be quoted, but the French government had apparently deemed it a violation of the laws of war. The next convoy to France or Barcelona would bear him with it as a prisoner to be tried by a military commission. Bonaparte was quite capable of shooting him, both from personal rancour and as a proof of the most convincing sort to

Europe of British duplicity and wickedness, and during the last day or two Hornblower thought he had read as much in the eyes of his gaolers.

Just enough time had elapsed for the news of the *Sutherland*'s capture to have reached Paris and for Bonaparte's subsequent orders to have been transmitted to Rosas. The *Moniteur Universal* would have blazed out in a paean of triumph, declaring to the Continent that this loss of a ship of the line was clear proof that England was tottering to her fall like ancient Carthage; in a month or two's time presumably there would be another announcement to the effect that a traitorous servant of perfidious Albion had met his just deserts against a wall in Vincennes or Montjuich.

Hornblower cleared his throat nervously as he walked; he expected to feel afraid and was surprised that he did not. The thought of an abrupt and inevitable end of that sort did not alarm him as much as did his shapeless imaginings when he was going into action on his quarterdeck. In fact he could almost view it with relief, as putting an end to his worries about his wife Maria whom he had left pregnant, and to his jealous torments of longing for Lady Barbara who had married his admiral; in the eyes of England he would be regarded as a martyr whose widow deserved a pension. It would be an honourable end, then, which a man ought to welcome – especially a man like Hornblower whose persistent and unfounded disbelief in his own capacity left him continually frightened of professional disgrace and ruin.

And it would be an end of captivity, too. Hornblower had been a prisoner once before, for two heartbreaking years in Ferrol, but with the passing of time he had forgotten the misery of it until his new experience. In those days, too, he had never known the freedom of his own quarterdeck, and had never tasted the unbounded liberty – the widest freedom on earth – of being a captain of a ship. It was torture now to be a prisoner, even with the liberty to look upon the sky and the sea. A caged lion must fret behind his bars in the same way as Hornblower fretted against his confinement. He felt suddenly sick and ill through restraint. He clenched his fists and only by an effort prevented himself from raising them above his head in a gesture of despair.

Then he took hold of himself again, with an inward sneer at his childish weakness. To distract himself he looked out again to the blue sea which he loved, the row of black cormorants silhouetted against the grey cliff, the gulls wheeling against the blue sky. Five miles out he could see the topsails of His Majesty's frigate *Cassandra* keeping sleepless watch over the four French ships huddled for shelter under the guns of Rosas, and beyond them he could see the royals of the *Pluto* and the *Caligula* – Admiral Leighton, the unworthy husband of his beloved Lady Barbara, was flying his flag in the *Pluto*, but he refused to let that thought worry him – where they awaited an accession of strength from

the Mediterranean fleet before coming in to destroy the ships which
had captured him. He could rely upon the British to avenge his defeat.
Martin, the vice-admiral with the Toulon blockading squadron, would
see to it that Leighton did not make a hash of this attack, powerful as
might be the guns of Rosas.

He looked along the ramparts at the massive twenty-four-pounders
mounted there. The bastions at the angles carried forty-two-pounders –
colossal pieces. He leaned over the parapet and looked down; it was a
sheer drop from there of twenty-five feet to the bottom of the ditch,
and along the bottom of the ditch itself ran a line of stout palisades,
which no besieging army could damage until he had sapped right up to
the lip of the ditch. No hurried, extemporised attack could carry the
citadel of Rosas. A score of sentries paced the ramparts, even as did he;
in the opposite face he could see the massive gates with the portcullis
down, where a hundred men of the grand guard were always ready to
beat back any surprise attack which might elude the vigilance of the
twenty sentinels.

Down there, in the body of the place, a company of infantry was being
put through its drill – the shrill words of command were clearly audible
to him up here. It was Italian which was being spoken; Bonaparte had
attempted his conquest of Catalonia mainly with the foreign auxiliaries
of his empire, Italians, Neapolitans, Germans, Swiss, Poles. The uniforms of the infantry down there were as ragged as the lines they were
forming; the men were in tatters, and even the tatters were not homo-
geneous – the men wore white or blue or grey or brown according to
the resources of the depots which had originally sent them out. They
were half starved, poor devils, as well. Of the five or six thousand men
based on Rosas the ones he could see were all that could be spared for
military duty; the others were all out scouring the countryside for food
– Bonaparte never dreamed of trying to feed the men whom he compelled to serve him, just as he only paid them, as an afterthought, a year or
two in arrears. It was amazing that his ramshackle Empire had endured
so long – that was the clearest proof of the incompetence of the various
kingdoms who had pitted their strength against it. Over on the other
side of the Peninsula the French Empire was at this very minute putting
out all its strength against a man of real ability and an army which knew
what discipline was. On the issue of that struggle depended the fate of
Europe. Hornblower was convinced that the redcoats with Wellington
to lead them would be successful; he would have been just as certain
even if Wellington were not his beloved Lady Barbara's brother.

Then he shrugged his shoulders. Not even Wellington would destroy
the French Empire quickly enough to save him from trial and execution. Moreover, the time allowed him for his day's exercise was over
now. The next items in his monotonous programme would be to visit

the sick in the casemate, and then the prisoners in the storeroom – by
the courtesy of the commandant he was allowed ten minutes for each,
before being shut up again in his room, drearily to attempt to re-read
the half-dozen books which were all that the garrison of Rosas possessed,
or to pace up and down, three steps each way, or to lie huddled on his
bed wondering about Maria and the child that was to be born in the
New Year, and torturing himself with thoughts of Lady Barbara.

II

Hornblower awoke that night with a start, wondering what it was that
had awakened him. A moment later he knew, when the sound was repeated. It was the dull thud of a gun fired on the ramparts above his
head. He leaped from his bed with his heart pounding, and before his
feet touched the floor the whole fortress was in a turmoil. Overhead
there were guns firing. Somewhere else, outside the body of the fortress,
there were hundreds of guns firing; through the barred windows of his
room came a faint flickering as the flashes were reflected down from the
sky. Immediately outside his door drums were beating and bugles were
pealing as the garrison was called to arms – the courtyard was full of the
sounds of nailed boots clashing on the cobbles.

That tremendous pulsation of artillery which he could hear could
mean only one thing. The fleet must have come gliding into the bay in
the darkness, and now he could hear the rolling of its broadsides as it
battered the anchored ships. There was a great naval battle in progress
within half a mile of him, and he could see nothing of it. It was utterly
maddening. He tried to light his candle, but his trembling fingers could
do nothing with his flint and steel. He dashed the tinderbox to the floor,
and, fumbling in the darkness, he dragged on his coat and trousers and
shoes and then beat upon the door madly with his fists. The sentry
outside was Italian, he knew, and he spoke no Italian – only fluent
Spanish and bad French.

'Officier! Officier!' he shouted, and then he heard the sentry call for
the sergeant of the guard, and the measured step of the sergeant as he
came up. The clatter of the garrison's falling in under arms had already
died away.

'What do you want?' asked the sergeant's voice – at least so Hornblower fancied, for he could not understand what was said.

'Officier! Officier!' roared Hornblower, beating still on the heavy door.
The artillery was still rolling terrifically outside. Hornblower went on
pounding on the door even until he heard the key in the lock. The door

swung open and he blinked at the light of a torch which shone into his
eyes. A young subaltern in a neat white uniform stood there between
the sergeant and the sentry.

'Qu'est-ce-que monsieur désire?' he asked – he at least understood
French, even if he spoke it badly. Hornblower fumbled to express himself in an unfamiliar tongue.

'I want to see!' he stammered. 'I want to see the battle! Let me go on
to the walls.'

The young officer shook his head reluctantly; like the other officers
of the garrison, he felt a kindly feeling towards the English captain who
– so rumour said – was so shortly to be conducted to Paris and shot.

'It is forbidden,' he said.

'I will not escape,' said Hornblower; desperate excitement was
loosening his tongue now. 'Word of honour – I swear it! Come with me,
but let me see! I want to see!'

The officer hesitated.

'I cannot leave my post here,' he said.

'Then let me go alone. I swear I will stay on the walls. I will not try
to escape.'

'Word of honour?' asked the subaltern.

'Word of honour. Thank you, sir.'

The subaltern stood aside, and Hornblower dashed out of his room,
down the short corridor to the courtyard, and up the ramp which led
to the seaward bastion. As he reached it, the forty-two-pounder mounted
there went off with a deafening roar, and the long tongue of orange flame
nearly blinded him. In the darkness the bitter powder smoke engulfed
him. Nobody in the groups bending over the guns noticed him, and he
ran down the steep staircase to the curtain wall, where, away from the
guns, he could see without being blinded.

Rosas Bay was all a-sparkle with gun flashes. Then, five times in
regular succession, came the brilliant red glow of a broadside, and each
glow lit up a stately ship gliding in rigid line ahead past the anchored
French ships. The *Pluto* was there; Hornblower saw her three decks,
her ensign at the peak, her admiral's flag at the mizzen, her topsails set
and her other canvas furled. Leighton would be there, walking his
quarterdeck – thinking of Barbara, perhaps. And that next astern was
the *Caligula*. Bolton would be stumping about her deck revelling in the
crash of her broadsides. She was firing rapidly and well – Bolton was a
good captain, although a badly educated man. The words 'Oderint dum
metuant' – the Caesar Caligula's maxim – picked out in letters of gold
across the *Caligula*'s stern had meant nothing to Bolton until Hornblower translated and explained them to him. At this very moment, perhaps, those letters were being defaced and battered by the French shot.

But the French squadron was firing back badly and irregularly. There was no sudden glow of broadsides where they lay anchored, but only an irregular and intermittent sparkle as the guns were loosed off anyhow. In a night action like this, and after a sudden surprise, Hornblower would not have trusted even an English seaman with independent fire. He doubted if as many as one-tenth of the French guns were being properly served and pointed. As for the heavy guns pealing away beside him from the fortress, he was quite certain they were doing no good to the French cause and possibly some harm. Firing at half a mile in the darkness, even from a steady platform and with large-calibre guns, they were as likely to hit friend as foe. It had well repaid Admiral Martin to send in Leighton and his ships in the moonless hours of the night, risking all the navigational perils of the bay.

Hornblower choked with emotion and excitement as his imagination called up the details of what would be going on in the English ships – the leadsman chanting the soundings with disciplined steadiness, the heave of the ship to the deafening crash of the broadside, the battle lanterns glowing dimly in the smoke of the lower decks, the squeal and rattle of the gun trucks as the guns were run up again, the steady orders of the officers in charge of sections of guns, the quiet voice of the captain addressing the helmsmen. He leaned far over the parapet in the darkness, peering down into the bay.

A whiff of wood smoke came to his nostrils, sharply distinct from the acrid powder smoke which was drifting by from the guns. They had lit the furnaces for heating shot, but the commandant would be a fool if he allowed his guns to fire red-hot shot in these conditions. French ships were as inflammable as English ones, and just as likely to be hit in a close battle like this. Then his grip tightened on the stonework of the parapet, and he stared and stared again with aching eyes towards what had attracted his notice. It was the tiniest, most subdued little red glow in the distance. The English had brought in fire ships in the wake of their fighting squadron. A squadron at anchor like this was the best possible target for a fire ship, and Martin had planned his attack well in sending in his ships of the line first to clear away guard boats and beat down the French fire and occupy the attention of the crews. The red glow suddenly increased, grew brighter and brighter still, revealing the hull and masts and rigging of a small brig; still brighter it grew as the few daring spirits who remained on board flung open hatches and gunports to increase the draught. The tongues of flame which soared up were visible even to Hornblower on the ramparts, and they revealed to him, too, the form of the *Turenne* alongside her – the one French ship which had emerged from the previous battle with all her masts. Whoever the young officer in command of the fire ship might be, he was a man with a cool head and determined will, thus to select the most profitable target of all.

Hornblower saw points of fire begin to ascend the rigging of the *Turenne* until she was outlined in red like some setpiece in a firework display. Sudden jets of flame showed where powder charges on her deck were taking fire; and then the whole set-piece suddenly swung round and began to drift before the gentle wind as the burnt cables gave way. A mast fell in an upward torrent of sparks, strangely reflected in the black water all round. As once the sparkle of gunfire in the other French ships began to die away as the crews were called from their guns to deal with the drifting menace, and a slow movement of the shadowy forms lit by the flames revealed that their cables had been cut by officers terrified of death by fire.

Then suddenly Hornblower's attention was distracted to a point closer in to shore, where the abandoned wreck of the *Sutherland* lay beached. There, too, a red glow could be seen, growing and spreading momentarily. Some daring party from the British squadron had boarded her and set her on fire, too, determined not to leave even so poor a trophy in the hands of the French. Farther out in the bay three red dots of light were soaring upwards slowly, and Hornblower gulped in sudden nervousness lest an English ship should have caught fire as well, but he realised next moment that it was only a signal – three vertical red lanterns – which was apparently the prearranged recall, for with their appearance the firing abruptly ceased. The blazing wrecks lit up now the whole of this corner of the bay with a lurid red in whose light could be distinctly seen the other French ships, drifting without masts or anchors towards the shore. Next came a blinding flash and a stunning explosion as the magazine of the *Turenne* took fire. For several seconds after the twenty tons of gunpowder had exploded Hornblower's eyes could not see nor his mind think; the blast of it had shaken him, like a child in the hands of an angry nurse, even where he stood.

He became aware that daylight was creeping into the bay, revealing the ramparts of Rosas in hard outlines, and dulling the flames from the wreck of the *Sutherland*. Far out in the bay, already beyond gunshot of the fortress, the five British ships of the line were standing out to sea in their rigid line-ahead. There was something strange about the appearance of the *Pluto*; it was only at his second glance that Hornblower realised that she had lost her main topmast – clear proof that one French shot at least had done damage. The other ships revealed no sign of having received any injury during one of the best-managed affairs in the long history of the British Navy. Hornblower tore his gaze from his vanishing friends to study the field of battle. Of the *Turenne* and the fire ship there was no sign at all; of the *Sutherland* there only remained a few blackened timbers emerging from the water, with a wisp of smoke suspended above them. Two ships of the line were on the rocks to the westward of the fortress, and French seamanship would never make them seaworthy again. Only the three-decker was left, battered and mastless, swinging to the anchor which had checked her on the very edge of the surf. The next easterly gale would see her, too, flung ashore and useless. The British Mediterranean fleet would in the future have to dissipate none of its energies in a blockade of Rosas.

Here came General Vidal, the governor of the fortress, making his rounds with his staff at his heels, and just in time to save Hornblower from falling into a passion of despair at watching the English squadron disappear over the horizon.

'What are you doing here?' demanded the General, checking at the sight of him. Under the sternness of his expression could be read the kindly pity which Hornblower had noticed in the faces of all his enemies when they began to suspect that a firing party awaited him.

'The officer of the grand guard allowed me to come up here,' explained Hornblower in his halting French. 'I gave him my parole of honour not to try to escape. I will withdraw it again now, if you please.'

'He had no business to accept it, in any case,' snapped the General, but with that fateful kindliness still apparent. 'You wanted to see the battle, I suppose?'

'Yes, General.'

'A fine piece of work your companions have done.' The General shook his head sadly. 'It will not make the government in Paris feel any better disposed towards you, I fear, Captain.'

Hornblower shrugged his shoulders; he had already caught the infection of that gesture during his few days' sojourn among Frenchmen. He noted, with a lack of personal interest which seemed odd to him even then, that this was the first time that the Governor had hinted openly at danger threatening him from Paris.

'I have done nothing to make me afraid,' he said.

'No, no, of course not,' said the Governor hastily and out of countenance, like a parent denying to a child that a prospective dose of medicine would be unpleasant.

He looked round for some way of changing the subject, and fortunate chance brought one. From far below in the bowels of the fortress came a muffled sound of cheering – English cheers, not Italian screeches.

'That must be those men of yours, Captain,' said the General, smiling again. 'I fancy the new prisoner must have told them by now the story of last night's affair.'

'The new prisoner?' demanded Hornblower.

'Yes, indeed. A man who fell overboard from the admiral's ship – the *Pluto*, is it not? – and had to swim ashore. Ah, I suspected you would be interested, Captain. Yes, off you go and talk to him. Here, Dupont, take charge of the captain and escort him to the prison.'

Hornblower could hardly spare the time in which to thank his captor, so eager was he to interview the new arrival and hear what he had to say. Two weeks as a prisoner had already had their effect in giving him a thirst for news. He ran down the ramp, Dupont puffing beside him, across the cobbled court, in through the door which a sentry opened for him at a gesture from his escort, down the dark stairway to the iron-studded door where stood two sentries on duty. With a great clattering of keys the doors were opened for him and he walked into the room.

It was a wide, low room – a disused storeroom, in fact – lit and ventilated only by a few heavily barred apertures opening into the fortress ditch. It stank of closely confined humanity and it was at present filled with a babel of sound as what was left of the crew of the *Sutherland* plied questions at someone hidden in the middle of the crowd. At Hornblower's entrance the crowd fell apart and the new prisoner came forward; he was naked save for his duck trousers and a long pigtail hung down his back.

'Who are you?' demanded Hornblower.

'Phillips, sir. Maintopman in the *Pluto*.'

His honest blue eyes met Hornblower's gaze without a sign of flinching. Hornblower could guess that he was neither a deserter nor a spy – he had borne both possibilities in mind.

'How did you come here?'

'We was settin' sail, sir, to beat out o' the bay. We'd just seen the old *Sutherland* take fire, an' Cap'n Elliott he says to us, he says, sir, "Now's the time, my lads. Top'sls and to'gar'ns." So up we went aloft, sir, an' I'd just taken the earring o' the main to'garn'n when down came the mast, sir, an' I was pitched off into the water. So was a lot o' my mates, sir, but just then the Frenchy which was burnin' blew up, an' I think the wreckage killed a lot of 'em, sir, 'cos I found I was alone, an' *Pluto* was gone away, an' so I swum for the shore, an' there was a lot of Frenchies what I think had swum from the burning Frenchy an' they took me to some sojers an' the sojers brought me here, sir. There was a orficer what arst me questions – it'd 'a made you laugh, sir, to hear him trying to speak English – but I wasn't sayin' nothin', sir. An' when they see that they puts me in here along with the others, sir. I was just telling 'em about the fight, sir. There was the old *Pluto*, an' *Caligula*, sir, an'—'

'Yes, I saw it,' said Hornblower, shortly. 'I saw that *Pluto* had lost her main topmast. Was she knocked about much?'

'Lor' bless you, sir, no, sir. We hadn't had half a dozen shot come aboard, an' they didn't do no damage, barrin' the one that wounded the Admiral.'

'The Admiral!' Hornblower reeled a little as he stood, as though he had been struck. 'Admiral Leighton, d'you mean?'

'Admiral Leighton, sir.'

'Was – was he badly hurt?'

'I dunno, sir. I didn't see it meself, o' course, sir, seein' as how I was on the main deck at the time. Sailmaker's mate, he told me, sir, that the Admiral had been hit by a splinter. Cooper's mate told *him*, sir, what helped to carry him below.'

Hornblower could say no more for the present. He could only stare at the kindly stupid face of the sailor before him. Yet even in that moment he could take note of the fact that the sailor was not in the least moved by the wounding of his Admiral. Nelson's death had put the whole fleet into mourning, and he knew of half a dozen other flag officers whose death or whose wounding would have brought tears into the eyes of the men serving under him. If it had been one of those, the man would have told of the accident to him before mentioning his own mis-adventures. Hornblower had known before that Leighton was not beloved by his officers, and here was a clear proof that he was not beloved by his men either. But perhaps Barbara had loved him. She had at least married him. Hornblower forced himself to speak, to bear him-self naturally.

'That will do,' he said, curtly, and then looked round to catch his coxswain's eye. 'Anything to report, Brown?'

'No, sir. All well, sir.'

Hornblower rapped on the door behind him to be let out of prison, to be conducted by his guard back to his room again, where he could walk up and down, three steps each way, his brain seething like a pot on a fire. He only knew enough to unsettle him, to make him anxious. Leighton had been wounded, but that did not mean that he would die. A splinter wound – that might mean much or little. Yet he had been carried below. No admiral would have allowed that, if he had been able to resist – not in the heat of a fight, at any rate. His face might be lacerated or his belly torn open – Hornblower, shuddering, shook his mind free from the memories of all the horrible wounds he had seen received on shipboard during twenty years' service. But, coldblood-edly, it was an even chance that Leighton would die – Hornblower had signed too many casualty lists to be unaware of the chances of a wounded man's recovery.

If Leighton were to die, Barbara would be free again. But what had that to do with him, a married man – a married man whose wife was pregnant? She would be no nearer to him, not while Maria lived. And yet it assuaged his jealousy to think of her as a widow. But then perhaps she would marry again, and he would have to go once more through all the torment he had endured when he had first heard of her marriage to Leighton. In that case he would rather Leighton lived – a cripple, perhaps mutilated or impotent; the implications of that train of thought drove him into a paroxysm of too-rapid thinking from which he only emerged after a desperate struggle for sanity.

In the cold reaction which followed he sneered at himself for a fool. He was the prisoner of a man whose empire extended from the Baltic to Gibraltar. He told himself he would be an old man, that his child and Maria's would be grown up before he regained his liberty. And then with a sudden shock he remembered that he might soon be dead – shot for violation of the laws of war. Strange how he could forget that possibility. Sneering, he told himself that he had a coward's mind which could leave the imminence of death out of its calculations because the possibility was too monstrous to bear contemplation.

There was something else he had not reckoned upon lately, too. If Bonaparte did not have him shot, if he regained his freedom, even then he still had to run the gauntlet of a court martial for the loss of the *Sutherland*. A court martial might decree for him death or disgrace or ruin; the British public would not hear lightly of a British ship of the line surrendering, however great the odds against her. He would have liked to ask Phillips, the seaman from the *Pluto*, about what had been said in the fleet regarding the *Sutherland*'s action, whether the general verdict had been one of approval or not. But of course it would be impossible to ask; no captain could ask a seaman what the fleet thought of him, even if there was a chance of hearing the truth – which, too, was doubtful. He was compassed about with uncertainties – the uncertainties of his imprisonment, of the possibility of his trial by the French, of his future court martial, of Leighton's wound. There was even an uncertainty regarding Maria; she was pregnant – would the child be a girl or a boy, would he ever see it, would anyone raise a finger to help her, would she be able to educate the child properly without his supervision?

Once more the misery of imprisonment was borne in upon him. He grew sick with longing for his liberty, for his freedom, for Barbara and for Maria.

III

Hornblower was walking next day upon the ramparts again; the sentries with their loaded muskets stood one each end of the sector allotted to him, and the subaltern allotted to guard him sat discreetly against the parapet so as not to break in upon the thoughts which preoccupied him. But he was too tired to think much now – all day and nearly all night yesterday he had paced his room, three paces up and three paces back, with his mind in a turmoil. Exhaustion was saving him now, and he could think no more.

He welcomed as a distraction a bustle at the main gate, the turning out of the guard, the opening of the gate, and the jingling entrance of a coach drawn by six fine horses. He stood and watched the proceedings with all the interest of a captive. There was an escort of fifty mounted men in the cocked hats and blue-and-red uniforms of Bonaparte's gendarmerie, coachmen and servants on the box, an officer dismounting hurriedly to open the door. Clearly the new arrival must be a man of importance. Hornblower experienced a faint feeling of disappointment when there climbed out of the coach not a Marshal with plumes and feathers, but just another officer of gendarmerie. A youngish man with a bullet black head, which he revealed as he held his cocked hat in his hand while stooping to descend; the star of the Legion of Honour on his breast; high black boots with spurs. Hornblower wondered idly why a colonel of gendarmerie who was obviously not crippled should arrive in a coach instead of on horseback. He watched him go clinking across the courtyard to the Governor's headquarters.

Hornblower's walk was nearly finished when one of the young French aides-de-camp of the Governor approached him on the ramparts and saluted.

'His Excellency sends you his compliments, sir, and he would be glad if you could spare him a few minutes of your time as soon as it is convenient to you.'

Addressed to a prisoner, as Hornblower told himself bitterly, these words might as well have been 'Come at once.'

'I will come now, with the greatest of pleasure,' said Hornblower, maintaining the solemn farce.

Down in the Governor's office the colonel of gendarmerie was standing conversing alone with His Excellency; the Governor's expression was sad.

'I have the honour of presenting to you, Captain,' he said, turning, 'Colonel Jean-Baptiste Caillard, Grand Eagle of the Legion of Honour, and one of His Imperial Majesty's personal aides-de-camp. Colonel, this is Captain Horatio Hornblower, of His Britannic Majesty's Navy.'

The Governor was clearly worried and upset. His hands were fluttering and he stammered a little as he spoke, and he made a pitiful muddle of his attempt on the aspirates of Hornblower's name. Hornblower bowed, but as the colonel remained unbending he stiffened to attention. He could recognise that type of man at once – the servant of a tyrant, and in close personal association with him, modelling his conduct not on the tyrant's, but on what he fancied should be the correct behaviour of a tyrant, far out-Heroding Herod in arbitrariness and cruelty. It might be merely a pose – the man might be a kind husband and the loving father of a family – but it was a pose which might have unpleasant results for anyone in his power. His victims would suffer in his attempt to prove, to himself as well as to others, that he could be more stern, more unrelenting – and therefore naturally more able – than the man who employed him.

Caillard ran a cold eye over Hornblower's appearance.

'What is he doing with that sword at his side?' he asked of the Governor.

'The admiral returned it to him on the day of the battle,' explained the Governor hastily. 'He said—'

'It doesn't matter what he said,' interrupted Caillard. 'No criminal as guilty as he can be allowed a weapon. And a sword is the emblem of a gentleman of honour, which he most decidedly is not. Take off that sword, sir.'

Hornblower stood appalled, hardly believing he had understood. Caillard's face wore a fixed mirthless smile which showed white teeth, below the black moustache which lay like a gash across his olive face.

'Take off that sword,' repeated Caillard, and then, as Hornblower made no movement, 'If Your Excellency will permit me to call in one of my gendarmes, I will have the sword removed.'

At the threat Hornblower unbuckled his belt and allowed the weapon to fall to the ground; the clatter rang loud in the silence. The sword of honour which the Patriotic Fund had awarded him ten years ago for his heading of the boarding party which took the *Castilla* lay on the floor, jerked half out of its scabbard. The hiltless tang and the battered places on the sheath where the gold had been torn off bore mute witness to the lust for gold of the Empire's servants.

'Good!' said Caillard. 'Now will Your Excellency have the goodness to warn this man of his approaching departure?'

'Colonel Caillard,' said the Governor 'has come to take you and your first lieutenant, Mistaire – Mistaire Bush, to Paris.'

'Bush?' blazed out Hornblower, moved as not even the loss of his sword could move him. 'Bush? That is impossible. Lieutenant Bush is seriously wounded. It might easily be fatal to take him on a long journey at present.'

'The journey will be fatal to him in any case,' said Caillard, still with the mirthless smile and the gleam of white teeth.

The Governor wrung his hands.

'You cannot say that, Colonel. These gentlemen have still to be tried. The Military Commission has yet to give its verdict.'

'These gentlemen, as you call them, Your Excellency, stand condemned out of their own mouths.'

Hornblower remembered that he had made no attempt to deny, while the admiral was questioning him and preparing his report, that he had been in command of the *Sutherland* the day she wore French colours and her landing party stormed the battery at Llanza. He had known the ruse to be legitimate enough, but he had not reckoned on a French emperor determined upon convincing European opinion of the perfidy of England and cunning enough to know that a couple of resounding executions might well be considered evidence of guilt.

'The colonel,' said the Governor to Hornblower 'has brought his coach. You may rely upon it that Mistaire Bush will have every possible comfort. Please tell me which of your men you would like to accompany you as your servant. And if there is anything which I can provide which will make the journey more comfortable, I will do so with the greatest pleasure.'

Hornblower debated internally the question of the servant. Polwheal, who had served him for years, was among the wounded in the casemate. Nor, he fancied, would he have selected him in any case; Polwheal was not the man for an emergency – and it was just possible that there might be an emergency. Latude had escaped from the Bastille. Was not there a faint chance that he might escape from Vincennes? Hornblower thought of Brown's bulging muscles and cheerful devotion.

'I would like to take my coxswain, Brown, if you please,' he said.

'Certainly. I will send for him and have your present servant pack your things with him. And with regard to your needs for the journey?'

'I need nothing,' said Hornblower. At the same time as he spoke he cursed himself for his pride. If he were ever to save himself and Bush from the firing party in the ditch at Vincennes he would need gold.

'Oh, I cannot allow you to say that,' protested the Governor. 'There may be some few comforts you would like to buy when you are in France. Besides, you cannot deprive me of the pleasure of being of assistance to a brave man. Please do me the favour of accepting my purse. I beg you to, sir.'

Hornblower fought down his pride and took the proffered wallet. It was of surprising weight and gave out a musical chink as he took it.

'I must thank you for your kindness,' he said. 'And for all your courtesy while I have been your prisoner.'

'It has been a pleasure to me, as I said,' replied the Governor. 'I want to wish you the – the very best of luck on your arrival in Paris.'

'Enough of this,' said Caillard. 'My orders from His Majesty call for the utmost expedition. Is the wounded man in the courtyard?'

The Governor led the way out, and the gendarmes closed up round Hornblower as they walked towards the coach. Bush was lying there on a stretcher, strangely pale and strangely wasted out there in the bright light. He was feebly trying to shield his eyes from the sun; Hornblower ran and knelt beside him.

'They're going to take us to Paris, Bush,' he said.

'What, you and me, sir?'

'Yes.'

'It's a place I've often wanted to see.'

The Italian surgeon who had amputated Bush's foot was plucking at Hornblower's sleeve and fluttering some sheets of paper. These were instructions, he explained in faulty Italian French, for the further treatment of the stump. Any surgeon in France would understand them. As soon as the ligatures came away the wound would heal at once. He had put a parcel of dressings into the coach for use on the journey. Hornblower tried to thank him, but was interrupted when the surgeon turned away to supervise the lifting of Bush, stretcher and all, into the coach. It was an immensely long vehicle, and the stretcher just fitted in across one door, its ends on the two seats.

Brown was there now, with Hornblower's valise in his hand. The coachman showed him how to put it into the boot. Then a gendarme opened the other door and stood waiting for Hornblower to enter. Hornblower looked up at the ramparts towering above him; no more than half an hour ago he had been walking there, worn out with doubt. At least one doubt was settled now. In a fortnight's time perhaps they would all be settled, after he had faced the firing party at Vincennes. A spurt of fear welled up within him at the thought, destroying the first momentary feeling almost of pleasure. He did not want to be taken to Paris to be shot; he wanted to resist. Then he realised that resistance would be both vain and undignified, and he forced himself to climb into the coach, hoping that no one had noticed his slight hesitation.

A gesture from the sergeant of gendarmerie brought Brown to the door as well, and he came climbing in to sit apologetically with his officers. Caillard was mounting a big black horse, a spirited, restless creature which champed at its bit and passaged feverishly about. When he had settled himself in the saddle the word was given, and the horses were led round the courtyard, the coach jolting and heaving over the cobbles, out through the gate and down to the road which wound under the guns of the fortress. The mounted gendarmerie closed up round the coach, a whip cracked, and they were off at a slow trot, to the jingling of the harness and the clattering of the hoofs and the creaking of the leatherwork.

Hornblower would have liked to have looked out of the windows at the houses of Rosas village going by – after three weeks' captivity the change of scene allured him – but first he had to attend to his wounded lieutenant.

'How is it going, Bush?' he asked, bending over him.

'Very well, thank you, sir,' said Bush.

There was sunlight streaming in through the coach windows now, and here a succession of tall trees by the roadside threw flickering shadows over Bush's face. Fever and loss of blood had made Bush's face less craggy and gnarled, drawing the flesh tight over the bones so that he looked unnaturally younger, and he was pale instead of being the mahogany brown to which Hornblower was accustomed. Hornblower thought he saw a twinge of pain cross Bush's expression as the coach lurched on the abominable road.

'Is there anything I can do?' he asked, trying hard to keep the helplessness out of his voice.

'Nothing, thank you, sir,' whispered Bush.

'Try and sleep,' said Hornblower.

Bush's hand which lay outside the blanket twitched and stirred and moved towards him; he took it and he felt a gentle pressure. For a few brief seconds Bush's hand stroked his feebly, caressing it as though it was a woman's. There was a glimmer of a smile on Bush's drawn face with its closed eyes. During all the years they had served together it was the first sign of affection either had shown for the other. Bush's head turned on the pillow, and he lay quite still, while Hornblower sat not daring to move for fear of disturbing him.

The coach had slowed to a walk – it must be breasting the long climb which carried the road across the roots of the peninsula of Cape Creux. Yet even at that speed the coach lurched and rolled horribly; the surface of the road must be utterly uncared for. The sharp ringing of the hoofs of the escorts' horses told that they were travelling over rock, and the irregularity of the sound was a clear indication of the way the horses were picking their way among the holes. Framed in the windows Hornblower could see the gendarmes in their blue uniforms and cocked hats jerking and swaying about with the rolling of the coach. The presence of fifty gendarmes as an escort was not a real indication of the political importance of himself and Bush, but only a proof that even here, only twenty miles from France, the road was unsafe for small parties – a little band of Spanish guerilleros was to be found on every inaccessible hill-top.

But there was always a chance that Claros or Rovira with their Catalan miqueletes a thousand strong might come swooping down on the road from their Pyrenean fastnesses. Hornblower felt hope surging up within him at the thought that at any moment, in that case, he might find himself a free man again. His pulse beat faster and he crossed and uncrossed his knees restlessly – with the utmost caution so as not to disturb Bush. He did not want to be taken to Paris to face a mockery of a trial. He did not want to die. He was beginning to fret himself into a fever, when common sense came to his rescue and he compelled himself to sink into a stolid indifference.

Brown was sitting opposite him, primly upright with his arms folded. Hornblower almost grinned, sympathetically, at sight of him.

Brown was actually self-conscious. He had never in his life before, presumably, had to be at such close quarters with a couple of officers. Certainly he must be feeling awkward at having to sit in the presence of two such lofty individuals as a captain and a first lieutenant. For that matter, it was at least a thousand to one that Brown had never been inside a coach before, had never sat on leather upholstery with a carpet under his feet. Nor had he had any experience in gentlemen's service, his duties as captain's coxswain being mainly disciplinary and executive. There was something comic about seeing Brown, with the proverbial adaptability of the British seaman, aping what he thought should be the manners of the gentleman's gentleman, and sitting there as if butter would not melt in his mouth.

The coach lurched again, quickening its pace and the horses broke from a walk into a trot. They must be at the top of the long hill now, with a long descent before them, which would bring them back to the seashore somewhere near Llanza, where he had stormed the battery under protection of the tricolour flag. It was an exploit he had been proud of – still was, for that matter. He had never dreamed for one moment that it would lead him to Paris and a firing party. Through the window on Bush's side he could see the rounded brown slopes of the Pyrenees soaring upwards; on the other side, as the coach swung sickeningly round a bend, he caught a glimpse of the sea far below, sparkling in the rays of the afternoon sun. He craned his neck to look at it, the sea which had played him so many scurvy tricks and which he loved. He thought, with a little catch in his throat, that this would be the last day on which he would ever see it. Tonight they would cross the frontier; tomorrow they would plunge into France, and in ten days, a fortnight, he would be rotting in his grave at Vincennes. It would be hard to leave this life, even with all its doubts and uncertainties, to lose the sea with its whims and its treacheries, Maria and the child, Lady Barbara—

Those were white cottages drifting past the windows, and on the side towards the sea, perched on the grassy cliff, was the battery of Llanza. He could see a sentry dressed in blue and white; stooping and looking upwards he could see the French flag at the top of the flagstaff – Bush, here, had hauled it down not so many weeks ago. He heard the coachman's whip crack and the horses quickened their pace; it was still eight miles or so to the frontier and Caillard must be anxious to cross before dark. The mountains, bristling here with pines, were hemming the road in close between them and the sea. Why did not Claros or Rovira come to save him? At every turn of the road there was an ideal site for an ambush. Soon they would be in France and it would be too late. He had to struggle again to remain passive. The prospect of crossing into France seemed to make his fate far more certain and imminent.

It was growing dark fast – they could not be far now from the frontier.

Hornblower tried to visualise the charts he had often handled, so as to remember the name of the French frontier town, but his mind was not sufficiently under control to allow it. The coach was coming to a standstill; he heard footsteps outside, heard Caillard's metallic voice saying 'In the name of the Emperor,' and an unknown voice say 'Passez, passez, monsieur.' The coach lurched and accelerated again; they were in France now. Now the horses' hoofs were ringing on cobblestones. There were houses, one or two lights to be seen. Outside the houses there were men in all kinds of uniforms, and a few women picking their way among them, dressed in pretty costumes with caps on their heads. He could hear laughter and joking. Then abruptly the coach swerved to the right and drew up in the courtyard of an inn. Lights were appearing in plenty in the fading twilight. Someone opened the door of the coach and drew down the steps for him to descend.

IV

Hornblower looked round the room to which the innkeeper and the sergeant of gendarmerie had jointly conducted them. He was glad to see a fire burning there, for he was stiff and chilled with his long inactivity in the coach. There was a truckle bed against one wall, a table with a white cloth already spread. A gendarme appeared at the door, stepping slowly and heavily – he was the first of the two who were carrying the stretcher. He looked round to see where to lay it down, turned too abruptly, and jarred it against the jamb of the wall.

'Careful with that stretcher!' snapped Hornblower, and then, remembering he had to speak French 'Attention! Mettez le brancard là. Doucement!'

Brown came and knelt over the stretcher.

'What is the name of this place?' asked Hornblower of the innkeeper.

'Cerbère. Hôtel Iéna, monsieur,' answered the innkeeper, fingering his leather apron.

'Monsieur is allowed no speech with anyone whatever,' interposed the sergeant. 'He will be served, but he must address no speech to the inn servants. If he has any wishes, he will speak to the sentry outside his door. There will be another sentry outside his window.'

A gesture of his hand called attention to the cocked hat and the musket barrel of a gendarme, darkly visible through the glass.

'You are too amiable, monsieur,' said Hornblower.

'I have my orders. Supper will be served in half an hour.'

'I would be obliged if Colonel Caillard would give orders for a surgeon to attend Lieutenant Bush's wounds at once.'

'I will ask him, sir,' said the sergeant, escorting the innkeeper from the room.

Bush, when Hornblower bent over him, seemed somehow a little better than in the morning. There was a little colour in his cheeks and more strength in his movements.

'Is there anything I can do, Bush?' asked Hornblower.

'Yes—'

Bush explained the needs of sick-room nursing. Hornblower looked up at Brown, a little helplessly.

'I am afraid it'll call for two of you, sir, because I'm a heavy man,' said Bush apologetically. It was the apology in his tone which brought Hornblower to the point of action.

'Of course,' he said with all the cheerfulness he could bring into his voice. 'Come on, Brown. Lift him from the other side.'

After the business was finished, with no more than a single half-stifled groan from Bush, Brown displayed more of the astonishing versatility of the British seaman.

'I'll wash you, sir, shall I? An' you haven't had your shave today, have you, sir?'

Hornblower sat and watched in helpless admiration the deft movements of the burly sailor as he washed and shaved his first lieutenant. The towels were so well arranged that no single drop of water fell on the bedding.

'Thank 'ee, Brown, thank 'ee,' said Bush, sinking back on his pillow.

The door opened to admit a little bearded man in a semi-military uniform carrying a leather case.

'Good evening, gentlemen,' he said, sounding all his consonants in the manner which Hornblower was yet to discover was characteristic of the Midi. 'I am the surgeon, if you please. And this is the wounded officer? And these are the hospital notes of my confrère at Rosas? Excellent. Yes, exactly. And how are you feeling, sir?'

Hornblower had to translate, limpingly, the surgeon's question to Bush, and the latter's replies. Bush put out his tongue, and submitted to having his pulse felt, and his temperature gauged by a hand thrust into his shirt.

'So,' said the surgeon. 'And now let us see the stump. Will you hold the candle for me here, if you please, sir?'

He turned back the blankets from the foot of the stretcher, revealing the little basket which guarded the stump, laid the basket on the floor and began to remove the dressings.

'Would you tell him, sir,' asked Bush 'that my foot which isn't there tickles most abominably, and I don't know how to scratch it?'

The translation taxed Hornblower's French to the utmost, but the surgeon listened sympathetically.

'That is not at all unusual,' he said. 'And the itchings will come to a natural end in course of time. Ah, now here is the stump. A beautiful stump. A lovely stump.'

Hornblower, compelling himself to look, was vaguely reminded of the knuckle end of a roast leg of mutton; the irregular folds of flesh were caught in by half-healed scars, but out of the scars hung two ends of black thread.

'When Monsieur le Lieutenant begins to walk again,' explained the surgeon 'he will be glad of an ample pad of flesh at the end of the stump. The end of the bone will not chafe—'

'Yes, exactly,' said Hornblower, fighting down his squeamishness.

'A very beautiful piece of work,' said the surgeon. 'As long as it heals properly and gangrene does not set in. At this stage the surgeon has to depend on his nose for his diagnosis.'

Suiting the action to the word the surgeon sniffed at the dressings and at the raw stump.

'Smell, monsieur,' he said, holding the dressings to Hornblower's face. Hornblower was conscious of the faintest whiff of corruption.

'Beautiful, is it not?' said the surgeon. 'A fine healthy wound and yet every evidence that the ligatures will soon free themselves.'

Hornblower realised that the two threads hanging out of the scars were attached to the ends of the two main arteries. When corruption inside was complete the threads could be drawn out and the wounds allowed to heal; it was a race between the rotting of the arteries and the onset of gangrene.

'I will see if the ligatures are free now. Warn your friend that I shall hurt him a little.'

Hornblower looked towards Bush to convey the message, and was shocked to see that Bush's face was distorted with apprehension.

'I know,' said Bush. 'I know what he's going to do – sir.'

Only as an afterthought did he say that 'sir'; which was the clearest proof of his mental preoccupation. He grasped the bedclothes in his two fists, his jaw set and his eyes shut.

'I'm ready,' he said through his clenched teeth.

The surgeon drew firmly on one of the threads and Bush writhed a little. He drew on the other.

'A-ah,' gasped Bush, with sweat on his face.

'Nearly free,' commented the surgeon. 'I could tell by the feeling of the threads. Your friend will soon be well. Now let us replace the dressings. So. And so.' His dexterous plump fingers rebandaged the stump, replaced the wicker basket, and drew down the bed coverings.

'Thank you, gentlemen,' said the surgeon, rising to his feet and brushing his hands one against the other. 'I will return in the morning.'

'Hadn't you better sit down, sir,' came Brown's voice to Hornblower's ears as though from a million miles away, after the surgeon had withdrawn. The room was veiled in grey mist which gradually cleared away as he sat, to reveal Bush lying back on his pillow and trying to smile, and Brown's homely honest face wearing an expression of acute concern.

'Rare bad you looked for a minute, sir. You must be hungry, I expect, sir, not having eaten nothing since breakfast, like.'

It was tactful of Brown to attribute this faintness to hunger, to which all flesh might be subject without shame, and not merely to weakness in face of wounds and suffering.

'That sounds like supper coming now,' croaked Bush from the stretcher, as though one of a conspiracy to ignore their captain's feebleness.

The sergeant of gendarmerie came clanking in, two women behind him bearing trays. The women set the table deftly and quickly, their eyes downcast, and withdrew without looking up, although one of them smiled at the corner of her mouth in response to a meaning cough from Brown which drew a gesture of irritation from the sergeant. The latter cast one searching glance round the room before shutting and locking the door with a clashing of keys.

'Soup,' said Hornblower, peering into the tureen which steamed deliciously. 'And I fancy this is stewed veal.'

The discovery confirmed him in his notion that Frenchmen lived exclusively on soup and stewed veal – he put no faith in the more vulgar notions regarding frogs and snails.

'You will have some of this broth, I suppose, Bush?' he continued. He was talking desperately hard now to conceal the feeling of depression and unhappiness which was overwhelming him. 'And a glass of this wine? It has no label – let's hope for the best.'

'Some of their rotgut claret, I suppose,' grunted Bush. Eighteen years of war with France had given most Englishmen the notion that the only wines fit for men to drink were port and sherry and Madeira, and that Frenchmen only drank thin claret which gave the unaccustomed drinker the bellyache.

'We'll see,' said Hornblower as cheerfully as he could. 'Let's get you propped up first.'

With his hand behind Bush's shoulders he heaved him up a little; as he looked round helplessly, Brown came to his rescue with pillows taken from the bed, and between them they settled Bush with his head raised and his arms free and a napkin under his chin. Hornblower brought him a plate of soup and a piece of bread.

'M'm,' said Bush, tasting. 'Might be worse. Please, sir, don't let yours get cold.'

Brown brought a chair for his captain to sit at the table, and stood in an attitude of attention beside it; there was another place laid, but his action proclaimed as loudly as words how far it was from his mind to sit with his captain. Hornblower ate, at first with a distaste and then with increasing appetite.

'Some more of that soup, Brown,' said Bush. 'And my glass of wine, if you please.'

The stewed veal was extraordinarily good, even to a man who was accustomed to meat he could set his teeth in.

'Dash my wig,' said Bush from the bed. 'Do you think I could have some of that stewed veal, sir? This travelling has given me an appetite.'

Hornblower had to think about that. A man in a fever should be kept on a low diet, but Bush could not be said to be in a fever now, and he had lost a great deal of blood which he had to make up. The yearning look on Bush's face decided him.

'A little will do you no harm,' he said. 'Take this plate to Mr Bush, Brown.'

Good food and good wine – the fare in the *Sutherland* had been repulsive, and at Rosas scanty – tended to loosen their tongues and make them more cheerful. Yet it was hard to unbend beyond a certain unstated limit. The awful majesty surrounding a captain of a ship of the line lingered even after the ship had been destroyed; more than that, the memory of the very strict reserve which Hornblower had maintained during his command acted as a constraint. And to Brown a first lieutenant was in a position nearly as astronomically lofty as a captain; it was awesome to be in the same room as the two of them, even with the help of making-believe to be their old servant. Hornblower had finished his cheese by now, and the moment which Brown had been dreading had arrived.

'Here, Brown,' he said rising, 'sit down and eat your supper while it's still hot.'

Brown now, at the age of twenty-eight, had served His Majesty in His Majesty's ships from the age of eleven, and during that time he had never made use at table of other instruments than his sheath knife and his fingers; he had never eaten off china, nor had he drunk from a wineglass. He experienced a nightmare sensation as if his officers were watching him with four eyes as large as footballs the while he nervously picked up a spoon and addressed himself to this unaccustomed task. Hornblower realised his embarrassment in a clairvoyant flash. Brown had thews and sinews which Hornblower had often envied; he had a stolid courage in action with Hornblower could never hope to rival. He could knot and splice, hand, reef, and steer, cast the lead or pull an oar, all of them far better than his captain. He could go aloft on a black night in a howling storm without thinking twice about it, but the sight of a knife and fork made his hands tremble. Hornblower thought about how Gibbon would have pointed the moral epigrammatically in two vivid antithetical sentences.

Humiliation and nervousness never did any good to a man – Hornblower knew that if anyone ever did. He took a chair unobtrusively over beside Bush's stretcher and sat down with his back almost turned to the table, and plunged desperately into conversation with his first lieutenant while the crockery clattered behind him.

'Would you like to be moved into the bed?' he asked, saying the first thing which came into his head.

'No, thank you, sir,' said Bush. 'Two weeks now I've slept in the stretcher. I'm comfortable enough, sir, and it'd be painful to move me, even if – if—'

Words failed Bush to describe his utter determination not to sleep in the only bed and leave his captain without one.

'What are we going to Paris for, sir?' asked Bush.

'God knows,' said Hornblower. 'But I have a notion that Boney himself wants to ask us questions.'

That was the answer he had decided upon hours before in readiness for this inevitable question; it would not help Bush's convalescence to know the fate awaiting him.

'Much good will our answers do him,' said Bush, grimly. 'Perhaps we'll drink a dish of tea in the Tuileries with Maria Louisa.'

'Maybe,' answered Hornblower. 'And maybe he wants lessons in navigation from you. I've heard he's weak at mathematics.'

That brought a smile. Bush notoriously was no good with figures and suffered agonies when confronted with a simple problem in spherical trigonometry. Hornblower's acute ears heard Brown's chair scrape a little; presumably his meal had progressed satisfactorily.

'Help yourself to the wine, Brown,' he said, without turning round.

'Aye aye, sir,' said Brown cheerfully.

There was a whole bottle of wine left as well as some in the other. This would be a good moment for ascertaining if Brown could be trusted with liquor. Hornblower kept his back turned to him and struggled on with his conversation with Bush. Five minutes later Brown's chair scraped again more definitely, and Hornblower looked round.

'Had enough, Brown?'

'Aye aye, sir. A right good supper.'

The soup tureen and the dish of stew were both empty; the bread had disappeared all save the heel of the loaf; there was only a morsel of cheese left. But one bottle of wine was still two-thirds full – Brown had contented himself with a half bottle at most, and the fact that he had drunk that much and no more was the clearest proof that he was safe as regards alcohol.

'Pull the bellrope, then.'

The distant jangling brought in time the rattling of keys to the door, and in came the sergeant and the two maids; the latter set about clearing the tables under the former's eye.

'I must get something for you to sleep on, Brown,' said Hornblower.

'I can sleep on the floor, sir.'

'No, you can't.'

Hornblower had decided opinions about that; there had been occasions as a young officer when he had slept on the bare planks of a ship's deck, and he knew their unbending discomfort.

'I want a bed for my servant,' he said to the sergeant.

'He can sleep on the floor.'

'I will not allow anything of the kind. You must find a mattress for him.'

Hornblower was surprised to find how quickly he was acquiring the ability to talk French; the quickness of his mind enabled him to make the best use of his limited vocabulary and his retentive memory had stored up all sorts of words, once heard, and was ready to produce them from the subconscious part of his mind as soon as the stimulus of necessity was applied.

The sergeant had shrugged his shoulders and rudely turned his back.

'I shall report your insolence to Colonel Caillard tomorrow morning,' said Hornblower hotly. 'Find a mattress immediately.'

It was not so much the threat that carried the day as long-ingrained habits of discipline. Even a sergeant of French gendarmerie was accustomed to yielding deference to gold lace and epaulettes and an authoritative manner. Possibly the obvious indignation of the maids at the suggestion that so fine a man should be left to sleep on the floor may have weighed with him too. He called to the sentry at the door and told him to bring a mattress from the stables where the escort were billeted. It was only a palliasse of straw when it came, but it was something infinitely more comfortable than bare and draughty boards, all the same. Brown looked his gratitude to Hornblower as the mattress was spread out in the corner of the room.

'Time to turn in,' said Hornblower, ignoring it, as the door was locked behind the sergeant. 'Let's make you comfortable, first, Bush.'

It was some obscure self-conscious motive which made Hornblower select from his valise the embroidered nightshirt over which Maria's busy fingers had laboured lovingly – the nightshirt which he had brought with him from England for use should it happen that he should dine and sleep at a Governor's or on board the flagship. All the years he had been a captain he had never shared a room with anyone save Maria, and it was a novel experience for him to prepare for bed in sight of Bush and Brown, and he was ridiculously self-conscious about it, regardless of the fact that Bush, white and exhausted, was already lying back on his pillow with drooping eyelids, while Brown modestly stripped off his trousers with downcast eyes, wrapped himself in the cloak which Hornblower insisted on his using, and curled himself up on his palliasse without a glance at his superior.

Hornblower got into bed.

'Ready?' he asked, and blew out the candle; the fire had died down to embers which gave only the faintest red glow in the room. It was the beginning of one of those wakeful nights which Hornblower had grown by now able to recognise in advance. The moment he blew out the candle and settled his head on the pillow he knew he would not be able to sleep until just before dawn. In his ship he would have gone up on deck or walked his stern gallery; here he could only lie grimly immobile. Sometimes a subdued crackling told how Brown was turning over on his straw mattress; once or twice Bush moaned a little in his feverish sleep.

Today was Wednesday. Only sixteen days ago and Hornblower had been captain of a seventy-four, and absolute master of the happiness of five hundred seamen. His least word directed the operations of a gigantic engine of war; the blows it had dealt had caused an imperial throne to totter. He thought regretfully of night-time aboard his ship, the creaking of the timbers and the singing of the rigging, the impassive quartermaster at the wheel in the faint light of the binnacle and the officer of the watch pacing the quarterdeck.

Now he was a nobody; where once he had minutely regulated five hundred men's lives he was reduced to chaffering for a single mattress for the only seaman left to him; police sergeants could insult him with impunity; he had to come and to go at the bidding of someone he despised. Worse than that – Hornblower felt the hot blood running under his skin as the full realisation broke upon him again – he was being taken to Paris as a criminal. Very soon indeed, in some cold dawn, he would be led out into the ditch at Vincennes to face a firing party. Then he would be dead. Hornblower's vivid imagination pictured the impact of the musket bullets upon his breast, and he wondered how long the pain would last before oblivion came upon him. It was not the oblivion that he feared, he told himself – indeed in his present misery he almost looked forward to it. Perhaps it was the finality of death, the irrevocableness of it.

No, that was only a minor factor. Mostly it was instinctive fear of a sudden and drastic change to something completely unknown. He remembered the night he had spent as a child in the inn at Andover, when he was going to join his ship next day and enter upon the unknown life of the Navy. That was the nearest comparison – he had been frightened then, he remembered, so frightened he had been unable to sleep; and yet 'frightened' was too strong a word to describe the state of mind of someone who was quite prepared to face the future and could not be readily blamed for this sudden acceleration of heartbeat and prickling of sweat!

A moaning sigh from Bush, loud in the stillness of the room, distracted him from his analysis of his fear. They were going to shoot Bush, too. Presumably they would lash him to a stake to have a fair shot at him – curious how, while it was easy to order a party to shoot an upright figure, however helpless, every instinct revolted against shooting a helpless man prostrate on a stretcher. It would be a monstrous crime to shoot Bush, who, even supposing his captain were guilty, could have done nothing except obey orders. But Bonaparte would do it. The necessity of rallying Europe round him in his struggle against England was growing ever more pressing. The blockade was strangling the Empire of the French as Antaeus had been strangled by Hercules. Bonaparte's unwilling allies – all Europe, that was to say, save Portugal and Sicily – were growing restive and thinking about defection; the French people themselves, Hornblower shrewdly guessed, were by now none too enamoured of this King Stork whom they had imposed on themselves. It would not be sufficient for Bonaparte merely to say that the British fleet was the criminal instrument of a perfidious tyranny; he had said that for a dozen years. The mere announcement that British naval officers had violated the laws of war would carry small enough weight, too. But to try a couple of officers and shoot them would be a convincing gesture, and the perverted statement of facts issued from Paris might help to sustain French public opinion – European public opinion as well – for another year or two in its opposition to England.

But it was bad luck that the victims should be Bush and he. Bonaparte had had a dozen British naval captains in his hands during the last few years, and he could have trumped up charges against half of them. Presumably it was destiny which had selected Hornblower and Bush to suffer. Hornblower told himself that for twenty years he had been aware of a premonition of sudden death. It was certain and inevitable now. He hoped he would meet it bravely, go down with colours flying; but he mistrusted his own weak body. He feared that his cheeks would be pale and his teeth chatter, or worse still, that his heart would weaken so that he would faint before the firing party had done their work. That would be a fine opportunity for a mordant couple of lines in the *Moniteur Universel* – fine reading for Lady Barbara and Maria.

If he had been alone in the room he would have groaned aloud in his misery and turned over restlessly. But as it was he lay grimly rigid and silent. If his subordinates were awake they would never be allowed to guess that he was awake, too. To divert his mind from his approaching execution he cast round in search of something else to think about, and new subjects presented themselves in swarms. Whether Admiral

Leighton were alive or dead, and whether, if the latter were the case, Lady Barbara Leighton would think more often or less often about Hornblower, her lover; how Maria's pregnancy was progressing; what was the state of British public opinion regarding the loss of the *Sutherland*, and, more especially, what Lady Barbara thought about his surrendering – there were endless things to think and worry about; there was endless flotsam bobbing about in the racing torrent of his mind. And the horses stamped in the stable, and every two hours he heard the sentries being changed outside window and door.

V

Dawn was not fully come, the room was only faintly illuminated by the grey light, when a clash of keys and a stamping of booted feet outside the door heralded the entrance of the sergeant of gendarmerie.

'The coach will leave in an hour's time,' he announced. 'The surgeon will be here in half an hour. You gentlemen will please be ready.'

Bush was obviously feverish; Hornblower could see that at his first glance as he bent over him, still in his embroidered silk nightshirt. But Bush stoutly affirmed that he was not ill.

'I'm well enough, thank you, sir,' he said; but his face was flushed and yet apprehensive, and his hands gripped his bedclothes. Hornblower suspected that the mere vibration of the floor as he and Brown walked about the room was causing pain to the unhealed stump of his leg.

'I'm ready to do anything you want done,' said Hornblower.

'No, thank you, sir. Let's wait till the doctor comes, if you don't mind, sir.'

Hornblower washed and shaved in the cold water in the wash-hand stand jug; during the time which had elapsed since he had left the *Sutherland* he had never been allowed hot. But he yearned for the cold shower bath he had been accustomed to take under the jet of the wash-deck pump; his skin seemed to creep when he stopped to consider it, and it was a ghoulish business to make shift with washing glove and soap, wetting a few inches at a time. Brown dressed himself unobtrusively in his own corner of the room, scurrying out like a mouse to wash when his captain had finished.

The doctor arrived with his leather satchel.

'And how is he this morning?' he asked, briskly; Hornblower saw a shade of concern pass over his face as he observed Bush's evident fever.

He knelt down and exposed the stump, Hornblower beside him. The limb jerked nervously as it was grasped with firm fingers; the doctor took Hornblower's hand and laid it on the skin above the wound.

'A little warm,' said the doctor. It was hot to Hornblower's touch. 'That may be a good sign. We shall know now.'

He took hold of one of the ligatures and pulled at it. The thing came gliding out of the wound like a snake.

'Good!' said the doctor. 'Excellent!'

He peered closely at the debris entangled in the knot, and then bent to examine the trickle of pus which had followed the ligature out of the wound.

'Excellent,' repeated the doctor.

Hornblower went back in his mind through the numerous reports which surgeons had made to him regarding wounded men, and the verbal comments with which they had amplified them. The words 'laudable pus' came up in his mind; it was important to distinguish between the drainage from a wound struggling to heal itself and the stinking ooze of a poisoned limb. This was clearly laudable pus, judging by the doctor's comments.

'Now for the other one,' said the doctor. He pulled at the remaining ligature, but all he got was a cry of pain from Bush – which seemed to go clean through Hornblower's heart – and a convulsive writhing of Bush's tortured body.

'Not quite ready,' said the doctor. 'I should judge that it will only be a matter of hours, though. Is your friend proposing to continue his journey today?'

'He is under orders to continue it,' said Hornblower in his limping French. 'You would consider such a course unwise?'

'Most unwise,' said the doctor. 'It will cause him a great deal of pain and may imperil the healing of the wound.'

He felt Bush's pulse and rested his hand on his forehead.

'Most unwise,' he repeated.

The door opened behind him to reveal the gendarmerie sergeant.

'The carriage is ready.'

'It must wait until I have bandaged this wound. Get outside,' said the doctor testily.

'I will go and speak to the Colonel,' said Hornblower.

He brushed past the sergeant who tried too late to intercept him, into the main corridor of the inn, and out into the courtyard where stood the coach. The horses were being harnessed up, and a group of gendarmes were saddling their mounts on the farther side. Chance dictated that Colonel Caillard should be crossing the courtyard, too, in his blue and red uniform and his gleaming high boots, the star of the Legion of Honour dancing on his breast.

'Sir,' said Hornblower.

'What is it now?' demanded Caillard.

'Lieutenant Bush must not be moved. He is very badly wounded and a crisis approaches.'

The broken French came tumbling disjointedly from Hornblower's lips.

'I can do nothing in contravention of my orders,' said Caillard. His eyes were cold and his mouth hard.

'You were not ordered to kill him,' protested Hornblower.

'I was ordered to bring you and him to Paris with the utmost dispatch. We shall start in five minutes.'

'But, sir— Cannot you wait even today?'

'Even as a pirate you must be aware of the impossibility of disobeying orders,' said Caillard.

'I protest against those orders in the name of humanity.'

That was a melodramatic speech, but it was a melodramatic moment, and in his ignorance of French Hornblower could not pick and choose his words. A sympathetic murmur in his ear attracted his notice, and, looking round, he saw the two aproned maids and a fat woman and the innkeeper all listening to the conversation with obvious disapproval of Caillard's point of view. They shut themselves away behind the kitchen door as Caillard turned a terrible eye upon them, but they had granted Hornblower a first momentary insight into the personal unpopularity which Imperial harshness was causing to develop in France.

'Sergeant,' said Caillard abruptly. 'Put the prisoners into the coach.'

There was no hope of resistance. The gendarmes carried Bush's stretcher into the courtyard and perched it up on the seats, with Brown and Hornblower running round it to protect it from unnecessary jerks. The surgeon was scribbling notes hurriedly at the foot of the sheaf of notes regarding Bush's case which Hornblower had brought from Rosas. One of the maids came clattering across the courtyard with a steaming tray which she passed in to Hornblower through the open window. There was a platter of bread and three bowls of a black liquid which Hornblower was later to come to recognise as coffee – what blockaded France had come to call coffee. It was no pleasanter than the infusion of burnt crusts which Hornblower had sometimes drunk on shipboard during a long cruise without the opportunity of renewing cabin stores, but it was warm and stimulating at that time in the morning.

'We have no sugar, sir,' said the maid apologetically.

'It doesn't matter,' answered Hornblower, sipping thirstily.

'It is a pity the poor wounded officer has to travel,' she went on. 'These wars are terrible.'

She had a snub nose and a wide mouth and big black eyes – no one could call her attractive, but the sympathy in her voice was grateful to a man who was a prisoner. Brown was propping up Bush's shoulders and holding a bowl to his lips. He took two or three sips and turned his head away. The coach rocked as two men scrambled up on to the box.

'Stand away, there!' roared the sergeant.

The coach lurched and rolled and wheeled round out of the gates, the horses' hoofs clattering loud on the cobbles, and the last Hornblower saw of the maid was the slight look of consternation on her face as she realised that she had lost the breakfast tray for good.

The road was bad, judging by the way the coach lurched; Hornblower heard a sharp intake of breath from Bush at one jerk. He remembered what the swollen and inflamed stump of Bush's leg looked like; every jar must be causing him agony. He moved up the seat to the stretcher and caught Bush's hand.

'Don't you worry yourself, sir,' said Bush. 'I'm all right.'

Even while he spoke Hornblower felt him grip tighter as another jolt caught him unexpectedly.

'I'm sorry, Bush,' was all he could say; it was hard for the captain to speak at length to the lieutenant on such personal matters as his regret and unhappiness.

'We can't help it, sir,' said Bush, forcing his peaked features into a smile.

That was the main trouble, their complete helplessness. Hornblower realised that there was nothing he could say, nothing he could do. The leather-scented stuffiness of the coach was already oppressing him, and he realised with horror that they would have to endure this jolting prison of theirs for another twenty days, perhaps, before they should reach Paris. He was restless and fidgety at the thought of it, and perhaps his restlessness communicated itself by contact to Bush, who gently withdrew his hand and turned his head to one side, leaving his captain free to fidget within the narrow confines of the coach.

Still there were glimpses of the sea to be caught on one side, and of the Pyrenees on the other. Putting his head out of the window Hornblower ascertained that their escort was diminished today. Only two troopers rode ahead of the coach, and four clattered behind at the heels of Caillard's horse. Presumably their entry into France made any possibility of a rescue far less likely. Standing thus, his head awkwardly protruding through the window, was less irksome than sitting in the stuffiness of the carriage. There were the vineyards and the stubble fields to be seen, and the swelling heights of the Pyrenees receding into the blue distance. There were people, too – nearly all women, Hornblower noted – who hardly looked up from their hoeing to watch the coach and its escort bowling along the road. Now they were passing a party of uniformed soldiers – recruits and convalescents, Hornblower guessed, on their way to their units in Catalonia – shambling along the road more like sheep than soldiers. The young officer at their head saluted the glitter of the star on Caillard's chest and eyed the coach curiously at the same time.

Strange prisoners had passed along that road before him; Alvarez, the heroic defender of Gerona, who died on a wheelbarrow – the only bed granted him – in a dungeon on his way to trial, and Toussaint l'Ouverture, the negro hero of Hayti, kidnapped from his sunny island and sent to die, inevitably, of pneumonia in a rocky fortress in the Jura; Palafox of Zaragoza, young Mina from Navarre – all victims of the tyrant's Corsican rancour. He and Bush would only be two more items in a list already notable. D'Enghien, who had been shot in Vincennes six years ago, was of the blood-royal, and his death had caused a European sensation, but Bonaparte had murdered plenty more. Thinking of all those who had preceded him made Hornblower gaze more yearningly from the carriage window, and breathe more deeply of the free air.

Still in sight of sea and hills – Mount Caingou still dominating the background – they halted at a posting inn beside the road to change horses. Caillard and the escort took new mounts; four new horses were harnessed up to the coach, and in less than a quarter of an hour they were off again, breasting the steep slopes before them with renewed strength. They must be averaging six miles to the hour at least, thought Hornblower, his mind beginning to make calculations. How far Paris might be he could only guess – five or six hundred miles, he fancied. From seventy to ninety hours of travel would bring them to the capital, and they might travel eight, twelve, fifteen hours a day. It might be five days, it might be twelve days, before they reached Paris – vague enough figures. He might be dead in a week's time, or he might still be alive in three weeks. Still alive! As Hornblower thought those words he realised how greatly he desired to live; it was one of those moments when the Hornblower whom he observed so dispassionately and with faint contempt suddenly blended with the Hornblower who was himself, the most important and vital person in the whole world. He envied the bent old shepherd in the distance with the plaid rug over his shoulders, hobbling over the hillside bent over his stick.

Here was a town coming – there were ramparts, a frowning citadel, a lofty cathedral. They passed through a gateway and the horses' hoofs rang loudly on cobblestones as the coach threaded its way through narrow streets. Plenty of soldiers here, too; the streets were filled with variegated uniforms. This must be Perpignan, of course, the French base for the invasion of Catalonia. The coach stopped with a jerk in a wider street where an avenue of plane trees and a flagged quay bordered a little river, and, looking upward, Hornblower read the sign 'Hôtel de la Poste et du Perdrix. Route Nationale 9. Paris 849'. With a rush and bustle the horses were changed, Brown and Hornblower were grudgingly allowed to descend and stretch their stiff legs before returning to attend to Bush's wants – they were few enough in his present fever. Caillard and the gendarmes were snatching a hasty meal – the latter at tables outside the inn, the former visible through the windows of the front room. Someone brought the prisoners a tray with slices of cold meat, bread, wine, and cheese. It had hardly been handed into the coach when the escort climbed upon their horses again, the whip cracked and they were off. The coach heaved and dipped like a ship at sea as it mounted first one hump-backed bridge and then another, before the horses settled into a steady trot along the wide straight road bordered with poplars.

'They waste no time,' said Hornblower, grimly.

'No sir, that they don't,' agreed Brown.

Bush would eat nothing, shaking his head feebly at the offer of bread and meat. All they could do for him was to moisten his lips with wine, for he was parched and thirsty; Hornblower made a mental note to remember to ask for water at the next posting house, and cursed himself for forgetting anything so obvious up to now. He and Brown shared the food, eating with their fingers and drinking turn and turn about from the bottle of wine, Brown apologetically wiping the bottle's mouth with the napkin after drinking. And as soon as the food was finished Hornblower was on his feet again craning through the carriage window, watching the countryside drifting by. A thin chill rain began, soaking his scanty hair as he stood there, wetting his face and even running in trickles down his neck, but still he stood there, staring out at freedom.

The sign of the inn where they stopped at nightfall read 'Hôtel de la Poste de Sigean. Route Nationale 9. Paris 805. Perpignan 44'. This place Sigean was no more than a sparse village, straggling for miles along the high road, and the inn was a tiny affair, smaller than the posting stables round the other three sides of the courtyard. The staircase to the upper rooms was too narrow and winding for the stretcher to be carried up them; it was only with difficulty that the bearers were able to turn with it into the salon which the innkeeper reluctantly yielded to them. Hornblower saw Bush wincing as the stretcher jarred against the sides of the door.

'We must have a surgeon at once for the lieutenant,' he said to the sergeant.

'I will inquire for one.'

The innkeeper here was a surly brute with a squint; he was ungracious about clearing his best sitting-room of its spindly furniture, and bringing beds for Hornblower and Brown, and producing the various articles they asked for to help make Bush comfortable. There were no wax candles nor lamps; only tallow dips which stank atrociously.

'How's the leg feeling?' asked Hornblower, bending over Bush.

'All right, sir,' said Bush, stubbornly, but he was so obviously fever-ish and in such obvious pain that Hornblower was anxious about him.

When the sergeant escorted in the maid with the dinner he asked, sharply:

'Why has the surgeon not come?'

'There is no surgeon in this village.'

'No surgeon? The lieutenant is seriously ill. Is there no – no apothe-cary?'

Hornblower used the English word in default of French.

'The cow-doctor went across the hills this afternoon and will not be back tonight. There is no one to be found.'

The sergeant went out of the room, leaving Hornblower to explain the situation to Bush.

'All right,' said the latter, turning his head on the pillow with the feeble gesture which Hornblower dreaded. Hornblower nerved himself.

'I'd better dress that wound of yours myself,' he said. 'We might try cold vinegar on it, as they do in our service.'

'Something cold,' said Bush, eagerly.

Hornblower pealed at the bell, and when it was eventually answered he asked for vinegar and obtained it. Not one of the three had a thought for their dinner cooling on the side table.

'Now,' said Hornblower.

He had a saucer of vinegar beside him, in which lay the soaking lint, and the clean bandages which the surgeon at Rosas had supplied were at hand. He turned back the bedclothes and revealed the bandaged stump. The leg twitched nervously as he removed the bandages; it was red and swollen and inflamed, hot to the touch for several inches above the point of amputation.

'It's pretty swollen here, too, sir,' whispered Bush. The glands in his groin were huge.

'Yes,' said Hornblower.

He peered at the scarred end, examined the dressing he had re-moved, with Brown holding the light. There had been a slight oozing from the point where the ligature had been withdrawn yesterday; much of the rest of the scar was healed and obviously healthy. There was only the other ligature which could be causing this trouble; Hornblower knew that if it were ready to come out it was dangerous to leave it in. Cautiously he took hold of the silken thread. The first gentle touch of it conveyed to his sensitive fingers a suggestion that it was free. It moved distinctly for a quarter of an inch and, judging by Bush's quiescence, it caused him no sudden spasm of pain. Hornblower set his teeth and pulled; the thread yielded very slowly, but it was obviously free, and no longer attached to the elastic artery. He pulled steadily against a yielding resistance. The ligature came slowly out of the wound, knot and all. Pus followed it in a steady trickle, only slightly tinged with blood. The thing was done.

The artery had not burst, and clearly the wound was in need of the free drainage open to it now with the withdrawal of the ligature.

'I think you're going to start getting well now,' he said, aloud, making himself speak cheerfully. 'How does it feel?'

'Better,' said Bush. 'I think it's better, sir.'

Hornblower applied the soaking lint to the scarred surface. He found his hands trembling, but he steadied them with an effort as he bandaged the stump – not an easy job, this last, but one which he managed to complete in adequate fashion. He put back the wicker shield, tucked in the bedclothes, and rose to his feet. The trembling was worse than ever now, and he was shaken and sick, which surprised him.

'Supper, sir?' asked Brown. 'I'll give Mr Bush his.'

Hornblower's stomach resisted a protest at the suggestion of food. He would have liked to refuse, but that would have been too obvious a confession of weakness in front of a subordinate.

'When I've washed my hands,' he said loftily.

It was easier to eat than he had expected, when he sat down to force himself. He managed to choke down enough mouthfuls to make it appear as if he had eaten well, and with the passage of the minutes the memory of the revolting task on which he had been engaged became rapidly less clear. Bush displayed none of the appetite nor any of the cheerfulness which had been noticeable last night; that was the obvious result of his fever. But with free drainage to his wound it could be hoped that he would soon recover. Hornblower was tired now, as a result of his sleepless night the night before, and his emotions had been jarred into a muddle by what he had had to do; it was easier to sleep tonight, waking only at intervals to listen to Bush's breathing, and to sleep again reassured by the steadiness and tranquillity of the sound.

VI

After that day the details of the journey became more blurred and indistinct – up to that day they had had all the unnatural sharpness of a landscape just before rain. Looking back at the journey, what was easiest to remember was Bush's convalescence – his steady progress back to health from the moment that the ligature was withdrawn from his wound. His strength began to come back fast, so that it would have been astonishing to anyone who did not know of his iron constitution and of the Spartan life he had always led. The transition was rapid between the time when his head had to be supported to allow him to drink and the time when he could sit himself up by his own unaided strength.

Hornblower could remember those details when he tried to, but all the rest was muddled and vague. There were memories of long hours spent at the carriage window, when it always seemed to be raining, and the rain wetted his face and hair. Those were hours spent in a sort of melancholy; Hornblower came to look back on them afterwards in the same way as someone recovered from insanity must look back on the blank days in the asylum. All the inns at which they stayed and the doctors who had attended to Bush were confused in his mind. He could remember the relentless regularity with which the kilometre figures displayed at the posting stations indicated the dwindling distance between them and Paris – Paris 525, Paris 383, Paris 287; somewhere at that point they changed from Route Nationale No. 9 to Route Nationale No. 7. Each day was bringing them nearer to Paris and death, and each day he sank farther into apathetic melancholy. Issoire, Clermont-Ferrand, Moulins; he read the names of the towns through which they passed without remembering them.

Autumn was gone now, left far behind down by the Pyrenees. Here winter had begun. Cold winds blew in melancholy fashion through the long avenues of leafless trees, and the fields were brown and desolate. At night he was sleeping heavily, tormented by dreams which he could not remember in the morning; his days he spent standing at the carriage window staring with sightless eyes over a dreary landscape where the chill rain fell. It seemed as if he had spent years consecutively in the leathery atmosphere of the coach, with the clatter of the horses' hoofs in his ears, and, visible in the tail of his eye, the burly figure of Caillard riding at the head of the escort close to the offside hind wheel.

During the bleakest afternoon they had yet experienced it did not seem as if Hornblower would be roused from his stupor even by the sudden unexpected stop which to a bored traveller might provide a welcome break in the monotony of travel. Dully, he watched Caillard ride up to ask the reason; dully, he gathered from the conversation that one of the coach horses had lost a shoe and gone dead lame. He watched with indifference the unharnessing of the unfortunate brute, and heard without interest the unhelpful answers of a passing travelling salesman with a pack-mule of whom Caillard demanded the whereabouts of the nearest smith. Two gendarmes went off at a snail's pace down a side track, leading the crippled animal; with only three horses the coach started off again towards Paris.

Progress was slow, and the stage was a long one. Only rarely before had they travelled after dark, but here it seemed that night would over-

take them long before they could reach the next town. Bush and Brown
were talking quite excitedly about this remarkable mishap – Hornblower
heard their cackle without noticing it, as a man long resident beside a
waterfall no longer hears the noise of the fall. The darkness which was
engulfing them was premature. Low black clouds covered the whole sky,
and the note of the wind in the trees carried with it something of menace.
Even Hornblower noted that, nor was it long before he noticed something else, that the rain beating upon his face was changing to sleet, and
then from sleet to snow; he felt the big flakes upon his lips, and tasted
them with his tongue. The gendarme who lit the lamps beside the
driver's box revealed to them through the windows the front of his
cloak caked thick with snow, shining faintly in the feeble light of the
lamp. Soon the sound of the horses' feet was muffled and dull, the wheels
could hardly be heard, and the pace of the coach diminished still further
as it ploughed through the snow piling in the road. Hornblower could
hear the coachman using his whip mercilessly upon his weary animals –
they were heading straight into the piercing wind, and were inclined to
take every opportunity to flinch away from it.

Hornblower turned back from the window to his subordinates inside
the coach – the faint light which the glass front panel allowed to enter
from the lamps was no more than enough to enable him just to make out
their shadowy forms. Bush was lying huddled under all his blankets;
Brown was clutching his cloak round him, and Hornblower for the first
time noticed the bitter cold. He shut the coach window without a word,
resigning himself to the leathery stuffiness of the interior. His dazed
melancholy was leaving him without his being aware of it.

'God help sailors,' he said cheerfully, 'on a night like this.'

That drew a laugh from the others in the darkness – Hornblower
just caught the note of pleased surprise in it which told him that they
had noticed and regretted the black mood which had gripped him during
the last few days, and were pleased with this first sign of his recovery.
Resentfully he asked himself what they expected of him. They did not
know, as he did, that death awaited him and Bush in Paris. What was
the use of thinking and worrying, guarded as they were by Caillard and
six gendarmes? With Bush a hopeless cripple, what chance was there of
escape? They did not know that Hornblower had put aside all thought
of escaping by himself. If by a miracle he had succeeded, what would
they think of him in England when he arrived there with the news that
he had left his lieutenant to die? They might sympathise with him, pity
him, understand his motive – he hated the thought of any of that;
better to face a firing party at Bush's side, never to see Lady Barbara
again, never to see his child. And better to spend his last few days in
apathy than in fretting. Yet the present circumstances, so different from
the monotony of the rest of the journey, had stimulated him. He laughed

and chatted with the others as he had not done since they had left Béziers.

The coach crawled on through the darkness with the wind shrieking overhead. Already the windows on one side were opaque with the snow which was plastered upon them – there was not warmth enough within the coach to melt it. More than once the coach halted, and Hornblower, putting his head out, saw that they were having to clear the horses' hoofs of the snow balled into ice under their shoes.

'If we're more than two miles from the next post house,' he announced, sitting back again 'we won't reach it until next week.'

Now they must have topped a small rise, for the horses were moving quicker, almost trotting, with the coach swaying and lurching over the inequalities of the road. Suddenly from outside they heard an explosion of shouts and yells.

'Hé, hé, hé!'

The coach swung round without warning, lurching frightfully, and came to a halt leaning perilously over to one side. Hornblower sprang to the window and looked out. The coach was poised perilously on the bank of a river; Hornblower could see the black water sliding along almost under his nose. Two yards away a small rowing boat, moored to a post, swayed about under the influence of wind and stream. Otherwise there was nothing to be seen in the blackness. Some of the gendarmes had run to the coach horses' heads; the animals were plunging and rearing in their fright at the sudden apparition of the river before them.

Somehow in the darkness the coach must have got off the road and gone down some side track leading to the river here; the coachman had reined his horses round only a fraction of a second before disaster threatened. Caillard was sitting his horse blaring sarcasms at the others.

'A fine coachman you are, God knows. Why didn't you drive straight into the river and save me the trouble of reporting you to the sous-chef of the administration? Come along, you men. Do you want to stay here all night? Get the coach back on the road, you fools.'

The snow came driving down in the darkness, the hot lamps sizzling continuously as the flakes lighted on them. The coachman got his horses under control again, the gendarmes stood back, and the whip cracked. The horses plunged and slipped, pawing for a footing, and the coach trembled without stirring from the spot.

'Come along, now!' shouted Caillard. 'Sergeant, and you, Pellaton, take the horses. You other men get to the wheels! Now, altogether. Heave! Heave!'

The coach lurched a scant yard before halting again. Caillard cursed wildly.

'If the gentlemen in the coach would descend and help,' suggested one of the gendarmes 'it would be better.'

'They can, unless they would rather spend the night in the snow,' said Caillard; he did not condescend to address Hornblower directly. For a moment Hornblower thought of telling him that he would see him damned first – there would be some satisfaction in that – but on the other hand he did not want to condemn Bush to a night of discomfort merely for an intangible self-gratification.

'Come on, Brown,' he said, swallowing his resentment, and he opened the door and they jumped down into the snow.

Even with the coach thus lightened, and with five men straining at the spokes of the wheels, they could make no progress. The snow had piled up against the steep descent to the river, and the exhausted horses plunged uselessly in the deep mass.

'God, what a set of useless cripples!' raved Caillard. 'Coachman, how far is it to Nevers?'

'Six kilometres, sir.'

'You mean you think it's six kilometres. Ten minutes ago you thought you were on the right road and you were not. Sergeant, ride into Nevers for help. Find the mayor, and bring every able-bodied man in the name of the Emperor. You, Ramel, ride with the sergeant as far as the high road, and wait there until he returns. Otherwise they'll never find us. Go on, sergeant, what are you waiting for? And you others, tether your horses and put your cloaks on their backs. You can keep warm digging the snow away from that bank. Coachman, come off that box and help them.'

The night was incredibly dark. Two yards from the carriage lamps nothing was visible at all, and with the wind whistling by they could not hear, as they stood by the coach, the movements of the men in the snow. Hornblower stamped about beside the coach and flogged himself with his arms to get his circulation back. Yet this snow and this icy wind were strangely refreshing. He felt no desire at the moment for the cramped stuffiness of the coach. And as he swung his arms an idea came to him, which checked him suddenly in his movements, until, ridiculously afraid of his thoughts being guessed, he went on stamping and swinging more industriously than ever. The blood was running hot under his skin now, as it always did when he was making plans – when he had outmanoeuvred the *Natividad*, for instance, and when he had saved the *Pluto* in the storm off Cape Creux.

There had been no hope of escape without the means of transporting a helpless cripple; now, not twenty feet from him, there was the ideal means – the boat which rocked to its moorings at the river bank. On a night like this it was easy to lose one's way altogether – except in a boat on a river; in a boat one had only to keep shoving off from shore to allow the current to carry one away faster than any horse could travel in these conditions. Even so, the scheme was utterly hare-brained. For how many days would they be able to preserve their liberty in the heart of France, two able-bodied men and one on a stretcher? They would freeze, starve – possibly even drown. But it was a chance, and nothing nearly as good would present itself (as far as Hornblower could judge from his past observations) between now and the time when the firing party at Vincennes would await them. Hornblower observed with mild interest that his fever was abating as he formed his resolve; and he was sufficiently amused at finding his jaw set in an expression of fierce resolution to allow his features to relax into a grim smile. There was always something laughable to him in being involved in heroics.

Brown came stamping round the coach and Hornblower addressed him, contriving with great effort to keep his voice low and yet matter-of-fact.

'We're going to escape down the river in that boat, Brown,' he said.

'Aye aye, sir,' said Brown, with no more excitement in his voice than if Hornblower had been speaking of the cold. Hornblower saw his head in the darkness turn towards the nearly visible figure of Caillard, pacing restlessly in the snow beside the coach.

'That man must be silenced,' said Hornblower.

'Aye aye, sir.' Brown meditated for a second before continuing. 'Better let me do that, sir.'

'Very good.'

'Now, sir?'

'Yes.'

Brown took two steps towards the unsuspecting figure.

'Here,' he said. 'Here, you.'

Caillard turned and faced him, and as he turned he received Brown's fist full on his jaw, in a punch which had all Brown's mighty fourteen stone behind it. He dropped in the snow, with Brown leaping upon him like a tiger, Hornblower behind him.

'Tie him up in his cloak,' whispered Hornblower. 'Hold on to his throat while I get it unbuttoned. Wait. Here's his scarf. Tie his head up in that first.'

The sash of the Legion of Honour was wound round and round the wretched man's head. Brown rolled the writhing figure over and with his knee in the small of his back tied his arms behind him with his neckcloth. Hornblower's handkerchief sufficed for his ankles – Brown strained the knot tight. They doubled the man in two and bundled him into his cloak, tying it about him with his swordbelt. Bush, lying on his stretcher in the darkness of the coach, heard the door open and a heavy load drop upon the floor.

'Mr Bush,' said Hornblower – the formal 'Mr' came naturally again now the action had begun again – 'We are going to escape in the boat.'

'Good luck, sir,' said Bush.

'You're coming too. Brown, take that end of the stretcher. Lift. Starboard a bit. Steady.'

Bush felt himself lifted out of the coach, stretcher and all, and carried down through the snow.

'Get the boat close in,' snapped Hornblower. 'Cut the moorings. Now, Bush, let's get these blankets round you. Here's my cloak, take it as well. You'll obey orders, Mr Bush. Take the other side, Brown. Lift him into the stern-sheets. Lower away. Bow thwart, Brown. Take the oars. Right. Shove off. Give way.'

It was only six minutes from the time when Hornblower had first conceived the idea. Now they were free, adrift on the black river, and Caillard was gagged and tied into a bundle on the floor of the coach. For a fleeting moment Hornblower wondered whether Caillard would suffocate before being discovered, and he found himself quite indifferent in the matter. Bonaparte's personal aides-de-camp, especially if they were colonels of gendarmerie as well, must expect to run risks while doing the dirty work which their situation would bring them. Meanwhile he had other things to think about.

'Easy!' he hissed at Brown. 'Let the current take her.'

The night was absolutely black; seated on the stern thwart he could not even see the surface of the water overside. For that matter, he did not know what river it was. But every river runs to the sea. The sea! Hornblower writhed in his seat in wild nostalgia at a vivid recollection of sea breezes in the nostrils and the feel of a heaving deck under his feet. Mediterranean or Atlantic, he did not know which, but if they had fantastic luck they might reach the sea in this boat by following the river far enough, and the sea was England's and would bear them home, to life instead of death, to freedom instead of imprisonment, to Lady Barbara, to Maria and his child.

The wind shrieked down on them, driving snow down his neck – thwarts and bottom boards were thick with snow. He felt the boat swing round under the thrust of the wind, which was in his face now instead of on his cheek.

'Turn her head to wind, Brown,' he ordered 'and pull slowly into it.'

The surest way of allowing the current a free hand with them was to try to neutralise the effect of the wind – a gale like this would soon blow them on shore, or even possibly blow them upstream; in this blackness it was impossible to guess what was happening to them.

'Comfortable, Mr Bush?' he asked.

'Aye aye, sir.'

Bush was faintly visible now, for the snow had driven up already against the grey blankets that swathed him and could just be seen from where Hornblower sat, a yard away.

'Would you like to lie down?'

'Thank you, sir, but I'd rather sit.'

Now that the excitement of the actual escape was over, Hornblower found himself shivering in the keen wind without his cloak. He was about to tell Brown that he would take one of the sculls when Bush spoke again.

'Pardon, sir, but d'you hear anything?'

Brown rested on his oars, and they sat listening.

'No,' said Hornblower. 'Yes, I do, by God!'

Underlying the noise of the wind there was a distant monotonous roaring.

'H'm,' said Hornblower, uneasily.

The roar was growing perceptibly louder; now it rose several notes in the scale, suddenly, and they could distinguish the sound of running water. Something appeared in the darkness beside the boat; it was a rock nearly covered, rendered visible in the darkness by the boiling white foam round it. It came and was gone in a flash, the clearest proof of the speed with which the boat was travelling.

'Jesus!' said Brown in the bows.

Now the boat was spinning round, lurching, jolting. All the water was white overside, and the bellowing of the rapid was deafening. They could do no more than sit and cling to their seat as the boat heaved and jerked. Hornblower shook himself free from his dazed helplessness, which seemed to have lasted half an hour and probably lasted no more than a couple of seconds.

'Give me a scull,' he snapped at Brown. 'You fend off port side. I'll take starboard.'

He groped in the darkness, found a scull, and took it from Brown's hand; the boat spun, hesitated, plunged again. All about them was the roar of the rapid. The starboard side of the boat caught on a rock; Hornblower felt icy water deluge his legs as it poured in over the side behind him. But already he was thrusting madly and blindly with his scull against the rock, he felt the boat slip and swing, he thrust so that the swing was accentuated, and next moment they were clear, wallowing sluggishly with the water up to the thwarts. Another rock slid hissing past, but the roar of the fall was already dwindling.

'Christ!' said Bush, in a mild tone contrasting oddly with the blasphemy. 'We're through!'

'D'you know if there's a bailer in the boat, Brown?' demanded Hornblower.

'Yessir, there was one at my feet when I came on board.'

'Find it and get this water out. Give me your other scull.'

Brown splashed about in the icy water in a matter piteous to hear as he groped for the floating wooden basin.

'Got it, sir,' he reported, and they heard the regular sound of the water being scooped overside as he began work.

In the absence of the distraction of the rapids they were conscious of the wind again now, and Hornblower turned the boat's bows into it and pulled slowly at the sculls. Past experience appeared to have demonstrated conclusively that this was the best way to allow the current a free hand to take the boat downstream and away from pursuit. Judging by the speed with which the noise of the rapid was left behind the current of this river was very fast indeed – that was only to be expected, too, for all the rain of the past few days must have brought up every river brim full. Hornblower wondered vaguely again what river this was, here in the heart of France. The only one with whose name he was acquainted and which it might possibly be was the Rhône, but he felt a suspicion that the Rhône was fifty miles or so farther eastward. This river presumably had taken its origin in the gaunt Cevennes whose flanks they had turned in the last two days' journey. In that case it would run northward, and must presumably turn westward to find the sea – it must be the Loire or one of its tributaries. And the Loire fell into the Bay of Biscay below Nantes, which must be at least four hundred miles away. Hornblower's imagination dallied with the idea of a river four hundred miles long, and with the prospect of descending it from source to mouth in the depth of winter.

A ghostly sound as if from nowhere brought him back to earth again. As he tried to identify it it repeated itself more loudly and definitely, and the boat lurched and hesitated. They were gliding over a bit of rock which providence had submerged to a depth sufficient just to scrape their keel. Another rock, foam covered, came boiling past them close overside. It passed them from stern to bow, telling him what he had no means of discovering in any other way in the blackness, that in this reach the river must be running westward, for the wind was in the east and he was pulling into it.

'More of those to come yet, sir,' said Bush – already they could hear the growing roar of water among rocks.

'Take a scull and watch the port side, Brown,' said Hornblower.

'Aye aye, sir. I've got the boat nearly dry,' volunteered Brown, feeling for the scull.

The boat was lurching again now, dancing a little in the madness of the river. Hornblower felt bow and stern lift successively as they dropped over what felt like a downward step in the water; he reeled as he stood, and the water remaining in the bottom of the boat surged and splashed against his ankles. The din of the rapid in the darkness round them was tremendous; white water was boiling about them on either side. The boat swung and pitched and rolled. Then something invisible struck the port side amidships with a splintering crash. Brown tried unavailingly to shove off, and Hornblower swung round and with his added strength forced the boat clear. They plunged and rolled again; Hornblower, feeling in the darkness, found the gunwale stove in, but apparently only the two upper strakes were damaged – chance might have driven that rock through below the water line as easily as it had done above it. Now the keel seemed to have caught; the boat heeled hideously, with Bush and Hornblower falling on their noses, but she freed herself and went on through the roaring water. The noise was dying down again and they were through another rapid.

'Shall I bail again, sir?' asked Brown.

'Yes. Give me your scull.'

'Light on the starboard bow, sir!' interjected Bush.

Hornblower craned over his shoulder. Undoubtedly it was a light, with another close beside it, and another farther on, barely visible in the driving snow. That must be a village on the river bank, or a town – the town of Nevers, six kilometres, according to the coachman, from where they had embarked. They had come four miles already.

'Silence now!' hissed Hornblower. 'Brown, stop bailing.'

With those lights to guide him in the darkness, stable, permanent things in this insane world of infinite indefiniteness, it was marvellous how he felt master of his fate once more. He knew again which was upstream and which was down – the wind was still blowing downstream. With a touch of the sculls he turned the boat downstream, wind and current sped her along fast and the lights were gliding by rapidly. The snow stung his face – it was hardly likely there would be anyone in the town to observe them on a night like this. Certainly the boat must have come down the river faster than the plodding horses of the gendarmes whom Caillard had sent ahead. A new roaring of water caught his ear, different in timbre from the sound of a rapid. He craned round again to see the bridge before them silhouetted in white against the blackness by reason of the snow driven against the arches. He tugged wildly, first at one scull and then at both, heading for the centre of an arch; he felt the bow dip and the stern heave as they approached – the water was banked up above the bridge and rushed down through the arches in a long sleek black slope. As they whirled under Hornblower bent to his sculls, to give the boat sufficient way to carry her through the eddies which his seaman's instinct warned him would await them below the piers. The crown of the arch brushed his head as he pulled – the floods had risen as high as that. The sound of rushing water echoed strangely under the stonework for a second, and then they were through, with Hornblower tugging madly at the sculls.

One more light on the shore, and then they were in utter blackness again, their sense of direction lost.

'Christ!' said Bush again, this time with utter solemnity, as Hornblower rested on his sculls. The wind shrieked down upon them, blinding them with snow. From the bows came a ghostly chuckle.

'God help sailors,' said Brown 'on a night like this.'

'Carry on with the bailing, Brown, and save your jokes for afterwards,' snapped Hornblower. But he giggled, nevertheless, even in despite of the faint shock he experienced at hearing the lower deck cracking jokes to a captain and a first lieutenant. His ridiculous habit of laughing insanely in the presence of danger or hardship was already ready to master him, and he giggled now, while he dragged at the oars and fought against the wind – he could tell by the way the blades dragged through the water that the boat was making plenty of leeway. He only stopped giggling when he realised with a shock that it was hardly more than two hours back that he had first uttered the prayer about God helping sailors on a night like this. It seemed like a fortnight ago at least that he had last breathed the leathery stuffiness of the inside of the coach.

The boat grated heavily over gravel, caught, freed itself, bumped again, and stuck fast. All Hornblower's shoving with the sculls would not get her afloat again.

'Nothing to do but shove her off,' said Hornblower, laying down his sculls.

He stepped over the side into the freezing water, slipping on the stones, with Brown beside him. Between them they ran her out easily, scrambled on board, and Hornblower made haste to seize the sculls and pull her into the wind. Yet a few seconds later they were aground again. It was the beginning of a nightmare period. In the darkness Hornblower could not guess whether their difficulties arose from the action of the wind in pushing them against the bank, or from the fact that the river was sweeping round in a great bend here, or whether they had strayed into a side channel with scanty water. However it was, they were continually having to climb out and shove the boat off. They slipped and plunged over the invisible stones; they fell waist deep into unseen pools, they cut themselves and bruised themselves in this mad game of blind man's buff with the treacherous river. It was bitterly cold now; the sides of the boat were glazed with ice. In the midst of his struggles with the boat Hornblower was consumed with anxiety for Bush, bundled up in cloak and blankets in the stern.

'How is it with you, Bush?' he asked.

'I'm doing well, sir,' said Bush.

'Warm enough?'

'Aye aye, sir. I've only one foot to get wet now, you know, sir.'

He was probably being deceitfully cheerful, thought Hornblower, standing ankle deep in rushing water and engaged in what seemed to be an endless haul of the boat through invisible shallows. Blankets or no blankets, he must be horribly cold and probably wet as well, and he was a convalescent who ought to have been kept in bed. Bush might die out here this very night. The boat came free with a run, and Hornblower staggered back waist deep in the chill water. He swung himself in over the swaying gunwale while Brown, who apparently had been completely submerged, came spluttering in over the other side. Each of them grabbed a scull in their anxiety to have something to do while the wind cut them to the bone.

The current whirled them away. Their next contact with the shore was among trees – willows, Hornblower guessed in the darkness. The branches against which they scraped volleyed snow at them, scratched them and whipped them, held the boat fast until by feeling round in the darkness they found the obstruction and lifted it clear. By the time they were free of the willows Hornblower had almost decided that he would rather have rocks if he could choose and he giggled again, feebly, with his teeth chattering. Naturally, they were among rocks again quickly enough; at this point apparently there was a sort of minor rapid down which the river rolled among rocks and banks of stones.

Already Hornblower was beginning to form a mental picture of the river – long swift reaches alternating with narrow and rock-encumbered stretches, looped back and forth at the whim of the surrounding country. This boat they were in had probably been built close to the spot where they had found her, had been kept there as a ferry boat, probably by farming people, on the clear reach where they had started, and had probably never been more than half a mile from her moorings before. Hornblower, shoving off from a rock, decided that the odds were heavily against her ever seeing her moorings again.

Below the rapid they had a long clear run – Hornblower had no means of judging how long. Their eyes were quick now to pick out the snow-covered shore when it was a yard or more away, and they kept the boat clear. Every glimpse gave them a chance to guess at the course of the river compared with the direction of the wind, so that they could pull a few lusty strokes without danger of running aground as long as there was no obstructions in mid-channel. In fact, it had almost stopped snowing – Hornblower guessed that what little snow was being flung at them by the wind had been blown from branches or scooped from drifts. That did not make it any warmer; every part of the boat was coated with ice – the floorboards were slippery with it except where his heels rested while rowing.

Ten minutes of this would carry them a mile or more – more for certain. He could not guess at all how long they had been travelling, but he could be sure that with the countryside under thick snow they were well ahead of any possible pursuit, and the longer this wonderful rock-free reach endured the safer they would be. He tugged away fiercely, and Brown in the bows responded, stroke for stroke.

'Rapids ahead, sir,' said Bush at length.

Resting on his oar Hornblower could hear, far ahead, the familiar roar of water pouring over rocks; the present rate of progress had been too good to last, and soon they would be whirling down among rocks again, pitching and heaving.

'Stand by to fend off on the port side, Brown,' he ordered.

'Aye aye, sir.'

Hornblower sat on his thwart with his scull poised; the water was sleek and black overside. He felt the boat swing round. The current seemed to be carrying her over to one side, and he was content to let her go. Where the main mass of water made its way was likely to be the clearest channel down the rapid. The roar of the fall was very loud now.

'By God!' said Hornblower in sudden panic, standing up to peer ahead.

It was too late to save themselves – he had noticed the difference in the sound of the fall only when they were too close to escape. Here there was no rapid like those they had already descended, not even one much worse. Here there was a rough dam across the river – a natural transverse ledge, perhaps, which had caught and retained the rocks rolled down in the bed, or else something of human construction. Hornblower's quick brain turned these hypotheses over even as the boat leaped at the drop. Along its whole length water was brimming over the obstruction; at this particular point it surged over in a wide swirl, sleek at the top, and plunging into foaming chaos below. The boat heaved sickeningly over the summit and went down the slope like a bullet. The steep steady wave at the foot was as unyielding as a brick wall as they crashed into it.

Hornblower found himself strangling under the water, the fall still roaring in his ears, his brain still racing. In nightmare helplessness he was scraped over the rocky bottom. The pressure in his lungs began to hurt him. It was agony – agony. Now he was breathing again – one single gulp of air like fire in his throat as he went under again, and down to the rocks at the bottom until his breast was hurting worse than before. Then another quick breath – it was as painful to breathe as it was to strangle. Over and down, his ears roaring and his head swimming. The grinding of the rocks of the river bed over which he was scraped was louder than any clap of thunder he had ever heard. Another gulp of air – it was as if he had been anticipating it, but he had to force himself to make it, for he felt as if it would be easier not to, easier to allow this agony in his breast to consume him.

Down again, to the roar and torment below the surface. His brain, still working like lightning, guessed how it was with him. He was caught in the swirl below the dam, was being swept downstream on the surface, pushed into the undertow and carried up again along the bottom, to be spewed up and granted a second in which to breathe before being carried round again. He was ready this time to strike out feebly, no more than three strokes, sideways, at his next breathing space. When he was next sucked down the pain in his breast was inconceivably greater and blending with that agony was another just as bad of which he now became conscious – the pain of the cold in his limbs. It called for every scrap of his resolution to force himself to take another breath and to continue his puny effort sideways when the time came for it. Down again; he was ready to die, willing, anxious to die, now, so that this pain would stop. A bit of board had come into his hand, with nails protruding from one end. That must be a plank from the boat, shattered to fragments and whirling round and round with him, eternally. Then his resolution flickered up once more. He caught a gulp of air as he rose to the surface, striking out for the shore, waiting in apprehension to be dragged down. Marvellous; he had time for a second breath, and a third. Now he wanted to live, so heavenly were these painless breaths he was taking. But he was so tired, and so sleepy. He got to his feet, fell as the water swept his legs away again from under him, splashed and struggled in mad panic, scrambling through the shallows on his hands and knees. Rising, he took two more steps, before falling with his face in the snow and his feet still trailing in the rushing water.

He was roused by a human voice bellowing apparently in his ear. Lifting his head he saw a faint dark figure a yard or two away, bellowing with Brown's voice.

'Ahoy! Cap'n, Cap'n! Oh, Cap'n!'

'I'm here,' moaned Hornblower, and Brown came and knelt over him.

'Thank God, sir,' he said, and then, raising his voice 'The cap'n's here, Mr Bush.'

'Good!' said a feeble voice five yards away.

At that Hornblower fought down his nauseating weakness and sat up. If Bush were still alive he must be looked after at once. He must be naked and wet, exposed in the snow to this cutting wind. Hornblower reeled to his feet, staggered, clutched Brown's arm, and stood with his brain whirling.

'There's a light up there, sir,' said Brown, hoarsely. 'I was just goin' to it if you hadn't answered my hail.'

'A light?'

Hornblower passed his hands over his eyes and peered up the bank. Undoubtedly it was a light shining faintly, perhaps a hundred yards away. To go there meant surrender – that was the first reaction of Hornblower's mind. But to stay here meant death. Even if by a miracle they could light a fire and survive the night here they would be caught next morning – and Bush would be dead for certain. There had been a faint chance of life when he planned the escape from the coach, and now it was gone.

'We'll carry Mr Bush up,' he said.

'Aye aye, sir.'

They plunged through the snow to where Bush lay.

'There's a house just up the bank, Bush. We'll carry you there.'

Hornblower was puzzled by his ability to think and to speak while he felt so weak; the ability seemed unreal, fictitious.

'Aye aye, sir.'

They stooped and lifted him up between them, linking hands under his knees and behind his back. Bush put his arms round their necks; the flannel nightshirt dripped a further stream of water as they lifted him. Then they started trudging, knee deep in the snow, up the bank towards the distant light.

They stumbled over obstructions hidden in the snow. They slipped and staggered. Then they slid down a bank and fell, all together, and Bush gave a cry of pain.

'Hurt, sir?' asked Brown.

'Only jarred my stump. Captain, leave me here and send down help from the house.'

Hornblower could still think. Without Bush to burden them they might reach the house a little quicker, but he could imagine all the delays that would ensue after they had knocked at the door – the explanations which would have to be made in his halting French, the hesitation and the time-wasting before he could get a carrying party started off to find Bush – who meanwhile would be lying wet and naked in the snow. A quarter of an hour of it would kill Bush, and he might be exposed for twice as long as that. And there was the chance that there would be no one in the house to help carry him.

'No,' said Hornblower cheerfully. 'It's only a little way. Lift, Brown.'

They reeled along through the snow towards the light. Bush was a heavy burden – Hornblower's head was swimming with fatigue and his arms felt as if they were being dragged out of their sockets. Yet somehow within the shell of his fatigue the inner kernel of his brain was still active and restless.

'How did you get out of the river?' he asked, his voice sounding flat and unnatural in his ears.

'Current took us to the bank at once, sir,' said Bush, faintly surprised. 'I'd only just kicked my blankets off when I touched a rock, and there was Brown beside me hauling me out.'

'Oh,' said Hornblower.

The whim of a river in flood was fantastic; the three of them had been within a yard of each other when they entered the water, and he had been dragged under while the other two had been carried to safety. They could not guess at his desperate struggle for life, and they would never know of it, for he would never be able to tell them about it. He felt for the moment a bitter sense of grievance against them, resulting from his weariness and his weakness. He was breathing heavily, and he felt as if he would give a fortune to lay down his burden and rest for a couple of minutes; but his pride forbade, and they went on through the snow, stumbling over the inequalities below the surface. The light was coming near at last.

They heard a faint inquiring bark from a dog.

'Give 'em a hail, Brown,' said Hornblower.

'Ahoy!' roared Brown. 'House ahoy!'

Instantly two dogs burst into a clamorous barking.

'Ahoy!' yelled Brown again, and they staggered on. Another light flashed into view from another part of the house. They seemed to be in some kind of garden now; Hornblower could feel plants crushing under his feet in the snow, and the thorns of a rose tree tore at his trouser leg. The dogs were barking furiously. Suddenly a voice came from a dark upper window.

'Who is there?' it asked in French.

Hornblower prodded at his weary brain to find words to reply.

'Three men,' he said. 'Wounded.'

That was the best he could do.

'Come nearer,' said the voice, and they staggered forward, slipped down an unseen incline, and halted in the square of light cast by the big lighted window in the ground floor, Bush in his nightshirt resting in the arms of the bedraggled other two.

'Who are you?'

'Prisoners of war,' said Hornblower.

'Wait one moment, if you please,' said the voice politely.

They stood shuddering in the snow until a door opened near the lighted window, showing a bright rectangle of light and some human silhouettes.

'Come in, gentlemen,' said the polite voice.

VII

The door opened into a stone-flagged hall; a tall thin man in a blue coat with a glistening white cravat stood there to welcome them, and at his side was a young woman, her shoulders bare in the lamplight. There were three others, too – maidservants and a butler, Hornblower fancied vaguely, as he advanced into the hall under the burden of Bush's weight.

On a side table the lamplight caught the ivory butts of a pair of pistols, evidently laid there by their host on his deciding that his nocturnal visitors were harmless. Hornblower and Brown halted again for a moment, ragged and dishevelled and daubed with snow, and water began to trickle at once to the floor from their soaking garments; and Bush was between them, one foot in a grey worsted sock sticking out under the hem of his flannel nightshirt. Hornblower's constitutional weakness almost overcame him again and he had to struggle hard to keep himself from giggling as he wondered how these people were explaining to themselves the arrival of a nightshirted cripple out of a snowy night.

At least his host had sufficient self-control to show no surprise.

'Come in, come in,' he said. He put his hand to a door beside him and then withdrew it. 'You will need a better fire than I can offer you in the drawing-room. Felix, show the way to the kitchen – I trust you gentlemen will pardon my receiving you there? This way, sirs. Chairs, Felix, and send the maids away.'

It was a vast, low-ceilinged room, stone-flagged like the hall. Its grateful warmth was like Paradise; in the hearth glowed the remains of a fire and all round them kitchen utensils winked and glittered. The woman without a word piled fresh billets of wood upon the fire and set to work with bellows to work up a blaze. Hornblower noticed the glimmer of her silk dress; her piled-up hair was golden, nearly auburn.

'Cannot Felix do that, Marie, my dear? Very well, then. As you will,' said their host. 'Please sit down, gentlemen. Wine, Felix.'

They lowered Bush into a chair before the fire. He sagged and wavered in his weakness, and they had to support him; their host clucked in sympathy.

'Hurry with those glasses, Felix, and then attend to the beds. A glass of wine, sir? And for you, sir? Permit me.'

The woman he had addressed as 'Marie' had risen from her knees, and withdrew silently; the fire was crackling bravely amid its battery of roasting spits and cauldrons. Hornblower was shivering uncontrollably, nevertheless, in his dripping clothes. The glass of wine he drank was of no help to him; the hand he rested on Bush's shoulder shook like a leaf.

'You will need dry clothes,' said their host. 'If you will permit me, I will—'

He was interrupted by the re-entrance of the butler and Marie, both of them with their arms full of clothes and blankets.

'Admirable!' said their host. 'Felix, you will attend these gentlemen. Come, my dear.'

The butler held a silken nightshirt to the blaze while Hornblower and Brown stripped Bush of his wet clothes and chafed him with a towel.

'I thought I should never be warm again,' said Bush, when his head came out through the collar of the nightshirt. 'And you, sir? You shouldn't have troubled about me. Won't you change your clothes now, sir? I'm all right.'

'We'll see you comfortable first,' said Hornblower. There was a fierce perverse pleasure in neglecting himself to attend to Bush. 'Let me look at that stump of yours.'

The blunt seamed end still appeared extraordinarily healthy. There was no obvious heat or inflammation when Hornblower took it in his hand, no sign of pus exuding from the scars. Felix found a cloth in which Hornblower bound it up, while Brown wrapped him about in a blanket.

'Lift him now, Brown. We'll put him into bed.'

Outside in the flagged hall they hesitated as to which way to turn, when Marie suddenly appeared from the left-hand door.

'In here,' she said; her voice was a harsh contralto. 'I have had a bed made up on the ground floor for the wounded man. I thought it would be more convenient.'

One maid – a gaunt old woman, rather – had just taken a warming pan from between the sheets; the other was slipping a couple of hot bottles into the bed. Hornblower was impressed by Marie's practical forethought. He tried with poor success to phrase his thanks in French while they lowered Bush into bed and covered him up.

'God, that's good, thank you, sir,' said Bush.

They left him with a candle burning at his bedside – Hornblower was in a perfect panic now to strip off his wet clothes before that roaring kitchen fire. He towelled himself with a warm towel and slipped into a warm woollen shirt; standing with his bare legs toasting before the blaze he drank a second glass of wine. Fatigue and cold fell away from him, and he felt exhilarated and lightheaded as a reaction. Felix crouched before him tendering him a pair of trousers, and he stepped into them and suffered Felix to tuck in his shirt tails and button him up – it was the first time since childhood that he had been helped into his trousers, but this evening it seemed perfectly natural. Felix crouched again to put on his socks and shoes, stood to buckle his stock and help him on with waistcoat and coat.

'Monsieur le Comte and Madame la Vicomtesse await monsieur in the drawing room,' said Felix – it was odd how, without a word of explanation, Felix had ascertained that Brown was of a lower social level. The very clothes he had allotted to Brown indicated that.

'Make yourself comfortable here, Brown,' said Hornblower.

'Aye aye, sir,' said Brown, standing at attention with his black hair in a rampant mass – only Hornblower had had an opportunity so far of using a comb.

Hornblower stepped in to look at Bush, who was already asleep, snoring faintly at the base of his throat. He seemed to have suffered no ill effects from his immersion and exposure – his iron frame must have grown accustomed to wet and cold during twenty-five years at sea. Hornblower blew out the candle and softly closed the door, motioning to the butler to precede him. At the drawing-room door Felix asked Hornblower his name, and when he announced him Hornblower was oddly relieved to hear him make a sad hash of the pronunciation – it made Felix human again.

His host and hostess were seated on either side of the fire at the far end of the room, and the Count rose to meet him.

'I regret,' he said, 'that I did not quite hear the name which my major-domo announced.'

'Captain Horatio Hornblower, of His Britannic Majesty's ship *Sutherland*,' said Hornblower.

'It is the greatest pleasure to meet you, Captain,' said the Count, side-stepping the difficulty of pronunciation with the agility to be expected of a representative of the old régime. 'I am Lucien Antoine de Ladon, Comte de Graçay.'

The men exchanged bows.

'May I present you to my daughter-in-law? Madame la Vicomtesse de Graçay.'

'Your servant, ma'am,' said Hornblower, bowing again, and then felt like a graceless lout because the English formula had risen to his lips by the instinct the action prompted. He hurriedly racked his brains for the French equivalent, and ended in a shamefaced mumble of 'Enchanté.'

The Vicomtesse had black eyes in the maddest contrast with her nearly auburn hair. She was stoutly – one might almost say stockily – built, and was somewhere near thirty years of age, dressed in black silk which left sturdy white shoulders exposed. As she curtseyed her eyes met his in complete friendliness.

'And what is the name of the wounded gentleman whom we have the honour of entertaining?' she asked; even to Hornblower's unaccustomed ear her French had a different quality from the Count's.

'Bush,' said Hornblower, grasping the import of the question with an effort. 'First lieutenant of my ship. I have left my servant, Brown, in the kitchen.'

'Felix will see that he is comfortable,' interposed the Count. 'What of yourself, Captain? Some food? A glass of wine?'

'Nothing, thank you,' said Hornblower. He felt in no need of food in this mad world, although he had not eaten since noon.

'Nothing, despite the fatigues of your journey?'

There could hardly be a more delicate allusion than that to Hornblower's recent arrival through the snow, drenched and battered.

'Nothing, thank you,' repeated Hornblower.

'Will you not sit down, Captain?' asked the Vicomtesse.

They all three found themselves chairs.

'You will pardon us, I hope,' said the Count 'if we continue to speak French. It is ten years since I last had occasion to speak English, and even then I was a poor scholar, while my daughter-in-law speaks none.'

'Bush,' said the Vicomtesse. 'Brown. I can say those names. But your name, Captain, is difficult. Orrenblor – I cannot say it.'

'Bush! Orrenblor!' exclaimed the Count, as though reminded of something. 'I suppose you are aware, Captain, of what the French newspapers have been saying about you recently?'

'No,' said Hornblower. 'I should like to know, very much.'

'Pardon me, then.'

The Count took up a candle and disappeared through a door; he returned quickly enough to save Hornblower from feeling too self-conscious in the silence that ensued.

'Here are recent copies of the *Moniteur*,' said the Count. 'I must apologise in advance, Captain, for the statements made in them.'

He passed the newspapers over to Hornblower, indicating various columns in them. The first one briefly announced that a dispatch by semaphore just received from Perpignan informed the Ministry of Marine that an English ship of the line had been captured at Rosas. The next was the amplification. It proclaimed in triumphant detail that the hundred-gun ship *Sutherland* which had been committing acts of piracy in the Mediterranean had met a well-deserved fate at the hands of the Toulon fleet directed by Admiral Cosmao. She had been caught unawares and overwhelmed, and had 'pusillanimously hauled down the colours of perfidious Albion under which she had committed so many dastardly crimes'. The French public was assured that her resistance had been of the poorest, it being advanced in corroboration that only one French ship had lost a topmast during the cannonade. The action took place under the eyes of thousands of the Spanish populace, and would be a salutary lesson to those few among them who, deluded by English lies or seduced by English gold, still cherished notions of resistance to their lawful sovereign King Joseph.

Another article announced that the infamous Captain Hornblower and his equally wicked lieutenant Bush had surrendered in the *Sutherland*, the latter being one of the few wounded in the encounter. All those peace-loving French citizens who had suffered as a result of their piratical depredations could rest assured that a military court would inquire immediately into the crimes these two had committed. Too long had the modern Carthage sent forth her minions to execute her vile plans with impunity! Their guilt would soon be demonstrated to a world which would readily discriminate between the truth and the vile lies which the poisoned pens in Canning's pay so persistently poured forth.

Yet another article declared that as a result of Admiral Cosmao's great victory over the *Sutherland* at Rosas English naval action on the coasts of Spain had ceased, and the British army of Wellington, so imprudently exposed to the might of the French arms, was already suffering seriously from a shortage of supplies. Having lost one vile accomplice in the person of the detestable Hornblower, perfidious Albion was about to lose another on Wellington's inevitable surrender.

Hornblower read the smudgy columns in impotent fury. 'A hundred-gun ship', forsooth, when the *Sutherland* was only a seventy-four and almost the smallest of her rate in the list! 'Resistance of the poorest'! 'One topmast lost'! The *Sutherland* had beaten three bigger ships into wrecks and had disabled a fourth before surrendering. 'One of the few wounded'! Two-thirds of the *Sutherland*'s crew had given life or limb, and with his own eyes he had seen the blood running from the scuppers of the French flagship. 'English naval action had ceased'! There was not a hint that a fortnight after the capture of the *Sutherland* the whole French squadron had been destroyed in the night attack on Rosas Bay.

His professional honour had been impugned; the circumstantial lies had been well told, too – that subtle touch about only one topmast being lost had every appearance of verisimilitude. Europe might well believe that he was a poltroon as well as a pirate, and he had not the slightest chance of contradicting what had been said. Even in England such reports must receive a little credit – most of the *Moniteur*'s bulletins, especially the naval ones, were reproduced in the English press. Lady Barbara, Maria, his brother captains, must all be wondering at the present moment just how much credence should be given to the *Moniteur*'s statements. Accustomed as the world might be to Bonaparte's exaggerations people could hardly be expected to realise that in this case everything said – save for the bare statement of his surrender – had been completely untrue. His hands shook a little with the passion that consumed him, and he was conscious of the hot flush in his cheeks as he looked up and met the eyes of the others. It was hard to grope for his few French words while he was so angry.

'He is a liar!' he spluttered at length. 'He dishonours me!'

'He dishonours everyone,' said the Count, quietly.

'But this – but this,' said Hornblower, and then gave up the struggle to express himself in French. He remembered that while he was in captivity in Rosas he had realised that Bonaparte would publish triumphant bulletins regarding the capture of the *Sutherland*, and it was only weakness to be enraged by them now that he was confronted by them.

'Will you forgive me,' asked the Count ' if I change the subject and ask you a few personal questions?'

'Certainly.'

'I presume you have escaped from an escort which was taking you to Paris?'

'Yes,' said Hornblower.

'Where did you escape?'

Hornblower tried to explain that it was at a point where a by-road ran down to the river's edge, six kilometres on the farther side of Nevers. Haltingly, he went on to describe the conditions of his escape, the silencing of Colonel Caillard, and the wild navigation of the river in the darkness.

'That must have been about six o'clock, I presume?' asked the Count.

'Yes.'

'It is only midnight now, and you have come twenty kilometres. There is not the slightest chance of your escort seeking you here for some time. That is what I wanted to know. You will be able to sleep in tranquillity tonight, Captain.'

Hornblower realised with a shock that he had long taken it for granted that he would sleep in tranquillity, at least as far as immediate recapture was concerned; the atmosphere of the house had been too friendly for him to feel otherwise. By way of reaction, he began to feel doubts.

'Are you going to – to tell the police we are here?' he asked; it was infernally difficult to phrase that sort of thing in a foreign language and avoid offence.

'On the contrary,' said the Count. 'I shall tell them, if they ask me, that you are not here. I hope you will consider yourself among friends in this house, Captain, and that you will make your stay here as long as is convenient to you.'

'Thank you, sir. Thank you very much,' stammered Hornblower.

'I may add,' went on the Count 'that circumstances – it is too long a story to tell you – make it quite certain that the authorities will accept my statement that I know nothing of your whereabouts. To say nothing of the fact that I have the honour to be mayor of this commune and so represent the government, even though my *adjoint* does all the work of the position.'

Hornblower noticed his wry smile as he used the word 'honour', and tried to stammer a fitting reply, to which the Count listened politely. It was amazing, now Hornblower came to think about it, that chance should have led him to a house where he was welcomed and protected, where he might consider himself safe from pursuit, and sleep in peace. The thought of sleep made him realise that he was desperately tired, despite his excitement. The impassive face of the Count, and the friendly face of his daughter-in-law, gave no hint as to whether or not they too were tired; for a moment Hornblower wrestled with the problem which always presents itself the first evening of one's stay in a strange house – whether the guest should suggest going to bed or wait for a hint from his host. He made his resolve, and rose to his feet.

'You are tired,' said the Vicomtesse – the first words she had spoken for some time.

'Yes,' said Hornblower.

'I will show you your room, sir. Shall I ring for your servant? No?' said the Count.

Out in the hall, after Hornblower had bowed good night, the Count indicated the pistols still lying on the side table.

'Perhaps you would care to have those at your bedside?' he asked politely. 'You might feel safer?'

Hornblower was tempted, but finally he refused the offer. Two pistols would not suffice to save him from Bonaparte's police should they come for him.

'As you will,' said the Count, leading the way with a candle. 'I loaded them when I heard your approach because there was a chance that you were a party of réfractaires – young men who evade the conscription by hiding in the woods and mountains. Their number has grown considerably since the latest decree anticipating the conscription. But I quickly realised that no gang meditating mischief would proclaim its proximity with shouts. Here is your room, sir. I hope you will find here everything you require. The clothes you are wearing appear to fit so tolerably that perhaps you will continue to wear them tomorrow? Then I shall say good night. I hope you will sleep well.'

The bed was deliciously warm as Hornblower slid into it and closed the curtains. His thoughts were pleasantly muddled; disturbing memories of the appalling swoop of the little boat down the long black slope of water at the fall, and of his agonised battle for life in the water, were overridden by mental pictures of the Count's long, mobile face and of Caillard bundled in his cloak and dumped down upon the carriage floor. He did not sleep well, but he could hardly be said to have slept badly.

VIII

Felix entered the next morning bearing a breakfast tray, and he opened the bed curtains while Hornblower lay dazed in his bed. Brown followed Felix, and while the latter arranged the tray on the bedside table he applied himself to the task of gathering together the clothes which Hornblower had flung down the night before, trying hard to assume the unobtrusive deference of a gentleman's servant. Hornblower sipped

gratefully at the steaming coffee, and bit into the bread; Brown recollected another duty and hurried across to open the bedroom curtains.

'Gale's pretty nigh dropped, sir,' he said. 'I think what wind there's
left is backing southerly, and we might have a thaw.'

Through the deep windows of the bedroom Hornblower could see
from his bed a wide landscape of dazzling white, falling steeply away
down to the river which was black by contrast, appearing like a black
crayon mark on white paper. Trees stood out starkly through the snow
where the gale had blown their branches bare; down beside the river
the willows there – some of them stood in the flood, with white foam at
their feet – were still domed with white. Hornblower fancied he could
hear the rushing of water, and was certain that he could hear the regular
droning of the fall, the tumbling water at whose foot was just visible over
the shoulder of the bank. Far beyond the river could be seen the snow-
covered roofs of a few small houses.

'I've been in to Mr Bush already, sir,' said Brown – Hornblower felt
a twinge of remorse at being too interested in the landscape to have a
thought to spare for his lieutenant – 'and he's all right an' sends you his
best respects, sir. I'm goin' to help him shave after I've attended to you,
sir.'

'Yes,' said Hornblower.

He felt deliciously languorous. He wanted to be idle and lazy. The
present was a moment of transition between the miseries and dangers
of yesterday and the unknown activities of today, and he wanted that
moment to be prolonged on and on indefinitely; he wanted time to
stand still, the pursuers who were seeking him on the other side of
Nevers to be stilled into an enchanted rigidity while he lay here free
from danger and responsibility. The very coffee he had drunk contributed to his ease by relieving his thirst without stimulating him to
activity. He sank imperceptibly and delightfully into a vague day-dream;
it was hateful of Brown to recall him to wakefulness again by a respectful shuffling of his feet.

'Right,' said Hornblower resigning himself to the inevitable.

He kicked off the bedclothes and rose to his feet, the hard world of the
matter-of-fact closing round him, and his day-dreams vanishing like
the cloud-colours of a tropical sunrise. As he shaved, and washed in the
absurdly small basin in the corner, he contemplated grimly the prospect
of prolonged conversation in French with his hosts. He grudged the
effort it would involve, and he envied Bush his complete inability to
speak any other tongue than English. Having to exert himself today
loomed as large to his selfwilled mind as the fact that he was doomed to
death if he were caught again. He listened absentmindedly to Bush's
garrulity when he went in to visit him, and did nothing at all to satisfy
his curiosity regarding the house in which they had found shelter, and

the intentions of their hosts. Nor was his mood relieved by his pitying contempt for himself at thus working off his ill temper on his unoffending lieutenant. He deserted Bush as soon as he decently could and went off in search of his hosts in the drawing room.

The Vicomtesse alone was there, and she made him welcome with a smile.

'M. de Graçay is at work in his study,' she explained. 'You must be content with my entertaining you this morning.'

To say even the obvious in French was an effort for Hornblower, but he managed to make the suitable reply, which the lady received with a smile. But conversation did not proceed smoothly, with Hornblower having laboriously to build up his sentences beforehand and to avoid the easy descent into Spanish which was liable to entrap him whenever he began to think in a foreign tongue. Nevertheless, the opening sentences regarding the storm last night, the snow in the fields, and the flood, elicited for Hornblower one interesting fact – that the river whose roar they could hear was the Loire, four hundred miles or more from its mouth in the Bay of Biscay. A few miles upstream lay the town of Nevers; a little way downstream the large tributary, the Allier, joined the Loire, but there was hardly a house and no village on the river in that direction for twenty miles as far as Pouilly – from whose vineyards had come the wine they had drunk last night.

'The river is only as big as this in winter,' said the Vicomtesse. 'In summer it dwindles away to almost nothing. There are places where one can walk across it, from one bank to the other. Then it is blue, and its banks are golden, but now it is black and ugly.'

'Yes,' said Hornblower.

He felt a peculiar tingling sensation down his thighs and calves as the words recalled his experience of the night before, the swoop over the fall and the mad battle in the flood. He and Bush and Brown might easily all be sodden corpses now, rolling among the rocks at the bottom of the river until the process of corruption should bring them to the surface.

'I have not thanked you and M. de Graçay for your hospitality,' he said, picking his words with care. 'It is very kind of the Count.'

'Kind? He is the kindest man in the whole world. I can't tell you how good he is.'

There was no doubting the sincerity of the Count's daughter-in-law as she made this speech; her wide humorous mouth parted and her dark eyes glowed.

'Really?' said Hornblower – the word 'vraiment' slipped naturally from his lips now that some animation had come into the conversation.

'Yes, really. He is good all the way through. He is sweet and kind, by nature and not – not as a result of experience. He has never said a

word to me, not once, not a word, about the disappointment I have
caused him.'

'You, madame?'

'Yes. Oh, isn't it obvious? I am not a great lady – Marcel should not
have married me. My father is a Normandy peasant, on his own land,
but a peasant all the same, while the Ladons, Counts of Graçay, go back
to – to Saint Louis, or before that. Marcel told me how disappointed
was the Count at our marriage, but I should never have known of it
otherwise – not by word or by action. Marcel was the eldest son then,
because Antoine had been killed at Austerlitz. And Marcel is dead, too –
he was wounded at Aspern – and I have no son, no child at all, and the
Count has never reproached me, never.'

Hornblower tried to make some kind of sympathetic noise.

'And Louis-Marie is dead as well now. He died of fever in Spain. He
was the third son, and M. de Graçay is the last of the Ladons. I think
it broke his heart, but he has never said a bitter word.'

'The three sons are all dead?' said Hornblower.

'Yes, as I told you. M. de Graçay was an émigré – he lived in your
town of London with his children for years after the Revolution. And
then the boys grew up and they heard of the fame of the Emperor – he
was First Consul then – and they all wanted to share in the glory of
France. It was to please them that the Count took advantage of the amnesty and returned here – this is all that the Revolution has left of his
estates. He never went to Paris. What would he have in common with
the Emperor? But he allowed his sons to join the army, and now they are
all dead, Antoine and Marcel and Louis-Marie. Marcel married me
when his regiment was billeted in our village, but the others never
married. Louis-Marie was only eighteen when he died.'

'Terrible!' said Hornblower.

The banal word did not express his sense of the pathos of the story,
but it was all he could think of. He understood now the Count's statement of the night before that the authorities would be willing to accept
his bare word that he had seen nothing of any escaped prisoners. A
great gentleman whose three sons had died in the Imperial service would
never be suspected of harbouring fugitives.

'Understand me,' went on the Vicomtesse. 'It is not because he
hates the Emperor that he makes you welcome here. It is because he is
kind, because you needed help – I have never known him to deny help to
anyone. Oh, it is hard to explain, but I think you understand.'

'I understand,' said Hornblower, gently.

His heart warmed to the Vicomtesse. She might be lonely and unhappy; she was obviously as hard as her peasant upbringing would
make her, and yet her first thought was to impress upon this stranger
the goodness and virtue of her father-in-law. With her nearly-red hair

and brown eyes she was a striking-looking woman, and her skin had a thick creaminess which enhanced her looks; only a slight irregularity of feature and the wideness of her mouth prevented her from being of dazzling beauty. No wonder the young subaltern in the Hussars – Hornblower took it for granted that the dead Vicomte de Graçay had been a subaltern of Hussars – had fallen in love with her during the dreary routine of training, and had insisted on marrying her despite his father's opposition. Hornblower thought he would not find it hard to fall in love with her himself if he were mad enough to allow such a thing to happen while his life was in the hands of the Count.

'And you?' asked the Vicomtesse. 'Have you a wife in England? Children?'

'I have a wife,' said Hornblower.

Even without the handicap of a foreign language it was difficult to describe Maria to a stranger; he said that she was short and dark, and he said no more. Her red hands and dumpy figure, her loyalty to him which cloyed when it did not irritate – he could not venture on a fuller description lest he should betray the fact that he did not love her, and he had never betrayed it yet.

'So that you have no children either?' asked the Vicomtesse again.

'Not now,' said Hornblower.

This was torment. He told of how little Horatio and little Maria had died of smallpox in a Southsea lodging, and then with a gulp he went on to say that there was another child due to be born in January next.

'Let us hope you will be home with your wife then,' said the Vicomtesse. 'Today you will be able to discuss plans of escape with my father-in-law.'

As if this new mention of his name had summoned him, the Count came into the room on the tail of this sentence.

'Forgive my interrupting you,' he said, even while he returned Hornblower's bow, 'but from my study window I have just seen a gendarme approaching this house from a group which was riding along the river bank. Would it be troubling you too much, Captain, to ask you to go into Monsieur Bush's room for a time? I shall send your servant in to you, too, and perhaps then you would be good enough to lock the door. I shall interview the gendarme myself, and you will only be detained for a few minutes, I hope.'

A gendarme! Hornblower was out of the room and was crossing over to Bush's door before this long speech was finished, while M. de Graçay escorted him thither, unruffled, polite, his words unhurried. Bush was sitting up in bed as Hornblower entered, but what he began to say was broken off by Hornblower's abrupt gesture demanding silence. A moment later Brown tapped at the door and was admitted, Hornblower carefully locking the door after him.

'What is it, sir?' whispered Bush, and Hornblower whispered an explanation, still standing with his hand on the handle, stooping to listen.

He heard a knocking on the outer door, and the rattling of chains as Felix went to open it. Feverishly he tried to hear the ensuing conversation, but he could not understand it. But the gendarme was speaking with respect, and Felix in the flat passionless tones of the perfect butler. He heard the tramp of booted feet and the ring of spurs as the gendarme was led into the hall, and then all the sounds died away with the closing of a door upon them. The minutes seemed like hours as he waited. Growing aware of his nervousness he forced himself to turn and smile at the others as they sat with their ears cocked, listening.

The wait was too long for them to preserve their tension; soon they relaxed, and grinned at each other, not with hollow mirth as Hornblower's had been at the start. At last a renewed burst of sound from the hall keyed them up again, and they stayed rigid listening to the penetrating voices. And then they heard the clash of the outside door shutting, and the voices ceased. Still it was a long time before anything more happened – five minutes – ten minutes, and then a tap on the door startled them as though it were a pistol shot.

'Can I come in, Captain?' said the Count's voice.

Hurriedly Hornblower unlocked the door to admit him, and even then he had to stand and wait in feverish patience, translating awkwardly while the Count apologised to Bush for intruding upon him, and made polite inquiries about his health and whether he slept well.

'Tell him I slept nicely, if you please, sir,' said Bush.

'I am delighted to hear it,' said the Count. 'Now in the matter of this gendarme—'

Hornblower brought forward a chair for him. He would not allow it to be thought that his impatience overrode his good manners.

'Thank you, Captain, thank you. You are sure I will not be intruding if I stay? That is good of you. The gendarme came to tell me—'

The narrative was prolonged by the need for interpreting to Bush and Brown. The gendarme was one of those posted at Nevers; every available man in that town had been turned out shortly before midnight by a furious Colonel Caillard to search for the fugitives. In the darkness they had been able to do little, but with the coming of the dawn Caillard had begun a systematic search of both banks of the river, seeking for traces of the prisoners and making inquiries at every house and cottage along the banks. The visit of the gendarme had been merely one of routine – he had come to ask if anything had been seen of three escaped Englishmen, and to give warning that they might be in the vicinity. He had been perfectly satisfied with the Count's assurance upon the point. In fact, the gendarme had no expectation of finding the Englishmen alive. The search had already revealed a blanket, one of those which had been used by the wounded Englishman, lying on the bank down by the Bec d'Allier, which seemed a sure indication that their boat had capsized, in which case, with the river in flood, there could be no doubt that they had been drowned. Their bodies would be discovered somewhere along the course of the river during the next few days. The gendarme appeared to be of the opinion that the boat must have upset somewhere in the first rapid they had encountered, before they had gone a mile, so madly was the river running.

'I hope you will agree with me, Captain, that this information is most satisfactory,' added the Count.

'Satisfactory!' said Hornblower. 'Could it be better?'

If the French should believe them to be dead there would be an end to the pursuit. He turned and explained the situation to the others in English, and they endeavoured with nods and smiles to indicate to the Count their gratification.

'Perhaps Bonaparte in Paris will not be satisfied with this bald story,' said the Count. 'In fact I am sure he will not, and will order a further search. But it will not trouble us.'

'Thank you, sir,' said Hornblower, and the Count made a deprecatory gesture.

'It only remains,' he said 'to make up our minds about what you gentlemen would find it best to do in the future. Would it be officious of me to suggest that it might be inadvisable for you to continue your journey while Lieutenant Bush is still unwell?'

'What does he say, sir?' asked Bush – the mention of his name had drawn all eyes on him. Hornblower explained.

'Tell his lordship, sir,' said Bush 'that I can make myself a jury leg in two shakes, an' this time next week I'll be walking as well as he does.'

'Excellent!' said the Count, when this had been translated and expurgated for him. 'And yet I cannot see that the construction of a wooden leg is going to be of much assistance in our problem. You gentlemen might grow beards, or wear disguises. It was in my mind that by posing as German officers in the Imperial service you might, during your future journey, provide an excuse for your ignorance of French. But a missing foot cannot be disguised; for months to come the arrival of a stranger without a foot will recall to the minds of inquisitive police officers the wounded English officer who escaped and was believed to be drowned.'

'Yes,' said Hornblower. 'Unless we could avoid all contact with police officers.'

'That is quite impossible,' said the Count with decision. 'In this French Empire there are police officers everywhere. To travel you will need horses certainly, a carriage very probably. In a journey of a hundred leagues horses and a carriage will bring you for certain to the notice of the police. No man can travel ten miles along a road without having his passport examined.'

The Count pulled in perplexity at his chin; the deep parentheses at the corners of his mobile mouth were more marked than ever.

'I wish,' said Hornblower 'that our boat had not been destroyed last night. On the river, perhaps—'

The idea came up into his mind fully formed and as it did so his eyes met the Count's. He was conscious afresh of a strange sympathy between him and the Count. The same idea was forming in the Count's mind, simultaneously – it was not the first time that he had noticed a similar phenomenon.

'Of course!' said the Count 'the river! How foolish of me not to think of it. As far as Orleans the river is unnavigable; because of the winter floods the banks are practically deserted save at the towns, and there are few of those, which you could pass at night if necessary, as you did at Nevers.'

'Unnavigable, sir?'

'There is no commercial traffic. There are fishermen's boats here and there, and there are a few others engaged in dredging sand from the river bed. That is all. From Orleans to Nantes Bonaparte has been making efforts to render the river available to barges, but I understand he has had small success. And above Briare the new lateral canal carries all the traffic, and the river is deserted.'

'But could we descend it, sir?' persisted Hornblower.

'Oh yes,' said the Count, meditatively. 'You could do so in summer in a small rowing boat. There are many places where it would be difficult, but never dangerous.'

'In summer!' exclaimed Hornblower.

'Why, yes. You must wait until the lieutenant here is well, and then you must build your boat – I suppose you sailors can build your own boat? You cannot hope to start for a long time. And then in January the river usually freezes, and in February come the floods, which last until March. Nothing could live on the river then – especially as it would be too cold and wet for you. It seems to be quite necessary that you should give me the pleasure of your company until April, Captain.'

This was something entirely unexpected, this prospect of waiting for four months the opportunity to start. Hornblower was taken by surprise; he had supposed that a few days, three or four weeks at most, would see them on their way towards England again. For ten years he had never been as long as four months consecutively in the same place – for that matter during those ten years he had hardly spent four months on shore altogether. His mind sought unavailingly for alternatives. To go by road undoubtedly would involve horses, carriages, contact with all sorts of people. He could not hope to bring Bush and Brown successfully through. And if they went by river they obviously would have to wait; in four months Bush could be expected to make a complete recovery, and with the coming of summer they would be able to dispense with the shelter of inns or houses, sleeping on the river bank, avoiding all intercourse with Frenchmen, drifting downstream until they reached the sea.

'If you have fishing rods with you,' supplemented the Count, 'anyone observing you as you go past the towns will look on you as a fishing party out for the day. For some reason which I cannot fully analyse a fresh water fisherman can never be suspected of evil intent – except possibly by the fish.'

Hornblower nodded. It was odd that at that very moment he too had been visualising the boat drifting downstream, with rods out, watched by incurious eyes from the bank. It was the safest way of crossing France which he could imagine.

And yet – April? His child would be born. Lady Barbara might have forgotten that he ever existed.

'It seems monstrous,' he said, 'that you should be burdened with us all through the winter.'

'I assure you, Captain, your presence will give the greatest pleasure both to Madame la Vicomtesse and myself.'

He could only yield to circumstances.

IX

Lieutenant Bush was watching Brown fastening the last strap of his new wooden leg, and Hornblower, from across the room, was watching the pair of them.

''Vast heaving,' said Bush. 'Belay.'

Bush sat on the edge of his bed and moved his leg tentatively.

'Good,' he said. 'Give me your shoulder. Now, heave and wake the dead.'

Hornblower saw Bush rise and stand; he watched his lieutenant's expression change to one of hurt wonderment as he clung to Brown's burly shoulders.

'God!' said Bush feebly, 'how she heaves!'

It was the giddiness only to be expected after weeks of lying and sitting. Evidently to Bush the floor was pitching and tossing, and, judging by the movement of his eyes, the walls were circling round him. Brown stood patiently supporting him as Bush confronted this unexpected phenomenon. Hornblower saw Bush set his jaw, his expression hardening as he battled with his weakness.

'Square away,' said Bush to Brown. 'Set a course for the captain.'

Brown began walking slowly towards Hornblower, Bush clinging to him, the leather-tipped end of the wooden leg falling with a thump on the floor at each effort to take a stride with it – Bush was swinging it too high, while his sound leg sagged at the knee in its weakness.

'God!' said Bush again. 'Easy! Easy!'

Hornblower rose in time to catch him and to lower him into the chair, where Bush sat and gasped. His big white face, already unnaturally pale through long confinement, was whiter than ever. Hornblower remembered with a pang the old Bush, burly and self-confident, with a face which might have been rough-hewn from a solid block of wood; the Bush who feared nothing and was prepared for anything. This Bush was frightened of his weakness. It had not occurred to him that he would have to learn to walk again – and that walking with a wooden leg was another matter still.

'Take a rest,' said Hornblower, 'before you start again.'

Desperately anxious as Bush had been to walk, weary as he was of helplessness, there were times during the next few days when Hornblower had to give him active encouragement while he was learning to walk. All the difficulties that arose had been unforeseen by him, and depressed him out of proportion to their importance. It was a matter of some days before he mastered his giddiness and weakness, and then as as soon as he was able to use the wooden leg effectively they found all manner of things wrong with it. It was none too easy to find the most suitable length, and they discovered to their surprise that it was a matter of some importance to set the leather tip at exactly the right angle to the shaft – Brown and Hornblower between them, at a work-table in the stable yard, made and remade that wooden leg half a dozen times. Bush's bent knee, on which his weight rested when he walked, grew sore and inflamed; they had to pad the kneecap, and remake the socket to fit, more than once, while Bush had to take his exercise in small amounts until the skin over his kneecap grew calloused and more accustomed to its new task. And when he fell – which was often – he caused himself frightful agony in his stump, which was hardly healed; with his knee bent at right angles the stump necessarily bore the brunt of practically any fall, and the pain was acute.

But teaching Bush to walk was one way of passing the long winter days, while orders from Paris turned out the conscripts from every depot round, and set them searching once more for the missing English prisoners. They came on a day of lashing rain, a dozen shivering boys and a sergeant, wet through, and made only the poorest pretence at searching the house and its stabling – Hornblower and Bush and Brown were safe enough behind the hay in an unobtrusive loft. The conscripts were given in the kitchen a better meal by the servants than they had enjoyed for some time, and marched off to prosecute their inquiries elsewhere – every house and village for miles round was at least visited.

After that the next occurrence out of the ordinary was the announcement in Bonaparte's newspapers that the English captain and lieutenant, Hornblower and Bush, had met a well-deserved fate by being drowned in the Loire during an attempt to escape from an escort which was conducting them to their trial; undoubtedly (said the bulletin) this had saved the miscreants from the firing party which awaited them for the purpose of exacting the penalty of their flagrant piracy in the Mediterranean.

Hornblower read the announcement with mixed feelings when the Count showed it to him; not every man has the privilege of reading his own obituary. His first reaction was that it would make their escape considerably easier, seeing that the police would no longer be on the watch for them. But that feeling of relief was swamped by a wave of other feelings. Maria in England would think herself a widow, at this very moment when their child was about to be born. What would it mean to her? Hornblower knew, only too acutely, that Maria loved him as dearly as a woman could love a man, although he only admitted it to himself at moments like this. He could not guess what she would do when she believed him dead. It would be the end of everything she had lived for. And yet she would have a pension, security, a child to cherish. She might set herself, unconsciously, to make a new life for herself. In a clairvoyant moment Hornblower visualised Maria in deep mourning, her mouth set in prim resignation, the coarse red skin of her cheeks wet with tears, and her red hands nervously clasping and unclasping. She had looked like that the summer day when little Horatio and little Maria had been buried in their common grave.

Hornblower shuddered away from the recollection. Maria would at least be in no need of money; the British press would see that the government did its duty there. He could guess at the sort of articles which would be appearing in reply to this announcement of Bonaparte's, the furious indignation that a British officer should be accused of piracy, the openly expressed suspicions that he had been murdered in cold blood and had not died while attempting to escape, the clamour for reprisals. To this day a British newspaper seldom discussed Bonaparte without recalling the death of another British naval captain, Wright, who was said to have committed suicide in prison in Paris. Everyone in England believed that Bonaparte had had him murdered – they would believe the same in this case. It was almost amusing that nearly always the most effective attacks on the tyrant were based on actions on his part which were either trivial or innocent. The British genius for invective and propaganda had long discovered that it paid better to exploit trivialities rather than inveigh broadly against policies and principles; the newspapers would give more space to a condemnation of Bonaparte for causing the death of a single naval officer than to a discussion of the criminal nature of, say, the invasion of Spain, which had resulted in the wanton slaughter of some hundreds of thousands of innocent people.

And Lady Barbara would read that he was dead, too. She would be sorry – Hornblower was prepared to believe that – but how deep her sorrow would be he could not estimate at all. The thought called up all the flood of speculations and doubts which lately he had been trying to forget – whether she cared for him at all or not, whether or not her husband had survived his wound, and what he could do in the matter in any event.

'I am sorry that this announcement seems to cause you so much distress,' said the Count, and Hornblower realised that his expression had been anxiously studied during the whole reading. He had for once been caught off his guard, but he was on guard again at once. He made himself smile.

'It will make our journey through France a good deal easier,' he said.

'Yes. I thought the same as soon as I read it. I can congratulate you, Captain.'

'Thank you,' said Hornblower.

But there was a worried look in the Count's face; he had something more to say and was hesitating to say it.

'What are you thinking about, sir?' asked Hornblower.

'Only this— Your position is in one way more dangerous now. You have been pronounced dead by a government which does not admit mistakes – cannot afford to admit them. I am afraid in case I have done you a disservice in so selfishly accepting the pleasure of your company. If you are recaptured you *will* be dead; the government will see that you die without further attention being called to you.'

Hornblower shrugged his shoulders with a carelessness quite un-assumed for once.

'They were going to shoot me if they caught me. This makes no difference.'

He dallied with the notion of a modern government dabbling in secret murder, for a moment was inclined to put it aside as quite impossible, as something one might believe of the Turks or perhaps even of the Sicilians, but not of Bonaparte, and then he realised with a shock that it was not at all impossible, that a man with unlimited power and much at stake, with underlings on whose silence he could rely, could not be expected to risk appearing ridiculous in the eye of his public when a mere murder would save him. It was a sobering thought, but he made himself smile again, bravely.

'You have all the courage characteristic of your nation, Captain,' said the Count. 'But this news of your death will reach England. I fear that Madame Orrenblor will be distressed by it?'

'I am afraid she will.'

'I could find means of sending a message to England – my bankers can be trusted. But whether it would be advisable is another matter.'

If it were known in England that he was alive it would be known in France, and a stricter search would be instituted for him. It would be terribly dangerous. Maria would draw small profit from the knowledge that he was alive if that knowledge were to cause his death.

'I think it would not be advisable,' said Hornblower.

There was a strange duality in his mind; the Hornblower for whom he could plan so coolly, and whose chances of life he could estimate so closely, was a puppet of the imagination compared with the living, flesh-and-blood Hornblower whose face he had shaved that morning. He knew by experience now that only when a crisis came, when he was swimming for his life in a whirlpool, or walking a quarterdeck in the heat of action, that the two blended together – that was the moment when fear came.

'I hope, Captain,' said the Count, 'that this news has not disturbed you too much?'

'Not at all, sir,' said Hornblower.

'I am delighted to hear it. And perhaps you will be good enough to give Madame la Vicomtesse and myself the pleasure of your company again tonight at whist, you and Mr Bush?'

Whist was the regular way of passing the evening. The Count's delight in the game was another bond of sympathy between him and Hornblower. He was not a player of the mathematical variety, as was Hornblower. Rather did he rely upon a flair, an instinctive system of tactics. It was marvellous how often his blind leads found his partner's short suit and snatched tricks from the jaws of the inevitable, how often he could decide intuitively upon the winning play when confronted by a dilemma. There were rare evenings when this faculty would desert him, and when he would sit with a rueful smile losing rubber after rubber to the remorseless precision of his daughter-in-law and Hornblower. But usually his uncanny telepathic powers would carry him triumphantly through, to the exasperation of Hornblower if they had been opponents, and to his intense satisfaction if they had been partners – exasperation at the failure of his painstaking calculations, or satisfaction of their complete vindication.

The Vicomtesse was a good, well-taught player of no brilliance whose interest in the game, Hornblower suspected, was entirely due to her devotion to her father-in-law. It was Bush to whom these evenings of whist were a genuine penance. He disliked card games of any sort – even the humble vingt-et-un – and in the supreme refinement of whist he was hopelessly at a loss. Hornblower had cured him of some of his worst habits – of asking, for instance, 'What are trumps?' halfway through every hand – had insisted on his counting the cards as they fell, on his learning the conventional leads and discards, and by so doing had made of him a player whose presence three good players could just tolerate rather than miss their evening's amusement; but the evenings to him were periods of agonised, hard-breathing concentration, of flustered mistakes and shamefaced apology – misery made no less acute by the fact that conversation was carried on in French in which he could never acquire any facility. Bush mentally classed together French, whist, and spherical trigonometry as subjects in which he was too old ever to make any further progress, and which he would be content, if he were allowed, to leave entirely to his admired captain.

For Hornblower's French was improving rapidly, thanks to the need for continual use of the language. His defective ear would never allow him to catch the trick of the accent – he would always speak with the tonelessness of the foreigner – but his vocabulary was widening and his grammar growing more certain and he was acquiring a fluency in the idiom which more than once earned him a pretty compliment from his host. Hornblower's pride was held in check by the astonishing fact that below stairs Brown was rapidly acquiring the same fluency. He was living largely with French people, too – with Felix and his wife the housekeeper, and their daughter Louise the maid, and, living over the stables across the yard, the family of Bertrand, who was Felix's brother and incidentally the coachman; Bertrand's wife was the cook, with two daughters to help her in the kitchen, while one of her young sons was footman under Felix and the other two worked in the stables under their father.

Hornblower had once ventured to hint to the Count that the presence of himself and the others might well be betrayed to the authorities by one of all these servants, but the Count merely shook his head with a serene confidence that could not be shaken.

'They will not betray me,' he said, and so intense was his conviction on the point that it carried conviction to Hornblower – and the better he came to know the Count the more obvious it became that no one who knew him well would ever betray him. And the Count added with a wry smile –

'You must remember, too, Captain, that here I *am* the authorities.'

Hornblower could allow his mind to subside into security and sloth again after that – a sense of security with a fantastic quality about it that savoured of a nightmare. It was unreal to be mewed for so long within four walls, deprived of the wide horizons and the endless variety of the sea. He could spend his mornings tramping up and down the stable yard, as though it were a quarterdeck and as though Bertrand and his sons chattering about their duties were a ship's crew engaged on their morning's deck-washing. The smell of the stables and the land winds which came in over the high walls were a poor substitute for the keen freshness of the sea. He spent hours in a turret window of the house, with a spyglass which the Count found for him, gazing round the country-side; the desolate vineyards in their winter solitude, the distant towers of Nevers – the ornate Cathedral tower and the graceful turrets of the Gonzaga palace; the rushing black river, its willows half submerged – the ice which came in January and the snow which three times covered the blank slopes that winter were welcome variations of the monotonous landscape; there were the distant hills and the near-by slopes; the trace of the valley of the Loire winding off into the unknown, and of the valley of the Allier coming down to meet it – to a landsman's eye the prospect from the turret window would have been delightful, even perhaps in the lashing rain that fell so often, but to a seaman and a prisoner it was re-volting. The indefinable charm of the sea was wanting, and so were the mystery and magic and freedom of the sea. Bush and Brown, noting the black bad temper in which Hornblower descended from the turret window after a sitting with his spyglass, wondered why he spent his time in that fashion. He wondered why himself, but weakly he could not stop himself from doing so. Specially marked was his bad temper when the Count and his daughter-in-law went out riding, returning flushed and healthy and happy after some brisk miles of the freedom for which he craved – he was stupidly jealous, he told himself, angrily, but he was jealous all the same.

He was even jealous of the pleasure Bush and Brown took in the building of the new boat. He was not a man of his hands, and once the design of the boat had been agreed upon – its fifteen feet of length and four feet of beam and its flat bottom, he could contribute nothing towards the work except unskilled labour. His subordinates were far more expert with tools than he was, with plane and saw and drill, and characteristi-cally found immense pleasure in working with them. Bush's childish delight in finding his hands, softened by a long period of convalescence, forming their distinguishing callouses again, irritated him. He envied them the simple creative pleasure which they found in watching the boat grow under their hands in the empty loft which they had adopted as a workshop – more still he envied Brown the accuracy of eye he displayed, working with a spokeshave shaping the sculls without any of the apparatus of templates and models and stretched strings which Hornblower would have found necessary.

They were black days, all that winter of confinement. January came, and with it the date when his child would be born; he was half mad with the uncertainty of it all, with his worry about Maria and the child, with the thought that Barbara would think him dead and would forget him.

Even the Count's sweetness of temper and unvarying courtesy irritated him as soon as it began to cloy. He felt he would give a year of his life to hear him make a tart rejoinder to one of Bush's clumsy speeches; the impulse to be rude to the Count, to fire up into a quarrel with him even though – or perhaps because – he owed him his life, was sometimes almost irresistible, and the effort of self-control tried his temper still further. He was surfeited with the County's unwearying goodness, even with the odd way in which their thoughts ran so frequently together; it was queer, even uncanny, to see in the Count so often what seemed like reflections of himself in a mirror. It was madder still to remember that he had felt similar ties of sympathy, sometimes with the wickedest man he had ever known – with el Supremo in Central America.

El Supremo had died for his crime on a scaffold at Panama; Hornblower was worried by the thought that the Count was risking the guillotine at Paris for his friend's sake – it was mad to imagine any parallelism between the careers of el Supremo and the Count, but Hornblower was in a mad mood. He was thinking too much and he had too little to do, and his over-active brain was racketing itself to pieces. There was insanity in indulging in ridiculous mystic speculations about spiritual relationships between himself and the Count and el Supremo, and he knew it. Only self-control and patience were necessary, he told himself, to come safely through these last few weeks of waiting, but his patience seemed to be coming to an end, and he was so weary of exerting self-control.

It was the flesh that saved him when his spirit grew weak. One afternoon, descending from a long and maddening sitting with his telescope in the turret, he met the Vicomtesse in the upper gallery. She was at her boudoir door, about to enter, and she turned and smiled at him as he approached. His head was whirling; somehow his exasperation and feverishness drive him into holding out both his hands to her, risking a rebuff, risking everything, in his longing for some kind of comfort, something to ease this unbearable strain. She put her hands in his, smiling still, and at the touch self-possession broke down. It was madness to yield to the torrent of impulses let loose, but madness was somehow sweet. They were inside the room now, and the door was closed. There was sweet, healthy, satisfying flesh in his arms. There were no doubts nor uncertainties; no mystic speculations. Now blind instinct could take charge, all the bodily urges of months of celibacy. Her lips were ripe and rich and ready, the breasts which he crushed against him were hillocks of sweetness. In his nostrils was the faint intoxicating scent of womanhood.

Beyond the boudoir was the bedroom; they were there now and she was yielding to him. Just as another man might have given way to drink,

might have stupefied his brain in beastly intoxication, so Hornblower
numbed his own brain with lust and passion. He forgot everything, and
he cared for nothing, in this mad lapse from self-control.

And she understood his motives, which was strange, and she did not
resent them, which was stranger still. As his passion ebbed away, he
could see her face again clearly, and her expression was tender and
detached and almost maternal. She was aware of his unhappiness as she
had been aware of his lust for that splendid body of hers. She had given
him her body because of his crying need for it, as she might have given
a cup of water to a man dying of thirst. Now she held his head to her
breast, and stroked his hair, rocking a little as though he were a child,
and murmuring little soothing words to him. A tear fell from her eye
on to Hornblower's temple. She had come to love this Englishman, but
she knew only too well that it was not love which had brought him into
her arms. She knew of the wife and child in England, she guessed at the
existence of the other woman whom he loved. It was not the thought of
them which brought the tears to her eyes; it was the knowledge that
she was not any part of his real life, that this stay of his on the banks of
the Loire was as unreal to him as a dream, something to be endured
until he could escape again to the sea, into the mad world which to him
was sanity, where every day he would encounter peril and discomfort.
These kisses he was giving her meant nothing to him compared with
the business of life, which was war – the same war which had killed her
young husband, the wasteful, prodigal, beastly business which had
peopled Europe with widows and disfigured it with wasted fields and
burned villages. He was kissing her as a man might pat his dog's head
during an exciting business deal.

Then Hornblower lifted his face to hers again, and read the tragedy
in her eyes. The sight of her tears moved him inexpressibly. He stroked
her cheek.

'Oh my dear,' he said in English, and then began to try to find French
words to express what he wanted to say. Tenderness was welling up
within him. In a blinding moment of revelation he realised the love she
bore him, and the motives which had brought her submissively into his
arms. He kissed her mouth, he brushed away the splendid red hair from
her pleading eyes. Tenderness re-awoke passion; and under his caresses
her last reserve broke down.

'I love you!' she sighed, her arms about him. She had not meant to
admit it, either to him or to herself. She knew that if she gave herself to
him with passion he would break her heart in the end, and that he did
not love her, not even now, when tenderness had replaced the blind
lust in his eyes. He would break her heart if she allowed herself to love
him; for one more second she had that clairvoyance before she let herself
sink into the self-deception which she knew in the future she would not

believe to be self-deception. But the temptation to deceive herself into thinking he loved her was overwhelming. She gave herself to him passionately.

X

The affair thus consummated seemed, to Hornblower's mind at least, to clear the air like a thunderstorm. He had something more definite to think about now than mystic speculations; there was Marie's loving kindness to soothe him, and for counter-irritant there was the pricking of his conscience regarding his seduction of his host's daughter-in-law under his host's roof. His uneasiness lest the Count's telepathic powers should enable him to guess at the secret he shared with Marie, the fear lest someone should intercept a glance or correctly interpret a gesture, kept his mind healthily active.

And the love-affair while it ran its course brought with it a queer unexpected happiness. Marie was everything Hornblower could desire as a mistress. By marriage she was of a family noble enough to satisfy his liking for lords, and yet the knowledge that she was of peasant birth saved him from feeling any awe on that account. She could be tender and passionate, protective and yielding, practical and romantic; and she loved him so dearly, while at the same time she remained reconciled to his approaching departure and resolute to help it on in every way, that his heart softened towards her more and more with the passage of the days.

That departure suddenly became a much nearer and more likely possibility – by coincidence it seemed to come up over the horizon from the hoped-for into the expected only a day or two after Hornblower's meeting with Marie in the upper gallery. The boat was finished, and lay, painted and equipped, in the loft ready for them to use; Brown kept it filled with water from the well and proudly announced that it did not leak a drop. The plans for their journey to the sea were taking definite shape. Fat Jeanne the cook baked biscuit for them – Hornblower came triumphantly into his own then, as the only person in the house who knew how ship's biscuit should be baked, and Jeanne worked under his supervision.

Anxious debate between him and the Count had ended in his deciding against running the risk of buying food while on their way unless compelled; the fifty pounds of biscuit which Jeanne baked for them (there was a locker in the boat in which to store it) would provide the three of them with a pound of bread each day for seventeen days, and there was

a sack of potatoes waiting for them, and another of dried peas; and
there were long thin Arles sausages – as dry as sticks, and, to Hornblower's mind, not much more digestible, but with the merit of staying
eatable for long periods – and some of the dry cod which Hornblower
had come to know during his captivity at Ferrol, and a corner of bacon;
taken all in all – as Hornblower pointed out to the Count who was inclined to demur – they were going to fare better on their voyage down
the Loire than they had often fared in the ships of His Majesty King
George. Hornblower, accustomed for so long to sea voyages, never
ceased to marvel at the simplicity of planning a river trip thanks to the
easy solution of the problem of water supply; overside they would have
unlimited fresh water for drinking and washing and bathing – much
better water, too, as he told the Count again, than the stinking green
stuff, alive with animalculae, doled out at the rate of four pints a head a
day, with which people in ships had to be content.

He could anticipate no trouble until they neared the sea; it was only
with their entry into tidal waters that they would be in any danger. He
knew how the French coast swarmed with garrisons and customs officers
– as a lieutenant under Pellew he had once landed a spy in the salt
marshes of Bourgneuf – and it would be under their noses that they would
have to steal a fishing boat and make their way to sea. Thanks to the
Continental system, and the fear of English descents, and precautions
against espionage, tidal waters would be watched closely indeed. But
he felt he could only trust to fortune – it was hard to make plans against
contingencies which might take any shape whatever, and besides, those
dangers were weeks away, and Hornblower's newly contented mind was
actually too lazy to devote much thought to them. And as he grew fonder
of Marie, too, it grew harder to make plans which would take him away
from her. His attachment for her was growing even as strong as that.

It was left to the Count to make the most helpful suggestion of all.

'If you would permit me,' he said, one evening, 'I would like to tell
you of an idea I have for simplifying your passage through Nantes.'

'It would give me pleasure to hear it, sir,' said Hornblower – the
Count's long-winded politeness was infectious.

'Please do not think,' said the Count, 'that I wish to interfere in any
way in the plans you are making, but it occurred to me that your stay
on the coast might be made safer if you assumed the role of a high official
of the customs service.'

'I think it would sir,' said Hornblower, patiently, 'but I do not
understand how I could do it.'

'You would have to announce yourself, if necessary, as a Dutchman,'
said the Count. 'Now that Holland is annexed to France and King
Louis Bonaparte has fled, it is to be presumed that his employés will join
the Imperial service. I think it is extremely likely that, say, a colonel of

Dutch douaniers should visit Nantes to learn how to perform his duties – especially as it was over the enforcement of customs regulations that Bonaparte and his brother fell out. Your very excellent French would be just what might be expected of a Dutch customs officer, even though – please pardon my frankness – you do not speak quite like a native Frenchman.'

'But – but—' stammered Hornblower; it really seemed to him that the Count's customary good sense had deserted him ' – it would be difficult, sir—'

'Difficult?' smiled the Count. 'It might be dangerous, but, if you will forgive my contradicting you so directly, it would hardly be difficult. In your English democracy you perhaps have had no opportunity of seeing how much weight an assured manner and a uniform carry with them in a country like this, which has already made the easy descent from an autocracy to a bureaucracy. A colonel of douaniers on the coast can go anywhere, command anything. He never has to account for himself – his uniform does that for him.'

'But I have no uniform, sir,' said Hornblower, and before the words were out of his mouth he guessed what the Count was going to say.

'We have half a dozen needlewomen in the house,' smiled the Count, 'from Marie here to little Christine, the cook's daughter. It would be odd if between them they could not make uniforms for you and your assistants. I might add that Mr Bush's wound, which we all so much deplore, will be an actual advantage if you adopt the scheme. It is exactly consonant with Bonaparte's methods to provide for an officer wounded in his service by giving him a position in the customs. Mr Bush's presence with you would add a touch of – shall we say realism? – to the effect produced by your appearance.'

The Count gave a little bow to Bush, in apology for thus alluding to Bush's crippled condition, and Bush returned it awkwardly from his chair in bland ignorance of at least two-thirds of what had been said.

The value of the suggestion was obvious to Hornblower at once, and for days afterwards the women in the house were at work cutting and stitching and fitting, until the evening came when the three of them paraded before the Count in their neat coats of blue piped with white and red, and their rakish képis – it was the making of these which had taxed Marie's ingenuity most, for the képi was still at that time an unusual headdress in the French government services. On Hornblower's collar glittered the eight-pointed stars of colonel's rank, and the top of his képi bore the gold-lace rosette; as the three of them rotated solemnly before the Count the latter nodded approvingly.

'Excellent,' he said, and then hesitated. 'There is only one addition which I can think of to add realism. Excuse me a moment.'

He went off to his study, leaving the others looking at each other, but he was back directly with a little leather case in his hand which he proceeded to open. Resting on the silk was a glittering cross of white enamel, surmounted by a golden crown and with a gold medallion in the centre.

'We must pin this on you,' he said. 'No one reaches colonel's rank without the Legion of Honour.'

'Father!' said Marie – it was rare that she used the familiar mode of address with him – 'that was Louis-Marie's.'

'I know, my dear, I know. But it may make the difference between Captain Hornblower's success or – or failure.'

His hands trembled a little, nevertheless, as he pinned the scarlet ribbon to Hornblower's coat.

'Sir – sir, it is too good of you,' protested Hornblower.

The Count's long, mobile face, as he stood up, was sad, but in a moment he had twisted it into his usual wry smile.

'Bonaparte sent it to me,' he said, 'after – after my son's death in Spain. It was a posthumous award. To me of course it is nothing – the trinkets of the tyrant can never mean anything to a Knight of the Holy Ghost. But because of its sentimental value I should be grateful if you would endeavour to preserve it unharmed and return it to me when the war is over.'

'I cannot accept it, sir,' said Hornblower, bending to unpin it again, but the Count checked him.

'Please, Captain,' he said, 'wear it, as a favour to me. It would please me if you would.'

More than ever after his reluctant acceptance did Hornblower's conscience prick him at the thought that he had seduced this man's daughter-in-law while enjoying his hospitality, and later in the evening when he found himself alone with the Count in the drawing room the conversation deepened his sense of guilt.

'Now that your stay is drawing to an end, Captain,' said the Count, 'I know how much I shall miss your presence after you have gone. Your company has given me the very greatest pleasure.'

'I do not think it can compare with the gratitude I feel towards you, sir,' said Hornblower.

The Count waved aside the thanks which Hornblower was endeavouring awkwardly to phrase.

'A little while ago we mentioned the end of the war. Perhaps there will come an end some day, and although I am an old man perhaps I shall live to see it. Will you remember me then, and this little house beside the Loire?'

'Of course, sir,' protested Hornblower. 'I could never forget.'

He looked round the family drawing room, at the silver candelabra, the old-fashioned Louis Seize furniture, the lean figure of the Count in his blue dress-coat.

'I could never forget you, sir,' repeated Hornblower.

'My three sons were all young when they died,' said the Count. 'They were only boys, and perhaps they would not have grown into men I could have been proud of. And already when they went off to serve Bonaparte they looked upon me as an old-fashioned reactionary for whose views they had only the smallest patience – that was only to be expected. If they had lived through the wars we might have become better friends later. But they did not, and I am the last Ladon. I am a lonely man, Captain, lonely under this present régime, and yet I fear that when Bonaparte falls and the reactionaries return to power I shall be as lonely still. But I have not been lonely this winter, Captain.'

Hornblower's heart went out to the lean old man with the lined face sitting opposite him in the uncomfortable armchair.

'But that is enough about myself, Captain,' went on the Count. 'I wanted to tell you of the news which has come through – it is all of it important. The salute which we heard fired yesterday was, as we thought, in honour of the birth of an heir to Bonaparte. There is now a King of Rome, as Bonaparte calls him, to sustain the Imperial throne. Whether it will be any support I am doubtful – there are many Bonapartists who will not, I fancy, be too pleaséd at the thought of the retention of power indefinitely in a Bonaparte dynasty. And the fall of Holland is undoubted – there was actual fighting between the troops of Louis Bonaparte and those of Napoleon Bonaparte over the question of customs enforcement. France now extends to the Baltic – Hamburg and Lubeck are French towns like Amsterdam and Leghorn and Trieste.'

Hornblower thought of the cartoons in the English newspapers which had so often compared Bonaparte with the frog who tried to blow himself up as big as an ox.

'I fancy it is symptomatic of weakness,' said the Count. 'Perhaps you do not agree with me? You do? I am glad to have my suspicions confirmed. More than that; there is going to be war with Russia. Already troops are being transferred to the East, and the details of a new conscription were published at the same time as the proclamation of a King of Rome. There will be more refractories than ever hiding about the country now. Perhaps Bonaparte will find he has undertaken a task beyond his strength when he comes to grips with Russia.'

'Perhaps so,' said Hornblower. He had not a high opinion of Russian military virtues.

'But there is more important news still,' said the Count. 'There has at last been published a bulletin of the Army of Portugal. It was dated from Almeida.'

It took a second or two for Hornblower to grasp the significance of this comment, and it only dawned upon him gradually, along with the endless implications.

'It means,' said the Count, 'that your Wellington has beaten Bonaparte's Masséna. That the attempt to conquer Portugal has failed, and that the whole of the affairs of Spain are thrown into flux again. A running sore has been opened in the side of Bonaparte's empire, which may drain him of his strength – at what cost to poor France one can hardly imagine. But of course, Captain, you can form a more reliable opinion of the military situation than I can, and I have been presumptous in commenting on it. Yet you have not the facilities which I have of gauging the moral effect of this news. Wellington has beaten Junot, and Victor and Soult. Now he has beaten Masséna, the greatest of them all. There is only one man now against whom European opinion can measure him, and that is Bonaparte. It is not well for a tyrant to have rivals in prestige. Last year how many years of power would one have given Bonaparte if asked? Twenty? I think so. Now in 1811 we change our minds. Ten years, we think. In 1812 we may revise our estimate again, and say five. I myself do not believe the Empire as we know it will endure after 1814 – Empires collapse at a rate increasing in geometrical progression, and it will be your Wellington who will pull this one down.'

'I hope sincerely you are right, sir,' said Hornblower.

The Count was not to know how disturbing this mention of Wellington was to his audience; he could not guess that Hornblower was daily tormented by speculations as to whether Wellington's sister was widowed or not, whether Lady Barbara Leighton, née Wellesley, ever had a thought to devote to the naval captain who had been reported dead. Her brother's triumphs might well occupy her mind to the exclusion of everything else, and Hornblower feared that when at last he should reach England she would be far too great a lady to pay him any attention at all. The thought irked him.

He went to bed in a peculiarly sober mood, his mind busy with problems of the most varying nature – from speculations about the approaching fall of the French Empire to calculations regarding the voyage down the Loire which he was about to attempt. Lying awake, long after midnight, he heard his bedroom door quietly open and close; he lay rigid, instantly conscious of a feeling of faint distaste at this reminder of the intrigue which he was conducting under a hospitable roof. Very gently, the curtains of his bed were drawn open, and in the darkness he could see, through half-opened eyes, a shadowy ghost bending over him. A gentle hand found his cheek and stroked it; he could no longer sham sleep, and he pretended to wake with a start.

'It is Marie, 'Oratio,' said a voice, softly.

'Yes,' said Hornblower.

He did not know what he should say or do – for that matter he did not know what he wanted. Mostly he was conscious of Marie's imprudence in thus coming to his room, risking discovery and imperilling everything. He shut his eyes as though still sleepy, to gain time for consideration; the hand ceased to stroke his cheek. Hornblower waited for a second or two more, and was astonished to hear the slight click of the latch of the door again. He sat up with a jerk. Marie had gone, as silently as she had come. Hornblower continued to sit up, puzzling over the incident, but he could make nothing of it. Certainly he was not going to run any risks by going to seek Marie in her room and asking for explanations; he lay down again to think about it, and this time, with its usual capriciousness, sleep surprised him in the midst of his speculations, and he slept soundly until Brown brought him his breakfast coffee.

It took him half the morning to nerve himself for what he foresaw to be a very uncomfortable interview; it was only then that he tore himself away from a last inspection of the boat, in Bush's and Brown's company, and climbed the stairs to Marie's boudoir and tapped at the door. He entered when she called, and stood there in the room of so many memories – the golden chairs with their oval backs upholstered in pink and white, the windows looking out on the sunlit Loire, and Marie in the window-seat with her needlework.

'I wanted to say "good morning",' he said at length, as Marie did nothing to help him out.

'Good morning,' said Marie. She bent her head over her needlework – the sunshine through the windows lit her hair gloriously – and spoke with her face concealed. 'We only have to say "good morning" today, and tomorrow we shall say "goodbye".'

'Yes,' said Hornblower stupidly.

'If you loved me,' said Marie, 'it would be terrible for me to have you go, and to know that for years we should not meet again – perhaps for ever. But as you do not, then I am glad that you are going back to your wife and your child, and your ships, and your fighting. That is what you wanted, and I am pleased that you should have it all.'

'Thank you,' said Hornblower.

Still she did not look up.

'You are the sort of man,' she went on, 'whom women love very easily. I do not expect that I shall be the last. I don't think that you will ever love anybody, or know what it is to do so.'

Hornblower could have said nothing in English in reply to these two astonishing statements, and in French he was perfectly helpless. He could only stammer.

'Goodbye,' said Marie.

'Goodbye, madame,' said Hornblower, lamely.

His cheeks were burning as he came out into the upper hall, in a condition of mental distress in which humiliation only played a minor part. He was thoroughly conscious of having acted despicably, and of having been dismissed without dignity. But he was puzzled by the other remarks Marie had made. It had never occurred to him that women loved him easily. Maria – it was odd, that similarity of names, Maria and Marie – loved him, he knew; he had found it a little tiresome and disturbing. Barbara had offered herself to him, but he had never ventured to believe that she had loved him – and had she not married someone else? And Marie loved him; Hornblower remembered guiltily an incident of a few days ago, when Marie in his arms had whispered hotly, 'Tell me you love me,' and he had answered with facile kindness, 'I love you, dear.' 'Then I am happy,' answered Marie. Perhaps it was a good thing that Marie knew now that he was lying, and had made easy his retreat. Another woman with a word might have sent him and Bush to prison and death – there were women capable of it.

And this question of his never loving anyone; surely Marie was wrong about that. She did not know the miseries of longing he had been through on Barbara's account, how much he had desired her and how much he still desired her. He hesitated guiltily here, wondering whether his desire would survive gratification. That was such an uncomfortable thought that he swerved away from it in a kind of panic. If Marie had merely revengefully desired to disturb him she certainly had achieved her object; and if on the other hand she had wanted to win him back to her she was not far from success either. What with the torments of remorse and his sudden uneasiness about himself Hornblower would have returned to her if she had lifted a finger to him, but she did not.

At dinner that evening she appeared young and lighthearted, her eyes sparkling and her expression animated, and when the Count lifted his glass for the toast of 'a prosperous voyage home' she joined in with every appearance of enthusiasm. Hornblower was glum beneath his forced gaiety. Only now, with the prospect of an immediate move ahead of him, had he become aware that there were decided arguments in favour of the limbo of suspended animation in which he had spent the past months. Tomorrow he was going to leave all this certainty and safety and indifferent negativeness. There was physical danger ahead of him; that he could face calmly and with no more than a tightening of the throat, but besides that there was the resolution of all the doubts and uncertainties which had so troubled him.

Hornblower was suddenly aware that he did not so urgently desire his uncertainties to be resolved. At present he could still hope. If Leighton were to declare that Hornblower had fought at Rosas contrary to the spirit of his orders; if the court martial were to decide that the *Sutherland* had not been fought to the last gasp – and courts martial were chancy affairs; if – if – if. And there was Maria with her cloying sweetness awaiting him, and the misery of longing for Lady Barbara, all in contrast with the smoothness of life here with the Count's unruffled politeness and the stimulus of Marie's healthy animalism. Hornblower had to force a smile as he lifted his glass.

XI

The big green Loire was shrinking to its summer level. Hornblower had seen its floods and its ice come and go, had seen the willows at its banks almost submerged, but now it was back safely in its wide bed, with a hint of golden-brown gravel exposed on either bank. The swift green water was clear now, instead of turbid, and under the blue sky the distant reaches were blue as well, in charming colour contrast with the springtime emerald of the valley and the gold of the banks.

The two sleek dun oxen, patient under the yoke, had dragged the travois-sledge down to the water's edge in the first early light of dawn, Brown and Hornblower walking beside to see that the precious boat balanced on it came to no harm, and Bush stumping breathlessly behind them. The boat slid gently into the water, and under Bush's supervision the stable hands loaded her with the bags of stores which they had carried down. The faint morning mist still lay in the valley, and wreathed over the surface of the water, awaiting the coming of the sun to drink it up. It was the best time for departure, the mist would shield them from inquisitive persons who might be unduly curious at the sight of the expedition starting off. Up at the house farewells had all been said – the Count as unruffled as ever, as though it were usual for him to rise at five in the morning, and Marie smiling and calm. In the stable yard and the kitchen there had been tears; all the women had lamented Brown's going, weeping unashamed and yet laughing through their tears as he laughed and joked in the voluble French which he had acquired, and as he smacked their broad posteriors. Hornblower wondered how many of them Brown had seduced that winter, and how many Anglo-French children would be born next autumn as a result.

'Remember your promise to return after the war,' the Count had said to Hornblower. 'Marie will be as delighted to see you as I shall be.'

His smile had conveyed no hint of a hidden meaning – but how much did he guess, or know? Hornblower gulped as he remembered.

'Shove off,' he rasped. 'Brown, take the sculls.'

The boat scraped over the gravel, and then floated free as the current took her, dancing away from the little group of stable hands and the stolid oxen, vague already in the mist. The rowlocks creaked and the boat swayed to Brown's pulls; Hornblower heard the noises, and felt

Bush seated in the stern beside him, but for some seconds he saw nothing. There was a mist about him far denser than the reality.

The one mist cleared with the other, as the sun came breaking through, warm on Hornblower's back. High up the bank on the opposite side was the orchard at which Hornblower had often gazed from his window; it was marvellous now under its load of blossom. Looking back, he saw the château shining in the sun. The turrets at the corners had been added, he knew, no more than fifty years ago by a Comte de Graçay with a rococo taste for the antique, but they looked genuine enough at a distance. It was like a fairy castle in the pearly light, a dream castle; and already the months he had spent there seemed like a dream too, a dream from which he regretted awakening.

'Mr Bush,' he said sharply. 'I'll trouble you to get out your rod and make an appearance of fishing. Take a slower stroke, Brown.'

They went drifting on down the noble river, blue in the distance and green overside, clear and transparent, so that they could actually see the bottom passing away below them. It was only a few minutes before they reached the confluence of the Allier, itself a fine river almost the size of the Loire, and the united stream was majestically wide, a hundred and fifty fathoms at least from bank to bank. They were a long musket shot from land, but their position was safer even than that implied, for from the water's edge on either side stretched an extensive no-man's-land of sand and willow which the periodic floods kept free from human habitations and which was only likely to be visited by fishermen and laundering housewives.

The mist had entirely vanished now, and the hot sun bore with all the promise of one of those splendid spring days of central France. Hornblower shifted in his seat to make himself more comfortable. The hierarchy of this, his new command, was topheavy. A proportion of one seaman to one lieutenant and one captain was ludicrous. He would have to exercise a great deal of tact to keep them all three satisfied – to see that Brown was not made resentful by having all the work to do and yet that discipline was not endangered by a too democratic division of labour. In a fifteen-foot boat it would be difficult to keep up the aloof dignity proper to a captain.

'Brown,' he said. 'I've been very satisfied with you so far. Keep in my good books and I'll see you're properly rewarded when we get back to England. There'll be a warrant for you as master's mate if you want it.'

'Thank 'ee, sir. Thank 'ee very kindly. But I'm happy as I am, beggin' your pardon, sir.'

He meant he was happy in his rating as a coxswain, but the tone of his voice implied more than that. Hornblower looked at him as he sat with his face turned up to the sun, pulling slowly at the sculls. There was a blissful smile on his face – the man was marvellously happy. He had been well fed and well housed for months, with plenty of women's society, with light work and no hardship. Even now there was a long prospect ahead of him of food better than he had ever known before he entered France, of no harder work than a little gentle rowing, of no need ever to turn out on a blustering night to reef topsails. Twenty years of the lower deck in King George's Navy, Hornblower realised, must make any man form the habit of living only in the present. Tomorrow might bring a flogging, peril, sickness, death; certainly hardship and probably hunger, and all without the opportunity of lifting a finger to ward off any of these, for any lifting of a finger would make them all more certain. Twenty years of being at the mercy of the incalculable, and not merely in the major things of life but in the minor ones, must make a fatalist of any man who survived them. For a moment Hornblower felt a little twinge of envy of Brown, who would never know the misery of helplessness, or the indignity of indecision.

The river channel here was much divided by islands each bordered by a rim of golden gravel; it was Hornblower's business to select what appeared to be the most navigable channel – no easy task. Shallows appeared mysteriously right in the centre of what had seemed to be the main stream; over these the clear green water ran faster and faster and shallower and shallower until the bottom of the boat was grating on the pebbles. Sometimes the bank would end there with astonishing abruptness, so that one moment they were in six inches of rushing water and the next in six feet of transparent green, but more than once now they found themselves stuck fast, and Brown and Hornblower, trousers rolled to the knee, had to get out and haul the boat a hundred yards over a barely covered bank before finding water deep enough. Hornblower thanked his stars that he had decided on having the boat built flat-bottomed – a keel would have been a hampering nuisance.

Then they came to a dam, like the one which had brought them disaster in the darkness during their first attempt to navigate the river. It was half natural, half artificial, roughly formed of lumps of rock piled across the river bed, and over it the river poured in fury at a few points.

'Pull over to the bank there, Brown,' snapped Hornblower as his coxswain looked to him for orders.

They ran the boat up on to the gravel just above the dam, and Hornblower stepped out and looked downstream. There was a hundred yards of turbulent water below the dam; they would have to carry everything down. It took three journeys on the part of Hornblower and Brown to carry all their stores to the point he chose for them to re-enter the river – Bush with his wooden leg could only just manage to stumble over the uneven surface unladen – and then they addressed themselves to the business of transporting the boat. It was not easy; there was a colossal difference between dragging the boat through shallows even an inch deep only and carrying her bodily. Hornblower contemplated the task glumly for some seconds before plunging at it. He stooped and got his hands underneath.

'Take the other side, Brown. Now – lift.'

Between them they could just raise it; they had hardly staggered a yard with it before all the strength was gone from Hornblower's wrists and fingers and the boat slipped to the ground again. He avoided Brown's eye and stooped again, exasperated.

'Lift!' he said.

It was impossible to carry the heavy boat that way. He had no sooner lifted it than he was compelled to drop it again.

'It's no go, sir,' said Brown gently. 'We'll have to get her upon our backs, sir. That's the only way.'

Hornblower heard the respectful murmur as if from a long distance.

'If you take the bows, beggin' your pardon, sir, I'll look after the stern. Here, sir, lift t'other way round. Hold it, sir, 'till I can get aft. Right, sir. Ready. Lift!'

They had the boat up on their backs now, stooping double under the heavy load. Hornblower, straining under the lighter bows, thought of Brown carrying the much heavier stern, and he set his teeth and vowed to himself that he would not rest until Brown asked to. Within five seconds he was regretting his vow. His breath was coming with difficulty and there were stabbing pains in his chest. It grew harder and harder to take the trouble to attend to the proper placing of his feet as he stumbled over the uneven surface. Those months in the Château de Graçay had done their work in making him soft and out of condition; for the last few yards of the portage he was conscious of nothing save the overwhelming weight on his neck and shoulders and his difficulty of breathing. Then he heard Bush's bluff voice.

'Right, sir. Let me get hold, sir.'

With the small but welcome help that Bush could afford he was able to disengage himself and lower the boat to the ground; Brown was standing over the stern gasping, and sweeping the sweat off his forehead with his forearm. Hornblower saw him open his mouth to make a remark, presumably regarding the weight of the boat, and then shut it again when he remembered that now he was under discipline again and must only speak when spoken to. And discipline, Hornblower realised, required that he himself should display no sign of weakness before his subordinates – it was bad enough that he should have had to receive advice from Brown as to how to lift the boat.

'Take hold again, Brown, and we'll get her into the water,' he said, controlling his breathing with a vast effort.

They slid the boat in, and heaved the stores on board again. Hornblower's head was swimming with the strain; he thought longingly of
his comfortable seat in the stern, and then put the thought from him.

'I'll take the sculls, Brown,' he said.

Brown opened and shut his mouth again, but he could not question
explicit orders. The boat danced out over the water, with Hornblower
at the sculls happy in the rather baseless conviction that he had demonstrated that a captain in the King's Navy was the equal even in physical
strength of any mere coxswain, however Herculean his thews.

Once or twice that day shallows caught them out in midstream which
they were unable to pass without lightening the boat to a maximum
extent. When Hornblower and Brown, ankle-deep in rushing water,
could drag the boat no farther, Bush had to get out too, his wooden leg
sinking in the sand despite its broad leather sole, and limp downstream
to the edge of the shallows and wait until the others dragged the lightened boat up to him – once he had to stand holding the bag of bread and
the roll of bedding before they could tug the boat over the shallows, and
on that occasion they had to unstrap his wooden leg, help him in, and
then tug the leg free from the sand, so deeply had it sunk. There was
another portage to be made that day, fortunately not nearly such a long
one as the first; altogether there was quite enough interest in the day's
journey to keep them from growing bored.

On that big lonely river it was almost like travelling through an uninhabited country. For the greater part of the day there was hardly a soul
in sight. Once they saw a skiff moored to the bank which was obviously
used as a ferry-boat, and once they passed a big waggon ferry – a flat-
bottomed scow which was moored so as to swing itself across the river
by the force of the current, pendulum-fashion on long mooring ropes.
Once they passed a small boat engaged in the task of dredging sand for
building purposes from the river bed; there were two weather-beaten
men on board, hard at work with small hand dredgers on poles, which
they scraped over the bottom and emptied into the boat. It was a nervous
moment as they approached them, Bush and Brown with their orna-
mental fishing rods out, Hornblower forcing himself to do no more
with the sculls than merely keep the boat in midstream. He had thought,
as they drifted down, of giving orders to Bush and Brown regarding the
instant silencing of the two men if they appeared suspicious, but he
checked himself. He could rely on their acting promptly without warning, and his dignity demanded that he should betray none of the apprehension which he felt.

But the apprehension was quite baseless. There was no curiosity in
the glances which the two sand dredgers threw in them, and there was
cordiality in their smiles and in their polite 'Bonjour, messieurs'.

'Bonjour,' said Hornblower and Brown – Bush had the sense to keep shut the mouth which would instantly have betrayed them, and devoted his attention instead to his rod. Clearly boats with fishing parties on board were just common enough on the Loire to escape comment; and, besides, the intrinsic innocence of fishing as a pastime shielded them from suspicion, as Hornblower and the Count had agreed long before. And nobody could ever dream that a small boat in the heart of France was manned by escaped prisoners of war.

The commonest sight of all along the river was the women washing clothes, sometimes singly, sometimes in little groups whose gossiping chatter floated out to them distinctly over the water. The Englishmen could hear the 'clop clop clop' of the wooden beaters smacking the wet clothes on the boards, and could see the kneeling women sway down and up as they rinsed them in the current; most of the women looked up from their work and gave them a glance as they drifted by, but it was never more than a long glance, and often not as much. In time of war and upheaval there were so many possible explanations for the women not to know the occupants of the boat that their inability did not trouble them.

Of the roaring rapids such as had nearly destroyed them once before, they saw nothing; the junction of the Allier, and the cessation of the winter floods, accounted for that. The rock-strewn sand bars represented the sites of winter rapids and were far easier to navigate, or rather to circumvent. In fact, that were no difficulties at all. Even the weather was benign, a lovely clear day of sunshine, comfortably warm, lighting up the changing panorama of gold and blue and green. Brown basked in it all unashamedly, and the hard-bitten Bush took his ease whenever the peacefulness of it caught him napping; in Bush's stern philosophy mankind – naval mankind at at least – was born to sorrow and difficulty and danger, and any variation from such a state of affairs must be viewed with suspicion and not enjoyed too much lest it should have to be paid for at compound interest. It was too good to be true, this delightful drifting down the river, as morning wore into noon and noon into prolonged and dreamy afternoon, with a delicious lunch to eat of a cold paté (a parting gift from fat Jeanne) and a bottle of wine.

The little towns, or rather villages, which they passed were all perched up high on the distant banks beyond the flood limits; Hornblower, who already knew by heart the brief itinerary and table of distances which the Count had made out for him, was aware that the first town with a bridge was at Briare, which they could not reach until late evening. He had intended to wait above the town until nightfall and then to run through in the darkness, but as the day wore on his resolve steadily hardened to push on without waiting. He could not analyse his motives. He was aware that it was a very remarkable thing from him to do, to run into danger, even the slightest, when urged neither by the call of duty nor the thirst for distinction. Here the only benefit would be the saving of an hour or two's time. The Nelsonian tradition to 'lose not an hour' was grained deeply into him, but it was hardly that which influenced him.

Partly it was his innate cross-grainedness. Everything had gone so supremely well. Their escape from their escort had been almost miraculous, the coincidence which had brought them to the Château de Graçay, where alone in all France they could have found safety, was more nearly miraculous still. Now this voyage down the river bore every promise of easy success. His instinctive reaction to all this unnatural prosperity was to put himself into the way of trouble – there had been so much trouble in his life that he felt uneasy without it.

But partly he was being driven by devils. He was morose and cantankerous. Marie was being left behind, and he was regretting that more with every yard that divided them. He was tormented by the thought of the shameful part he had played, and by memories of the hours they had spent together; sentimentally he was obsessed with longing for her. And ahead of him lay England where they thought him dead, where Maria would by now have reconciled herself to her loss and would be doubly and painfully happy with him in consequence, and where Barbara would have forgotten him, and where a court martial to inquire into his conduct awaited him. He thought grimly that it might be better for everyone if he *were* dead; he shrank a little from the prospect of returning to England as one might shrink from a cold plunge, or as he shrank from the imminent prospect of danger. That was the ruling motive. He had always forced himself to face danger, to advance bravely to meet it. He had always gulped down any pill which life had presented to him, knowing that any hesitation would give him a contempt for himself more bitter still. So now he would accept no excuse for delay.

Briare was in sight now, down at the end of the long, wide reach of the river. Its church tower was silhouetted against the evening sky, and its long straggling bridge stood out black against the distant silver of the water. Hornblower at the sculls looked over his shoulder and saw all this; he was aware of his subordinates' eyes turned inquiringly upon him.

'Take the sculls, Brown,' he growled.

They changed places silently, and Bush handed over the tiller to him with a puzzled look – he had been well aware of the design to run past bridges only at night. There were two vast black shapes creeping over the surface of the river down there, barges being warped out of the lateral canal on one side and into the canal of Briare on the other by way of a channel across the river dredged for the purpose. Hornblower stared forward as they approached under the impulse of Brown's steady strokes. A quick examination of the water surface told him which arch of the bridge to select, and he was able to discern the tow-ropes and warps of the barges – there were teams of horses both on the bridge and on the banks, silhouetted clearly against the sky as they tugged at the ropes to drag the bulky barges across the rushing current.

Men were looking at them now from the bridge, and there was just sufficient gap left between the barges to enable the boat to slip between without the necessity to stop and make explanations.

'Pull!' he said to Brown, and the boat went careering headlong down the river. They slid under the bridge with a rush, and neatly rounded the stern of one of the barges; the burly old man at the tiller, with a little grandchild beside him, looked down at them with a dull curiosity as they shot by. Hornblower waved his hand gaily to the child – excitement was a drug which he craved, which always sent his spirits high – and looked up with a grin at the other men on the bridge and on the banks. Then they were past, and Briare was left behind.

'Easy enough, sir,' commented Bush.

'Yes,' said Hornblower.

If they had been travelling by road they certainly would have been stopped for examination of their passports; here on the unnavigable river such a proceeding occurred to no one. The sun was low now, shining right into his eyes as he looked forward, and it would be dark in less than an hour. Hornblower began to look out for a place where they could be comfortable for the night. He allowed one long island to slide past them before he saw the ideal spot – a tiny hummock of an island with three willow trees, the green of the central part surrounded by a broad belt of golden brown where the receding river had left the gravel exposed.

'We'll run the boat aground over there, Brown,' he announced. 'Easy. Pull starboard. Pull both. Easy.'

It was not a very good landing. Hornblower, despite his undoubted ability in handling big ships, had much to learn regarding the behaviour of flat-bottomed boats amid the shoals of a river. There was a black eddy, which swung them round; the boat had hardly touched bottom before the current had jerked her free again. Brown, tumbling over the bows, was nearly waist deep in water and had to grab the painter and brace himself against the current to check her. The tactful silence which ensued could almost be felt while Brown tugged the boat up to the gravel again – Hornblower, in the midst of his annoyance, was aware of Bush's restless movement and thought of how his first lieutenant would have admonished a midshipman guilty of such a careless piece of work. It made him grin to think of Bush bottling up his feelings, and the grin made him forget his annoyance.

He stepped out into the shallow water and helped Brown run the lightened boat farther up the bank, checking Bush when he made to step out too – Bush could never accustom himself to seeing his captain at work while he sat idle. The water was no more than ankle-deep by the time he allowed Bush to disembark; they dragged the boat up as far as she could go and Brown made fast the painter to a peg driven securely into the earth, as a precaution in case any unexpected rise in the water level should float the boat off. The sun had set now in the flaming west, and it was fast growing dark.

'Supper,' said Hornblower. 'What shall we have?'

A captain with strict ideas of discipline would merely have announced what they should eat, and would certainly not have called his subordinates into consultation, but Hornblower was too conscious of the top-heavy organisation of his present ship's company to be able to maintain appearances to that extent. Yet Bush and Brown were still oppressed by a life-long experience of subordination and could not bring themselves to proffer advice to their captain; they merely fidgeted and stood silent, leaving it to Hornblower to decree that they should finish off the cold paté with some boiled potatoes. Once the decision was made, Bush proceeded to amplify and interpret his captain's original order, just as a good first lieutenant should.

'I'll handle the fire here,' he said. 'There ought to be all the driftwood we need, Brown. Yes, an' I'll want some sheer-legs to hang the pan over the fire – cut me three off those trees, there.'

Bush felt it in his bones that Hornblower was meditating taking part in the preparation of supper, and could not bear the thought. He looked up at his captain half appealingly, half defiantly. A captain should not merely never be seen doing undignified work, but he should be kept in awful isolation, screened away in the mysterious recesses of his cabin. Hornblower left them to it, and wandered off round the tiny island, looking over at the distant banks and the far houses, fast disappearing in the growing twilight. It was a shock to discover that the pleasant green which carpeted most of the island was not the grass he had assumed it to be, but a bank of nettles, knee high already despite the earliness of the season. Judging by his language, Brown on the other side had just made the same discovery while seeking fuel with his feet bare.

Hornblower paced the gravel bank for a space, and on his return it was an idyllic scene which met his eyes. Brown was tending the little fire which flickered under the pot swinging from its tripod, while Bush, his wooden leg sticking stiffly out in front of him, was peeling the last of the potatoes. Apparently Bush had decided that a first lieutenant could share menial work with the sole member of the crew without imperilling discipline. They all ate together, wordless but friendly, beside the dying fire; even the chill air of the evening did not cool the feeling of comradeship of which each was conscious in his own particular way.

'Shall I set a watch, sir?' asked Bush, as supper ended.

'No,' said Hornblower.

The minute additional security which would be conferred by one of them staying awake would not compare with the discomfort and inconvenience of everyone losing four hours' sleep each night.

Bush and Brown slept in cloak and blanket on the bare soil, probably, Hornblower anticipated, most uncomfortably. For himself there was a mattress of cut nettles cunningly packed under the boat cover which Brown had prepared for him on the most level part of the gravel spit, presumably at a grave cost in stings. He slept on it peacefully, the dew wetting his face and the gibbous moon shining down upon it from the starry sky. Vaguely he remembered, in a troubled fashion, the stories of the great leaders of men – Charles XII especially – who shared their men's coarse fare and slept like them on the bare ground. For a second or two he feared he should be doing likewise, and then his common sense overrode his modesty and told him that he did not need to have recourse to theatrical tricks to win the affections of Bush and Brown.

XII

Those days on the Loire were pleasant, and every day was more pleasant than the one preceding. For Hornblower there was not merely the passive pleasure of a fortnight's picnic, but there was the far more active one of the comradeliness of it all. During his ten years as a captain his natural shyness had reinforced the restrictions surrounding his position, and had driven him more and more in upon himself until he had grown unconscious of his aching need for human companionship. In that small boat, living at close quarters with the others, and where one man's misfortune was everyone's, he came to know happiness. His keen insight made him appreciate more than ever the sterling good qualities of Bush, who was secretly fretting over the loss of his foot, and the inactivity to which that loss condemned him, and the doubtfulness of his future as a cripple.

'I'll see you posted as captain,' said Hornblower, on the only occasion on which Bush hinted at his troubles, 'if it's my last act on earth.'

He thought he might possibly contrive that, even if disgrace awaited him personally in England. Lady Barbara must still remember Bush and the old days in the *Lydia*, and must be aware of his good qualities as Hornblower was himself. An appeal to her, properly worded – even from a man broken by court martial – might have an effect, and might set turning the hidden wheels of Government patronage. Bush deserved post rank more than half the captains he knew on the list.

Then there was Brown with his unfailing cheerfulness. No one could judge better than Hornblower the awkwardness of Brown's position, living in such close proximity to two officers. But Brown always could find the right mixture of friendliness and deference; he could laugh gaily when he slipped on a rounded stone and sat down in the Loire, and he could smile sympathetically when the same thing happened to Hornblower. He busied himself over the jobs of work which had to be done, and never, not even after ten days' routine had established something like a custom, appeared to take it for granted that his officers would do their share. Hornblower could foresee a great future for Brown, if helped by a little judicious exertion of influence. He might easily end as a captain, too – Derby and Westcott had started on the lower deck in the same fashion. Even if the court martial broke him Hornblower could do something to help him. Elliott and Bolton at least would not desert him entirely, and would rate Brown as midshipman in their ships if he asked them to do with special earnestness.

In making these plans for the future of his friends, Hornblower could bring himself to contemplate the end of the voyage and the inevitable court martial with something like equanimity; for the rest, during those golden days, he was able to avoid all thought of their approaching end. It was a placid journey through a placid limbo. He was leaving behind him in the past the shameful memory of his treatment of Marie, and the troubles to come were still in the future; for once in his life he was able to live in the lotus-eating present.

All the manifold little details of the journey helped towards this desirable end – they were so petty and yet temporarily so important. Selecting a course between the golden sandbanks of the river; stepping out overside to haul the boat over when his judgment was incorrect; finding a lonely island on which to camp at night, and cooking supper when one was found; drifting past the gravel dredgers and the rare fishing parties; avoiding conspicuous behaviour while passing towns; there were always trifles to occupy the mind. There were the two nights when it rained, and they all slept huddled together under the shelter of a blanket stretched between willow trees – there had been a ridiculous pleasure about waking up to find Bush snoring beside him with a protective arm across him.

There was the pageantry of the Loire – Gien with its château-fortress high on its terraces, and Sully with its vast rounded bastions, and Château-Neuf-sur-Loire, and Jargeau. Then for miles along the river they were in sight of the gaunt square towers of the cathedral of Orleans – Orleans was one of the few towns with an extensive river front, past which they had to drift unobtrusively and with special care at its difficult bridges. Orleans was hardly out of sight before they reached Beaugency with its interminable bridges of countless arches and its strange square tower. The river was blue and gold and green. The rocks above Nevers were succeeded by the gravel banks of the middle reaches, and now the gravel gave way to sand, golden sand amid the shimmering blue of the river whose water was a clear green overside. All the contrasted greens delighted Hornblower's eyes, the green of the never-ending willows, of the vineyards and the cornfields and the meadows.

They passed Blois, its steeply-humped bridge crowned by the pyramid whose inscription proclaimed the bridge to be the first public work of the infant Louis XV, and Chaumont and Amboise, their lovely châteaux towering above the river, and Tours – an extensive water front to sidle past here, too – and Langeais. The wild desolation of the island-studded river was punctuated everywhere by towers and châteaux and cathedrals on the distant banks. Below Langeais the big placid Vienne entered the river on their left, and appeared to convey some of its own qualities to the united stream, which was now a little slower and more regular in its course, its shallows becoming less and less frequent. After Saumur and the innumerable islands of Les Ponts de Cé, the even bigger Maine came in on their right, and finally deprived the wild river of all the character-istics which had endeared it to them. Here it was far deeper and far slower, and for the first time they found the attempt to make the river available for commercial traffic successful here – they had passed numerous traces of wasted work on Bonaparte's part higher up.

But below the confluence of the Maine the groynes and dykes had withstood the winter floods, and the continual erosion had piled up long beaches of golden sand on either bank, and had left in the centre a deep channel navigable to barges – they passed several working their way up to Angers from Nantes. Mostly they were being towed by teams of mules, but one or two were taking advantage of a westerly wind to make the ascent under vast gaff-mainsails. Hornblower stared hungrily at them, for they were the first sails he had seen for months, but he put aside all thought of stealing one. A glance at their clumsy lines assured him that it would be more dangerous to put to sea, even for a short distance, in one of those than in the cockleshell boat they had already.

That westerly wind that brought the barges up brought something else with it, too. Brown, diligently tugging at the sculls as he forced the boat into it, suddenly wrinkled his nose.

'Begging your pardon, sir,' he said, 'I can smell the sea.'

They sniffed at the breeze, all three of them.

'By God, you're right, Brown,' said Bush.

Hornblower said nothing, but he had smelt the salt as well, and it had brought with it such a wave of mixed feelings as to leave him with-out words. And that night after they had camped – there were just as many desolate islands to choose from, despite the changes in the river – Hornblower noticed that the level of the water had risen perceptibly above where it had stood when they beached the boat. It was not flood water like the time when after a day of heavy rain their boat had nearly floated during the night; on this evening above Nantes there had been no rain, no sign of it, for three days. Hornblower watched the water creep up at a rate almost perceptible, watched it reach a maximum, dally there for a space, and then begin to sink. It was the tide. Down at Paimbœuf at the mouth there was a rise and fall of ten or twelve feet, at Nantes one of four or six; up here he was witnessing the last dying effort of the banked-up sea to hold the river back in its course.

There was a strange emotion in the thought. They had reached tide-water at last, the habitat on which he had spent more than half his life; they had travelled from sea to sea, from the Mediterranean to what was at least technically the Atlantic; this same tide he was witnessing here washed also the shores of England, where were Barbara, and Maria, and his unknown child, and the Lords Commissioners of the Admiralty. But more than that. It meant that their pleasant picnic on the Loire was over. In tidal water they could not hope to move about with half the freedom they had known inland; strange faces and new arrivals would be scanned with suspicion, and probably the next forty-eight hours or so would determine whether he was to reach England to face a court martial or be recaptured to face a firing squad. Hornblower knew that moment the old sensation of excitement, which he called fear to himself – the quickened heart beat, the dampening palms, the tingling in the calves of his legs. He had to brace himself to master these symptoms before returning to the others to tell them of his observations.

'High water half an hour back, sir?' repeated Bush in reply.

'Yes.'

'M'm,' said Bush.

Brown said nothing, as accorded with his position in life, but his face bore momentarily the same expression of deep cogitation. They were both assimilating the fact, in the manner of seamen. Hornblower knew that from now on, with perhaps a glance at the sun but not necessarily with a glance at the river, they would be able to tell offhand the state of the tide, producing the information without a thought by the aid of a subconscious calculating ability developed during a lifetime at sea. He could do the same himself – the only difference between them was that he was interested in the phenomenon while they were indifferent to it or unaware of it.

XIII

For their entrance into Nantes Hornblower decided that they must wear their uniforms as officials of the customs service. It called for long and anxious thought to reach this decision, a desperately keen balancing of chances. If they arrived in civilian clothes they would almost certainly be questioned, and in that case it would be almost impossible to explain their lack of papers and passports, whereas in uniform they might easily not be questioned at all, and if they were a haughty demeanour might still save them. But to pose as a colonel of douaniers would call for histrionic ability on the part of Hornblower, and he mistrusted himself – not his ability, but his nerve. With remorseless self-analysis he told himself that he had played a part for years, posing as a man of rigid imperturbability when he was nothing of the kind, and he asked himself why he could not pose for a few minutes as a man of swaggering and overbearing haughtiness, even under the additional handicap of having to speak French. In the end it was in despite of his doubts that he reached his decision, and put on the neat uniform and pinned the glittering Legion of Honour on his breast.

As always, it was the first moment of departure which tried him most – getting into the sternsheets of the boat and taking the tiller while Brown got out the sculls. The tension under which he laboured was such that he knew that, if he allowed it, the hand that rested on the tiller would tremble, and the voice which gave the orders to Brown would quaver. So he carried himself with the unbending rigidity which men were accustomed to see in him, and he spoke with the insensitive harshness he always used in action.

Under the impulse of Brown's sculls the river glided away behind them, and the city of Nantes came steadily nearer. Houses grew thicker and thicker on the banks, and then the river began to break up into several arms; to Hornblower the main channel between the islands was made obvious by the indications of traces of commercial activity along the banks – traces of the past, largely, for Nantes was a dying town, dying of the slow strangulation of the British blockade. The lounging idlers along the quays, the deserted warehouses, all indicated the dire effects of war upon French commerce.

They passed under a couple of bridges, with the tide running strongly, and left the huge mass of the ducal château to starboard; Hornblower forced himself to sit with careless ease in the boat, as though neither courting nor avoiding observation; the Legion of Honour clinked as it swung upon his breast. A side glance at Bush suddenly gave him enormous comfort and reassurance, for Bush was sitting with a masklike immobility of countenance which told Hornblower that he was nervous too. Bush could go into action and face an enemy's broadside with an honest indifference to danger, but this present situation was trying his nerves severely, sitting watched by a thousand French eyes, and having to rely upon mere inactivity to save himself from death or imprisonment. The sight was like a tonic to Hornblower. His cares dropped from him, and he knew the joy and thrill of reckless bravery.

Beyond the next bridge the maritime port began. Here first were the fishing boats – Hornblower looked keenly at them, for he had in mind to steal one of them. His experience under Pellew in the blockading squadron years ago was serving him in good stead now, for he knew the ways of those fishing boats. They were accustomed to ply their trade among the islands of the Breton coast, catching the pilchards which the French persisted in calling 'sardines', and bringing their catch up the estuary to sell in the market at Nantes. He and Bush and Brown between them could handle one of those boats with ease, and they were seaworthy enough to take them safely out to the blockading squadron, or to England if necessary. He was practically certain that he would decide upon such a plan, so that as they rowed by he sharply ordered Brown to pull more slowly, and he turned all his attention upon them.

Below the fishing boats two American ships were lying against the quay, the Stars and Stripes fluttering jauntily in the gentle wind. His attention was caught by a dreary clanking of chains – the ships were being emptied of their cargoes by gangs of prisoners, each man staggering bent double under a bag of grain. That was interesting. Hornblower looked again. The chain gangs were under the charge of soldiers – Hornblower could see the shakos and the flash of the musket barrels – which gave him an insight into who the poor devils might be. They were military criminals, deserters, men caught sleeping at their posts, men who had disobeyed an order, all the unfortunates of the armies Bonaparte maintained in every corner of Europe. Their sentences condemned them to 'the galleys' and as the French Navy no longer used galleys in which they could be forced to tug at the oars, they were now employed in all the hard labour of the ports; twice as lieutenant in Pellew's *Indefatigable* Hornblower had seen picked up small parties of desperate men who had escaped from Nantes in much the same fashion as he himself proposed now to do.

And then against the quay below the American ships they saw something else, something which caused them to stiffen in their seats. The tricolour here was hoisted above a tattered blue ensign, flaunting a petty triumph.

'*Witch of Endor*, ten-gun cutter,' said Bush hoarsely. 'A French frigate caught her on a lee shore off Noirmoutier last year. By God, isn't it what you'd expect of the French? It's eleven months ago and they're still wearing French colours over British.'

She was a lovely little ship; even from where they were they could see the perfection of her lines – speed and seaworthiness written all over her.

'The Frogs don't seem to have over-sparred her the way you'd expect 'em to,' commented Bush.

She was ready for sea, and their expert eyes could estimate the area of the furled mainsail and job. The high graceful mast nodded to them, almost imperceptibly, as the cutter rocked minutely beside the quay. It was as if a prisoner were appealing to them for aid, and the flapping colours, tricolour over blue ensign, told a tragic story. In a sudden rush of impulse Hornblower put the helm over.

'Lay us alongside the quay,' he said to Brown.

A few strokes took them there; the tide had turned some time ago and they headed against the flood. Brown caught a ring and made the painter fast, and first Hornblower, nimbly, and then Bush, with difficulty, mounted the stone steps to the top of the quay.

'Suivez-nous,' said Hornblower to Brown, remembering at the last moment to speak French.

Hornblower forced himself to hold up his head and walk with a swagger; the pistols in his side pockets bumped reassuringly against his hips, and his sword tapped against his thigh. Bush walked beside him, his wooden leg thumping with measured stride on the stone quay. A passing group of soldiers saluted the smart uniform, and Hornblower returned the salute nonchalantly, amazed at his new coolness. His heart was beating fast, but ecstatically he knew he was not afraid. It was worth running this risk to experience this feeling of mad bravery.

They stopped and looked at the *Witch of Endor* against the quay. Her decks were not of the dazzling whiteness upon which an English first lieutenant would have insisted, and there was a slovenliness about her standing rigging which was heartbreaking to contemplate. A couple of men were moving lackadaisically about the deck under the supervision of a third.

'Anchor watch,' muttered Bush. 'Two hands and a master's mate.'

He spoke without moving his lips, like a naughty boy in school, lest some onlooker should read his words and realise that he was not speaking French.

'Everyone else on shore, the lubbers,' went on Bush.

Hornblower stood on the quay, the tiny breeze blowing round his ears, soldiers and sailors and civilians walking by, the bustle of the unloading of the American ships noisy in the distance. Bush's thoughts were following on the heels of his own. Bush was aware of the temptation Hornblower was feeling, to steal the *Witch of Endor* and to sail her to England – Bush would never have thought of it himself, but years of service under his captain made him receptive of ideas, however fantastic.

Fantastic was the right word. Those big cutters carried a crew of sixty men, and the gear and tackle were planned accordingly. Three men – one a cripple – could not even hope to be able to hoist the big mainsail, although it was just possible that the three of them might handle her under sail in the open sea in fair weather. It was that possibility which had given rise to the train of thought, but on the other hand there was all the tricky estuary of the Loire between them and the sea; and the French, Hornblower knew, had removed the buoys and navigation marks for fear of an English raid. Unpiloted they could never hope to find their way through thirty-five miles of shoals without going aground, and besides, there were batteries at Paimbœuf and St Nazaire to prohibit unauthorised entrance and exit. The thing was impossible – it was sheer sentimentality to think of it, he told himself, suddenly self-critical again for a moment.

He turned away and strolled up towards the American ships, and watched with interest the wretched chain gangs staggering along the gang planks with their loads of grain. The sight of their misery sickened him; so did the bullying sergeants who strutted about in charge of them. Here, if anywhere, he told himself, was to be found the nucleus of that rising against Bonaparte which everyone was expecting. All that was needed was a desperate leader – that would be something worth reporting to the Government when he reached home. Farther down the river yet another ship was coming up to the port, her topsails black against the setting sun, as, with the flood behind her, she held her course closehauled to the faint southerly breeze. She was flying the Stars and Stripes – American again. Hornblower experienced the same feeling of exasperated impotence which he had known in the old days of his service under Pellew. What was the use of blockading a coast, and enduring all the hardships and perils of that service, if neutral vessels could sail in and out with impunity? Their cargoes of wheat were officially non-contraband, but wheat was of as vital importance to Bonaparte as ever was hemp, or pitch, or any other item on the contraband list – the more wheat he could import, the more men he could draft into his armies. Hornblower found himself drifting into the eternal debate as to whether America, when eventually she became weary of the indignities of neutrality, would turn her arms against England or France – she had actually been at war with France for a short time already, and it was much to her interest to help pull down the imperial despotism, but it was doubtful whether she would be able to resist the temptation to twist the British lion's tail.

The new arrival, smartly enough handled, was edging in now to the quay. A backed topsail took the way off her, and the warps creaked round the bollards. Hornblower watched idly, Bush and Brown beside him. As the ship was made fast, a gang plank was thrown to the quay, and a little stout man made ready to walk down it from the ship. He was in civilian clothes, and he had a rosy round face with a ridiculous little black moustache with upturned ends. From his manner of shaking hands with the captain, and from the very broken English which he was speaking, Hornblower guessed him to be the pilot.

The pilot! In that moment a surge of ideas boiled up in Hornblower's mind. It would be dark in less than an hour, with the moon in its first quarter – already he could see it, just visible in the sky high over the setting sun. A clear night, the tide about to ebb, a gentle breeze, southerly with a touch of east. A pilot available on the one hand, a crew on the other. Then he hesitated. The whole scheme was rash to the point of madness – beyond that point. It must be ill-digested, unsound. His mind raced madly through the scheme again, but even as it did so he was carried away by the wave of recklessness. There was an intoxication about throwing caution to the winds which he had forgotten since his boyhood. In the tense seconds which were all he had, while the pilot was descending the gang plank and approaching them along the quay, he had formed his resolution. He nudged his two companions, and then stepped forward and intercepted the fat little pilot as he walked briskly past them.

'Monsieur,' he said. 'I have some questions to ask you. Will you kindly accompany me to my ship for a moment?'

The pilot noted the uniform, the star of the Legion of Honour, the assumed manner.

'Why, certainly,' he said. His conscience was clear; he was guilty of no more than venal infringements of the Continental system. He turned and trotted alongside Hornblower. 'You are a newcomer to this port, Colonel, I fancy?'

'I was transferred here yesterday from Amsterdam,' answered Hornblower shortly.

Brown was striding along at the pilot's other elbow; Bush was bringing up the rear, gallantly trying to keep pace with them, his wooden leg thumping the pavement. They came up to the *Witch of Endor*, and made their way up her gang plank to her deck; the officer there looked at them with a little surprise. But he knew the pilot, and he knew the customs uniform.

'I want to examine one of your charts, if you please,' said Hornblower. 'Will you show us the way to the cabin?'

The mate had not a suspicion in the world. He signed to his men to go on with their work and led the way down the brief companion to the after cabin. The mate entered, and politely Hornblower thrust the pilot in next, before him. It was a tiny cabin, but there was sufficient room to be safe when they were at the farther end. He stood by the door and brought out his two pistols.

'If you make a sound,' he said, and excitement rippled his lips into a snarl, 'I will kill you.'

They simply stood and stared at him, but at last the pilot opened his mouth to speak – speech was irrepressible with him.

'Silence!' snapped Hornblower.

He moved far enough into the room to allow Brown and Bush to enter after him.

'Tie 'em up,' he ordered.

Belts and handkerchiefs and scarves did the work efficiently enough; soon the two men were gagged and helpless, their hands tied behind them.

'Under the table with 'em,' said Hornblower. 'Now, be ready for the two hands when I bring 'em down.'

He ran up on deck.

'Here, you two,' he snapped. 'I've some questions to ask you. Come down with me.'

They put down their work and followed him meekly, to the cabin where Hornblower's pistols frightened them into silence. Brown ran on deck for a generous supply of line with which to bind them and to make the lashings of the other two more secure yet. Then he and Bush – neither of them had spoken as yet since the adventure began -- looked to him for further orders.

'Watch 'em,' said Hornblower. 'I'll be back in five minutes with a crew. There'll be one more man at least to make fast.'

He went up to the quay again, and along to where the gangs of galley slaves were assembling, weary after their day's work of unloading. The ten chained men under the sergeant whom he addressed looked at him with lack-lustre eyes, only wondering faintly what fresh misery this spruce colonel was bringing them.

'Sergeant,' he said. 'Bring your party down to my ship. There is work for them there.'

'Yes, Colonel,' said the sergeant.

He rasped an order at the weary men, and they followed Hornblower down the quay. Their bare feet made no sound, but the chain which ran from waist to waist clashed rhythmically with their stride.

'Bring them down on to the deck,' said Hornblower. 'Now come down into the cabin for your orders.'

It was all so easy, thanks to that uniform and star. Hornblower had to try hard not to laugh at the sergeant's bewilderment as they disarmed him and tied him up. It took no more than a significant gesture with Hornblower's pistol to make the sergeant indicate in which pocket was the key of the prisoners' chain.

'I'll have these men laid out under the table, if you please, Mr Bush,' said Hornblower. 'All except the pilot. I want him òn deck.'

The sergeant and the mate and the two hands were laid out, none too gently, and Hornblower went out on deck while the others dragged the pilot after him; it was nearly quite dark now, with only the moon shining. The galley slaves were squatting listlessly on the hatchcoaming. Hornblower addressed them quietly. Despite his difficulty with the language, his boiling excitement conveyed itself to them.

'I can set you men free,' he said. 'There will be an end of beatings and slavery if you will do what I order. I am an English officer, and I am going to sail this ship to England. Does anyone not want to come?'

There was a little sigh from the group; it was as if they could not believe they were hearing aright – probably they could not.

'In England,' went on Hornblower, 'you will be rewarded. There will be a new life awaiting you.'

Now at last they were beginning to understand that they had not been brought on board the cutter for further toil, that there really was a chance of freedom.

'Yes, sir,' said a voice.

'I am going to unfasten your chain,' said Hornblower. 'Remember this. There is to be no noise. Sit still until you are told what to do.'

He fumbled for the padlock in the dim light, unlocked it and snapped it open – it was pathetic, the automatic gesture with which the first man lifted his arms. He was accustomed to being locked and unlocked daily, like an animal. Hornblower set free each man in turn, and the chain clanked on the deck; he stood back with his hands on the butts of his pistols ready in case of trouble, but there was no sign of any. The men stood dazed – the transition from slavery to freedom had taken no more than three minutes.

Hornblower felt the movement of the cutter under his feet as the wind swung her; she was bumping gently against the fends-off hung between her and the quay. A glance over the side confirmed his conclusions – the tide had not yet begun to ebb. There were still some minutes to wait, and he turned to Brown, standing restless aft of the mainmast with the pilot sitting miserably at his feet.

'Brown,' he said quietly, 'run down to our boat and bring me my parcel of clothes. Run along now – what are you waiting for?'

Brown went unhappily. It seemed dreadful to him that his captain should waste precious minutes over recovering his clothes, and should even trouble to think of them. But Hornblower was not as mad as he might appear. They could not start until the tide turned, and Brown might as well be employed fetching clothes as standing fidgeting. For once in his life Hornblower had no intention of posing before his subordinates. His head was clear despite his excitement.

'Thank you,' he said, as Brown returned, panting with the canvas bag. 'Get me my uniform coat out.'

He stripped off his colonel's tunic and put on the coat which Brown held for him, experiencing a pleasant thrill as his fingers fastened the buttons with their crown and anchor. The coat was sadly crumpled, and the gold lace bent and broken, but still it was a uniform, even though the last time he had worn it was months ago when they had been capsized in the Loire. With this coat on his back he could no longer be accused of being a spy, and should their attempt result in failure and recapture it would shelter both himself and his subordinates. Failure and recapture were likely possibilities, as his logical brain told him, but secret murder now was not. The stealing of the cutter would attract sufficient public attention to make that impossible. Already he had bettered his position – he could not be shot as a spy nor be quietly strangled in prison. If he were recaptured now he could only be tried on the old charge of violation of the laws of war, and Hornblower felt that his recent exploits might win him sufficient public sympathy to make it impolitic for Bonaparte to press even that charge.

It was time for action now. He took a belaying pin from the rail, and walked up slowly to the seated pilot, weighing the instrument meditatively in his hand.

'Monsieur,' he said, 'I want you to pilot this ship out to sea.'

The pilot goggled up at him in the faint moonlight.

'I cannot,' he gabbled. 'My professional honour – my duty—'

Hornblower cut him short with a menacing esture of the belaying pin.

'We are going to start now,' he said. 'You can give instructions or not, as you choose. But I tell you this, monsieur. The moment this ship touches ground, I will beat your head into a paste with this.'

Hornblower eyed the white face of the pilot – his moustache was lopsided and ridiculous now after his rough treatment. The man's eyes were on the belaying pin with which Hornblower was tapping the palm of his hand, and Hornblower felt a little thrill of triumph. The threat of a pistol bullet through the head would not have been sufficient for this imaginative southerner. But the man could picture so clearly the crash of the belaying pin upon his skull, and the savage blows which would beat him to death, that the argument Hornblower had selected was the most effective one.

'Yes, monsieur,' said the pilot, weakly.

'Right,' said Hornblower. 'Brown, lash him to the rail, there. Then we can start. Mr Bush, will you take the tiller, if you please?'

The necessary preparations were brief; the convicts were led to the halliards and the ropes put in their hands, ready to haul on the word of command. Hornblower and Brown had so often before had experience in pushing raw crews into their places, thanks to the all-embracing activities of the British press-gangs, and it was good to see that Brown's

French, eked out by the force of his example, was sufficient for the occasion.

'Cut the warps, sir?' volunteered Brown.

'No. Cast them off,' snapped Hornblower.

Cut warps left hanging to the bollards would be a sure proof of a hurried and probably illegal departure; to cast them off meant possibly delaying inquiry and pursuit by a few more minutes, and every minute of delay might be precious in the uncertain future. The first of the ebb was tightening the ropes now, simplifying the business of getting away from the quay. To handle the tiny fore-and-aft rigged ship was an operation calling for little either of the judgment or of the brute strength which a big square-rigger would demand, and the present circumstances – the wind off the quay and the ebbing tide – made the only precaution necessary that of casting off the stern warp before the bow, as Brown understood as clearly as Hornblower. It happened in the natural course of events, for Hornblower had to fumble in the dim light to disentangle the clove hitches with which some French sailor had made fast, and Brown had completed his share long before him. The push of the tide was swinging the cutter away from the quay. Hornblower, in the uncertain light, had to time his moment for setting sail, making allowance for the unreliability of his crew, the eddy along the quayside, the tide and the wind.

'Hoist away,' said Hornblower, and then, to the men, 'Tirez.'

Mainsail and job rose, to the accompaniment of the creaking of the blocks. The sails flapped, bellied, flapped again. Then they filled, and Bush at the tiller – the cutter steered with a tiller, not a wheel – felt a steady pressure. The cutter was gathering way; she was changing from a dead thing to a live. She heeled the tiniest fraction to the breeze with a subdued creaking of her cordage, and simultaneously Hornblower heard a little musical chuckle from the bows as her forefoot bubbled through the water. He picked up the belaying pin again, and in three strides was at the pilot's side, balancing the instrument in his hand.

'To the right, monsieur,' gabbled the individual. 'Keep well to the right.'

'Port your helm, Mr Bush. We're taking the starboard channel!' said Hornblower, and then, translating the further hurried instructions of the pilot. 'Meet her! Keep her at that!'

The cutter glided on down the river in the faint moonlight. From the bank of the river she must make a pretty picture – no one would guess that she was not setting forth on some quite legitimate expedition.

The pilot was saying something else now; Hornblower bent his ear to listen. It had regard to the advisability of having a man at work with the lead taking soundings, and Hornblower would not consider it for a moment. There were only Brown and himself who could do that, and they both might be wanted at any moment in case it should be necessary for the cutter to go about – moreover, there would be bound to be a muddle about fathoms and metres.

'No,' said Hornblower. 'You will have to do your work without that. And my promise still holds good.'

He tapped his palm with the belaying pin, and laughed. That laugh surprised him, it was so blood-curdling in its implications. Anyone hearing it would be quite sure that Hornblower was determined upon clubbing the pilot to death if they went aground. Hornblower asked himself if he were acting and was puzzled to discover that he could not answer the question. He could not picture himself killing a helpless man – and yet he could not be sure. This fierce, relentless determination that consumed him was something new to him, just as it always was. He was aware of the fact that once he had set his hand to a scheme he never allowed any consideration to stop his carrying it through, but he always looked upon himself as fatalistic or resigned. It was always startling to detect in himself qualities which he admired in other men. But it was sufficient, and satisfactory, for the moment, to know that the pilot was quite sure that he would be killed in an unpleasant fashion if the cutter should touch ground.

Within half a mile it was necessary to cross to the other side – it was amusing to note how this vast estuary repeated on a grand scale the characteristics of the upper river, where the clear channel serpentined from shore to shore between the sandbanks. At the pilot's warning Hornblower got his motley crew together in case it might be necessary to go about, but the precaution was needless. Closehauled, and with the tide running fast behind her, the cutter glided across, Hornblower and Brown at the sheets, and Bush at the tiller demonstrating once more what an accomplished seaman he was. They steadied her with the wind again over her quarter, Hornblower anxiously testing the direction of the wind and looking up at the ghostly sails.

'Monsieur,' pleaded the pilot. 'Monsieur, these cords are tight.'

Hornblower laughed again, horribly.

'They will serve to keep you awake, then,' he said.

His instinct had dictated the reply; his reason confirmed it. It would be best to show no hint of weakness towards this man who had it in his power to wreck everything – the more firmly the pilot was convinced of his captor's utter pitilessness the less chance there was of his playing them false. Better that he should endure the pain of tight ligatures than that three men should risk imprisonment and death. And suddenly Hornblower remembered the four other men – the sergeant and the mate and the two hands – who lay gagged and bound in the cabin. They must be highly uncomfortable, and probably fairly near to suffocation. It could not be helped. No one could be spared for a moment from the deck to go below and attend them. There they must lie until there was no hope of rescue for them.

He found himself feeling sorry for them, and put the feeling aside. Naval history teemed with stories of recaptured prizes, in which the prisoners had succeeded in overpowering weak prize crews. He was going to run no risk of that. It was interesting to note how his mouth set itself hard at the thought, without his own volition; and it was equally interesting to observe how his reluctance to go home and face the music reacted contrariwise upon his resolution to see this affair through. He did not want to fail, and the thought that he might be glad of failure because of the postponement of the settlement of his affairs only made him more set in his determination not to fail.

'I will loosen the cords,' he said to the pilot, 'when we are off Noirmoutier. Not before.'

XIV

They were off Noirmoutier at dawn, with the last dying puff of wind. The grey light found them becalmed and enwreathed in a light haze which drifted in patches over the calm surface of the sea, awaiting the rising of the sun to dissipate it. Hornblower looked round him as the details became more clear. The galley slaves were all asleep on the foredeck, huddled together for warmth like pigs in a sty, with Brown squatting on the hatch beside them, his chin on his hand. Bush still stood at the tiller, betraying no fatigue after his sleepless night; he held the tiller against his hip with his wooden leg braced against a ring bolt. Against the rail the pilot drooped in his bonds; his face which yesterday had been plump and pink was this morning drawn and grey with pain and fatigue.

With a little shudder of disgust Hornblower cut him loose.

'I keep my promise, you see,' he said, but the pilot only dropped to the deck, his face distorted with pain, and a minute later he was groaning with the agony of returning circulation.

The big mainsail boom came inboard with a clatter as the sail flapped.

'I can't hold the course, sir,' said Bush.

'Very well,' said Hornblower.

He might have expected this. The gentle night wind which had wafted them down the estuary was just the sort to die away with the dawn, leaving them becalmed. But had it held for another half hour, had they made another couple of miles of progress, they would be far safer. There lay Noirmoutier to port, and the mainland astern; through the shredding mist he could make out the gaunt outlines of the semaphore station on the mainland – sixteen years ago he had been second in command of the landing party which Pellew had sent ashore to destroy it. The islands were all heavily garrisoned now, with big guns mounted, as a consequence of the incessant English raids. He scanned the distance which separated them from Noirmoutier, measuring it with his eye – they were out of big-gun range, he fancied, but the tide might easily drift them in closer. He even suspected, from what he remembered of the set of the tides, that there was danger of their being drifted into the Bay of Bourgneuf.

'Brown,' he called, sharply, 'Wake those men up. Set them to work with the sweeps.'

On either side of every gun was a thole for a sweep, six on each side of the ship; Brown shoved his blear-eyed crew into their positions and showed them how to get out the big oars, with the long rope joining the looms.

'One, two, three, pull!' shouted Brown.

The men put their weight on the oars; the blades bubbled ineffectively through the still water.

'One, two, three, pull! One, two, three, pull!'

Brown was all animation, gesticulating, running from man to man beating time with his whole body. Gradually the cutter gathered way, and as she began to move the oar blades began to bite upon the water with more effect.

'One, two, three, pull!'

It did not matter that Brown was counting time in English, for there was no mistaking his meaning, nor the meaning of the convulsive movements of his big body.

'Pull!'

The galley slaves sought for foothold on the deck as they tugged; Brown's enthusiasm was infectious, so that one or two of them even raised their voices in a cracked cheer as they leaned back. Now the cutter was perceptibly moving; Bush swung the tiller over, felt the rudder bite, and steadied her on her course again. She rose and fell over the tiny swell with a clattering of blocks.

Hornblower looked away from the straining men over the oily sea. If he had been lucky he might have found one of the ships of the blockading squadron close inshore – often they would come right in among the islands to beard Bonaparte. But today there was no sail in sight. He studied the grim outlines of the islands for signs of life. Even as he looked the gallows-like arms of the semaphore station on the mainland sprang up to attention. They made no further movement, and Hornblower guessed that they were merely announcing the operators' readiness to receive a message from the station farther inshore invisible to him – he could guess the purport of the message. Then the arms started signalling, moving jerkily against the blue sky, transmitting a brief reply to the interior. Another period of quiescence, and then Hornblower saw the signal arms swing round towards him – previously they had been nearly in profile. Automatically he turned towards Noirmoutier, and he saw the tiny speck of the flag at the masthead there dip in acknowledgement. Noirmoutier was ready to receive orders from the land. Round and round spun the arms of the semaphore; up and down went the flag in acknowledgement of each sentence.

Near the foot of the mast appeared a long jet of white smoke, rounding off instantly into a ball, and one after the other four fountains of water leaped from the glassy surface of the sea as a shot skipped over it, the dull report following after. The nearest fountain was a full half mile away, so that they were comfortably out of range.

'Make those men pull!' roared Hornblower to Brown.

He could guess what would be the next move. Under her sweeps the cutter was making less than a mile in the hour, and all day long they would be in danger, unless a breeze came, and his straining eyes could see no hint of a breeze on the calm surface of the sea, nor in the vivid blue of the morning sky. At any moment boats crowded with men would be putting off towards them – boats whose oars would move them far faster than the cutter's sweeps. There would be fifty men in each, perhaps a gun mounted in the bows as well. Three men with the doubtful aid of a dozen galley slaves could not hope to oppose them.

'Yes I can, by God,' said Hornblower to himself.

As he sprang into action he could see the boats heading out from the tip of the island, tiny dots upon the surface of the sea. The garrison must have turned out and bundled into the boats immediately on receiving the order from the land.

'Pull!' shouted Brown.

The sweeps groaned on the tholes, and the cutter lurched under the impulse.

Hornblower had cleared away the aftermost six-pounder on the port side. There was shot in the locker under the rail, but no powder.

'Keep the men at work, Brown,' he said, 'and watch the pilot.'

'Aye aye, sir,' said Brown.

He stretched out a vast hand and took hold of the pilot's collar, while Hornblower dived into the cabin. One of the four prisoners there had writhed and wriggled his way to the foot of the little companion – Hornblower trod on him in his haste. With a curse he dragged him out of the way; as he expected there was a hatchway down into the lazarette. Hornblower jerked it open and plunged through; it was nearly dark, for the only light was what filtered through the cabin skylight and down the hatchway, and he stumbled and blundered upon the piled-up stores inside. He steadied himself; whatever the need for haste there was no profit in panic. He waited for his eyes to grow accustomed to the darkness, while overhead he could hear Brown still bellowing and the sweeps still groaning on the tholes. Then in the bulkhead before him he saw what he sought, a low doorway with a glass panel, which must indicate the magazine – the gunner would work in there by the light of a lantern shining through.

He heaved the piled-up stores out of his way, sweating in his haste and the heat, and wrenched open the door. Feeling about him in the tiny space, crouching nearly double, his hands fell upon four big hogsheads of gunpowder. He fancied he could feel the grittiness of gunpowder under his feet; any movement on his part might start a spark and blow the cutter to fragments – it was just like the French to be careless with explosives. He sighed with relief when his fingers encountered the paper containers of ready charges. He had hoped to find them but there had always been the chance that there were no cartridges available, and he had not been enamoured of the prospect of using a powder-ladle. He loaded himself with cartridges and backed out of the tiny magazine to the cabin, and sprang up on deck again, to the clear sunshine.

The boats were appreciably nearer, for they were no longer black specks but boats, creeping beetle-like over the surface towards them, three of them, already spaced out in their race to effect a recapture. Hornblower put down his cartridges upon the deck. His heart was pounding with his exertions and with excitement, and each successive effort that he made to steady himself seemed to grow less successful. It was one thing to think and plan and direct, to say, 'Do this,' or 'Go there,' and it was quite another to have success dependent upon the cunning of his own fingers and the straightness of his own eye.

His sensations were rather similar to those he experienced when he had drunk a glass of wine too many – he knew clearly enough what he had to do, but his limbs were not quite as ready as usual to obey the orders of his brain. He fumbled more than once as he rigged the train-tackle of the gun.

That fumbling cured him; he rose from the task shaking his unsteadiness from him like Christian losing his burden of sin. He was cool now, set completely on the task in hand.

'Here, you,' he said to the pilot.

The pilot demurred for a moment, full of fine phrases regarding the impossibility of training a gun upon his fellow countrymen, but a sight of the alteration in Hornblower's expression reduced him to instant humble submission. Hornblower was unaware of the relentless ferocity of his glance, being only conscious of a momentary irritation at anyone crossing his will. But the pilot had thought that any further delay would lead to Hornblower's killing him, pitilessly – and the pilot may have been right. Between them they laid hold of the train-tackle and ran the gun back. Hornblower took out the tampion and went round to the breech; he twirled the elevating screw until his eye told him that the gun was at the maximum elevation at which it could be run out. He cocked the lock, and then, crouching over the gun so that the shadow of his body cut off the sunlight, jerked the lanyard. The spark was satisfactory.

He ripped open a cartridge, poured the powder into the muzzle of the gun, folded the paper into a wad, and rammed the charge home with the flexible rammer. A glance towards the boats showed that they were still probably out of range, so that he was not pressed for time. He devoted a few seconds to turning over the shot in the locker, selecting two or three of the roundest, and then strolled across the deck to the starboard-side locker and made a selection from there. For long-range work with a six-pounder he did not want shot that bounced about during its passage up the gun and was liable to fly off God-knew-where when it emerged. He rammed his eventual selection well down upon the wad – at this elevation there was no need for a second wad – and, ripping open a second cartridge, he primed the breach.

'Allons!' he snapped at the pilot, and then ran the gun up. Two men were the barest minimum crew for a six-pounder, but Hornblower's long slight body was capable of exerting extraordinary strength at the behest of his mind.

With a handspike he trained the gun round aft as far as possible. Even so, the gun did not point towards the leading boat, which lay far abaft the beam; the cutter would have to yaw to fire at her. Hornblower straightened himself up in the sunlight. Brown was chanting hoarsely at the galley slaves almost in his ear, and the aftermost sweep had been working right at his elbow, and he had not noticed either, so intent had he been on his task. For the cutter to yaw meant losing a certain amount of distance; he had to balance that certain loss against the chances of hitting a boat with a six-pounder ball at two thousand yards. It would not pay at present; it would be better to wait a little, for the range to shorten, but it was an interesting problem, even though it could have no exact solution in consequence of the presence of an unknown, which was the possibility of the coming of a wind.

Of that there was still no sign, long and anxiously though Hornblower stared over the glassy sea. As he looked round he caught the eye of Bush at the tiller directed anxiously at him – Bush was awaiting the order to yaw. Hornblower smiled at him and shook his head, resuming his study of the horizon, the distant islands, the unbroken expanse to seaward where lay freedom. A seagull was wheeling overhead, dazzling white against the blue, and crying plaintively. The cutter was nodding a little in the faint swell.

'Beggin' your pardon, sir,' said Brown in his ear. 'Beggin' your pardon, sir – Pull! – These men can't go on much longer, sir. Look at that one over there on the starboard side, sir – Pull!'

There could be no doubt of it; the men were swaying with fatigue as they reached forward with the long sweeps. Dangling from Brown's hand was a length of knotted cord; clearly he had already been using the most obvious argument to persuade them to work.

'Give 'em a bit of a rest, sir, and summat to eat an' drink, an' they'll go on all right, sir. Pull, you bastards! They haven't had no breakfast, sir, nor no supper yesterday.'

'Very good,' said Hornblower. 'You can rest 'em and get 'em fed. Mr Bush! Let her come slowly round.'

He bent over the gun, oblivious at once to the clatter of the released sweeps as the galley slaves ceased work, just as he was oblivious that he himself had not eaten or drunk or slept since yesterday. At the touch of the tiller and with her residual way the cutter turned slowly. The black mass of a boat appeared in the V of the dispart sight, and he waved his hand to Bush. The boat had disappeared again, and came back into his field of vision as Bush checked the turn with the tiller, but not quite in alignment with the gun. Hornblower eased the gun round with the handspike until the aim was true, drew himself up, and stepped out of the way of the recoil, lanyard in hand. Of necessity, he was far more doubtful of the range than of the direction, and it was vital to observe the fall of the shot. He took note of the motion of the cutter on the swell, waited for the climax of the roll, and jerked the lanyard. The gun roared out and recoiled past him; he sprang sideways to get clear of the smoke. The four seconds of the flight of the shot seemed to stretch out indefinitely, and than at last he saw the jet of water leap into brief existence, fully two hundred yards short and a hundred yards to the right. That was poor shooting.

He sponged out the gun and reloaded it, called the pilot to him with an abrupt gesture, and ran the gun out again. It was necessary, he realised, to get acquainted with the weapon if he wanted to do any fancy shooting with it, so that he made no alteration in elevation, endeavoured to lay the gun exactly as before, and jerked the lanyard at as nearly the same instant of the roll as possible. This time it appeared that the elevation was correct, for the shot pitched well up to the boat, but it was out to the right again, fifty yards off at least. It seemed likely that the gun, therefore, had a tendency to throw to the right. He trained the gun round a trifle to the left, and, still without altering the elevation, fired again. Too far to the left, and two hundred yards short again.

Hornblower told himself that a variation of two hundred yards in the fall of shot from a six-pounder at full elevation was only to be expected, and he knew it to be true, but that was cold comfort to him. The powder varied from charge to charge, the shot were never truly round, quite apart from the variations in atmospheric conditions and in the temperature of the gun. He set his teeth, aimed and fired again. Short, and a trifle to the left. It was maddening.

'Breakfast, sir,' said Brown at his elbow.

Hornblower turned abruptly, and there was Brown with a tray, bearing a basin of biscuit, a bottle of wine, a jug of water, a pewter mug; the sight made Hornblower realise that he was intensely hungry and thirsty.

'What about you?' asked Hornblower.

'We're all right, sir,' said Brown.

The galley slaves were squatting on the deck wolfing bread and drinking water; so was Bush, over by the tiller. Hornblower discovered that his tongue and the roof of his mouth were dry as leather – his hands shook as he mixed water with wine and gulped it down. Beside the cabin skylight lay the four men who had been left in bonds in the cabin. Their hands were free now, although their feet were still bound. The sergeant and one of the seamen were noticeably pale.

'I took the liberty of bringing 'em up, sir,' said Brown. 'Those two was pretty nigh dead, 'cause o' their gags, sir. But they'll be all right soon, I fancy, sir.'

It had been thoughtless cruelty to leave them bound, thought Hornblower. But going back in his mind through the events of the night he could not think of any time until now when any attention could have been spared for them. In war there was always plenty of cruelty.

'These beggars,' said Brown, indicating the galley slaves, 'wanted to throw the sojer overboard when they saw 'im, sir.'

He grinned widely, as though that were very amusing. The remark opened a long vista of thought, regarding the miseries of the life of a galley slave and the brutalities of their guards.

'Yes,' said Hornblower, gulping down a morsel of biscuit and drinking again. 'You had better set 'em all to work at the sweeps.'

'Aye aye, sir. I had the same idea, beggin' your pardon, sir. We can have two watches with all these men.'

'Arrange it as you like,' said Hornblower, turning back to the gun.

The nearest boat was appreciably nearer now; Hornblower judged it advisable to make a small reduction in the elevation, and this time the shot pitched close to the boat, almost among the oars on one side, apparently.

'Beautiful, sir!' said Bush beside the tiller.

Hornblower's skin was prickling with sweat and powder smoke. He took off his gold-laced coat, suddenly conscious of the heavy weight of the pistols in the side pocket; he proffered them to Bush, but the latter shook his head and grinned, pointing to the bell-mouthed blunderbuss

on the deck beside him. That would be a far more efficacious weapon if
there was trouble with their motley crew. For an exasperated moment
Hornblower wondered what to do with the pistols, and finally laid them
handy in the scuppers before sponging out and reloading the gun. The
next shot was a close one, too – apparently the small reduction of range
had had a profound effect on the accuracy of the gun. Hornblower saw
the shot pitch close to the bows of the boat; it would be a matter of
pure chance at that range if he scored an actual hit, for no gun could be
expected to be accurate to fifty yards.

'Sweeps are ready, sir,' said Brown.

'Very good. Mr Bush, kindly lay a course so that I can keep that boat
under fire.'

Brown was a pillar of strength. He had had rigged only the three foremost sweeps on each side, setting six men to work on them. The others
were herded together forward, ready to relieve the men at work when
they were tired – six sweeps would only just give the big cutter steerage
way, but continuous slow progress was preferable to an alternation of
movement and passivity. What arguments he had used to persuade the
four Frenchmen who were not galley slaves to work at the sweeps Hornblower judged it best not to inquire – it was sufficient that they were
there, their feet hobbled, straining away at the sweeps while Brown gave
them the time, his knotted rope's end dangling from his fist.

The cutter began to creep through the blue water again, the rigging
rattling at each tug on the sweeps. To make the chase as long as possible
she should have turned her stern to her pursuers, instead of keeping
them on her quarter. But Hornblower had decided that the chance of
scoring a hit with the gun was worth the loss in distance – a decision of
whose boldness he was painfully aware and which he had to justify.
He bent over the gun and aimed carefully, and this time the shot flew
wide again. Watching the splash from the rail Hornblower felt a surge
of exasperation. For a moment he was tempted to hand the gun over to
Bush, for him to try his hand, but he put the temptation aside. In the
face of stark reality, without allowing false modesty to enter into the
debate, he could rely on himself to lay a gun better than Bush could.

'Tirez!' he snapped at the pilot, and between them they ran the gun
up again.

The pursuing boats, creeping black over the blue sea, had shown no
sign so far of being dismayed by the bombardment to which they were
being subjected. Their oars kept steadily at work, and they maintained
resolutely a course which would cut the *Witch of Endor*'s a mile or so
farther on. They were big boats, all three of them, carrying at least a
hundred and fifty men between them – only one of them need range
alongside to do the business. Hornblower fired again and then again,
doggedly, fighting down the bitter disappointment at each successive

miss. The range was little over a thousand yards now, he judged – what he would call in an official report 'long cannon shot'. He hated those black boats creeping onward, immune, threatening his life and liberty, just as he hated this cranky gun which would not shoot the same two rounds running. The sweat was making his shirt stick to him, and the powder-grains were irritating his skin.

At the next shot there was no splash; Hornblower could see no sign of its fall anywhere. Then he saw the leading boat swing half round, and her oars stop moving.

'You've hit her, sir,' called Bush.

Next moment the boat straightened on her course again, her oars hard at work. That was disappointing – it had hardly been likely that a ship's long boat could survive a direct hit from a six-pounder ball without injury to her fighting ability, but it was possible, all the same. Hornblower felt for the first time a sense of impending failure. If the hit he had scored with such difficulty was of no avail, what was the sense in continuing the struggle? Then, doggedly, he bent over the gun again, staring along the sights to allow for the small amount of right-hand bias which the gun exhibited. Even as he looked he saw the leading boat cease rowing again. She wavered and then swung round, signalling wildly to the other boats. Hornblower trained the gun round upon her and fired again and missed, but he could see that she was perceptibly lower in the water. The other boats drew up alongside her, evidently to transfer her crew.

'Port a point, Mr Bush!' yelled Hornblower – already the group of boats was out of the field of fire of the gun, and yet was far too tempting a mark to ignore. The French pilot groaned as he helped to run the gun up, but Hornblower had no time for his patriotic protests. He sighted carefully, and fired. Again there was no sign of a splash – the ball had taken effect, but presumably upon the boat which had already been hit, for immediately afterwards the other two drew away from their water-logged fellow to resume the pursuit.

Brown was changing over the men at the sweeps – Hornblower remembered now that he had heard him cheering hoarsely when he had scored his hit – and Hornblower found a second in which to admire his masterful handling of the men, prisoners of war and escaping slaves alike. There was time for admiration, but no time for envy. The pursuers were changing their tactics – one boat was heading straight at them, while the other, diverging a little, was still heading to intercept them. The reason was soon obvious, for from the bows of the former boat came a puff of smoke, and a cannon-ball raised a splash from the surface of the water on the cutter's quarter and skipped past the stern.

Hornblower shrugged his shoulders at that – a three-pounder boat gun, fired from a platform far more unsteady even than the *Witch of*

Endor, could hardly do them any harm at that range, and every shot meant delay in the pursuit. He trained his gun round upon the intercepting boat, fired, and missed. He was already taking aim again before the sound of the second shot from the boat gun reached his ears, and he did not trouble to find out where the ball went. His own shot fell close to its target, for the range was shortening and he was growing more experienced with the gun and more imbued with the rhythm of the long Atlantic swell which rocked the *Witch of Endor*. Three times he dropped a shot so close to the boat that the men at the oars must have been wetted by the splashes – each shot deserved to be a hit, he knew, but the incalculable residuum of variables in powder and ball and gun made it a matter of chance just where the ball fell in a circle of fifty-yards radius, however well aimed. Ten guns properly controlled, and fired together in a broadside, would do the business, but there was no chance of firing ten guns together.

There was a crash from forward, a fountain of splinters from the base of a stanchion, and a shot scarred the deck diagonally close beside the fore hatchway.

'No you don't,' roared Brown, leaping forward with his rope's end. 'Keep pulling, you bastard!'

He jerked the scared galley slave who had dropped his sweep – the shot must have missed him by no more than a yard – back into position.

'Pull!' he shouted, standing, magnificent in his superb physique, right in the midst of them, the weary ones lying on the deck, the others sweating at the sweeps, the knotted rope swinging from his hand. He was like a lion tamer in a cage. Hornblower could see there was no need for him and his pistols, and he bent again, this time with a real twinge of envy, over his gun.

The boat which was firing at them had not closed in at all – if anything she had fallen a trifle back – but the other one was far nearer by now. Hornblower could see the individual men in her, the dark heads and the brown shoulders. Her oars were still for the moment, and there was some movement in her, as if they were re-arranging the men at the oars. Now she was in motion again, and moving far faster, and heading straight at them. The officer in charge, having worked up as close as this, had double-banked his oars so as to cover the last, most dangerous zone with a rush, pouring out the carefully conserved energy of his men prodigally in his haste to come alongside.

Hornblower estimated the rapidly diminishing range, twirled the elevating screw, and fired. The shot hit the water ten yards from her bows and must have ricochetted clean over her. He sponged and loaded and rammed – a miss-fire now, he told himself, would be fatal, and he forced himself to go through the routine with all the exactness he had employed before. The sights of the gun were looking straight at the bows of the boat, it was point-blank range. He jerked the lanyard and sprang instantly to reload without wasting time by seeing where the shot went. It must have passed close over the heads of the men at the oars, for when he looked along the sights again there she was, still heading straight at him. A tiny reduction in elevation, and he stepped aside the jerked the lanyard. He was dragging at the train tackles before he could look again. The bows of the boat had opened like a fan. In the air above her there was a black dot – a water breaker, presumably, sent flying like a football by the impact of the shot, which had hit clean and square upon her stem at water level. Her bows were lifted a little out of the water, the loose strakes spread wide, and then they came down again and the water surged in, and she was gunwale deep in a flash, her bottom smashed, presumably, as well as her bows, by the passage of the shot.

Brown was cheering again, and Bush was capering as well as he could with a wooden leg while steering, and the little French pilot at his side pulling in his breath with a sharp hissing noise. There were black dots on the surface of the blue water where men struggled for their lives – it must be bitter cold and they would die quickly, those who could not find support on the shattered hull, but nothing could be done to help them. Already they had more prisoners than they could conveniently handle, and any delay would bring the other boat alongside them.

'Keep the men at work!' said Hornblower, harshly, to Brown, and unnecessarily. Then he bent to reload the gun once more.

'What course, sir?' asked Bush, from the tiller. He wanted to know if he should steer so as to allow fire to be opened on the third boat, which had ceased firing now and was pulling hastily towards the wreck.

'Keep her as she is,' snapped Hornblower. He knew perfectly well that the boat would not annoy them further; having seen two of her fellows sunk and being of necessity vastly overcrowded she would turn back sooner than maintain the contest. And so it proved. After the boat had picked up the survivors they saw her swing round and head towards Noirmoutier, followed by a derisive cheer from Brown.

Hornblower could look round him now. He walked aft to the taffrail beside Bush – it was curious how much more natural it felt to be there than at the gun – and scanned the horizon. During the fight the cutter had made very decided progress under her sweeps. The mainland was lost in the faint haze; Noirmoutier was already far behind. But there was still no sign of a breeze. They were still in danger – if darkness should find them where boats could reach them from the islands a night attack would tell a very different story. They needed every yard they could gain, and the men must go on slaving at the sweeps all through the day, all through the night too, if necessary.

He was conscious now that he ached in every joint after the frantic

exertions of serving the gun the whole morning, and he had had a whole
night without sleep – so had Bush, so had Brown. He felt that he stank
of sweat and smoke, and his skin tingled with powder grains. He wanted
rest, yet automatically he walked over to make the gun secure again, to
put the unused cartridges out of harm's way, and to repocket the pistols
which he noticed reproaching his carelessness from the scuppers.

XV

At midnight, and not before, a tiny breeze came whispering over the
misty surface of the water, at first merely swinging over the big mainsail
and setting the rigging chattering, but then breathing more strongly until
the sails could catch it and hold it, filling out in the darkness until
Hornblower could give the word for the exhausted men at the sweeps to
abandon their labour and the cutter could glide on with almost imperceptible motion, so slowly, that there was hardly a bubble at her bows,
yet even at that faster than the sweeps had moved her. Out of the east
came that breath of wind, steady even though feeble; Hornblower could
feel hardly any pull as he handled the mainsheet, and yet the cutter's
big area of canvas was able to carry her graceful hull forward over the
invisible surface as though in a dream.

It was like a dream indeed – weariness and lack of sleep combined to
make it so for Hornblower, who moved about his tasks in a misty
unreality which matched the misty darkness of the sea. The galley slaves
and prisoners could lie and sleep – there was no fear of trouble from
them at present, when they had spent ten hours out of the last twenty
pulling at the sweeps with hands which by nightfall were running with
blood, but there was no sleep for him nor for Bush and Brown. His
voice sounded strange and distant in his own ears, like that of a stranger
speaking from another room, as he issued his orders; the very hands
with which he held the ropes seemed not to belong to him. It was as if
there was a cleavage between the brain with which he was trying to
think and the body which condescended to obey him.

Somewhere to the northwest lay the fleet which maintained its un-
sleeping watch over Brest; he had laid the cutter on a northwesterly
course with the wind comfortably on her quarter, and if he could not
find the Channel fleet he would round Ushant and sail the cutter to
England. He knew all this – it made it more like a dream than ever that
he could not believe it although he knew it. The memory of Marie de
Graçay's upper boudoir, or of his battle for life in the floodwater of the
Loire, was far more real to him than this solid little ship whose deck he

trod and whose mainsheet he was handling. Setting a course for Bush to steer was like playing a make-believe game with a child. He told himself desperately that this was not a new phenomenon, that often enough before he had noticed that although he could dispense with one night's sleep without missing it greatly, on the second in succession his imagination began to play tricks with him, but it did not help to clear his mind.

He came back to Bush at the tiller, when the faint binnacle light made the lieutenant's face just visible in the darkness; Hornblower was even prepared to enter into conversation in exchange for a grasp at reality.

'Tired, Mr Bush?' he asked.

'No, sir. Of course not. But how is it with you, sir?'

Bush had served with his captain through too many fights to have an exaggerated idea of his strength.

'Well enough, thank you.'

'If this breeze holds, sir,' said Bush, realising that this was one of the rare occasions when he was expected to make small talk with his captain, 'we'll be up to the fleet in the morning.'

'I hope so,' said Hornblower.

'By God, sir,' said Bush, 'what will they say of this in England?'

Bush's expression was rapt. He was dreaming of fame, of promotion, for his captain as much as for himself.

'In England?' said Hornblower vaguely.

He had been too busy to dream any dreams himself, to think about what the British public, sentimental as always, would think of an escaping British captain retaking almost single-handed a captured ship of war and returning in her in triumph. And he had seized the *Witch of Endor* in the first place merely because the opportunity had presented itself, and because it was the most damaging blow he could deal the enemy; since the seizure he had been at first too busy, and latterly too tired, to appreciate the dramatic quality of his action. His distrust of himself, and his perennial pessimism regarding his career, would not allow him to think of himself as dramatically successful. The unimaginative Bush could appreciate the potentialities better than he could.

'Yes, sir,' said Bush, eagerly – even with tiller and compass and wind claiming so much of his attention he could be loquacious at this point – 'It'll look fine in the *Gazette*, this recapture of the *Witch*. Even the *Morning Chronicle*, sir—'

The *Morning Chronicle* was a thorn in the side of the government, ever ready to decry a victory or make capital of a defeat. Hornblower remembered how during the bitter early days of his captivity at Rosas he had worried about what the *Morning Chronicle* would say regarding his surrender of the *Sutherland*.

He felt sick now, suddenly. His mind was active enough now. Most of its vagueness must have been due, he told himself, because he had been refusing in cowardly fashion to contemplate the future. Until this night everything had been uncertain – he might have been recaptured at any moment, but now, as sure as anything could be at sea, he would see England again. He would have to stand his trial for the loss of the *Sutherland*, and face a court martial, after eighteen years of service. The court might find him guilty of not having done his utmost in the presence of the enemy, and for that there was only one penalty, death – that Article of War did not end, as others did, with the mitigating words 'or such less penalty—'. Byng had been shot fifty years before under that Article of War.

Absolved on that account, the wisdom of his actions in command of the *Sutherland* might still be called into question. He might be found guilty of errors of judgment in hazarding his ship in a battle against quadruple odds, and be punished by anything from dismissal from the service, which would make him an outcast and a beggar, down to a simple reprimand which would merely wreck his career. A court martial was always a hazardous ordeal from which few emerged unscathed – Cochrane, Sydney Smith, half a dozen brilliant captains had suffered damage at the hands of a court martial, and the friendless Captain Hornblower might be the next.

And a court martial was only one of the ordeals that awaited him. The child must be three months old now; until this moment he had never been able to think clearly about the child – boy or girl, healthy or feeble. He was torn with anxiety for Maria – and yet, gulping at the pill of reality, he forced himself to admit that he did not want to go back to Maria. He did not want to. It had been in mad jealousy of the moment, when he heard of Lady Barbara's marriage to Admiral Leighton, that the child had been conceived. Maria in England, Marie in France – his conscience was in a turmoil about both of them, and underlying the turmoil was an unregenerate hunger for Lady Barbara which had remained quiescent during his preoccupation but which he knew would grow into an unrelenting ache, an internal cancer, the moment his other troubles ceased, if ever they did.

Bush was still babbling away happily beside him at the tiller. Hornblower heard the words, and attached no meaning to them.

'He – h'm," he said. 'Quite so.'

He could find no satisfaction in the simple pleasures Bush had been in ecstasy about – the breath of the sea, the feeling of a ship's deck underfoot – not now, not with all these bitter thoughts thronging his mind. The harshness of his tone checked Bush in the full career of his artless and unwonted chatter, and the lieutenant pulled himself up abruptly. Hornblower thought it was absurd that Bush should still cherish any affection for him after the cutting cruelty with which he

sometimes used him. Bush was like a dog, thought Hornblower bitterly –
too cynical for the moment to credit Bush with any perspicacity at all –
like a dog, coming fawning to the hand that beat him. Hornblower
despised himself as he walked forward again to the mainsheet, to a long,
long, period of a solitary black hell of his own.

There was just the faintest beginning of daylight, the barest pearly
softening of the sombreness of night, a greyness instead of a blackness
in the haze, when Brown came aft to Hornblower.

'Beggin' your pardon, sir, but I fancy I see the loom of something
out there just now. On the port bow, sir – there, d'you see it, sir?'

Hornblower strained his eyes through the blackness. Perhaps there
was a more solid nucleus to the black mist out there, a tiny something.
It came and went as his eyes grew tired.

'What d'you make of it, Brown?'

'I thought it was a ship, sir, when I first saw it, but in this haze,
sir—'

There was a faint chance she might be a French ship of war – it was
about as likely as to find the king unguarded when leading from a suit
of four to an ace. Much the most likely chance was that she was an
English ship of war, and the next most likely that she was a merchantman. The safest course was to creep down upon her from the windward,
because the cutter, lying nearer the wind than any square-rigged ship
could do, could escape if necessary the way she came, trusting to the
mist and darkness and surprise to avoid being disabled before she got
out of range.

'Mr Bush, I fancy there's a sail to leeward. Put the cutter before the
wind and run down to her, if you please. Be ready to go about if I give
the word. Jib-sheet, Brown.'

Hornblower's head was clear again now, in the face of a possible
emergency. He regretted the quickening of his pulse – uncertainty always had that effect. The cutter steadied upon her new course, creeping
before the wind over the misty water, mainsail boom far out to port.
Hornblower experienced a moment's doubt in case Bush was sailing
her by the lee, but he would not allow himself to call a warning – he
knew he could trust a sailor of Bush's ability not to risk a gibe in an
emergency of this sort. He strained his eyes through the darkness; the
mist was patchy, coming and going as he looked, but that was a ship
without any doubt. She was under topsails alone – that made it almost
certain that she was an English ship of war, one of the fleet which maintained unceasing watch over Brest. Another patch of mist obscured her
again, and by the time they had run through it she was appreciably
nearer, and dawn was at hand – her sails were faint grey in the growing
light. Now they were close upon her.

Suddenly the stillness was rent by a hail, high-pitched, penetrating, its purity of quality almost unspoilt by the speaking trumpet – the voice which uttered it was trained in clarity in Atlantic gales.

'Cutter ahoy! What cutter's that?'

At the sound of the English speech Hornblower relaxed. There was no need now to go about, to claw to windward, to seek shelter in the mist. But on the other hand all the unpleasantness of the future which he had been visualising were certain now. He swallowed hard, words failing him for the moment.

'What cutter's that?' repeated the hail, impatiently.

Unpleasant the future might be; he would fly his colours to the last, and, if his career were ending, he would end it with a joke.

'His Britannic Majesty's armed cutter *Witch of Endor*, Captain Horatio Hornblower. What ship's that?'

'*Triumph*, Captain Sir Thomas Hardy – *what* did you say that cutter was?'

Hornblower grinned to himself. The officer of the watch in the strange sail had begun his reply automatically; it was only after he had stated the names of his ship and captain that it had suddenly dawned upon him that the cutter's statement was quite incredible. The *Witch of Endor* had been a prize to the French for nearly a year, and Captain Horatio Hornblower had been dead six months.

Hornblower repeated what he had said before; both Bush and Brown were chuckling audibly at a joke which appealed to them forcibly indeed.

'Come under my lee, and no tricks, or I'll sink you,' hailed the voice.

From the cutter they could hear the guns being run out in the *Triumph*; Hornblower could picture the bustle on board, hands being turned up, the captain being called – Sir Thomas Hardy must be Nelson's late flag captain at Trafalgar, two years Hornblower's senior in the captains' list. Hornblower had known him as a lieutenant, although since then their paths had hardly crossed. Bush eased the cutter under the stern of the two-decker, and brought her to the wind under her lee. Dawn was coming up fast now, and they could see the details of the ship, as she lay hove to, rolling in the swell, and a long shuddering sigh burst from Hornblower's breast. The sturdy beauty of the ship, the two yellow streaks along her sides, checkered with black gunports, the pendant at the main, the hands on the deck, the red coats of the marines, the boatswain's voice roaring at dilatory seamen – all the familiar sights and sounds of the Navy in which he had grown up moved him inexpressibly at this moment, the end of his long captivity and flight.

The *Triumph* had launched a boat, which came dancing rapidly over to them, and a young midshipman swung himself dexterously on board, dirk at his hip, arrogant suspicion on his face, four seamen at his back with pistols and cutlasses.

'What's all this?' demanded the midshipman. His glance swept the cutter's deck, observing the sleepy prisoners rubbing their eyes, the wooden-legged civilian at the tiller, the bareheaded man in a King's coat awaiting him.

'You call me "sir",' barked Hornblower, as he had done to midshipmen ever since he became a lieutenant.

The midshipman eyed the gold-laced coat – undoubtedly it was trimmed in the fashion of the coat of a captain of more than three years' seniority, and the man who wore it carried himself as though he expected deference.

'Yes, sir,' said the midshipman, a little abashed.

'That is Lieutenant Bush at the tiller. You will remain here with these men under his orders, while I go to interview your captain.'

'Aye aye, sir,' said the midshipman, stiffening to attention.

The boat bore Hornblower to the *Triumph*'s side; the coxswain made the four-finger gesture which indicated the arrival of a captain, but marines and side-boys were not in attendance as Hornblower went up the side – the Navy could not risk wasting her cherished compliments on possible impostors. But Hardy was there on deck, his huge bulk towering over everyone round him; Hornblower saw the expression of his beefy face alter as he saw him.

'Good God, it's Hornblower all right,' said Hardy, striding forward, with his hand outstretched. 'Welcome back, sir. How do you come here, sir? How did you retake the *Witch*? How—'

What Hardy wanted to say was, 'How have you risen from the grave?' but such a question seemed to savour of impoliteness. Hornblower shook hands, and trod gratefully the quarterdeck of a ship of the line once more. His heart was too full for speech, or his brain was too numb with fatigue, and he could make no reply to Hardy's questioning.

'Come below to my cabin,' said Hardy, kindly – phlegmatic though he was, he still could just appreciate the other's difficulty.

There was more ease in the cabin, sitting on the cushioned locker under the portrait of Nelson that hung on the bulkhead, and with the timbers groaning faintly all round, and the blue sea visible through the great stern window. Hornblower told a little of what had happened to him – not much, and not in detail; only half a dozen brief sentences, for Hardy was not a man with much use for words. He listened with attention pulling at his whiskers, and nodding at each point.

'There was a whole *Gazette*,' he remarked, 'about the attack in Rosas Bay. They brought Leighton's body back for burial in St Paul's.'

The cabin swam round Hornblower; Hardy's homely face and magnificent whiskers vanished in a mist.

'He was killed, then?' Hornblower asked.

'He died of his wounds at Gibraltar.'

So Barbara was a widow – had been one for six months now.

'Have you heard anything of my wife?' asked Hornblower. The question was a natural one to Hardy, little use though he himself had for women; and he could see no connection between it and the preceding conversation.

'I remember reading that she was awarded a Civil List pension by the government when the news of – of your death arrived.'

'No other news? There was a child coming.'

'None that I know of. I have been four months in this ship.'

Hornblower's head sunk on his breast. The news of Leighton's death added to the confusion of his mind. He did not know whether to be pleased or sorry about it. Barbara would be as unattainable to him as ever, and perhaps there would be all the jealous misery to endure of her re-marriage.

'Now,' said Hardy. 'Breakfast?'

'There's Bush and my coxswain in the cutter,' said Hornblower. 'I must see that all is well with them first.'

XVI

A midshipman came into the cabin as they ate breakfast.

'The fleet's in sight from the masthead, sir,' he reported to Hardy.

'Very good.' As the midshipman went out again Hardy turned back to Hornblower. 'I must report your arrival to His Lordship.'

'Is he still in command?' asked Hornblower, startled. It was a surprise to him that the government had left Admiral Lord Gambier in command of the Channel Fleet for three years, despite the disastrous waste of opportunity at the Basque Roads.

'He hauls down his flag next month,' said Hardy, gloomily. Most officers turned gloomy when discussing 'Dismal Jimmy'. 'They white-washed him at the court martial, and had to leave him his full three years.'

A shade of embarrassment appeared in Hardy's expression; he had let slip the mention of a court martial to a man who soon would endure the same ordeal.

'I supposed they had to,' said Hornblower, his train of thought following that of his fellow captain as he wondered if there would be any whitewash employed at his trial.

Hardy broke the embarrassed silence which followed.

'Would you care to come on deck with me?' he asked.

Over the horizon to leeward was appearing a long line of ships, closehauled. They were in rigid, regular line, and as Hornblower watched they went about in succession in perfect order, as if they were chained together. The Channel Fleet was at drill – eighteen years of drill at sea had given them their unquestioned superiority over any other fleet in the world.

'*Victory*'s in the van,' said Hardy, handing his glass to Hornblower. 'Signal midshipman! "*Triumph* to flag. Have on board—".'

Hornblower looked through the glass while Hardy dictated his message. The three-decker with her admiral's flag at the main was leading the long line of ships, the broad stripes on her side glistening in the sunlight. She had been Jervis's flagship at St Vincent, Hood's in the Mediterranean, Nelson's at Trafalgar. Now she was Dismal Jimmy's – a tragedy if ever there was one. Signal-hoists were soaring up to her yardarms; Hardy was busy dictating replies.

'The Admiral is signalling for you to go on board, sir,' he said at last, turning back to Hornblower. 'I trust you will do me the honour of making use of my barge?'

The *Triumph*'s barge was painted primrose yellow picked out with black, and so were the oarblades; her crew wore primrose-coloured jumpers with black neckcloths. As Hornblower took his seat, his hand still tingling from Hardy's handclasp, he reminded himself gloomily that he had never been able to afford to dress his barge's crew in a fancy rig-out; he always felt sore on the point. Hardy must be a wealthy man with his Trafalgar prize money and his pension as Colonel of Marines. He contrasted their situations – Hardy, a baronet, moneyed, famous, and he himself poor, undistinguished, and awaiting trial.

They piped the side for him in the *Victory*, as Admiralty regulations laid down – the marine guard at the present, the side-boys in white gloves to hand him up, the pipes of the boatswain's mates all a-twittering; and there was a captain on the quarterdeck ready to shake hands with him – odd, that was to Hornblower, seeing that soon he would be on trial for his life.

'I'm Calendar, Captain of the Fleet,' he said. 'His Lordship is below, waiting for you.'

He led the way below, extraordinarily affable.

'I was first of the *Amazon*,' he volunteered, 'when you were in *Indefatigable*. Do you remember me?'

'Yes,' said Hornblower. He had not risked a snub by saying so first.

'I remember you plainly,' said Calendar. 'I remember hearing what Pellew had to say about you.'

Whatever Pellew said about him would be favourable – he had owed his promotion to Pellew's enthusiastic recommendation – and it was pleasant of Calendar to remind him of it at this crisis of his career.

Lord Gambier's cabin was not nearly as ornate as Captain Hardy's had been – the most conspicuous item of furniture therein was the big brass-bound Bible lying on the table. Gambier himself, heavy-jowled, gloomy, was sitting by the stern window dictating to a clerk who withdrew on the arrival of the two captains.

'You can make your report verbally, sir, for the present,' said the Admiral.

Hornblower drew a deep breath and made the plunge. He sketched out the strategic situation at the moment when he took the *Sutherland* into action against the French squadron off Rosas. Only a sentence or two had to be devoted to the battle itself – these men had fought in battles themselves and could fill in the gaps. He described the whole crippled mass of ships drifting helpless up Rosas Bay to where the guns of the fortress awaited them, and the gunboats creeping out under oars.

'One hundred and seventeen killed,' said Hornblower. 'One hundred and forty-five wounded, of whom forty-four died before I was removed from Rosas.'

'My God!' said Calendar. It was not the deaths in hospital which called forth the exclamation – that was a usual proportion – but the total casualty list. Far more than half the crew of the *Sutherland* had been put out of action before surrendering.

'Thompson in the *Leander* lost ninety-two out of three hundred, my lord,' he said. Thompson had surrendered the *Leander* to a French ship of the line off Crete after a defence which had excited the admiration of all England.

'I was aware of it,' answered Gambier. 'Please go on, Captain.'

Hornblower told of how he witnessed the destruction of the French squadron, of how Caillard arrived to take him to Paris, of his escape, first from his escort and then from drowning. He made only a slight mention of Count de Graçay and of his voyage down the Loire – that was not an admiral's business – but he descended to fuller details when he told of his recapture of the *Witch of Endor*. Details here were of importance, because in the course of the manifold activities of the British Navy it might easily happen that a knowledge of harbour arrangements at Nantes and of the navigational difficulties of the lower Loire might be useful.

'Good God Almighty, man,' said Calendar, 'how can you be so coldblooded about it? Weren't you—'

'Captain Calendar,' interrupted Gambier, 'I have requested you before not to allude to the Deity in that blasphemous fashion. Any repetition will incur my serious displeasure. Kindly continue, Captain Hornblower.'

There was only the brush with the boats from Noirmoutier to be described now. Hornblower continued, formally, but this time Gambier himself interrupted him.

'You say you opened fire with a six-pounder,' he said. 'The prisoners were at the sweeps, and the ship had to be steered. Who laid the gun?'

'I did, my lord. The French pilot helped me.'

'M'm. And you frightened 'em off?'

Hornblower confessed that he had succeeded in sinking two out of the three boats sent against him. Calendar whistled his surprise and admiration, but the hard lines in Gambier's face only set harder still.

'Yes?' he said. 'And then?'

'We went on under sweeps until midnight, my lord, and then we picked up a breeze. We sighted *Triumph* at dawn.'

There was silence in the cabin, only broken by the noises on deck, until Gambier stirred in his chair.

'I trust, Captain,' he said, 'that you have given thanks to the Almighty for these miraculous preservations of yours. In all these adventures I can see the finger of God. I shall direct my chaplain at prayers this evening to make a special mention of your gratitude and thankfulness.'

'Yes, my lord.'

'Now you will make your report in writing. You can have it ready by dinner time – I trust you will give me the pleasure of your company at dinner? I will then be able to enclose it in the packet I am about to despatch to Their Lordships.'

'Yes, my lord.'

Gambier was still thinking deeply.

'*Witch of Endor* can carry the despatches,' he said. Like every admiral the world over, his most irritating and continuous problem was how to collect and disseminate information without weakening his main body by detachments; it must have been an immense relief to him to have the cutter drop from the clouds, as it were, to carry these despatches. He went on thinking.

'I will promote this lieutenant of yours, Bush, into her as Commander,' he announced.

Hornblower gave a little gasp. Promotion to Commander meant almost certain post rank within the year, and it was this power of promotion which constituted the most prized source of patronage an Admiral in command possessed. Bush deserved the step, but it was surprising that Gambier should give it to him – Admirals generally had some favourite lieutenant, or some nephew or some old friend's son awaiting the first vacancy. Hornblower could imagine Bush's delight at the news that he was at last on his way to becoming an admiral himself if he lived long enough.

But that was not all, by no means all. Promotion of a captain's first lieutenant was a high compliment to the captain himself. It set the seal of official approval on the captain's proceedings. This decision of Gambier's was a public – not merely a private – announcement that Hornblower had acted correctly.

'Thank you, my lord, thank you,' said Hornblower.

'She is your prize, of course,' went on Gambier. 'Government will have to buy her on her arrival.'

Hornblower had not thought of that. It meant at least a thousand pounds in his pocket.

'That coxswain of yours will be in clover,' chuckled Calendar. 'He'll take all the lower deck's share.'   ◊

That was true, too. Brown would have a quarter of the value of the *Witch of Endor* for himself. He could buy a cottage or land and set up in business on his own account if he wished to.

'*Witch of Endor* will wait until your report is ready,' announced Gambier. 'I will send my secretary in to you. Captain Calendar will provide you with a cabin and the necessities you lack. I hope you will continue to be my guest until I sail for Portsmouth next week. It would be best, I think.'

The last words were a delicate allusion to that aspect of the matter which had occupied most of Hornblower's thoughts on his arrival, and which had not as yet been touched upon – the fact that he must undergo court martial for the loss of the *Sutherland*, and was of necessity under arrest until that time. By old-established custom he must be under the supervision of an officer of equal rank while under arrest; there could be no question of sending him home in the *Witch of Endor*.

'Yes, my lord,' said Hornblower.

Despite all Gambier's courtesy and indulgence towards him, despite Calendar's open admiration, he still felt a constriction of the throat and a dryness of the mouth at the thought of that court martial; they were symptoms which persisted even when he tried to settle down and compose his report with the aid of the competent young clergyman who made his appearance in the cabin to which Calendar conducted him.

'Arma virumque cano,' quoted the Admiral's secretary after the first halting sentences – Hornblower's report naturally began with the battle of Rosas. 'You begin in medias res, sir, as every good epic should.'

'This is an official report,' snapped Hornblower. 'It continues to the last report I made Admiral Leighton.'

His tiny cabin only allowed him to walk three paces each way, and crouching nearly double at that – some unfortunate lieutenant had been turned out to make room for him. In a flagship, even in a big three-decker like the *Victory*, the demand for cabins always greatly exceeded the supply, what with the Admiral, and the Captain of the Fleet, and the flag lieutenant, and the secretary, and the chaplain, and the rest of the staff. He sat down on the breech of the twelve-pounder beside the cot.

'Continue, if you please,' he ordered. ' "Having regard to these conditions, I therefore proceeded—" '

It was finished in the end – it was the third time that morning that

Hornblower had recounted his adventures, and they had lost all their savour for him now. He was dreadfully tired – his head drooped forward at his breast as he squatted on the gun, and then he woke with a snort. He was actually falling asleep while he sat.

'You are tired, sir,' said the secretary.

'Yes.'

He forced himself to wake up again. The secretary was looking at him with eyes shining with admiration, positive hero-worship. It made him feel uncomfortable.

'If you will just sign this, sir, I will attend to the seal and the super-scription.'

The secretary slipped out of the chair and Hornblower took the pen and dashed off his signature to the document on whose evidence he was soon to be tried for his life.

'Thank you, sir,' said the secretary, gathering the papers together.

Hornblower had no more attention to spare for him. He threw himself face downward on to the cot, careless of appearances. He went rushing giddily down a tremendous slope into blackness – he was snoring before the secretary had reached the door, and he never felt the touch of the blanket with which the secretary returned, five minutes later, tiptoeing up to the cot to spread it over him.

XVII

Something enormously painful was recalling Hornblower to life. He did not want to return. It was agony to wake up, it was torture to feel unconsciousness slipping away from him. He clung to it, tried to re-capture it, unavailingly. Remorselessly it eluded him. Somebody was gently shaking his shoulder, and he came back to complete conscious-ness with a start, and wriggled over to see the Admiral's secretary bending over him.

'The Admiral will dine within the hour, sir,' he said. 'Captain Calendar thought you might prefer to have a little time in which to prepare.'

'Yes,' grunted Hornblower. He fingered instinctively the long stubble on his unshaven chin. 'Yes.'

The secretary was standing very stiff and still, and Hornblower looked up at him curiously. There was an odd, set expression on the secretary's face, and he held a newspaper imperfectly concealed behind his back.

'What's the matter?' demanded Hornblower.

'It is bad news for you, sir,' said the secretary.

'What news?'

Hornblower's spirits fell down into the depths of despair. Perhaps Gambier had changed his mind. Perhaps he was going to be kept under strict arrest, tried, condemned, and shot. Perhaps—

'I remembered having seen this paragraph in the *Morning Chronicle* of three months ago, sir,' said the secretary. 'I showed it to his Lordship, and to Captain Calendar. They decided it ought to be shown to you as early as possible. His Lordship says—'

'What is the paragraph?' demanded Hornblower, holding out his hand for the paper.

'It is bad news, sir,' repeated the secretary, hesitatingly.

'Let me see it, damn you.'

The secretary handed over the newspaper, one finger indicating the paragraph.

'The Lord giveth, the Lord taketh away,' he said. 'Blessed be the name of the Lord.'

It was a very short paragraph.

We regret to announce the death in childbed, on the seventh of this month, of Mrs Maria Hornblower, widow of the late Captain Horatio Hornblower, Bonaparte's martyred victim. The tragedy occurred in Mrs Hornblower's lodgings at Southsea, and we are given to understand that the child, a fine boy, is healthy.

Hornblower read it twice, and he began on it a third time. Maria was dead, Maria the tender, the loving.

'You can find consolation in prayer, sir—' said the secretary, but Hornblower paid no attention to what the secretary said.

He had lost Maria. She had died in childbed, and having regard to the circumstances in which the child had been engendered, he had as good as killed her. Maria was dead. There would be no one, no one at all to welcome him now on his return to England. Maria would have stood by him during the court martial and, whatever the verdict, she would never have believed him to be at fault. Hornblower remembered the tears wetting her coarse red cheeks when she had last put her arms round him to say goodbye. He had been a little bored by the formality of an affectionate goobye, then. He was free now – the realisation came creeping over him like cold water in a warm bath. But it was not fair to Maria. He would not have bought his freedom at such a price. She had earned by her own devotion his attention, his kindness, and he would have given them to her uncomplainingly for the rest of his life. He was desperately sorry that she was dead.

'His Lordship instructed me, sir,' said the secretary 'to inform you of his sympathy in your bereavement. He told me to say that he would not take it amiss if you decided not to join him and his guests at dinner but sought instead the consolation of religion in your cabin.'

'Yes,' said Hornblower.

'Any help which I can give, sir—'

'None,' said Hornblower.

He continued to sit on the edge of the cot, his head bowed, and the secretary shuffled his feet.

'Get out of here,' said Hornblower, without looking up.

He sat there for some time, but there was no order in his thoughts; his mind was muddled. There was a continuous undercurrent of sadness, a hurt feeling indistinguishable from physical pain, but fatigue and excitement and lack of sleep deprived him of any ability to think clearly. Finally with a desperate effort he pulled himself together. He felt as if he was stifling in the stuffy cabin; he hated his stubby beard and the feelings of dried sweat.

'Pass the word for my servant,' he ordered the sentry at his door.

It was good to shave off the filthy beard, to wash his body in cold water, to put on clean linen. He went up on deck, the clean sea air rushing into his lungs as he breathed. It was good, too, to have a deck to pace, up and down, up and down, between the slides of the quarterdeck carronades and the line of ringbolts in the deck, with all the familiar sounds of shipboard life as a kind of lullaby to his tired mind. Up and down he walked, up and down, as he had walked so many hours before, in the *Indefatigable*, and the *Lydia*, and the *Sutherland*. They left him alone; the officers of the watch collected on the other side of the ship and only stared at him unobtrusively, politely concealing their curiosity about this man who had just heard of the death of his wife, who had escaped from a French prison, who was waiting his trial for surrendering his ship – the first captain to strike his colours in a British ship of the line since Captain Ferris in the *Hannibal* at Algecira. Up and down he walked, the goodly fatigue closing in upon him again until his mind was stupefied with it, until he found that he could hardly drag one foot past the other. Then he went below to the certainty of sleep and oblivion. But even in his sleep tumultuous dreams came to harass him – dreams of Maria, against which he struggled, sweating, knowing that Maria's body was now only a liquid mass of corruption; nightmares of death and imprisonment; and, ever-recurring, dreams of Barbara smiling to him on the farther side of the horrors that encompassed him.

From one point of view the death of his wife was of benefit to Hornblower during those days of waiting. It provided him with a good excuse for being silent and unapproachable. Without being thought impolite he could find a strip of deck and walk by himself in the sunshine.

Gambier could walk with the captain of the fleet or the flag captain, little groups of lieutenants and warrant officers could walk together, chatting lightly, but they all kept out of his way; and it was not taken amiss that he should sit silent at the Admiral's dinner table and hold himself aloof at the Admiral's prayer meetings.

Had it not been so he would have been forced to mingle in the busy social life of the flagship, talking to officers who would studiously avoid all reference to the fact that shortly they would be sitting as judges on him at his court martial. He did not have to join in the eternal technical discussions which went on round him, stoically pretending that the responsibility of having surrendered a British ship of the line sat lightly on his shoulders. Despite all the kindness with which he was treated, he felt a pariah. Calendar could voice open admiration for him, Gambier could treat him with distinction, the young lieutenants could regard him with wide-eyed hero-worship, but they had never hauled down their colours. More than once during his long wait Hornblower found himself wishing that a cannonball had killed him on the quarter-deck of the *Sutherland*. There was no one in the world who cared for him now – the little son in England, in the arms of some unknown foster-mother, might grow up ashamed of the name he bore.

Suspecting, morbidly, that the others would treat him like an outcast if they could, he anticipated them and made an outcast of himself, bitterly proud. He went through all that period of black reaction by himself, without companionship, during those last days of Gambier's tenure of command, until Hood came out in the *Britannia* to take over the command, and, amid the thunder of salutes, the *Victory* sailed for Portsmouth. There were headwinds to delay her passage; she had to beat up the Channel for seven long days before at last she glided into Spithead and the cable roared out through the hawse-hole.

Hornblower sat in his cabin – he felt no interest in the green hills of the Isle of Wight nor in the busy prospect of Portsmouth. The tap which came at his cabin door heralded, he supposed, the arrival of the orders regarding his court martial.

'Come in!' he said, but it was Bush who entered, stumping along on his wooden leg, his face wreathed in smiles, his arms burdened with packages and parcels.

At the sight of that homely face Hornblower's depression evaporated like mist. He found himself grinning as delightedly as Bush, he wrung his hand over and over again, sat him down in the only chair, offered to send drinks for him, all trace of self-consciousness and reserve disappearing in the violence of his reaction.

'Oh, I'm well enough, sir, thank you,' said Bush, in reply to Hornblower's questions. 'And this is the first chance I've had of thanking you for my promotion.'

'Don't thank me,' said Hornblower, a trace of bitterness creeping back into his voice. 'You must thank his Lordship.'

'I know who I owe it to, all the same,' said Bush, sturdily. 'They're going to post me as captain this week. They won't give me a ship – not with this leg of mine – but there's the dockyard job at Sheerness waiting for me. I should never be captain if it weren't for you, sir.'

'Rubbish,' said Hornblower. The pathetic gratitude in Bush's voice and expression made him feel uncomfortable.

'And how is it with you, sir?' asked Bush, regarding him with anxious blue eyes.

Hornblower shrugged his shoulders.

'Fit and well,' he said.

'I was sorry to hear about Mrs Hornblower, sir,' said Bush.

That was all he needed to say on that subject. They knew each other too well to have to enlarge on it.

'I took the liberty, sir,' said Bush, hastily, 'of bringing you out your letters – there was a good deal waiting for you.'

'Yes?' said Hornblower.

'This big package is a sword, I'm sure, sir,' said Bush. He was cunning enough to think of ways of capturing Hornblower's interest.

'Let's open it, then,' said Hornblower, indulgently.

A sword it was, sure enough, with a gold-mounted scabbard and a gold hilt, and when Hornblower drew it the blue steel blade bore an inscription in gold inlay. It was the sword 'of one hundred guineas' value' which had been presented to him by the Patriotic Fund for his defeat of the *Natividad* in the *Lydia*, and which he had left in pawn with Duddingstone the ship's chandler at Plymouth, as a pledge for payment for captain's stores when he was commissioning the *Sutherland*.

'A sight too much writing on this for me,' Duddingstone had complained at the time.

'Let's see what Duddingstone has to say,' said Hornblower, tearing open the note enclosed in the package.

SIR,

It was with great emotion that I read today of your escape from the Corsican's clutches and I cannot find words to express my relief that the reports of your untimely death were unfounded, nor my admiration of your exploits during your last commission. I cannot reconcile it with my conscience to retain the sword of an officer so distinguished, and have therefore taken the liberty of forwarding the enclosed to you, hoping that in consequence you will wear it when next you enforce Britannia's dominion of the seas.

Your obedient and humble servant to command.

                              J. DUDDINGSTONE.

'God bless my soul!' said Hornblower.

He let Bush read the note; Bush was a captain and his equal now, as well as his friend, and there was no disciplinary objection to allowing him to know to what shifts he had been put when commissioning the *Sutherland*. Hornblower laughed a little self-consciously when Bush looked up at him after reading the note.

'Our friend Duddingstone,' said Hornblower, 'must have been very moved to allow a pledge for forty guineas to slip out of his fingers.' He spoke cynically to keep the pride out of his voice, but he was genuinely moved. His eyes would have grown moist if he had allowed them.

'I'm not surprised, sir,' said Bush, fumbling among the newspapers beside him. 'Look at this, sir, and at this. Here's the *Morning Chronicle* and the *Times*. I saved them to show you, hoping you'd be interested.'

Hornblower glanced at the columns indicated; somehow the gist of them seemed to leap out at him without his having to read them. The British press had let itself go thoroughly. As even Bush had foreseen, the fancy of the British public had been caught by the news that a captain whom they had imagined to be foully done to death by the Corsican tyrant had succeeded in escaping, and not merely in escaping, but in carrying off a British ship of war which had been for months a prize to the Corsican. There were columns in praise of Hornblower's daring and ability. A passage in the *Times* caught Hornblower's attention and he read it more carefully. 'Captain Hornblower still has to stand his trial for the loss of the *Sutherland*, but, as we pointed out in our examination of the news of the battle of Rosas Bay, his conduct was so well advised and his behaviour so exemplary on that occasion, whether he was acting under the orders of the late Admiral Leighton or not, that, although the case is still *sub judice*, we have no hesitation in predicting his speedy reappointment.'

'Here's what the *Anti-Gallican* has to say, sir,' said Bush.

What the *Anti-Gallican* had to say was very like what the other newspapers had said; it was beginning to dawn upon Hornblower that he was famous. He laughed uncomfortably again. All this was a most curious experience and he was not at all sure that he liked it. Cold-bloodedly he could see the reason for it. Lately there had been no naval officer prominent in the affections of the public – Cochrane had wrecked himself by his intemperate wrath after the Basque Roads, while six years had passed since Hardy had kissed the dying Nelson; Collingwood was dead and Leighton too, for that matter – and the public always demanded an idol. Like the Israelites in the desert, they were not satisfied with an invisible object for their devotion. Chance had made him the public's idol, and presumably government were not sorry, seeing how much it would strengthen their position to have one of their own men suddenly popular. But somehow he did not like it; he was not used to fame, he distrusted it, and his ever-present personal modesty made him feel it was all a sham.

'I hope you're pleased, sir,' said Bush, looking wonderingly at the struggle on Hornblower's face.

'Yes. I suppose I am,' said Hornblower.

'The Navy bought the *Witch of Endor* yesterday at the Prize Court!' said Bush, searching wildly for news which might delight this odd captain of his. 'Four thousand pounds was the price, sir. And the division of the prize money where the prize has been taken by an incomplete crew is governed by an old regulation – I didn't know about it, sir, until they told me. It was made after that boat's crew from *Squirrel*, after she foundered, captured the Spanish plate ship in '97. Two-thirds to you, sir – that's two thousand six hundred pounds. And a thousand to me and four hundred for Brown.'

'H'm,' said Hornblower.

Two thousand six hundred pounds was a substantial bit of money – a far more concrete reward than the acclamation of a capricious public.

'And there's all these letters and packets, sir,' went on Bush, anxious to exploit the propitious moment.

The first dozen letters were all from people unknown to him, writing to congratulate him on his success and escape. Two at least were from madmen, apparently – but on the other hand two were from peers; even Hornblower was a little impressed by the signatures and the coroneted notepaper. Bush was more impressed still when they were passed over to him to read.

'That's very good indeed, sir, isn't it?' he said. 'There are some more here.'

Hornblower's hand shot out and picked one letter out of the mass offered him the moment he saw the handwriting, and then when he had taken it he stood for a second holding it in his hand, hesitating before opening it. The anxious Bush saw the hardening of his mouth and the waning of the colour in his cheeks; watched him while he read, but Hornblower had regained his self-control and his expression altered no farther.

LONDON,
129 BOND STREET.
3rd June 1811.

DEAR CAPTAIN HORNBLOWER,

It is hard for me to write this letter, so overwhelmed am I with pleasure and surprise at hearing at this moment from the Admiralty that you are free and well. I hasten to let you know that I have your son here in my care. When he was left orphaned after the lamented death of your wife I ventured to take charge of him and make myself responsible for his upbringing, while my brothers Lords Wellesley and Wellington consented to act as his godfathers at his baptism, whereat he was consequently given the names Richard Arthur Horatio. Richard is a fine healthy boy with a wonderful resemblance to his father and he has already endeared himself greatly to me, to such an extent that I shall be conscious of a great loss when the time comes for you to take him away from me. Let me assure you that I shall look upon it as a pleasure to continue to have charge of Richard until that time, as I can easily guess that you will be much occupied with affairs on your arrival in England. You will be very welcome should you care to call here to see your son, who grows in intelligence every day. It will give pleasure not only to Richard, but to

> Your firm friend,
> BARBARA LEIGHTON.

Hornblower nervously cleared his throat and re-read the letter. There was too much crowded in it for him to have any emotion left. Richard Arthur Horatio Hornblower, with two Wellesleys as godfathers, and growing in intelligence every day. There would be a great future ahead of him, perhaps. Up to that moment Hornblower had hardly thought about the child – his paternal instincts had hardly been touched by any consideration of a child he had never seen; and they further were warped by memories of the little Horatio who had died of smallpox in his arms so many years ago. But now he felt a great wave of affection for the unknown little brat in London who had managed to endear himself to Barbara.

And Barbara had taken him in charge; possibly because, widowed and childless, she had sought for a convenient orphan to adopt – and yet it might be because she still cherished memories of Captain Hornblower, whom at the time she had believed to be dead at Bonaparte's hands.

He could not bear to think about it any more. He thrust the letter into his pocket – all the others he had dropped on the deck – and with immobile face he met Bush's gaze again.

'There are all these other letters, sir,' said Bush, with masterly tact.

They were letters from great men and from madmen – one contained an ounce of snuff as a token of some eccentric squire's esteem and regard – but there was only one which caught Hornblower's attention. It was from some Chancery Lane lawyer – the name was unfamiliar – who wrote, it appeared, on hearing from Lady Barbara Leighton that the presumption of Captain Hornblower's death was unfounded. Previously he had been acting under the instructions of the Lords Commissioners of the Admiralty to settle Captain Hornblower's estate, and working in conjunction with the Prize Agent at Port Mahon. With the consent of the Lord Chancellor, upon the death intestate of Mrs Maria Hornblower, he had been acting as trustee to the heir, Richard Arthur Horatio Hornblower, and had invested for the latter in the Funds the proceeds of the sale of Captain Hornblower's prizes after the deduction of expenses. As Captain Hornblower would see from the enclosed account, there was the sum of three thousand two hundred and ninety-one pounds six and fourpence invested in the Consolidated Fund, which would naturally revert to him. The lawyer awaited his esteemed instructions.

The enclosed accounts, which Hornblower was about to thrust aside, had among the innumerable six and eightpences and three and fourpences one set of items which caught his eye – they dealt with the funeral expenses of the late Mrs Hornblower, and a grave in the cemetery of the church of St Thomas à Beckett, and a headstone, and fees for gravewatchers; it was a ghoulish list which made Hornblower's blood run a little colder. It was hateful. More than anything else it accentuated his loss of Maria – he would only have to go on deck to see the tower of the church where she lay.

He fought down the depression which threatened to overmaster him once more. It was at least a distraction to think about the news in that lawyer's letter, to contemplate the fact that he owned three thousand odd pounds in the Funds. He had forgotten all about those prizes he had made in the Mediterranean before he came under Leighton's command. Altogether that made his total fortune nearly six thousand pounds – not nearly as large as some captains had contrived to acquire, but handsome enough. Even on half-pay he would be able to live in comfort now, and educate Richard Arthur Horatio properly, and take his place in a modest way in society.

'The captains' list has changed a lot since we saw it last, sir,' said Bush, and he was echoing Hornblower's train of thought rather than breaking into it.

'Have you been studying it?' grinned Hornblower.

'Of course, sir.'

Upon the position of their names in that list depended the date of their promotion to flag rank – year by year they would climb it as death or promotion eliminated their seniors, until one day, if they lived long enough, they would find themselves admirals, with admirals' pay and privileges.

'It's the top half of the list which has changed most, sir,' said Bush. 'Leighton was killed, and Ball died at Malta, and Troubridge was lost at sea – in Indian waters, sir – and there's seven or eight others who've gone. You're more than half-way up now.'

Hornblower had held his present rank eleven years, but with each coming year he would mount more slowly, in proportion to the decrease in number of his seniors, and it would be 1825 or so before he could fly his flag. Hornblower remembered the Count de Graçay's prediction that the war would end in 1814 – promotion would be slower in peace time. And Bush was ten years older than he, and only just beginning the climb. Probably he would never live to be an admiral, but then Bush was perfectly content with being a captain. Clearly his ambition had never soared higher than that; he was fortunate.

'We're both of us very lucky men, Bush,' said Hornblower.

'Yes, sir,' agreed Bush, and hesitated before going on. 'I'm giving evidence at the court martial, sir, but of course you know what my evidence'll be. They asked me about it at Whitehall, and they told me that what I was going to say agreed with everything they knew. You've nothing to fear from the court martial, sir.'

XVIII

Hornblower told himself often during the next twenty-four hours that he had nothing to fear from the court martial, and yet it was nervous work waiting for it – to hear the repeated twitter of pipes and stamping of marines' boots overhead as the compliments were given to the captains and admirals who came on board to try him, to hear silence close down on the ship as the court assembled, and to hear the sullen boom of the court martial gun as the court opened, and the click of the cabin-door latch as Calendar came to escort him before his judges.

Hornblower remembered little enough afterwards of the details of the trial – only a few impressions stood out clearly in his memory. He could always recall the flash and glitter of the gold lace on the coats of the semicircle of officers sitting round the table in the great cabin of the *Victory*, and the expression on Bush's anxious, honest face as he declared that no captain could have handled a ship with more skill and determination than Hornblower had handled *Sutherland* at Rosas Bay. It was a neat point which Hornblower's 'friend' – the officer the Admiralty had sent to conduct his defence – made when his question brought out the fact that just before the surrender Bush had been completely incapacitated by the loss of his foot, so that he bore no responsibility whatever for the surrender and had no interest in presenting as good a case as possible. There was an officer who read, seemingly for an eternity, long extracts from depositions and official reports, in a spiritless mumble – the greatness of the occasion apparently made him nervous and affected his articulation, much to the annoyance of the President of the Court. At one point the President actually took the paper from him, and himself read, in his nasal tenor, Admiral Martin's pronouncement that the *Sutherland*'s engagement had certainly made the eventual destruction of the French squadron more easy, and in his opinion was all that had made it possible. There was an awkward moment when a discrepancy was detected between the signal logs of the *Pluto* and *Caligula*, but it passed away in smiles when someone reminded the Court that signal midshipmen sometimes made mistakes.

During the adjournment there was an elegant civilian in buff and blue, with a neat silk cravat, who came into Hornblower with a good many questions. Frere, his name was, Hookham Frere – Hornblower had a vague acquaintance with the name. He was one of the wits who wrote in the *Anti-Gallican*, a friend of Canning's, who for a time had acted as ambassador to the patriot government of Spain. Hornblower was a little intrigued by the presence of someone deep in cabinet secrets, but he was too preoccupied, waiting for the trial to re-open, to pay much attention to him or to answer his questions in detail.

And it was worse when all the evidence had been given, and he was waiting with Calendar while the Court considered its decision. Hornblower knew real fear, then. It was hard to sit apparently unmoved, while the minutes dragged by, waiting for the summons to the great cabin, to hear what his fate would be. His heart was beating hard as he went in, and he knew himself to be pale. He jerked his head erect to meet his judges' eyes, but the judges in their panoply of blue and gold were veiled in a mist which obscured the whole cabin, so that nothing was visible to Hornblower's eyes save for one little space in the centre – the cleared area in the middle of the table before the President's seat, where lay his sword, the hundred-guinea sword presented by the Patriotic Fund. That was all Hornblower could see – the sword seemed to hang there in space, unsupported. And the hilt was towards him; he was not guilty.

'Captain Hornblower,' said the President of the Court – that nasal tenor of his had a pleasant tone – 'This Court is of the unanimous opinion that your gallant and unprecedented defence of His Majesty's ship *Sutherland*, against a force so superior, is deserving of every praise the country and this Court can give. Your conduct, together with that of the officers and men under your command, reflects not only the highest honour on you, but on the country at large. You are therefore most honourably acquitted.'

There was a little confirmatory buzz from the other members of the Court, and a general bustle in the cabin. Somebody was buckling the hundred-guinea sword to his waist; someone else was patting his shoulder. Hookham Frere was there, too, speaking insistently.

'Congratulations, sir. And now, are you ready to accompany me to London? I have had a post chaise horsed and waiting this last six hours.'

The mists were only clearing slowly; everything was still vague about him as he allowed himself to be led away, to be escorted on deck, to be handed down into the barge alongside. Somebody was cheering. Hundreds of voices were cheering. The *Victory*'s crew had manned the yards and were yelling themselves hoarse. All the other ships at anchor there were cheering him. This was fame. This was success. Precious few other captains had ever been cheered by all the ships in a fleet like this.

'I would suggest that you take off your hat, sir,' said Frere's voice in his ear, 'and show how much you appreciate the compliment.'

He took off his hat and sat there in the afternoon sun, awkwardly in the sternsheets of the barge. He tried to smile, but he knew his smile to be wooden – he was nearer tears than smiles. The mists were closing round him again, and the deep-chested bellowing was like the shrill piping of children in his ears.

The boat rasped against the wall. There was more cheering here, as they handed him up. People were thumping him on the shoulder, wringing his hand, while a blaspheming party of marines forced a passage for him to the post chaise with its horses restless amid the din, Then a clatter of hoofs and a grinding of wheels, and they were flying out of the yard, the postilion cracking his whip.

'A highly satisfactory demonstration of sentiment, on the part of the public and of the armed forces of the Crown,' said Frere, mopping his face.

Hornblower suddenly remembered something, which made him sit up, tense.

'Stop at the church!' he yelled to the postilion.

'Indeed, sir, and might I ask why you gave that order? I have the express commands of His Royal Highness to escort you to London without losing a moment.'

'My wife is buried there,' snapped Hornblower.

But the visit to the grave was unsatisfactory – was bound to be with Frere fidgeting and fuming at his elbow, and looking at his watch. Hornblower pulled off his hat and bowed his head by the grave with its carved headstone, but he was too much in a whirl to think clearly. He tried to murmur a prayer – Maria would have liked that, for she was always pained by his free thinking. Frere clucked with impatience.

'Come along, then,' said Hornblower, turning on his heel and leading the way back to the post chaise.

The sun shone gloriously over the countryside as they left the town behind them, lighting up the lovely green of the trees and the majestic rolling Downs. Hornblower found himself swallowing hard. This was the England for which he had fought for eighteen long years, and as he breathed its air and gazed round him he felt that England was worth it.

'Damned lucky for the Ministry,' said Frere, 'this escape of yours. Something like that was needed. Even though Wellington's just captured Almeida the mob was growing restive. We had a ministry of all the talents once – now it's a ministry of no talent. I can't imagine why Castlereagh and Canning fought that duel. It nearly wrecked us. So did Gambier's affair at the Basque Roads. Cochrane's been making a thorough nuisance of himself in the House ever since. Has it ever occurred to you that you might enter parliament? Well, it will be time enough to discuss that when you've been to Downing Street. It's sufficient at present that you've given the mob something to cheer about.'

Mr Frere seemed to take much for granted – for instance, that Hornblower was wholeheartedly on the government side, and that Hornblower had fought at Rosas Bay and had escaped from France solely to maintain a dozen politicians in office. It rather damped Hornblower's spirits. He sat silent, listening to the rattle of the wheels.

'H.R.H. is none too helpful,' said Frere. 'He didn't turn us out when he assumed the Regency, but he bears us no love – the Regency Bill didn't please him. Remember that, when you see him tomorrow. He likes a bit of flattery, too. If you can make him believe that you owe your success to the inspiring examples both of H.R.H. *and* of Mr Spencer Perceval you will be taking the right line. What's this? Horndean?'

The postilion drew the horses to a halt outside the inn, and ostlers came running with a fresh pair.

'Sixty miles from London,' commented Mr Frere. 'We've just time.'

The inn servants had been eagerly questioning the postilion, and a knot of loungers – smocked agricultural workers and a travelling tinker – joined them, looking eagerly at Hornblower in his blue and gold. Someone else came hastening out of the inn; his red face and silk cravat and leather leggings seemed to indicate him as the local squire.

'Acquitted, sir?' he asked.

'Naturally, sir,' replied Frere at once. 'Most honourably acquitted.'

'Hooray for Hornblower!' yelled the tinker, throwing his hat into the air. The squire waved his arms and stamped with joy, and the farm hands echoed the cheer.

'Down with Boney!' said Frere. 'Drive on.'

'It is surprising how much interest has been aroused in your case,' said Frere a minute later. 'Although naturally one would expect it to be greatest along the Portsmouth Road.'

'Yes,' said Hornblower.

'I can remember,' said Frere, 'when the mob were howling for Wellington to be hanged, drawn and quartered – that was after the news of Cintra. I thought we were gone then. It was his court of inquiry which saved us as it happened, just as yours is going to do now. Do you remember Cintra?'

'I was commanding a frigate in the Pacific at the time,' said Hornblower, curtly.

He was vaguely irritated – and he was surprised at himself at finding that he neither liked being cheered by tinkers nor flattered by politicians.

'All the same,' said Frere, 'it's just as well that Leighton was hit at Rosas. Not that I wished him harm, but it drew the teeth of that gang. It would have been them or us otherwise, I fancy. His friends counted twenty votes on a division. You know his widow, I've heard?'

'I have that honour.'

'A charming woman for those who are partial to that type. And most influential as a link between the Wellesley party and her late husband's.'

'Yes,' said Hornblower.

All the pleasure was evaporating from his success. The radiant afternoon sunshine seemed to have lost its brightness.

'Petersfield is just over the hill,' said Frere. 'I expect there'll be a crowd there.'

Frere was right. There were twenty or thirty people waiting at the Red Lion, and more came hurrying up, all agog to hear the result of the court martial. There was wild cheering at the news, and Mr Frere took the opportunity to slip in a good word for the government.

'It's the newspapers,' grumbled Frere, as they drove on with fresh horses. 'I wish we could take a lead out of Boney's book and only allow 'em to publish what we think they ought to know. Emancipation – Reform – naval policy – the mob wants a finger in every pie nowadays.'

Even the marvellous beauty of the Devil's Punch Bowl was lost on Hornblower as they drove past it. All the savour was gone from life. He was wishing he was still an unnoticed naval captain battling with Atlantic storms. Every stride the horses were taking was carrying him nearer to Barbara, and yet he was conscious of a sick, vague desire that he was returning to Maria, dull and uninteresting and undisturbing. The crowd that cheered him at Guildford – market day was just over – stank of sweat and beer. He was glad that with the approach of evening Frere ceased talking and left him to his thoughts, depressing though they were.

It was growing dark when they changed horses again at Esher.

'It is satisfactory to think that no footpad or highwayman will rob us,' laughed Frere. 'We have only to mention the name of the hero of the hour to escape scot free.'

No footpad or highwayman interfered with them at all, as it happened. Unmolested they crossed the river at Putney and drove on past the more frequent houses and along the dark streets.

'Number Ten Downing Street, postie,' said Frere.

What Hornblower remembered most vividly of the interview that followed was Frere's first sotto voce whisper to Perceval – 'He's safe' – which he overheard. The interview lasted no more than ten minutes, formal on the one side, reserved on the other. The Prime Minister was not in a talkative mood apparently – his main wish seemed to be to inspect this man who might perhaps do him an ill turn with the Prince Regent or with the public. Hornblower formed no very favourable impression either of his ability or of his personal charm.

'Pall Mall and the War Office next,' said Frere. 'God, how we have to work!'

London smelt of horses – it always did, Hornblower remembered, to men fresh from the sea. The lights of Whitehall seemed astonishingly bright. At the War Office there was a young Lord to see him, someone whom Hornblower liked at first sight. Palmerston was his name, the Under Secretary of State. He asked a great many intelligent questions regarding the state of opinion in France, the success of the last harvest, the manner of Hornblower's escape. He nodded approvingly when Hornblower hesitated to answer when asked the name of the man who had given him shelter.

'Quite right,' he said. 'You're afraid some damned fool'll blab it out and get him shot. Some damned fool probably would. I'll ask you for it if ever we need it badly, and you will be able to rely on us then. And what happened to these galley slaves?'

'The first lieutenant in the *Triumph* pressed them for the service, my lord.'

'So they've been hands in a King's ship for the last three weeks? I'd rather be a galley slave myself.'

Hornblower was of the same opinion. He was glad to find someone in high position with no illusions regarding the hardships of the service.

'I'll have them traced and brought home if I can persuade your superiors at the Admiralty to give 'em up. I can find a better use for 'em.'

A footman brought in a note which Palmerston opened.

'His Royal Highness commands your presence,' he announced. 'Thank you, Captain. I hope I shall again have the pleasure of meeting you shortly. This discussion of ours has been most profitable. And the Luddites have been smashing machinery in the north, and Sam Whitbread has been raising Cain in the House, so that your arrival is most opportune. Good evening, Captain.'

It was those last words which spoilt the whole effect. Lord Palmerston planning a new campaign against Bonaparte won Hornblower's respect, but Lord Palmerston echoing Frere's estimate of the political results of Hornblower's return lost it again.

'What does His Royal Highness want of me?' he asked of Frere, as they went down the stairs together.

'That's to be a surprise for you,' replied Frere archly.

'You may even have to wait until tomorrow's levee to find out. It isn't often Prinny's sober enough for business at this time in the evening.

Probably he's not. You may find tact necessary in your interview with him.'

It was only this morning, thought Hornblower, his head whirling, that he had been sitting listening to the evidence at his court martial. So much had already happened today. He was surfeited with new experiences. He was sick and depressed. And Lady Barbara and his little son were in Bond Street, not a quarter of a mile away.

'What time is it?' he asked.

'Ten o'clock. Young Pam keeps late hours at the War Office. He's a glutton for work.'

'Oh,' said Hornblower.

God only knew at what hour he would escape from the palace. He would certainly have to wait until tomorrow before he called at Bond Street. At the door a coach was waiting, coachmen and footmen in the royal red liveries.

'Sent by the Lord Chamberlain,' explained Frere. 'Kind of him.'

He handed Hornblower in through the door and climbed after him.

'Ever met His Royal Highness?' he went on.

'No.'

'But you've been to Court?'

'I have attended two levees. I was presented to King George in '98.'

'Ah! Prinny's not like his father. And you know Clarence, I suppose?'

'Yes.'

The carriage had stopped at a doorway brightly lit with lanterns; the door was opened, and a little group of footmen were awaiting to hand them out. There was a glittering entrance hall, where somebody in uniform and powder and with a white staff ran his eyes keenly over Hornblower.

'Hat under your arm,' he whispered. 'This way, please.'

'Captain Hornblower. Mr Hookham Frere,' somebody announced.

It was an immense room, dazzling with the light of its candles; a wide expanse of polished floor, and at the far end a group of people bright with gold lace and jewels. Somebody came over to them, dressed in naval uniform – it was the Duke of Clarence, pop-eyed and pineapple-headed.

'Ah, Hornblower,' he said, hand held out, 'welcome home.'

Hornblower bowed over the hand.

'Come and be presented. This is Captain Hornblower, sir.'

'Evenin', Captain.'

Corpulent, handsome, and dissipated, weak and sly, was the sequence of impressions Hornblower received as he made his bow. The thinning curls were obviously dyed; the moist eyes and the ruddy pendulous cheeks seemed to hint that His Royal Highness had dined well, which was more than Hornblower had.

'Everyone's been talkin' about you, Captain, ever since your cutter – what's its name, now? – came in to Portsmouth.'

'Indeed, sir?' Hornblower was standing stiffly at attention.

'Yas. And, damme, so they ought to. So they ought to, damme, Captain. Best piece of work I ever heard of – good as I could have done myself. Here, Conyngham, make the presentations.'

Hornblower bowed to Lady This and Lady That, to Lord Somebody and to Sir John Somebody-else. Bold eyes and bare arms, exquisite clothes and blue Garter-ribbons, were all the impressions Hornblower received. He was conscious that the uniform made for him by the *Victory's* tailor was a bad fit.

'Now let's get the business done with,' said the Prince. 'Call those fellows in.'

Someone was spreading a carpet on the floor, someone else was bearing in a cushion on which something winked and sparkled. There was a little procession of three solemn men in red cloaks. Someone dropped on one knee to present the Prince with a sword.

'Kneel, sir,' said Lord Conyngham to Hornblower.

He felt the accolade and heard the formal words which dubbed him knight. But when he rose, a little dazed, the ceremony was by no means over. There was a ribbon to be hung over his shoulder, a star to be pinned on his breast, a red cloak to be draped about him, a vow to be repeated and signatures written. He was being invested as a Knight of the Most Honourable Order of the Bath, as someone loudly proclaimed. He was Sir Horatio Hornblower, with a ribbon and star to wear for the rest of his life. At last they took the cloak from his shoulders again and the officials of the order withdrew.

'Let me be the first to congratulate you, Sir Horatio,' said the Duke of Clarence, coming forward, his kindly imbecile face wreathed in smiles.

'Thank you, sir,' said Hornblower. The broad star thumped his chest as he bowed again.

'My best wishes, Colonel,' said the Prince Regent.

Hornblower was conscious of all the eyes turned on him at that speech; it was that which warned him that the Prince was not making a slip regarding his rank.

'Sir?' he said, inquiringly, as seemed to be expected of him.

'His Royal Highness,' explained the Duke, 'has been pleased to appoint you one of his Colonels of Marines.'

A Colonel of Marines received pay to the amount of twelve hundred pounds a year, and did no duty for it. It was an appointment given as a reward to successful captains, to be held until they reached flag rank. Six thousand pounds he had already, Hornblower remembered. Now he had twelve hundred a year in addition to his captain's half pay at least.

He had attained financial security at last, for the first time in his life. He had a title, a ribbon and star. He had everything he had ever dreamed of having, in fact.

'The poor man's dazed,' laughed the Regent loudly, delighted.

'I am overwhelmed, sir,' said Hornblower, trying to concentrate again on the business in hand. 'I hardly know how to thank your Royal Highness.'

'Thank me by joining us at hazard. Your arrival interrupted a damned interesting game. Ring that bell, Sir John, and let's have some wine. Sit here beside Lady Jane, Captain. Surely you want to play? Yes, I know about you, Hookham. You want to slip away and tell John Walter that I've done my duty. You might suggest at the same time that he writes one of his damned leaders and has my Civil List raised – I work hard enough for it, God knows. But I don't see why you should take the captain away. Oh, very well then, damn it. You can go if you want to.'

'I didn't imagine,' said Frere, when they were safely in the coach again, 'that you'd care to play hazard. *I* wouldn't, not with Prinny, if he were using his own dice. Well, how does it feel to be Sir Horatio?'

'Very well,' said Hornblower.

He was digesting the Regent's allusion to John Walter. This was the editor of the *Times*, he knew. It was beginning to dawn upon him that his investiture as Knight of the Bath and appointment as Colonel of Marines were useful pieces of news. Presumably their announcement would have some influence politically, too – that was the reason for haste. They would convince doubting people that the government's naval officers were achieving great things – it was almost as much a political move to make him a knight as was Bonaparte's scheme to shoot him for violating the laws of war. The thought took a great deal of the pleasure out of it.

'I took the liberty,' said Frere, 'of engaging a room for you at the Golden Cross. You'll find them expecting you; I had your baggage sent round. Shall I stop the coach there? Or do you want to visit Fladong's first?'

Hornblower wanted to be alone; the idea of visiting the naval coffee house tonight – for the first time in five years – had no appeal for him, especially as he felt suddenly selfconscious in his ribbon and star. Even at the hotel it was bad enough, with host and boots and chambermaid all unctuously deferential with their 'Yes, Sir Horatio,' and 'No, Sir Horatio,' making a procession out of lighting him up to his room, and fluttering round him to see that he had all he wanted, when all he wanted now was to be left in peace.

There was little enough peace for him, all the same, when he climbed into bed. Resolutely as he put out of his mind all recollection of the wild doings of the day, he could not stop himself thinking about the fact that tomorrow he would be seeing his son and Lady Barbara. He spent a restless night.

XIX

'Sir Horatio Hornblower,' announced the butler, holding open the door for him.

Lady Barbara was there; it was a surprise to see her in black – Hornblower had been visualising her as dressed in the blue gown she had worn when last he had seen her, the grey-blue which matched her eyes. She was in mourning now, of course, for Leighton had been dead less than a year still. But the black dress suited her well – her skin was creamy white against it. Hornblower remembered with a strange pang the golden tang of her cheeks in those old days on board the *Lydia*.

'Welcome,' she said, her hands outstretched to him. They were smooth and cool and delicious – he remembered their touch of old. 'The nurse will bring Richard directly. Meanwhile, my heartiest congratulations on your success.'

'Thank you,' said Hornblower. 'I was extremely lucky, ma'am.'

'The lucky man,' said Lady Barbara, 'is usually the man who knows how much to leave to chance.'

While he digested this statement he stood awkwardly looking at her. Until this moment he had forgotten how Olympian she was, what self-assurance – kindly self-assurance – she had, which raised her to inaccessible heights and made him feel like a loutish schoolboy. His knighthood must appear ridiculously unimportant to her, the daughter of an earl, the sister of a marquis and of a viscount who was well on his way towards a dukedom. He was suddenly acutely conscious of his elbows and hands.

His awkwardness only ended with the opening of the door and the entrance of the nurse, plump and rosy in her ribboned cap, the baby held to her shoulder. She dropped a curtsey.

'Hullo, son,' said Hornblower, gently.

He did not seem to have much hair yet, under his little cap, but there were two startling brown eyes looking out at his father; nose and chin and forehead might be as indeterminate as one would expect in a baby, but there was no ignoring those eyes.

'Hullo, baby,' said Hornblower, gently, again.

He was unconscious of the caress in his voice. He was speaking to

Richard as years before he had spoken to little Horatio and little Maria. He held up his hands to the child.

'Come to your father,' he said.

Richard made no objections. It was a little shock to Hornblower to feel how tiny and light he was – Hornblower, years ago, had grown used to older children – but the feeling passed immediately.

'There, baby, there,' said Hornblower.

Richard wriggled in his arms, stretching out his hands to the shining gold fringe of his epaulette.

'Pretty?' asked Hornblower.

'Da!' said Richard, touching the threads of bullion.

'That's a man!' said Hornblower.

His old skill with babies had not deserted him. Richard gurgled happily in his arms, smiled seraphically as he played with him, kicked his chest with tiny kicks through his dress. The good old trick of bowing the head and pretending to butt Richard in the stomach had its never-failing success. Richard gurgled and waved his arms in ecstasy.

'What a joke!' said Hornblower. 'Oh, what a joke!'

Suddenly remembering, he looked round at Lady Barbara. She had eyes only for the baby, her serenity strangely exalted, her smile tender. He thought then that she was moved by her love for the child. Richard noticed her too.

'Goo!' he said, with a jab of an arm in her direction.

She came nearer, and Richard reached over his father's shoulder to touch her face.

'He's a fine baby,' said Hornblower.

'O' course he's a fine babby,' said the wet nurse, reaching for him. She took it for granted that godlike fathers in glittering uniforms would only condescend to notice their children for ten seconds consecutively, and would need to be instantly relieved of them at the end of that time.

'He's a saucy one,' said the wet nurse, the baby back in her arms. He wriggled there, those big brown eyes of his looking from Hornblower to Barbara.

'Say "bye bye",' said the nurse. She held up his wrist and waved his fat fist at them. 'Bye bye.'

'Do you think he's like you?' asked Barbara, as the door closed behind the nurse and baby.

'Well—' said Hornblower, with a doubtful grin.

He had been happy during those few seconds with the baby, happier than he had been for a long long time. The morning up to now had been one of black despondency for him. He had told himself that he had everything heart could desire, and some inner man within him had replied that he wanted none of it. In the morning light his ribbon and star had appeared gaudy gew-gaws. He never could contrive to feel proud of himself; there was something vaguely ridiculous about the name 'Sir Horatio Hornblower', just as he always felt there was something vaguely ridiculous about himself.

He had tried to comfort himself with the thought of all the money he had. There was a life of ease and security before him; he would never again have to pawn his gold-hilted sword, nor feel self-conscious in good society about the pinchbeck buckles on his shoes. And yet the prospect was frightening now that it was certain. There was something of confinement about it, something reminiscent of those weary weeks in the Château de Graçay – how well he remembered how he fretted there. Unease and insecurity, which had appeared such vast evils when he suffered under them, had something attractive about them now, hard though that was to believe.

He had envied brother captains who had columns about themselves in the newspapers. Surfeit in that way was attained instantaneously, he had discovered. Bush and Brown would love him neither more nor less on account of what the *Times* had to say about him; he would scorn the love of those who loved him more – and he had good reason to fear that there would be rivals who would love him less. He had received the adulation of crowds yesterday; that did not heighten his good opinion of crowds, and he was filled with a bitter contempt for the upper circle that ruled those crowds. Within him the fighting man and the humanitarian both seethed with discontent.

Happiness was a Dead Sea fruit that turned to ashes in the mouth, decided Hornblower, generalising recklessly from his own particular experience. Prospect, and not possession, was what gave pleasure, and his cross-grainedness would deprive him, now that he had made that discovery, even of the pleasure in prospect. He misdoubted everything so much. Freedom that could only be bought by Maria's death was not a freedom worth having; honours granted by those that had the granting of them were no honours at all; and no security was really worth the loss of insecurity. What life gave with one hand she took back with the other. The political career of which he had once dreamed was open to him now, especially with the alliance of the Wellesley faction, but he could see with morbid clarity how often he would hate it; and he had been happy for thirty seconds with his son, and now, more morbidly still, he asked himself cynically if that happiness could endure for thirty years.

His eyes met Barbara's again, and he knew she was his for the asking. To those who did not know and understand, who thought there was romance in his life when really it was the most prosaic of lives, that would be a romantic climax. She was smiling at him, and then he saw her lips tremble as she smiled. He remembered how Marie had said he was a man whom women loved easily, and he felt uncomfortable at being reminded of her.

The
Commodore

I

Captain Sir Horatio Hornblower sat in his bath, regarding with distaste his legs dangling over the end. They were thin and hairy, and recalled to his mind the legs of the spiders he had seen in Central America. It was hard to think about anything except his legs, seeing how much they were forced upon his attention by their position under his nose as he sat in this ridiculous bath; they hung out at one end while his body protruded from the water at the other. It was only the middle portion of him, from his waist to above his knees, which was submerged, and that was bent almost double. Hornblower found it irritating to have to take a bath in this fashion, although he tried not to allow it to irritate him, and he strove desperately to dismiss from his mind recollections of thousands of more comfortable baths taken on the deck of a ship, under a wash-deck pump which threw over him unlimited quantities of stimulating sea-water. He seized his soap and flannel, and began viciously to wash those parts of himself above the surface, and as he did so water slopped in quantities over the side on to the polished oak floor of his dressing-room. That meant trouble for a housemaid, and in Hornblower's present mood he was glad to cause trouble.

He rose awkwardly to his feet in the bath, water flying in all directions, soaped and washed off the middle of himself, and yelled for Brown. Brown came in at once from the bedroom, although a good servant would have sensed his master's mood and delayed for a second or two so as to be sworn at. He hung a warm towel over Hornblower's shoulders, dexterously preventing the ends from dipping into the water as Hornblower stepped out of the soapy mess and walked across the floor, leaving upon it a trail of drops and wet footprints. Hornblower towelled himself and stared gloomily through the door into the bedroom at the clothes which Brown had laid out for him there.

'It's a lovely morning, sir,' said Brown.

'God damn your eyes,' said Hornblower.

He would have to put on that damned suit of buff and blue, the varnished boots and the gold fob; he had never worn that suit before, and he had hated it when the tailor tried it on him, hated it when his wife admired it, and he supposed he would go on hating it for the rest of his days and still have to wear it. His hatred was a double one, firstly a

159

simple, blind, unreasoning hatred, and secondly a hatred for a suit which he was quite sure did not properly set off his looks, making him appear absurd instead of merely plain. He pulled the two-guinea linen shirt over his head, and then with infinite trouble dragged the tight buff trousers up over his legs. They fitted him like a skin, and it was only when they were fully on, and Brown had slipped behind him and hauled the waistband taut, that he realised that he had not yet put on his stockings. To take the trousers off again would be to admit a mistake, and he refused to do so, ripping out another oath at Brown's suggestion. Philosophically Brown knelt and rolled up the tight trouser legs, but they would not roll even as far as the knee, making it hopeless to try to put on the long stockings.

'Cut the tops off the damned things!' spluttered Hornblower.

Brown, kneeling on the floor, rolled a protesting eye up at him, but what he saw in Hornblower's face cut short anything he had in mind to say. In disciplined silence Brown obeyed orders, bringing the scissors from the dressing-table. Snip, snip, snip! The tops of the stockings fell to the floor, and Hornblower put his feet into the mutilated ends and felt the first satisfaction of the day as Brown rolled down the trousers over them. The fates might be against him, by God, but he would show them that he still had a will of his own. He crammed his feet into the varnished boots and refrained from swearing at their tightness – he remembered guiltily that he had been weak with the fashionable bootmaker and had not insisted on comfort, not with his wife standing by to see that the dictates of fashion were obeyed.

He stumped across to the dressing-table and tied his neck-cloth, and Brown buckled his stock. The ridiculous thing brushed his ears as he turned his head and his neck felt as if it were being stretched to double its length. He had never been more uncomfortable in his life; he would never draw an easy breath while wearing this damned choker which Brummell and the Prince Regent had made fashionable. He slipped on the flowered waistcoat – blue sprigged with pink – and then the broadcloth coat, buff, with big blue buttons; the inside of the pocket flaps and the reverse of the lapels and collar were of a matching blue. For twenty years Hornblower had worn nothing except uniform, and the image that the mirror reflected back to his jaundiced eyes was unnatural, grotesque, ridiculous. Uniform was comforting – no one could blame him if it did not suit him, because he had to wear it. But with civilian clothes he was presumed to display his own taste and choice – even though he was a married man – and people could laugh at him for what he wore. Brown attached the gold watch to the fob, and forced it into the pocket. It made an unsightly bulge there, over his belly, but Hornblower furiously put aside the idea of going without a watch so as to allow his clothes to fit better. He stuffed into his sleeve the linen handkerchief which Brown handed him after shaking scent on to it, and then he was ready.

'That's a beautiful suit, sir,' said Brown.

'Beautiful rubbish!' said Hornblower.

He stumped back across the dressing-room and knocked on the farther door.

'Come in,' said his wife's voice.

Barbara was still sitting in her bath, her legs dangling over the edge just as his own had done.

'How handsome you look, dear,' said Barbara. 'It's a refreshing change to see you out of uniform.'

Even Barbara, the nicest woman in the world, was not free of the besetting sin of womankind, approving of change merely because it was change; but Hornblower did not answer her as he answered Brown.

'Thank you,' he said, trying desperately to sound gracious as he said it.

'My towel, Hebe,' said Barbara. The little negro maid came gliding forward, and wrapped her up as she stepped out of the hip-bath.

'Venus rises from the waves,' said Hornblower gallantly. He was doing his best to fight down the feeling of awkwardness which possessed him when he saw his wife naked in the presence of another woman, even though Hebe was a mere servant, and coloured.

'I expect,' said Barbara, standing while Hebe patted the towel to her skin to dry her, 'the village has already heard of this strange habit of ours of taking baths every day. I can hardly imagine what they think of it.'

Hornblower could imagine; he had been a village boy himself, once. Barbara threw off the towel and stood naked again for a moment as Hebe passed her silk shift over her head. Women, once the barriers were down, really had no sense of decency, and Barbara in that transparent shift was even more shocking than when she was naked. She sat at the dressing-table and set to work to cream her face while Hebe brushed her hair; there were a myriad pots and jars on the dressing-table and Barbara took ingredients from one after the other as though compounding a witches' brew.

'I'm glad to see,' said Barbara, inspecting her reflection closely, 'that the sun is shining. It is well to have a fine day for this morning's ceremony.'

The thought of the ceremony had been in Hornblower's mind ever since he woke up; it could not be said that he disliked the prospect, but he was not comfortable about it. It would be the first landmark in a new way of life, and Hornblower felt a not unnatural distrust of his own reactions to the change. Barbara was studying the reflection of his face in her mirror.

'Welcome to the new Squire of Smallbridge,' she said, and smiled, turning towards him.

The smile transformed not only her expression but Hornblower's whole mental outlook as well. Barbara ceased to be the great lady, the earl's daughter with the bluest blood of the aristocracy in her veins, whose perfect poise and aplomb always afflicted Hornblower with the diffidence he detested; instead she became the woman who had stood unfrightened beside him upon the shot-torn decks of the *Lydia* in the Pacific, the woman who throbbed with love in his arms, the beloved companion and the companionable lover. Hornblower's heart went out to her on the instant. He would have taken her in his arms and kissed her if it had not been that Hebe was in the room. But Barbara's eyes met his and read in them what was in his mind. She smiled another smile at him; they were in perfect accord, with secrets shared between them, and the world was a brighter place for both of them.

Barbara pulled on a pair of white silk stockings, and knotted above her knees the scarlet silk garters. Hebe stood ready with her gown, and Barbara dived into it. The gown flapped and billowed as Barbara made her way into it, and then at last she emerged, her arms waving as they pushed into the sleeves, and her hair tousled. No one could be a great lady in those conditions, and Hornblower loved her more dearly than ever. Hebe settled the gown about her mistress, and hung a lace cape over her shoulders ready for the final adjustment of her hair. When the last pin had been inserted, the last curl fixed in place, the shoes eased upon her feet by a grovelling Hebe with a shoehorn, Barbara devoted her attention to settling on her head the vast hat with the roses and ribbons.

'And what is the time, my dear?' she asked.

'Nine o'clock,' said Hornblower, hauling his watch with an effort from out of the tense fob-pocket in the front of his trousers.

'Excellent,' said Barbara, reaching for the long white silk gloves which had come to her by devious smugglers' routes from Paris. 'Hebe, Master Richard will be ready now. Tell nurse to bring him to me. And I think, dear, that your ribbon and star would be in the spirit of this morning's occasion.'

'At my own front door?' protested Hornblower.

'I fear so,' said Barbara. She wagged her head with its pyramid of roses, and this time it was not so much a smile that she bestowed upon him as a grin, and all Hornblower's objections to wearing his star evaporated on the spot. It was a tacit admission that she attached no more importance, as far as he and she were concerned, to the ceremony of welcoming him as the new Squire of Smallbridge, than Hornblower himself. It was as if an augur winked.

In his bedroom Hornblower took the red ribbon of the Bath and the Star from the drawer in his wardrobe, and Brown found for him the dog-skin gloves which he tugged on as he walked down the stairs. A scared housemaid dropped him a curtsey; in the hall stood Wiggins the butler with Hornblower's tall beaver hat, and beside him John the footman in the new livery which Barbara had chosen. And here came Barbara with Richard in his nurse's arms. Richard's curls were pomaded into stiff decorum. The nurse set him down and twitched his petticoats and his lace collar into position, and Hornblower hastened to take one of his hands while Barbara took the other; Richard was not yet sufficiently accustomed to standing on his feet and was liable to go down on all fours in a way which might not suit the dignity of this morning's ceremony. Wiggins and John threw open the door, and the three of them, Barbara and Hornblower with Richard between them, walked out to the head of the steps above the driveway, Hornblower remembering just in time to clap the tall hat on his head before crossing the threshold.

It seemed as if every inhabitant of Smallbridge were formed up below them. On one side was the parson with a herd of children; in front the four tenant farmers in ill-fitting broadcloth with their labourers in their smocks, and on the other side a cluster of women in aprons and bonnets. Behind the children the ostler at the Coach and Horses stuck a fiddle under his chin and played a note; the parson waved a hand and the children burst into shrill piping –

'See-ee the *conk*-ring he-ee-ee-ee-ero comes,
Sow-ow-ow-ow-ound the *trum*-pets, bee-ee-ee-eat the drums!'

Obviously this was meant for Hornblower, and he took off his hat and stood awkwardly; the tune meant nothing to his tone-deaf ear, but he could distinguish some of the words. The chorus came to a ragged end, and the parson took a step forward.

'Your Ladyship,' he began, 'Sir Horatio. Welcome in the name of the village. Welcome, Sir Horatio, with all the glory you have won in the war against the Corsican tyrant. Welcome, Your Ladyship, wife of the hero before us, sister of the hero commanding our valiant army now in Spain, daughter of the highest nobility in the land! Welcome—'

'Man!' yelled Richard unexpectedly. 'Da-da!'

The parson took the interruption without flinching; already well in his stride he continued to mouth out his fulsome sentences, telling of the joy the village of Smallbridge felt at finding itself in the ownership of a famous sailor. Hornblower was distracted from the discourse by the necessity of holding on tight to Richard's hand – if Richard once got loose he evidently would go down on all fours and throw himself down the steps to make a closer acquaintance with the village children. Hornblower looked out over the lush green of the park; beyond it rose the massive curves of the Downs, and to one side the tower of Smallbridge church rose above the trees. On that side, too, an orchard was in full bloom, exquisitely lovely. Park and orchard and church were all his;

he was the Squire, a landed gentleman, owner of many acres, being welcomed by his tenantry. Behind him was his house, full of his servants; on his breast the ribbon and star of an order of chivalry; and in London Coutts & Company had in their vaults a store of golden guineas which were his as well. This was the climax of a man's ambition. Fame, wealth, security, love, a child – he had all that heart could desire. Hornblower, standing at the head of the steps while the parson droned on, was puzzled to find that he was still not happy. He was irritated with himself in consequence. He ought to be running over with pride and joy and happiness, and yet here he was contemplating the future with faint dismay; dismay at thought of living on here, and positive distaste at the thought of spending the fashionable season in London, even though Barbara would be beside him all the time.

These disorderly thoughts of Hornblower's were suddenly broken into. Something had been said which should not have been said, and as the parson was the only person speaking, he must have said it, although he was still droning along in obvious ignorance of any blunder. Hornblower stole a glance at Barbara; her white teeth showed for a moment against her lower lip, clear proof of her vexation to anyone who knew her well. Otherwise she was exhibiting the stoical calm of the British upper classes. What was it that had been said to upset her? Hornblower raked through his subconscious memory to recall the words the parson had been using, and which he had heard without attending. Yes, that was it. The stupid fool had spoken about Richard as though he were the child of both of them. It irritated Barbara unbearably to have her stepson taken to be her own child, and the more fond she grew of him the more it irritated her, curiously enough. But it was hard to blame the parson for his mistake: when a married pair arrives with a sixteen-months-old baby it is only natural to assume it to be their child.

The parson had finished now, and an awkward pause had already begun. Clearly something must be said in reply, and it was Hornblower's business to say it.

'Ha – h'm,' said Hornblower – he had still not been married long enough to Barbara to have completely mastered that old habit – while he groped wildly for something to say. He ought to have been ready for this, of course; he ought to have been preparing a speech instead of standing day-dreaming. 'Ha – h'm. It is with pride that I look over this English countryside—'

He managed to say all that was necessary. The Corsican tyrant. The yeomen stock of England. The King and the Prince Regent. Lady Barbara. Richard. When he finished there was another awkward pause while people looked at each other, before one of the farmers stepped forward.

'Three cheers for 'Er Ladyship!'

Everyone cheered, to Richard's astonishment, expressed in a loud yell.

'Three cheers for Sir Horatio! One, two, three an' a tiger!'

There was nothing left to do now, except to withdraw gracefully into the house again and leave the tenantry to disperse. Thank God it was all over, anyway. John the footman stood at what he obviously thought was attention in the hall. Hornblower made a weary mental note to teach him to keep his elbows into his sides. If he were going to employ a footman he would make a good footman out of him. Here came the nurse, swooping down to find out how wet Richard had made himself. And here came the butler, hobbling along with a letter on a salver. Hornblower felt a rush of blood into his face as he saw the seal; that seal and that thick linen paper were only used by the Admiralty, as far as he knew. It was months, and it seemed like years, since he had last received any letter from the Admiralty. He snatched the letter from the salver, and only by the mercy of Providence remembered to glance at Barbara in apology, before breaking the seal.

THE LORDS COMMISSIONERS OF THE ADMIRALTY,
WHITEHALL.
10th April, 1812.

SIR,

I am commanded by the Lords Commissioners to inform you that their Lordships desire to employ you immediately as Commodore with a Captain under you on a service which their Lordships consider worthy of an officer of your seniority and standing. You are hereby directed and required, therefore, to inform their Lordships through me as speedily as possible as to whether or not you will accept this appointment, and in the event of your accepting it you are further directed and required to present yourself in person at this office without delay in order to receive verbally their Lordships' instructions and also those of any other Minister of State whom it may be judged necessary you should address.

Your obed't servant,
E. NEPEAN, *Secy. to the*
Lords Commissioners of the Admiralty.

Hornblower had to read the letter twice – the first time it conveyed no meaning to him at all. But at the second reading the glorious import of the letter burst in upon him. The first thing he was conscious of was that this life here in Smallbridge or in Bond Street need not continue. He was free of all that; he could take a bath under a wash-deck pump instead of in a damned hip-bath with a kettleful of water in it; he could walk his own deck, breathe the sea air, take off these damned tight trousers and never put them on again, receive no deputations, speak to no damned tenants, never smell another pigsty or smack another horse's back. And that was only the first thing; the second was that he was being offered appointment as Commodore – a Commodore of the first class, too, with a captain under him, so that he would be like an Admiral. He would have a broad pendant flying at the mainmasthead, compliments and honours – not that they mattered, but they would be outward signs of the trust reposed in him, of the promotion that was his. Louis at the Admiralty must have a good opinion of him, clearly, to appoint him Commodore when he was hardly more than half-way up the captains' list. Of course, that phrase about 'worthy of his seniority and standing' was merely formula, justifying the Admiralty in anticipation in putting him on half-pay should he decline; but – those last words, about consulting with Ministers of State, had enormous import. They meant that the mission to be entrusted to him would be one of responsibility, of international importance. Waves of excitement broke over him.

He hauled out his watch. Ten-fifteen – the day was still young by civilian standards.

'Where's Brown?' he snapped at Wiggins.

Brown materialised miraculously in the background – not too miraculously, perhaps; the whole house must be aware, of course, that the master had received a letter from the Admiralty.

'Get out my best uniform and my sword. Have the horses put-to in the chariot. You had better come with me, Brown – I shall want you to drive. Have my things for the night ready and yours too.'

The servants scattered in all directions, for not merely must the weighty orders of the master be obeyed, but this was an affair of State and doubly important in consequence. So that as Hornblower came out of his preoccupation Barbara was standing there alone.

God, he had forgotten all about her in his excitement, and she was aware of it. She was drooping a little, and one corner of her mouth was down. Their eyes met then, and that corner of her mouth went up for a moment, but then it went down again.

'It's the Admiralty,' explained Hornblower lamely. 'They'll appoint me Commodore with a captain under me.'

It was a pity that Hornblower could see her try to appear pleased.

'That's a high compliment,' she said. 'No more than you deserve, my dear, all the same. You must be pleased, and I am too.'

'It will take me away from you,' said Hornblower.

'Darling, I have had six months with you. Six months of the kind of happiness you have given me is more than any woman deserves. And you will come back to me.'

'Of course I will,' said Hornblower.

II

This was typical April weather. It had been miraculously sunny during the ceremony at the foot of the steps of Smallbridge House, but it had rained torrentially once already during the twenty-mile drive to London. Then the sun had reappeared, had warmed and dried them; but now as they crossed Wimbledon Common the sky was black again, and the first drops began to drive into their faces. Hornblower pulled his cloak about him and rebuttoned the collar. His cocked hat with its gold lace and button lay on his knees under the sheltering tent of the cloak; cocked hats worn for long in the rain accumulated pools of water in both crown and brim and were pulled out of shape.

Now it came, wind and rain, shrieking down from the west in un-believable contrast with the delightful weather of only half an hour before. The near-side horse had the full brunt of it and was inclined to shirk its work in consequence. Brown laid the whiplash on its glisten-ing haunch and it threw itself into the collar in a fresh spasm of energy. Brown was a good whip – he was good at everything. He had been the best captain's coxswain Hornblower had ever known, he had been a loyal subordinate during the escape from France, and he had made himself into the best manservant heart could desire. Now he sat here, tolerant of the driving rain, the slippery leather of the reins grasped in a big brown hand; hand and wrist and forearm acted like a spring to maintain that subtle pressure upon the horses' mouths – not enough pressure to interfere in the least with their work, but enough to give them confidence on the slippery road, and to have them under control in any emergency. They were pulling the chariot over the muddy macadam up the steep ascent of Wimbledon Common with a whole-heartedness they never displayed for Hornblower.

'Would you like to go to sea again, Brown?' asked Hornblower. The mere fact that he allowed himself to make this unnecessary speech was proof of how much Hornblower was lifted out of himself with excite-ment.

'I'd like it main well, sir,' said Brown shortly.

Hornblower was left to guess what Brown really meant – whether his curtness was just the English way of concealing enthusiasm, or whether Brown was merely being in polite agreement with his master's mood.

The rain from Hornblower's wet hair was trickling down his neck now inside his collar. He ought to have brought a sou'-wester with him. He hunched himself together on the padded leather seat, resting his two hands on the hilt of the sword belted round his waist – the hundred-guinea sword given him by the Patriotic Fund. With the sword vertical his hands held the heavy wet cloak away from the cocked hat on his

knees. Another little rivulet coursed down inside his clothes and made
him squirm. By the time the shower had passed he was thoroughly
damp and uncomfortable, but here once more came the glorious sun.
The raindrops in the gorse and the brambles shone like diamonds; the
horses steamed; larks resumed their song far overhead, and Hornblower
threw open his cloak and wiped his damp hair and neck with his handkerchief. Brown eased the horses to a walk at the crest of the hill to
breathe them before the brisk descent.

'London, sir,' he said.

And there it was. The rain had washed the smoke and dust out of the
air so that even at that distance the gilt cross and bell over St Paul's
gleamed in the sunshine. The church spires, dwarfed by the dome, stood
out with unnatural clarity. The very roof-tops were distinct. Brown
clicked his tongue at the horses and they broke once more into a trot,
rattling the chariot down the steep descent into Wandsworth, and Hornblower pulled out his watch. It was no more than two o'clock, ample
time to do business. Even though his shirt was damp inside his coat this
was a far better day than he had anticipated when he sat in his bath
that morning.

Brown drew the horses to a halt outside the Admiralty, and a ragged
urchin appeared who guarded the wheel so that it did not muddy Hornblower's cloak and uniform as he climbed down from the chariot.

'At the Golden Cross, then, Brown,' said Hornblower, fumbling
for a copper for the urchin.

'Aye aye, sir,' said Brown, wheeling the horses round.

Hornblower carefully put on his cocked hat, settled his coat more
smoothly, and centred the buckle of his sword-belt. At Smallbridge
House he was Sir Horatio, master of the house, lord of the manor, auto-
crat undisputed, but now he was just Captain Hornblower going in to
see the Lords of the Admiralty. But Admiral Louis was all cordiality.
He left Hornblower waiting no more than three minutes in the anteroom
– no longer than would be necessary to get rid of his visitor of the
moment – and he shook hands with obvious pleasure at the sight of him;
he rang the bell for a clerk to take Hornblower's wet cloak away, and
with his own hands he pulled up a chair for him beside the vast fire
which Louis maintained summer and winter since his return from the
command of the East Indian Station.

'Lady Barbara is well, I trust?' he asked.

'Very well, thank you, sir,' said Hornblower.

'And Master Hornblower?'

'Very well too, sir.'

Hornblower was mastering his shyness rapidly. He sat farther back
in his chair and welcomed the heat of the fire. That was a new portrait
of Collingwood on the wall; it must have replaced the old one of Lord

Barham. It was pleasant to note the red ribbon and the star and to look down at his own breast and to see that he wore the same decoration.

'And yet you left domestic bliss at the first moment you received our letter?'

'Of course, sir.'

Hornblower realised that perhaps it might be more profitable not to be natural; it might be better to adopt a pose, to appear reluctant to take up his professional duties, or to make it look as if he were making a great personal sacrifice for his country, but for the life of him he could not do it. He was too pleased with his promotion, too full of curiosity regarding the mission the Admiralty had in mind for him. Louis' keen eyes were studying him closely, and he met their gaze frankly.

'What is it you plan for me, sir?' he asked; he would not even wait for Louis to make the first move.

'The Baltic,' said Louis.

So that was it. The two words terminated a morning of wild specula-tion, tore up a wide cobweb of possibilities. It might have been anywhere in the world; Java or Jamaica, Cape Horn or the Cape of Good Hope, the Indian Ocean or the Mediterranean, anywhere within the twenty-five-thousand-mile circuit of the world where the British flag flew. And it was going to be the Baltic; Hornblower tried to sort out in his mind what he knew about the Baltic. He had not sailed in northern waters since he was a junior lieutenant.

'Admiral Keats is commanding there, isn't he?'

'At the moment, yes. But Saumarez is replacing him. His orders will be to give you the widest latitude of discretion.'

That was a curious thing to say. It hinted at diversion of command, and that was inherently vicious. Better a bad commander-in-chief than a divided command. To tell a subordinate that his superior was under orders to grant him wide discretion was a dangerous thing to do, unless the subordinate was a man of superlative loyalty and common sense. Hornblower gulped at that moment – he had honestly forgotten temporarily that he was the subordinate under consideration; maybe the Admiralty credited him with 'superlative loyalty and common sense'.

Louis was eyeing him curiously.

'Don't you want to hear the size of your command?' he asked.

'Yes, of course,' answered Hornblower, but he did not mind very much. The fact that he was going to command something was much more important than what he was going to command.

'You'll have the *Nonsuch*, seventy-four,' said Louis. 'That will give you a ship of force should you need one. For the rest you'll have all the small stuff we can scrape together for you – *Lotus* and *Raven*, sloops; two bomb-ketches, *Moth* and *Harvey*, and the cutter *Clam*. That's all so far, but by the time you sail we might have some more ready for you. We want you to be ready for all the inshore work that may come your way. There's likely to be plenty.'

'I expect so,' said Hornblower.

'Don't know whether you'll be fighting for the Russians or against them,' mused Louis. 'Same with the Swedes. God knows what's building up, up there. But His Nibs'll tell you all about that.'

Hornblower looked a question.

'Your revered brother-in-law, the most noble the Marquis Wellesley, K.P., His Britannic Majesty's Secretary of State for Foreign Affairs. We call him His Nibs for short. We'll walk across and see him in a minute. But there's something else important to settle. Who d'you want for captain in *Nonsuch*?'

Hornblower gasped at that. This was patronage on a grand scale. He had sometimes appointed midshipmen and surgeon's mates; a parson of shady record had once hungrily solicited him for nomination as chaplain in his ship, but to have a say in the appointment of a captain of a ship of the line was something infinitely more important than any of these. There were a hundred and twenty captains junior to Hornblower, men of most distinguished record, whose achievements were talked of with bated breath in the four quarters of the world, and who had won their way to that rank at the cost of their blood and by the performance of feats of skill and daring unparalleled in history. Certainly half of these, perhaps more, would jump at the suggestion of the command of a seventy-four. Hornblower remembered his own joy at his appointment to *Sutherland* two years ago. Captains on half-pay, captains with shore appointments eating out their hearts with waiting for a sea command, it was in his power to change the whole life and career of one of these. Yet there was no hesitation about his decision. There might be more brilliant captains available, captains with more brains, but there was only one man that he wanted.

'I'll have Bush,' he said, 'if he's available.'

'You can have him,' said Louis, with a nod. 'I was expecting you to ask for him. That wooden leg of his won't be too serious a handicap, you think?'

'I don't think so,' said Hornblower. It would have been irksome in the extreme to go to sea with any other captain than Bush.

'Very well, then,' said Louis, looking round at the clock on the wall. 'Let's walk across and see His Nibs, if you've no objection.'

III

Hornblower sat in his private sitting-room in the Golden Cross inn.
There was a fire burning, and on the table at which he sat there were
no fewer than four wax candles lighted. All this luxury – the private
sitting-room, the fire, the wax candles – gave Hornblower uneasy
delight. He had been poor for so long, he had had to scrape and econo-
mise so carefully all his life, that recklessness with money gave him this
queer dubious pleasure, this guilty joy. His bill tomorrow would con-
tain an item of at least half a crown for light, and if he had been content
with rush dips the charge would not have been more than twopence.
The fire would be a shilling, too. And you could trust an innkeeper to
make the maximum charges to a guest who obviously could afford them,
a Knight of the Bath, with a servant, and a two-horse chariot. Tomorrow's bill would be nearer two guineas than one. Hornblower
touched his breast pocket to reassure himself that his thick wad of one-
pound notes was still there. He could afford to spend two guineas a day.

Reassured, he bent again to the notes which he had made during his
interview with the Foreign Secretary. They were in irregular order,
jotted down as first one thing and then another had come into Wellesley's
mind. It was quite clear that not even the Cabinet knew for certain
whether the Russians were going to fight Bonaparte or r t. No, that
was the wrong way to put it. Nobody knew whether Bonaparte was going
to fight the Russians or not. However much ill will the Czar bore towards
the French – and obviously it was great – he would not fight unless he
had to, unless Bonaparte deliberately attacked him. Certainly the Czar
would make every possible concession rather than fight, at least at
present while he was still trying to build up and reorganise his army.

'It's hard to think Boney will be mad enough to pick a quarrel,'
Wellesley had said, 'when he can get practically all he wants without
fighting.'

But if there was going to be war it was desirable that England should
have a striking force in the Baltic.

'If Boney chases Alexander out of Russia, I want you to be on hand
to pick him up,' said Wellesley. 'We can always find a use for him.'

Kings in exile were at least useful figureheads for any resistance that
might still be maintained by countries which Bonaparte had overrun.
Under her protecting wing England had the rulers of Sicily and Sardinia,
the Netherlands and Portugal and Hesse, all of them helping to keep
alive hope in the bosoms of their former subjects now ground beneath
the tyrant's heel.

'So much depends on Sweden,' was another remark of Wellesley's.
'No one can guess what Bernadotte will do. Russia's conquest of Finland

has irritated the Swedes, too. We try and point out to them that of the two Bonaparte's the worse menace to 'em. He's at the mouth of the Baltic, while Russia's only at the top. But it can't be comfortable for Sweden, having to choose between Russia and Bonaparte.'

That was a pretty tangle, one way and the other – Sweden ruled by a Crown Prince who only three years before had been a French general, and some sort of connection by marriage with Bonaparte at that; Denmark and Norway in the tyrant's hands, Finland newly conquered by Russia, and the south shore of the Baltic swarming with Bonaparte's troops.

'He has army camps at Danzig and Stettin,' Wellesley had said, 'and South German troops echelonned all the way back to Berlin, to say nothing of the Prussians and the Austrians and the other allies.'

With Europe at his feet Bonaparte was able to drag in his train the armies of his late enemies; if he were to make war upon Russia it seemed as though a substantial part of his army would be foreigners – Italians and South Germans, Prussians and Austrians, Dutchmen and Danes.

'There are even Spaniards and Portuguese, they tell me,' said Wellesley. 'I hope they have enjoyed the recent winter in Poland. You speak Spanish, I understand?'

Hornblower had said 'Yes.'

'And French too?'

'Yes.'

'Russian?'

'No.'

'German?'

'No.'

'Swedish? Polish? Lithuanian?'

'No.'

'A pity. But most of the educated Russians speak French better than Russian, they tell me – although in that case, judging by the Russians I have met, they must be very ignorant of their own language. And we have a Swedish interpreter for you – you will have to arrange with the Admiralty how he will be rated in the ship's book – I believe that is the correct nautical expression.'

It was typical of Wellesley to put in that little sneer. He was an ex-Governor-General of India, and the present Foreign Secretary, a man of blue blood and of the height of fashion. In those few words he had been able to convey all his sublime ignorance and his consequent sublime contempt for matters nautical, as well as the man of fashion's feeling of lordly superiority over the uncouth seadog, even when the seadog in question happened to be his own brother-in-law. Hornblower had been a little nettled, and was still feeling sufficiently above himself to endeavour to irritate Wellesley in return.

'You are a master of all trades, Richard,' he said evenly.

It was just as well to remind the man of fashion that the seadog was closely enough related to be entitled to use the Christian name, and, in addition to that, it might annoy the Marquis to suggest he had anything to do with a trade.

'Not of yours, Hornblower, I'm afraid. Never could learn all those ports and starboards and back-your-lees and things of that sort. One has to learn those as a schoolboy, like hic, haec, hoc.'

It was hard to prick the Marquis's sublime complacency; Hornblower turned away from that memory back to serious business. The Russians had a fair navy, as many as fourteen ships of the line, perhaps, at Reval and Kronstadt; Sweden nearly as many. The German and Pomeranian ports swarmed with French privateers, and an important part of Hornblower's duty would be to help protect British shipping from these wolves of the sea, for the Swedish trade was vital to England. From the Baltic came the naval stores that enabled England to rule the sea – the tar and the turpentine, the pine trees for masts, cordage and timber, rosin and oil. If Sweden were to ally herself with Bonaparte against Russia, the Swedish contribution to the trade – far more than half – would be lost, and England would have to struggle along with the little that could be gleaned from Finland and Estonia, convoyed through the Baltic in the teeth of the Swedish Navy, and somehow got out through the Sound even though Bonaparte was master of Denmark. Russia would want those stores for her own navy, and she must be persuaded, one way or another, to part with enough to maintain the British Navy at sea.

It was as well that England had not come to the rescue of Finland when Russia had attacked her; if she had, there would be far less chance of Russia going to war with Bonaparte. Diplomacy backed by force might perhaps protect Sweden from allying herself with Bonaparte, and might make the Baltic trade safe and might open the North German coastline to raids against Bonaparte's communications – under that sort of pressure, if by any miracle Bonaparte should sustain a reverse, even Prussia might be persuaded to change sides. That would be another of Hornblower's tasks, to help woo Sweden from her hereditary distrust of Russia, and to woo Prussia from her enforced alliance with France, while at the same time he must do nothing to imperil the Baltic trade. A false step could mean ruin.

Hornblower laid his notes down on the table and stared unseeing at the wall across the room. Fog and ice and shoals in the Baltic; the Russian Navy and the Swedish Navy and the French privateers; the Baltic trade and the Russian alliance and the attitude of Prussia; high politics and vital commerce; during the next few months the fate of Europe, the history of the world, would be balanced on a knife-edge, and the responsibility would be his. Hornblower felt the quickening of his pulses, the tensing of his muscles, which he had known of old at the prospect of danger. Nearly a year had gone by since the last time he had experienced those symptoms, when he had entered the great cabin of the *Victory* to hear the verdict of the court martial which might have condemned him to death. He felt he did not like this promise of peril, this prospect of enormous responsibility; he had visualised nothing like this when he drove up at noon that day so gaily to receive his orders. It would be for this that he would be leaving Barbara's love and friendship, the life of a country squire, the tranquillity and peace of his newly-won home.

Yet even while he sat there, almost despairing, almost disconsolate, the lure of the problems of the future began to make itself felt. He was being given a free hand by the Admiralty – he could not complain on that score. Reval froze in December; Kronstadt often in November. While the ice lasted he would have to base himself farther down the Baltic. Did Lubeck ever freeze? In any case it would be better to— Hornblower abruptly pushed his chair back from the table, quite unconscious of what he was doing. For him to think imaginatively while sitting still was quite impossible; he could do it for no longer than he could hold his breath; such a comparison was the more apt because if he was compelled to sit still when his brain was active he exhibited some of the characteristic symptoms of slow strangulation – his blood pressure mounted, and he thrashed about restlessly.

Tonight there was no question of having to sit still; having pushed back his chair he was able to pace up and down the room, from the table to the window and back again, a walk quite as long and perhaps more free from obstacles than he had known on many a quarterdeck. He had hardly begun when the sitting-room door opened quietly and Brown peered in through the crack, his attention attracted by the sound of the chair scraping on the floor. For Brown one glance was enough. The Captain had begun to walk, which meant that he would not be going to bed for a very long time.

Brown was an intelligent man who used his brains on this job of looking after the Captain. He closed the door again quietly, and waited a full ten minutes before entering the room. In ten minutes Hornblower had got well into the swing of his walk and his thoughts were pursuing a torrential course from which they could not easily be diverted. Brown was able to creep into the room without distracting his master – indeed, it would be very hard to say if Hornblower knew he entered or not. Brown, timing his moves accurately against the Captain's crossings of the room, was able to reach the candles and snuff them – they had begun to gutter and to smell horribly – and then to reach the fireplace and put more coal on the fire, which had died down to red embers. Then he was able to make his way out of the room and settle down to a long wait; usually the Captain was a considerate master who would not dream of keeping his servant up late merely eventually to put his master to bed. It was because Brown was aware of this that he did not resent the fact that tonight Hornblower had forgotten for once to tell him he might go to bed.

Up and down the room walked Hornblower, with a regular, measured stride, turning with his foot two inches from the wainscoting under the window on one side, and on the other with his hip just brushing the end of the table as he turned. Russians and Swedes, convoys and privateers, Stockholm and Danzig, all these gave him plenty to think about. It would be cold in the Baltic, too, and he would have to make plans for conserving his crews' health in cold weather. And the first thing he must do, the moment his flotilla was assembled, must be to see that in every vessel there was an officer who could be relied upon to read and transmit signals correctly. Unless communications were good all discipline and organisation was wasted and he might as well not try to make any plans at all. Bomb-ketches had the disadvantage of—

At this point Hornblower was distracted by a knocking at the door.

'Come in,' he rasped.

The door opened slowly, and revealed to his gaze both Brown and a scared innkeeper in a green baize apron.

'What is it?' snapped Hornblower. Now that he had halted in his quarter-deck walk he was suddenly aware that he was tired; much had happened since the Squire of Smallbridge had been welcomed by his tenants that morning, and the feeling in his legs told him that he must have been doing a fair amount of walking.

Brown and the innkeeper exchanged glances, and then the innkeeper took the plunge.

'It's like this, sir,' he began, nervously. 'His Lordship is in number four just under this sitting-room, sir. His Lordship's a man of hasty temper, sir, beggin' your pardon, sir. He says – beggin' your pardon again, sir – he says that two in the morning's late enough for anyone to walk up and down over his head. He says—'

'Two in the morning?' demanded Hornblower.

'It's nearer three, sir,' interposed Brown, tactfully.

'Yes, sir, it struck the half-hour just when he rang for me the second time. He says if only you'd knock something over, or sing a song, it wouldn't be so bad. But just to hear you walking up and down, sir— His Lordship says it makes him think about death and Judgment Day. It's too regular, like. I told him who you was, sir, the first time he rang. And now—'

Hornblower had come to the surface by now, fully emerged from the wave of thought that had engulfed him. He saw the nervous gesticulations of the innkeeper, caught between the devil of this unknown Lordship downstairs and the deep sea of Captain Sir Horatio Hornblower upstairs, and he could not help smiling – in fact it was only with an effort that he prevented himself from laughing outright. He could visualise the whole ludicrous business, the irascible unknown peer down below, the innkeeper terrified of offending one or other of his two wealthy and influential guests, and as a crowning complication Brown stubbornly refusing to allow until the last possible moment any intrusion upon his master's deliberations. Hornblower saw the obvious relief in the two men's faces when he smiled, and that really made him laugh this time. His temper had been short of late and Brown had expected an explosion, while the wretched innkeeper never expected anything else – innkeepers never looked for anything better than tantrums from the people fate compelled them to entertain. Hornblower remembered damning Brown's eyes without provocation only that very morning: Brown was not quite as clever as he might be, for this morning Hornblower had been fretting as an unemployed naval officer doomed to country life, while this evening he was a Commodore with a flotilla awaiting him and nothing in the world could upset his temper – Brown had not allowed for that.

'My respects to His Lordship,' he said. 'Tell him that the march of doom will cease from this moment. Brown, I shall go to bed.'

The innkeeper fled in huge relief down the stairs, while Brown seized a candlestick – the candle in it was burned down to a stump – and lit his master through into the bedroom. Hornblower peeled off his coat with the epaulettes of heavy bullion, and Brown caught it just in time to save it falling to the floor. Shoes and shirt and trousers followed, and Hornblower pulled on the magnificent nightshirt which was laid out on the bed; a nightshirt of solid China silk, brocaded, with faggoting at the cuffs and neck, for which Barbara had sent a special order all the way to the East through her friends in the East India Company. The blanket-wrapped brick in the bed had cooled a good deal, but had diffused its warmth gratefully over much of the area; Hornblower snuggled down into its mild welcome.

'Good night, sir,' said Brown, and darkness rushed into the room from out of the corners as he extinguished the candle. Tumultuous dreams rushed with it. Whether asleep or awake – next morning Hornblower could not decide which – his mind was turning over all through the rest of the night the endless implications of this coming campaign in the Baltic, where his life and his reputation and his self-respect would be once more at stake.

IV

Hornblower sat forward on the seat of the coach and peered out of the window.

'Wind's veering nor'ard a little,' he said. 'West-by-north now, I should say.'

'Yes, dear,' said Barbara patiently.

'I beg your pardon, dear,' said Hornblower, 'I interrupted you. You were telling me about my shirts.'

'No. I had finished telling you about those, dear. What I was saying was that you must not let anyone unpack the flat sea-chest until the cold weather comes. Your sheepskin coat and your big fur cloak are in it, with plenty of camphor, and they'll be safe from moth just as they are. Have the chest put straight below when you go on board.'

'Yes, dear.'

The coach was clattering over the cobbles of Upper Deal. Barbara stirred a little and took Hornblower's hand in hers again.

'I don't like talking about furs,' she said. 'I hope – oh, I hope so much – that you'll be back before the cold weather comes.'

'So do I, dear,' said Hornblower, with perfect truth.

It was gloomy and dark inside the coach, but the light from the window shone on Barbara's face, illuminating it like a saint's in church. The mouth beneath the keen aquiline nose was set firm; there was nothing soft about the grey-blue eyes. No one could tell from Lady Barbara's expression that her heart was breaking; but she had slipped off her glove, and her hand was twining feverishly in Hornblower's.

'Come back to me, dear. Come back to me!' said Barbara softly.

'Of course I will,' said Hornblower.

For all her patrician birth, for all her keen wit, for all her iron self-control, Barbara could say foolish things just like any blowsy wife of any ordinary seaman. It made Hornblower love her more dearly than ever that she should say pathetically 'come back to me,' as if he had power over the French or Russian cannon-balls that would be aimed at him. Yet in that moment a horrible thought shot up in Hornblower's mind, like a bloated corpse rising to the surface from the ooze at the bottom of the sea. Lady Barbara had seen a husband off to war once before, and he had not returned. He had died under the surgeon's knife at Gibraltar after a splinter had torn open his groin in the battle of Rosas Bay. Was Barbara thinking of that dead husband now, at this moment? Hornblower shuddered a little at the thought, and Barbara, despite the close sympathy that always existed between them, misinterpreted the movement.

'My darling,' she said, 'my sweet.'

She brought her other hand up and touched his cheek, and her lips sought his. He kissed her, fighting down the dreadful doubt that assailed him. He had contrived for months not to be jealous of the past – he was annoyed with himself for allowing it to happen at this time of all times, and his annoyance added to the devil's brew of emotions within him. The touch of her lips won him over; his heart came out to her, and he kissed her with all the passion of his love, while the coach lurched unstably over the cobbles. Barbara's monumental hat threatened to come adrift; she had to withdraw from his arms to set it straight and to restore herself to her normal dignity. She was aware of, even if she had misinterpreted, the turmoil in Hornblower's soul, and she deliberately began a new line of conversation which would help them both to recover their composure ready for their imminent appearance in public again.

'I am pleased,' she said, 'whenever I think of the high compliment the government is paying you in giving you this new appointment.'

'I am pleased that you are pleased, dear,' said Hornblower.

'Hardly more than half-way up the captains' list, and yet they are giving you this command. You will be an admiral *in petto*.'

She could have said nothing that could calm Hornblower more effectively. He grinned to himself at Barbara's mistake. She was trying to say that he would be an admiral on a small scale, in miniature, *en petit* as it would be phrased in French. But *en petit* meant nothing like *in petto*, all the same. *In petto* was Italian for 'in the breast'; when the Pope appointed a cardinal *in petto* it meant that he intended to keep the appointment to himself for a time without making it public. It tickled Hornblower hugely to hear Barbara guilty of a solecism of that sort. And it made her human again in his eyes, of the same clay as his own. He warmed to her afresh, with tenderness and affection supplementing passion and love.

The coach came to a stop with a lurch and a squeaking of brakes, and the door opened. Hornblower jumped out and handed Barbara down before looking round him. It was blowing half a gale, west-by-north, undoubtedly. This morning it had been a strong breeze, southwesterly, so that it was both veering and strengthening. A little more northing in the wind and they would be weather-bound in the Downs until it backed again. The loss of an hour might mean the loss of days. Sky and sea were grey, and there were whitecaps a-plenty. The East India convoy was visible at anchor some way out – as far as they were concerned the wind had only to veer a trifle more for them to up-anchor and start down-Channel. There was other shipping to the northward, and presumably the *Nonsuch* and the flotilla were there, but without a glass it was too far to tell ship from ship. The wind whipped round his ears and forced him to hold his hat on tightly. Across the cobbled street was the jetty with a dozen Deal luggers riding to it.

Brown stood waiting for orders while the coachman and footman were hauling the baggage out of the boot.

'I'll have a hoveller take me out to the ship, Brown,' said Hornblower. 'Make a bargain for me.'

He could have had a signal sent from the castle to the *Nonsuch* for a boat, but that would consume precious time. Barbara was standing beside him, holding on to her hat; the wind flapped her skirt round her like a flag. Her eyes were grey this morning – if sea and sky had been blue her eyes would have been blue too. And she was making herself smile at him.

'If you are going out to the ship in a lugger, dear,' she said, 'I could come too. The lugger could bring me back.'

'You will be wet and cold,' said Hornblower. 'Closehauled and with this wind it will be a rough passage.'

'Do you think I mind?' said Barbara, and the thought of leaving her tore at his heartstrings again.

Brown was back again already, and with him a couple of Deal boatmen, handkerchiefs bound round their heads and ear-rings in their ears; their faces, burned by the wind and pickled by the salt, a solid brown like wood. They laid hold of Hornblower's sea-chests and began to carry them as if they were feathers towards the jetty; in nineteen years of war innumerable officers had had their chests carried down to Deal jetty. Brown followed them, and Hornblower and Lady Barbara brought up the rear, Hornblower clutching tenaciously the leather portfolio containing his 'most secret' orders.

'Morning, Captain.' The captain of the lugger knuckled his forehead to Hornblower. 'Morning, Your Ladyship. All the breeze anyone wants today. Still, you'll be able to weather the Goodwins, Captain, even with those unweatherly bombs of yours. Wind's fair for the Skaw once you're clear of the Downs.'

So that was military secrecy in this England; this Deal hoveller knew just what force he had and whither he was bound – and tomorrow, as likely as not, he would have a rendezvous in mid-Channel with a French chasse-marée, exchanging tobacco for brandy and news for news. In three days Bonaparte in Paris would know that Hornblower had sailed for the Baltic with a ship of the line and a flotilla.

'Easy with them cases!' roared the lugger captain suddenly. 'Them bottles ain't made o' iron!'

They were lowering down into the lugger the rest of his baggage from the jetty; the additional cabin stores which Barbara had ordered for him and whose quality she had checked so carefully, a case of wine, a case of provisions, and the parcel of books which was her special present to him.

'Won't you take a seat in the cabin, Your Ladyship?' asked the lugger

captain with queer untutored politeness. ''Twill be a wet run out to
Nonsuch.'

Barbara caught Hornblower's eye and refused politely; Hornblower
knew those stuffy, smelly cabins of old.

'A tarpaulin for Your Ladyship, then.'

The tarpaulin was fastened round Barbara's shoulders, and hung
round her to the deck like a candle extinguisher. The wind was still
pulling at her hat, and she put up her hand and with a single gesture
snatched it from her head and drew it inside the tarpaulin. The brisk
wind blew her hair instantly into streamers, and she laughed, and with a
shake of her head set her whole mane flying in the wind. Her cheeks
flushed and her eyes sparkled, just as Hornblower could remember her
in the old days when they rounded the Horn in *Lydia*. Hornblower
wanted to kiss her.

'Cast off, there! Hands to the halliard!' roared the captain, coming
aft and casually holding the tiller against his hip. The hands strained
at the tackle, and the mainsail rose foot by foot; the lugger made a
sternboard away from the jetty.

'Lively with that sheet, now, Ge-arge!'

The captain hauled the tiller over, and the lugger checked herself,
spun on her keel, and dashed forward, as handy as a horse in the hands
of a skilful rider. As she came out from the lee of the jetty the wind took
hold of her and laid her over, but the captain put down the tiller and
Ge-arge hauled aft on the sheet until the sail was like a board, and the
lugger, closehauled – dramatically so to anyone unfamiliar with her
type – plunged forward into the teeth of the gale, with the spray flying
aft from her port bow in sheets. Even in the sheltered Downs there was
enough of a sea running to make the lugger lively enough as she met it,
pitch following roll as each wave passed under her from port bow to
starboard quarter.

Hornblower suddenly realised that this was the moment when he
should be seasick. He could not remember the start of any previous
voyage when he had not been sick, and the motion of this lively little
lugger should find him out if anything would. It was interesting that
nothing of the sort was happening; Hornblower noticed with deep
amazement that the horizon forward showed up above the boat's bow,
and then disappeared as the lugger stood up on her stern, without his
feeling any qualm at all. It was not so surprising that he had retained his
sea-legs; after twenty years at sea it was not easy to lose them, and he
stood swaying easily with the boat's quick motion; he only lost his sea-
legs when he was really dizzy with seasickness, and that dread plague
showed no sign of appearing. At the start of previous voyages he had
always been worn out with the fatigues of fitting out and commissioning,
of course, short of sleep and worn down with anxieties and worries

and ready to be sick even without going to sea. As Commodore he had had none of these worries; the Admiralty and the Foreign Office and the Treasury had heaped orders and advice upon him, but orders and responsibility were not nearly as harassing as the petty worries of finding a crew and dealing with dockyard authorities. He was perfectly at ease.

Barbara was having to hold on tightly, and now that she looked up at him she was obviously not quite as comfortable inside as she might be; she was filled with doubts if with nothing else. Hornblower felt both amusement and pride; it was pleasant to be newly at sea and yet not sick, and it was more pleasant still to be doing something better than Barbara, who was so good at everything. He was on the point of teasing her, of vaunting his own immunity, when common sense and his tenderness for his wife saved him from such an incredible blunder. She would hate him if he did anything of the sort – he could remember with enormous clarity how much he hated the whole world when he was being seasick. He did his best for her.

'You're fortunate not to be sick, my dear,' he said. 'This motion is lively, but then you always had a good stomach.'

She looked at him, with the wind whipping her tousled hair; she looked a trifle dubious, but Hornblower's words had heartened her. He made a very considerable sacrifice for her, one she would never know about.

'I envy you, dear,' he said. 'I'm feeling the gravest doubts about myself, as I always do at the beginning of a voyage. But you are your usual happy self.'

Surely no man could give a better proof of his love for his wife, than that he should not only conceal his feeling of superiority but that he should even for her sake pretend to be seasick when he was not. Barbara was all concern at once.

'I am sorry, dearest,' she said, her hand on his shoulder. 'I hope so much you do not have to give way. It would be most inconvenient for you at this moment of taking up your command.'

The stratagem was working; with something important to think about other than the condition of her stomach Barbara was forgetting her own qualms.

'I hope I shall last out,' said Hornblower; he tried to grin a brave reluctant grin, and although he was no actor Barbara's wits were sufficiently dulled not to see through him. Hornblower's conscience pricked him when he saw that this stolid mock-heroism of his was making her fonder of him than ever. Her eyes were soft for him.

'Stand by to go about!' bellowed the captain of the lugger, and Hornblower looked up in surprise to see that they were close up under the stern of the *Nonsuch*. She had some canvas showing forward and her mizzen-topsail backed so as to set her across the wind a trifle and give the lugger a lee on her starboard side. Hornblower flung back his boat cloak and stood clear so that he could be seen from the quarterdeck of the *Nonsuch*; for Bush's sake, if for no other reason, he did not want to come on board without due warning. Then he turned to Barbara.

'It's time to say goodbye, dear,' he said.

Her face was without expression, like that of a marine under inspection.

'Goodbye, dearest,' she said. Her lips were cold, and she did not incline towards him to offer them, but stood stiffly upright. It was like kissing a marble statue. Then she melted suddenly. 'I'll cherish Richard, darling. Our child.'

Barbara could have said nothing to endear her more to Hornblower. He crushed her hands in his.

The lugger came up into the wind, her canvas volleying, and then she shot into the two-decker's lee. Hornblower glanced up; there was a bos'un's chair dangling ready to lower to the lugger.

'Belay that chair!' he yelled, and then to the captain, 'Lay us alongside.'

Hornblower had no intention of being swung up to the deck in a bos'un's chair; it was too undignified a way of taking up his new command to be swung aboard legs dangling. The lugger surged beside the big ship; the painted ports were level with his shoulder, and beneath him boiled the green water confined between the two vessels. This was a nervous moment. If he were to miss his footing and fall into the sea so that he would have to be hauled in wet and dripping it would be far more undignified than any entrance in a bos'un's chair. He let fall his cloak, pulled his hat firmly on to his head, and hitched his sword round out of his way. Then he leaped across the yard-wide gap, scrambling upwards the moment fingers and toes made contact. It was only the first three feet which were difficult; after that the tumble-home of the *Nonsuch*'s side made it easy. He was even able to pause to collect himself before making the final ascent to the entry-port and to step down to the deck with all the dignity to be expected of a Commodore.

Professionally speaking, this was the highest moment of his career up to now. As a captain he had grown accustomed to a captain's honours, the bos'un's mates twittering on their pipes, the four side-boys and the marine sentries. But now he was a Commodore taking up his command; there were six side-boys with their white gloves, there was the whole marine guard and the marine band, a long double lane of bos'un's mates with their pipes, and at the end of the lane a crowd of officers in full dress. As he set his foot on the deck the drums beat a ruffle in competition with the bos'un's calls, and then the fifes of the band struck up 'Heart of oak are our ships, Jolly tars are our men—' With his hand at the salute Hornblower strode up the lane of bos'un's mates and side-boys; all this was peculiarly exhilarating despite his efforts to tell himself that these outward signs of the dignity of his position were mere childish baubles. He had to check himself, or his face would have borne a stupid ecstatic grin; it was with difficulty that he forced himself to assume the stern composure a Commodore should display. There was Bush at the end of the lane, saluting stiffly, and standing effortlessly despite his wooden leg, and it was so pleasant to see Bush that he had to fight down his grin all over again.

'Good morning, Captain Bush,' he said, as gruffly as he knew how, and offering his hand with all he could manage of formal cordiality.

'Good morning, sir.'

Bush brought down his hand from the salute and grasped Hornblower's, trying hard to act his part, as if there was no friendship in this handshake but mere professional esteem. Hornblower noted that his hand was as hard as ever – promotion to captain's rank had not softened it. And try as he would Bush could not keep his face expressionless. The blue eyes were alight with pleasure, and the craggy features kept softening into a smile as they escaped from his control. It made it harder than ever for Hornblower to remain dignified.

Out of the tail of his eye Hornblower saw a seaman hauling briskly at the main signal halyards. A black ball was soaring up the mast, and as it reached the block a twitch of the seaman's wrist broke it out. It was the Commodore's broad pendant, hoisted to distinguish the ship he was in, and as the pendant broke out a puff of smoke forward and a loud bang marked the first gun of the salute which welcomed it. This was the highest, the greatest moment of all – thousands upon thousands of naval officers could serve all their lives and never have a distinguishing pendant hoisted for them, never hear a single gun fired in their honour. Hornblower could not help smiling now. His last reserve was broken down; he met Bush's eye and he laughed outright, and Bush laughed with him. They were like a pair of schoolboys exulting over a successful bit of mischief. It was extraordinarily pleasant to be aware that Bush was not only pleased at serving with him again, but was also pleased just because Hornblower was pleased.

Bush glanced over the port-side rail, and Hornblower looked across with him. There was the rest of the squadron, the two ugly bomb-ketches, the two big ship-rigged sloops, and the graceful little cutter. There were puffs of smoke showing at the sides of each of them, blown to nothingness almost instantly by the wind, and then the boom of the shots as each ship saluted the pendant, firing gun for gun, taking the time from the Commodore. Bush's eyes narrowed as he looked them over, observing whether everything was being done decently and in order, but his face lapsed into a grin again as soon as he was sure. The last shot of the salute was fired; eleven rounds from each ship. It was interesting to work out that the mere ceremony of hoisting his pendant had cost his country fifty pounds or so, at a time when she was fighting for her life against a tyrant who dominated all Europe. The twitter of the pipes brought the ceremony to an end; the ship's company took up their duties again, and the marines sloped arms and marched off, their boots sounding loud on the deck.

'A happy moment, Bush,' said Hornblower.

'A happy moment indeed, sir.'

There were presentations to be made; Bush brought forward the ship's officers one by one. At first sight one face was like another, but Hornblower knew that in a short period of crowded living each individual would become distinct, his peculiarities known to the limit of boredom.

'We shall come to know each other better, I hope, gentlemen,' said Hornblower, phrasing his thought politely.

A whip at the main yardarm was bringing up his baggage from the lugger, with Brown standing by to supervise – he must have come on board by an unobtrusive route, through a gun-port presumably. So the lugger and Barbara must still be alongside. Hornblower walked to the rail and peered over. True enough. And Barbara was standing just as he had left her, still, like a statue. But that must have been the last parcel swung up by the ship; Hornblower had hardly reached the side when the lugger cast off from the *Nonsuch*'s chains, hoisted his big mainsail and wheeled away as effortlessly as a gull.

'Captain Bush,' said Hornblower, 'we shall get under way immediately, if you please. Make a signal to the flotilla to that effect.'

V

'I'll put the pistols in this locker, sir,' said Brown, completing the unpacking.

'Pistols?' said Hornblower.

Brown brought the case over to him; he had only mentioned them because he knew that Hornblower was not aware of the pistols' existence. It was a beautiful mahogany case, velvet-lined; the first thing to catch the eye inside was a white card. It bore some words in Barbara's handwriting – 'To my dear husband. May he never need to use them, but if he must then may they serve him well, and at least may they remind him of his loving wife, who will pray every day for his safety, for his happiness, and for his success.' Hornblower read the words twice before he put the card down to examine the pistols. They were beautiful weapons, of bright steel inlaid with silver, double-barrelled, the butts of ebony, giving them a perfect balance in the hand. There were two copper tubes in the case to open next; they merely contained pistol bullets, each one cast flawlessly, a perfect sphere. The fact that the makers had gone to the trouble of casting special bullets and including them in the case recalled Hornblower's attention to the pistols. Inside the barrels were bright spiral lanes; they were rifled pistols, then. The next copper box in the case contained a number of discs of thin leather impregnated with oil; these would be for wrapping up the bullet before inserting it into the barrel, so as to ensure a perfect fit. The brass rod and the little brass mallet would be for hammering the bullets home. The little brass cup must be a measure of the powder charge. It was small, but that was the way to ensure accuracy – a small powder charge, a heavy ball, and a true barrel. With these pistols he could rely on himself to hit a small bull's-eye at fifty yards, as long as he held true.

But there was one more copper box to open. It was full of little square bits of copper sheet, very thin indeed. He was puzzled at the sight of them; each bit of copper had a bulge in the centre, where the metal was especially thin, making the black contents just visible through it. It dawned slowly upon Hornblower that these must be the percussion caps he had heard vaguely about recently. To prove it he laid one on his desk and tapped it sharply with the brass mallet. There was a sharp crack, a puff of smoke from under the mallet, and when he lifted up the latter he could see that the cap was rent open, and the desk was marked with the stain of the explosion.

He looked at the pistols again. He must have been blind, not to have noticed the absence of flint and priming pan. The hammer rested on what appeared at first sight to be a simple block of metal, but this pivoted at a touch, revealing a shallow cavity below it clearly intended to receive a cap. At the base of the cavity was a small hole which must communicate with the breech end of the barrel. Put a charge in the pistol, put a cap in the cavity, and fix it firm with the metal block. Now snap the hammer down upon the block. The cap explodes; the flame passes through the hole into the charge and the pistol is fired. No haphazard arrangement of flint and priming; rain or spray could never put these pistols out of action. Hornblower guessed there would not be a misfire once in a hundred shots. It was a wonderful present – it was very thoughtful indeed of Barbara to buy them for him. Heaven only knew what they must have cost; some skilled workman must have laboured for months over the rifling of those four barrels, and the copper caps – five hundred of them, every one hand-made – must have cost a pretty penny of themselves. But with those two pistols loaded he would have four men's lives in his hands; on a fine day with two flint-lock double-barrelled pistols he would expect one misfire, if not two, and if it were raining or there was spray flying it would be remarkable if he could fire a single shot. To Hornblower's mind the rifling was not as important as the percussion caps; in the usual shipboard scuffle when pistols were likely to be used accuracy was not important, for one generally pressed the muzzle against one's adversary's stomach before pulling the trigger.

Hornblower laid the pistols in their velvet nests and mused on. Dear Barbara. She was always thinking for him, trying to anticipate his wants, but something more than that as well. These pistols were an example of the way she tried to satisfy wants of his that he was not aware of. She had lifted her eyebrows when he had said that Gibbon would be all the reading material he would need on this commission, and she had bought and packed a score of other books for him; one of them, he could see from here, was this new poem in the Spenserian stanza, 'Childe Harold' (whatever that might mean) by the mad peer Lord Byron. Everyone had been talking about it just before his departure; he must admit he was glad of the chance to read it, although he would never have dreamed of buying it for himself. Hornblower looked back over a life of Spartan self-denial with a twinge of queer regret that it should have ended, and then he got angrily out of his chair. In another moment he would be wishing he were not married to Barbara, and that was perfect nonsense.

He could tell, down here in his cabin, that the *Nonsuch* was still closehauled to the strong northwesterly breeze; she was lying over to it so steadily that there was little roll in her motion, although she was pitching deeply as she met the short North Sea rollers. The tell-tale compass over his head showed that she was making good her course for the Skaw; the whole cabin was resonant with the harping of the taut rigging transmitted through the timbers of the ship, while she creaked positively thunderously as she pitched, loud enough to make conversation difficult. There was one frame that made a noise like a pistol shot at one particular moment of each pitch, and he had already grown so used to the sound as to be able to anticipate it exactly, judging it by the ship's motion.

He had been puzzled for a space by a peculiar irregular thud over his head; in fact, he had been so piqued at his inability to account for it that he had put on his hat and gone up on the quarterdeck to find out. There was nothing in sight on the deck which seemed likely to have made that rhythmical noise, no pump at work, nobody beating out oakum – even if it were conceivable that such a thing could be done on the quarterdeck of a ship of the line; there were only Bush and the officers of the watch, who immediately froze into inconspicuous immobility when the great man appeared on the companion. Heaven only knew what made that thumping; Hornblower began to wonder if his ears had deceived him and if the noise really came from a deck below. He had to make a pretence of having come on deck for a purpose –

interesting to find that even Commodore, First Class, still had to sink to such subterfuges – and he began to stride up and down the weather side of the quarterdeck, hands behind him, head bowed forward, in the old comfortable attitude. Enthusiasts had talked or written of pleasures innumerable, of gardens or women, wine or fishing; it was strange that no one had ever told of the pleasure of walking a quarterdeck.

But what was it that had made that slow thumping noise? He was forgetting why he had come upon deck. He darted covert glances from under his brows as he walked up and down and still saw nothing to account for it. The noise had not been audible since he came on deck, but still curiosity consumed him. He stood by the taffrail and looked back at the flotilla. The trim ship-rigged sloops were beating up against the strong breeze without difficulty, but the bomb-ketches were not so comfortable. The absence of a foremast, the huge triangular fore-sail, made it hard to keep them from yawing, even in a wind. Every now and then they would put their stumpy bowsprits down and take the green sea in over their bows.

He was not interested in bomb-ketches. He wanted to know what had been thumping the deck over his head when he was in his cabin, and then common sense came to help him fight down his ridiculous self-consciousness. Why should not a Commodore ask a simple question about a simple subject? Why in the world had he even hesitated for a moment? He swung round with determination.

'Captain Bush!' he called.

'Sir!' Bush came hastening aft to him, his wooden leg thumping the deck.

That was the noise! With every second step Bush took, his wooden leg with its leather button came down with a thump on the planking. Hornblower certainly could not ask the question he had just been forming in his mind.

'I hope I shall have the pleasure of your company at dinner this evening,' said Hornblower, thinking rapidly.

'Thank you, sir. Yes, sir. Yes indeed,' said Bush. He beamed with pleasure at the invitation so that Hornblower felt positively hypocritical as he made his way down into the cabin to supervise the last of his unpacking. Yet it was as well that he had been led by his own peculiar weaknesses to give that invitation instead of spending the evening, as he would otherwise have done, dreaming about Barbara, calling up in his mind the lovely drive through springtime England from Smallbridge to Deal, and making himself as miserable at sea as he had managed to make himself on land.

Bush would be able to tell him about the officers and men of the *Nonsuch*, who could be trusted and who must be watched, what was the material condition of the ship, if the stores were good or bad, and all the hundred other things he needed to know. And tomorrow, as soon as the weather moderated, he would signal for 'All Captains', and so make the acquaintance of his other subordinates, and size them up, and perhaps begin to convey to them his own particular viewpoints and theories, so that when the time came for action there would be need for few signals and there would be common action directed speedily at a common objective.

Meanwhile, there was one more job to be done immediately; the present would be the best time, he supposed with a sigh, but he was conscious of a faint distaste for it even as he applied himself to it.

'Pass the word for Mr Braun – for my clerk,' he said to Brown, who was hanging up the last of the uniform coats behind the curtain against the bulkhead.

'Aye aye, sir,' said Brown.

It was odd that his clerk and his coxswain should have names pro-nounced in identical fashion; it was that coincidence which had led him to add the unnecessary last three words to his order.

Mr Braun was tall and spare, fair, youngish, and prematurely bald, and Hornblower did not like him, although typically he was more cordial to him than he would have been if he had liked him. He offered him the cabin chair while he himself sat back on the locker, and when he saw Mr Braun's eyes resting curiously on the case of pistols – Barbara's gift – he condescended to discuss it with him as a conversational pre-liminary, pointing out the advantages of the percussion caps and the rifled barrels.

'Very good weapons indeed, sir,' said Mr Braun, replacing them in their velvet case.

He looked across the cabin at Hornblower, the dying light which came through the stern windows shining on his face and reflected in curious fashion from his pale-green eyes.

'You speak good English,' said Hornblower.

'Thank you, sir. My business before the war was largely with England. But I speak Russian and Swedish and Finnish and Polish and German and French just as well. Lithuanian a little. Estonian a little because it is so like Finnish.'

'But Swedish is your native language, though?'

Mr Braun shrugged his thin shoulders.

'My father spoke Swedish. My mother spoke German, sir. I spoke Finnish with my nurse, and French with one tutor and English with another. In my office we spoke Russian when we did not speak Polish.'

'But I thought you were a Swede?'

Mr Braun shrugged his shoulders again.

'A Swedish subject, sir, but I was born a Finn. I thought of myself as a Finn until three years ago.'

So Mr Braun was one more of these stateless individuals with whom all Europe seemed to be peopled nowadays – men and women without a country, Frenchmen, Germans, Austrians, Poles who had been uprooted by the chances of war and who dragged out a dreary existence in the hope that some day another chance of war would re-establish them.

'When Russia took advantage of her pact with Bonaparte,' explained Mr Braun, 'to fall upon Finland, I was one of those who fought. What use was it? What could Finland do against all the might of Russia? I was one of the fortunate ones who escaped. My brothers are in Russian gaols at this very minute if they are alive, but I hope they are dead. Sweden was in revolution – there was no refuge for me there, even though it had been for Sweden that I was fighting. Germany, Denmark, Norway were in Bonaparte's hands, and Bonaparte would gladly have handed me back to oblige his new Russian ally. But I was in an English ship, one of those to which I sold timber, and so to England I came. One day I was the richest man in Finland where there are few rich men, and the next I was the poorest man in England where there are many poor.'

The pale-green eyes reflected back the light again from the cabin window, and Hornblower realised anew that his clerk was a man of disquieting personality. It was not merely the fact that he was a refugee, and Hornblower, like everybody else, was surfeited with refugees and their tales of woe although his conscience pricked him about them – the first ones had begun to arrive twenty years ago from France, and ever since then there had been an increasing tide from Poland and Italy and Germany. Braun's being a refugee was likely to prejudice Hornblower against him from the start, and actually had done so, as Hornblower admitted to himself with his usual fussy sense of justice. But that was not the reason that Hornblower did not like him. There was less reason even than that – there was no reason at all.

It was irksome to Hornblower to think that for the rest of this commission he would have to work in close contact with this man. Yet the Admiralty orders in his desk enjoined upon him to pay the closest attention to the advice and information which he would receive from Braun, 'a gentleman whose acquaintance with the Baltic countries is both extensive and intimate.' Even this evening it was a great relief when Bush's knock at the cabin door, heralding his arrival for dinner, freed Hornblower from the man's presence. Braun slid unobtrusively out of the cabin with a bow to Bush; every line of his body indicated the pose – whether forced or natural Hornblower could not guess – of the man who has seen better days resignedly doing menial duties.

'How do you find your Swedish clerk, sir?' asked Bush.

'He's a Finn, not a Swede.'

'A Finn? You don't say, sir! It'd be better not to let the men know that.'

Bush's own honest face indicated a disquietude against which he struggled in vain.

'Of course,' said Hornblower.

He tried to keep his face expressionless, to conceal that he had completely left out of account the superstition that prevailed about Finns at sea. In a sailor's mind every Finn was a warlock who could conjure up storms by lifting his finger, but Hornblower had quite failed to think of the shabby-genteel Mr Braun as that kind of Finn, despite those unwholesome pale-green eyes.

VI

'Eight bells, sir.'

Hornblower came back to consciousness not very willingly; he suspected he was being dragged away from delightful dreams, although he could not remember what they were.

'Still dark, sir,' went on Brown remorselessly, 'but a clear night. Wind steady at west-by-north, a strong breeze. The sloops an' the flotilla in sight to looard, an' we're hove to, sir, under mizzen-t's'l, maint'mast stays'l an' jib. An' here's your shirt, sir.'

Hornblower swung his legs out of his cot and sleepily pulled off his nightshirt. He was minded at first just to put on those few clothes which would keep him warm on deck, but he had his dignity as Commodore to remember, and he wanted to establish a reputation as a man who was never careless about any detail whatever. He had left orders to be called now, a quarter of an hour before it was really necessary, merely to be able to do so. So he put on uniform coat and trousers and boots, parted his hair carefully in the flickering light of the lantern Brown held, and put aside the thought of shaving. If he came on deck at four in the morning newly shaved everyone would guess that he had been at pains regarding his appearance. He clapped on his cocked hat, and struggled into the pea-jacket which Brown held for him. Outside his cabin door the sentry snapped to attention as the great man appeared. On the half-deck, a group of high-spirited youngsters coming off watch subsided into awed and apprehensive silence at the sight of the Commodore, which was a fit and proper thing to happen.

On the quarterdeck it was as raw and unfriendly as one might expect before dawn in the Kattegat on a spring morning. The bustle of calling the watch had just subsided; the figures which loomed up in the darkness and hurriedly moved over to the port side, leaving the starboard side clear for him, were unrecognisable. But the thump of Bush's wooden leg was unmistakable.

'Captain Bush!'

'Sir?'

'What time is sunrise this morning?'

'Er – about five-thirty, sir.'

'I don't want to know about what time it will be. I asked, "What time is sunrise?"'

A second's silence while the crestfallen Bush absorbed this rebuke, and then another voice answered.

'Five-thirty-four, sir.'

That was that fresh-faced lad, Carlin, the second lieutenant of the ship. Hornblower would have given something to be sure whether Carlin really knew when sunrise was, or whether he was merely guessing, taking a chance that his Commodore would not check his figures. As for Bush, it was bad luck on him that he should be rebuked publicly, but he should have known what time was sunrise, seeing that last night Hornblower had been making plans with him based on that very point. And it would do the discipline of the rest of the force no harm if it were known that the Commodore spared no one, not even the captain of a ship of the line, his best friend.

Hornblower took a turn or two up and down the deck. Seven days out from the Downs, and no news. With the wind steady from the westward, there could be no news – nothing could have got out from the Baltic, or even from Gothenburg. He had not seen a sail yesterday after rounding the Skaw and coming up the Kattegat. His last news from Sweden was fifteen days old, then, and in fifteen days anything could happen. Sweden might have easily changed from unfriendly neutrality to open hostility. Before him lay the passage of the Sound, three miles wide at its narrowest point; on the starboard side would be Denmark, undoubtedly hostile under Bonaparte's domination whether she wanted to be or not. On the port side would be Sweden, and the main channel up the Sound lay under the guns of Helsingborg. If Sweden were England's enemy the guns of Denmark and Sweden – of Elsinore and of Helsingborg – might easily cripple the squadron as they ran the gauntlet. And retreat would always be perilous and difficult, if not entirely cut off. It might be as well to delay, to send in a boat to discover how Sweden stood at the present moment.

But on the other hand, to send in a boat would warn Sweden of his presence. If he dashed in now, the moment there was light enough to see the channel, he might go scathless, taking the defences by surprise even if Sweden were hostile. His vessels might be knocked about, but with the wind west-by-north, in an ideal quarter, even a crippled ship could struggle along until the Sound widened and they would be out of range. If Sweden's neutrality were still wobbling it would do no harm to let her see a British squadron handled with boldness and decision, nor for her to know that a British force were loose in the Baltic able to threaten her shores and ravage her shipping. Should Sweden turn hostile he could maintain himself one way or the other in the Baltic through the summer – and in a summer anything might happen – and with good fortune might fight his way out again in the autumn. There certainly were arguments in favour of temporising and delay and communicating with the shore, but there were more cogent arguments still in favour of prompt action.

The ship's bell struck one sharp note; hardly more than an hour before dawn, and already over there to leeward there was a hint of grey in the sky. Hornblower opened his mouth to speak, and then checked himself. He had been about to issue a sharp order, consonant with the tenseness of the moment and with the accelerated beating of his pulse; but that was not the way he wanted to behave. While he had time to think and prepare himself he could still pose as a man of iron nerves.

'Captain Bush!' he managed to make himself drawl the words, and to give his orders with an air of complete indifference. 'Signal all vessels to clear for action.'

'Aye aye, sir.'

Two red lights at the main yardarm and a single gun; that was the night signal for danger from the enemy which would send all hands to quarters. It took several seconds to bring a light for the lanterns; by the time the signal was acknowledged the *Nonsuch* was well on the way to being cleared for action – the watch below turned up, the decks sanded and the fire-pumps manned, guns run out and bulkheads knocked down. It was still a pretty raw crew – Bush had been through purgatory trying to get his ship manned – but the job could have been worse done. Now the grey dawn had crept up over the eastern sky, and the rest of the squadron was just visible as vessels and not as solid nuclei in the gloom, but it was still not quite light enough to risk the passage. Hornblower turned to Bush and Hurst the first lieutenant.

'If you please,' he drawled, dragging out every word with all the nonchalance he could muster, 'I will have the signal bent ready for hoisting, "Proceed to leeward in the order of battle".'

'Aye aye, sir.'

Everything was done now. This last two minutes of waiting in inactivity, with nothing left to do, were especially trying. Hornblower was about to walk up and down, when he remembered that he must stand still to maintain his pose of indifference. The batteries on shore might have their furnaces alight, to heat shot red-hot; there was a possibility that in a few minutes the whole force of which he was so proud might be no more than a chain of blazing wrecks. Now it was time.

'Hoist,' said Hornblower. 'Captain Bush, I'll trouble you to square away and follow the squadron.'

'Aye aye, sir,' said Bush.

Bush's voice hinted at suppressed excitement; and it came to Hornblower, with a blinding flash of revelation, that his pose was ineffective with Bush. The latter had learned, during years of experience, that when Hornblower stood still instead of walking about, and when he drawled out his words as he was doing at present, then in Hornblower's opinion there was danger ahead. It was an intensely interesting discovery, but there was no time to think about it, not with the squadron going up the Sound.

Lotus was leading. Vickery, her commander, was the man Hornblower had picked out as the captain with the steadiest nerves who could be trusted to lead without flinching. Hornblower would have liked to have led himself, but in this operation the rear would be the post of danger – the leading ships might well get through before the gunners on shore could get to their guns and find the range – and the *Nonsuch* as the most solidly built and best able to endure fire must come last so as to be able to succour and tow out of action any disabled ship. Hornblower watched *Lotus* set topsails and courses and square away. The cutter *Clam* followed – she was the feeblest of all; a single shot might sink her, and she must be given the best chance of getting through. Then the two ugly bomb-ketches, and then the other sloop, *Raven*, just ahead of *Nonsuch*; Hornblower was not sorry to have the opportunity to watch how her commander, Cole, would behave in action. *Nonsuch* followed, driving hard with the strong breeze on her starboard quarter. Hornblower watched Bush shaking the wind out of the mizzen-topsail so as to keep exact station astern of the *Raven*. The big two-decker seemed a lumbering clumsy thing compared with the grace and elegance of the sloops.

That was Sweden in sight now, Cape Kullen, now on the port bow.

'A cast of the log, if you please, Mr Hurst.'

'Aye aye, sir.'

Hornblower thought Hurst looked a little sidelong at him, unable to conceive why any sane man should want a cast of the log at a moment when the ship was about to risk everything; but Hornblower wanted to know how long the strain was likely to endure, and what was the use of being a Commodore if one could not then indulge one's whims? A midshipman and a couple of quartermasters came running aft with log and glass; the speed of the ship was sufficient to make the quartermaster's arms vibrate as he held the reel above his head.

'Nigh on nine knots, sir,' reported the midshipman to Hurst.

'Nigh on nine knots, sir,' reported Hurst to Hornblower.

'Very good.'

It would be a full eight hours, then, before they were beyond Saltholm and comparatively out of danger. There was the Danish coast on the starboard bow now, just visible in the half-light; the channel was narrowing fast. Hornblower could imagine sleepy sentries and lookouts peering from their posts at the hardly visible sails, and calling to their sergeants, and the sergeants coming sleepily to see for themselves and then hastening away to tell their lieutenants and then the drums beating to arms and the gunners running to their pieces. On the Danish side they would make ready to fire, for there were the minions of Bonaparte, and any sail was likely to be an enemy. But on the Swedish side? What had Bernadotte decided during the last few days? Was Bonaparte's Marshal still neutral, or had he at last made up his mind to throw the weight of Sweden on the side of his native land?

There were the low cliffs of Elsinore, and there were the steeples of Helsingborg in plain view to port, and the fortress above the town. *Lotus*, nearly a mile ahead, must be into the narrows. Hornblower levelled his glass at her; her yards were bracing round for the turn, and still no shot had been fired. *Clam* was turning next – please God the clumsy bomb-ketches did not misbehave. Ah! There it was. The heavy dull boom of a gun, and then the sullen roar of a salvo. Hornblower turned his glass to the Swedish coast. He could see no smoke there. Then to the Danish side. Smoke was evident, although the brisk wind was dispersing it fast. Under Bush's orders the helmsman was putting the wheel over a spoke or two, in readiness for the turn; Elsinore and Helsingborg were suddenly surprisingly near. Three miles wide was the channel, and Vickery in *Lotus* was carrying out his orders correctly, and keeping well to the port side of the fairway, two miles from Denmark, and only a mile from Sweden, with every vessel following exactly in his track. If the Swedish guns came into action and were well handled, they could deal the squadron some shrewd blows. Three jets of water from the surface of the sea on the starboard beam; although the eye could not see the ball that made them it was easy to imagine one could, as it skipped over the surface, but the last jet was a full cable's length from the side. The Swedish guns were still not firing; Hornblower wished he could tell whether it was because the Swedish gunners were taken by surprise or because they were under orders not to fire.

Elsinore was abaft the beam now, and the channel was opening wide. Hornblower shut his telescope with a snap, and a decided feeling of anticlimax. He could hardly imagine now what he had been worrying about. Calling up in his mind's eye the chart that he had so anxiously studied, he calculated that it would be an hour before they were in range of the shore again, where the fairway lay close in to the Swedish island of Hven – however that was pronounced in these barbarous northern tongues. This latter thought made him glance round. Braun was at his station on the quarterdeck, in attendance on the Commodore, as he should be. With his hands on the rail he was gazing over at the Swedish shore; Hornblower could not see his face, but every line of the man's figure disclosed rapt attention. The poor devil of an exile was looking longingly on the shores on which he could never hope to set foot. The world was full of exiles, but Hornblower felt sorry for this one.

Here came the sun, peeping between two Swedish hills as they opened up the valley. It was full daylight, with every promise of a fine day. The minute warmth of the sun, as the shadow of the mizzen-rigging ran across the quarterdeck, suddenly awoke in Hornblower the knowledge that he was stiff and chilled with having made himself stand still so long. He took a turn or two along the quarterdeck, restoring his circulation, and the fresh knowledge was borne in upon him that he wanted his breakfast. Glamorous visions of steaming cups of coffee danced momentarily in his mind's eye, and it was with a sense of acute disappointment that he remembered that, with the ship cleared for action and all fires out, there was no chance of hot food at all. So acute was the disappointment that he realised guiltily that his six months ashore had made him soft and self-indulgent; it was with positive distaste that he contemplated the prospect of breakfasting off biscuit and cold meat, and washing them down with ship's water which already had obviously been kept a long time in cask.

The thought reminded him of the men standing patiently at their guns. He wished Bush would remember about them, too. Hornblower could not possibly interfere in the details of the internal management of the ship – he would do more harm than good if he were to try – but he yearned to give the orders which were running through his mind. He tried for a moment to convey his wishes to Bush telepathically, but Bush seemed unreceptive, just as Hornblower expected. He walked over to the lee side as though to get a better view of the Swedish coast, stopping within two yards of Bush.

'Sweden still seems to be neutral,' he said, casually.

'Yes, sir.'

'We shall know better when we reach Hven – God knows how one's supposed to pronounce that. We must pass close under the guns there; the fairway's that side.'

'Yes, sir, I remember.'

'But there's nearly an hour before we come to it. I shall have a bite of breakfast brought up to me here. Will you join me, Captain?'

'Thank you, sir. I shall be delighted.'

An invitation of that sort from a Commodore was as good as a command to a captain. But Bush was far too good an officer to dream of eating food when his men could not do so. Hornblower could see in his

face his struggle against his nervous but impractical desire to have his
crew at their guns every moment of this tense time; Bush, after all, was
new to command and found his responsibility heavy. But good sense
won him over in the end.

'Mr Hurst. Dismiss the watch below. Half an hour for them to get
their breakfast.'

That was exactly the order Hornblower had wanted him to give – but
the pleasure at having brought it about did not in Hornblower's mind
counterbalance the annoyance at having had to make a bit of casual
conversation, and now there would have to be polite small talk over the
breakfast. The tense silence of the ship at quarters changed to the bustle
of dismissing the watch; Bush bawled orders for chairs and a table to be
brought up to the quarterdeck, and fussed over having them set up just
where the Commodore would like them. A glance from Hornblower to
Brown sufficed to spread the table with the delicacies suitable for the
occasion which Brown could select from the stores Barbara had sent
on board – the best hard bread money could buy; butter in a stone crock,
not nearly rancid yet; strawberry jam; a heavily smoked ham; a smoked
mutton ham from an Exmoor farm; Cheddar and Stilton cheese;
potted char. Brown had had a brilliant idea, and squeezed some of the
dwindling store of lemons for lemonade in order to disguise the flavour
of the ship's water; he knew that Hornblower was quite incapable of
drinking beer, even small beer, at breakfast time – and beer was the
only alternative.

Bush ran an appreciative eye over the loaded table, and at Hornblower's invitation sat down with appetite. Bush had been poor, too,
most of his life, with a host of indigent female relations dependent on his
pay. He was not yet surfeited with luxury. But Hornblower's characteristic cross-grainedness had got the better of him; he had wanted coffee,
and he could not have coffee, and so he wanted nothing at all. Even
lemonade was a mere mockery; he ate resentfully. It seemed to him that
Bush, spreading potted char liberally on a biscuit and eating with all the
appetite one might expect of him after a night on deck, was doing so
deliberately to annoy him. Bush cocked an eye at him across the table
and thought better of his first idea of making an appreciative comment on
the food. If his queer Commodore chose to be in a bad mood it was best
to leave him in it – Bush was better than a wife, thought Hornblower,
his acute perceptions noting the gesture.

Hornblower pulled out his watch as a reminder to Bush of the next
thing to be done.

'Call the watch below. Dismiss the watch on deck for breakfast,'
ordered Bush.

It was strange – dramatic, presumably, would be the right word – to
be sitting here in this Baltic sunshine, breakfasting at leisure while no

more than three miles away the hordes of the tyrant of Europe could only gaze at them impotently. Brown was offering cigars; Bush cut the end off his with the big sailor's clasp-knife which he brought out of a side pocket, and Brown brought the smouldering slow match from the tub beside the quarterdeck carronades to give them a light. Hornblower breathed in the smoke luxuriously and found it impossible to maintain his evil humour, now with the sun shining, his cigar drawing well, and the advanced guard of a million French soldiers three miles distant. The table was whipped away from between them and he stretched his legs. Even Bush did the same – at least, he sat farther back instead of perching on the edge of his chair; his wooden leg stuck out straight before him although the other one remained decorously bent. The *Nonsuch* was still thrashing along gloriously under plain sail, heeling a little to the wind, with the green sea creaming joyously under her bows. Hornblower pulled at his cigar again in strange spiritual peace. After his recent discontent it was like the unbelievable cessation of toothache.

'Hven nearly within random shot, sir,' reported the first lieutenant.

'Call all hands to quarters,' ordered Bush, with a glance at Hornblower.

But Hornblower sat on tranquilly. He felt suddenly quite certain that the guns on Hven would not open fire, and he did not want to throw away ungratefully the cigar which had served him so well. Bush took a second glance at him and decided to sit still too. He hardly deigned to spare a glance for Hven as it came up under the lee bow and passed away under the lee quarter. Hornblower thought of Saltholm and Amager lying ahead; that would be the time of greatest danger, for both islands were in Danish hands and the twelve-fathom channel passed between them and close to both of them. But there was plenty of time to finish this cigar. It was with sincere regret that he drew the last puff, rose slowly to his feet, and sauntered to the lee rail to pitch the end carefully overside.

The sudden swoop of his squadron in the grey dawn had taken the Elsinore garrison by surprise, but there could be no surprise for Saltholm and Amager. They could see his ships in this clear weather a dozen miles away, and the gunners would have ample time to make all preparations to receive them. He looked ahead down the line of vessels.

'Make a signal to *Moth*,' he snapped over his shoulder, "Keep better station".'

If the line were to straggle it would be the longer exposed to fire. The land was in plain sight through his glass; it was lucky that Saltholm was low-lying so that its guns had only poor command. Copenhagen must be only just out of sight, below the horizon to starboard. Vickery was taking *Lotus* exactly down the course Hornblower had laid down for him in his orders. There was the smoke bursting out from Saltholm.

There was the boom of the guns – a very irregular salvo. He could see no sign of damage to the ships ahead. *Lotus* was firing back; he doubted if her popgun nine-pounders could hit at that range, but the smoke might help to screen her. All Saltholm was covered with smoke now, and the boom of the guns across the water was in one continuous roll like a drum. They were still out of range of Amager at present; Vickery was wearing ship now for the turn. Bush very sensibly had leadsmen in the chains.

'By the mark seven!'

Seven fathoms was ample, with the tide making. Brown against green – those were the batteries on Saltholm, dimly visible in the smoke; young Carlin on the maindeck was pointing out the target to the port-side twelve-pounders.

'By the deep six, and half six!'

A sudden tremendous crash, as the port-side battery fired all together. The *Nonsuch* heaved with the recoil, and as she did so came the leadsman's cry.

'And a half six!'

'Starboard your helm,' said Bush. 'Stand by, the starboard guns!'

Nonsuch poised herself for the turn; as far as Hornblower could tell, not a shot had been fired at her at present.

'By the mark five!'

They must be shaving the point of the shoal. There were the Amager batteries in plain sight – the starboard-side guns, with the additional elevation due to the heel of the ship, should be able to reach them. Both broadsides together, this time, an ear-splitting crash, and the smoke from the starboard guns billowed across the deck, bitter and irritant.

'And a half five!'

That was better. God, *Harvey* was hit. The bomb-ketch, two cables' lengths ahead of *Nonsuch*, changed in a moment from a fighting vessel to a wreck. Her towering mainmast, enormous for her size, had been cut through just above her deck; mast and shrouds, and the huge area of canvas she carried, were trailing over her quarter. Her stumpy mizzen-topmast had gone as well, hanging down from the cap. *Raven*, as her orders dictated, swept past her, and *Harvey* lay helpless as *Nonsuch* hurtled down upon her.

'Back the maintops'l,' roared Bush.

'Stand by with the heaving-line, there!' said Hurst.

'And a half five!' called the leadsman.

'Helm-a-lee,' said Bush, and then in the midst of the bustle the starboard broadside bellowed out again, as the guns bore on the Amager batteries, and the smoke swept across the decks. *Nonsuch* heaved over; her backed topsail caught the wind and checked her way as she recovered. She hovered with the battered *Harvey* close alongside. Hornblower could see Mound, her captain, directing the efforts of her crew from his station at the foot of her mizzenmast. Hornblower put his speaking-trumpet to his lips.

'Cut that wreckage away, smartly, now.'

'Stand by for the line!' shouted Hurst.

The heaving-line, well thrown, dropped across her mizzen shrouds, and Mound himself seized it; Hurst dashed below to superintend the passing across of the towline, which lay on the lower gundeck all ready to be passed out of an after gun-port. A splintering crash forward told that one shot at least from Amager had struck home on *Nonsuch*. Axes were cutting furiously at the tangle of shrouds over the *Harvey*'s side; a group of seamen were furiously hauling in the three-inch line from *Nonsuch* which had been bent on the heaving-line. Another crash forward; Hornblower swung round to see that a couple of foremast shrouds had parted at the chains. With the *Nonsuch* lying nearly head to wind neither port-side nor starboard-side guns bore to make reply, but Carlin had a couple of guns' crews hard at work with hand-spikes heaving the two foremost guns round – it would be as well to keep the batteries under fire so as not to allow them to indulge in mere target practice. Hornblower turned back; *Nonsuch*'s stern was almost against *Harvey*'s quarter, but some capable officer already had two spars out from the stern gallery to boom her off. The big cable itself was on its way over now; as Hornblower watched he saw *Harvey*'s men reach and grasp it.

'We'll take you out stern first, Mr Mound,' yelled Hornblower through his speaking-trumpet – there was no time to waste while they took the cable forward. Mound waved acknowledgement.

'Quarter less five,' came the voice of the leadsman; the leeway which the two vessels were making was carrying them down on the Saltholm shoals.

On the heels of the cry came the bang-bang of the two guns which Carlin had brought to bear on the Amager batteries, and following that came the howl of shot passing overhead. There were holes in main and mizzen-topsails – the enemy were trying to disable *Nonsuch*.

'Shall I square away, sir?' came Bush's voice at Hornblower's side.

Mound had taken a turn with the cable's end round the base of the *Harvey*'s mizzenmast, which was stepped so far aft as to make a convenient point to tow from. He was waving his arms to show that all was secure, and his axemen were hacking at the last of the mainmast shrouds.

'Yes, Captain.' Hornblower hesitated before dropping a word of advice on a matter which was strictly Bush's business. 'Take the strain slowly, or you'll part the tow or pluck that mizzenmast clear out of her. Haul your headsails up to starboard, then get her slowly under way before you brace up your maintops'l.'

'Aye aye, sir.'

Bush showed no resentment at Hornblower's telling him what to do, for he knew very well that Hornblower's advice was something more valuable than gold could ever buy.

'And if I were doing it I'd keep the towline short – stern first, with nothing to keep her under control, *Harvey*'ll tow better that way.'

'Aye aye, sir.'

Bush turned and began to bellow his orders. With the handling of the headsails the *Nonsuch* turned away from the wind, and instantly Carlin brought his guns into action again. The ship was wrapped in smoke and in the infernal din of the guns. Shots from Amager were still striking home or passing overhead, and in the next interval of comparative silence the voice of the leadsman made itself heard.

'And a half four!'

The sooner they were away from these shoals the better. Fore- and mizzen-topsails were filling slightly, and the headsails were drawing. The towline tightened, and as the ears recovered from the shock of the next broadside they became aware of a vast creaking as the cable and the bitts took the strain – on the *Nonsuch*'s quarterdeck they could overhear *Harvey*'s mizzenmast creaking with the strain. The ketch came round slowly, to the accompaniment of fierce bellowings at *Nonsuch*'s helmsman, as the two-decker wavered at the pull across her stern. It was all satisfactory; Hornblower nodded to himself – if Bush were stealing glances at him (as he expected) and saw that nod it would do no harm.

'Hands to the braces!' bellowed Bush, echoing Hornblower's thoughts. With fore- and mizzen-topsails trimmed and drawing well *Nonsuch* began to increase her speed, and the ketch followed her with as much docility as could be expected of a vessel with no rudder to keep her straight. Then she sheered off in ugly fashion to starboard before the tug of the line pulled her straight again to a feu de joie of creaks. Hornblower shook his head at the sight, and Bush held back his order to brace up the maintopsail.

'Starboard your helm, Mr Mound!' shouted Hornblower through his speaking-trumpet. Putting *Harvey*'s rudder over might have some slight effect – the behaviour of every ship being towed was an individual problem. Speed was increasing, and that, too, might affect *Harvey*'s behaviour for better or worse.

'By the mark five!'

That was better. And *Harvey* was behaving herself, too. She was yawing only very slightly now; either the increase in speed or the putting over of the rudder was having its effect.

'That's well done, Captain Bush,' said Hornblower pompously.

'Thank you, sir,' said Bush, and promptly ordered the maintopsail to be braced up.

'By the deep six!'

They were well off the Saltholm shoal, then, and Hornblower suddenly realised that the guns had not fired for some time, and he had heard nothing of any more firing from Amager. They were through the channel, then, out of range of the batteries, at a cost of only a single spar knocked away. There was no need to come within range of any other hostile gun – they could round Falsterbo well clear of the Swedish batteries.

'By the deep nine!'

Bush was looking at him with that expression of puzzled admiration which Hornblower had seen on his face before. Yet it had been easy enough. Anyone could have foreseen that it would be best to leave to the *Nonsuch* the duty of towing any cripples out of range, and, once that was granted, anyone would have the sense to have a cable roused out and led aft ready to undertake the duty instantly, with heaving-lines and all the other gear to hand, and anyone would have posted *Nonsuch* last in the line, both to endure the worst of the enemy's fire and to be in position to run down to a cripple and start towing without delay. Anyone could have made those deductions – it was vaguely irritating that Bush should look like that.

'Make a general signal to heave to,' said Hornblower. 'Captain Bush, stand by, if you please, to cast off the tow. I'll have *Harvey* jury rigged before we round Falsterbo. Perhaps you'll be good enough to send a party on board to help with the work.'

And with that he went off below. He had seen all he wanted both of Bush and of the world for the present. He was tired, drained of his energy. Later there would be time enough to sit at his desk and begin the weary business of – 'Sir, I have the honour to report –' There would be dead and wounded to enumerate, too.

VII

His Britannic Majesty's seventy-four-gun ship *Nonsuch* was out of sight of land in the Baltic. She was under easy sail, running before that persistent westerly wind, and astern of her, like a couple of ugly ducklings following their portly mother, came the two bomb-ketches. Far out to starboard, only just in sight, was the *Lotus*, and far out to port was the *Raven*. Beyond the *Raven*, unseen from the *Nonsuch*, was the *Clam*; the four ships made a visual chain which could sweep the narrow neck of the Baltic, from Sweden to Rügen, from side to side. There was still no news; in spring, with the melting of the ice, the whole traffic of the

Baltic was outwards, towards England and Europe, and with this westerly wind so long prevailing little was astir. The air was fresh and keen, despite the sunshine, and the sea was silver-grey under the dappled sky.

Hornblower gasped and shuddered as he took his bath under the wash-deck pump. For fifteen years he had served in tropical and Mediterranean waters; he had had lukewarm seawater pumped over him far more often than he could remember, and this Baltic water, chilled by the melting ice in the gulfs of Bothnia and Finland, and the snow-water of the Vistula and the Oder, was still a shock to him. There was something stimulating about it, all the same, and he pranced grotesquely under the heavy jet, forgetful – as he always was while having his bath – of the proper dignity of a Commodore. Half a dozen seamen, working in leisurely fashion under the direction of the ship's carpenter at replacing a shattered gun-port, stole wondering glances at him. The two seamen at the pump, and Brown standing by with towel and dressing-gown, preserved a proper solemnity of aspect, close under his eye as they were.

Suddenly the jet ceased; a skinny little midshipman was standing saluting his naked Commodore. Despite the gravity of addressing so great a man the child was round-eyed with wonder at this fantastic behaviour on the part of an officer whose doings were a household word.

'What is it?' said Hornblower, water streaming off him. He could not return the salute.

'Mr Montgomery sent me, sir. *Lotus* signals, "Sail to leeward", sir.'

'Very good.'

Hornblower snatched the towel from Brown, but the message was too important for time to be wasted drying himself, and he ran up the companion still wet and naked, with Brown following with his dressing-gown. The officer of the watch touched his hat as Hornblower appeared on the quarterdeck – it was like some old fairy story, the way everybody rigidly ignored the Commodore's lack of clothes.

'New signal from *Lotus*, sir. "Chase has tacked. Chase is on the port tack, bearing east-by-north, half east".'

Hornblower leaped to the compass; only the topsails of the *Lotus* were in sight from the deck as he took the bearing by eye. Whatever that sail was, he must intercept it and gather news. He looked up to see Bush hastening on deck, buttoning his coat.

'Captain Bush, I'll trouble you to alter course two points to starboard.'

'Aye aye, sir.'

'*Lotus* signalling again, sir. "Chase is a ship. Probably British merchantman".'

'Very good. Set all sail, Captain Bush, if you please."

'Aye aye, sir.'

The pipes shrilled through the ship, and four hundred men went pouring up the ratlines to loose the royals and set studding-sails. Hornblower raised a professional eye to watch the operation, carried out under a storm of objurgation from the officer of the watch. The still clumsy crew was driven at top speed by the warrant officers through the evolution, and it was hardly completed before there was a yell from the masthead.

'Sail on the starboard bow!'

'Must be the ship *Lotus* can see, sir,' said Bush. 'Masthead there! What can you see of the sail?'

'She's a ship, sir, closehauled an' coming up fast. We're headin' to meet her."

'Hoist the colours, Mr Hurst. If she was beating up for the Sound, sir, she would have tacked whether she saw *Lotus* or not.'

'Yes,' said Hornblower.

A shriek came from the masthead, where one of the midshipmen of the watch, an urchin who had not yet mastered his changing voice, had run up with a glass.

'British colours, sir!'

Hornblower remembered he was still wet and naked; at least, he was still wet in those parts of him which did not offer free play for the wind to dry him. He began to dab at these inner corners with the towel he still held, only to be interrupted again.

'There she is!' said Bush; the ship's upper sails were over the horizon, in view from the deck.

'Lay a course to pass her within hail, if you please,' said Hornblower.

'Aye aye, sir. Starboard a point, Quartermaster. Get those stuns'ls in again, Mr Hurst.'

The ship they were approaching held her course steadily; there was nothing suspicious about her, not even the fact that she had gone about immediately on sighting *Lotus.*

'Timber from the South Baltic, I expect, sir,' said Bush, training his glass. 'You can see the deck cargo now.'

Like most ships bound out of the Baltic her decks were piled high with timber, like barricades along the bulwarks.

'Make the merchant ships' private signal if you please, Captain,' said Hornblower.

He watched the reply run up the ship's halliards.

'A – T – numeral – five – seven, sir,' read Hurst through his glass. 'That's the correct reply for last winter, and she won't have received the new code yet.'

'Signal her to heave to,' said Hornblower.

With no more delay than was to be expected of a merchant ship, unadept at reading signals, and with a small crew, the ship backed her maintopsail and lay-to. The *Nonsuch* came hurtling down upon her.

'That's the yellow Q she's hoisting now, sir,' said Hurst, suddenly. 'The fever flag.'

'Very good. Heave to, Captain Bush, if you please.'

'Aye aye, sir. I'll keep to wind'ard of her, too, if you've no objection, sir.'

The *Nonsuch* laid her topsails to the mast and rounded-to, rocking in the gentle trough of the waves a pistol-shot to windward Hornblower took his speaking-trumpet.

'What ship's that?'

'*Maggie Jones* of London. Eleven days out from Memel!'

In addition to the man at the wheel there were only two figures visible on the poopdeck of the *Maggie Jones*; one of them, wearing white duck trousers and a blue coat, was obviously the captain. It was he who was answering by speaking-trumpet.

'What's that yellow flag for?'

'Smallpox. Seven cases on board, and two dead. First case a week ago.'

'Smallpox, by God!' muttered Bush. A frightful mental picture came up before his mind's eye, of what smallpox would do, let loose in his precious *Nonsuch*, with nine hundred men crammed into her restricted space.

'Why are you sailing without convoy?'

'None available at Memel. The rendezvous for the trade's off Langeland on the twenty-fourth. We're beating up for the Belt now.'

'What's the news?' Hornblower had waited patiently during all these interminable sentences before asking that question.

'The Russian embargo still holds, but we're sailing under licence.'

'Sweden?'

'God knows, sir. Some say they've tightened up their embargo there.'

A curious muffled howl came from below decks in the *Maggie Jones* at the moment, just audible in the *Nonsuch*.

'What's that noise?' asked Hornblower.

'One of the smallpox cases, sir. Delirious. They say the Czar's meeting Bernadotte next week for a conference somewhere in Finland.'

'Any sign of war between France and Russia?'

'None that I could see in Memel.'

That delirious patient must be very violent for his shrieks to reach Hornblower's ears at this distance against the wind. Hornblower heard them again. Was it possible for one man to make all that noise? It sounded more like a muffled chorus to Hornblower. Hornblower felt a sudden wave of suspicion surging up within him. The white-trousered figure on the *Maggie Jones*'s poop was altogether too glib, too professional in his talk. A naval officer might possibly discuss the chances of war in the Baltic as coldly as this man was doing, but a merchant captain would put more feeling in his words. And more than one man was making that noise in her forecastle. The captain could easily have offered his information about the Czar's meeting with Bernadotte as a red herring to distract Hornblower's attention from the cries below deck. Something was wrong.

'Captain Bush,' said Hornblower, 'send a boat with a boarding-party over to that ship.'

'Sir!' protested Bush, wildly. 'Sir – she has smallpox on board – sir! Aye aye, sir.'

Bush's protests died an uneasy death at the look on Hornblower's face. Bush told himself that Hornblower knew as well as he did the frightful possibilities of the introduction of smallpox into *Nonsuch*. Hornblower knew the chances he was taking. And one more look at Hornblower's face told Bush that the decision had not been an easy one.

Hornblower put the trumpet to his lips again.

'I'm sending a boat to you,' he shouted. It was hard at twenty yards' distance to detect any change in the manner of the man he was addressing, especially when hampered with a speaking-trumpet, but Hornblower thought he could see the captain start a little. Certainly there was a decided pause before he answered.

'As you wish, sir. I have warned you of smallpox. Could you send a surgeon and medicines?'

That was exactly what he should have said. But all the same, there was that suspicious pause before answering, as if the man had been taken by surprise and had searched round in his mind for the best reply to make. Bush was standing by, with misery in his face, hoping that Hornblower would countermand his order, but Hornblower made no sign. Under the orders of the boatswain the whaler rose to the pull of the tackles, was swayed outboard, and dropped into the sea. A midshipman and a boat's crew dropped down into her, sulkily. They would have gone cheerfully to board an armed enemy, but the thought of a loathsome disease unmanned them.

'Push off,' ordered the officer of the watch, after a last glance at Hornblower. The whaler danced over the waves towards the *Maggie Jones*, and then Hornblower saw the captain dash his speaking-trumpet to the deck and look round wildly as though for some means of escape.

'Stay hove-to, or I'll sink you,' roared Hornblower, and with a gesture of despair the captain stood still, drooping in defeat.

The whaler hooked on to the *Maggie Jones*'s main-chains and the midshipman led his party on to the decks with a rush. There was no sign of any opposition offered, but as the seamen ran aft there was the sudden pop of a pistol, and Hornblower saw the midshipman bending over the writhing, white-trousered body of the captain. He found himself taking an oath that he would break that midshipman, court martial him, ruin him, and have him begging his bread in the gutter if he had wantonly killed the captain. Hornblower's hunger and thirst for news, for facts, for information, was so intense that the thought of the captain escaping him by death roused him to ferocious bitterness.

'Why the devil didn't I go myself?' he demanded of no one in particular. 'Captain Bush, I'll be obliged if you'll have my barge called away."

'But the smallpox, sir—'

'Smallpox be damned. And there's none on board that ship.'

The midshipman's voice came across the water to them.

'*Nonsuch* ahoy! She's a prize. Taken yesterday by a French privateer.'

'Who's that captain I was speaking to?' demanded Hornblower.

'A renegade Englishman, sir. He shot himself as we came on board.'

'Is he dead?'

'Not yet, sir.'

'Mr Hurst,' said Bush, 'send the surgeon over. I'll give him one minute to get his gear together. I want that renegade's life saved so that we can see how he looks at a yardarm.'

'Send him in my barge,' said Hornblower, and then, through the speaking-trumpet, 'Send the prisoners and the ship's officers over to me.'

'Aye aye, sir.'

'And now I'll get some clothes on, by God,' said Hornblower; he had only just realised that he had been standing naked on the quarterdeck for an hour or more – if he had obeyed his first impulse and gone over in his barge he would have boarded the *Maggie Jones* without a stitch on.

The captain and the two mates were ushered down into Hornblower's cabin, where he and Bush questioned them eagerly, the chart of the Baltic spread out before him.

'We heard that renegade tell you the truth, sir,' said the captain. 'We were ten days out from Memel, bound for the Belt, when he pounced on us yesterday – big ship-rigged privateer, ten guns a side, flush-decked. Name *Blanchefleur*, whatever way you say it. What the Frogs call a corvette. French colours. They put a prize crew on board under that renegade – Clarke's his name, sir – an' I think we were headed for Kiel when you caught us. They shut us up in the lazarette. God, how we yelled, hoping you'd hear us.'

'We heard you,' said Bush.

'How were things at Memel when you left?' demanded Hornblower.

The captain's face wrinkled; if he had been French he would have shrugged his shoulders.

'The same as ever. Russian ports are still closed to us, but they'll give anyone a licence to trade who asks for it. It's the same with the Swedes on the other side.'

'What about war between Bonaparte and Russia?'

This time the tangle of doubt really made the captain shrug.

'Everyone's talking about it, but nothing definite yet. Soldiers everywhere. If Boney really fights 'em he'll find 'em as ready as Russians ever are.'

'Do you think he will?'

'I wish you'd tell *me*, sir. I don't know. But it was true what Clarke told you, sir. The Czar and Bernadotte are meeting soon. Perhaps you can guess what that means. It means nothing to a plain man like me, sir. There have been so many of these meetings and conferences and congresses.'

So there it was; Sweden and Russia were still in the equivocal position of being nominal enemies of England and nominal allies of Bonaparte, pretending to make war, pretending to be at peace, half belligerent, half neutral, in the strange manner which seemed to have become fashionable nowadays. It was still doubtful whether Bonaparte would take the tremendous step of waging war on Russia. No one could analyse Bonaparte's motives. One might think that he would do better for himself by turning all his vast resources towards finishing off the war in Spain and endeavouring to strike down England before attempting the conquest of the East; but on the other hand a swift decisive blow at Russia might free him from the menace of a powerful and doubtfully friendly nation at his back. Bonaparte had conquered so often; he had struck down every nation in Europe – except England – and it hardly seemed likely that Russia could withstand the impact of his massed forces. With Russia beaten he would have no enemies left on the mainland at all. There would only be England left to oppose him, singlehanded. It was comforting that England had not taken active measures in support of Finland when Russia attacked her, all the same. That made a working alliance with Russia far more practicable now.

'Now tell me more about this *Blanchefleur*,' said Hornblower, bending over the chart.

'She nabbed us off Rügen, sir. Sassnitz bore so'west, eight miles. You see, sir—'

Hornblower listened to the explanation with attention. A twenty-gun corvette under a good French captain was a serious menace loose in the Baltic. With the trade beginning to move on the melting of the ice it would be his first duty to capture her or drive her into port and blockade her. A ship of that force would be able to put up a good fight even against one of his sloops. He hoped he could entrap her, for she would be far too fast for *Nonsuch* to overhaul her in a stern chase. She was sending her prizes into Kiel, for there they could dispose of the prisoners, pick up a French crew, and start the hazardous voyage round Denmark to the west – Bonaparte needed naval stores, with ships of war building in every port from Hamburg to Trieste.

'Thank you, gentlemen,' he said. 'I'll not detain you longer. Captain Bush, we'll talk to the prisoners next.'

But there was little to learn from the seamen of the captured prize crew, even though they were brought in separately for questioning. Four of them were Frenchmen; Hornblower conducted his own examination of them, with Bush looking on admiringly. Bush had already succeeded in forgetting all the little French he had so painfully learned during his enforced sojourn in France. Two were Danes, and two were Germans; Mr Braun was called in to interpret while they were questioned. They were all experienced seamen, and as far as Hornblower could gather they had all been driven to take service in the *Blanchefleur* sooner than be conscripted into Bonaparte's navy or army. Even though they were faced with what might well be a lifetime in an English prison the Frenchmen refused any offer to serve in the British Navy, but the others accepted immediately Braun put the suggestion to them. Bush rubbed his hands at acquiring four prime seamen in this fashion to help fill his chronically undermanned ships. They had picked up a little French in the *Blanchefleur*, and they would soon pick up enough English in the *Nonsuch* or the *Lotus*; certainly they would under the stimulus of a rope's end handled by an experienced petty officer.

'Take 'em away and read 'em in, Mr Hurst,' said Bush, rubbing his hands again. 'Now, sir, shall we take a look at that damned renegade Englishman?'

Clarke was lying on the maindeck of the *Nonsuch*, to which he had been hoisted from the boat by a tackle at the yardarm, and the surgeon was still bending over him. He had tried to blow out his brains, but he had only succeeded in shattering his lower jaw. There was blood on his blue coat and on his white trousers, and his whole head was swathed in bandages, and he lay tossing in agony on the canvas sheet in which he had been hoisted. Hornblower peered down at him. The features he could see, chalk white so that the tan looked like a coat of dirt, were pinched and refined and weak, a thin nose and hollow cheeks, brown eyes like a woman's, with scanty sandy eyebrows above them. What little hair Hornblower could see was scanty and sandy too. Hornblower wondered what combination of circumstances could have led him into betraying his country and taking service with Bonaparte. Hatred of imprisonment, perhaps – Hornblower had known what it was to be a prisoner, in Ferrol and Rosas and in France. Yet that over-refined face did not seem to indicate the sort of personality that would fret itself to pieces in confinement. It might have been a woman, perhaps, who had driven him or led him to this, or he might be a deserter from the Navy who had fled to escape punishment – it would be interesting to see if his back was scarred with the cat-o'-nine-tails. He might perhaps be an Irishman, one of those fanatics who in their desire to hurt England refused to see that the worst England had ever done to Ireland would be nothing compared with what Bonaparte would do to her if she were once in his power.

Whatever might be the case, he was a man of ability and quick wit. As soon as he had seen that *Lotus* had cut him off from escape to the mainland he had resolutely taken the only course that gave him any chance of safety. He had steered the *Maggie Jones* as innocently as kiss-your-hand up to *Nonsuch*; that suggestion of smallpox had been an ingenious one, and his conversation by speaking-trumpet had been very nearly natural.

'Is he going to live?' asked Bush of the surgeon.

'No, sir. The mandible is extensively comminuted on both sides – I mean his jaw is shattered, sir. There is some splintering of the maxilla as well, and his tongue – the whole glossopharyngeal region, in fact – is in rags. The haemorrhage may prove fatal – in other words the man may bleed to death, although I do not think he will, now. But I do not think anything on earth can stop mortification – gangrene, in other words, sir – which in this area will prove immediately fatal. In any event the man will die of inanition, of hunger and thirst that is to say, even if we could keep him alive for a while by injections per rectum.'

It was ghoulish to smile at the surgeon's pomposity, to make the inevitable light speech.

'It sounds as if nothing could save him, then.'

It was a human life they were discussing.

'We must hang him, sir, before he dies,' said Bush, turning to Hornblower. 'We can convene a court martial—'

'He cannot defend himself,' replied Hornblower.

Bush spread his hands in a gesticulation which for him was vastly eloquent.

'What defence has he to offer, sir? We have all the evidence we need. The prisoners have supplied it apart from the obvious facts.'

'He might be able to rebut the evidence if he could speak,' said Hornblower. It was an absurd thing to say. There could be no possible doubt of Clarke's guilt – his attempt at suicide proved it even if nothing else did; but Hornblower knew perfectly well that he was quite incapable of hanging a man who was physically unable to make any defence.

'He'll slip through our fingers if we wait, sir.'

'Then let him.'

'But the example to the men, sir—'

'No, no, no,' flared Hornblower. 'What sort of example would it be to the men to hang a dying man – a man who would not know what was being done to him, for that matter?'

It was horrible to see the faint play of expression in Bush's face. Bush was a kindly man, a good brother to his sisters and a good son to his mother, and yet there was that hint of the lust of cruelty, the desire for a hanging. No, that was not quite fair. What Bush lusted for was revenge – revenge on a traitor who had borne arms against their common country.

'It would teach the men not to desert, sir,' said Bush, still feebly raising arguments. Hornblower knew – he had twenty years of experience – how every British captain was plagued by desertion, and spent half his waking hours wondering first how to find men and second how to retain them.

'It might,' said Hornblower, 'but I doubt it very much.'

He could not imagine any good being done, and he certainly could picture the harm, if the men were forced to witness a helpless man, one who could not even stand on his feet, being noosed about the neck and swung up to the yardarm.

Bush still hankered for blood. Even though he had no more to say, there was still a look in his face, there were still protests trembling on his lips.

'Thank you, Captain Bush,' said Hornblower. 'My mind is made up.'

Bush did not know, and might never learn, that mere revenge, object-less, retaliatory, was always stale and unprofitable.

VIII

The *Blanchefleur* would most likely still be hovering round the island of Rügen. Cape Arcona would be a profitable haunt – shipping coming down the Baltic from Russian and Finnish ports would make a landfall there, to be easily snapped up, hemmed in between the land and the two-fathom shoal of the Adlergrund. She would not know of the arrival of a British squadron, nor guess that the immediate recapture of the *Maggie Jones* had so quickly revealed her presence here.

'I think that is all perfectly plain, gentlemen?' said Hornblower, looking round his cabin at his assembled captains.

There was a murmur of assent. Vickery of the *Lotus* and Cole of the *Raven* were looking grimly expectant. Each of them was hoping that it would be his ship that would encounter the *Blanchefleur* – a successful single-ship action against a vessel of so nearly equal force would be the quickest way to be promoted captain from commander. Vickery was young and ardent – it was he who had commanded the boats at the cutting-out of the *Sevres* – and Cole was grey-headed and bent. Mound, captain of the *Harvey*, and Duncan, captain of the *Moth*, were both of them young lieutenants; Freeman, of the cutter *Clam*, swarthy and with long black hair like a gypsy, was of a different type; it would be less surprising to hear he was captain of a smuggling craft than captain of a King's ship. It was Duncan who asked the next question.

'If you please, sir, is Swedish Pomerania neutral?'

'Whitehall would be glad to know the answer to that question, Mr Duncan,' said Hornblower, with a grin. He wanted to appear stern and aloof, but it was not easy with these pleasant boys.

They grinned back at him; it was with a curious pang that Hornblower realised that his subordinates were already fond of him. He thought, guiltily, that if they only knew all the truth about him they might not like him so much.

'Any other questions, gentlemen? No? Then you can return to your ships and take your stations for the night.'

At dawn when Hornblower came on deck there was a thin fog over the surface of the sea; with the dropping of the westerly wind the cold water flowing out from the melting ice-packs of the Gulf of Finland had an opportunity of cooling the warm damp air and condensing its moisture into a cloud.

'It could be thicker, sir, but not much,' grumbled Bush. The foremast was visible from the quarterdeck, but not the bowsprit. There was only a faint breeze from the north, and the *Nonsuch*, creeping along before it, was very silent, pitching hardly at all on the smooth sea, with a rattle of blocks and cordage.

'I took a cast with the deep-sea lead at six bells, sir,' reported Montgomery. 'Ninety-one fathoms. Grey mud. That'll be the Arcona deep, sir.'

'Very good, Mr Montgomery,' said Bush. Hornblower was nearly sure that Bush's curt manner to his lieutenants was modelled on the manner Hornblower used to employ towards him when he was first lieutenant.

'Nosing our way about with the lead,' said Bush, disgustedly. 'We might as well be a Dogger Bank trawler. And you remember what the prisoners said about the *Blanchefleur*, sir? They have pilots on board who know these waters like the palms of their hands.'

Groping about in a fog in shoal waters was not the sort of exercise for which a big two-decker was designed, but the *Nonsuch* had a special value in this campaign. There were few ships this side of the Sound which could match her in force; under her protection the flotilla could cruise wherever necessary. Danes and Swedes and Russians and French had plenty of small craft, but when *Nonsuch* made her appearance they were powerless to hinder.

'If you please, sir,' said Montgomery, touching his hat. 'Isn't that gunfire which I can hear?'

Everybody listened, enwrapped in the clammy fog. The only noises to be heard were those of the ship, and the condensed fog dripping

from the rigging to the deck. Then a flat-sounding thud came faintly
to their ears.

'That's a gun, sir, or my name's not Sylvanus Montgomery!'

'From astern,' said Hornblower.

'Beg your pardon, sir, but I thought it was on the port bow.'

'Damn this fog,' said Bush.

If the *Blanchefleur* once had warning of the presence of a British
squadron in pursuit of her, and then got away, she would vanish like a
needle in a haystack. Hornblower held up a wetted finger and glanced
into the binnacle.

'Wind's north,' he said. 'Maybe nor'nor'east.'

That was comforting. To leeward, the likely avenue of escape, lay
Rügen and the coast of Swedish Pomerania, twenty miles away. If
Blanchefleur did not slip through the net he had spread she would be
hemmed in.

'Set the lead going, Mr Montgomery,' said Bush.

'Aye aye, sir.'

'There's another gun!' said Hornblower. 'On the port bow, sure
enough.'

A wild yell from the masthead.

'Sail ho! Sail right ahead!'

The mist was thinner in that direction. Perhaps as much as a quarter
of a mile away could be seen the thinnest, palest ghost of a ship creeping
through the fog across the bows.

'Ship-rigged, flush-decked,' said Bush. 'That's the *Blanchefleur*,
sure as a gun!'

She vanished as quickly as she had appeared, into a thicker bank of
fog.

'Hard-a-starboard!' roared Bush. 'Hands to the braces!'

Hornblower was at the binnacle, taking a hurried bearing.

'Steady as you go!' he ordered the helmsman. 'Keep her at
that!'

In this gentle breeze the heavily sparred privateer would be able to
make better speed than a clumsy two-decker. All that could be hoped for
would be to keep *Nonsuch* up to windward of her to head her off if she
tried to break through the cordon.

'Call all hands,' said Bush. 'Beat to quarters.'

The drums roared through the ship, and the hands came pouring up
to their stations.

'Run out the guns,' continued Bush. 'One broadside into her, and
she's ours.'

The trucks roared as three hundred tons of metal were run out. At
the breech of every gun there clustered an eager group. The linstocks
smouldered sullenly.

'Masthead, there! Stay awake!' pealed Bush, and then more quietly to Hornblower, 'He may double back and throw us off the scent.'

There was always the possibility of the masthead being above this thin fog – the lookout in *Nonsuch* might catch a glimpse of the *Blanchefleur*'s topmasts when nothing could be seen from the deck.

For several minutes there was no more sound save for the cry of the leadsman; *Nonsuch* rolled gently in the trough of the waves, but it was hard to realise in the mist that she was making headway.

'By the mark twenty!' called the leadsman.

Before he had uttered the last word Hornblower and Bush had turned to glance at each other; up to that moment their subconscious minds had been listening to the cries without their consciousness paying any attention. But 'by the mark' meant that now there was at most twenty fathoms under them.

'Shoaling, sir,' commented Bush.

Then the masthead lookout yelled again.

'Sail on the lee quarter, sir!'

Bush and Hornblower sprang to the rail, but in the clinging fog there was nothing to be seen.

'Masthead, there! What d'you see?'

'Nothin' now, sir. Just caught a glimpse of a ship's royals, sir. There they are again, sir. Two points – three points abaft the port beam.'

'What's her course?'

'Same as ours, sir. She's gone again now.'

'Shall we bear down on her, sir?' asked Bush.

'Not yet,' said Hornblower.

'Stand to your guns on the port side!' ordered Bush.

Even a distant broadside might knock away a spar or two and leave the chase helpless.

'Tell the men not to fire without orders,' said Hornblower. 'That may be *Lotus*.'

'So it may, by God,' said Bush.

Lotus had been on *Nonsuch*'s port beam in the cordon sweeping down towards Rügen. Someone had undoubtedly been firing – that must have been *Lotus*, and she would have turned in pursuit of the *Blanchefleur*, which could bring her into just the position where those royals had been seen; and the royals of two ship-rigged sloops, seen through mist, would resemble each other closely enough to deceive the eye even of an experienced seaman.

'Wind's freshening, sir,' commented Hurst.

'That's so,' said Bush. 'Please God it clears this fog away.'

Nonsuch was perceptibly leaning over to the freshening breeze. From forward came the cheerful music of the sea under the bows.

'By the deep eighteen!' called the leadsman.

Then twenty voices yelled together.

'There she is! Sail on the port beam! That's *Lotus*!'

The fog had cleared in this quarter, and there was *Lotus* under all sail, three cables' lengths away.

'Ask her where's the chase,' snapped Bush.

'Sail – last – seen – ahead,' read off the signal midshipman, glass to eye.

'Much use that is to us,' Bush grumbled.

There were enough streaks of fog still remaining to obscure the whole circle of the horizon, even though there was a thin watery sunshine in the air, and a pale sun – silver instead of gold – visible to the eastward.

'There she is!' suddenly yelled someone at the masthead. 'Hull down on the port quarter!'

'Stole away, by God!' said Hurst. 'She must have put up her helm the moment she saw us.'

The *Blanchefleur* was a good six miles away, with only her royals visible from the deck of the *Nonsuch*, heading downwind under all sail. A string of signal flags ran up *Lotus*'s mast, and a gun from her called attention to the urgency of her signal.

'She's seen her too,' said Bush.

'Wear ship, Captain Bush, if you please. Signal "general chase".'

Nonsuch came round on the other tack, amid the curses of the officers hurled at the men for their slowness. *Lotus* swung round with her bow pointing straight at *Blanchefleur*. With the coast of Pomerania ahead, *Nonsuch* to windward, and *Lotus* and *Raven* on either side, *Blanchefleur* was hemmed in.

'*Raven* must be nearly level with her over there, sir,' said Bush, rubbing his hands. 'And we'll pick the bombs up again soon, wherever they got to in the fog.'

'By the deep fourteen!' chanted the leadsman.

Hornblower watched the man in the chains, whirling the lead with practised strength, dropping it in far ahead, reading off the depth as the ship passed over the vertical line, and then hauling in ready for a fresh cast. It was tiring work, continuous severe exercise; moreover, the leadsman was bound to wet himself to the skin, hauling in a hundred feet of dripping line. Hornblower knew enough about life below decks to know that the man would have small chance of ever getting his clothes dry again; he could remember as a midshipman in Pellew's *Indefatigable* being at the lead that wild night when they went in and destroyed the *Droits de l'homme* in the Biscay surf. He had been chilled to the bone that night, with fingers so numb as almost to be unable to feel the difference between the markers – the white calico and the leather with a hole in it and all the others. He probably could not heave the lead now if he tried, and he was quite sure he could not remember the arbitrary order of the markers. He hoped Bush would have the humanity and the common sense to see that his leadsmen were relieved at proper intervals, and given special facilities for drying their clothes, but he could not interfere directly in the matter. Bush was personally responsible for the interior economy of the ship and would be quite rightly jealous of any interference; there were crumpled roseleaves in the bed even of a Commodore.

'By the mark ten!' called the leadsman.

'*Raven* in sight beyond the chase, sir,' reported a midshipman. 'Heading to cut her off.'

'Very good,' said Hornblower.

'Rügen in sight, too, sir,' said Bush. 'That's Stubbenkammer, or whatever they call it – a white cliff, anyway.'

Hornblower swung his glass round the horizon; fate was closing in on the *Blanchefleur*, unless she took refuge in the waters of Swedish Pomerania. And that was clearly what she was intending to do. Bush had the chart spread out before him and was taking bearings on the distant white streak of the Stubbenkammer. Hornblower studied the chart, looked over at the distant ships, and back at the chart again. Stralsund was a fortress – it had stood more than one siege lately. If *Blanchefleur* got in there she would be safe if the Swedes saw fit to protect her. But the rest of the coast ahead was merely shoals and sandbanks; a couple of bays had water enough for coasting vessels – there were batteries marked in the chart to defend their entrances. Something might be attempted if *Blanchefleur* ran in one of those – she was probably of light enough draught – but it would be hopeless if she reached Stralsund.

'Signal *Lotus*,' he said, ' "Set course to cut chase off from Stralsund".'

In the course of the interminable war every aid to navigation had disappeared. There was not a buoy left to mark the deep-water channel – the Bodden, the chart called it – up to Stralsund. Vickery in the *Lotus* would have to look lively with the lead as he found his way into it.

'By the mark seven!' called the leadsman; *Nonsuch* was in dangerously shoal water already; Bush was looking anxious.

'Shorten sail, if you please, Captain Bush.'

There was no chance of *Nonsuch* overhauling *Blanchefleur*, and if they were going to run aground they might as well do so as gently as possible.

'Chase is hauling her wind, sir,' said Hurst.

So she was; she was clearly giving up the attempt to reach Stralsund. That was thanks to Vickery, who had gone charging with gallant reck-lessness under full sail through the shoals to head her off.

'*Raven*'ll have a chance at her if she holds that course long!' said Bush in high excitement.

'Chase is going on the other tack!' said Hurst.

'And a half five!' called the leadsman.

Bush was biting his lips with anxiety; his precious ship was entangling herself among the shoals on a lee shore, and there was only thirty-three feet of water under her now.

'Heave to, Captain Bush,' said Hornblower. There was no reason to run any farther now until they could see what *Blanchefleur* intended. *Nonsuch* rounded-to and lay with her port bow breasting the gentle swell. The sun was pleasantly warm.

'What's happened to *Raven*?' exclaimed Bush.

The sloop's foretopmast, with yard and sail and everything, had broken clear off and was hanging down in a frightful tangle among her headsails.

'Aground, sir,' said Hurst, glass to eye.

The force with which she had hit the sand had snapped her topmast clean off.

'She draws eight feet less than us, sir,' said Bush, but all Hornblower's attention was directed again to *Blanchefleur*. Obviously she was finding her way up a channel to the shelter of Hiddensoe. On the chart there was a single sounding marked there, a laconic '2½'. Fifteen feet of water, and a battery at the head of the long peninsula. *Blanchefleur* could reckon herself safe if the Swedes would defend her. On the horizon to windward Hornblower saw the queer topsails of the bomb-ketches; Duncan and Mound, after blundering about in the fog, must have caught sight of *Nonsuch* while on their way to the rendezvous off Cape Arcona.

'Send the boats to assist *Raven*, if you please, Captain Bush,' said Hornblower.

'Aye aye, sir.'

Hoisting longboat and cutter off their chocks and overside was an evolution calling for a couple of hundred hands. Pipes squealed and the bos'un's cane stirred up the laggards. The sheaves squeaked in the blocks, bare feet stamped the decks, and even *Nonsuch*'s massive bulk heeled a little with the transfer of weight. Hornblower betook himself to his telescope again.

Blanchefleur had found herself a curious anchorage. She lay between the main island of Rügen and the long narrow strip of Hiddensoe; the latter was more of a sandspit than an island, a thread of sand-dunes emerging from the yellow shallows. In fact *Blanchefleur*'s spars were still in plain sight against the background of the low mud cliffs of Rügen; it was only her hull which was concealed by the dunes of Hiddensoe lying like a long curving breakwater in front of her. On one end of Hiddensoe was a battery – Hornblower could see the silhouettes of the guns, black against the green of the grass-grown embrasures – which covered one entrance to the tiny roadstead; at the other end the breaking waves showed that there was not water enough even for a ship's longboat to pass. The squadron had succeeded in cutting off the privateer's escape into Stralsund, but it seemed as if she were just as safe where she was now, with miles of shoals all round her and a battery to protect her; any attempt to cut her out must be made by the ship's boats, rowing in plain view for miles through the shallows, then through a narrow channel under the guns of the battery, and finally bringing out the prize under the same guns and over the unknown shoals. That was not a tempting prospect; he could land marines on the seaward front of Hiddensoe and try to storm the battery by brute force, but the attempt would be inviting a bloody repulse if there were no surprise to cover the assaulting party. Besides, the battery's garrison would be Swedes, and he did not want to shed Swedish blood – Sweden was only a nominal enemy, but any vigorous action on his part might easily make her an active one. Hornblower remembered the paragraphs of his instructions which bore on this very point.

As if in echo to his thoughts the signal midshipman saluted with a new report.

'Signal from *Lotus*, sir.'

Hornblower read the message written in crude capitals on the slate.

'Flags of truce coming out from Stralsund. Have allowed them to pass.'

'Acknowledge,' said Hornblower.

What the devil did that mean? One flag of truce he could expect, but Vickery was reporting two at least. He swung his glass over to where Vickery had very sensibly anchored *Lotus*, right between *Blanchefleur*'s refuge and any possible succour from Stralsund. There were one – two – three small sails heading straight for the *Nonsuch*, having just rounded *Lotus*. They were all of them of the queer Baltic rig, like Dutchmen with a foreign flavour – rounded bows and lee-boards and big gaff-mainsails. Closehauled, with the white water creaming under their blunt bows and the spray flying in sheets even in this moderate breeze, they were clearly being sailed for all they were worth, as if it were a race.

'What in God's name?' said Bush, training his glass on them.

It might be a ruse to gain time. Hornblower looked round again at the spars of *Blanchefleur* above the sandspit. She had furled everything and was riding at anchor.

'White above yellow and blue, sir,' said Bush, still watching the approaching boats. 'That's Swedish colours under a flag of truce.'

Hornblower turned his glass on the leader and confirmed Bush's decision.

'The next one, sir—' Bush laughed apologetically at his own innocence, '– I know it's strange, sir, but it looks just like the British ens'n under a flag of truce.'

It was hard to believe; and it was easy to make a mistake in identifying a small boat's flag at that distance. But Hornblower's glass seemed to show the same thing.

'What do you make of that second boat, Mr Hurst?'

'British colours under white, sir,' said Hurst without hesitation.

The third boat was some long way astern, and her colours were not so easy to make out.

'French, I think, sir,' said Hurst, but the leading boat was approaching fast now.

It was a tall portly gentleman who was swung up on to the deck in the bos'un's chair, clinging to his cocked hat. He wore a blue coat with gold buttons and epaulettes, and he hitched his sword and his stock into position before laying the hat – a fore-and-aft one with a white plume and a Swedish cockade – across his chest in a sweeping bow.

'Baron Basse,' he said.

Hornblower bowed.

'Captain Sir Horatio Hornblower, Commodore commanding this squadron.'

Basse was a heavily jowled man with a big hook-nose and a cold grey eye; and it was obvious that he could only guess faintly at what Hornblower said.

'You fight?' he asked, with an effort.

'I am in pursuit of a privateer under French colours,' said Hornblower, and then, realising the difficulty of making himself understood when he had to pick his words with diplomatic care: 'Here, where's Mr Braun?'

The interpreter came forward with a brief explanation of himself in Swedish, and Hornblower watched the interplay of glances between the two. They were clearly the deadliest political enemies, meeting here on the comparatively neutral ground of a British man-o'-war. Basse brought out a letter from his breast pocket and passed it to Braun, who glanced at it and handed it to Hornblower.

'That is a letter from the Governor-General of Swedish Pomerania,' he explained, 'saying that this gentleman, the Baron Basse, has his full confidence.'

'I understand,' said Hornblower.

Basse was already talking rapidly to Braun.

'He says,' explained Braun, 'that he wants to know what you will do.'

'Tell him,' said Hornblower, 'that that depends on what the Swedes do. Ask him if Sweden is neutral.'

Obviously the reply was not a simple 'yes' or 'no'. Basse offered a lengthy explanation.

'He says that Sweden only wants to be at peace with all the world,' said Braun.

'Tell him that that means neutrality, then, and neutrality has obligations as well as privileges. There is a ship-of-war under French colours there. She must be warned that her presence in Swedish waters can only be tolerated for a limited time, and I must be informed of what the time-limit is.'

Basse's heavy face showed considerable embarrassment at Braun's translation of Hornblower's demand. He worked his hands violently as he made his reply.

'He says he cannot violate the laws of international amity,' said Braun.

'Say that that is exactly what he is doing. That ship cannot be allowed to use a Swedish port as a base of operations. She must be warned to leave, and if she will not, then she must be taken over and a guard put in her to make sure she does not slip away.'

Basse positively wrung his hands as Braun spoke to him, but any reply he was going to make was cut short by Bush's salute to Hornblower.

'The French flag of truce is alongside, sir. Shall I allow them to send someone on board?'

'Oh yes,' said Hornblower testily.

The new figure that came in through the entry-port was even more decorative than Basse, although a much smaller man. Across his blue coat lay the watered red silk ribbon of the Legion of Honour, and its star glittered on his breast. He, too, swept off his hat in an elaborate bow.

'The Count Joseph Dumoulin,' he said, speaking French, 'Consul-General in Swedish Pomerania of His Imperial and Royal Majesty Napoleon, Emperor of the French, King of Italy, Protector of the Confederation of the Rhine, Mediator of the Swiss Republic.'

'Captain Hornblower,' said Hornblower. He was suddenly excessively cautious, because his government had never recognised those resounding titles which Dumoulin had just reeled off. In the eyes of King George and his ministers, Napoleon, Emperor of the French, was merely General Bonaparte in his personal capacity, and Chief of the French Government in his official one. More than once British officers had found themselves in serious trouble for putting their names to documents – cartels and the like – which bore even incidental references to the Empire.

'Is there anyone who can speak French?' asked Dumoulin politely. 'I regret bitterly my complete inability to speak English.'

'You can address yourself to me, sir,' said Hornblower, 'and I should be glad of an explanation of your presence in this ship.'

'You speak admirable French, sir,' said Dumoulin. 'Ah, of course I remember. You are the Captain Hornblower who made the sensational escape from France a year ago. It is a great pleasure to meet a gentleman of such renown.'

He bowed again. It gave Hornblower a queer self-conscious pleasure to find that his reputation had preceded him even into this obscure corner of the Baltic, but it irritated him at the same time, as having nothing to do with the urgent matter in hand.

'Thank you,' he said, 'but I am still waiting for an explanation of why I have the honour of this visit.'

'I am here to support M. le Baron in his statement of the belligerent position of Swedish Pomerania.'

Braun interpreted, and Basse's embarrassment perceptibly increased.

'Boat with English colours alongside, sir,' interrupted Bush.

The man who came on board was immensely fat, and dressed in a sober black civilian suit.

'Hauptmann,' he said, bending himself at the waist; he spoke English with a thick German accent. 'His Britannic Majesty's consular agent at Stralsund.'

'What can I do for you, Mr Hauptmann?' asked Hornblower, trying not to allow himself to grow bewildered.

'I have come,' said Hauptmann – actually what he said was 'I haf gome' – 'to help explain to you the position here in Swedish Pomerania.'

'I see no need for explanation,' said Hornblower. 'If Sweden is neutral, then that privateer must be either forced to leave or taken into custody. If Sweden is a belligerent, then my hands are free and I can take whatever steps I think proper.'

He looked round at his audience. Braun began to translate into Swedish.

'What was it you said, Captain?' asked Dumoulin.

Desperately Hornblower plunged into a French translation, and the curse of Babel descended upon the *Nonsuch*. Everyone tried to speak at once; translation clashed with expostulation. Clearly, what Basse wanted was the best of both worlds, to make both France and England believe Sweden was friendly. What Dumoulin wanted was to make sure that *Blanchefleur* would be enabled to continue her depredations among British shipping. Hornblower looked at Hauptmann.

'Come with me for a minute, please,' said Hauptmann. He put his fat hand on Hornblower's shrinking arm and led him across the quarter-deck out of earshot.

'You are a young man,' said Hauptmann, 'and I know you naval officers. You are all headstrong. You must be guided by my advice. Do nothing in a hurry, sir. The international situation here is tense, very tense indeed. A false move may mean ruin. An insult to Sweden might mean war, actual war, instead of pretending war. You must be careful what you do.'

'I am always careful,' snapped Hornblower, 'but do you expect me to allow that privateer to behave as if this were Brest or Toulon?'

Braun came over to them.

'Baron Basse asks me to say to you, sir, that Bonaparte has two hundred thousand men on the borders of Pomerania. He wants me to say that one cannot offend the master of an army that size.'

'That bears out what I say, Captain,' said Hauptmann.

Here came Dumoulin, and Basse after him – no one would trust any one of his colleagues to be alone with the British captain for a moment. Hornblower's tactical instinct came to his rescue; the best defensive is a vigorous local offensive. He turned on Hauptmann.

'May I ask, sir, how His Majesty maintains a consular agent in a port whose neutrality is in doubt?'

'It is necessary because of the need for licences to trade.'

'Are you accredited to the Swedish Government by His Majesty?'

'No, sir. I am accredited by His Bavarian Majesty.'

'His *Bavarian* Majesty?'

'I am a subject of His Bavarian Majesty.'

'Who happens to be at war with His Britannic Majesty,' said Hornblower dryly. The whole tangle of Baltic politics, of hole-and-corner hostilities and neutralities, was utterly beyond unravelling. Hornblower listened to everyone's pleas and expostulations until he could bear it no longer; his impatience grew at length apparent to his anxious interviewers.

'I can form no conclusion at present, gentlemen,' said Hornblower. 'I must have time to think over the information you have given me. Baron Basse, as representative of a governor-general, I fancy you are entitled to a seventeen-gun salute on leaving this ship?'

The salutes echoed over the yellow-green water as the officials went over the side. Seventeen guns for Baron Basse. Eleven for Dumoulin, the Consul-General. Hauptmann, as a mere consular agent, rated only five, the smallest salute noticed in naval ceremonial. Hornblower stood at the salute as Hauptmann went down into his boat, and then sprang into activity again.

'Signal for the captains of *Moth*, *Harvey*, and *Clam* to come on board,' he ordered abruptly.

The bomb-vessels and the cutter were within easy signalling distance now; there were three hours of daylight left, and over there the spars of the French privateer still showed over the sand-dunes of Hiddensoe as though to taunt him.

IX

Hornblower swung himself up over the side of the *Harvey* where Lieutenant Mound stood at attention to welcome him with his two boatswain's mates twittering their pipes. The bang of a gun, coming unexpectedly and not a yard from him, made him jump. As the Commodore was shifting his broad pendant from one ship to another (there it was breaking out at the lofty masthead of the *Harvey*) it was the correct moment for another salute, which they were firing off with one of the four six-pounders which *Harvey* carried aft.

'Belay that nonsense,' said Hornblower.

Then he felt suddenly guilty. He had publicly described the Navy's beloved ceremonial as nonsense – just as extraordinary, he had applied the term to a compliment which ought to have delighted him as it was only the second time he had received it. But discipline had not apparently suffered, although young Mound was grinning broadly as he gave the order to cease firing.

'Square away and let's get going, Mr Mound,' said Hornblower.

As the *Harvey* filled her sails and headed diagonally for the shore with *Moth* close astern, Hornblower looked round him. This was a new experience for him; in twenty years of service he had never seen action in a bomb-vessel. Above him towered the enormous mainmast (they had made a good job of replacing the spar shot away in the Sound) which had to make up in the amount of canvas it carried for the absence of a foremast. The mizzenmast, stepped far aft, was better proportioned to the diminutive vessel. The prodigious forestay necessary for the security of the mainmast was an iron chain, curiously incongruous amid the hempen rigging. The waist of the ketch was forward – that was the absurd but only way of describing her design – and there, on either side of her midline, were the two huge mortars which accounted for her quaint build. Hornblower knew that they were bedded upon a solid mass of oak against her kelson; under the direction of a gunner's mate four hands were laying out the immense thirteen-inch shells which the mortars fired. The bos'un's mate with another party had passed a cable out from a starboard gun-port, and, having carried it forward, were securing it to the anchor hanging at the cathead. That was the 'spring'; Hornblower had often attached a spring to his cable as a practice evolution, but had never used one in action before. Close beside him in the portside main-chains a hand was heaving the lead; Hornblower thought to himself that nine-tenths of the time he had spent in the Baltic the lead had been going, and presumably that would be the case for the rest of this commission.

'And a half three!' called the leadsman. These bomb-ketches drew less than nine feet.

Over there *Raven* was preparing to kedge off the shoal on which she was aground. Hornblower could see the cable, black against the water. She had already cleared away the raffle of her wrecked foretopmast. *Clam* was creeping out beyond her; Hornblower wondered if her gypsy-looking captain had fully grasped the complex instructions given him.

Mound was standing beside him, conning the ship. He was the only commissioned officer; a midshipman and two master's mates kept watches, and the two latter were standing wide-legged aft measuring with sextants the vertical angle subtended by *Blanchefleur*'s spars. Hornblower could sense through the vessel an atmosphere of light-heartedness, only to be expected when the captain was only twenty years old. Discipline was bound to be easier in these small craft – Hornblower had often heard crabbed captains of vast seniority bewailing the fact.

'Quarter less three!' called the leadsman.

Seventeen feet of water.

'We are within range now, sir,' said Mound.

'Those mortars of yours are more accurate when firing at less than extreme range, though, aren't they?'

'Yes, sir. And I would prefer to have a little to spare, too, in case they can shift anchorage.'

'Leave yourself plenty of room to swing, though. We know nothing of these shoals.'

'Aye aye, sir.'

Mound swung round for a final glance at the tactical situation; at the spars of the *Blanchefleur* above the dunes where she was anchored far up the lagoon, the battery at the end of the spit, *Clam* taking up a position where she could see up the lagoon from a point just out of range of the battery, and *Lotus* waiting beyond the entrance to cut off escape in case by any miracle the *Blanchefleur* should be able to claw her way out to windward and make a fresh attempt to reach Stralsund. Mound kept on reaching for his trouser pockets and then hastily refraining from putting his hands in, when he remembered the Commodore was beside him – an odd gesture, and he did it every few seconds.

'For God's sake, man,' said Hornblower, 'put your hands in your pockets and leave off fidgeting.'

'Aye aye, sir,' said Mound, a little startled. He plunged his hands in gratefully, and hunched his shoulders into a comfortable slouch, pleasantly relaxed. He took one more look round before calling to the midshipman standing by the cathead forward.

'Mr Jones. Let go!'

The anchor cable roared out briefly as the crew of the ketch raced aloft to get in the canvas.

The *Harvey* swung slowly round until she rode bows upwind, pointing nearly straight at the invisible *Blanchefleur.* The *Moth,* Hornblower saw, anchored nearly abreast of her sister ship.

Mound moved with a deceptive appearance of leisureliness about the business of opening fire. He took a series of bearings to make sure that the anchor was holding. At a word from him a seaman tied a white rag to the 'spring' where it lay on the deck as it passed forward to the capstan, and Mound fished in his pocket, brought out a piece of chalk, and marked a scale on the deck beside the rag.

'Mr Jones,' he said, 'take a turn on the capstan.'

Four men at the capstan turned it easily. The white rag crept along the deck as the spring was wound in. The spring passed out through an after gun-port and was attached to the anchor far forward; pulling on it pulled the stern of the vessel round so that she lay at an angle to the wind, and the amount of the angle was roughly indicated by the movement of the white rag against the scale chalked on the deck.

'Carry on, Mr Jones,' said Mound, taking a rough bearing of the *Blanchefleur*'s spars. The capstan clanked as the men at the bars spun it round.

'Steady!' called Mound, and they stopped.

'One more pawl,' said Mound, sighting very carefully now for *Blanchefleur*'s mainmast.

Clank! went the capstan as the men momentarily threw their weight on the bars.

'One more!'

Clank!

'I think that's right, sir,' said Mound. The *Harvey*'s centre line was pointing straight at *Blanchefleur.* 'Of course the cables stretch and the anchor may drag a little, but it's easy enough to maintain a constant bearing by paying out or taking in on the spring.'

'So I understand,' said Hornblower.

He was familiar with the theory of the bomb-vessel; actually he was intensely interested in and excited at the prospect of the approaching demonstration. Ever since, at a desperate moment, he had tried to hit a small boat at long range with a six-pounder shot from the *Witch of Endor,* Hornblower had been conscious that naval gunnery was an art which should be improved if it were possible. At present it was chancy, literally hit-or-miss. Mortar-fire from a bomb-vessel was the uttermost refinement of naval gunnery, brought to a high degree of perfection, although it was only a bastard offshoot. The high trajectory and the low muzzle velocity of the projectile, and the avoidance of the disturbing factor of irregularities in the bore of the gun, made it possible to drop the shell with amazing accuracy.

'If you'll excuse me, sir,' said Mound, 'I'll go forrard. I like to cut my fuses myself.'

'I'll come with you,' said Hornblower.

The two mortars were like big cauldrons in the eyes of the bomb-ketch.

'Eleven hundred yards,' said Mound. 'We'll try a pound and three-quarters of powder, Mr Jones.'

'Aye aye, sir.'

The powder was made up in cartridges of a pound, half a pound, and a quarter of a pound. The midshipman tore open one of each size, and poured the contents into the starboard-side mortar, and pressed it home with an enormous wad of felt. Mound had a measuring rule in his hand, and was looking up at the sky in a calculating way. Then he bent over one of the big shells, and with a pair of scissors he cut the fuse with profound care.

'One and eleven sixteenths, sir,' he said, apologetically. 'Don't know why I decided on that. The fuse burns at different speeds according to the weather, and that seems right for now. Of course we don't want the shell to burst in the air, but if you have too long a fuse some Frog may get to it and put it out before it bursts.'

'Naturally,' said Hornblower.

The big shell was lifted up and placed in the muzzle of the mortar; a few inches down the bore narrowed abruptly, leaving a distinct step inside, on which the bold belt round the shell rested with reassuring solidity. The curve of the thirteen-inch shell, with the fuse protruding, was just level with the rim of the muzzle.

'Hoist the red swallowtail,' called Mound, raising his voice to reach the ears of the master's mate aft.

Hornblower turned and looked through his glass at *Clam*, anchored in the shallows a couple of miles away. It was under his personal super-vision that this code of signals had been arranged, and he felt a keen anxiety that it should function correctly. Signals might easily be mis-understood. A red swallowtail mounted to the *Clam*'s peak.

'Signal acknowledged, sir,' called the master's mate.

Mound took hold of the smouldering linstock, and applied it to the fuse of the shell. After a moment the fuse took fire, spluttering feebly.

'One, two, three, four, five,' counted Mound, slowly, while the fuse still spluttered. Apparently he left himself a five-second margin in case the fuse burnt unsatisfactorily and had to be relit.

Then he pressed the linstock into the touch-hole of the mortar, and it went off with a roar. Standing immediately behind the mortar, Horn-blower could see the shell rise, its course marked by the spark of the burning fuse. Up and up it went, higher and higher, and then it dis-appeared as it began its downward flight at right angles now to the line of sight. They waited, and they waited, and nothing more happened.

'Miss,' said Mound. 'Haul down the red swallowtail.'

'White pendant from *Clam*, sir,' called the master's mate.

'That means "range too great",' said Mound. 'A pound and a half of powder this time, please, Mr Jones.'

Moth had two red swallowtails hoisted, and two were hoisted in reply by *Clam*. Hornblower had foreseen the possibility of confusion, and had settled that signals to do with *Moth* should always be doubled. Then there would be no chance of *Harvey* making corrections for *Moth*'s mistakes, or vice versa. *Moth*'s mortar roared out, its report echoing over the water. From the *Harvey* they could see nothing of the flight of the shell.

'Double yellow flag from *Clam*, sir.'

'That means *Moth*'s shell dropped short,' said Mound. 'Hoist our red swallowtail.'

Again he fired the mortar, again the spark of the fuse soared towards the sky and disappeared, and again nothing more happened.

'White pendant from *Clam*, sir.'

'Too long again?' said Mound, a little puzzled. 'I hope they're not cross-eyed over there.'

Moth fired again, and was rewarded by a double white pendant from *Clam*. This shell had passed over, when her preceding one had fallen short. It should be easy for *Moth* to find the target now. Mound was checking the bearing of the target.

'Still pointing straight at her,' he grumbled. 'Mr Jones, take one half a quarter-pound from that pound and a half.'

Hornblower was trying to imagine what the captain of the *Blanchefleur* was doing at that moment on his own side of the sandspit. Probably until the very moment when the bomb-ketches opened fire he had felt secure, imagining that nothing except a direct assault on the battery could imperil him. But now shells must be dropping quite close to him, and he was unable to reply or defend himself in any active way. It would be hard for him to get under way; he had anchored his ship at the far end of the long, narrow lagoon. The exit near him was shoal water too shallow even for a skiff – as the breakers showed – and with the wind as it was at present it was impossible for him to try to beat up the channel again closer to the battery. He must be regretting having dropped so far to leeward before anchoring; presumably he had done so to secure himself the better from the claws of a cutting-out attack. With boats or by kedging he might be able to haul his ship slowly up to the battery, near enough for its guns to be able to keep the bomb-ketches out of mortar range.

'Red swallowtail at the dip, sir!' reported the master's mate excitedly.

That meant that the shell had fallen short but close.

'Put in two pinches more, Mr Jones,' said Mound.

Moth's mortar roared out again, but this time they saw the shell burst, apparently directly above the *Blanchefleur*'s mastheads. They saw the big ball of smoke, and the sound of the explosion came faintly back to them on the wind. Mound shook his head gravely; either Duncan over there had not cut his fuse correctly or it had burnt away more rapidly than usual. Two blue flags at *Clam*'s peak indicated that the fall of *Moth*'s shot had been unobserved – the signalling system was still functioning correctly. Then Mound bent his gangling body over and applied the linstock to fuse and touch-hole. The mortar roared; some freak of ballistics sent a fragment of blazing wad close over Hornblower's head, making him duck while the smoke billowed round him, but as he looked up again he just caught sight of the spark of the fuse high up against the sky, poised at the top of its trajectory, before it disappeared from sight in its swift downward swoop. Hornblower, Mound, Jones, the whole mortar's crew stood waiting tensely for the shell to end its flight. Then over the rim of the sand-dune they saw a hint of white smoke, and the sound of the bursting shell came back to them directly afterwards.

'I think we've hit her, sir,' said Mound, with elaborate carelessness.

'Black ball at *Clam*'s masthead, sir!' shouted the master's mate.

That meant a hit. A thirteen-inch shell, soaring that immense distance into the air, had come plunging down on to *Blanchefleur*'s decks and had exploded. Hornblower could not imagine what destruction it might cause.

'Both mortars together, now,' snapped Mound, throwing aside all lackadaisical pose. 'Jump to it, you men.'

Two white pendants at the dip from *Clam* meant that *Moth*'s next shot had fallen close but too far. Then both of *Harvey*'s mortars roared – the little ketch dipped and plunged as the violence of the recoil forced her bows down. Up went the black ball to *Clam*'s masthead.

'Another hit!' exulted Mound.

Blanchefleur's topmasts, seen over the dunes, suddenly began to separate. She was turning round – her desperate crew was trying to tow her or kedge her back up the channel.

'Please God we wreck her before she gets away!' said Mound. 'Why in hell doesn't *Moth* fire?'

Hornblower watched him closely; the temptation to fire his mortars the moment they were loaded, without waiting for *Moth* to take her turn, was powerful indeed, but to yield to it meant confusion for the observer over in *Clam* and eventual losing of all control. *Moth* fired, and two black balls at *Clam*'s masthead showed that she, too, had scored a hit. But *Blanchefleur* had turned now; Hornblower could see the tiniest, smallest movement of her topmast against the upper edge of the dunes, only a yard or two at most. Mound fired his two mortars, and even while the shells were in the air his men leaped to the capstan and flung themselves on the bars. Clank – clank! Twice the pawl slipped over the ratchet as they hauled in on the spring and swung the ketch round to keep her mortars trained on the target. At that instant *Blanchefleur*'s foretopmast fell from view. Only main and mizzen were in sight now.

'Another hit, by God!' shouted Hornblower, the words forced from him like a cork from a popgun. He was as excited as a schoolboy; he found he was jumping up and down on the deck. The foremast gone; he tried to picture the frightful destruction those shells must be causing, crashing down on the frail wooden decks. And there was smoke visible over the crest of the dunes too, more than could be accounted for by the bursting of the shells, and blacker, too. Probably she was on fire. Mizzen-mast and mainmast came into line again – *Blanchefleur* was swinging across the channel. She must be out of control. Perhaps a shell had hit the cable out to the kedge, or wrecked the towing boats.

Moth fired again; and two red swallowtails at the dip showed that her shells had fallen close and short – *Blanchefleur* must have swerved appreciably across the channel. Mound had noticed it, and was increasing the propelling charge in his mortars. That was smoke; undoubtedly it was smoke eddying from *Blanchefleur*. She must be on fire. And from the way she lay, stationary again – Hornblower could see that her topmasts made no movement at all to the sand-dunes – she must have gone aground. Mound fired again, and they waited. There went the mizzen-topmast, leaning over slowly, and the maintopmast disappeared as well. There was nothing to see now, except the smoke rising ever more thickly. Mound looked at Hornblower for orders.

'Better keep on firing,' said Hornblower, thickly. Even if the crew were roasting alive in her it was his duty to see that *Blanchefleur* was utterly destroyed. The mortars roared out again, and the shells made their steep ascent, climbing upwards for ten full seconds before swooping down again. *Clam* signalled 'close and over'. *Moth* fired again, and *Clam* signalled a hit for her; Hornblower's inner eye was seeing mental pictures of the shells plunging from the sky in among the crew of the *Blanchefleur* as they laboured amid the flames to save their ship, burning, dismasted, and aground. It took only the briefest interval of time for those pictures to form, for the moment the signal was seen in *Clam* Mound bent to fire the mortars, and yet the fuses had not taken fire when the sound of a violent explosion checked him. Hornblower whipped his glass to his eye; an immense gust of smoke showed over the sand-dunes, and in the smoke Hornblower thought he could make out flying specks – corpses or fragments of the ship, blown into the air by the explosion. The fire, or one of *Moth*'s last shells, had reached *Blanchefleur*'s magazines.

'Signal to *Clam*, Mr Mound,' said Hornblower. ' "What do you see of the enemy?" '

They waited for the answer.

' "Enemy – totally – destroyed", sir,' read off the master's mate, and the crew gave a ragged cheer.

'Very good, Mr Mound. I think we can leave these shallows now before daylight goes. Hang out the recall, if you please, with *Clam*'s number and *Lotus*'s number.'

This watery northern sunshine was deceptive. It shone upon one but it gave one no heat at all. Hornblower shivered violently for a moment – he had been standing inactive, he told himself, upon the *Harvey*'s deck for some hours, and he should have worn a greatcoat. Yet that was not the real explanation of the shudder, and he knew it. The excitement and interest had died away, leaving him gloomy and deflated. It had been a brutal and cold-blooded business, destroying a ship that had no chance of firing back at him. It would read well in a report, and brother officers would tell each other of Hornblower's new achievement, destroying a big French privateer in the teeth of the Swedes and the French amid shoals innumerable. Only he would know of this feeling of inglorious anticlimax.

X

Bush wiped his mouth on his table napkin with his usual fussy attention to good manners.

'What do you think the Swedes'll say, sir?' he asked, greatly daring. The responsibility was none of his, and he knew by experience that Hornblower was likely to resent being reminded that Bush was thinking about it.

'They can say what they like,' said Hornblower, 'but nothing they can say can put *Blanchefleur* together again.'

It was such a cordial reply compared with what Hornblower might have said that Bush wondered once more what it was which had wrought the change in Hornblower – whether his new mellowness was the consequence of success, of recognition of promotion, or of marriage. Hornblower was inwardly debating that very question at that very moment as well, oddly enough, and he was inclined to attribute it to advancing years. For a few moments he subjected himself to his usual pitiless self-analysis, almost morbidly intense. He knew he had grown blandly tolerant of the fact that his hair was thinning, and turning grey over his temples – the first time he had seen a gleam of pink scalp as he combed his hair he had been utterly revolted, but by now he had at least grown accustomed to it. Then he looked down the double row of young faces at his table, and his heart warmed to them. Without a doubt, he was growing paternal, coming to like young people in a way new to him; he suddenly became aware, for that matter, that he was growing to like people young or old, and was losing – temporarily at least, said his cautious spirit – that urgent desire to get away by himself and torture himself.

He raised his glass.

'I give you a toast, gentlemen,' he said, 'to the three officers whose careful attention to duty and whose marked professional ability resulted in the destruction of a dangerous enemy.'

Bush and Montgomery and the two midshipmen raised their glasses and drank with enthusiasm, while Mound and Duncan and Freeman looked down at the tablecloth with British modesty; Mound, taken unawares, was blushing like a girl and wriggling uncomfortably in his chair.

'Aren't you going to reply, Mr Mound?' said Montgomery. 'You're the senior.'

'It was the Commodore,' said Mound, eyes still on the tablecloth. 'It wasn't us. He did it all.'

'That's right,' agreed Freeman, shaking his gypsy locks.

It was time to change the subject, thought Hornblower, sensing the approach of an awkward gap in the conversation after this spell of mutual congratulation.

'A song, Mr Freeman. We have all of us heard that you sing well. Let us hear you.'

Hornblower did not add that it was from a Junior Lord of the Admiralty that he had heard about Freeman's singing ability, and he concealed the fact that singing meant nothing to him. Other people had this strange desire to hear music, and it was well to gratify the odd whim.

There was nothing self-conscious about Freeman when it came to singing: he simply lifted his chin, opened his mouth, and sang.

> When first I looked in Chloe's eyes
> Sapphire seas and summer skies –

An odd thing this music was. Freeman was clearly performing some interesting and difficult feat; he was giving decided pleasure to these others (Hornblower stole a glance at them), but all he was doing was to squeak and to grunt in different fashions, and drag out the words in an arbitrary way – and such words. For the thousandth time in his life Hornblower gave up the struggle to imagine just what this music was which other people liked so much. He told himself, as he always did, that for him to make the attempt was like a blind man trying to imagine colour.

Chloe is my o-o-o-only love!

Freeman finished his song, and everyone pounded on the table in genuine applause.

'A very good song, and very well sung,' said Hornblower.

Montgomery was trying to catch his eye.

'Will you excuse me, sir?' he said. 'I have the second dogwatch.'

That sufficed to break up the party; the three lieutenants had to return to their own ships, Bush wanted to take a look round on deck, and the two midshipmen, with a proper appreciation of the insignificance of their species, hastened to offer their thanks for their entertainment and take their departure. That was quite the right sort of party, thought Hornblower, watching them go – good food, lively talk, and a quick ending. He stepped out into the stern gallery, stooping carefully to avoid the low cove overhead. At six o'clock in the evening it was still broad daylight; the sun had not nearly set, but was shining into the gallery from right aft, and a faint streak beneath it showed where Bornholm lay just above the horizon.

The cutter, her mainsail pulled aft as flat as a board, passed close beneath him as she turned closehauled under the stern with the three lieutenants in the sternsheets going back to their ships – the wind was northwesterly again. The young men were skylarking together until one of them caught sight of the Commodore up in the stern gallery, and then they promptly stiffened into correct attitudes. Hornblower smiled at himself for having grown fond of those boys, and he turned back into the cabin again to relieve them of the strain of being under his eye. Braun was waiting for him.

'I have read through the newspapers, sir,' he said. *Lotus* had intercepted a Prussian fishing-boat that afternoon, and had released her after confiscating her catch and taking these newspapers from her.

'Well?'

'This one is the *Königsberger Hartunsche Zeitung*, sir, published under French censorship, of course. This front page is taken up with the meeting at Dresden. Bonaparte is there with seven kings and twenty-one sovereign princes.'

'Seven kings?'

'The kings of Holland, Naples, Bavaria, Württemberg, Westphalia, Saxony, and Prussia, sir,' read Braun. 'The Grand Dukes of—'

'No need for the rest of the list,' said Hornblower. He peered at the ragged sheets and found himself, as usual, thinking what a barbaric language German was. Bonaparte was clearly trying to frighten someone

– it could not be England, who had faced Bonaparte's wrath without flinching for a dozen years. It might be his own subjects, all the vast mass of western Europe which he had conquered. But the obvious person for Bonaparte to try to cow was the Czar of Russia. There were plenty of good reasons why Russia should have grown restive under the bullying of her neighbour, and this supreme demonstration of Bonaparte's power was probably designed to frighten her into submission.

'Is there anything about troop movements?' asked Hornblower.

'Yes, sir. I was surprised at the freedom with which they were mentioned. The Imperial Guard is at Dresden. There's the First, the Second,' – Braun turned the page – 'and the Ninth Army Corps all mentioned. They are in Prussia – headquarters Danzig – and Warsaw.'

'Nine army corps,' reflected Hornblower. 'Three hundred thousand men, I suppose.'

'There's a paragraph here which speaks of Murat's reserve cavalry. It says, "there are forty thousand men, superbly mounted and equipped". Bonaparte reviewed them.'

An enormous mass of men was obviously accumulating on the frontier between Bonaparte's Empire and Russia. Bonaparte would have the Prussian and Austrian armies under his orders too. Half a million men – six hundred thousand men – the imagination failed to grasp the figures. A vast tide of humanity was piling up here in eastern Europe. If Russia failed to be impressed by the threat, it was hard to believe that anything could survive the onrush of such a mass of men. The doom of Russia appeared to be sealed; she must either submit or be destroyed. No continental nation yet had successfully opposed Bonaparte, although every single one had felt the violence of his attack; only England still withstood him, and Spain still fought on although his armies had ravaged every village and every valley in the unhappy peninsula.

Doubt came back into Hornblower's mind. He could not see that Bonaparte would derive any benefit from the conquest of Russia proportionate to the effort needed, or even proportionate to the slight risk involved. Bonaparte ought to be able to find a far more profitable employment for the men and the money. Probably there would be no war. Russia would submit, and England would face a Europe every square mile of which would be in the tyrant's hands. And yet –

'This one is the *Warsaw Gazette*, sir,' went on Braun. 'A little more official, from the French point of view, even than the other one, although it's in the Polish language. Here is a long article about Russia. It speaks of "the Cossack menace to Europe". It calls Alexander "the barbarian ruler of a barbarian people". "The successor of Genghis Khan." It says that "St Petersburg is the focus of all the potential anarchy of Europe" – "a menace to the peace of the world" – "deliberately hostile to the benefits conferred upon the world by the French people".'

'And that must be published with Bonaparte's consent,' commented Hornblower, half to himself, but Braun was still deep in the article.

' "The wanton ravisher of Finland",' read Braun, more than half to himself. He raised his green eyes from the sheet. There was a gleam of hatred in them that startled Hornblower; it reminded him of what he was in a fair way to forget, that Braun was a penniless exile on account of Russia's attack on Finland. Braun had taken service with England, but that was at a time when Russia was at least England's nominal enemy. Hornblower made a mental note that it might be as well not to trust Braun with any confidential business regarding Russia; of her own free will Russia would never restore Finnish independence, and there was always the chance that Bonaparte might do so – that he might restore what Bonaparte would call Finnish independence, for what that was worth. There were still people who might be deceived by Bonaparte's professions, despite his record of deceit and broken faith, of cruelty and robbery.

Braun would bear watching, thought Hornblower – that would be something more to bear in mind, as if he did not have enough worries or carry enough responsibility already. He could joke with Bush about the Swedes and the Russians, but secretly anxiety was gnawing at him. The Swedes might well be exasperated by the destruction of the *Blanchefleur* in Pomeranian waters. That might be the last straw; Bernadotte might at this very moment be contemplating wholehearted alliance with Bonaparte and war with England. The prospect of the enmity of Sweden as well as that of France might easily break down Russia's resolution. English might find herself with the whole world in arms against her as a result of Hornblower's action. A fine climax that would be to his first independent command. Those cursed brothers of Barbara's would sneer in superior fashion at his failure.

Hornblower shook himself with an effort out of this nightmare, to find that Braun was obviously still in his. The hatred in his eyes, the intensity of his expression were quite startling. And then someone knocked on the cabin door and Braun came out of his dream and slipped instantly into his old attitude of attentive deference.

'Come in,' shouted Hornblower.

It was one of the midshipmen of the watch.

'Mr Montgomery sent me with this signal from *Raven*, sir.'

He held out the slate; it was scrawled with the words written on it by the signal officer.

Have met Swedish vessel desirous of speaking with Commodore.

'I'll come on deck,' said Hornblower. 'Ask the captain if he'll be kind enough to come too.'

'The cap'n's on deck, sir.'

'Very good.'

Bush and Montgomery and half a dozen officers had their glasses trained towards the topsails of the *Raven* at her station far out on the port beam as the squadron swept up the Baltic. There was still an hour of daylight left.

'Captain Bush,' said Hornblower, 'I'd be obliged if you would have the helm put up and run down towards her.'

'Aye aye, sir.'

'And signal for the squadron to take up night stations, if you please.'

'Aye aye, sir.'

Nonsuch heaved her ponderous self about, lying over as she took the wind abeam while the watch hauled aft on the starboard braces.

'There's a sail just astern of *Raven*, sir,' said Montgomery. 'Looks like a brig. A Swede from the cut of her tops'ls, sir. One of those Baltic traders you see in Leith Roads.'

'Thank you,' said Hornblower.

It would not be long before he heard what the news was. It might well be – it probably would be – something desperately unpleasant. Some new load of responsibility for his shoulders, for certain, even if it told of no actual disaster. He found himself envying Montgomery his simple duties of officer of the watch, with nothing more to do than simply obey orders and keep an eye on the weather, with the blessed obligation of having to refer all important decisions to a superior. Hornblower made himself stand still on the quarterdeck, his hands clasped behind him, as *Nonsuch* and the brig approached each other, as first the brig's courses and then her hull came up over the horizon. To the west the sky was a flaming crimson, but twilight lingered on as the brig came up into the wind.

'Captain Bush,' said Hornblower, 'will you heave to, if you please? They are putting a boat overside.'

He would not display vulgar curiosity by staring at the boat as it was launched, or by looking down into it as it came alongside; he paced peacefully up and down the quarterdeck in the lovely evening, looking in every direction save towards the boat, while the rest of the officers and the men chattered and stared and speculated. Yet Hornblower, for all his air of sublime indifference, turned to face the entry-port at the exact moment when the visitor was coming in over the side. The first thing Hornblower saw was a fore-and-aft cocked hat with a white plume that seemed familiar, and then under the hat appeared the heavy face and portly form of Baron Basse. He laid the hat across his chest to make his bow just as he had done before.

'Your servant, sir,' said Hornblower, saluting stiffly. He was handicapped by the fact that although he could remember Basse very well, and could have described him to perfection, he did not remember his name. He turned to the midshipman of the watch. 'Pass the word for Mr Braun.'

The Swedish gentleman was saying something, but what it was Hornblower could not imagine.

'I beg your pardon, sir,' said Hornblower, and Basse repeated what he said, with no more success at conveying his meaning. He began once more laboriously, but cut himself short when he saw Hornblower distractedly looking away from him towards the entry-port. Hornblower was doing his best to be polite, but he could see a bearskin headdress coming in at the entry-port, and that was too intriguing a sight for him possibly to withstand its attraction. A big bearskin cap with a red plume, a bristling red moustache, a scarlet tunic, a red sash, a profusion of gold lace, blue pantaloons with a red stripe, high boots, a sword whose golden hilt glowed strangely in the fading light; that was the uniform of the Guards, surely. The wearer of the uniform was undersized for a guardsman, but he certainly knew his ceremonial; his hand was at the salute to the quarterdeck as he came in through the entry-port, and then he strode forward on short legs and brought his heels together in a smart Guards salute to Hornblower.

'Good evening, sir,' he said. 'You are Captain Sir Horatio Hornblower?'

'Yes,' said Hornblower.

'May I introduce myself? I am Colonel Lord Wychwood, of the First Guards.'

'Good evening,' said Hornblower coolly. As Commodore he was decidedly senior to a Colonel, and he could afford to be cool while waiting on events. He supposed that he would soon hear the explanation of this arrival of a Colonel of the Grenadier Guards in full regimentals in the middle of the Baltic Sea.

'I have despatches,' said Lord Wychwood, fumbling in the breast of his tunic, 'from our Ambassador at Stockholm for you, sir.'

'Let us go to my cabin, sir,' said Hornblower. He darted a glance at Basse.

'You have already made the acquaintance of Baron Basse, I understand? He has messages for you, too.'

'Then perhaps the Baron will be kind enough to come below as well. If you gentlemen will be kind enough to allow me to precede you, I will show the way.'

Braun interpreted ceremoniously as Hornblower headed the procession. In the darkened cabin Brown hastened to bring lamps and brought forward chairs; Wychwood lowered himself into his with all the caution demanded by his tight overalls.

'You've heard what Boney's done?' he began.

'I have heard nothing recently.'

'He sent fifty thousand troops into Swedish Pomerania the moment he got the news of what you did off Stralsund.'

'Indeed?'

'They acted in their usual style. Vandamme was in command. He began by fining the municipality of Stralsund a hundred thousand francs for not greeting his arrival with the ringing of the church bells. He interrupted the service at the church of the Holy Ghost so as to lay hold of the communion plate. He seized the Governor-General and threw him into gaol. The troops were out of hand because the garrison of Rügen tried to oppose their crossing. There was looting and murder and rape all through Rügen. The Baron here escaped in a fishing-boat. All the other officials and the troops are prisoners.'

'So Boney is at war with Sweden now?'

Wychwood shrugged his shoulders; everyone in the Baltic seemed to shrug shoulders when it was a matter of having to make a downright statement regarding peace and war.

'The Baron here can tell you about that,' said Wychwood. They turned their glance towards the Baron, who began a voluble explanation in Swedish; Braun, standing against the bulkhead, translated.

'He says that the question of peace and war lies with the Crown Prince, His Royal Highness Charles John, who used to be known as Marshal Bernadotte. His Royal Highness is not in Sweden at the moment. He is visiting the Czar in Russia.'

'I expect that's what these despatches I have for you are about, sir,' said Wychwood. He produced a large canvas envelope, heavily sealed, and handed it over. Hornblower tore it open and read the contents.

EMBASSY OF HIS BRITANNIC MAJESTY AT STOCKHOLM.

20th May, 1812.

SIR,

The bearer of this despatch, Colonel Lord Wychwood First Guards, will inform you as to the political situation here. It is to be hoped that Bonaparte's invasion of Swedish Pomerania will bring about a declaration of war on the part of the Swedish government. It is therefore necessary that all possible aid should be given to Swedish officials who wish to communicate with H.R.H. the Crown Prince. You are therefore directed and required to use all diligence and despatch to escort or convey any such officials on their way to Russia. You are further directed and required to make all use of this opportunity to enable Lord Wychwood to open communication with the Russian government so as to assure H.I.M. the Czar of the full support of His Majesty's forces by land and sea in the event of war between H.I.M. and the French government. You will further make all use of any opportunity which may present itself to you to further good relations between H.M. and H.I.M.

Your obed't servant,

H. L. MERRY, *H.B.M.'s Ambassador
to the Court of Stockholm.*

CAPTAIN SIR HORATIO HORNBLOWER, K.B.,
Commodore Commanding the British Squadron in the Baltic.

Hornblower read the orders through twice, carefully. There was an important decision to be made. Merry had no business giving orders, and especially had no business to give orders in the explicit 'directed and required' wording which was the cherished prerogative of his naval superiors. An Ambassador was an important official – to a naval officer in foreign waters the most important official after the Lords of Admiralty – but he could only request and advise, not give orders. If Hornblower should follow Merry's instructions and the matter turn out ill he would have no excuse to plead to the Admiralty. Yet on the other hand Hornblower knew only too well that if he were to ignore Merry's letter there would be bitter complaints sent to London.

Hornblower recalled his Admiralty orders to himself; they gave him wide discretion as to how he should behave towards the northern powers. Merry's letter relieved him of no responsibility. He could allow Wychwood and Basse to proceed in the Swedish brig, or he could convey them himself; the point at issue was whether the news of Bonaparte's latest aggression should be conveyed by a British squadron or not. Bearers of bad tidings were always unpopular – a ridiculous detail to have to bear in mind, but an important one. The two potentates might feel exasperated at being reminded of the meddling British Navy, bringing trouble to everyone. On the other hand, the presence of a British squadron far up the Baltic, at the very gates of St Petersburg, might be a salutary reminder of the length of England's arm. Submission to Bonaparte on the part of Sweden and Russia must mean war, real actual war, with England this time; Bonaparte would be satisfied with nothing less. The sight of British topsails on the horizon, the knowledge that war would mean instant blockade, instant capture of every ship that ventured out, constant harassing of all their shores, might be a powerful argument at their councils. Bonaparte might be at their frontiers, but England would be at their doors. Hornblower made his decision.

'Gentlemen,' he said, 'I think it is my duty to convey you to Russia in this squadron. I can offer you the hospitality of this ship, if you would be kind enough to accept it.'

XI

Despite the fact that he was a peer and a guardsman, despite his little red moustache and his funny popeyes and his ludicrous appearance in uniform, Wychwood was a shrewd and experienced man of the world. At thirty-five he had visited two-thirds of the Courts of Europe, he was familiar with their intrigues, knew their weaknesses and their strengths, the military power of which they could dispose, their prejudices and their traditions. He sat (at Hornblower's invitation) in Hornblower's cabin while a brisk westerly wind sent the squadron rolling and pitching up the Baltic. Basse was incapacitated in his berth with seasickness, so that they were not embarrassed by his presence – Wychwood's cheeks were a little pale as well, and his manner occasionally hinted at an inward preoccupation, but he controlled himself manfully.

'Boney's weakness,' said Wychwood, 'is that he thinks all the opposition in the world can be dissolved by force. Often he's right, of course; you have only to look back at his career to see that. But sometimes he is wrong. People would rather fight – would rather die – than be slaves to his will any longer.'

'Spain showed that,' said Hornblower.

'Yes. But with Russia it still may be different. Russia is the Czar, much more definitely than Spain was the Bourbon monarchy. If Alexander chooses to submit to Boney's threats, Russia will submit. Alexander's swallowed insults enough already.'

'He's swallowed other things besides insults,' said Hornblower dryly.

'Finland, you mean? That's perfectly true. And all the other Baltic provinces, Lithuania and Courland and so on. You know better than I do how much difference that makes to the security of St Petersburg – I find it hard to blame him for it. At home, of course, his attack on Finland roused a good deal of feeling. I hope they forget it if he becomes our ally.'

'And what are the chances of that?'

'God knows. If he can be sure of the Swedish alliance he may fight. And that depends on whether Bernadotte is willing to submit to having Pomerania taken away from him.'

'Bonaparte made a false step there,' said Hornblower.

'Yes, by God! The British colours are like a red rag to a bull to him. You have only to show them to get him to charge. The way you destroyed that ship – what was her name? – the *Blanchefleur* under his very nose must have driven him crazy. If anything makes the Swedes fight, it'll be that.'

'Let's hope it does,' said Hornblower, decidedly comforted.

He knew he had taken a bold step when he went in to destroy the *Blanchefleur*; if the subsequent political repercussions should be unfavourable he might well be called to account. His only justification would be the final event; a more cautious man would have held back and contented himself with keeping the privateer under observation. Probably that would have resulted in her slipping clean away the first foggy night, to resume her ravages among British shipping, but no man could be held responsible for fog. And if Sweden became an active enemy all England would clamour for the head of the officer they deemed responsible. Yet come what might he could not but feel that he had taken the best course in proving that England had the power to strike and would not hesitate to use it. There were few occasions in history when timidity was wise.

They were bringing further news to St Petersburg, too. Wellington was on the offensive in Spain; in two desperate strokes he had cleared his front by storming Ciudad Rodrigo and Badajoz, and now was ready to strike into the heart of the Peninsula. The knowledge that a large part of Bonaparte's army was hotly engaged in the South might bring firmness to the councils of the North.

His brother-in-law was an Earl now – another victory or two would make him a Duke, reflected Hornblower. Barbara would be proud of him, and to Hornblower that was another reason for him to dread failure for himself; Barbara had a high standard of comparison. But she would understand. She would know how high were the stakes he was playing for in the Baltic – as high as those her brother was playing for in Spain; she would know what moral courage was needed to make the kind of decisions he had made. She would be considerate; and at that moment Hornblower told himself that he did not want his wife to have to be considerate on his account. The thought revolted him, drove him to make his excuses to Wychwood and plunge out on deck, into the pouring rain under the grey sky, to walk the quarterdeck while the other officers eyed him askance and kept well clear of him. There was not a soul in the squadron who had not heard that only fools crossed the Commodore's hawse when he was walking the deck.

The brisk wind was chill, even in late May, here in the North Baltic; the squadron pitched and rolled over the short steep waves, leaden-hued under the leaden sky, as it drove ever northward towards the Gulf of Finland, towards Russia, where the destiny of the world hung in the balance. The night was hardly darker than the day, up here in the sixtieth degree of north latitude, when the sky cleared, for the sun was barely hidden below the horizon and the moon shone coldly in the pale twilight as they drove past Hoghland and hove to in sight of Lavansaari so as to approach Kronstadt after sunrise.

Braun was on deck early, leaning against the rail, craning over in fact; that faint grey smear on the horizon to the northward was his native land, the Finland of lake and forest which the Czar had just conquered and from which he was a hopeless exile. Hornblower noted the dejection of the poor devil's pose and was sorry for him, even in the keen excitement of anticipation regarding the reception they might be accorded. Bush came bustling up, in all the glory of epaulettes and sword, darting eager glances over the deck and aloft to make quite sure that everything in the ship was ready to bear the inspection of an unfriendly power.

'Captain Bush,' said Hornblower, 'I'd be obliged if you would square away for Kronstadt.'

'Aye aye, sir.'

Hornblower would have liked to have asked if the arrangements for saluting were properly in train, but he forbore. He could trust Bush with any routine duty, and he had to be very careful not to interfere with the working of the ship. He was glad that so far he had never forgotten to make use of the polite forms of request when giving orders to Bush, who was his equal in substantive rank. 'I'd be obliged' and 'if you please' still came strangely enough to his lips as a preface to an order.

He turned his back on the dawn and trained his glass aft on the squadron; they were squaring away and taking up their stations astern in succession, the two sloops, and then the two bomb-vessels, and the cutter last.

'General signal,' he snapped, ' "Keep better station".'

He wanted his squadron to come up the difficult channel in exact, regular order, like beads on a string. Out of the tail of his eye he saw Basse and Wychwood come on deck, and he ignored them.

'Make that signal again,' he rasped, 'with *Harvey's* number.'

Harvey was yawing slightly from her course; young Mound had better keep a sharp eye on his helmsman, or he would be in trouble. To starboard, where the wide shoals extended from the Oranienbaum shore, there were buoys to mark the limits of the channel, which serpentined back and forth in unpredictable fashion. If ever he had to penetrate this channel as an enemy he would find it a tricky business. There were the low grey fortifications of Kronstadt on the port bow; a turn in the channel sent the *Nonsuch* heading directly for them, so that in the event of fighting the fire of the guns there would enfilade the whole line. Then the channel swung back again, and then it straightened out so that all ships would be forced to pass close under the guns of Kronstadt. Through his glass Hornblower made out the blue and white flag of Imperial Russia flying above the grey walls.

'Make the signal "anchor",' said Hornblower to the signal midshipman, and then he darted a meaning glance at Bush, who nodded. He had everything ready. The ship crept forward, closer and closer under the guns.

'Haul down,' said Hornblower, and the signal to anchor came down in a flash, putting the order into force at that moment. Six cables roared through six hawseholes. In the six ships a thousand men poured aloft, and the canvas vanished as though by magic as the ships swung round to their cables.

'Pretty fair,' said Hornblower to himself, realising, with an inward smile at his own weakness, that no evolution could ever be carried out to his perfect satisfaction. Forward the saluting gun began to crash out its marks of respect for the Russian flag; Hornblower saw a puff of smoke from the fortress and then the sound of the first gun of the return salute reached his ears. Eleven guns; they recognised his broad pendant, then, and knew what compliments were due to a Commodore. Here came the doctor's boat to give them pratique; the doctor was a man with a large black beard who spoke limping French. His visit was a good opportunity to test Braun's ability to speak Russian – Braun translated with facility Hornblower's declaration that there was no infectious disease on board. Everyone in the ship was a little excited at this visit to Russia, and crowded the side to look down at the Russian boat's crew, seated in their boat with the bowman hooking on to the chains, but they appeared no different from any other boat's crew – much the same kind of coloured shirts and ragged trousers and bare feet, and they handled their craft capably enough. It was Bush who drove the *Nonsuch*'s crew from the side; he was hotly indignant about their blatant curiosity and the noise they made.

'Chattering like a herd of monkeys,' said Bush indignantly to the first lieutenant. 'Making more noise than a tree full of jackdaws. What'll these Russians think of us? Set the men to work and keep 'em at it.'

In these conditions of doubtful neutrality it would be best for the first contact with the shore to be made by Basse. At least ostensibly the squadron had come to Kronstadt merely to bring him with his news to the Swedish Crown Prince. Hornblower had his barge hoisted out and sent Basse away in it, and the boat returned without him but with no other information. Basse had landed at the jetty, and the barge, in accordance with Hornblower's orders, had immediately returned. Apart from the salute and the doctor's visit the Russian Empire chose to ignore the British squadron's existence.

'What sort of people do they think we are?' grumbled Bush fretting, as usual, at inaction. Bush knew as well as Hornblower that in all matters of diplomacy it was best to display no eagerness at all, but he could not force himself to appear calm as Hornblower could. He gave a meaning glance at Hornblower's full uniform and ribbon and star, donned so as to be ready for any official occasion whatever; he wanted Hornblower to proceed on shore to call on the local governor and put the whole situation to the test, but Hornblower was obstinate. He was waiting for an invitation. England had survived the storm in Europe so far without a Russian alliance, and future relations would be simplified if Russia were to make the first advances now – provided she did make them. His squadron was present merely to bring Basse to report to Bernadotte; if the Russian Government chose to take advantage of his presence to approach him, well and good. Otherwise he would have to devise some other plan.

'The telegraph hasn't ceased working since Basse reached shore,' commented Bush, glass to eye. The three gaunt black arms of the semaphore on the top of the fortress were whirling busily round transmitting messages to the next station higher up the bay. Otherwise there was almost nothing to be seen; across the low land of the island were visible a few masts to mark the site of the naval dockyard; two or three merchant ships swung at anchor in that direction, and a few fishing-boats plied their trade.

'There goes a boat!' said Montgomery suddenly.

A smart pinnace was shooting out from the direction of the dockyard heading across the channel almost directly away from *Nonsuch*.

'Russian Imperial colours,' said Bush. 'Can anyone see who's on board?'

But the pinnace was too far away for any details to be visible by telescope.

'I think I can see gold lace,' said Carlin, doubtfully.

'Much good that is,' said Bush. 'A blind man would guess there was gold lace in a Russian navy pinnace at Kronstadt.'

The pinnace passed away into the distance, quartering across the broad channel until her white sail dwindled to a speck.

'Call me if anything happens, if you please, Captain Bush,' said Hornblower.

He went off below to his cabin; Brown relieved him of his heavy full-dress coat with the epaulettes, and, once more alone, he began to fidget about the cabin. He opened the case of pistols which Barbara had given him, read the card inside it – the last word he had received from her – and shut the case again. He stepped out into the stern gallery and returned to the cabin. The realisation that he was worried annoyed him; he took down Archdeacon Coxe's travels from the bookshelf and set himself seriously to read the Archdeacon's intensely wearisome remarks about the condition of Russia, in the endeavour to inform himself more fully about the northern powers. But the words made sheer nonsense to him; he took up the slim volume of 'Childe Harold' instead.

'Bombast and fustian,' he said to himself, flipping through the pages.

He heard six bells strike; it was still no later than eleven in the morning, and he could not possibly dine before two. He got up from his chair and made himself lie on his cot, shut his eyes and grimly clenched his hands and tried to force himself to doze. He could not possibly go up on deck again and walk up and down, as he wanted to – that would be a public admission that he was restless and nervous. The minutes passed on leaden feet; he felt he had never felt so caged and unhappy before in his life.

Eight bells went, and he heard the watch relieved; it was like an eternity before he heard a bustle on the half-deck outside and someone knocked on the door. Hornblower settled himself in an attitude of complete relaxation on his cot.

'Come in!' he called, and he blinked and peered at the midshipman as if he had just awakened from a sound sleep.

'Boat heading towards us, sir,' said the midshipman.

'I'll come up,' said Hornblower. 'Pass the word for my cox'n.'

Brown helped him into his dress-coat, and he reached the deck while the boat was still some distance off.

'The same pinnace that we saw before, sir,' commented Hurst.

The pinnace came into the wind, and took in her mainsail while the bowman hailed the ship in Russian.

'Where's Mr Braun?' said Hornblower.

The hail was repeated, and Braun translated.

'He is asking permission to hook on to us, sir. And he says he has a message for you.'

'Tell him to come alongside,' said Hornblower. This dependence upon an interpreter always irritated him.

The boat's crew was smart, dressed in something like a uniform with blue shirts and white trousers, and in the stern-sheets, ready to mount the side, was an officer in military uniform, frogged across the breast in Hussar fashion. The Hussar came clumsily up the side, and glanced round, saluting the mass of gold lace which awaited him. Then he produced a letter, which he offered with a further explanation in Russian.

'From His Imperial Majesty the Czar,' translated Braun with a catch in his voice.

Hornblower took the letter; it was addressed in French –

M. LE CHEF D'ESCADRE LE CAPITAINE SIR HORNBLOWER, VAISSEAU BRITANNIQUE NOONSUCH.

Apparently the Czar's secretary, however competent he might be in other ways, was shaky regarding both British titles and spelling. The letter within was written in French as well – it was pleasant to be able to translate without Braun's assistance.

THE IMPERIAL PALACE OF PETERHOF
GRAND MARSHALATE OF THE IMPERIAL COURT.
30th May, 1812.

SIR,

I am commanded by His Imperial Majesty the Emperor of All the Russias to express to you His Imperial Majesty's pleasure at hearing of your arrival in His Imperial Majesty's waters. His Imperial Majesty and His Royal Highness the Prince of Sweden further command you to dinner at this palace today at four o'clock accompanied by your staff. His Excellency the Minister of Marine has put at your disposal a boat which will convey you and your party direct to the quay, and the officer who conveys this letter to you will serve as your guide.

Accept, sir, the assurances of my highest consideration,

KOTCHUBEY, *Grand Marshal of the Court.*

'I am invited to dinner with the Czar and Bernadotte,' said Hornblower to Bush; he handed over the letter, and Bush looked at it wisely with his head on one side as if he could read French.

'You're going, I suppose, sir?'

'Yes.'

It would hardly be tactful to begin his first encounter with the Russian and Swedish authorities by refusing an Imperial and a royal command.

Hornblower suddenly glanced round to find half the officers of the ship hanging on his words. This public discussion of his affairs was not in the least dignified, and detracted vastly from the pomp and mystery which should surround a Commodore. He had fallen sadly away from his old standards.

'Have none of you anything better to do than stand about and gape?' he bellowed, rounding on the herd. 'I can find mastheads even for senior officers if necessary.'

They began to slink away in gratifying fright, each one doing his best to avoid catching his eye as he glowered round him. That was a very desirable result. Then he became aware that the Hussar had yet another letter in his hand. He took it from him and glanced at the superscription.

'Here, Colonel, this is for you,' he said, handing it to Wychwood before turning back to Bush. 'The Czar and Bernadotte are at Peterhof – the palace is marked on the chart, on the Oranienbaum shore over there. You will be in command in my absence, of course.'

Bush's face reflected a complexity of emotions; Hornblower knew that he was remembering other occasions when Hornblower had left him in command, to go on shore to beard a mad tyrant on the coast of Central America, or to undertake some harebrained adventure on the coast of France.

'Aye aye, sir,' said Bush.

'I have to take my staff,' said Hornblower. 'Who do you think would care to dine with the Czar?'

He could afford to be jocose with Bush, who held the same substantive rank as himself – especially after his recent assertion of his dignity.

'You'll need Braun, I suppose, sir?'

'I suppose so.'

Dinner with the Czar would be a notable experience for any young officer, something he would be able to yarn about for the rest of his life. Good service could be rewarded by an invitation; and at the same time some future Admiral might gain invaluable experience.

'I'll take Hurst,' decided Hornblower; there were not the makings of an Admiral in the first lieutenant, but discipline demanded that he be included in the party. 'And young Mound, if you'll signal for him. And a midshipman. Who do you suggest?'

'Somers is the brightest, sir.'

'The fat one? Very good, I'll take him. Have you been invited, too, Colonel?'

'I have, sir,' answered Wychwood.

'We must be there at four. How long will it take to arrive?'

He looked at the Hussar, who did not understand him, and then looked round for Braun, who had left the deck, which was perfectly infuriating. When Hornblower had turned on the idling crowd he had not meant Braun to go, of course. It was just like Braun with his mock-humble pose to take his chief literally. Hornblower angrily ordered the word to be passed for him, and fumed until he came up again; yet when he came there was small satisfaction to be derived from his services, for when Hornblower's question was translated to the Hussar the latter merely raised his eyes to the sky and shrugged his shoulders before offering the information – translated by Braun – that it might be two hours and it might be four. As a soldier the Hussar would make no estimate of the time necessary for a journey by boat.

'We mustn't be late for a royal command, damn it,' said Hornblower. 'We'll leave in half an hour.'

Hornblower came punctually to the ship's side to find the others awaiting him, young Somers' plump cheeks empurpled with the constriction of his stock, Hurst and Mound uncomfortable in their full dress, Braun stiffly uniformed.

'Carry on,' said Hornblower.

Young Somers went first in accordance with the age-old rule of the junior getting first into a boat, and Braun followed him. Braun's lifted arm, as he went over the side, pulled up his tight coat for a moment, and his waistcoat with it. Something flashed momentarily into view at his waistband; something black – Hornblower's eyes were resting on it at that moment. It must have been the butt of a pistol, the barrel of it pushed into the waistband of his breeches, round by his hip where the bulge would be least noticeable. The fellow was wearing his sword, of course. Hornblower began to wonder why he should take a pistol. But Mound and Hurst had followed him down by this time, and Wychwood was heaving himself over, in his scarlet tunic and bearskin. The Hussar should go next, so that the Commodore should descend last, but he was hanging back with misplaced politeness, bowing and making way for the Commodore.

'After you, sir,' said Hornblower to his deaf ears.

Hornblower had positively to stamp his foot to compel the ignorant soldier to precede him, and then he swung himself over to the shrilling of the pipes of the boatswain's mates and the rigid salutes of the ship's officers. He dropped into the sternsheets, encumbered with his boat-cloak. There was a tiny cabin forward, where he joined Wychwood and Hurst. Mound and the warrant officers and the Hussar kept themselves discreetly in the stern. The coxswain yelled some strange order and the boat cast off, the lugsail was hoisted and they headed over to the Oranien-baum shore.

From where he sat Hornblower could see Braun sitting stiffly in the sternsheets. That business of the pistol was rather curious. Presumably he had fears of attack or arrest on shore as a recent rebel, and wished to have the means to defend himself. But not even the Russians would lay hands on an English officer, in a British uniform. That was a big pistol butt; a black one too. Hornblower suddenly moved uneasily on his locker, uncrossed his knees and recrossed them. That was one of the pistols Barbara had given him the butt of which he had seen in Braun's waistband. He remembered the shape of the ebony butt too well to be mistaken about it.

The presence of a thief on board a ship was always upsetting and disturbing; theft was so easy and suspicion could be spread so wide, although that was not true in this case. It would still be a nasty business accusing Braun of the crime and punishing him for it. An English-made rifled pistol with percussion caps – presumably the very first of its kind to reach Russia – would command a fabulous price at the Russian Court. Braun could reasonably expect to obtain two or three hundred guineas for it. And yet even with all his prejudice against him he could not believe Braun capable of petty theft.

The coxswain suddenly shouted a new order, and the pinnace came about on the other tack; the dipping lug with which she was equipped had to be taken in and reset when she tacked, and Hornblower watched the evolution with professional interest. The Russian sailors were smart and handy enough, but that was to be expected of the crew of the pinnace specially attached to the service of the Russian Admiralty. The

Nonsuch was already far astern, hull down. A buoy made its appearance close alongside, and passed away astern, the rapidity of its passage proof of the speed the pinnace was making through the water.

'We're heading sou'west now, sir,' commented Hurst; 'we're out of the fairway.'

He climbed up out of the little cabin and peered ahead.

'Land right ahead, sir,' he reported, 'but no sign of any palace.'

'I know nothing about the Peterhof,' remarked Wychwood. 'I was in Czarskoe Selo and the old Winter Palace as a subaltern on Wilson's staff before Tilsit. The Peterhof's one of the lesser palaces; I expect they chose it for this meeting so that Bernadotte could arrive direct by sea.'

It was quite futile to debate what would be the result of this evening's meeting, and yet the temptation was overwhelming. The minutes slipped by until the coxswain shouted a new order. The lugsail came down, and the piles of a jetty came into sight beside the pinnace as she rounded-to. Lines were thrown out and the pinnace drew in beside a broad companionway run-down into the water from the top of the jetty. This time the Russian officer's politeness was not misplaced. First out of a boat and last in, in order of seniority, was the etiquette of the Navy; Hornblower ducked out of the little cabin, stepped on to the companionway and began to walk up, hurriedly making sure that his cocked hat was on straight and his sword properly slung. As he reached the top someone shouted an order; there was a guard of twenty soldiers drawn up there, grenadiers in bearskins and blue coats. They put their left arms across their breasts as they presented arms in a fashion that appeared back-handed to a man accustomed to receiving salutes from the Royal Marines. Yet the uniforms and the pose seemed strangely familiar; Hornblower realised that he was being reminded of the wooden soldiers that young Richard had been playing with – a box of German soldiers smuggled out of the continental blockade and presented to him by one of Barbara's diplomatic friends. Of course the Russian Army was organised on the German model, and German uniforms had been introduced by Peter III. Hornblower stiffly returned the salute of the officer of the guard, standing at attention long enough for the rest of the party to catch him up; the Hussar spoke rapidly to Braun in Russian.

'There are carriages waiting for us, sir,' Braun interpreted.

Hornblower could see them at the end of the jetty, two big open landaus, with fine horses to each; in the drivers' seats sat coachmen pigtailed and powdered wearing red coats – not the scarlet of the British Army or of the British royal liveries, but a softer, strawberry red. Footmen similarly dressed stood at the horses' heads and at the carriage doors.

'Senior officers go in the first carriage,' explained Braun.

Hornblower climbed in, with Wychwood and Hurst after him; with an apologetic smile the Hussar followed them and sat with his back to the horses. The door shut. One footman leaped up beside the coachman and the other sprang up behind, and the horses dashed forward. The road wound through a vast park, alternate sweeps of grass and groves of trees; here and there fountains threw lofty jets of water at the sky, and marble naiads posed by marble basins. Occasional turns in the road opened up beautiful vistas down the terraced lawns; there were long flights of marble steps and beautiful little marble pavilions, but also, at every turning, beside every fountain and every pavilion, there were sentries on guard, stiffly presenting arms at the carriages whirled by.

'Every Czar for the last three generations has been murdered,' remarked Wychwood. 'It's only the women who die in their beds. Alexander is taking precautions.'

The carriage turned sharply again and came out on a broad, gravelled parade ground; on the farther side Hornblower just had time to see the palace, a rambling rococo building of pink and grey stone with a dome at either end, before the carriage drew up at the entrance to the salute of a further guard, and a white-powdered footman opened the doors. With a few polite words in Russian the Hussar led the party forward up a flight of pink marble steps and into a lofty anteroom. A swarm of servants came forward to take their boat-cloaks; Hornblower remembered to put his cocked hat under his arm and the others followed his example. The folding doors beyond were thrown open, and they went towards them, to be received by a dignified official whose coat was of the same Imperial red where the colour was visible through the gold lace. He wore powder and carried in his hand a gold-tipped ebony stave.

'Kotchubey,' he said, speaking fair French. 'Grand Marshal of the Palace. Commodore Hornblower? Lord Wychwood?'

They bowed to him, and Hornblower presented the others; he saw the Grand Marshal run an all-embracing eye over their uniforms to make sure that nothing unworthy of the Court of the Czar would penetrate farther into the palace. Then he turned back to Hornblower and Wychwood.

'His Excellency the Minister of Marine would be honoured if Commodore Hornblower would grant him time for a short interview.'

'I am at His Excellency's service,' said Hornblower, 'but I am here at the command of His Imperial Majesty.'

'That is very good of you, sir. There will be time before His Imperial Majesty appears. And His Excellency the Minister of Foreign Affairs would be honoured by Lord Wychwood's attention for a few minutes in a similar way.'

'I am at His Excellency's service,' said Wychwood. For a man of his experience his French was remarkably poor.

'Thank you,' said Kotchubey.

He turned, and three more officers of the Court approached at his gesture. They wore less gold lace than Kotchubey, and from the gold keys embroidered on their lapels Hornblower knew them to be chamberlains. There were further introductions, more bows.

'Now if you have the kindness to accompany me, sir—' said Kotchubey to Hornblower.

Two chamberlains took charge of the junior officers, one took charge of Wychwood, and Kotchubey led Hornblower away. Hornblower gave one last glance at his party. Even the stolid Hurst, even the deliberately languid Mound, wore rather scared expressions at being abandoned by their captain like this in an Imperial palace. Hornblower was reminded of children being handed over by their parents to a strange nurse. But Braun's expression was different. His green eyes were glowing with excitement, and there was a new tenseness about his features, and he was casting glances about him like a man preparing himself for some decisive action. Hornblower felt a wave of misgiving break over him; during the excitement of setting foot in Russia he had forgotten about Braun, about the stolen pistol, about everything connected with him. He wanted time to think, and yet Kotchubey was hurrying him away and allowing him no time. They walked through a magnificent room – Hornblower was only just conscious of its furniture, pictures, and statuary – and through folding doors beyond, which were opened for them by two of the footmen who seemed to be present in hundreds. The corridor was wide and lofty, more like a picture gallery than a corridor, but Kotchubey only went a few yards along it. He stopped abruptly at an inconspicuous door, from before which two more footmen stepped with alacrity at his approach. The door opened straight upon a steep winding stairway; half-way up there was another door, this one guarded by four burly soldiers in pink uniforms with high boots and baggy breeches whom Hornblower recognised as the first Cossacks he had ever seen in the flesh. They nearly jammed the narrow stairways as they drew back against the wall to make way; Hornblower had to push past them. Kotchubey scratched upon the door and instantly opened it, immediately drawing Hornblower after him with a gesture as though he were a conspirator.

'Sir Hornblower,' he announced, having shut the door. The big man in the vaguely naval uniform, with epaulettes and a string of orders across his breast, must be the Minister of Marine; he came forward cordially, speaking fair French and with a courtly apology for not speaking English. But in the far corner of the room was another figure, tall and slender, in a beautiful light-blue uniform. He was strikingly handsome, but as though he came from another world; the ivory pallor of his cheeks, accentuated by his short black side-whiskers, was more unnatural than unhealthy. He made no move as he sat stiffly upright in the dark corner, his finger-tips resting on a low table before him, and neither of the Russian officials gave any overt sign of acknowledging his presence, but Hornblower knew that it was the Czar; thinking quickly, he realised that if the Czar's own officials pretended the Czar was not there, then he could do no less. He kept his eyes on the Minister of Marine's.

'I trust,' said the latter, 'that I see you in good health?'

'Thank you,' said Hornblower. 'I am in the best of health.'

'And your squadron?'

'That is in the best of health too, Your Excellency.'

'Does it need anything?'

Hornblower had to think quickly again. On the one hand was the desire to appear utterly independent, but on the other there was the nagging knowledge that water would soon be running short. Every commanding officer, whether of ships or squadron, carried always at the back of his mind the vital, urgent need for renewing his ship's drinking water. And a Minister of Marine – even a Russian one – must be aware of that.

'Firewood and water, as always,' said Hornblower, 'would be of the greatest convenience.'

'I shall inquire if it is convenient to send a water-boat to your squadron tomorrow morning,' said the Minister.

'I thank Your Excellency,' said Hornblower, wondering what he would be asked to do in exchange.

'You have been informed, sir,' said the Minister, changing the subject so obviously that Hornblower could only attribute it to nervousness at having the Czar listening to the conversation 'of Bonaparte's occupation of Swedish Pomerania?'

'Yes, Your Excellency.'

'And what is your opinion of that transaction?'

Hornblower delayed his answer while he sorted out his thoughts and worked out the French phrases.

'Typical Bonapartism,' he said. 'He tolerates neutrality on the part of weak powers only while he can profit by it. The moment he finds it inconveniences him, he treacherously sends forward his army, and on the heels of the army march all the plagues of Bonapartism, terror and famine and misery. The gaol, the firing party, and the secret police. The bankers and the merchants are stripped of all they possess. The men are thrust into the ranks of his army, and the women – all the world knows what happens to the women.'

'But do you not believe his object was merely plunder?'

'No, Your Excellency – although plunder is always useful to Bonaparte's top-heavy finances. He overran Pomerania the moment it was apparent that its usefulness as a neutral base for his privateers had ceased with the appearance of my squadron.'

Inspiration came to Hornblower at that moment; his expression must have changed, for as he hesitated the Minister prompted him with obvious interest.

'Monsieur was going to say—?'

'Bonaparte controls the whole Baltic coast now as far as the frontiers of His Imperial Majesty's dominions. That would be most convenient to him in one particular event, Your Excellency. In the event of his deciding to launch an attack on Russia.' Hornblower threw into those words all the power of speech that he could muster, and the Minister nodded – Hornblower did not dare, much as he wanted to, to throw a glance at the Czar to see what effect his words had on him.

'Bonaparte would never feel easy in his mind regarding his communications while Pomerania was Swedish so long as there was a British fleet in the Baltic. It could be too good a base for an attack on his rear, convoyed by my squadron. He has eliminated that danger now – he can march an army against St Petersburg, should he attack Russia, without fear of its being cut off. It is one more threat to His Imperial Majesty's dominions.'

'And how serious do you consider his threats to be regarding Russia, sir?'

'Bonaparte's threats are always serious. You know his methods, Your Excellency. A demand for concessions, and when the concessions are granted then new demands, each one more weakening than the one before, until either the object of his attentions is too weak to oppose him further or is at least so weakened as to make armed resistance fatal. He will not rest until all his demands are granted; and what he demands is nothing short of the dominion of the world, until every nation is in bondage to him.'

'Monsieur is very eloquent.'

'I am eloquent because I speak from the heart, Your Excellency. For nineteen years, since my boyhood, I have served my country against the monstrous power which overshadows Europe.'

'And with what effect has your country fought?'

'My country is still free. In the history of the world that counts for much. And now it counts for more. England is striking back. Portugal, Sicily, are free too, thanks to England. Her armies are marching into Spain even while I am speaking to you here, Your Excellency. Soon Bonaparte will be defending the very frontiers of his boasted Empire against them. We have found the weak spot in the vast structure; we are probing into it, on to the very foundations, and soon the whole elaborate mass will crumble into ruin.'

The little room must be very warm; Hornblower found himself sweating in his heavy uniform.

'And here in the Baltic?'

'Here England has penetrated too. Not one of Bonaparte's ships will move from today without my permission. England is ready with her support. She is ready to pour in money and arms to help any power that will withstand the tyrant. Bonaparte is ringed in from the South and the West and the North. There is only the East left to him. That is where he will strike and that is where he must be opposed.'

It was the handsome, pale young man in the dark corner of the room to whom these remarks were really addressed. The Minister of Marine had a far smaller stake on the board of international politics than did his master. Other kings in war risked a province or two, risked their dignity or their fame, but the Czar of Russia, the most powerful and autocratic of them all, risked his life, and there was no gainsaying that. A word from the Czar might send a nobleman to Siberia; another word might set half a million men on the move to war; but if either move were a false one the Czar would pay for it with his life. A military defeat, a momentary loss of control over his courtiers or his guards, and the Czar was doomed, first to dethronement and then to inevitable murder. That had been the fate of his father, of his grandfather, and of his great-grandfather. If he fought and was unsuccessful; if he did not fight and lost his prestige there would be a silken scarf round his throat or a dozen swords between his ribs.

An ormolu clock on a bracket on the wall struck in silvery tones.

'The hour strikes, you see, Your Excellency,' said Hornblower. He was shaking with the excitement that boiled within him. He felt weak and empty.

'The hour strikes indeed,' answer the Minister. He was clearly struggling desperately not to glance back at the Czar. 'As regards the clock, I regret it deeply, as it reminds me that if I detain you longer you will be late for the Imperial reception.'

'I must certainly not be late for that,' said Hornblower.

'I must thank you for the clear way in which you have stated your views, Captain. I shall have the pleasure of meeting you at the reception. His Excellency the Grand Marshal will show you the way to the Tauride Hall.'

Hornblower bowed, still keeping his eyes from wavering towards the Czar, but he contrived to back from the room without either turning his back on the Czar or making his precaution too obvious. They squeezed past the Cossacks on the stairs down to the ground floor again.

'This way, if you please, sir.'

XII

Footmen opened two more huge doors, and they entered a vast room, the lofty ceiling soaring into a dome far above their heads. The walls were a mass of marble and gold, and grouped in the hall was a crowd of people, the men in uniforms of all the colours of the rainbow, the women in Court dresses with plumes and trains. Orders and jewels reflected the light of innumerable candles.

A group of men and women, laughing and joking in French, opened their ranks to admit Hornblower and the Grand Marshal.

'I have the honour to present—' began the latter. It was a prolonged introduction; the Countess of This, and the Baroness of That, and the Duchess of the Other, beautiful women, some of them bold-eyed and some of them languid. Hornblower bowed and bowed again, the Star of the Bath thumping his chest each time he straightened up.

'You will partner the Countess Canerine at dinner, Captain,' said the Grand Marshal, and Hornblower bowed again.

'Delighted,' he said.

The Countess was the boldest-eyed and most beautiful of them all; under the arches of her brows her eyes were dark and liquid and yet with a consuming fire within them. Her face was a perfect oval, her complexion like rose petals, her magnificent bosom white as snow above the low décolleté of her Court dress.

'As a distinguished stranger,' went on the Grand Marshal, 'you will take precedence immediately after the Ambassadors and Ministers. Preceding you will be the Persian Ambassador, His Excellency Gorza Khan.'

The Grand Marshal indicated an individual in turban and diamonds; it was a bit of blessed good fortune that he was the most easily identified person in the whole crowd, seeing that Hornblower would have to follow him. Everyone else in the group looked with even greater interest at this English captain who was being accorded such distinction; the Countess rolled a considering eye upon him, but the Grand Marshal interrupted the exchange of glances by continuing the introductions. The gentlemen returned Hornblower's bows.

'His Imperial Majesty,' said the Grand Marshal, filling in the gap in the conversation when the introductions were completed, 'will be wearing the uniform of the Simonouski Guards.'

Hornblower caught sight of Wychwood across the room, his bearskin under his arm and Basse at his side, being introduced to another group. They exchanged nods, and Hornblower returned, a little distractedly, to the conversation of his own group. The Countess was asking him about his ship, and he tried to tell her about *Nonsuch*. Through the far

doors there was filing a double line of soldiers, tall young men in breast-
plates that shone like silver – that probably were silver – with silver
helmets with waving white plumes.

'The Chevalier Guard,' explained the Countess, 'all young men of
noble birth.'

She looked at them with distinct approval; they were forming against
the walls at intervals of two or three yards, each standing like a silver
statue as soon as he reached his post. The crowd was moving slowly
away from the centre of the room, leaving it clear. Hornblower wondered
where the rest of his officers were; he looked round, and realised that
there was a further crowd of uniformed individuals in the gallery
which ran at first-floor level three-quarters of the way round the dome
over his head. That would be where the lesser people could look down
on the doings of the great. He saw Hurst and Mound leaning against the
balustrade. Behind them young Somers, his low-crowned hat in his
hand, was talking with elaborate pantomime to a trio of pretty girls,
who were holding weakly on to each other as they laughed. Heaven only
knew what language Somers was trying to talk, but he was evidently
making himself agreeable.

It was Braun that Hornblower was worried about; yet what with the
violence of his reaction after his speech-making, and the chatter and
glitter around him, and the sultry glances of the Countess, it was hard
to think. Hornblower had to drive himself to keep his mind on his subject. The pistol in Braun's waistband – the fierce intensity of Braun's
expression – that gallery up there. He could fit the piece of the puzzle
together if only he were left undistracted for a moment.

'The Prince of Sweden will make his entry with His Imperial Majesty,'
the Countess was saying.

The Prince of Sweden! Bernadotte, the initiator of a new dynasty, the
supplanter of Gustavus, for whom Braun had risked life and fortune.
Alexander had conquered Finland; Bernadotte had abandoned it to
him. The two men whom Braun had most reason to hate in the whole
world were probably Alexander and Bernadotte. And Braun was armed
with a double-barrelled pistol, a rifled pistol with percussion caps that
never missed fire and which carried true for fifty yards. Hornblower
swept the gallery with his eyes. There he was, at the far end, standing
unobtrusively between two pillars. Something must be done at once.
The Grand Marshal was chattering affably with a couple of courtiers,
and Hornblower turned to him, abandoning the Countess and breaking
rudely into the conversation with the only excuse that he could think of.

'Impossible!' said the Grand Marshal, glancing at the clock. 'His Imperial Majesty and His Royal Highness enter in three and a half minutes.'

'I'm sorry,' said Hornblower. 'I regret it deeply, but I must—it is
absolutely necessary – it is urgent—'

Hornblower fairly danced with anxiety, and the gesture reinforced the argument he had already advanced. The Grand Marshal stood weighing the relative undesirability of interrupting a Court ceremony and offending someone who, as the recent interview showed, might have the ear of the Czar.

'Go out through that door, then, sir,' he said reluctantly at length, pointing, 'and please, sir, come back without calling attention to yourself.'

Hornblower fled, sidling rapidly but as unobtrusively as possible through the groups of people to the door; he slipped through it and glanced round desperately. The broad staircase to the left must lead up to the gallery. He grasped the scabbard of his sword to keep it from tripping him up and ran up the stairs two at a time; the one or two footmen whom he passed hardly spared him a glance. The gallery was crowded, although the dresses were not as beautiful nor the uniforms as brilliant. Hornblower hurried along towards the end where he had seen Braun; he took long strides while doing his best to look like a nonchalant stroller. Mound caught his eye – Hornblower could not spare the time to say anything, dared not risk saying a word, but he put all the meaning into his glance that he could, hoping that Mound would follow him. Down below he heard the sound of doors being thrown open, and the babble of conversation stopped abruptly. A loud harsh voice announced 'L'Empéreur! L'Impératrice! Le Prince Royal de Suède!'

Braun stood there between the two pillars, glancing down. His hand was at his waist; he was drawing the pistol. There was only one silent way to stop him. Hornblower whipped out his sword – the hundred-guinea gold-hilted sword, the gift of the Patriotic Fund, with an edge like a razor – and he slashed at the wrist of the hand that held the pistol. With the tendons severed the fingers opened nervelessly and the pistol fell heavily on the carpeted floor while Braun turned in gaping surprise, looking first at the blood spouting from his wrist and then at Hornblower's face. Hornblower put the point of the blade at his breast; he could lunge and kill him on the instant, and every line in his expression must have attested the genuineness of his determination to do so if necessary, for Braun uttered no sound, made no movement. Somebody loomed up at Hornblower's shoulder; it was Mound, thank God.

'Look after him,' whispered Hornblower. 'Tie that wrist up! Get him out of here somehow.'

He glanced over the railing. A little crowd of royalty was advancing through the huge doors opposite and below him – Alexander in his light-blue uniform; a tall swarthy man with a huge nose who must be Bernadotte; a number of women, two with crowns who must be the Empress and Empress-Mother, and the rest in plumes. Braun would have had the easiest shot heart could desire. All round the vast room the Court was

making obeisance, the men bowing low and the women curtseying; as
Hornblower looked they rose all together, plumes and uniforms like a
breaking wave of flowers. Hornblower tore his eyes from the spectacle,
sheathed his sword, and picked up the pistol from the floor, stuffing it
down into his waistband. Mound, his eternal nonchalance replaced by
swift catlike movements, had his long arms round Braun, who was
leaning against him. Hornblower snatched out his handkerchief and put
it in Mound's hand, but there was not time to do more. He turned away
and hastened back along the gallery. The lesser courtiers up here had
straightened up from their bows and their curtseys and were beginning
to look around them again and resume their conversation. It was lucky
that at the moment of crisis they had had no eyes or ears for anything
save the royal party. Hurst and Somers were about to start talking to
the women again when Hornblower caught their eyes.

'Go back there to Mound,' he said. 'He needs your help.'

Then he walked quickly down the stairs again, found the door into
the audience hall, and pushed past the footman on guard there. A glance
showed him the position of the group he had left, and he sidled round
to it and took up his position at the Countess's side. The royal party was
making the circle of the room, making the usual conventional remarks to
distinguished individuals, and it was only a matter of a few minutes
before they reached Hornblower. The Grand Marshal presented him,
and Hornblower, his head swimming with his recent excitement so
that he felt as if he was in a nightmare, bowed to each crowned head in
turn and to Bernadotte.

'It is a pleasure to meet Commodore Hornblower,' said Alexander
pleasantly. 'We have all of us heard of his exploits.'

'Your Majesty is too kind,' gulped Hornblower.

Then the royal group passed on, and Hornblower turned to meet the
Countess's glance again. The fact that the Czar had addressed a few
words to him personally evidently confirmed her suspicions that he was
a man of potential influence, and there was a considering look in her
eyes.

'Will you be making a long stay in Russia?' she asked.

It was very hard, during this period of intense reaction, to keep his
mind on anything. All he wanted to do was to sit down and rest quietly.
He flogged his mind into making a polite rejoinder, and when the men
of the party began to ply him with questions about the British Navy
and about maritime affairs in general he tried to answer sensibly, but it
was a forlorn hope.

Footmen were rolling in long buffet tables, glittering with gold and
silver; Hornblower forced himself to watch keenly, so as to commit no
breach of etiquette. To one side the royal party had taken their seats,
Empresses and Czar in armchairs and the princes and princesses in

upright chairs, and everyone had to be careful always to face in that direction so as not to commit the heinous crime of letting royalty see a human back. People were beginning to take food from the buffets, and, try as he would, Hornblower could see no sign at all of any attention to precedence. But there was the Persian Ambassador munching something from a gold plate, so that he was justified in making a move in the same direction. Yet all the same this was the most curious dinner he had ever attended, with everyone standing up except royalty; and royalty, he could see, were eating nothing at all.

'May I offer you my arm, Countess?' he said, as the group began to drift towards a buffet.

The courtiers by dint of long practice had seemingly mastered the art of eating while standing up and while holding their hats under their arms, but it was not easy. His dangling sword was liable to trip him, too, and that infernal pistol in his waistband was digging uncomfortably into his side. The footmen serving at the buffets understood no French, and the Countess came to Hornblower's rescue with an order.

'That is caviare,' she explained to him, 'and this is vodka, the drink of the people, but I think you will find that the two are admirably suited to each other.'

The Countess was right. The grey, unappetising-looking stuff was perfectly delicious. Hornblower sipped cautiously at the vodka, and in his present highly strung condition hardly noticed the fierce bite of the liquor; but there was no doubt that vodka and caviare blended together exquisitely. He felt the warm glow of the alcohol inside him, and realised that he was desperately hungry. The buffet was covered with foods of all kinds, some being kept warm in chafing dishes, some cold; under the tutelage of the Countess, Hornblower went a fair way towards tackling them all. There was a dish apparently of stewed mushrooms that was excellent, slices of smoked fish, an unidentifiable salad, some varieties of cheese, eggs both hot and cold, a sort of ragoût of pork. There were other liquors as well, and Hornblower ate and drank with his spirits rising momentarily, playing his part in the conversation and feeling more and more warmly grateful to the Countess. It might be a queer way to have dinner, but Hornblower thought he had never tasted such delicious food. His head began to whirl with the liquor; he knew that danger signal of old, although this time he did not resent it quite so bitterly as usual, and he checked himself in the midst of a laugh in time not to be too unrestrained. Laughter, chatter, and bright lights; this was one of the jolliest parties he had ever attended – he felt as if it had been someone else who had slashed Braun's wrist open with a sword an hour ago. Hornblower replaced his lovely porcelain plate on the buffet, among the gold dishes, and wiped his mouth with one of the silken napkins that lay there. He was comfortably replete, with the gratifying sensation of having eaten just too much and having drunk just enough; he supposed coffee would be served soon, and a cup of coffee was all he needed to complete his internal gratification.

'I have dined extremely well,' he said to the Countess.

The most remarkable expression passed over the Countess's face. Her eyebrows rose, and she opened her mouth to say something and then shut it again. She was smiling and puzzled and distressed all at the same time. She again started to speak, but her words were cut short by the ceremonial opening of yet another pair of doors from which twenty or thirty footmen emerged to form an avenue leading into the next room. Hornblower became conscious that the royal party had risen from their chairs and were falling into formation, and the complete cessation of conversation told Hornblower that some specially solemn moment had arrived. Couples were moving about the room like ships jockeying for position. The Countess laid her hand on his arm with a gentle pressure as if to lead him. By George, a procession was forming behind the royal party! There went the Persian Ambassador, a smiling girl on his arm. Hornblower just had time to lead his own partner forward to join the procession next, and after two or three more couples had joined behind him the procession began to move forward, its tail being steadily length-ened as it went. Hornblower kept his eyes on the Persian Ambassador before him; they passed down the avenue of footmen, and entered the next room.

The procession was breaking off to left and to right in alternate couples as though in a country dance; the Persian Ambassador went to the left, and Hornblower was ready to go to the right without the prompting of the gesture of the Grand Marshal, who was standing there ready to direct anyone in doubt. It was another enormous room, lit by what seemed to be hundreds of cut-glass chandeliers dangling from the roof, and all down the length of it ran a vast table – miles long, it seemed, to Hornblower's disordered imagination – covered with gold plate and crystal and embanked with flowers. The table was shaped like a T with a very small crosspiece, and the royal party had already taken their seats at the head; behind every chair all the way down stood a white-wigged footman. It dawned upon Hornblower that dinner was about to begin; the food and drink which had been served in the domed hall had been something extra and introductory. Hornblower was ready to laugh at himself for his idiotic lack of comprehension at the same time as he was ready to groan with despair at the thought of having to eat his way through an Imperial dinner in his present distended condition.

Save for royalty, the men were standing at their chairs while the ladies sat; across the table the Persian Ambassador was bending affably over the young woman he had brought in, and the aigrette in his turban nodded and his diamonds flashed. The last woman took her seat, and then the men sat down together – not quite as simultaneously as marines presenting arms, but almost so. A babble of conversation began immediately, and almost immediately a golden soup-plate was put under Hornblower's nose and a golden soup tureen full of pink soup was offered to him for him to help himself from. He could not help glancing down the table; everyone had been given soup at the same moment – there must be two hundred footmen at least waiting at table.

'That is M. de Narbonne, the French Ambassador,' said the Countess, indicating with a glance a handsome young man across the table two places higher than the Persian Ambassador. 'Of course the Grand Marshal did not present you to him. And that is the Austrian Ambassador, and the Saxon Minister, and the Danish Minister, all your enemies officially. The Spanish Ambassador comes from Joseph Bonaparte, not from the Spanish partisan government which you recognise, so you could hardly be presented to him either. I don't believe there's a soul here except us Russians to whom it would be proper to present you.'

There was a cool, pleasant yellow wine in a tall glass before Hornblower, and he sipped it.

'My experience today,' he said, 'is that Russians are the most delightful people in the world, and Russian women the most charming and most beautiful.'

The Countess flashed a glance at him from her sultry eyes, and, it seemed to Hornblower, set his brains creeping about inside his skull. The golden soup-plate was whisked away and replaced by a golden dinner-plate. Another wine was poured into another glass before him – champagne. It effervesced just as his thoughts appeared to him to be doing. His footman spoke to him in Russian, apparently offering him a choice, and the Countess settled the problem without referring to him.

'As this is your first visit to Russia,' she explained, 'I could be sure that you have not yet tasted our Volga River trout.'

She was helping herself to one as she spoke, from a golden dish; Hornblower's footman was presenting another golden dish.

'A gold service looks very well,' said the Countess sadly, 'but it allows the food to grow unfortunately cold. I never use mine in my house save when I entertain His Imperial Majesty. As that is the case in most houses I doubt if His Imperial Majesty ever has a hot meal.'

The gold knife and fork with which Hornblower dissected his fish were heavy in his hands, and scraped oddly against the gold plate.

'You have a kind heart, madame,' he said.

'Yes,' said the Countess, with deep significance.

Hornblower's head whirled again; the champagne, so cold, so delicate, seemed perfectly adapted to put this right, and he drank of it thirstily.

A couple of fat little birds on toast followed the trout; they melted delicately in the mouth; some other wine followed the champagne. And there was a venison stew, and a cut of some roast which might be mutton but which was borne on Pegasus-wings of garlic beyond mundane speculation. Somewhere in the procession of food appeared a pink water ice, only the third or fourth which Hornblower had ever tasted.

'Foreign kickshaws,' said Hornblower to himself, but he enjoyed the food and had no prejudice against foreign cookery. Perhaps he said 'foreign kickshaws' to himself because that was what Bush would have said had he been eating the dinner. Or perhaps it was because he was a little drunk – Hornblower's persistent self-examination brought him to this startling conclusion with a shock, comparable with that received by a man walking into a stanchion in the dark. He must certainly not get drunk while he was representing his country, and he would be a fool to get drunk while in the imminent personal danger which surrounded him. He personally had brought an assassin to the palace, and if the fact ever leaked out it would go hard with him, especially if the Czar should become aware that the assassin was armed with a rifled pistol which was Hornblower's private property. Hornblower sobered still further when it came to him that he had forgotten all about his junior officers – he had left them trying to dispose of the wounded assassin, and what they would do with him was more than he could guess.

The Countess beside him was pressing his foot under the table; and a little electric thrill ran through him and his steadiness vanished once more. He smiled at her beatifically. She gave him a long look with lowered lids and then turned away to address a remark to her neighbour on her other side, a tactful hint for Hornblower to pay a little attention to the Baroness to whom he had hardly spoken a word. Hornblower plunged feverishly into conversation, and the general in the outlandish dragoon uniform on the far side of the Baroness joined in with a question about Admiral Keats, whose acquaintance he had made in 1807. The footman was offering a new dish; his hairy wrist was exposed between his cuff and his white glove, and that wrist was spotted with flea-bites. Hornblower remembered having read in one of the books he had been studying about the northern powers that the farther east one travelled the worse the vermin became – the Polish flea was bad, but the Russian flea was unbearable. If it was any worse than the Spanish flea, with which Hornblower had an intimate acquaintance, it must be a remarkably well-developed flea.

There must be hundreds – there must actually be thousands – of servants in this palace, and Hornblower could guess how closely they must be herded together. Having waged a ceaseless war against body-vermin for twenty years in crowded ships Hornblower was well aware of the difficulty of extermination. But while one part of his mind was discussing with the dragoon general the principles of seniority and selection in the British Navy another part was telling himself that he would greatly prefer not to be served by a flea-bitten footman. The conversation languished, and Hornblower turned back to the Countess.

'Do pictures interest monsieur very much?' she asked.

'Of course,' said Hornblower politely.

'The picture gallery in this palace is very fine. You have not seen it yet?'

'I have not yet had that pleasure.'

'This evening, after the royal party has retired, I could show it to you. Unless you would rather join one of the card tables?'

'I would much prefer to see pictures,' said Hornblower. His laugh rang a little loud even in his own ears.

'Then if, after the royal party has withdrawn, you are by the door on the far side of the room, I shall show you the way.'

'That will be delightful, madame.'

They were drinking toasts at the head of the table – for the first one everyone had to stand while they drank the health of the Prince of Sweden, and after that conversation perforce became disjointed with other toasts to be drunk, announced by a gigantic official with a colossal voice – Stentor with Hercules' frame, said Hornblower to himself, pleased with the classical touch – who stood behind the Czar's chair. Between toasts there was music; not orchestral music, but vocal music from an unaccompanied male choir, seemingly of hundreds of voices which filled the vast room with their din. Hornblower heard it with the faint but growing irritation of the completely tone-deaf. It was a relief when the music ceased and everyone stood once more while the royal party withdrew through a doorway near the head of the table, and no sooner had the door closed after them than the women went out too, ushered through the far door by Madame Kotchubey.

'A bientôt,' smiled the Countess, as she left him.

The men began to gather in groups along the table while footmen hastened in with coffee and cordials; Wychwood, his bearskin still under his arm, made his way round to Hornblower. His face was redder than ever; his eyes, if it were possible, stuck out even farther from his head.

'The Swedes'll fight if Russia will,' said Wychwood, in a grating whisper, 'I have that direct from Basse, who was with Bernadotte all day.'

Then he passed on and Hornblower heard his remarkable French being practised on a uniformed group higher up the table. The room was unbearably hot, presumably because of the infinity of candles alight in it; some of the men were already beginning to drift away through the door where the women had preceded them. Hornblower drank his coffee and rose to his feet, transferring his cocked hat once more from his knees to under his arm. The room he entered must have been the counterpart of the one in which the royal reception had been held, for it was domed too, and of similar proportions; Hornblower remembered the two domes he had seen when his carriage draw up to the palace. It was dotted with chairs and sofas and tables, round one of which a group of dowagers were already playing cards, and an elderly couple were playing backgammon at another. At the far end his eye instantly discerned the Countess, seated on a couch with her train spread beside her and her coffee cup and saucer in her hands, while she chatted with another woman; every line of the Countess's attitude proclaimed girlish innocence.

From the number of people already assembled it was clear that this was the meeting-place of the whole Court; presumably the hundreds of people who had perforce witnessed the royal reception from the gallery were permitted to descend and mingle with their betters after dining less elaborately. Young Mound was lounging towards him, his lean gangling body looking like an overgrown colt's.

'We have him in a side room aloft, sir,' he reported. 'He fainted with the loss of blood – we had to put a tourniquet on his arm to stop the bleeding. We bandaged him with half of Somers' shirt, and Somers and Mr Hurst are keeping guard over him.'

'Does anyone know about it?'

'No, sir. We got him into the room without anyone seeing us. I poured a glass of liquor over his coat and from the stink of him anyone'll think he's drunk.'

Mound was obviously a capable man in an emergency, as Hornblower had already suspected.

'Very good.'

'The sooner we get him away the better, sir,' said Mound, with a diffidence to be expected of a junior officer making suggestions to a senior.

'You're quite right,' said Hornblower, 'except that—'

Hornblower was still having to think quickly. It would hardly be possible, in any case, to leave at once, the moment dinner was over. It would not be polite. And there was the Countess over there, presumably watching them. If they were to leave now, immediately after conferring together – and breaking an engagement with her – she would be full of suspicion, as well as of the fury of a woman scorned. They simply could not leave immediately.

'We shall have to stay another hour at least,' he said. 'The conventions demand it. Go back and hold the fort for that time.'

'Aye aye, sir.'

Mound restrained himself in the nick of time from coming to attention as with the habit of years he had grown accustomed to do when uttering those words – further proof of the clearness of his head. He nodded and wandered off as if they had been merely discussing the weather, and Hornblower allowed his slow legs to carry him over towards the Countess.

She smiled at his approach.

'Princess,' she said, 'you have not met Commodore Hornblower? The Princess de Stolp.'

Hornblower bowed; the Princess was an elderly woman with a good deal left of what must have been marvellous beauty.

'The Commodore,' went on the Countess, 'has expressed a desire to see the picture gallery. Would you care to come with us, Princess?'

'No, thank you,' said the Princess. 'I fear I am too old for picture galleries. But go, my children, without me.'

'I would not like to leave you alone, here,' protested the Countess.

'Even at my age, I can boast that I am still never left long alone, Countess. Leave me, I beg you. Enjoy yourselves, children.'

Hornblower bowed again, and the Countess took his arm, and they walked slowly out. She pressed his arm, while footmen stood aside to allow them passage.

'The Italian pictures of the Cinque Cento are in the far gallery,' said the Countess as they came into the broad corridor. 'Would you care to see the more modern ones first?'

'As madame wishes,' said Hornblower.

Once through a door, once out of the ceremonial part of the palace, it was like a rabbit warren, narrow passages, innumerable staircases, an infinity of rooms. The apartment to which she led him was on the first floor; a sleepy maid who was awaiting her coming vanished into the room beyond as they came into the luxurious sitting-room. It was into the room beyond that the Countess called him, five minutes later.

XIII

Hornblower turned over in his cot with a groan; the effort of turning brought back the pain into his temples, although he moved very cautiously. He was a fool to have drunk so much – it was the first time he had had this sort of headache for half a dozen years. Yet it had been hard to avoid, just as everything else had been hard to avoid; he did not know what else he could have done, once events had him in their grip. He raised his voice and shouted for Brown – it hurt his head again to shout, and his voice was a hoarse croak. He heard the voice of the sentry at the door passing on the word, and with an infinity of effort he sat up and put his legs out of bed, determined that Brown should not find him prostrate.

'Bring me some coffee,' he said when Brown came in.

'Aye aye, sir.'

Hornblower continued to sit on the edge of his cot. Overhead he heard the raucous voice of Hurst blaring through the skylight, apparently addressing a delinquent midshipman.

'A fine young flibberty-gibbet *you* are,' said Hurst. 'Look at that brasswork! D'you call that bright? Where d'you keep your eyes? What's your division been doing this last hour? God, what's the Navy coming to, when warrants are given to young jackanapes who wouldn't keep their noses clear with a marline-spike! You call yourself a King's officer? You're more like a winter's day, short, dark, and dirty!'

Hornblower took the coffee Brown brought in.

'My compliments to Mr Hurst,' he croaked, 'and ask him kindly not to make so much noise over my skylight.'

'Aye aye, sir.'

The first satisfaction that day was to hear Hurst cut his tirade abruptly short. Hornblower sipped at the scalding coffee with some degree of pleasure. It was not surprising that Hurst should be in a bad temper today. He had been through a harassing evening the night before; Hornblower remembered Hurst and Mound carrying Braun, unconscious and reeking with spirits, into the carriage at the palace door. Hurst had been strictly sober, but apparently the mental strain of keeping guard over a secret assassin in the Czar's palace had been too much for his nerves. Hornblower handed his cup back to Brown to be refilled when Brown reappeared, and pulled his nightshirt over his head as he waited. Something caught his eye as he laid his nightshirt on his cot; it was a flea, leaping high out of the sleeve. In a wave of disgust he looked down at himself; his smooth round belly was pockmarked with flea-bites. That was a striking commentary on the difference between an Imperial palace and one of His Britannic Majesty's ships of the line. When Brown returned with his second cup of coffee Hornblower was still cursing fiercely both at Imperial uncleanness and at the dreary prospect of the nuisance of having to rid himself of vermin to which he was peculiarly susceptible.

'Take that grin off your face,' snapped Hornblower, 'or I'll send you to the grating to see if you grin there!'

Brown was not grinning; all that could be said about his expression was that he was too obviously not grinning. What irritated Hornblower was the knowledge that Brown was enjoying the superior and paternal state of mind of one who has not a headache while the man who is with him has.

His shower-bath restored some of Hornblower's peace of mind, and he put on clean linen, gave Brown orders for the disinfection of his clothes, and went up on deck, where the first person on whom he laid eyes was Wychwood, bleary-eyed and obviously with a far worse headache than he had himself. Yet the keen air of the Russian morning was invigorating and refreshing. The normal early-morning ship's routine, the sight of the rows of men holystoning the decks, the pleasant swish of the water over the planking, were comforting and restorative as well.

'Boat coming off to us, sir,' reported a midshipman to the officer of the watch.

It was the same pinnace as had taken them ashore yesterday, and it brought a naval officer with a letter in French –

His Excellency the Minister of the Imperial Marine presents his compliments to Commodore Sir Hornblower. His Excellency has given orders for a water-boat to be alongside the *Nonsuch* at eleven o'clock this morning.

A distinguished nobleman, M. le Comte du Nord, having expressed a desire to see one of His Britannic Majesty's Ships, His Excellency proposes to trespass upon Sir Hornblower's hospitality by visiting the *Nonsuch* at ten o'clock in company with the Comte du Nord.

Hornblower showed the letter to Wychwood, who confirmed his suspicions.

'That's Alexander,' he said. 'He used the title of Comte du Nord when he was travelling on the continent as Czarevitch. He'll be coming incognito, so that there'll be no need for royal honours.'

'Yes,' said Hornblower dryly, a little nettled at this soldier giving him advice beyond what he was asked for. 'But an Imperial Minister of Marine must rank with a First Lord of the Admiralty. That'll mean nineteen guns and all the other honours. Midshipman of the watch! My compliments to the captain, and I shall be very obliged if he will be good enough to come on deck.'

Bush heard the news with a low whistle, and instantly turned to sweep decks and rigging with his glance, anxious that his ship should be in the perfection of condition for this Imperial visit.

'How can we take in water,' asked Bush piteously, 'and be in a fit state for the Czar to come on board, sir? What will he think of us? Unless we water the flotilla first.'

'The Czar's a man of sense,' said Hornblower, briskly. 'Let's show him the hands at work. He doesn't know the difference between the mizzen-stay and the flying jib-boom, but he'll recognise efficient work if we show it to him. Start watering while he's on board.'

'And the food?' asked Bush. 'We'll have to offer him something, sir.'

Hornblower grinned at his anxiety.

'Yes, we'll offer him something.'

It was typical of Hornblower's contrary temperament that the more difficulties other people foresaw the more cheerful he became; the only person really capable of depressing Hornblower was Hornblower himself. His headache had left him completely, and he was positively smiling now at the thought of a busy morning. He ate his breakfast with appetite, and put on his full-dress uniform once more and came on deck to find Bush still fussing round the ship, with the crew all in clean white frocks and duck trousers, the accommodation ladder rigged, with hand-ropes as white as snow, the marines all pipeclayed and polished, the hammocks stowed in mathematical tiers. It was only when the midshipman of the watch reported a cutter approaching that he felt a little twinge of nervousness, a sudden catch in his breath, at the thought that the next few hours might have a decided bearing on the history of the world for years to come.

The calls of the boatswain's mates shrilled through the ship, and the ship's company fell in by divisions, officers to the front with epaulettes and swords, and Hornblower at the quarterdeck rail looked down at the assembly. British seamen on parade could not possibly rival the Prussian Guard in exactitude and uniformity, and to drill them into any approach to it would be likely to expel from them the very qualities that made them the valuable men they were; but any thinking man, looking down the lines of intelligent, self-reliant faces, could not fail to be impressed.

'Man the yards!' ordered Bush.

Another squeal from the pipes, and the topmen poured up the rigging in an orderly upward torrent, without a break in their speed as they hung back-downward from the futtock-shrouds, going hand-over-hand up the topgallant-shrouds like the trained gymnasts they were, running out along the yards like tight-rope walkers, each man taking up his position on the foot-ropes the moment he reached it.

Various emotions warred in Hornblower's breast as he watched. There was a momentary feeling of resentment that these men of his, the cream of the service, should be put through their paces like performing bears to gratify an Oriental monarch. Yet as the evolution was completed, when each man reached his place, as though by some magic a gust of wind had whirled a heap of dead leaves into the air and left them suspended in a pattern of exquisite symmetry, his resentment was swamped by artistic satisfaction. He hoped that Alexander, looking on, would have the sense to realise that these men could be relied upon to perform the same feat in any conditions, in a black night with a howling gale blowing, on a raging sea with the bowsprit stabbing at the invisible sky and the yardarms dipping towards the invisible sea.

The boatswain, looking with one eye over the starboard rail, gave an infinitesimal jerk of his head. A little procession of officers was coming up the accommodation ladder. The boatswain's mates put their calls to their lips. The sergeant-drummer of marines contrived to snap his fingers beside the seams of his trousers as he stood at attention, and the six side-drums roared out in a bold ruffle.

'Present arms!' bellowed Captain Norman, and the fifty muskets with fixed bayonets of the marines left the fifty scarlet shoulders and came down vertically in front of fifty rows of gleaming buttons, while the swords of the three marine officers swept in the graceful arc of the military salute.

Alexander, followed by two aides-de-camp, came slowly on board side by side with the Minister of Marine to whom nominally all this ceremony was dedicated. He put his hand to his hat-brim while the pipes died away in a final squeal, the drums completed their fourth ruffle, the first gun of the salute banged out forward, and the fifes and drums of the marine band burst into 'Hearts of Oak'. Hornblower walked forward and saluted.

'Good morning, Commodore,' said the Minister of Marine. 'Permit me to present you to the Comte du Nord.'

Hornblower saluted again, his face as expressionless as he could manage it even while he fought down a smile at Alexander's queer liking to be incognito.

'Good morning, Commodore,' said Alexander; with a shock Hornblower realised that he was speaking English of a sort. 'I hope our little visit does not discommode you too much?'

'Not in any way to compare with the honour done to the ship, sir,' said Hornblower, wondering as he said it whether 'sir' was the right way to address a Czar incognito. Apparently it sufficed.

'You may present your officers,' said Alexander.

Hornblower brought them up one by one, and they saluted and bowed with the uneasy stiffness to be expected of junior officers in the presence of a Czar of all the Russias, and an incognito one at that.

'I think you can give orders to prepare the ship for watering now, Captain,' said Hornblower to Bush, and then he turned back to Alexander. 'Would you care to see more of the ship, sir?'

'I would indeed,' said Alexander.

He lingered on the quarterdeck to watch the preparations begin. The topmen came pouring down from aloft; Alexander blinked in the sunlight with admiration as half a dozen hands came sliding down the mizzen-backstays and the mizzen-topsail halliards to land on their feet on the quarterdeck beside him. Under the petty officers' urging the men ran hither and thither about their tasks; it was a scene of activity like a disturbed ants' nest, but far more orderly and purposeful. The hatches were whipped off, the pumps made ready, tackles rigged at the yardarms, fenders dropped over the port side. Alexander stared at the sight of a half-company of marines tailing on to a fall and walking away with it in flat-footed rhythm.

'Soldiers and sailors too, sir,' explained Hornblower, deprecatingly, as he led the way below.

Alexander was a very tall man, an inch or two taller than Hornblower, and he bent himself nearly double as he crouched under the low deck beams below decks and peered about with short-sighted eyes. Hornblower took him forward along the lower gun-deck, where the head clearance was no more than five feet six inches; he showed him the midshipmen's berth, and the warrant officers' mess, all the unlovely details of the life of a sailor. He called away a group of seamen, had them unstow and sling their hammocks, and get into them, so that Alexander could see more clearly what twenty-two inches per man really meant, and he gave a graphic description of a whole deck full of hammocks swinging together in a storm, with the men packed in a solid mass. The grins of the men who made the demonstration were proof enough to Alexander not merely of the truth of what Hornblower was saying, but also of the high spirits of the men, far different from the patient uneducated peasants whom he was accustomed to see in the ranks of his army.

They peered down through the hatchway to see the working party down there breaking out the water casks and preparing the tiers for refilling, and a whiff of the stench of the orlop came up to them – bilgewater and cheese and humanity intermingled.

'You are an officer of long service, I believe, Commodore?' said Alexander.

'Nineteen years, sir,' said Hornblower.

'And how much of that time have you spent at sea?'

'Sixteen years, sir. For nine months I was a prisoner in Spain, and for six months in France.'

'I know of your escape from France. You went through much peril to return to this life.'

Alexander's handsome forehead was wrinkled as he puzzled over the fact that a man could spend sixteen years of his life living in these conditions and still be sane and healthy.

'How long have you held your present rank?'

'As Commodore, sir, only two months. But I have nine years' seniority as Captain.'

'And before that?'

'I was six years lieutenant, and four years midshipman.'

'Four years? You lived four years in a place like the midshipmen's berth you showed me?'

'Not quite as comfortable as that, sir. I was in a frigate nearly all the time, under Sir Edward Pellew. A battleship is not quite as crowded as a frigate, sir.'

Hornblower, watching Alexander closely, could see that he was impressed, and he could guess at the line of thought Alexander was following. The Czar was not so much struck by the miserable conditions of life on board ship – if he knew anything about his people at all he must be aware that nearly all of them lived in conditions a good deal worse – as by the fact that those conditions could train an officer of ability.

'I suppose it is necessary,' sighed Alexander, revealing for a moment the humane and emotional side of his nature which rumour had long hinted that he possessed.

By the time they came on deck again the water-boat was already alongside. Some of the *Nonsuch*'s hands were down on her decks, mingling with the Russians to help with the work. Working parties were swinging away lustily at the pumps, and the long snake-like canvas hoses pulsated at each stroke. Forward they were swaying up bundles of firewood, the men chanting as they hauled.

'Thanks to your generosity, sir,' said Hornblower, 'we will be able to keep the sea for four months if necessary without entering port.'

Luncheon was served in Hornblower's cabin to a party of eight, Hornblower, Bush, the two senior lieutenants, and the four Russians. Bush was sweating with nervousness at the sight of the inhospitable table; at the last moment he had drawn Hornblower aside and pleaded unavailingly for Hornblower to change his mind and serve some of his remaining cabin delicacies as well as the plain ship's fare. Bush could not get out of his mind the obsession that it was necessary to feed the Czar well; any junior officer entertaining an admiral would blast all his hopes of future promotion if he put the men's ration beef on the table, and Bush could only think in terms of entertaining admirals.

The Czar looked with interest at the battered pewter tureen which Brown set before Hornblower.

'Pea soup, sir,' explained Hornblower. 'One of the great delicacies of shipboard life.'

Carlin, of long habit, began to rap his biscuit on the table, stopped when he realised what he was doing, and then started rapping again, guiltily. He remembered the orders Hornblower had given, that everyone should behave as if no distinguished company were present; Hornblower had backed up those orders with the direct threat of punishment should they be forgotten, and Carlin knew that Hornblower did not threaten in that way without every intention of doing what he promised. Alexander looked at Carlin and then inquiringly at Bush beside him.

'Mr Carlin is knocking out the weevils, sir,' explained Bush, almost overcome with self-consciousness. 'If you tap gently they come out of their own accord, this way, you see, sir.'

'Very interesting,' said Alexander, but he ate no bread; one of his aides-de-camp repeated the experiment, peered down at the fat white weevils with black heads that emerged, and exploded into what must have been a string of Russian oaths – almost the first words he had said since boarding the ship.

The visitors, after this inauspicious beginning, gingerly tasted the soup. But in the British Navy pea soup, as Hornblower had remarked, was the best dish served; the aide-de-camp who had sworn at the weevils exclaimed with surprised gratification when he had tasted it, speedily consumed his plateful, and accepted another. There were only three dishes served as the next course, boiled salt ribs of beef, boiled salt-beef tongue, and boiled salt pork, with pickled cabbage to accompany the meat. Alexander studied the three dishes, and wisely accepted the tongue; the Minister of Marine and the aides-de-camp, at Hornblower's suggestion, took a mixed plateful, carved for them by Hornblower and Bush and Hurst. The once silent but now talkative aide-de-camp set himself to chew on the salt beef with a truly Russian appetite and found it a long hard struggle.

Brown was now serving rum.

'The life-blood of the Navy, sir,' said Hornblower, as Alexander studied his tumbler. 'May I offer you gentlemen a toast which we can all drink with the heartiest goodwill? The Emperor of All the Russias! Vive l'Empereur!'

All rose except Alexander to drink the toast, and they were hardly seated before Alexander was on his feet in turn.

'The King of Great Britain.'

The aide-de-camp's French broke down again when he tried to explain how deep an impression Navy rum made on him at this, his first encounter with it. Eventually he gave the clearest proof of his appreciation by draining his tumbler and holding it out for Brown to refill. As the table was cleared Alexander was ready with another toast.

'Commodore Sir Horatio Hornblower, and the British Royal Navy.'

As the glasses were drained Hornblower, looking round him, saw that he was expected to reply in form.

'The Navy,' he said. 'The guardian of the liberties of the world. The unswerving friend, the unremitting enemy. When the tyrant of Europe looks about him, seeking by fair means or foul to extend his dominion, it is the Navy that he finds in his path. It is the Navy which is slowly strangling that tyrant. It is the Navy which has baulked him at every turn, which is draining the life-blood from his boasted Empire and which will bring him down in ruin at the end. The tyrant may boast of un-broken victory on land, but he can only deplore unbroken defeat at sea. It is because of the Navy that every victory only leaves him weaker than before, forced, liked Sisyphus, to roll his rock once more up towards an unattainable summit. And one day that rock will crush him. May it be sooner rather than later!'

Hornblower ended his speech amid a little fierce murmur from the others at the table. He was in an exalted mood again; this present occasion for making a speech had taken him a little by surprise, but he had hoped when he had first heard of the intended visit of the Czar to have an opportunity sometime during the day of calling his attention once more to the aid which the British alliance could afford him. Alexander was young and impressionable. It was necessary to appeal to his emotions as well as to his intellect. Hornblower stole a glance at the Czar to see if he had attained his end; Alexander was sitting rapt in thought, his eyes looking down at the table. He raised them to meet Hornblower's with a smile, and Hornblower felt a wave of exultation, of sublime confidence that his plan had succeeded. He had had plain fare served at luncheon of set purpose; he had shown Alexander exactly how the Navy lived and slept and worked. The Czar could not be ignorant of the British Navy's glory, and Hornblower's intuitive mind told him that proof of the hardship of naval life would be a subtle appeal to the Czar's emotions; it would be hard to explain exactly how it would appeal, but Hornblower was sure of it. Alexander would be moved both to help men who won glory at such a cost and also would desire to have such tough fighters on his side.

Alexander was making a move to leave; the aide-de-camp hurriedly drained his fifth tumbler of rum, and it and its predecessors so worked upon him as to make him put his arm round Bush's shoulders as they came up on the quarterdeck and pat him on the back with wholehearted affection, while the long row of medals and orders on his chest jingled and clinked like tinkers working on pots and kettles. Bush, keenly aware of the eyes of the ship's company upon him, tried to writhe away from the embrace, but unavailingly. He was red in the face as he bawled the order for the manning of the yards, and sighed with evident relief as Alexander's departure down the accommodation ladder made it necessary for the aide-de-camp to follow him.

XIV

An easterly wind was not to be wasted. *Nonsuch* and the flotilla were heading back down the Gulf of Finland with all sail set, and the Commodore was walking the quarterdeck, turning over in his mind all the problems which beset a commander-in-chief. The problem of drinking water at least was settled; it would be two months easily, four months if necessary, before he had to worry about that. The mere fact that he had refilled his water casks would be some sort of justification for his having had dealings with the Court of St Petersburg should Downing Street or Whitehall take exception to his recent activities – Hornblower ran through in his mind the wording of his report, which had laid as much stress on the advantage gained in this fashion as on the desirability of having made contact with the Russian Government. He had a good case to plead. But—

Hornblower turned and looked back at the squadron.

'Make a signal to *Lotus*,' he ordered. ' "Why are you out of station?" '

The flags soared up the halliards, and Hornblower saw the sloop hurriedly correct her position.

'*Lotus* acknowledges the signal, sir,' reported the midshipman.

'Then make, "Why do you not reply to my question?" ' said Hornblower, harshly.

It was some seconds before any reply was visible.

'*Lotus* signals, "Inattention on the part of the officer of the watch", sir.'

'Acknowledge,' said Hornblower.

He had stirred up trouble there; Vickery would be raging at this public censure, and the officer of the watch in question would be regretting his inattention at this very moment. There would be no harm done and probably some good. But Hornblower was perfectly aware that he had only launched the censure because he wanted an excuse to postpone thinking about the next unpleasant matter on which he had to decide. He wondered to himself how many of the other reprimands he had seen dealt out – which he himself had received as a junior officer, for that matter – had been administered by harassed admirals as a distraction from more unpleasant thoughts. He himself had to think about the case of Braun.

The low shore of Finland was just visible to the northward; down on the maindeck Carlin had a division of guns at exercise, the men going through the drill of loading and running out. With the wind almost dead astern and studding-sails set *Nonsuch* was making good speed through the water – if the sea were to get up any more she would have to shorten sail so as to allow the bomb-ketches to keep up. A boatswain's mate forward was starting one of the hands with the foretopsail clewline, something altogether too thick to be used for that purpose. Hornblower was on the point, reluctantly, of interfering with the internal working of the ship when he saw a lieutenant intervene and save him the trouble. Some knowledge of his prejudices and desires had evidently filtered down through Bush to the junior officers. Hornblower watched the trio separate again about their business until there was absolutely no excuse for watching them any longer.

He simply had to think about Braun. The man had attempted to commit murder, and by the laws of England and the Articles of War he should die. But being the holder of a Navy Board warrant, it would call for a court of five post-captains to pass a death sentence on him, and there were not five post-captains within a hundred miles. Bush and Hornblower were the only ones, Vickery and Cole being merely commanders. By law, then, Braun should be kept under arrest until a competent court could be assembled to try him, unless – and here he had discretion – the good of the service, the safety of the ship, or the welfare of England demanded immediate action. In that case he could summon a court composed of whatever senior officers were available, try him, and hang him on the spot. The evidence would be overwhelming; his own and Mound's would suffice to hang Braun ten times over.

The need for summary action was not so apparent, nevertheless. Braun, languishing in the sick bay with a right hand he would never use again, and half dead with loss of blood, was certainly not going to start a mutiny among the hands, or set fire to the ship, or seduce the officers from their duty. But there must be the wildest tales flying round the lower deck already. Hornblower could not imagine how the hands would try to account for Braun being brought back from the Czar's palace badly wounded. There would be talk and gossip which sooner or later would reach the ears of Bonaparte's agents, and Hornblower knew Bonaparte's methods too well to doubt that he would make the utmost use of an opportunity to sow dissension between his enemies. Alexander would never forgive a country which had brought him within a hair's breadth of assassination. When the authorities at home should come to know of the incident they would be furious, and it was he, Hornblower, who would be the object of their fury. Hornblower thought of the report locked in his desk, marked 'Most Secret and Confidential' in which he had put down the facts. He could imagine that report being put in as evidence against him at a court martial, and he could imagine what view his brother captains who would be his judges would take of it.

For a moment Hornblower toyed with the idea of concealing the incident altogether, making no report about it at all, but he put the notion aside as impractical. Someone would talk. On the other hand, there was the clause in his orders which bound him to make the freest use of Braun's experience; that might cover him, and besides, the insertion of that clause implied that Braun had friends in authority who would be interested possibly in protecting him and certainly in protecting themselves, and who in consequence would not wish too public a scandal to be made. It was all very complex.

'Mr Montgomery,' said Hornblower, harshly, 'what sort of course do your quartermasters keep? Have 'em steer smaller than that, or I shall want an explanation from you.'

'Aye aye, sir,' said Montgomery.

At least he had done his part towards dragging Russia into war with Bonaparte – the last word he had received from Wychwood before leaving Kronstadt had been to the effect that Alexander had sent a defiant reply to Bonaparte's latest demands. Should war result, Bonaparte's main strength would have to be employed in the East for this summer, giving Wellington the opportunity to strike a blow in the South. But how much chance had Russia of withstanding the attack Bonaparte could launch against her? Every year for a dozen years had seen a great victory won by Bonaparte, one nation or another overthrown in a few weeks' campaign. Next winter might well see Russia beaten and as subservient to Bonaparte as Austria or Prussia were already; and Downing Street, faced by Russian hostility, would remember her previous dubious neutrality with regret, especially as Bonaparte would undoubtedly take advantage of a Russian defeat to overrun Sweden. So then the whole of Europe, from North Cape to the Dardanelles, would be leagued against England; she would be driven from her meagre foothold in Spain, and left to face the alternatives of continuing a struggle in which there was no prospect of any relief, or making a still more dangerous peace with a tyrant whose malignant ill will could never be appeased. In that case it would not be to any man's credit that he had contributed to the catastrophe of Russia's entry into the war.

Bush had come on deck, clearly sent for by Montgomery as officer of the watch. He was reading the deck log which Montgomery had inscribed on the slate, and he was studying the traverse board. Now he came stumping over to the starboard side of the quarterdeck to touch his hat to Hornblower.

'Reval – Tallinn as those Swedish charts call it, sir – bears south-east twenty-five miles by my reckoning, sir. That point of land to port is the north cape of Naissaar island, however it's pronounced.'

'Thank you, Captain Bush.'

Hornblower even felt the temptation to vent his ill temper on Bush; he could imagine keenly enough how Bush would wilt and the hurt look that would come into his face at a sarcastic gibe at his mispronunciation of foreign names and his selfconsciousness regarding it. Bush was always an easy target, and a satisfactory one from the point of view of readily apparent results. Hornblower dallied with the temptation while Bush stood before him awaiting orders. It was even amusing to keep him waiting like this; Hornblower suspected that Bush was nervously wondering what devilment he had in mind. Then in a wave of reaction Hornblower felt contempt for himself. It was bad enough that Vickery's unknown officer of the watch should at this moment be in trouble because his Commodore was worried about what to do with Braun; it was far worse that the faithful, capable Bush should be suffering mental unhappiness for the same reason.

'Lay a course for Königsberg, Captain Bush, if you please.'

'Aye aye, sir.'

So far did the reaction go that Hornblower went on to explain the motives that guided him in reaching this decision.

'Danzig and Königsberg and East Prussia are Bonaparte's base of operations. The army he has gathered in Poland is supplied by river and canal from there – by the Vistula and the Pregel and the Memel. We're going to see if we can put a spoke on Bonaparte's wheel.'

'Aye aye, sir.'

'I'll put the squadron through general evolutions this morning.'

'Aye aye, sir.'

Bush was simply beaming at this remarkable unbending of his unpredictable chief. He was a long-suffering individual; as second-in-command he would be justified in looking upon it as his right to be admitted to the Commodore's secret's. After all, a stray bullet, a falling spar, a stroke of disease might easily put him in command of the whole force. Yet he remained grateful for any scraps of information which Hornblower condescended to throw to him.

Nonsuch came round on the port tack as Bush and the sailing master decided on what course to steer. She lay over under her pyramids of canvas, the taut weather-rigging harping sharply to the wind, and Hornblower moved over from the starboard side to port, the windward side, as was his right. He looked back at the rest of the squadron, each vessel bracing sharp up in succession, following in the leader's wake, *Lotus* and *Raven*, *Moth* and *Harvey*. *Clam* was not with them – she had been kept at Kronstadt to follow with any news Wychwood might be able to pick up – but five vessels were quite enough to exercise at manoeuvres.

'Bring me the signal book,' ordered Hornblower.

Flags raced up the halliards, each signal a chain of black balls, like beads on a string, until it was broken out, but in the other ships keen eyes were watching through telescopes, reading the flags even before they were broken out, and anxious officers were ordering the replies to be bent on ready to hoist without a moment's delay. The squadron tacked in succession, wore together on a line of bearing, came to the wind again in succession into line ahead. They reduced sail in conformity with the leader – every ship sending every possible hand aloft to get in courses or topgallants the moment Hornblower's intentions became clear – and they made sail again. They reefed topsails, double-reefed them, shook them out again. They hove-to, hoisted out their boats manned with armed boarding parties, and hoisted the boats in again. Resuming their course they opened their ports, ran out their guns, secured them again, and then ran them out and secured them again. A fresh signal mounted *Nonsuch*'s halliards, headed by *Raven*'s number.

'Commodore to Captain. Why did you not obey my order?'

Hornblower's glass had detected that *Raven* had not fully secured her guns – she had not bolted her gun-ports so as to open them more quickly if the order should come, but Hornblower could see the ports opening slightly with the roll of the ship; moreover, judging by the little of the action of the guns' crew that he could see she had not un-coupled and stowed her train-tackles, giving her a clear five seconds' start over the other ships. It was foolish of Cole to try an old trick like that, and one so easily detected; it was right that *Raven's* shame should be proclaimed to the rest of the squadron. Half the object of manoeuvres was to sharpen the captains' wits; if they could manage to outguess the Commodore, well and good, for there would be more likelihood of their outguessing a Frenchman should they meet one.

Raven hastily secured gun-ports and train-tackles; to rub the lesson in Hornblower waited until he was sure the order had just been passed on her decks and then sent up the signal for running out the guns. The counter-order following so quickly upon the order caught *Raven* unready – Hornblower could imagine the cursing officers on her main-deck – and she was seven full seconds behind any other ship in hoisting the 'evolution completed' signal. There was no need to comment on the fact, however – everybody in the *Raven* would be aware of what had happened and a further reprimand might weaken Cole's authority over his ship's company.

It was an active busy morning for all hands in the squadron, and Hornblower, looking back to the time when he was a midshipman, could well imagine the sigh of relief that must have gone round when at noon he signalled for the order of sailing and gave the men a chance to get their dinners. He watched the *Nonsuch's* crew form up to receive their ration of spirits; the eager, skylarking hands each carrying his wooden piggin; the guard over the grog tub – the latter with its painted inscription 'The King, God bless him'; Montgomery and two master's mates watching the issue. Hornblower saw one hand come up to the tub and be indignantly hustled away; evidently he was a defaulter who had been sentenced to lose his ration and who had nevertheless tried to obtain it. Such an attempt would earn a man at least two dozen lashes in some ships, but, judging by Montgomery's actions, it would mean no more than a further deprivation or a spell at the pumps or perhaps a turn at cleaning out the heads.

The liveliness and high spirits of everyone were reassuring. He could rely on these men to fight as desperately as any occasion could demand; equally important, he could rely on them to endure the long tedious days of beating about at sea, the wearisome monotony of life in a ship of the line, without more complaint than one need expect. But he must drop a hint to Bush to see that this happy condition endured. A hornpipe competition – theatricals – something of that sort would be necessary soon, unless there should happen to be enough action to keep the men's minds busy. And with that decision he turned and went below, having managed, as a result of this morning's activity, to drive out of his own mind any worry about what to do with Braun when the latter should recover from his wounds. After all, he might yet die.

Besides, there were the charts of the Frisches Haff and the approaches to Königsberg to study, and plans to be made for assailing Bonaparte's communications in the neighbourhood, should that be possible. If this fair wind should persist he had no more than three days in which to think out some method of attack there. He had the charts got out for him and he pored over them, irritably calling for lamps to light his dim cabin so as to make it possible to read the little figures scattered over them. The soundings were fantastically complex, and the problem of studying them was not made easier by the fact that he had three different charts to study – a Swedish one with the soundings marked in Swedish feet, a new French one with the soundings in metres, and only a sketchy English one in fathoms. It was a toilsome business comparing them, and perfectly unsatisfactory in the end, seeing that they did not agree.

Yet the desirability of striking a blow there was perfectly obvious. In roadless Poland and East Prussia the only way of distributing provisions and munitions to Bonaparte's swelling armies was by water. His main advanced base was Danzig, whence the troops in Central Poland could be supplied by the Vistula. But the large forces in East Prussia and in Eastern Poland were dependent on the other river systems, radiating from Königsberg and Elbing on the Frisches Haff. This Frisches Haff, a long narrow lagoon almost cut off from the Baltic by a long sandspit, would quite obviously be the scene of extensive barge traffic from Elbing to Königsberg. Fifty miles long, a dozen miles wide, shallow – three or four fathoms at most – with the narrow entrance guarded by the guns of the fortress of Pillau, from the French point of view it would be a perfectly safe route for water-borne supplies, sheltered both from storms and from the English. Danzig was the best objective, of course, for a stroke anywhere along this Baltic coast, but Danzig·was safe, several miles from the sea up the Vistula, and heavily fortified to boot. If it took Bonaparte and a hundred thousand men three months to capture Danzig Hornblower was not likely to effect anything against the place with a couple of hundred marines. Danzig was impregnable to him. For that matter, so were Königsberg and Elbing. But it was the communications between them that he wanted to break; no more than that need be done. The wind was fair, too – a Roman would look on that as a good omen.

XV

This was an ideal night in which to reconnoitre the entrance to the Frisches Haff. Overcast, so that not much light came from the summer sky with the sun only just below the horizon, and a strong breeze blowing – the sloop Hornblower had just quitted had single-reefed her topsails earlier in the evening. A strong breeze and a choppy sea meant that there would be far less chance of guard-boats – guard-boats manned by landsmen – rowing a close watch over this boom that Hornblower was setting out to investigate.

But at the same time Hornblower was suffering considerable personal inconvenience from the choppy sea. The cutter in whose sternsheets he sat was rearing and plunging, standing first on her bows and then on her stern, with the spray flying across her in a continuous sheet, so that a couple of hands had to bale all the time. The spray was finding its way remorselessly through the interstices of his boat-cloak, so that he was wet and cold, and the cold and the violent motion inevitably turned his mind towards seasickness. His stomach felt as uneasy as his body felt uncomfortable. In the darkness he could not see Vickery, beside him at the tiller, nor Brown tending the sheet, and he felt a poor sort of relief at the thought that his pallor and uneasiness were not apparent to them. Unlike some victims he had met he could never be seasick unselfconsciously, he told himself bitterly, and then with his usual rasping self-analysis he told himself that that should not surprise him, seeing that he was never unselfconscious at all.

He shifted his position in the stern of the cutter, and clutched his cloak more tightly round him. The Germans and Frenchmen guarding Pillau had as yet no knowledge that an English squadron was so close to them; it was less than an hour ago that he had come up in the darkness with the two sloops, leaving Nonsuch and the bomb-vessels over the horizon. A soft-hearted senior officer in Königsberg might easily hesitate before giving orders that a guard-boat should toilsomely row guard up and down the boom on such a blustery night, and even if the orders were given there was every chance that the petty officer in charge of the boat might shirk his duty – especially as there could not be much love lost between the French who would occupy the higher ranks and the Germans who would fill the lower ones.

A low warning cry came from the lookout in the bows, and Vickery put down his tiller a trifle, bringing the cutter closer to the wind. She rose over a crest, and then as she came down in the trough a dark object appeared close overside, dimly visible in the darkness in a flurry of foam.

'A cable, sir,' reported Vickery. 'An' there's the boom, right ahead.'

On the heaving surface of the sea just ahead could be seen a faint hint of blackness.

'Lay me alongside it,' said Hornblower, and Vickery turned up into the wind, and at his shouted order the lugsail came down and the cutter ranged herself against the boom. The wind was blowing not quite along it, so that there was a tiny lee on their side of the boom; on the far side the steep waves broke against it with a roar, but on this side the surface for a narrow space was smooth although covered with foam that reflected what little light made its way from the dark sky. The bowmen had hooked on to the cable just where it was secured to the boom.

Hornblower put off his cloak and left himself exposed to the spray which hurtled at him, poised himself for a leap, and sprang for the boom. As he landed on it a wave broke across it, sousing him to the skin, and he had to clutch desperately with fingers and toes to save himself from being washed off. He was riding an enormous tree trunk, floating on the surface with very little of itself exposed above the surface. With the best timber country in Europe to draw upon, and easy water transport available, it was, of course, certain that the French would select the heaviest trees possible to guard the entrance to the port. He clawed his way on all fours along the log, balancing in nightmare fashion on his pitching and rolling mount. An active topman, or Vickery for that matter, would probably walk upright, but then Hornblower wanted the evidence of his own senses regarding the boom, not a report at secondhand. The cable, when he reached it, was the largest he had ever seen in his life – a thirty-inch cable at least; the largest cable *Nonsuch* carried was only nineteen inches. He felt about the log with inquiring fingers while the icy water soused him to the ears, and found what he was expecting to find, one of the chain cables that attached this log to the next. It was a two-inch chain cable with a breaking strain of a hundred tons or so, heavily stapled down to the log, and further search immediately revealed another one. Presumably there were others below the surface, making four or five altogether. Even a ship of the line, charging down full tilt before the wind, would be hardly likely to break that boom, but would only cause herself desperate underwater damage. Peering through the spray, he could see the end of the next log and its cable; the gap was some ten feet only. The wind, blowing almost lengthwise along the boom,· had pushed it down to leeward as far as the cables would allow, boom and cables making a herring-bone with the cables as taut as could be.

Hornblower clawed his way back down the trunk, poised himself, and leaped for the boat. In the darkness, with the irregular motion of boom and boat in the choppy sea, it was hard to time the moment to jump, and he landed awkwardly across the gunwale with one leg in the sea, and Vickery hauled him into the boat without much dignity left him.

'Let her drop down to leeward,' ordered Hornblower. 'I want soundings taken at every log.'

Vickery handled the boat well. He kept her bows to the wind after shoving off, and with a couple of oars pulling steadily he manoeuvred her past each cable as the boat drifted to leeward. Brown stood amidships, balancing himself against the boat's extravagant plunges, while he took soundings with the awkward thirty-foot sounding pole. It called for a powerful man to handle that thing in this wind, but properly used it was quicker and far less noisy than a hand lead. Four fathoms – three and a half – four – the boom was laid right across the fairway, as was only to be expected. At the windward end it was not more than a couple of hundred yards – a cable's length – from the beach at Pillau, and Hornblower, staring into the night, more than suspected a supplementary boom from that shore which, overlapping this one, would compel any vessel entering to go about so as to make the turn. That meant that any ship trying to enter with hostile intentions would be sunk or set afire for certain by the heavy guns in Pillau.

They reached the leeward end of the boom; a stretch of clear water extended from here towards the sandspit – the Nehrung, to use the curious German word for it – which divided the Haff from the Baltic for twenty miles. The open stretch must be a quarter of a mile wide, but it was useless for navigation. Brown's pole recorded a depth of ten feet for a couple of soundings, and then the water shallowed to no more than six or eight.

Vickery put his hand on Hornblower's arm and pointed to the land. There was a nucleus of greater darkness there – a guard-boat beating out through the shallows to keep watch over the boom.

'Out oars,' said Hornblower. 'Get out to sea.'

There were thrum mats round the looms of the oars to muffle the noise they made against the thole-pins; the men put their backs into their work, and the cutter crept out to sea as the guard-boat continued its course. When the two boats were far enough apart for the sail to be invisible Hornblower gave orders for the lug to be set and they began the beat back to *Lotus*, with Hornblower shivering uncontrollably in his wet clothes, bitterly ashamed though he was that Vickery should be aware that his Commodore should shiver on account of a mere wet jacket which any tough seaman would think nothing of. It was irritating, though it was no more than was to be expected, that the first attempt to find *Lotus* in the darkness should be unsuccessful, and the cutter had to go about and reach to windward on the other tack before at last they picked up the loom of her in the night. When her hail reached their ears Brown made a speaking-trumpet of his hands.

'Commodore!' he shouted, and Vickery turned the cutter into the *Lotus*'s lee, and Hornblower went up the sloop's low side as the two came together. On the quarterdeck Vickery turned to him for orders.

'Haul up and make an offing, Mr Vickery,' said Hornblower. 'Make sure *Raven* follows us. We must be out of sight of land by dawn.'

Down in Vickery's tiny cabin, stripping off his wet clothes, with Brown hovering round him, Hornblower tried to make his dulled mind work on the problem before him. Brown produced a towel and Hornblower rubbed a little life into his chilled limbs. Vickery knocked and entered, coming, as soon as he had seen his ship on her proper course, to see that his Commodore had all that he needed. Hornblower straightened up after towelling his legs and hit his head with a crash against the deck beams; in this small sloop there was hardly more than five feet clearance. Hornblower let out an oath.

'There's another foot of headroom under the skylight, sir,' said Vickery, diplomatically.

The skylight was three feet by two, and standing directly beneath it Hornblower could just stand upright, and even then his hair brushed the skylight. And the lamp swung from a hook on a deck beam beside the aperture; an incautious movement on Hornblower's part brought his bare shoulder against it so that warm stinking oil ran out of the receiver on to his collarbone. Hornblower swore again.

'There's hot coffee being brought to you, sir,' said Vickery.

The coffee when it came was of a type which Hornblower had not tasted for years – a decoction of burnt bread with the merest flavouring of coffee – but at least it was warming. Hornblower sipped it and handed back the cup to Brown, and then took his dry shirt from the breech of the twelve-pounder beside him and struggled into it.

'Any further orders, sir?' asked Vickery.

'No,' replied Hornblower heavily; his head poked forward to make sure it did not hit the deck beams again. He tried to keep the disappointment and the bad temper out of his voice, but he feared he had not succeeded. It irked him to have to admit that there was no chance of any successful attempt against the Frisches Haff, and yet prudence, common sense, his whole instinct dictated such a decision. There was no breaking that boom, and there was no going round it, not in any of the vessels under his command. He remembered bitterly his unnecessary words to Bush about the desirability of raiding this area from the sea. If ever he needed a lesson in keeping his mouth shut he was receiving one now. The whole flotilla was expecting action, and he was going to disappoint them, sail away without doing anything at all. In future he would double lock his jaws, treble curb his unruly tongue, for if he had not talked so lightheartedly to Bush there would not be nearly so much harm done; Bush, in the absence of orders to the contrary, would naturally have discussed the future with his officers, and hope would be running high – everyone was expecting great things of the bold Hornblower (said he to himself with a sneer) whose reputation for ingenious daring was so tremendous.

Unhappy, he went back again over the data. At the sandspit end of the boom there was water enough for a flotilla of ship's boats to pass. He could send in three or four launches, with four-pounders mounted in the bows and with a hundred and fifty men on board. There was not much doubt that at night they could run past the boom, and, taking everyone in the lagoon by surprise, could work swift havoc on the coasting trade. Very likely they could destroy thousands of tons of shipping. But they would never get out again. The exit would be watched far too carefully; the batteries would be manned day and night, gunboats would swarm round the end of the boom, and even gunboats manned by landsmen, if there were enough of them, would destroy the flotilla. His squadron could ill afford to lose a hundred and fifty trained seamen – one-tenth of the total ships' complements – and yet a smaller force might well be completely wasted.

No; no destruction of coasters would be worth a hundred and fifty seamen. He must abandon the idea; as if symbolical of that decision he began to pull on the dry trousers Vickery had provided for him. And then, with one leg in and one leg out, the idea suddenly came to him, and he checked himself, standing in his shirt with his left leg bare and his right leg covered only from ankle to knee.

Mr Vickery,' he said, 'let's have those charts out again.'

'Aye aye, sir,' said Vickery.

There was eagerness and excitement in his voice at once, echoing the emotion which must have been obvious in Hornblower's tone – Hornblower took notice of it, and as he buckled his waistband he reaffirmed his resolution to be more careful how he spoke, for he must regain his reputation as a silent hero. He stared down at the charts which Vickery spread for him – he knew that Vickery was studying his face, and he took great care to show no sign whatever of reaching a decision one way or the other. When his mind was made up he said 'Thank you', in the flattest tone he could contrive, and then, suddenly remembering his most noncommittal exclamation, he cleared his throat.

'Ha – h'm,' he said, without any expression at all, and, pleased with the result, he repeated it and drew it out longer still, 'Ha-a-a-a-h'm.'

The bewildered look in Vickery's face was a great delight to him.

Next morning, back in his own cabin in *Nonsuch*, he took a mild revenge in watching the faces of his assembled captains as he laid the scheme before them. One and all, they thirsted for the command, hotly eager to risk life and liberty on a mission which might at first sight seem utterly harebrained. The two commanders yearned for the chance of promotion to post rank; the lieutenants hoped they might become commanders.

'Mr Vickery will be in command,' said Hornblower, and had further opportunity of watching the play of emotion over the faces of his audience. But as in this case everyone present had a right to know why he had been passed over, he gave a few words of explanation.

'The two captains of the bomb-vessels are irreplaceable; there are no other lieutenants with us who can use their infernal machines as well as they can. I don't have to explain to you why Captain Bush is irreplaceable. It was Mr Vickery who happened to go with me to investigate the boom, and so he happens to know more about the situation than Mr Cole, who's the other obvious candidate for the command.'

There was no harm in soothing Cole's feelings with an excuse like that, for no good end would be served by letting people guess that he would not trust Cole with any command out of his sight – poor old Cole, grey-haired and bowed, almost too old for his work, hoping against hope for promotion to captain. Hornblower had an uneasy feeling that Cole saw through the excuse, and had to comfort himself with the trite thought that no war can be fought without someone's feelings being hurt. He passed on hurriedly to the next point.

'Having settled that question, gentlemen, I would welcome your views on who else should go as Mr Vickery's subordinates. Mr Vickery first, as he is most concerned.'

When those details were settled the next step was to prepare the four boats for the expedition – *Nonsuch*'s launch and cutter, and the cutters from *Lotus* and *Raven*. A four-pounder in the eyes of the launch, a three-pounder in the eyes of each of the cutters; food, water, ammunition, combustibles for setting captures on fire. The crews that had been told off for the expedition were paraded and inspected, the seamen with pistols and cutlasses, the marines with muskets and bayonets. At the end of the day Vickery came back on board *Nonsuch* for a final confirmation of the future rendezvous.

'Good luck,' said Hornblower.

'Thank you, sir,' said Vickery.

He looked frankly into Hornblower's eyes.

'I have so much to thank you for, sir,' he added.

'Don't thank me, thank yourself,' said Hornblower testily.

He found it particularly irksome to be thanked for risking young Vickery's life. He calculated to himself that if he had married as a midshipman he might by now be the father of a son just Vickery's age.

At nightfall the squadron stood in towards the land. The wind was backing northerly a little, but it was still blowing a strong breeze, and although the night was not quite as overcast as the preceding one, there was every chance that the boats would slip through unobserved. Hornblower watched them go, just as two bells struck in the middle watch, and as they vanished into the greyness he turned away. Now he would have to wait. It interested him to discover once more that he would genuinely and sincerely have preferred to be in action himself, that he would rather be risking life and limb and liberty there in the Frisches Haff than be here safe at sea with nothing to do but await results. He looked on himself as a coward; he dreaded mutilation and he disliked the thought of death only less than that, so that it was a matter of peculiar interest to find that there were some things he disliked even more than danger. When a long enough time had elapsed for the boats to have passed the boom – or for them to have fallen into the hands of the enemy – Hornblower went below to rest for the brief interval before dawn, but he could only pretend to sleep, he could only hold himself down in his cot and prevent himself by sheer mental effort from tossing and turning. It was a positive relief to go out on the half-deck again when the sky began to grow lighter, to souse himself under the head-pump, and then to go up on the quarterdeck and drink coffee there, glancing the while over the starboard quarter where (with the ship hove-to on the port tack) lay Pillau and the entrance to the Haff.

The growing daylight revealed it all through Hornblower's glass. At random cannon-shot lay the yellow and green headland on which Pillau was set; the twin church steeples were clearly visible. The line of the boom showed up, lying across the entrance, marked by breaking waves and occasionally a glimpse of dark timber. Those dark mounds above the water's edge must be the batteries thrown up there to defend the entrance. On the other side lay the long line of the Nehrung, a yellowish green line of sandhills, rising and falling with minute variations of altitude as far as the eye could see, and beyond. But through the entrance there was nothing to see at all, nothing except grey water, flecked here and there with white where the shoals dotted the lagoon. The opposite shore of the Haff was too distant to be visible from the deck.

'Captain Bush,' ordered Hornblower, 'would you please be good enough to send an officer with good eyes to the masthead with a glass?'

'Aye aye, sir.'

Hornblower watched the young lieutenant dashing up the rigging, moving as fast as he could with his Commodore's eye on him, hanging back downward as he scaled the futtock-shrouds, going hand over hand up the topgallant-shrouds. Hornblower knew that in his present condition he could not do that without resting in the maintop for a space, and he also knew that his eyes were not as good as they were – not as good as the lieutenant's. He watched the lieutenant settle himself at the topgallant masthead, adjust his glass, and sweep the horizon, and he waited impatiently for a report. Unable to wait longer he grabbed his speaking-trumpet.

'Masthead, there! What do you see of the shore inside?'

'Nothing, sir. It's too hazy to see plain. But I can see no sails, sir.'

Maybe the garrison was laughing up their sleeves at him. Maybe the boats had fallen straight into their hands, and now they were amusing themselves watching the squadron beginning an endless wait for any further sight of the lost boats and seamen. Hornblower refused to allow himself to be pessimistic. He set himself to picture the state of affairs in the batteries and in the town, when the dawn revealed a British squadron lying-to just out of range. How the drums would beat and trumpets peal, as the troops were hurriedly turned out to guard against a possible landing. That was what must be going on at this very moment. The garrison, the French governor, must be still unaware as yet that wolves had slipped into their sheepfold, that British boat crews had penetrated into the waters of the Haff where no enemy had been seen since Danzig fell to the French five years back. Hornblower tried to comfort himself with thought of all the additional bustle that would develop as soon as the situation disclosed itself to the enemy; the messengers that would gallop with warnings, the gunboats that would be hastily warned, the coasters and barges which would seek the shelter of the nearest batteries – if batteries there were; Hornblower was willing to bet that there was none between Elbing and Königsberg, for none had been necessary so far.

'Masthead! Can't you see anything inshore?'

'No, sir – yes, sir. There's gunboats putting out from the town.'

Hornblower could see those himself, a flotilla of small two-masted vessels, rigged with the sprit-mainsails usual to small Baltic craft, putting out from Elbing. They were a little like Norfolk wherries. Presumably they each carried one heavy gun, a twenty-four-pounder possibly, mounted right up in the eyes of the boat. They anchored at intervals in the shoal water, obviously as a further protection to the boom in case of an attempt upon it. Four of them moved right across and anchored to guard the shallows between the boom and the Nehrung – not exactly locking the stable door after the horse had been stolen, decided Hornblower, rejecting the simile after it came to his mind; they were locking the stable door to prevent the thief getting out, if they knew as yet (which was highly doubtful) that there was a thief inside. The haziness was fast clearing; overhead the sky was almost blue and a watery sun was showing through.

'Deck, there! If you please, sir, there's a bit of smoke in sight now, right up the bay. Can't see more than that, sir, but it's black smoke and might be from a burning ship.'

Bush, measuring with his eye the dwindling distance between the ship and the boom, was giving orders to brace up and work a trifle farther out to sea again, and the two sloops conformed to the *Nonsuch*'s movements. Hornblower wondered whether or not he had put too much trust in young Mound with the bomb-ketches. Mound had an important rendezvous for next morning; with the *Moth* and the *Harvey* he was out of sight below the horizon. So far the garrison of Elbing had seen only the three British ships, and did not know of the existence of the ketches. That was well – as long as Mound carried out his orders correctly. Or a gale might blow up, or a shift of the wind might raise too much of a surf for the project Hornblower had in mind. Hornblower felt anxiety surge upon him. He had to force himself to relax, to appear composed. He permitted himself to walk the deck, but slowed down his nervous strides to a casual saunter.

'Deck, there! There's more smoke inshore, sir. I can see two lots of it, as if there were two ships on fire now.'

Bush had just given orders to back the maintopsail again, and as the ship hove-to he came across to Hornblower.

'It looks as if Vickery has caught something, doesn't it, sir?' he said, smiling.

'Let's hope so,' answered Hornblower.

There was no sign of any anxiety in Bush's expression; his craggy face denoted nothing more than fierce satisfaction at the thought of Vickery loose amidst the coasting trade. His sublime confidence began to reassure Hornblower until the latter suddenly realised that Bush was not really paying consideration to circumstances. Bush knew that Hornblower had planned this attack, and that was enough for him. In that case he could imagine no possibility of failure, and Hornblower found it profoundly irritating that this should be the case.

'Deck, there! There's two small sail heading across the bay close-hauled for the town. And I can't be sure yet, sir, but I think the second one is our cutter.'

'Our cutter it is, sir!' yelled another voice. Every idle hand in the ship was perched by now at the mastheads.

'That'll be Montgomery,' said Bush. He had fitted the toe of his wooden leg into the ring-bolt of the aftermost carronade tackle so that he could stand without effort on the gently heaving deck.

'She's caught her, sir!' yelled the voice from the masthead. 'Our cutter's caught her!'

'That's one lot of beef and bread that Boney won't get,' said Bush.

Very heavy destruction of the coastal shipping in the Haff might be some compensation for the loss of a hundred and fifty prime seamen. But it would be hard to convince Their Lordships of the Admiralty of that, if there was no certain evidence of the destruction.

'Deck, there! The two sail are parting company. Our cutter's going off before the wind. The other has her mains'l brailed up, I think, sir. Looks to me as if—'

The lieutenant's report terminated abruptly in mid-sentence.

'There she goes!' yelled another voice, and at the same moment there came a cheer from everyone aloft.

'She's blown up!' shouted the lieutenant, forgetting in his excitement even to add 'sir' to his words when addressing his Commodore. 'There's a pillar of smoke as high as a mountain! You can see it from the deck, I think.'

They certainly could – a mushroom-topped pillar of smoke, black and heavy, apparent as it reached above the horizon. It lasted a perceptible time before the wind blew it into strange ragged shapes and then dispersed it utterly.

'That wasn't beef and bread, by God!' said Bush, pounding his left palm with his right fist. 'That was powder! A bargeload of powder! Fifty tons of powder, by God!'

'Masthead! What of the cutter?'

'She's all right, sir. Doesn't look as if the explosion harmed her. She's hull-down from here already, sir.'

'Off after another one, please God,' said Bush.

The destruction of a powder barge was the clearest possible proof that Bonaparte was using the inland water route for the transport of military stores. Hornblower felt he had achieved something, even though Whitehall might not be fully convinced, and he found himself smiling with pleasure. He suppressed the smile as soon as he was aware of it, for his dignity demanded that triumph should leave him as unmoved as uncertainty.

'It only remains to get Vickery and the men out tonight, sir,' said Bush.

'Yes, that is all,' said Hornblower, as woodenly as he could manage.

The blowing up of the powder barge was the only sure proof they had that day in the *Nonsuch* of success in the Haff, although more than once the lookouts hesitatingly reported smoke on the horizon inside. As evening came on another string of gunboats made their appearance, from Königsberg presumably, and took up their stations along the boom. A column of troops could be seen for a space, too, the horizontal lines of blue coats and white breeches clearly visible even from the deck as they marched in to strengthen the defences of Pillau. The entrance into the Haff was going to be stoutly defended, obviously, if the British should attempt a coup de main.

In the evening Hornblower came up from below, where he had been making pretence at eating his dinner, and looked round him again although his senses had been so alert in his cabin that his glance told him nothing he did not know already. The wind was moderating with the dying of the day; the sun was on the point of setting, although there would be daylight for a couple of hours more at least.

'Captain Bush, I'd be obliged if you would send your best gun pointers to the lower gundeck starboard-side guns.'

'Aye aye, sir.'

'Have the guns cleared away and run out, if you please. Then I would like it if you would allow the ship to drop down within range of the batteries there. I want to draw their fire.'

'Aye aye, sir.'

Pipes twittered round the ship; bosun and bosun's mates roared out orders, and the hands ran to their stations. A long earthquake-tremor shook the ship as the massive twenty-four-pounders of the lower gun-deck ran thunderously out.

'Please see that the gun-captains are certain what their target is,' said Hornblower.

He knew how limited was the view afforded a man on the lower deck, looking through a gun-port only a yard or so above the water's edge, and he did not want the enemy to jump to the conclusion that the feint he was about to make was no more than a feint. The hands at the maintopsail lee brace, walking smartly down the deck, swung the big sail round and *Nonsuch* came to the wind and slowly gathered way.

'Port a little,' said Bush to the helmsman. 'Let her fall off. Meet her there! Steady as you go!'

'Steady as you go, sir,' echoed the helmsman, and then by a neat feat of facial gymnastics transferred his quid from his cheek to his mouth, and a moment later spat accurately into the spit-kid beside the wheel without transferring any of his attention from the leech of the maintopsail and the compass in the binnacle.

Nonsuch edged down steadily towards the entrance and the batteries. This was a ticklish business, coming down to be shot at. There was smoke as from a fire visible not far from the batteries; maybe it was merely rising from the cooking stoves of the garrison, but it might well be smoke from the furnaces for heating red-hot shot. But Bush was aware of that possibility when in action against coastal batteries, and had needed no warning. Every available man was standing by with fire buckets, and every pump and hose was rigged. Now he was measuring the range with his eye.

'A little closer, if you please, Captain Bush,' said Hornblower to prompt him, for to Hornblower it was obvious that they were still out of range. A fountain of water was visible for a moment on the surface of the choppy sea, two cables' lengths from the starboard bow.

'Not near enough yet, Captain Bush,' said Hornblower.

In the tense silence the ship moved on. A whole cluster of fountains sprang suddenly into existence close under the starboard quarter, one so close indeed that a hatful of water, flung by some freak wave and wind, hit Bush full in the face.

'God damn it to hell,' spluttered Bush, wiping his eyes.

That battery had no business to have come so close as that with that salvo. And there was no smoke near it either. Hornblower traversed his glass round, and gulped. It was another battery altogether which had fired, one farther to the left, and moreover one whose existence he had not suspected until that moment. Apparently the grass had grown over the parapets sufficiently to conceal it from quite close inspection; but it had unmasked itself a trifle too soon. If the officer commanding there had been patient for another ten minutes *Nonsuch* might have found herself in a difficult situation.

'That will do, Captain Bush,' said Hornblower.

'Full and by,' said Bush to the helmsman and then raised his voice. 'Lee braces, there!'

Nonsuch swung round, turning her starboard broadside towards the batteries, and, close-hauled, was now edging towards them far less rapidly. Hornblower pointed out the exact situation of the newly revealed battery to the midshipman of the watch, and then sent him flying below to carry the information to the guns.

'Keep your luff!' growled Bush to the helmsman.

'Keep your luff, sir.'

For a moment or two there were waterspouts leaping from the surface of the sea all round, and the loud noise of cannonballs passing through the air assaulted their ears. It was remarkable that they were not hit; at least, it was remarkable until Hornblower, glancing up, saw two elliptical holes in the mizzen-topsail. The shooting was poor, for there were at least twenty heavy guns firing at them, as Hornblower calculated from the smoke appearing on shore. He took careful note of the sites of the batteries – one never knew when such intelligence might be useful.

'Open fire, Captain, if you please,' said Hornblower, and before the polite ending of the sentence had passed his lips Bush had raised his speaking-trumpet and was repeating the order at the top of his lungs. The gunner's mate posted at the main hatchway relayed the message to the lower gundeck. There was a brief pause which Hornblower noted with pleasure, because it showed that the gun-captains were taking pains to train their guns on the target, and not merely jerking the lanyards the moment the word reached them. Then came a ragged crash; the ship trembled, and the smoke surged up and blew away to leeward. Through his glass Hornblower could see sand flying all round the masked battery. The seventeen twenty-four-pounders roared out again and again, the deck vibrating under Hornblower's feet with the concussion and with the rumble of the gun-tracks.

'Thank you, Captain Bush,' said Hornblower, 'you can put the ship about, now.'

Bush blinked at him momentarily, his fighting blood roused so that he had to stop and think before dealing with the new order.

'Aye aye, sir.' He raised his trumpet. 'Cease fire! Stand by to go about!'

The order was relayed to the guns, and the din died down abruptly, so that Bush's 'Hard-a-lee,' to the helmsman sounded unnecessarily loud.

'Mainsail haul!' bellowed Bush.

As *Nonsuch* went ponderously about, rising to an even keel with her canvas slatting, a further cluster of waterspouts, grouped closely together for the first time, rose from the surface of the sea on the starboard bow. If she had not made the sudden turn the shots might well have hit her. Hornblower might be a mutilated corpse lying on the quarterdeck with his guts strung out beside him at this moment.

Nonsuch had passed the wind, and the after sails were filling.

'Let go and haul!' yelled Bush. The forward sails filled as the hands came aft with the lee braces, and *Nonsuch* settled down on the new tack.

'Any further orders, sir?' asked Bush.

'That will do for the present.'

Close-hauled on the starboard tack the ship was drawing away fast from the land, beating out to where the two sloops were backing and filling while waiting for her. The people on shore must be exulting over having driven off a serious attack; probably some garrulous gunner was swearing that he had seen with his own eyes damaging hits striking home on the British intruder. They must be encouraged in the belief that something desperate was still being meditated in this neighbourhood.

'Midshipman?' said Hornblower.

Strings of coloured flags soared up *Nonsuch*'s halliards; it was good practice for the signal midshipman to try to spell out, 'The curfew tolls the knell of parting day', with the fewest possible number of flag hoists. With his telescope pointed the midshipman read off *Raven*'s reply.

'The—' he read '1 – o – w – must be "blowing". No, it's "lowing", whatever he means by that. H – e – r – d. Herd. Two – five. That's "wind", and "s". That's "winds". S – 1 – o –'

So Cole in the *Raven* was at least familiar with Gray's Elegy, and whoever was responsible for the flag hoists on board her was ingenious enough to use the code hoist for 'winds'. As Hornblower expected, he used the code hoist 'lee' for 'lea' as well, thereby saving one signal flag.

'The lowing herd winds slowly o'er the lee, sir,' reported the puzzled midshipman.

'Very good. Acknowledge.'

All these innumerable signals between battleship and sloops must be visible from the shore and exciting their interest. Hornblower sent up another signal under *Lotus*'s number – 'The ploughman homeward plods his weary way,' – only to receive the puzzled reply, 'Signal not understood'. Purvis, the first lieutenant of the *Lotus*, at present in command, was obviously not very bright, or perhaps not very well read.

What in the world, at that rate, he was making of all this, was beyond even Hornblower's imagination, although the thought of it brought a smile to his lips.

'Cancel the signal, then,' he ordered, 'and substitute "Report immediately number of red-haired married men on board".'

Hornblower waited until the reply came; he could have wished that Purvis had not been so literal-minded and had been able to think up an answer which should combine the almost incompatible qualities of deference and wit, instead of merely sending the bald reply 'Five'. Then he turned to business.

'Signal to both sloops,' he ordered. ' "Advance on boom in threatening manner avoiding action".'

In the dwindling daylight he watched the two vessels move down as though to attack. They wheeled, edged into the wind, and fell away again. Twice Hornblower saw a puff of smoke and heard, echoing over the water, the dull flat boom of a twenty-four-pounder as a gunboat tried the range. Then, while there was just light enough for the signal to be read, he hoisted, 'Discontinue the action after half an hour'. He had done all he could to attract the enemy's attention to this end of the bay, the only exit. The garrison ought to be quite certain now that the raiding boats would attempt to escape by this route. Probably the garrison would anticipate a rush in the first light of dawn, assisted by an attack by the big ships from outside. He had done all he could, and it only remained now to go to bed and spend the rest of the night in tranquillity if that were possible.

Naturally, it was impossible, with the fate of a hundred and fifty seamen at stake, with his own reputation for good fortune and ingenuity at stake. Half an hour after he had got into bed Hornblower found himself wishing that he had ordered three junior officers to join him in a game of whist until dawn. He dallied with the idea of getting up and doing so now, but put it aside in the certainty that if he should do so now everyone would know that he had tried to go to sleep and had failed. He could only turn over stoically and force himself to stay in bed until dawn came to release him.

When he came on deck the pearly mist of the Baltic morning was making the vague outline of visible objects vaguer yet. There was every promise of a fine day, wind moderate, backing a little. Bush was already on deck – Hornblower knew that, before he went up, because he had heard Bush's wooden leg thumping over his head – and at first sight of him Hornblower hoped that his own face did not show the same signs of sleeplessness and anxiety. They had at least the effect of bracing him up to conceal his own anxiety as he returned Bush's salute.

'I hope Vickery's all right, sir,' said Bush.

The mere fact that Bush ventured to address Hornblower at this time in the morning after so many years of service under him was the best possible proof of his anxiety.

'Oh yes,' said Hornblower, bluffly. 'I'll trust Vickery to get out of any scrape.'

That was a statement made in all sincerity; it occurred to Hornblower as he made it – what he had often thought before – that worry and anxiety were not really connected with the facts of the case. He had done everything possible. He remembered his profound study of the charts, his careful reading of the barometer, his painstaking – and now clearly successful – attempts to predict the weather. If he were compelled to bet, he would bet that Vickery was safe, and moreover he would judge the odds to be at least three to one. But that did not save him from being anxious, all the same. What did save him was the sight of Bush's nervousness.

'With this breeze there can't have been much surf, sir,' said Bush.

'Of course not.'

He had thought of that fifty times at least during the night, and he tried to look as if it had not been more than once. The mist was thin enough now to make the land just visible; the gunboats were still stationed along the boom, and he could see a belated guard-boat rowing along it.

'The wind's fair for the bomb-ketches, sir,' said Bush. 'They ought to have picked Vickery up by now and be on their way towards us.'

'Yes.'

Bush turned a searching eye aloft to make sure that the lookouts were at their posts and awake. It was twelve miles down the Nehrung, the long spit of sand that divided the Haff from the Baltic, that Mound with the bomb-ketches was going to pick up Vickery and his men. Vickery was going to land in the darkness on the Nehrung, abandon his boats, cross the sandspit, and rendezvous with Mound an hour before dawn. With their shallow draught the ketches would be safe among the shoals, so that they could send in their boats and bring Vickery off. Vickery's four ship's boats would all be lost, but that was a small price to pay for the destruction he must have caused, and Hornblower hoped that, what with the distraction of his own demonstrations off Pillau, and what with the fact that the possibility of Vickery abandoning his boats might easily never occur to the enemy's mind, Vickery would find no opposition on the Nehrung. Even if there were, the Nehrung was fifteen miles long and Vickery with a hundred and fifty determined men could be relied upon to break through any thin cordon of sentries or customs officials.

Yet if all had gone well the bomb-ketches ought to be in sight very soon. The next few minutes would be decisive.

'We couldn't have heard gunfire in the bay yesterday, sir,' said Bush, 'the wind being where it was. They may have met with any sort of armed vessel in the bay.'

'So they may,' said Hornblower.

'Sail ho!' yelled the masthead lookout. 'Two sail on the port beam! It's the bomb-ketches, sir.'

They might possibly be coming back, having been unable to pick up Vickery, but it was unlikely that in that case they would have returned so promptly. Bush was grinning broadly, with all his doubts at an end.

'I think, Captain,' said Hornblower, 'you might put the helm down and go to meet them.'

It would not be consonant with the dignity of a Commodore to hang out a signal of inquiry as the vessels closed to visual range, for it to be read the moment a telescope in the *Harvey* could distinguish the flags. But *Nonsuch* was making a good five knots, with the water lapping cheerfully under her bows, and *Harvey* was doing the same, so that it was only a matter of waiting a few more minutes.

'*Harvey*'s signalling, sir,' reported the midshipman. He read the flags and hurriedly referred to the code book, ' "seamen on board", sir.'

'Very good. Make, "Commodore to Captain. Come on board with Mr Vickery to make your report".'

There was not much longer to wait. As the two vessels came within hail they rounded-to, and *Harvey*'s gig dropped into the water and came bobbing across to *Nonsuch*. It was a weary Vickery who came up the side with Mound beside him; his face was grey, and below his eyes were marks like new scars as proof that he had not slept for three successive nights. He sat down gratefully when Hornblower gave him permission to do so as soon as they were in his cabin.

'Well?' said Hornblower. 'I'll hear you first, Vickery.'

'It went off very well, sir.' Vickery dragged a scrap of paper out of his pocket on which apparently he had kept notes. 'There was no trouble going past the boom on the night of the 15th. We saw nothing of the enemy. At dawn on the 16th we were off the mouth of the Königsberg river. There we took and destroyed the – the *Fried Rich*, coaster, of Elbing, about two hundred tons, seven of a crew, with a cargo of rye and live pigs. We burned her, and sent the crew ashore in their own boat. Then we caught the – the – *Blitzer*, also of Elbing, about one hundred tons, laden with grain. We burned her, too. Then the *Charlotte*, of Danzig. She was ship-rigged, four hundred tons, twenty-five crew, laden with general cargo of military stores – tents, stretchers, horseshoes, ten thousand stand of small arms; we burned her. Then the *Ritter Horse*, powder barge, about seventy tons. We blew her up.'

'We saw that, I think,' said Hornblower. 'That was *Nonsuch*'s cutter.'

'Yes, sir. That was all at this end of the bay. Then we bore down to
the westward. We caught the *Weece Ross* of Kolberg, two hundred tons.
She carried four six-pounders and showed fight, but Montgomery
boarded her over the bows and they threw down their arms. We had
two men wounded. We burned her. Then there was—'

'How many altogether?'

'One ship, sir. Eleven sail of coasting vessels. Twenty-four barges.
All destroyed.'

'Excellent,' said Hornblower. 'And then?'

'By then it was nigh on dark, sir. I anchored on the north side of the
bay until midnight. Then I ran over to the sand-spit. We found two
soldiers there, and made 'em prisoners. 'Twas easy enough crossing the
spit, sir. We burned a blue light and made contact with the *Harvey*.
They started taking us aboard at two a.m., and I was aboard at three, by
the first light. I went back and burned the boats before I embarked, sir.'

'Better still.'

The enemy, then, had not even the sorry compensation of the capture
of four ships' boats in exchange for the frightful destruction Vickery
had wrought. He turned to Mound.

'I have nothing particular to report, sir. Those waters are shoal,
without a doubt, sir. But I had no difficulty making my way to the rendezvous. After taking Mr Vickery's party on board we touched bottom,
sir. We had nearly a hundred extra hands on board an' must have been
drawing nigh on a foot more water. But we got off all right. I had the
men run from side to side to rock the vessel, an' I threw all aback an'
she came off.'

'I understand.'

Hornblower looked at Mound's expressionless face and smiled inwardly at his studied languid manner. Picking the way in the dark
through the shoals to the rendezvous must have been something of an
epic achievement. Hornblower could estimate the seamanship it called
for, but it was not in the tradition to lay stress on difficulties surmounted.
And a less reliable officer might have tried to suppress the fact that his
ship had touched ground once. It was to Mound's credit that he had not
done so.

'I shall call the attention of the Admiralty,' said Hornblower, trying
his best to combat the pomposity which persisted in making itself heard
in his voice, 'to the conduct of both of you officers. I consider it excellent. I shall, of course, require reports from you immediately in writing.'

'Aye aye, sir.'

Now that he was a Commodore Hornblower felt more sympathy
towards senior officers who had been pompous to him; he was pompous
himself – it was one way in which could be concealed the fact that he
had been anxious.

XVI

Hornblower was dining by himself. He had Gibbon securely wedged against the cheese-crock on the table before him, and his legs stretched out at ease under it. Today he was indulging himself extraordinarily with a half-bottle of wine, and the sea pie from which he was about to help himself smelt most appetising. It was one of those days when there was nothing wrong with the world at all, when he could allow himself to sway with the rhythm of the ship without any further thought, when food tasted good and wine delicious. He dug a spoon into the sea pie just at the moment when there was a knock on the door and a midshipman entered.

'*Clam* in sight to wind'ard, sir,' he said.

'Very good.'

Hornblower proceeded to transfer the sea pie from the dish to his plate, and as he spread out his helping to allow it to cool his mind began to rouse itself. *Clam* would be bringing news; she had been left at St Petersburg for the very purpose of waiting for news. Maybe Russia was at war with Bonaparte now. Or maybe Alexander had made the abject surrender which would be the only thing that could save him from war. Or maybe Alexander was dead, murdered by his officers as his father had been. It would be by no means the first time that a change in Russian policy had been ushered in by a palace revolution. Maybe – maybe anything, but the sea pie was growing cold. He applied himself to it, just as the midshipman knocked at the door again.

'*Clam* signals, "Have despatches for Commodore", sir.'

'How far off is she?'

'Hull-up to wind'ard, sir. We're running down to her.'

'Make, "Commodore to *Clam*. Send despatches on board as soon as practicable".'

'Aye aye, sir.'

There was nothing surprising about *Clam*'s message; the surprise would have been if she carried no despatches. Hornblower found himself shovelling sea pie into his mouth as if the faster he ate it the faster the despatches would come. He checked himself and took sips of his wine, but neither wine nor food had any attraction for him. Brown came in and served him with cheese, and he munched and told himself he had dined well. Cocking his ear to the noises on the deck overhead he could guess there was a boat coming alongside, and directly afterwards one more knock on the door heralded the arrival of Lord Wychwood. Hornblower rose for him, offered him a chair, offered him dinner, took over the bulky canvas-wrapped despatch which Wychwood handed him, and signed a receipt for it. He sat with it on his knee for a moment.

'Well,' said Wychwood, 'it's war.'

Hornblower could not allow himself to ask, 'War with whom?' He made himself wait.

'Alexander's done it, or rather Boney has. Boney crossed the Niemen with fifteen army corps ten days back. No declaration of war, of course. That's not the sort of courtesy one would expect of two potentates who have been blackguarding each other in every sheet in every language in Europe. War was inevitable the moment Alexander sent back his answer a month ago – the day before you left us. Now we'll see.'

'Who's going to win?'

Wychwood shrugged.

'I can't imagine Boney being beaten. And from what I've heard the Russian Army did not show to advantage last year in Finland despite their reorganisation. And Boney has half a million men marching on Moscow.'

Half a million men; the largest army the world had seen since Xerxes crossed the Hellespont.

'At least,' went on Wychwood, 'it will keep Boney busy all this summer. Next year we'll see – maybe he'll lose so many men his people will bear it no longer.'

'Let's hope so,' said Hornblower.

He took out his penknife and ripped open his despatch.

BRITISH EMBASSY,
ST PETERSBURG.
June 24th, 1812.

SIR,

The bearer of this despatch, Colonel Lord Wychwood, will inform you of affairs in this country and of the state of war which now exists between His Imperial Majesty the Czar and Bonaparte. You will, of course, take all necessary steps to render all the assistance in your power to our new ally. I am informed, and have reason to believe, that while the main body of Bonaparte's army is marching on Moscow, a very considerable detachment, believed to consist of the Prussian army corps and a French corps d'armée, the whole under the orders of Marshal Macdonald, Duke of Tarentum, altogether some 60,000 men, has been directed on the northern route towards St Petersburg. It is highly desirable that this army should be prevented from reaching its goal, and at the request of the Russian Imperial Staff I must call your attention to the possibility that your squadron may be able to give assistance at Riga, which the French must capture before continuing their march on St Petersburg. I wish to add my own advice to that of the Russian staff, and to press upon you as urgently as possible that you should give assistance at Riga for as long as may be compatible with your original orders.

In virtue of the powers granted me under the terms of my instructions, I must inform you that I consider it important to the national safety that the cutter *Clam*, at present under your command, shall be despatched to England in order to carry with the utmost rapidity the news of the outbreak of war. I trust and hope that you will raise no objection.

I have the honour to be, sir,

Etc., etc.,

> CATHCART, *His Britannic Majesty's Minister-*
> *Plenipotentiary and Ambassador*
> *Extraordinary to H.I.M.*

'Cathcart's a good man,' commented Wychwood, observing that Hornblower had completed his reading. 'Both as a soldier and as a diplomat he's worth two of Merry at Stockholm. I'm glad Wellesley sent him out.'

Certainly this despatch was better worded than the last Hornblower had received, nor did Cathcart presume to give orders to the Commodore.

'You will be going on in *Clam* to England,' said Hornblower. 'I must ask you to wait while I complete my own despatches for the Admiralty.'

'Naturally,' said Wychwood.

'It will only be a matter of minutes,' said Hornblower. 'Perhaps Captain Bush will entertain you while you are waiting. Doubtless there are many letters awaiting carriage to England. Meanwhile, I am sending my secretary back to England in *Clam* too. I shall put in your charge the papers relative to his case.'

Alone in his cabin, Hornblower opened his desk and found himself pen and ink. There was little enough to add to his official despatch. He read the last words – 'I wish most strongly to call Their Lordships' attention to the conduct and professional ability of Commander William Vickery and Lieutenant Percival Mound.' Then he began a new paragraph. 'I am taking the opportunity of the departure of *Clam* to England to forward this letter to you. In accordance with the recommendation of His Excellency Lord Cathcart, I shall proceed at once with the rest of my squadron to render all the assistance in my power to the Russian forces at Riga.' He thought for a moment of adding some conventional expression like, 'I trust this course of action will meet with Their Lordships' approval', and then put the notion aside. It meant nothing, was merely waste verbiage. He dipped his pen again and merely wrote, 'I have the honour to be, Your obed't servant, Horatio Hornblower, Captain and Commodore'.

He closed the letter, shouting for Brown as he did so. While he wrote the address – Edward Nepean, Esq., Secretary to the Lords Commissioners of the Admiralty – Brown brought him a candle and sealing wax, and he sealed the letter and laid it on one side. Then he took another sheet and began to write again.

H.M.S. *Nonsuch*, IN THE BALTIC.

MY DEAR WIFE,

The cutter waits for me to complete my correspondence for England, and I have only time to write these few lines to add to the other letters which have been awaiting an opportunity to make the voyage. I am in the best of health, and the progress of the campaign remains satisfactory. The great news of the outbreak of war between Bonaparte and Russia has just reached me. I hope that the event will prove this to be Bonaparte's worst mistake, but I can only anticipate long and costly fighting, with small possibility of my returning to your dear presence, at least until the freezing of the harbours makes further operations in these waters impracticable.

I trust most sincerely that you are well and happy, and that the rigours of the London season have not proved too trying for you. I like to think of the good air of Smallbridge restoring the roses to your cheeks, so that the vagaries of costumiers and milliners will not exact too excessive a toll of your health and peace of mind.

Also I trust that Richard is comporting himself towards you with the duty and obedience you expect, and that his teeth have continued to make their appearance with as little disturbance as possible. It would be a great delight to me if he were old enough to write to me himself, especially if that would give me further news of you; only a letter from you yourself could give me greater pleasure. It is my hope that soon letters will reach me from England, and that it will be my happiness to hear that all is well with you.

When next you see your brother, Lord Wellesley, I trust you will give him my duty and respects. For you I reserve my whole love.

Your affectionate husband,

HORATIO.

Wychwood took the letters Hornblower gave him, and wrote out a receipt on Bush's desk with Bush's pen. Then he held out his hand.

'Goodbye, sir,' he said, and hesitated; then, with a rush, he added, 'God knows how this war will turn out. I expect the Russians'll be beaten. But you have done more than any one man to bring the war about. You've done your whole duty, sir.'

'Thank you,' said Hornblower.

He was in a disturbed and unsettled mood; he stood on the quarterdeck of the *Nonsuch* while over his head the ensign was dipped in a parting salute to the *Clam*, and he watched the cutter sail off towards

England. He watched her until she was out of sight, while *Nonsuch* put up her helm and bore away for Riga and whatever new adventures awaited him there. He knew quite well what was the matter with him; he was homesick, plunged into a storm of emotional disturbance as he always was when he wrote home, and, oddly enough, Wychwood's last words added to his disturbance. They had reminded him of the terrible load of responsibility that he bore. The future of the world and the survival of his country would be profoundly affected by his doings. Should this Russian adventure end in defeat and disaster everyone anxious to shuffle off responsibility would blame him. He would be condemned as inept and shortsighted. He even found himself envying Braun, now on his way back to London under arrest and awaiting probable trial and possible execution, and he remembered with longing his petty troubles at Smallbridge; he smiled at himself when he recalled that his heaviest burden there had been to receive a deputation of welcome from the village. He thought of Barbara's ready sympathy, of the intense pleasure he had known when it first dawned upon him that Richard loved him, and enjoyed and looked forward to his company. Here he had to be content with Bush's unthinking loyalty and the precarious admiration of the young officers.

Recalling himself to reality, he forced himself to remember with what a bubble of excitement he had received his orders back to active service, the light heart with which he had left his child, the feeling of – there was no blinking the matter – emancipation with which he had parted from his wife. The prospect of once more being entirely his own master, of not having to defer to Barbara's wishes, of not being discommoded by Richard's teeth, had seemed most attractive then. And here he was complaining to himself about the burden of responsibility, when responsibility was the inevitable price one had to pay for independence; irresponsibility was something which, in the very nature of things, could not co-exist with independence.

This was all very well and logical, but there was no blinking the fact that he wished he were home; he could conjure up in imagination so vividly the touch of Barbara's hand on his own that it was an acute disappointment to realise that it was only in imagination. He wanted to have Richard on his knee again, shrieking with laughter over the colossal joke of having his nose pinched. And he did not want to imperil his reputation, his liberty, and his life in combined operations with these unpredictable Russians in a God-forsaken corner of the world like Riga. Yet then and there – his interest rousing itself spontaneously – he decided that he had better go below and reread the Sailing Directions for Riga; and a close study of the chart of Riga Bay might be desirable, too.

XVII

The Northern Continental summer had come speedily, as ever. Last week at Pillau there had still been a decided touch of winter in the air. Today, with Riga just over the horizon, it was full summer. This blazing heat would have done credit to the doldrums were it not for an invigorating quality which the tropics never knew. A brassy sun shone down from a cloudless sky, although there was just enough mist to leave the distant horizon undefined. There was a gentle two-knot breeze blowing, from the south-west just enough wind to give *Nonsuch* bare steerage-way with all her canvas set, studding-sails on both sides to the royals. The squadron was making the best speed it could, with *Lotus* hull-down on the starboard bow, *Raven* close astern, and the two bomb-ketches trailing far behind; even the clumsy *Nonsuch* could outsail them in the prevailing conditions.

Everything was very peaceful. Forward a party of seamen under the sailmaker's supervision were overhauling a mainsail for repair. In the waist another party was dragging a 'bear' up and down the deck – a huge coir mat weighted down with sand which could scrub the planking more effectively than holystones could do. On the quarterdeck the sailing-master was holding a class in navigation, his mates and the midshipmen standing round him in a semicircle, their sextants in their hands. Hornblower walked near enough to hear one of the midshipmen, a mere child whose voice had not broken, piping up a reply to the question just shot at him.

'The parallax of an object is measured by an arc of a vertical circle intercepted between a line extended from the centre of the earth and a line – and a line – a line—'

The midshipman suddenly became conscious of the awful proximity of the Commodore. His voice quavered and died away. So far he had been quoting Norie's *Epitome of Navigation* with word-perfect exactitude. It was young Gerard, nephew of the second lieutenant of the *Sutherland*, whom Bush had taken into his ship for the sake of his uncle, still languishing in a French prison. The sailing-master's brows drew together in a frown.

'Come, come, Mr Gerard,' he said.

Hornblower had a sudden mental picture of young Gerard bent over the breech of a gun while a lithe cane taught him at least the necessity of knowing Norie's *Epitome* by heart. He intervened in hurried pity.

' "Between a line extended from the centre of the earth",' he said, over Gerard's shoulder, ' "and a line extended from the eye of the observer, through the centre of the object." Is that correct, Mr Tooth?'

'Quite correct, sir,' said the sailing-master.

'I think Mr Gerard knew it all the time. Didn't you, youngster?'

'Y – yes, sir.'

'I thought so. I was just your age when I learned that same passage.'

Hornblower resumed his walk, hoping that he had saved Gerard's skinny posterior from punishment. A sudden scurrying by the midshipman of the watch to grab slate and pencil told him that one of the squadron was making a signal, and two minutes later the midshipman saluted him, message in hand.

'*Lotus* to Commodore. Land in sight bearing South.'

That would be Pitraga Cape, the southern headland of the entrance to the Gulf of Riga.

'Reply, "Heave to and await Commodore",' said Hornblower.

If the weather were not so thick the island of Oesel ought to be just in sight to the northward from the masthead. They were just passing the threshold of a new adventure. Some seventy miles ahead, at the bottom of the gulf, lay Riga, presumably even now being assailed by the armies of Bonaparte. With this mere pretence of a wind it would be a couple of days before he reached there. The fact that they were entering Russian waters again was making not the least ripple on the placid surface of the ship's life. Everything was progressing as before, yet Hornblower felt in his bones that many of the men now entering the Gulf of Riga would never come out from it, even if any should. Even with this hot sun blazing down upon him, under this radiant sky, Hornblower felt a sudden chill of foreboding which it was hard to throw off. He himself – it was curious to think that his dead body might be buried in Russia, of all places.

Someone – the Russians, or the Swedes, or the Finns – had buoyed effectively the channel that wound its way through the treacherous shallows of the Gulf of Finland. Even though the squadron had to anchor for the night a slight freshening and veering of the wind enabled them to ascend the whole gulf by the evening of the next day. They picked up a pilot at noon, a bearded individual who wore sea-boots and a heavy jacket even on this blazing day. He proved to be an Englishman, Carker by name, who had not set eyes on his native land for twenty-four years. He blinked at Hornblower like an owl when the latter began to fire questions at him regarding the progress of the war. Yes, some cavalry patrols of French and Prussians had shown themselves advancing towards Riga. The last news of the main campaign was of desperate fighting round Smolensk, and everyone was expecting Bonaparte to be beaten there. The town was preparing itself for a siege, he believed – at least, there were plenty of soldiers there, when he had left in his cutter yesterday, and there had been proclamations calling on the people to fight to the last, but no one could imagine the French making a serious attack on the place.

Hornblower turned away from him impatiently in the end, as a typical example of the uninformed civilian, with no real knowledge of affairs or appreciation of the seriousness of the situation. Livonia, having been for centuries the cockpit of northern Europe, had not seen an enemy during the last three generations, and had forgotten even the traditions of invasion. Hornblower had no intention at all of taking his squadron into the Dwina River (queer names these Russians used!) if there was a chance of his retreat being cut off, and he stared out through his glass at the low green shore when it came in sight at last from the deck. Almost right astern of the squadron the sun was lying on the horizon in a fiery bed of cloud, but there were two hours more of daylight left, and *Nonsuch* crept steadily closer to Riga. Bush came up to him and touched his hat.

'Pardon, sir, but do you hear anything? Gunfire, maybe?'

Hornblower strained his attention.

'Yes, gunfire, by God,' he said.

It was the lowest, faintest muttering, coming upwind from the distant shore.

'The Frogs have got there before us, sir,' said Bush.

'Be ready to anchor,' said Hornblower.

Nonsuch crept steadily on, gliding at three or four knots towards the land; the water around her was greyish yellow with the mud borne down by a great river. The mouth of the Dwina was only a mile or two ahead, and with the spring rains and the melting of the snows the river must be in full flood. The buoys of a middle-ground shoal enabled Hornblower to make sure of his position; he was coming within long cannon-shot of those flat green shores. As though standing in the yellow water there was a church visible on the starboard bow, with an onion-shaped dome surmounted by a cross which reflected back to him, even at that distance, the red glare of the sunset. That must be the village of Daugavgriva, on the left bank; if it were in French hands entrance to the river would be dangerous, perhaps impossible, as soon as they had big guns mounted there. Maybe they already had.

'Captain Bush,' said Hornblower, 'I'd be obliged if you would anchor.'

The cable roared out through the hawsehole, and *Nonsuch* swung round to the wind as the hands, pouring aloft, took in the sails. The rest of the squadron came up and prepared to anchor just when Hornblower was beginning to feel he had been too precipitate, or at least when he was regretting bitterly that night had come upon him before he could open communication with the shore.

'Call away my barge,' he ordered. 'Captain Bush, I am shifting to *Harvey*. You will assume command of the squadron during my absence.'

Mound was at the side to welcome him as he swung himself up over *Harvey*'s low freeboard.

'Square away, Mr Mound. We'll close the shore in the direction of that church. Set a good hand at work with the lead.'

The bomb-ketch, with anchor catted and ready to let go, stole forward over the still water. There was still plenty of light from the sky, for here in 57° North, within a few days of the solstice, the sun was not very far below the horizon.

'Moon rises in an hour's time, sir,' said Mound, 'three-quarters full.'

It was a marvellous evening, cool and invigorating. There was only the tiniest whisper of water round the bows of the ketch as she glided over the silvery surface; Hornblower felt that they only needed a few pretty women on board and someone strumming a guitar to make a yachting expedition of it. Something on shore attracted his attention, and he whipped his glass to his eye at the very moment when Mound beside him did the same.

'Lights on shore,' said Mound.

'Those are bivouac fires,' said Hornblower.

He had seen bivouac fires before – the fires of el Supremo's army in Central America, the fires of the landing force at Rosas. They sparkled ruddily in the twilight, in roughly regular lines. Traversing his glass round, Hornblower picked up further groups of lights; there was a dark space between one mass and the other, which Hornblower pointed out to Mound.

'That's no-man's-land between the two forces, I fancy,' he said. 'The Russians must be holding the village as an outwork on the left bank of the river.'

'Couldn't all those fires be French fires, sir?' asked Mound. 'Or Russian fires?'

'No,' said Hornblower. 'Soldiers don't bivouac if they can billet in villages with roofs over their heads. If two armies weren't in presence they'd all be comfortably asleep in the cottagers' beds and barns.'

There was a long pause while Mound digested this.

'Two fathoms, sir,' he said, at length. 'I'd like to bear up, if I may.'

'Very good. Carry on. Keep as close inshore as you think proper.'

The *Harvey* came round with the wind abeam, half a dozen hands hauling lustily on the mainsheet. There was the moon, rising round and red over the land; the dome of the church was silhouetted against it. A sharp cry came from the forward lookout.

'Boat ahead! Fine on the port bow, sir. Pulling oars.'

'Catch that boat if you can, Mr Mound,' said Hornblower.

'Aye aye, sir. Starboard two points! Clear away the gig. Boat's crew stand by!'

They could see the dim shape of the boat not far ahead; they could even see the splashes of the oars. It occurred to Hornblower that the rowers could not be men of much skill, and whoever was in charge was not very quick in the uptake if he wanted to avoid capture; he should have headed instantly for shoal water if he wanted to avoid capture, while as it was he tried to pit oars against sails – a hopeless endeavour even with that light breeze blowing. It was several minutes before they turned for the shore, and during that time their lead was greatly reduced.

'Hard-a-lee!' roared Mound. 'Away, gig!'

Harvey came into the wind, and as she lost her way the gig dropped into the water with the boat's crew falling into it.

'I want prisoners!' roared Hornblower at the departing boat.

'Aye aye, sir,' came the reply as the oars tore the water.

Under the impulse of the skilled oarsmen the gig rapidly was overtaking the strange boat; they could see the distance narrowing as the two boats disappeared in the faint light. Then they saw the orange-red flashes of half a dozen pistol-shots, and the faint reports reached them over the water directly after.

'Let's hope they're not Russians, sir,' said Mound.

The possibility had occurred to Hornblower as well, and he was nervous and uncomfortable, but he spoke bluffly –

'Russians wouldn't run away. They wouldn't expect to find Frenchmen at sea.'

Soon two boats, rowing slowly, emerged from the gloom.

'We've got 'em all, sir,' said a voice in reply to Mound's hail.

Five prisoners were thrust up on to the deck of the *Harvey*, one of them groaning with a pistol bullet through his arm. Someone produced a lantern and shone it on them, and Hornblower heaved a sigh of relief when he saw that the star which glittered on the breast of the leader was the Legion of Honour.

'I would like to know monsieur's name and rank,' he said, politely, in French.

'Jussey, chef de bataillon du corps de Génie des armées de l'Empereur.'

A major of engineers; quite an important capture. Hornblower bowed and presented himself, his mind working rapidly on the problem of how to induce the major to say all he knew.

'I regret very much the necessity of taking M. le chef de bataillon prisoner,' he said. 'Especially at the beginning of such a promising campaign. But good fortune may allow me the opportunity of arranging a cartel of exchange at an early date. I presume M. le chef de bataillon has friends in the French Army whom he would like informed of what has happened to him? I will take the opportunity of the first flag of truce to do so.'

'The Marshal Duke of Tarentum would be glad to hear,' said Jussey, brightening a little. 'I am on his staff.'

The Marshal Duke of Tarentum was Macdonald, the local French commander-in-chief – son of a Scottish exile who had fled after the

Young Pretender's rebellion – so that it seemed likely that Jussey was the chief engineer, a bigger catch than Hornblower had hoped for.

'It was extremely bad fortune for you to fall into our hands,' said Hornblower. 'You have no reason to suspect the presence of a British squadron operating in the bay.'

'Indeed I had none. Our information was to the contrary. These Livonians—'

So the French staff was obtaining information from Livonian traitors; Hornblower might have guessed it, but it was as well to be sure.

'Of course they are useless, like all Russians,' said Hornblower, soothingly. 'I suppose your Emperor has met with little opposition?'

'Smolensk is ours, and the Emperor marches on Moscow. It is our mission to occupy St Petersburg.'

'But perhaps passing the Dwina will be difficult?'

Jussey shrugged in the lamplight.

'I do not expect so. A bold push across the mouth of the river and the Russians will retreat the moment their flank is turned.'

So that was what Jussey was doing; reconnoitring for a suitable place to land a French force on the Russian side of the river mouth.

'A daring move, sir, worthy of all the great traditions of the French Army. But no doubt you have ample craft to transport your force?'

'Some dozens of barges. We seized them at Mitau before the Russians could destroy them.'

Jussey checked himself abruptly, clearly disturbed at realising how much he had said.

'Russians are always incompetent,' said Hornblower, in a tone of complete agreement. 'A prompt attack on your part, giving them no chance of steadying themselves, is of course your best plan of operations. But will you pardon me, sir, while I attend to my duties?'

There was no chance of wheedling anything more out of Jussey at the moment. But he had at least yielded up the vital information that the French had laid hands on a fleet of barges which the Russians had neglected, or been unable, to destroy, and that they planned a direct attack across the river mouth. By feigning entire indifference Hornblower felt that Jussey might be inveigled later into talking freely again. Jussey bowed, and Hornblower turned to Mound.

'We'll return to the squadron,' he said.

Mound gave the orders which laid the *Harvey*'s closehauled on the starboard tack – the French prisoners ducked hastily as the big mainsail boom swung over their heads, and the seamen bumped into them as they ran to the sheet. While Jussey and Hornblower had been talking two of the prisoners had cut off the sleeve of the wounded man and bandaged his arm; now they all squatted in the scuppers out of the way, while the *Harvey* crept back to where the *Nonsuch* lay at anchor.

XVIII

'Oars,' said Brown, and the barge's crew ceased to pull. 'In bows.'

The bow oarsman brought his oar into the boat and grabbed for the boathook, and Brown laid the barge neatly alongside the quay while the rushing Dwina river eddied about it. An interested crowd of the people of Riga watched the operation, and stared stolidly at Hornblower as he ran up the stone steps to road level, epaulettes, star, and sword all a-glitter in the scorching sunshine. Beyond the line of warehouses along the quay he was vaguely aware of a wide square surrounded by medieval stone buildings with high-pitched roofs, but he had no attention to spare for this his first close sight of Riga. There was the usual guard of honour to salute, the usual officer at its head, and beside it the burly figure of the Governor, General Essen.

'Welcome to the city, sir,' said Essen. He was a Baltic German, a descendant of those Knights of the Sword who had conquered Livonia from the heathen centuries before, and the French which he spoke had some of the explosive quality of the French spoken by an Alsatian.

An open carriage, to which were harnessed two spirited horses who pawed restlessly at the ground, awaited them, and the Governor handed Hornblower in and followed him.

'It is only the shortest distance to go,' he said, 'but we shall take this opportunity of letting the people see us.'

The carriage lurched and bounced frightfully over the cobbled streets; Hornblower had twice to straighten his cocked hat which was jerked sideways on his head, but he endeavoured to sit up straight and unconcerned as they dashed along narrow streets full of people who eyed them with interest. There was no harm in allowing the inhabitants of a beleaguered city the opportunity of seeing a British naval officer in full uniform – his presence would be a pledge that Riga was not alone in her hour of trial.

'The Ritterhaus,' explained Essen, as the coachman pulled up his horses outside a handsome old building with a line of sentries posted before it.

The reception awaited them, officers in uniform, a few civilians in black, and many, many women in gala dresses. Several of the officers Hornblower had already met at the conference that morning at Dwina Maude; Essen proceeded to present the more important of the rest of the company.

'His Excellency the Intendant of Livonia,' said Essen, 'and the Countess—'

'It has already been my great pleasure to meet the Countess,' interposed Hornblower.

'The Commodore was my partner at dinner at the Peterhof,' said the Countess.

She was as beautiful and as vivacious as ever; maybe, as she stood there with her hand on her husband's arm, her glance was not so sultry. She bowed to Hornblower with a polite indifference. Her husband was tall, bony, and elderly, with a thin moustache that drooped from his lip, and short-sighted eyes that he assisted with a quizzing glass. Hornblower bowed to him, endeavouring to behave as though this were only one more ordinary meeting. It was ridiculous to feel embarassed at this encounter, yet he was, and had to struggle to conceal it. Yet the beaky-nosed Intendant of Livonia eyed him with even more indifference than did his wife; most of the others who were presented to Hornblower were obviously delighted to meet the English naval officer, but the Intendant made no effort to hide the fact that to him, the direct representative of the Czar and an habitué of Imperial palaces, this provincial reception was tedious and uninteresting, and the guest of honour nobody of importance.

Hornblower had learned his lesson regarding the etiquette of a Russian formal dinner; the tables of hors d'oeuvres he knew now to be mere preliminaries. He tasted caviare and vodka once again, and the very pleasant combination of flavours called up a sudden host of memories. Without being able to prevent himself he glanced across at the Countess, and caught her eye as she stood chattering with half a dozen grave men in uniform. It was only for a moment, but that was long enough. Her glance seemed to tell him that she, too, was haunted by the same memories. Hornblower's head whirled a little, and he made a prompt resolve to drink nothing more that night. He turned and plunged hastily into conversation with the Governor.

'How delightfully complementary to each other are vodka and caviare,' he said. 'They are worthy to rank with those other combinations of food discovered by the pioneers of the gastronomic art. Eggs and bacon, partridge and Burgundy, spinach and – and—'

He fumbled for a French word for 'gammon', and the Governor supplied it, his little pig's eyes lighting up with interest in the midst of his big red face.

'You are a gastronome, sir?' he said.

The rest of the time before dinner passed easily enough then, with Hornblower well exercised in having to discuss food with someone to whom food was clearly a matter of deep interest. Hornblower drew a little on his imagination to describe the delicacies of the West Indies and of Central America; fortunately during his last period of leave he had moved in wealthy London circles with his wife and had eaten at several renowned tables, including that of the Mansion House, which gave him a solid basis of European experience with which to supplement his imagination. The Governor had taken advantage of the campaigns in which he had served to study the foods of the different countries. Vienna and Prague had fed him during the Austerlitz campaign; he had drunk resinated wine in the Seven Islands; he rolled up his eyes in ecstasy at the memory of frutti di mare consumed in Leghorn when he had served in Italy under Suvaroff. Bavarian beer, Swedish schnapps, Danzig goldwasser – he had drunk of them all, just as he had eaten Westphalian ham and Italian beccaficoes and Turkish rahat lakoum. He listened with rapt attention when Hornblower spoke of grilled flying-fish and Trinidad pepperpot, and it was with the deepest regret that he parted with Hornblower to take his place at the head of the dinner table; even then he persisted in calling Hornblower's attention to the dishes being served, leaning forward to address him across two ladies and the Intendant of Livonia, and when dinner was ended he apologised to Hornblower for the abrupt termination of the meal, complaining bitterly of the fact that he had to gulp his final glass of brandy because they were already nearly an hour late for the gala performance of the ballet where they were next due to go.

He walked heavily up the stone stairs of the theatre, his spurs ringing and his sword clattering as it trailed beside him. Two ushers led the way, and behind Hornblower and Essen walked the others of the inner circle, the Countess and her husband and two other officials and their wives. The ushers held open the door of the box, and Hornblower waited on the threshold for the ladies to enter.

'The Commodore will go first,' said Essen, and Hornblower plunged in. The theatre was brightly lighted, and parterre and gallery were crowded; Hornblower's entrance drew a storm of applause, which smote upon his ears and momentarily paralysed him as he stood there. A fortunate instinct prompted him to bow, first to one side and then to the other, as if he were an actor, as he said to himself. Then someone thrust a chair behind him and he sat down, with the rest of the party round him. Throughout the auditorium ushers immediately began to turn down the lamps, and the orchestra broke into the overture. The curtain rose to reveal a woodland scene, and the ballet began.

'A lively thing, this Madame Nicolas,' said the Governor in a penetrating whisper. 'Tell me if you like her. I can send for her after the performance if you desire.'

'Thank you,' whispered Hornblower in reply, feeling ridiculously embarrassed. The Countess was close on his other side and he was too conscious of her warmth to feel comfortable.

The music hurried on, and in the golden glow of the footlights the ballet went through its dazzling maze, skirts flying and feet twinkling. It was incorrect to say that music meant nothing to Hornblower; the monotonous beat of its rhythm, when he was compelled to listen to it for long, stirred something in the depths of him even while its guessed-at sweetness tormented his ear like a Chinese water torture. Five minutes of music left him dull and unmoved; fifteen minutes made him restless; an hour was sheer agony. He forced himself to sit still during the long ordeal, even though he felt he would gladly exchange his chair in the box for the quarterdeck of a ship in the hottest and most hopeless battle ever fought. He tried to shut his ears to the persistent insidious noise, to distract himself by concentrating his attention on the dancers, on Madame Nicolas as she pirouetted across the stage in her shimmering white, on the others as, chin on finger and the other hand supporting the elbow, they came down the stage a-tiptoe in alluring line. Yet it was of no avail, and his misery increased from minute to minute.

The Countess at his side was stirring, too. He knew, telepathically, what she was thinking about. The literature of all ages, from the *Ars Amatoria* to *Les Liaisons Dangereuses* told him theoretically of the effect of music and spectacles upon the feminine mind, and in violent revulsion he hated the Countess as much as he hated music. The only movement he made, as he sat there stoically enduring the tortures of the damned for the sake of his duty, was to shift his foot away out of reach of hers – he knew in his bones that she would endeavour to touch him soon, while her beaky-nosed husband with his quizzing glass sat just behind them. The entr'acte was only a poor respite; the music at least ceased, and he was able to stand, blinking a little as the thrown-open door of the box admitted a stream of light, and he bowed politely when the Governor presented a few latecomers who came to pay their respects to the British visitor. But in no time at all, it seemed, he was forced to seat himself again, while the orchestra resumed its maddening scraping, and the curtain rose on a new scene.

Then a distraction came. Hornblower was not sure when he first heard it; he might have missed the first premonitory shots in his determined effort to shut himself inside himself. He came out of his nightmare conscious of a new tension in the people round him; the boom of heavy artillery was very noticeable now – it even seemed as if the theatre itself were vibrating gently to the heavy concussions. He kept his head and neck still, and stole a glance out of the corner of his eye at the Governor beside him, but the Governor seemed to be still entirely engrossed in watching Mme Nicolas. Yet the firing was very heavy. Somewhere not very far away big guns were being fired rapidly and in large numbers. His first thought was for his ships, but he knew them to be safe, anchored at the mouth of the Dwina, and if the wind was still in the direction it was blowing when he entered the theatre Bush could get them out of harm's way whatever happened, even if Riga were taken by storm that very hour.

The audience was taking its cue from the Governor, and as he refused to allow the gunfire to distract him everyone made a brave attempt to appear unconcerned. But everyone in the box, at least, felt tightened nerves when rapid steps outside in the stone-flagged corridor, to the accompaniment of the ringing of spurs, heralded the entrance of an orderly officer, who came in and whispered hurriedly to the Governor. Essen dismissed him with a few words, and only when he had gone, and after a minute's interval which seemed like an hour, leaned over to Hornblower with the news.

'The French have tried to take Daugavgriva by a coup de main,' he explained. 'There is no chance of their succeeding.'

That was the village on the left bank of the Dwina, in the angle between the sea and the river, the natural first objective for a besieging force that was desirous of cutting off the town from all hope of relief by sea. It was nearly an island, with the Gulf of Riga covering one flank, and the mile-wide Dwina river covering the rear, while the rest was girt by marshes and ditches and protected by breastworks thrown up by the peasant labour called in from miles round. The French would be likely to try assault upon the place, because success would save them weeks of tedious siege operations, and they had no knowledge as yet of whether or not the Russians were able or willing to offer effective resistance. This was the first time Macdonald had encountered any serious opposition since he had begun his advance across Lithuania – the main Russian armies were contesting the road to Moscow in the neighbourhood of Smolensk. Hornblower had inspected the works that very morning, had observed the strength of the place and the steady appearance of the Russian grenadiers who garrisoned it, and had formed the conclusion that it was safe against anything except systematic siege. Yet he wished he could be as sublimely confident about it as the Governor was.

On the other hand, everything possible had already been done. If the village fell, it fell, and nothing more serious had happened than the loss of an outwork. If the attack were beaten off there could be no question of following up the success, not while Macdonald disposed of sixty thousand men and the Russians of fifteen thousand at most. Of course Macdonald was bound to attempt a coup de main upon Daugavgriva. It was interesting to speculate what would be his next move should the assault fail. He might march up the river and endeavour to force a passage above the town, although that meant plunging into a roadless tangle of marsh and attempting a crossing at a place where he would find no boats. Or he might try the other plan and use the boats which had fallen into his hands at Mitau to pass a force across the mouth of the river, leaving Daugavgriva untaken while he compelled the Russians in Riga to choose between coming out and fighting the landing party, or retreating towards St Petersburg, or being shut in completely in the town. It was hard to guess what he would decide on. Certainly Macdonald had sent out Jussey to reconnoitre the river mouth, and although he had lost his chief engineer in doing so he might still be tempted by the prospect of being able to continue immediately his advance on St Petersburg.

Hornblower came back to himself, delighted to find that he had missed in his abstraction some substantial amount of the ballet. He did not know how long his absent-mindedness had endured, but it must be, he thought, for some considerable time. The gunfire had ceased; either the assault had failed or had been completely successful.

At the very moment the door opened to admit another orderly officer with a whispered message for the Governor.

'The attack has been beaten off,' said Essen to Hornblower. 'Yakoulev reports his men have hardly suffered at all, and the front of the place is covered with French and German dead.'

That was to be expected, granted the failure of the attack. The losses would be dreadful in an unsuccessful assault. Macdonald had gambled, risking a couple of thousand lives against a speedy end to the siege, and he had lost. Yet an Imperial army would be exasperated rather than depressed by such a preliminary reverse. The defence could expect further vigorous attacks at any moment.

It was wonderful to discover that he had managed to sit through another whole ballet without noticing it. Here was another entr'acte, with the light shining into the box, and the opportunity to stand and stretch one's legs; it was even delightful to exchange polite banalities in French tinged with half the accents of Europe. When the entr'acte ended Hornblower was quite reconciled to reseating himself and bracing himself to endure one more ballet; yet the curtain had only just risen when he felt himself heavily nudged in the thigh by Essen, who rose and made his way out of the box with Hornblower at his heels.

'We may as well go and see,' said Essen, the moment they stood outside the closed door of the box. 'It would not have been well to get up and go when the firing began. But the people will not know now that we left in haste.'

Outside the theatre a troop of hussars sat their horses, while two grooms stood at the heads of two more horses, and Hornblower realised that he was committed to riding in his full-dress uniform. It was not the serious business it used to be, though; Hornblower thought with pleasure of his dozen reserve pairs of silk stockings stored away in *Nonsuch*. Essen climbed on to his horse, and Hornblower followed his example. The bright moon filled the square with light, as, with the escort following, they trotted clattering over the cobbles. Two turns and a moderate descent brought them to the big floating bridge that spanned the Dwina; the roadway over the pontoons drummed hollow beneath

the horses' hoofs. Across the river a road ran on the top of a high levée
beside the water; on the far side the land was cut and seamed with ditches
and ponds, around which twinkled innumerable camp-fires, and here
Essen halted and gave an order which sent the hussar officer and half
the escort riding ahead of them.

'I have no desire to be shot by my own men,' explained Essen.
'Sentries will be nervous, and riding into a village that has just suffered a
night attack will be as dangerous as storming a battery.'

Hornblower was too preoccupied to appreciate the point very much.
His sword and his ribbon and star and his cocked hat added to his usual
difficulty of retaining his seat on horseback, and he bumped ungracefully
in his saddle, sweating profusely in the cool night, and grabbing spasmodically at items of his equipment whenever he could spare a hand from
his reins. They were challenged repeatedly as they rode along, but
despite Essen's gloomy prognostication no jumpy sentry fired at them.
Finally they drew up in reply to another challenge at a point where the
dome of the church of Daugavgriva stood up black against the pale sky.
With the cessation of the noise of the horses' hoofs a fresh sound claimed
Hornblower's attention; a wailing clamour coloured by high agonised
screams; a whole chorus of groans and cries. The sentry passed them
through, and they rode forward into the village, and as they did so the
groans and screams were explained, for they passed on their left the
torch-lit field where the wounded were being treated – Hornblower had
a glimpse of a naked writhing body being held down on a table while
the surgeons bent over it in the glare of the torches like the familiars of
the Inquisition, while the whole field was carpeted with writhing and
groaning wounded. And this had been a mere outpost skirmish, a
trifling matter of a few hundred casualties on either side.

They dismounted at the door of the church and Essen led the way in,
returning the salute of the bearded grenadiers at the door. Candles
within made a bright pool of light in the midst of the surrounding gloom,
and at a table there sat a group of officers drinking tea from a samovar
which hissed beside them. They rose as the Governor entered, and
Essen made the introductions.

'General Diebitch. Colonel von Clausewitz – Commodore Sir Hornblower.'

Diebitch was a Pole, Clausewitz a German – the Prussian renegade
Hornblower had heard about previously, an intellectual soldier who had
decided that true patriotism lay in fighting Bonaparte regardless of
which side his country nominally assisted. They made their report in
French; the enemy had attempted at moonrise to storm the village without preparation, and had been bloodily repulsed. Prisoners had been
taken; some had captured an outlying cottage and had been cut off in the
counter-attack, and there were other isolated prisoners from various

units who had fallen into Russian hands at other points of the perimeter of the village.

'They have already been questioned, sir,' said Diebitch. Hornblower had the feeling that it would be an unpleasant experience to be a prisoner submitted to questioning at the hands of General Diebitch.

'Their statements were useful, sir,' added Clausewitz, producing a sheet of notes. Each prisoner had been asked what was his battalion, how many men there were in it, how many battalions in his regiment, what was his brigade and division and army corps. Clausewitz was in a fair way by now to reconstituting the whole organisation of the French part of the attacking army and to estimate its number fairly accurately.

'We know already the strength of the Prussian corps,' said Essen, and there was a moment's awkwardness while everyone avoided meeting Clausewitz's eye, for he had brought in that information.

'It is only half an hour before dawn, sir,' interposed Diebitch with more tact than could have been expected of a man of his countenance. 'Would you care to climb to the dome and see for yourself?'

The sky was brighter still by the time they had climbed the narrow stone stair in the thickness of the wall of the church and emerged into the open gallery that encircled it. The whole of the flat marshy country-side was revealed for their inspection, the ditches and the lakes, and the little Mitau river winding its way down from the far distance, through the village almost under the side of the church, to lose itself at the very angle where the vast Dwina entered the bay. The line of breastworks and abattis thrown up by the garrison to defend the left bank of the Dwina was plainly traced, and beyond them could be seen the scanty works which were all that the invaders had bothered to construct up to the moment. The smoke of a thousand cooking-fires drifted over the country.

'In my opinion, sir,' said Clausewitz deferentially, 'if the enemy should decide to proceed by regular siege that is where he will begin. He will trace his first parallel *there*, between the river and that pinewood and sap forward against the village, establishing his batteries on that neck of land *there*. After three weeks' work he could expect to bring his batteries forward on to the glacis and deliver a regular assault. He must effect the reduction of this village before proceeding to the attack on the town.'

'Perhaps,' said Essen.

Hornblower could not imagine a Napoleonic army of sixty thousand men in full march for St Petersburg condescending to spend three weeks in siege operations against an outwork without trying first every ex-temporary method, like the brusque assault of last night. He borrowed a telescope from one of the staff, and devoted his time to examining the maze of waterways and marshes that stretched before him, and then, walking round the dome along the gallery, he turned his attention to

the view of Riga, with its spires, beyond the huge river. Far off, well
down the channel, he could just see the masts of his own squadron,
where it swung at anchor at the point where the river blended with the
Gulf. Tiny specks of ships, minute in their present surroundings and
yet of such vast importance in the history of the world.

XIX

Hornblower was asleep in his cabin in the *Nonsuch* when the alarm was
given. Even while he was asleep – or perhaps it may be granted that he
woke occasionally without knowing it – his subconscious mind had been
taking note of conditions. At least, when he woke fully, he was already
vaguely aware of the changes that had occurred during the night. His
sleeping, or half-awakened, mind had noted the veering of the wind that
had swung *Nonsuch* round to her anchor, and the brief sharp rain squalls
that had pelted down on the deck. Certainly he had awakened to the
sharp cry of the watch on deck, and had heard the footsteps overhead
of the midshipman of the watch running to him with the news. He was
fully awake by the time the midshipman pounded on the door and burst
in.

'Rocket from *Raven*, sir.'

'Very good,' said Hornblower, swinging his legs out of his cot.

Brown, the good servant, was already in the cabin – God only knew
how he had picked up the warning – with a lighted lantern to hang on
the deck beam above, and he had trousers and coat ready for Hornblower to pull over his nightshirt. Hornblower rushed up to the dark
quarterdeck, cannoning into another hurrying figure as he did so.

'Damn your eyes!' said the figure, in Bush's voice, and then, 'I beg
your pardon, sir.'

The ship was alive with the twittering of the pipes as the hands were
summoned from their hammocks, and the maindeck resounded with
the drumming of bare feet. Montgomery, officer of the watch, was at the
starboard rail.

'*Raven* sent up a rocket, sir, two minutes back. Bearin' sou'-by-east.'

'Wind's west-by-north,' decided Bush, looking down into the tiny
light of the binnacle.

A westerly wind and a dark blustery night; ideal conditions for
Macdonald to try and push a force across the river mouth. He had
twenty big river barges, into which he could cram five thousand men
and a few guns; if he once managed to push a force of that size across
the river the Russian position would be hopelessly turned. On the other

hand, if he were to lose a force of that size – five thousand men killed or drowned or prisoners – it would be a staggering blow which might well give him pause and so gain time for the Russians. A fortified position, in the final analysis, was only a means of gaining time. Hornblower hoped most passionately that the French flotilla had been allowed to thrust its head well into the noose before Cole in the *Raven* gave the alarm.

A shout from the masthead claimed his attention.

'Gunfire to loo'ard, sir!'

From the deck they could just see a pinpoint of flame stab the darkness far to the westward, and then another one.

'That's too far to the west'ard,' said Hornblower to Bush.

'I'm afraid it is, sir.'

At anchor on the very edge of the shoals in that direction was the *Raven*; it was her light draught that had dictated her position there. Vickery in *Lotus* guarded the other bank of the river, while *Nonsuch* perforce still lay anchored in the fairway. All the armed boats of the squadron were rowing guard in the mouth of the river – a navy cutter with a three-pounder could be counted on to deal with a river barge, even if the latter did carry three hundred soldiers. But from the direction of the gunfire it looked as if Vickery had given the alarm prematurely. Another gun flashed to leeward; the wind prevented them from hearing the sound of it.

'Call my barge,' ordered Hornblower. He felt he could not stay here in useless suspense.

The boat pushed off from the *Nonsuch*, the men tugging at the oars to move the boat in the teeth of the wind. Brown, in the darkness beside Hornblower, felt his captain's restlessness and anxiety.

'Pull, you b—!' he shouted at the rowers. The boat crawled forward over the tossing water, with Brown standing in the sternsheets with his hand on the tiller.

''Nother gun, sir. Right ahead,' he reported to Hornblower.

'Very good.'

A tedious quarter of an hour followed, while the boat lurched and pitched over the steep little waves, and the hands slaved away at the oars. The wash of the seas overside and the groaning of the oars against the thole-pins made a monotonous accompaniment to Hornblower's racing thoughts.

'There's a whole lot o' guns firin' now, sir,' reported Brown.

'I can see them,' replied Hornblower.

The darkness was pierced by shot after shot; it was evident that the guard-boats were all clustered round a single victim.

'There's *Raven*, sir. Shall I make for her?'

'No. Steer for the firing.'

The dark shape of the sloop was just visible ahead; Brown put his helm over a little to lay the barge on a course that would take her past the sloop at a cable's length's distance, heading for the gunfire. They had drawn up abeam of the sloop when there came a flash and a roar from her side, and a shot howled close overhead.

'Jesus!' said Brown. 'Ain't the fools got eyes in their heads?'

Presumably the sloop had hailed the passing boat, and, receiving no reply – the hail being carried away by the wind – had incontinently fired. Another shot came from the *Raven*, and someone in the barge squawked with dismay. It was demoralising to be fired upon by one's own side.

'Turn towards her,' ordered Hornblower. 'Burn a blue light.'

At any moment the sloop might fire a full broadside, with every chance of blowing the barge out of the water. Hornblower took the tiller while Brown wrestled, cursing under his breath, with flint and steel and tinder. The hand pulling at the stroke oar said something to try to quicken his movements.

'Shut your mouth!' snapped Hornblower.

Everything was in a muddle, and the men knew it. Brown caught a spark on the tinder, jabbed the fuse of the blue light upon it, and then blew the fuse into a glow. A moment later the firework burst into an unearthly glare, lighting up the boat and the water round it, and Hornblower stood up so that his features and his uniform should be visible to the sloop. It was poor revenge to think of the consternation in the *Raven* when they saw that they had been firing on their own Commodore. Hornblower went up the sloop's side in a state of cold fury. Cole was there to receive him, of course.

'Well, Mr Cole?'

'Sorry I fired on you, sir, but you didn't answer my hail.'

'Did it occur to you that with this wind blowing I could not hear you?'

'Yes, sir. But we know the French are out. The boats fired on them an hour back, and half my crew is away in the boats. Supposing I were boarded by two hundred French soldiers? I couldn't take chances, sir.'

It was no use arguing with a man as jumpy and as nervous as Cole evidently was.

'You sent up the alarm rocket?'

'Yes, sir. I had to inform you that the barges were at sea.'

'You did that the first moment you knew?'

'Yes, sir. Of course, sir.'

'Did it occur to you that you would alarm the French as well?'

'I thought that was what you wanted, sir.'

Hornblower turned away in disgust. The man in his excitement had clean forgotten every order given him.

'Boat approaching from to wind'ard, sir,' reported someone, his white shirt just visible in the gathering dawn. Cole ran forward excitedly, with Hornblower striding after him, catching up to him as he stood at the knightheads staring at the boat.

'Boat ahoy!' yelled Cole through his speaking trumpet.

'Aye aye,' came the answering hail downwind. That was the correct reply for an approaching boat with officers on board. She was a ship's cutter under a dipping lugsail; as Hornblower watched she took in the sail with considerable clumsiness and came drooping down to the sloop under oars. Level with the bow she turned, clumsily again, and headed in to lie alongside the sloop. Hornblower could see she was crammed with men.

'Soldiers!' suddenly exclaimed Cole, pointing at the boat with an excited forefinger. 'Stand to your guns, men! Sheer off, there!'

Hornblower could see shakoes and crossbelts; it must be just the kind of vision Cole's imagination had been toying with all through the night. A reassuring English voice came back to them from overside.

'Avast, there! This is *Lotus*'s cutter with prisoners.'

It was Purvis's voice without a doubt. Hornblower walked to the waist and looked down. There was Purvis in the stern, and British seamen in check shirts at the oars, but every inch of space was filled with soldiers, sitting in attitudes of apprehension or dejection. Right up in the eyes of the boat, round the boat's gun, four red-coated marines held their muskets at the ready; that was the way Purvis had prepared to deal with any attempt by the prisoners to regain their freedom.

'Let 'em come up,' said Hornblower.

They climbed the side, greeted by the grinning seamen as they reached the deck, and stared round in the growing light. Purvis swung himself up and touched his hat to Hornblower.

'They're all Dutchmen, I think, sir. Not Frogs. We got 'em off the barge we caught. Had to fire into 'em a long time – just shot the barge to pieces, us an' the other boats. They're following us, sir, with the other prisoners.'

'You only caught one barge?'

'Yes, sir. The others ran for home the moment the rocket went up. But we got two hundred prisoners, I should think, an' we had to kill nigh on a hundred more.'

One single barge taken, with two hundred men, when Hornblower had hoped for a dozen barges at least and three thousand men! But Purvis in his innocence was obviously delighted with his capture.

'Here's one of their officers, sir.'

Hornblower turned on the blue-coated man who was wearily climbing over the side.

'Who are you, sir?' he asked in French, and after a moment's hesitation the officer replied haltingly in the same language.

'Lieutenant von Bulow, of the Fifty-first Regiment of Infantry.'

'French infantry?'

'Of the King of Prussia,' said the officer, sternly, with a Teutonic explosiveness in the word 'Prusse' which indicated his annoyance at the suggestion that he would be a Frenchman.

So Macdonald had not risked French lives in this highly dangerous venture; that was to be expected, of course. Bonaparte had made war largely at the expense of his allies for the last ten years.

'I will see that you are given refreshment,' said Hornblower, politely. 'Please order your men to sit down against the rail there.'

The officer barked the order. It was significant how at the first warning 'achtung' the dispirited soldiers came instantly to attention, standing stiff and straight. Most of them were wet and bedraggled, apparently having been in the water before surrendering. Hornblower gave orders for them to be fed, at the same time as the other boats came back downwind, each with its quota of prisoners. On the cramped decks of the *Raven* the two hundred prisoners made a fine show; Cole had the two foremost chase-guns run inboard and trained round upon them, a round of canister in each gun, the gun-captains posted with lighted matches ready to fire into them. Seamen, still grinning, went along their ranks handing out bread and beer.

'See how they eat, sir!' said Purvis. 'Look at that one, layin' into his biscuit like a wolf with a bone. God damme, it's gone a'ready. It's true what they say, sir, about Boney never feedin' his men.'

An Imperial army was wont to gather its food from the countryside as it marched; Macdonald's sixty thousand had been stationary now for over two weeks, and in a thinly populated country. They must be on short commons. Every day the siege of Riga could be prolonged would cost lives in plenty to Bonaparte, and although he was ever prodigal with lives there must come a time at last when he would have no more to spare, not even Prussian ones, or Italian ones. The greater the pity, then, that the whole division that had tried to pass the river had not been wiped out. Hornblower told himself that was his fault; he should not have entrusted any vital part of the operation to a nervous old woman like Cole. He ought instead to have stayed on board *Raven* himself. Yet it was hard to be sure of that; the other end of the line, which he had entrusted to Vickery in *Lotus*, was just as important, and it was desirable that he should be in the centre in *Nonsuch* to co-ordinate the activities of his two wings. If Vickery and Cole had had their positions interchanged — as would have to be done — although Vickery could have been relied upon not to spring the trap too soon could Cole have been relied upon to keep it closed? There might be five thousand Prussians on the farther bank of the Dwina at this moment if it had been up to Cole to head them off. Hornblower found himself wishing that he had known exactly which night Macdonald would make the attempt; he might as well have wished for the moon.

'Mr Cole,' said Hornblower, 'make a signal to *Nonsuch*, "Commodore to Captain. Am proceeding to Riga with prisoners." Then the guard-boats can return to their respective ships, and if you will kindly up anchor we'll start.'

XX

Hornblower was once more up in the gallery that encircled the dome of the church of Daugavgriva.

'You see what I was telling you about, sir,' said Clausewitz, pointing.

Out beyond the Russian works stretched a long line, brown against the green, the parapet of the trench the French had thrown up during the night. Macdonald must be a general with energy, for he had had this work done at the same time as he had sent the Prussians on their risky endeavour to cross the river, so that while one attempt had failed he had made a solid gain, profiting by the dark and rainy night to throw up this entrenchment far forward unobserved.

'That is his first parallel, sir, and in the centre of it is the battery he is constructing. And see there, sir? That is where he is sapping forward.'

Hornblower stared through his telescope. At a point towards the end of the face of the first parallel he could see something that looked like a wall constructed of bundles of timber. The guns in the Russian works far below him were firing at it; he could see earth flying as the shots struck round it. At the end of the wall of timber was something that looked strange – a sort of shield on wheels. He was studying it when he saw it moved out suddenly, leaving a narrow gap between it and the end of the timber wall, in which for a fleeting moment he saw a couple of men in blue uniforms. It was only a fleeting moment, for immediately the gap was filled with a new bundle of timber. Above the new bundle he could see the blades of spades rising and then disappearing; apparently the bundle of timber was hollow, barrel-shaped, and as soon as it was in position the men sheltering behind it set to work to fill it up with earth dug from behind it. Hornblower realised that he was witnessing the classic method of sapping towards an enemy's position with 'gabion' and 'fascine'. That big timber basket was a gabion, now being filled with earth. Farther back, under cover of the line of filled gabions, the besiegers were revetting their breastwork with fascines, six-foot bundles of wood, and farther back still they were building the whole thing solid with earth dug from a trench behind the breastwork. As he watched, the shield was suddenly pushed forward another yard, and another gabion was put in position; the French were three feet nearer the earthworks which guarded Daugavgriva. No, not a yard, a little less, because the sap was not pointing straight at its objective, but out at its flank so that it could not be enfiladed. Soon it would change its direction, and point towards the other flank, approaching the fortress in zigzag fashion, ruthlessly and remorselessly. Of all operations of war a scientific siege was the most certain if relief did not arrive from the outside.

'See there, sir!' said Clausewitz suddenly.

From behind a high embankment had suddenly emerged a long string of horses, looking like ants at that distance, but the white breeches of the men who led them showed up clearly in the sunshine. The horses were dragging a cannon, a big piece of artillery when its apparent size was compared with that of the horses. It crawled towards the battery in the centre of the first parallel, a myriad white-breeched specks attending it. The high breastwork of the first parallel screened the operation from the sight of the Russian gunners and shielded it from their fire. When the guns had all been brought into the battery, Hornblower knew, openings – 'embrasures' – would be made in the breastwork through which the guns would open fire on the village, silencing the return fire of the defence, and then hammering a breach; meanwhile the sap would be expanded into a wide trench, the 'second parallel', from which, or if necessary from a 'third parallel', the stormers would rush out to carry the breach.

'They will have that battery armed by tomorrow,' said Clausewitz. 'And look! There is another gabion put in place.'

Siege operations had the remorseless cold inevitability of the advance of a snake on a paralysed bird.

'Why do your guns not stop the work on the sap?' asked Hornblower.

'They are trying, as you see. But a single gabion is not an easy target to hit at this range, and it is only the end one which is vulnerable. And by the time the sap approaches within easy range their battery-fire will be silencing our guns.'

Another siege-gun had made its appearance from behind the high embankment, and was crawling towards the battery; its predecessor was at that moment being thrust finally into its position at the breastwork.

'Can you not bring your ships up, sir?' asked Clausewitz. 'See how the water comes close to their works there. You could shoot them to pieces with your big guns.'

Hornblower shook his head; the same idea had already occurred to him, for the long glittering arm of the Gulf of Riga which reached into the land there was very tempting. But there was less than a fathom of water in it, and even his shallow bomb-ketches drew nine feet – seven at least if he emptied them of all their stores save those necessary for the action.

'I would do so if I could,' said Hornblower, 'but at the present moment I can see no means of getting my guns into range.'

Clausewitz looked at him coldly, and Hornblower was conscious that goodwill between allies was a frail thing. Earlier that morning British and Russians had been the best of friends; Essen and Clausewitz had been thoroughly elated at the turning back of Macdonald's attempt to cross the river, and – like the unthinking junior officers in the squadron – had thought the annihilation of a half-battalion of Prussians a notable success, not knowing of the far more far-reaching plan which Hornblower had made and which Cole's nervousness had brought to almost naught. When affairs went well, allies were the best of friends, but in adversity each naturally tended to blame the other. Now that the French approaches were moving towards Daugavgriva he was asking why the Russian artillery did not stop them, and the Russians were asking why his ships' guns did not do the same.

Hornblower made his explanation as fully as he could, but Clausewitz turned an unsympathetic ear, and so did Essen when the matter came up for discussion as Hornblower was saying goodbye to him. It was a poor showing for a Navy whose boast was that nothing was impossible; Hornblower was irritable and snappy when he returned that afternoon to the *Nonsuch*, and he had no word for Bush who came hastily to greet him as he came up the side. His cabin was unfriendly and inhospitable to his jaundiced eye when he entered it, and it was 'make and mend' day on board, with the hands skylarking noisily on the deck, so that he knew that if he went up to walk the quarterdeck his train of thought would be continually interrupted. He toyed for a moment with the idea of ordering Bush to cancel his order for make and mend and instead to put the hands to some quiet labour. Everyone would know that it was because the Commodore wanted to walk the deck in peace, and might be properly impressed with his importance, but there was never a chance of his acting on the notion. He would not deprive the men of their holiday, and the thought of swelling his importance in their eyes acted as a positive deterrent.

Instead, he went out into the quarter gallery, and, bowed below the overhanging cove above, he tried to stride up and down its twelve-foot length. It was indeed a pity that he could not bring his ships' guns to bear on the siege-works. Heavy guns at close range would play havoc with the French breastworks. And behind the high dyke from which he had seen the guns being dragged must lie the French park and train – a few shells from the bomb-vessels would wreak havoc there, and if only he could get the ketches up the bay it would be easy to drop shells over the dyke. But over most of the bay there was only three or four feet of water, and nowhere more than seven. The thing was impossible, and the best thing he could do was to forget about it. To distract himself he stepped over the rail into the other quarter gallery, and peeped through the stern window into Bush's cabin. Bush was asleep on his cot, flat on his back with his mouth open, his hands spread wide at his sides and his wooden leg hanging in a becket against the bulkhead. Hornblower felt a twinge of annoyance that his captain should be sleeping so peacefully while he himself had so many cares on his shoulders. For two pins he would send a message in to Bush and wreck his nap for him. But he knew he would never do that, either. He could never bring himself to a wanton abuse of power.

He stepped back into his own quarter gallery, and as he did, as he stood with one leg suspended and with the rudder gudgeons creaking a little in their pintles in the stream below him, the idea came to him, so that he stood stock still for a space, with one leg in mid-air. Then he brought his leg over and walked into his cabin and shouted for a messenger.

'My compliments to the officer of the watch, and will he please signal to *Harvey* for Mr Mound to come on board at once.'

Mound came down into the cabin, young and expectant, and yet with his eagerness thinly overlaid with assumed nonchalance. It suddenly dawned upon Hornblower as he greeted him that that careless lackadaisical air of Mound's was assumed in imitation of himself. Hornblower realised that he was something of a hero – more than that, very much of a hero – to this young lieutenant who was paying him the sincerest flattery of imitation. It made him grin wryly to himself even while he motioned Mound to a chair, and then it was forgotten as he plunged into the vital discussion.

'Mr Mound, do you know of the progress of the French siege-works?'

'No, sir.'

'Then look at this chart with me. They have a line of trenches here, with a battery here. Their main flank and stores are behind a dyke, here. If we could bring the bomb-vessels up the bay we could shell them out of both places.'

'Shoal water, sir,' said Mound regretfully.

'Yes,' said Hornblower, and for the life of him he could not stop himself from making a dramatic pause before uttering the crucial word. 'But with camels we could reduce the draught.'

'Camels!' exclaimed Mound, and as he realised all the implications his face lit up. 'By George, sir, you're right.'

Camels are a means of reducing the draught of a ship – loaded vessels lashed tightly one on each side and them emptied, so as to raise the centre ship farther out of the water. Mound was already grappling with the details.

'There are lighters and barges in Riga, sir. They'll give us some, sure as a gun. Plenty of sand to ballast 'em, or we can fill 'em with water and pump 'em out. With two big lighters I could lessen *Harvey*'s draught by five feet easy – lift her clear out of the water for that matter. Those lighters are two hundred tons burden an' don't draw more than a couple of feet empty.'

A difficulty had occurred to Hornblower while Mound was speaking, one which he had not thought of before.

'How are you going to steer 'em all?' he demanded. 'They'll be unmanageable.'

'Rig a Danube rudder, sir,' replied Mound instantly. 'Make it big enough and you could steer anything with one.'

' "Give me a fulcrum and I will move the world",' quoted Hornblower.

'Exactly, sir. An' I'll pierce the lighters for sweeps. There'll be no beatin' to wind'ard any more than in a raft. I could put the men to work at once if you'll give the order, sir.'

Mound might have been a boy of ten instead of one of twenty from the eagerness of his voice. The languid calm was quite forgotten.

'I'll send a note to the Governor,' said Hornblower, 'asking for the loan of four lighters. I'll make it six, in case of accidents. Have your plans ready in an hour's time. You can draw upon this ship and the sloops for the materials and men you'll need.'

'Aye aye, sir.'

There was need for haste, for that every evening there came sullenly booming across the bay the sound of heavy guns firing, not the higher-pitched incisive growl of the field-pieces they had heard before, but the deep-toned roar of siege artillery; the enemy was trying a few shots with the first of the big guns dragged up into their battery. And the next morning, just as Hornblower came out on the quarterdeck, there was a sudden loud crash ashore, like a peal of thunder, to herald the opening salvo of the enemy. Its echoes had not died away before a more ragged salvo succeeded it, and then another more ragged still, and so on until the air was ceaselessly tormented by the loud reports, like a continuous thunderstorm from which the ear waited continually for relief that was not granted it. The masthead lookout reported a long smear of smoke drifted by the breeze across the countryside from the enemy's battery.

'Call away my barge,' said Hornblower.

At *Nonsuch*'s boat booms there already lay an assortment of the boats of the squadron, piled high with the stores which had been taken out of the two bomb-ketches. The barge danced over the water in the spark-ling dawn to where the bomb-ketches lay anchored, each with a lighter on either side. Duncan, captain of the *Moth*, was being rowed round the group in a jolly boat. He touched his hat as the barge approached.

'Morning, sir,' he said, and then instantly turned back to the work in hand, raising his speaking-trumpet to his lips. 'Too much by the bows! Take up the for'ard cable another pawl!'

Hornblower had himself rowed on to the *Harvey*, and leaped from his barge to the lighter on her starboard side – not much of a leap, because she was laden down with ballast – without bothering officers or men for compliments. Mound was standing on his tiny quarterdeck, testing with his foot the tension of the big cable – one of *Nonsuch*'s – which was frapped round his own ship and both lighters, two turns round each, forward and aft.

'Carry on, port side!' he yelled.

In each of the lighters a large working party was stationed, the men equipped with shovels for the most part extemporised out of wood. At Mound's order the men in the port-side lighter recommenced lustily shovelling the sand over the side. Clouds of it drifted astern on the faint wind. Mound tested the tension again.

'Carry on, starboard side!' he yelled again, and then, perceiving his Commodore approaching, he came to the salute.

'Good morning, Mr Mound,' said Hornblower.

'Good morning, sir. We have to do this part of it step by step, you see, sir. I have the old ketch so light she'll roll over in the cables if I give her the chance.'

'I understand, Mr. Mound.'

'The Russians were prompt enough sending out the lighters to us, sir.'

'Can you wonder?' replied Hornblower. 'D'you hear the French battery at work?'

Mound listened and apparently heard it for the first time. He had been engrossed too deeply in his work to pay any attention to it before; his face was unshaven and grey with fatigue, for his activity had not ceased since Hornblower had summoned him the afternoon before. In that time both ketches had been emptied of their stores, the cables roused out and got across to them, the lighters received and laid alongside in the dark, and each group of three vessels bound into a single mass with the cables hauled taut by the capstans.

'Excuse me, sir,' said Mound, and ran forward to examine the forward cable.

With the shovelling-out of the sand, hove overside by a hundred lusty pairs of arms, the lighters were rising in the water, lifting the ketch between them, cables and timber all a-creaking, and it was necessary to keep the cables taut as the rising of the lighters relieved the strain upon them. Hornblower turned aft to see what another working party were doing there. A large barrel half filled with water had been streamed out astern with a line to either quarter of the ketch, conducted in each case through a fair-lead to an extemporised windlass fixed to the deck. Paying out or heaving in on the lines would regulate the pull of the barrel, were the ketch under way, to one side or the other, exerting a powerful leverage. The barrel then was intended to undertake the duties of the rudder, which was already sufficiently high out of the water to be almost useless.

'It's only a contraption, sir,' said Mound, who had returned from forward. 'I had intended, as I told you, sir, to rig a Danube rudder. It was Wilson here who suggested this – I'd like to call your attention to him, sir. It'll be much more effective, I'm sure.'

Wilson looked up from his work with a gap-toothed grin.

'What's your rating?' asked Hornblower.

'Carpenter's mate, sir.'

'As good a one as I've known, sir,' interpolated Mound.

'What service?'

'Two commissions in the old *Superb*, sir. One in *Arethusa*, an' now this one, sir.'

'I'll make out an acting warrant for you as carpenter,' said Hornblower.

'Thankee, sir, thankee.'

Mound could easily have taken the whole credit for devising this jury rudder to himself if he had wished. Hornblower liked him all the more for not having done so. It was good for discipline and for the spirits of the men to reward good work promptly.

'Very good, Mr Mound. Carry on.'

Hornblower went back to his barge and rowed over to the *Moth*. The work here was a stage more advanced; so much sand had been shovelled out of the lighters that it was only with slow effort that the working parties could heave their shovelfuls over the side, shoulder-high. A wide streak of the *Moth*'s copper was already visible, so high was she riding.

'Watch your trim, Mr Duncan,' said Hornblower. 'She's canting a little to port.'

'Aye aye, sir.'

It called for some complicated adjustment of the cables, veering out and hauling in, to set *Moth* on an even keel again.

'She won't draw more'n two feet by the time we're finished with her, sir,' said Duncan exultantly.

'Excellent,' said Hornblower.

Duncan addressed himself to putting more men to work in the lighters, shovelling sand across from the inboard to the outboard sides, to ease the work of those actually heaving the sand over.

'Two hours more an' they'll be clear, sir,' reported Duncan. 'Then we'll only have to pierce the sides for sweeps.'

He glanced over at the sun, still not far above the horizon.

'We'll be ready for action half an hour before noon, sir,' he added.

'Put the carpenters to work piercing the sides now,' said Hornblower. 'So that you can rest your men and give them a chance to have breakfast. Then when they start again they can shovel through the ports and work quicker.'

'Aye aye, sir,'

Half an hour before noon seemed to be a more likely sort of estimate with that improvement in the programme, yet even if the completion of the work were delayed by two hours there would still be long hours of daylight left in which the blow could be struck. While the sides of the lighters were being pierced Hornblower called Duncan and Mound to him and went over their final orders with them.

'I'll be up in the church with the signalling party,' he said in conclusion. 'I'll see that you're properly supported. So good luck.'

'Thank you, sir,' they answered in unison. Excitement and anticipation masked their weariness.

So Hornblower had himself rowed over to the village, where a tiny jetty saved him and the signallers from splashing through the shallows; the roar of the bombardment and the counter-bombardment grew steadily louder as they approached. Diebitch and Clausewitz came to meet them as they mounted the jetty, and led the way towards the church. As they skirted the foot of the earthworks which ringed the village on its landward side Hornblower looked up and saw the Russian artillerymen working their guns, bearded soldiers, naked to the waist in the hot sun. An officer walked from gun to gun in the battery, pointing each piece in succession.

'There are few men in our artillery who can be trusted to lay a gun,' explained Clausewitz.

The village was already badly knocked about, great holes showing in the walls and roofs of the flimsy cottages of which it was composed. As they neared the church a ricocheting ball struck the church wall, sending a cloud of chips flying, and remaining embedded in the brickwork like a plum in a cake. A moment later Hornblower swung round to a sudden unusual noise to see his two midshipmen standing staring at the headless corpse of a seaman who a moment before had been walking at their heels. A ball flying over the earthworks had shattered his head to atoms and flung his body against them. Somers was eyeing with disgust the blood and brains which had spattered his white trousers.

'Come along,' said Hornblower.

In the gallery under the dome they could look down upon the siege. The zigzag approach trench was almost half-way towards the defences, the head of it almost obscured by flying earth as the Russians fired furiously upon it. But the central redoubt which covered the entrance to the village was in bad shape, its parapets battered into nothing more than mounds, a gun lying half buried beside its shattered carriage, although the other one was still being worked by a devoted little group. The whole of the French works were obscured by the thin pall of smoke which spread from the breaching battery, but the smoke was not so thick as to hide a column of infantry marching down towards the first parallel from the rear.

'They relieve the guard of the trenches at noon,' explained Clausewitz. 'Where are these boats of yours, sir?'

'Here they come,' said Hornblower.

They were creeping over the silvery water, fantastic in appearance, the ketches with their sails furled and the ugly bulks of the lighters beside them. The long clumsy sweeps, a dozen on each side, looked like the legs of a water-boatman on a pond, but far slower in movement as the toiling seamen who manned them tugged them through each successive endless stroke.

'Somers! Gerard!' said Hornblower, sharply. 'How are your signalling arrangements working out? Lash those blocks to the cornice up there. Come along, you haven't all day to get ready in.'

The midshipman and seamen addressed themselves to the business of making a signalling station up on the gallery. The blocks were lashed to the cornice and the halliards rove through them, the Russian staff watching the operation with interest. Meanwhile the bomb-ketches came crawling up the bay, painfully slowly under their sweeps, heading crabwise on account of the gentle breeze on their bow, before which they sagged away to leeward quite perceptibly to Hornblower's eye above them. No one among the enemy seemed to be paying them the least attention; Bonaparte's armies, lords of Europe from Madrid to Smolensk, had had few opportunities of becoming acquainted with bomb-ketches. The firing from the big battery went on steadily, pounding at the crumbling Russian earthworks below, with the Russians returning the fire with desperate energy.

The *Harvey* and the *Moth* came creeping in until they were quite close to shore; Hornblower through his glass could see minute figures moving in their bows, and knew they were dropping their anchors. The sweeps worked spasmodically, first on one side and then on the other – Hornblower up in the gallery, his heart beating fast, could well picture Mound and Duncan on their quarterdecks shouting their orders to the rowers as they manoeuvred themselves about like beetles pinned to a card. They were placing themselves in position to drop other anchors at the stern, so that by veering and hauling in on their cables they could swing themselves so as to be able to point their mortars anywhere along a wide arc. Clausewitz and the staff looked on uncomprehending, having no notion of the meaning of these manoeuvres. Hornblower saw the stern anchors let go, and could see little groups of men bending to work at the capstans; the bomb-ketches turned almost imperceptibly first this way and then that as their captains trained them round by the aid of the leading marks on the shore.

'There's the "ready" flag going up in *Harvey*,' said Hornblower, the glass at his eye.

The sheave in the block above his head shrilled noisily as the halliard ran over it, bearing the acknowledgement. A big puff of smoke suddenly spurted upwards from the *Harvey*'s bows; Hornblower at that distance could see nothing of the shell in its flight, and he waited nervously, compelling himself to search the whole area round about the battery to make sure of seeing the burst. And he saw nothing, nothing at all. Reluctantly he ordered hoisted the black cone for 'unobserved' and *Harvey* fired again. This time he could see the burst, a little volcano of smoke and fragments just beyond the battery.

'That was over, sir,' said Somers.

'Yes. Make that to *Harvey*.'

Duncan had anchored *Moth* by now, and was flying the signal of readiness. *Harvey*'s next shell fell square in the centre of the battery, and immediately afterwards *Moth*'s first shell did the same. At once the two ketches began a systematic bombardment of the battery, dropping shells into it in constant succession, so that there was not a moment when a fountain of smoke and earth was not apparent within its earthworks. It was a plain rectangular structure, without traverses or internal subdivisions, and there was no shelter for the men within it now that their enemy had found means to circumvent their earthworks. They only maintained their fire for a few seconds, and then Hornblower could see them running from their guns; the interior of the battery looked like a disturbed ants' nest. One of the big thirteen-inch shells landed full on the parapet, and the smoke clearing away revealed the breastwork blown flat, opening the interior of the battery to view from ground level in the village, and through the gap was visible the muzzle of a dismounted siege-gun, pointed skywards and helpless – a cheering sight for the defence. That was only the beginning. Gap after gap was blown in the earthworks; the whole interior was plastered with shells. At one moment there was a much bigger explosion than usual, and Hornblower guessed that an 'expense magazine' – the small store of gunpowder kept in the battery and continually replenished from the rear – had blown up. Down below him the defence had taken new heart, and every gun along the menaced front had reopened fire; it was a shot from the village, apparently, which hit the muzzle of the dismounted gun and flung it back upon the ground.

'Signal "cease fire",' said Hornblower.

Thirteen-inch shells were not munitions of war that could be readily obtained in the Baltic, and there was no purpose in wasting them upon a target which was silenced and at least made temporarily useless. And then came the countermove on the part of the attack, as he had expected. A battery of field artillery was coming over the distant slope, six guns, minute at that distance, jolting and swaying after their limbers. The country was still marshy, for the summer was not yet old enough to have dried up the fields, and the artillery, hock and axle-deep in the mire, made only slow progress.

'Signal for the target to change,' ordered Hornblower.

There was no means of observing the fall of the shells on the new target, for the bomb-ketches were dropping them just over the high dyke. It was a matter of chance should they do any destruction, but Hornblower could guess that the park and depots of an army of sixty thousand men conducting a first-class siege were likely to be both extensive and crowded; a few shells dropped there might do good. The first field battery was approaching the water's edge, the horses wheeling round to leave the guns jointing at the bomb-ketches at neat geometrical intervals.

'*Harvey* signals she's shifting target, sir,' reported Gerard.

'Very good.'

Harvey was firing at the field battery; it took her a little while to get the range, and field-guns, spaced far apart in a long thin line, were not a good target for mortars, even though the fall of the shells was now under direct observation. And a second battery was coming up on the flank of the first and – Hornblower's telescope could easily make them out across the narrow extremity of the bay – there were more guns coming into action to put the bomb-vessels under a cross-fire. One of *Harvey*'s shells burst close beside one of the guns, presumably killing every man serving it, but by chance leaving the gun itself still on its wheels. The other guns had opened fire, the smoke creeping lazily from their muzzles. Across the bay the other field batteries were coming into action, although at very long range for field artillery. There was no purpose in continuing to expose the bomb-ketches to the fire of the shore; Macdonald had two hundred field-guns, and there were only two bomb-ketches.

'Signal "Discontinue the action",' ordered Hornblower.

Now that he had given the word it seemed to him that he had waited over-long. It seemed ages before the bomb-ketches got their anchors hoisted, and Hornblower could see, as he waited anxiously, the splashes thrown up all round them by the shots from the shore. He saw the sweeps thrust out from the sides of the lighters take a grip on the water, swinging the vessels round, and then the white sails mounted the masts, and the queer craft sailed away out of range, making vast leeway which caused them to head crabwise aslant of their course. Hornblower turned away with relief to meet the eyes of the governor, who had been standing silently watching the whole operation through a vast telescope which he had mounted upon the shoulder of a patient orderly whose back must have ached with crouching.

'Excellent, sir,' said the Governor. 'I thank you, in the name of the Czar. Russia is grateful to you, sir, and so is the city of Riga.'

'Thank you, Your Excellency,' said Hornblower.

Diebitch and Clausewitz were awaiting his attention. They were eager to discuss future operations with him, and he had to listen to them. He dismissed his midshipmen and signalling party, hoping that Somers would have the sense to interpret the glance he threw him as a warning not to let his men get hold of any Lettish spirits while they were ashore. Then he resumed the conversation, which was continually interrupted by the coming and going of orderlies with messages, and hasty orders given in languages that he could not understand. But the results of those orders were soon apparent; two regiments of infantry came filing up through the village, with bayonets fixed, lined the earthworks, and then dashed out on the glacis with a yell. The heavy guns in the battery which should have torn them to pieces with grapeshot were all silent; Hornblower watched the sortie reach the approach trench almost without opposition; the men burst into it over the parapets, and hurriedly began to tear down the sandbags and gabions with which it was constructed, while down into the ruined battery came a French infantry force too late to stop them, even if they had been able to do so under the artillery fire of the besieged. In an hour the work was done, the approach trench levelled over large sections, the tools taken, spare gabions heaped together and set on fire.

'Thanks to you, sir,' said Clausewitz, 'the progress of the siege has been delayed by four days.'

Four days; and the French had all the rest of the year to continue pounding the defences. It was his duty, and the Russians', to maintain them as long as might be. There was something a little depressing about the prospect of trying to maintain this outwork while Bonaparte was marching, irresistibly, into the heart of Russia. Yet the game had to be played out to the end. He parted from his hosts feeling weary and disconsolate, a dark shadow overhanging any elation he might feel regarding the success – the success that had won four days – of his attack on the French. The pipes squealed as he came over the side of the *Nonsuch*: Captain Bush and the first lieutenant and the officer of the watch were on the quarterdeck to receive him.

'Good evening, Captain Bush. Would you be kind enough to hang out a signal for Mr Duncan and Mr Mound to repair on board here immediately?'

'Yes, sir.' Bush did not speak again for a second or two, but he did not turn away to obey. 'Yes, sir. Mound was killed.'

'What's that you say?'

'One of the last shots from the beach cut him in two, sir.'

Bush was trying to keep his expression harsh as usual, but it was obvious that he was deeply moved. Yet he had not grown as fond of Mound as had Hornblower. And in that one moment there came flooding over Hornblower all the torrent of regrets and doubts which he was to know for so long to come. If only he had ordered the bomb-ketches out of action earlier! Had he been wantonly reckless of human life in keeping them in action after the field batteries began to return fire? Mound had been one of the best young officers he had ever been fortunate enough to command. England had suffered a severe loss in his death, and so had he. But his feeling of personal loss was more acute still, and the thought of the finality of death oppressed him. The wave of torment was still breaking over him when Bush spoke again.

'Shall I signal for Duncan and *Harvey*'s first lieutenant, sir?'

'Yes, do that, if you please, Captain Bush.'

XXI

Hornblower was endeavouring to write a note in French to the Governor – a weary exercise. Sometimes it was words and sometimes it was phrases which were beyond his power to express in French, and each hitch meant retracing his steps and beginning the sentence again.

Despatches received at this moment from England – he was trying to say – inform me that the armies of His Majesty the King of Great Britain and Ireland have been successful in a great battle fought on the 14th of last month at Salamanca in Spain. Marshal Marmont, Duke of Ragusa, was wounded, and some ten thousand prisoners were captured. The British general, the Marquess of Wellington, is, according to the advices I have received, in full march for Madrid, which is certain to fall to him. The consequences of this battle cannot be estimated too highly.

Hornblower swore a little to himself; it was not for him to recommend to the Governor what action he should take regarding this news. But the fact that one of Bonaparte's armies had been thoroughly beaten, in a battle fought between equal numbers on a large scale, was of the highest importance. If he were Governor, he would fire salutes, post proclamations, do all that he could to revive the spirits of soldiers and civilians in their weary task of holding Riga against the French. And what it would mean to the main Russian army, now drawing together in the south to defend Moscow in one last desperate battle, it was impossible to estimate.

He signed and sealed the note, shouted for Brown, and handed it over to him for immediate despatch ashore. Beside him, in addition to the official despatches just received, lay a pile of fifteen letters all addressed to him in Barbara's handwriting; Barbara had written to him every week since his departure, and the letters had piled up in the Admiralty office awaiting the time when *Clam* should return with despatches, and he had opened only the last one to assure himself that all was well at home, and he picked it up again to reread it.

MY BELOVED HUSBAND,

This week the domestic news is quite overshadowed by the great news from Spain. Arthur has beaten Marmont and the whole usurping government in that country is in ruin. Arthur is to be made a Marquess. Was it in my first letter or in my second that I told you he had been made an Earl? Let us hope that soon I shall be writing to you that he has been made a Duke not because I wish my brother to be a Duke, but because that will mean another victory. All England is talking of Arthur this week, just as two weeks back all England was talking of Commodore Hornblower and his exploits in the Baltic.

The household here at Smallbridge is so much agog with all this news that our most important event bade fair to pass unnoticed. I refer to the breeching of Richard Arthur. He is in smallclothes now, and his petticoats are put away for ever. He is young for such a transformation, and Ramsbottom melted into tears at the passing of her baby; but if you could see him I think you would agree that he looks vastly well in his new clothes, at least until he can escape from supervision and indulge himself in his favourite recreation of digging holes in the ground in the shrubbery. He exhibits both physically and morally a partiality for the soil which appears odd in the son of such a distinguished sailor. When I have completed this letter I shall ring and send for him so that he can affix his mark, and I daresay he will add such grubby fingerprints as will further identify his signature.

Hornblower turned the page, and the grubby fingerprints were there, sure enough, along with the shaky X that Richard Arthur had scrawled under his stepmother's signature. Hornblower felt a desperate longing to see his son at that moment, happily muddy and spading away at his hole in the shrubbery, all-engrossed in the business of the moment with babyhood's sublime concentration of purpose. Above the X were the last few lines Barbara had written.

As always, it is my constant dream that my dear husband shall soon return victorious, when I shall be able to exert myself to increase his happiness in place of merely praying for it as I do now.

Hornblower refused to allow himself to grow sentimental, brutally strangling any emotion which he experienced. So now he had two brothers-in-law who were Marquesses, and one of them was a full General, while he himself was no more than a Knight of the Bath and – unless there should be an unusual casualty rate among his seniors – it would still be eight years before he became even a Rear Admiral, even if he should live so long and his career were not cut short by disciplinary action. He reached for the despatch which had been the first one he had opened, and read once more the passage which had the greatest bearing on the present moment.

Their Lordships desire me to call your particular notice to the fact that Government attaches the greatest importance to maintaining the defence of Riga as long as it is possible. They instruct me that they consider the safety of the squadron under your command as secondary compared with the prolongation of the siege and they charge you, on your peril, to do everything in your power to prevent the enemy from continuing his march on St Petersburg.

In other words, thought Hornblower, Riga must be defended to the last man – and ship – and they would shoot him if they thought he had not done his utmost. He shouted for his barge, locked his desk, seized his hat and, after a moment's hesitation, his pistols, and had himself rowed once more over to Daugavgriva.

The village was now a mere mass of ruins, save for the church, whose solid walls had withstood the flames that had swept the place and the continual storm of ricocheting shots which came over from the bombardment of the ramparts. The place stank of death, for the dead were many and the earth over them scanty. Trenches had been driven from cellar to cellar of the ruined houses to permit of safe passage through the village, and it was by way of these that he made his way to the church. From the gallery there the view was ominous. The besiegers' second parallel was completed, no more than two hundred yards from the defences, and the approaches were continuing their remorseless progress towards the ditch. The fire from the big battery was ceaseless, and there was but small reply from the ramparts; too many gunners had been killed and too many guns knocked to pieces, and guns and artillerymen were scarce, so that it was better to try to preserve the remainder to beat off the assault when it should come. Down at the water's edge on the besiegers' side a well-constructed battery displayed the guns that were ready to sweep the area where the bomb-ketches had anchored; there was no chance of repeating the surprise bombardment of the breaching battery which had prolonged the siege for days at the cost of Mound's life.

Clausewitz commented coolly on the situation to Hornblower as they

looked at all this through their glasses. To a doctrinaire soldier a siege
was an intellectual exercise. It was mathematically possible to calculate
the rate of progress of the approaches and the destructive effect of the
batteries, to predict every move and countermove in advance, and to
foretell within an hour the moment of the final assault. The time had
come, now that it was impossible to maintain fire upon the head of the
sap, to attempt to delay the progress of the besiegers by a sortie.

'But,' expostulated Hornblower, 'if the French know that a sortie is
due, will not they make preparations for it?'

'Yes,' said Clausewitz, his cold grey eyes expressionless.

'Would it not be better to surprise them?'

'Yes. But in a siege how is that to be done?'

'We surprised them with the bomb-vessels.'

'Yes. But now—'

Clausewitz indicated the battery which denied the end of the bay to
them.

'But still—' began Hornblower, and then bit off the sentence. There
was no purpose in being critical without having a helpful suggestion to
make at the same time. He turned his attention once more to the siege-
works, looking for inspiration, while the guns roared out below him.
They roared from farther up the river as well, where the French had
opened another front of attack on the Mitau suburb directly across the
river from Riga. The resources of the defence were being stretched very
thin, and Macdonald had locked his teeth, bulldog fashion, into the
siege and it would be hard to shake his hold. All the resources of Prussia
were being drawn upon to supply his army with stores for the siege, and
he had already proved that nothing would distract him from it, not
even the fact that the Lettish and Livonian and Lithuanian peasantry
had risen in revolt in his rear and had set all the country behind him in
a turmoil.

'The dead are beginning to come down the river,' said Clausewitz.
He had big white teeth that revealed themselves at the least provocation.
Hornblower looked at him without comprehension.

'From the fighting two weeks ago,' explained Clausewitz. 'At Vitebsk
and Smolensk two hundred miles to the south of us. Some of the corpses
have succeeded in making the journey. Russian corpses, many of them.
But French corpses too, and Bavarian corpses, and Westphalian corpses,
and Italian corpses – many Italians. It must have been a big battle.'

'Very interesting,' said Hornblower, scanning the siege-works again.
In the centre of the second parallel was a new battery, the fire from whose
guns would cut up any force attacking frontally in the hope of destroying
the works. It would be asking much of any sallying force to cross two
hundred yards of naked glacis in the teeth of such a fire and then storm
ditch and parapet. The flanks were secure, too, one guarded by the little

river and the other trending back towards the bay. The bay! The French batteries might be able to sweep the bay sufficiently effectively to prevent bomb-vessels anchoring there in daylight, but they would not be able to stop an infantry attack launched from boats at night. Then the parallel could be rushed at dawn from the flank. Hornblower turned to Clausewitz with the suggestion, and Clausewitz adopted it instantly. These Continental soldiers were always liable to forget about the sea when making their plans, but Clausewitz, Prussian though he was, was a man of sufficient elasticity of mind still to be able to see the merits of a plan based on command of the sea.

There was no time to be lost if the assault upon Daugavgriva were to be anticipated. The plan had to be given form instantly; timetables worked out, signals agreed upon, troops allocated for the landing and marched to the point where Hornblower could have boats' crews ready to man the river barges which were to carry the troops to the point selected for landing. Hornblower had to detail crews and officers, issue his orders, and make sure they were understood. Montgomery and Duncan, Purvis and Carlin, had to be sent for, brought up to the dome and shown the objectives to be aimed at – Hornblower fretted himself weary walking round the gallery while waiting for them to come ashore after he had sent for them. Mounted messengers, riding in hot haste, brought back a trio of Russian colonels to the gallery; it was their regiments which were detailed to make the landing. Hornblower explained to them in French, and then explained to his officers in English. Then he had the job of interpreting the questions which everyone wanted to ask. Half a dozen Russian subalterns, squatting on the floor of the gallery nursing pieces of board on which sheets of paper were pinned, wrote out the orders which Clausewitz dictated to them. Essen arrived in the midst of all the bustle; he had given his verbal consent at once to the proposed attack, and when, on his arrival, he found the preparations so far advanced, like a sensible man he left the elaboration of the details to the men who had devised the scheme. All this went on with the steady roar of the bombardment supplying a loud undertone to every conversation, while the Russian ramparts crumbled steadily under the hail of shot, and while the approach trenches crept steadily nearer.

It was before noon that Hornblower had made the suggestion to Clausewitz; it was eight in the evening, and the sun had set, before everything was completed, before Hornblower had had himself rowed to the Dwina mouth to inspect the boats which had been provided, and to watch the Russian grenadiers marching down to be herded into them.

'You understand your orders, Duncan?' asked Hornblower.

'Yes sir.'

'Let's see your watch. Set it by mine.'

'Aye aye, sir.'

'Mr Montgomery. Mr Purvis. Remember what I said about keeping the landing force together. You must strike all at once – no landing in driblets. Make sure the soldiers know the direction in which to advance when they land.'

'Aye aye, sir.'

'Good luck, then.'

'Thank you, sir.'

It was quite dark by the time Hornblower set foot again on the little jetty at Daugavgriva; dark, and there was a chilly breath in the air. So far had the year advanced since he had first cast anchor in Riga Bay. Midsummer had gone and autumn was at hand. He had to feel his way along the trenches and up to the church, and his legs felt hardly strong enough to carry him up the interminable dark stairs to the gallery. He had hardly sat down since the morning, and he had eaten nothing, and his head was swimming with fatigue and hunger. Clausewitz was still on duty, up in the gallery where the stars shone bravely down upon him, giving a light which seemed bright compared with the pitchy darkness of the stairs Hornblower had just climbed.

'The French seem unusually active tonight,' was Clausewitz's greeting to him. 'At dusk they changed the guard of their trenches.'

A string of bright orange flames suddenly lit up the French lines, and the roar of a salvo reached their ears.

'They are periodically spraying the ditch with grape,' explained Clausewitz, 'to hinder our repair parties. It is what is always done, but after half a dozen rounds they lose direction and range.'

If siege warfare was such a mechanical art, if every step was obvious and could be foreseen, there was always the chance of an original-minded general breaking the rules. In two days the breaches and approaches would be ripe for an assault – what was to prevent an assailant from making his attack a little prematurely and catching the defender off his guard? Hornblower made the suggestion to Clausewitz.

'It is always possible,' said Clausewitz, pontifically. 'But our trench guards are unusually strong tonight because of the sortie at dawn.'

Hornblower felt round in the gloom, and found one of the trusses of straw which had been carried up to the gallery in an endeavour to make this advanced headquarters more comfortable. He sat down gratefully, for his legs were actually trembling with fatigue. He wrapped his cloak closer round him against the chill of the night, and the thought of sleep became inexpressibly alluring. He stretched himself out on the crackling straw, and then heaved himself up on his elbow again to pinch up a wad of straw as a pillow.

'I shall rest a while,' he announced, and lay back and closed his eyes.

There was something more than mere fatigue about this desire for sleep. Asleep, he would be quit of this siege, of its stinks and perils and bitterness; he would be free of his responsibilities; he would not be plagued with the endless reports of Bonaparte's steady advance into the heart of Russia; he would no longer be tormented with the feeling of fighting a desperate and hopeless battle against an enemy who was bound, because of his colossal might, to prevail in the end. Oblivion awaited him if he could only sleep, oblivion, nepenthe, forgetfulness. Tonight he yearned to sink into sleep as a man might yearn to sink into the arms of his mistress. His nerves were curiously steady, despite the strain of the last few weeks – perhaps (such was his contrary nature) because of it. He settled himself down in the straw, and even the tumultuous dreams that assailed him were (as he was somehow aware) not nearly so serious as the thoughts from which he would have suffered had he been awake.

He awoke to Clausewitz's arm on his shoulder, and pieced himself back into the Hornblower who was aiding in the defence of Riga like a man fitting together a jigsaw puzzle.

'An hour before dawn,' said Clausewitz, still only a vague shadow in the brooding darkness.

Hornblower sat up; he was stiff, and had grown cold under the inadequate cover of his cloak. The landing force, if all had gone well, must be creeping up the bay now. It was too dark to see anything as he peered over the parapet of the gallery. Another shadow loomed up at his elbow and thrust something scalding hot into his hand – a glass of tea. He sipped it gratefully, feeling its warmth penetrate into his inner recesses. The faint report of a single musket-shot reached his ears, and Clausewitz began a remark to him which was cut short by a violent outburst of firing down in no-man's-land between the trench systems. The darkness was spangled with points of flame.

'Possibly patrols with a fit of nerves,' said Clausewitz, but the firing showed no signs of dying down. Instead, it grew in violence. There was a great spearhead of flame down below, pointing towards an irregular mass of flashes, where apparently a column was meeting a line. The flashes flared up and died away with the ragged volleys; soon cannon were contributing their orange flames, and immediately afterwards there was more fire as blazing combustibles – carcasses – were flung by attackers and defenders from the parapets to illuminate their enemies. From the bay arose a curving streak of yellow fire, soaring upwards towards the sky, and then bursting into scarlet stars.

'Thank God for that!' said Hornblower, but he kept the words to himself.

The landing party had reached their station a little ahead of their time, and somebody, English or Russian, had sensibly decided to launch the flank attack immediately upon seeing the firing ashore. Clausewitz turned and rapped out an order which sent an aide-de-camp hurrying down the stairs. At almost the same moment a messenger came running up, gabbling Russian so rapidly that Clausewitz, with his limited command of the language, had to make him repeat his words more slowly. When the message was delivered he turned to Hornblower.

'The enemy is in strong force, apparently intending to make a surprise attack. He might save two days if it were successful.'

A fresh tumult broke out down below; the landing party had encountered their first opposition, and the invisible landscape towards the shore was spangled with a new pattern of flashes. There was a desperate battle going on, where attackers and counter-attackers and the flank attack drove together; there was a faint light beginning to show now, enough to reveal Clausewitz, unshaven, and with his uniform covered with bits of straw in direct contrast with his usual spruce appearance. But still nothing could be seen of the fighting, save for vague smoke-clouds drifting in the semi-darkness. Hornblower was reminded of Campbell's lines in 'Hohenlinden' about the level sun at morn being unable to pierce the dun war-clouds. The clatter of musketry and the crash of artillery told of the bitter struggle, and once Hornblower heard a deep shout from many throats answered by a wild yell. That was when some attack met a counter-attack, presumably. Steadily the landscape grew brighter, and the messengers began to pour in.

'Shevstoff has stormed the battery guarding the shore,' said Clausewitz, exultantly.

Shevstoff was the general commanding the landing party. If he had stormed the battery the boats' crews would be able to effect an unmolested retreat, while the arrival of a messenger from him here in Daugavgriva meant that he was in full touch with the defenders, and presumably his force had executed its orders and fallen on the flank of the French position. The firing seemed to be dying away, even though the smoke still blended with the low ground-mist of autumn and kept everything concealed.

'Kladoff is in the approaches,' went on Clausewitz. 'His workmen are breaking down the parapets.'

The firing increased again, although now there was so much light that no flashes were visible. A frightful death-struggle was apparently going on, so desperate that the arrival of the Governor in the gallery attracted little attention from the group straining to see through the fog and smoke.

Essen gathered the details with a few quick questions to Clausewitz, and then he turned to Hornblower.

'I would have been here an hour ago,' he said, 'but I was detained by the arrival of despatches.'

Essen's massive countenance was gloomy; he took Hornblower's arm and drew him out of earshot of the junior staff officers.

'Bad news?' asked Hornblower.

'Yes. The worst. We have been beaten in a great battle outside Moscow, and Bonaparte is in the city.'

That was the worst of news indeed. Hornblower could foresee a future time when he supposed that battle would rank along with Marengo and Austerlitz and Jena, as a smashing victory which laid a nation low, and the entry into Moscow would rank with the occupation of Vienna and Berlin. A week or two more and Russia would sue for peace – if she had not begun to do so already – and England would be left alone, with the whole world in arms against her. Was there anything in the world that could stand against Bonaparte's craft and power? Even the British Navy? Hornblower forced himself to take the blow impassively, forced his face to bear no hint of his dismay.

'We shall fight it out here all the same,' he said.

'Yes,' said Essen, 'my men will fight to the last. So will my officers.'

There was almost a grin on his face as he jerked his head towards Clausewitz; that was a man who had his neck in a noose if ever a man had, fighting against his own country. Hornblower remembered Wellesley's hint to him that his squadron might well serve as a refuge for the Russian Court. His ships would be jammed with refugees fleeing from this, the last continental country in arms against Bonaparte.

The mist and smoke were thinning, and patches of the field of battle were visible now, and Hornblower and Essen turned their attention to the work in hand as if with relief from contemplating the future.

'Ha!' said Essen, pointing.

Portions of the approaches were in plain view, and here and there were jagged gaps in the parapets.

'Kladoff has carried out his orders, sir,' said Clausewitz.

Until those gaps were repaired, one by one, starting with the gap nearest the first parallel, no one would be able to reach the head of the sap, and certainly no strong force could use the approaches. Another two days had been won, decided Hornblower, gauging the amount of destruction with his eye – experience had brought him facility already in appreciating siege operations. There was still heavy firing going on as the rearguard covered the retreat of the sallying forces to the ramparts. Essen balanced his huge telescope on the shoulder of his aide-de-camp and pointed it down at the scene. Hornblower was looking through his own glass; the big barges which had brought the landing party were lying deserted on the beach, and the boats which were conveying back his crews which had manned them were already safely out of range. Essen's hand on his shoulder swung him round.

'See there, Commodore!' said Essen.

Hornblower's glass revealed to him in a flash the thing to which Essen had wanted to call his attention. Isolated infantrymen from the besiegers were ranging over no-man's-land on their way back to their own trenches and – Hornblower saw it done – they bayoneted the Russian wounded who lay heaped in their path. Perhaps it was only to be expected, in this long and bloody siege, that bitterness and ferocity should be engendered on this scale, especially among Bonaparte's hordes who had wandered over Europe for years now, since boyhood, living on what they could gather from the countryside, with the musket and bayonet as the only court of appeal. Essen was white with anger, and Hornblower tried to share his rage, but he found it difficult. That kind of atrocity was what he had come to expect. He was perfectly prepared to go on killing Bonaparte's soldiers and sailors, but he would not flatter himself that he was executing justice by killing one man because some other man had murdered his wounded allies.

Down in the shattered remains of the village, as he walked along the trenches, those of the wounded who had been fortunate enough to drag themselves back were receiving treatment. Shuddering, Hornblower told himself that perhaps those who had been bayoneted in no-man's-land were the lucky ones. He pushed past ranks of smoke-blackened and ragged Russian soldiers, talking with the noisy abandon of men who have just emerged from a hard-won victory.

XXII

Among the mass of long-delayed mail from England were great packets of printed pamphlets, in French and in German, a few even in Dutch and in Danish. They were appeals to Bonaparte's forces to desert his standard – not suggestions for mass desertions, but intended for the individual soldier, telling him that he could be sure of a welcome if he were to come over. They denied the statements that Bonaparte was continually making in his proclamations, to the effect that England confined her prisoners in floating hells of hulks, and that deserters were forced by ill-treatment to take service in England mercenary regiments. They offered a life of ease and security, with the honourable alternative, only if requested, of enlistment in the British forces, to those who wished to strike a blow against the tyrant. The French pamphlet was certainly well written, and presumably the others were too; maybe Canning, or that fellow – what was his name, now? – Hookham Frere, had had a hand in composing them.

The letter that accompanied the pamphlets, charging him to do his utmost to get them into the hands of Bonaparte's forces, had an interesting enclosure – a copy of a letter from Bonaparte to Marmont, intercepted presumably somewhere in Spain, in which the Emperor raged against this new evidence of British falseness and perfidy. He had seen some of the first pamphlets, apparently, and they had touched him on a sore spot. Judging by the wording of his letter, he was driven quite frantic at this attempt to seduce his men from their allegiance. If the violence of the Imperial reaction was any guide, then this method of warfare was likely to be effective. The usually well-fed and well-cared-for Prussians under Macdonald's command were on meagre rations now that the country round had been stripped bare by foragers; an offer of a life of well-fed ease combined with an appeal to their patriotism might bring in deserters in plenty. Hornblower mapped out in his mind a formal letter to the Governor in which he would suggest that a few pedlars be sent into the French camp ostensibly to sell luxuries but really to distribute these pamphlets. Here where Bonaparte's men were suffering real hardship and meeting with small success the appeal might carry more weight than with Bonaparte's main army in Moscow; Hornblower was inclined to distrust the flamboyant Russian bulletin about the burning of Moscow, and Alexander's fervent public declaration that he would never make peace while a Frenchman was on Russian soil. In Hornblower's opinion French morale was likely to be still high enough, and Bonaparte's strength still great enough, to force peace at the bayonet's point from Russia in the Russian capital, be the destruction of Moscow never so great – even as great as Moscow said it was.

Someone knocked at the door.

'Come in,' bellowed Hornblower, irritated at the interruption, for he had intended to spend all day catching up on his arrears of paper work.

'A letter from the beach, sir,' said the midshipman of the watch.

It was a brief note from the Governor with its point compressed into a single sentence –

I have some new arrivals in the city who I think will interest you if you can spare the time for a visit.

Hornblower sighed; his report to London would never be finished, apparently, but he could not ignore this invitation.

'Call away my barge,' he said to the midshipman, and turned to lock his desk.

God knew who these 'new arrivals' would be. These Russians were sometimes so portentously mysterious about trifles. It might be a fool's errand, but on the other hand he must find out what this new development was before sending off his despatch to England. As his barge danced over the water he looked over at the siege-lines; the battering guns were still volleying away – he had grown so used to the noise that he only noticed it when his attention was called to it – and the usual long pall of smoke lay over the flat country there.

Then the boat entered the mouth of the river and Daugavgriva's ruins were hidden from view save for the dome of the church where he had so often stood. Riga came steadily nearer and nearer, and they had to keep close to the bank to avoid the worst of the Dwina's rapid current, until at last the oars ceased and the barge slid against the steps of the river-wall. At the head of them waited the Governor with his staff and a spare horse for Hornblower.

'It is only a short ride,' said Essen, 'and one I think you will consider worth the making.'

Hornblower climbed on to his horse, with a nod of thanks to the groom who held its head, and then they all wheeled and dashed away through the clattering streets. A postern was opened for them in the eastern fortifications – so far no enemy had shown his face on this bank of the Dwina – and they rode out over a drawbridge spanning the ditch. On the glacis beyond the ditch was a large force of soldiers, squatting and lying in rank; as soon as the cavalcade appeared they came hastily to their feet, dressed their lines, and then, in obedience to a shrill chorus of bugles, presented arms, their regimental colours fluttering in the little breeze. Essen reined up, returning the salute.

'Well, what do you think of them, sir?' he asked Hornblower with a chuckle.

They were ragged soldiers – bare skin showed frequently in the ranks through holes in the blue or dirty grey uniforms. They were shambling, unsoldierly soldiers, too; any troops who had seen hard service might be ragged, but Hornblower, looking along the ranks, had the impression of voluntary dirt and disorder. Essen was still chuckling, and Hornblower looked the harder to find the reason for this mirth. Essen would not have brought him out here just to see ragged soldiers – Hornblower had seen enough of those in the past three months to last him the rest of his life. There were several thousand men, a strong brigade or a weak division; Hornblower glanced at the regimental standards to ascertain the number of units present, and then he nearly lost his precarious seat with surprise. Those flags were red and yellow, the national colours of Spain, and the moment this dawned upon him he realised that the ragged uniforms were the remains of the Bourbon white and blue he had come so much to hate ten years ago during his captivity at Ferrol. Not only that, but on the left of the line there was a single standard of silver and blue – the Portuguese flag, held aloft before a single shrunken battalion of scarecrows.

'I thought you would be surprised, sir,' said Essen, still chuckling.

'Who are these men?' asked Hornblower.

'Some of Bonaparte's willing allies,' replied Essen, ironically. 'They were in St Cyr's Corps at Polotsk. One day they found themselves on the very fringe of the outpost line, and fought their way down the river to join us. Come and meet their general.'

He urged his horse forward, and he and Hornblower cantered up to where a ragged officer sat a bony white horse at the head of an even worse-mounted staff.

'I have the honour to present,' said Essen, formally, 'His Excellency the Conde de los Altos – His Excellency Commodore Sir Horatio Hornblower.'

The Conde saluted; it took Hornblower a few moments to make himself think in Spanish – the last time he had used that language was during the abortive attack on Rosas, two years ago.

'It is highly gratifying to meet Your Excellency,' he said.

The Conde's expression revealed his startled pleasure at being addressed in his own tongue, and he replied rapidly.

'You are the English Admiral, sir?'

Hornblower did not see fit to enter into explanations regarding the difference between an Admiral and a Commodore. He merely nodded.

'I have asked that my men and the Portuguese be returned by sea to Spain, there to fight against Bonaparte on our own soil. They tell me that as this can only be done by sea your consent must be secured. You will grant it, of course, sir?'

That was asking a good deal. Five thousand men at four tons a man meant twenty thousand tons of shipping – a large convoy; it would be straining his powers for him to pledge his government to provide twenty thousand tons of shipping to carry the Spaniards from Riga to Spain. There never were enough ships. And there was also the question of the moral effect on the garrison of Riga if they were to see this seasonable reinforcement which had dropped from the clouds, so to speak, shipped away again as soon as it arrived. Yet on the other hand there was a chance that Russia might make peace with Bonaparte, and in that case the sooner these Spaniards were beyond the clutches of either country the better. Five thousand men would make a considerable army in Spain – where·the Spaniards were likely to do their best – while it was only a trifling force in this continental war of millions. But none of this was of nearly as much importance as the moral side. What would be the effect on the other unwilling allies of Bonaparte, the Prussians and the Austrians, the Bavarians and the Italians, when they heard not merely that a national contingent had fought its way to join the allies, but had been received with open arms, fêted and made much of, and finally shipped back to their native land with the least possible delay? Hornblower expected a tremendous revulsion of feeling among Bonaparte's satellites, especially if the Russians executed their determination to keep

on fighting through the winter. This might be the beginning of the
crumbling of Bonaparte's Empire.

'I shall be very happy to send you and your men to Spain as quickly
as it can be arranged,' he said. 'I will issue orders today for shipping to
be collected.'

The Conde was profuse in his thanks, but Hornblower had something
to add.

'There is one thing I ask in return,' he said, and the Conde's countenance fell a little.

'What is it, sir?' he asked. The embittered suspicion resulting from
years of being a victim of international double-dealing, of lies and
deception and threats – from Godoy's pitiful subterfuges to Bonaparte's
mailed-fisted bullying – showed instantly in his face.

'You signature to a proclamation, that is all. I shall endeavour to
circulate among Bonaparte's other forced allies the news of your joining
the cause of liberty, and I would like you to attest its truth.'

The Conde darted one more keen look at Hornblower before he agreed.

'I will sign it,' he said.

That immediate consent was a pretty compliment, first to Hornblower's obvious honesty of purpose, and second to the reputation the
Navy had acquired of always fulfilling its engagements.

'There is nothing more to be done, then,' said Hornblower 'save to
draw up the proclamation and to find ships for your forces.'

Essen was fidgeting in his saddle beside them while this conversation
was going on in Spanish; he clearly knew no word of that language and
was restless in consequence – Hornblower found it gratifying, for during
the past few months he had had to be an uncomprehending listener to so
many conversations in Russian and German. This was some slight
revenge.

'Has he told you about conditions in Bonaparte's army?' asked
Essen. 'Have you heard about the hunger and the disease?'

'Not yet,' said Hornblower.

The story came out rapidly, staccato, drawn from the Conde's lips
by explosive promptings from Essen. Bonaparte's army had been dying
on its feet long before it reached Moscow; hunger and disease had
thinned its ranks as Bonaparte hurried it by forced marches across the
desolated plains.

'The horses are nearly all dead already. There was only green rye
to give them,' said the Conde.

If the horses were dead it would be impossible to drag supplies in to
the main body of the army; it would have to scatter or starve, and as
long as the Russians had any sort of army in existence it would be impossible for the main body to scatter. As long as Alexander's nerve
held, as long as he maintained the struggle, there was still hope. It

began to seem certain that Bonaparte's army in Moscow had spent its strength, and the only way in which the French could bring fresh pressure upon Alexander would be by advancing upon St Petersburg with the army here before Riga. That made it more imperative still to hold on here. Hornblower felt considerable doubt as to Alexander's constancy if he were to lose both his capitals.

The wretched Spanish infantry had been standing presenting arms during all this long conversation, and Hornblower felt uncomfortable about them. He let his attention wander to them obviously, recalling the Conde to a sense of his duty. The Conde gave an order to his staff, and the colonels repeated it; the regiments ordered arms awkwardly and then stood easy, the latter to the manner born.

'His Excellency tells me,' said the Conde, 'that you have recently served in Spain, sir. What is the news of my country?'

It was not easy to give a thumbnail sketch of the complicated history of the Peninsula for the last four years, to a Spaniard who had been cut off from all news during that time. Hornblower did his best, glossing over the innumerable Spanish defeats, laying stress on the devotion and efficiency of the guerrilleros, and ending on a hopeful note as he told of Wellington's recent capture of Madrid. The Spanish staff pressed more and more closely round him as he spoke. For four long years, ever since the Spanish people had declared their will, ceasing to be subservient allies and becoming the most bitter enemies of the Empire, Bonaparte had seen to it these these Spanish troops of his, three thousand miles from home, had received not a single word which might tell them of the real situation in Spain. They had had only the lying Imperial bulletins on which to base their vague theories. It was a strange experience to talk to these exiles; Hornblower felt a curious sensation, as if there were an actual movement inside his brain, as he remembered the conditions in which he himself had learned of the Spanish change of front. That had been on the deck of the *Lydia*, in the uncharted tropical Pacific. For a few seconds his brain was a battleground of memories. The blue and gold of the Pacific, the heat and the storms and the fighting there, el Supremo and the Governor of Panama – he had to tear himself away from them to bring himself back to this parade ground on the shores of the Baltic.

An orderly officer was galloping madly towards them, the dust flying from beneath the ringing hoofs of his charger. He reined up before Essen with a perfunctory salute, the words of his message pouring from his lips before his hand had left his forehead. A word from the Governor sent him flying back whence he came, and Essen turned to Hornblower.

'The enemy is massing in his trenches,' he said. 'They are about to assault Daugavgriva.'

Essen began blaring orders to his staff; horses wheeled and pranced as spurs were struck into their sides and the cruel bits dragged their heads round. In a moment half a dozen officers were galloping in different directions with the messages flung at them.

'I'm going there,' said Essen.

'I shall come too,' said Hornblower.

Hornblower found it hard to stay in the saddle as his excited horse swung round beside the Governor's; he had to resettle himself, his hand on the pommel, and regain his lost stirrup as they clattered along. Essen turned his head with another order shouted to one of the few remaining orderlies accompanying them, and then spurred his horse yet again; as the brute sprang forward with increased speed the low muttering of the bombardment increased in intensity. They clattered through the streets of Riga, and the timber road-bed of the boat bridge roared under their horses' hoofs. The sweat was running from Hornblower's face in the clear autumn sunshine, his sword leaped against his thigh, and time and again his cocked hat rode precariously up his forehead and was only saved by a hurried grab at the last moment. Hornblower was conscious of the swirling water of the Dwina as they crossed the bridge, and then on his right hand as they galloped along the quays. The roar of the bombardment grew louder and louder, and then suddenly died away.

'It is the moment of the assault!' bellowed Essen, bending his clumsy body forward in an effort to get more speed out of his labouring horse.

Now they were in the village itself, among the ruins of the cottages, and here they met broken troops, stumbling back pell-mell, blue uniforms grey with dust, with cursing officers trying to rally them, and beating the stupefied men with the flats of their swords. Essen's voice blared out again, like a tuneless trumpet; he was waving his sword over his head and spurring forward into the press. At the sight of him the men began to rally, turning back to face the enemy, and instinctively closing together into line.

Down through the ruins came a disordered column of the enemy – it must have come up over the breach like a whirlwind. By now it was more of a mob than a column, officers capering at the head of their men, waving their hats and swords. A standard waved over them. The appearance of a formed line caused a momentary hesitation, and ragged firing broke out on both sides; Hornblower saw one of the capering officers fall dead as he called to his men to come on. He looked over at Essen, but he was still towering high in the smoke. Hornblower wheeled his horse towards the flank; his mind was working with the ecstatic speed of excitement, bullets were singing by him, and he knew that this was the crisis of the assault. Halt an attacking column for one moment, and then any trifle might turn the scale, and it would go back as fast as it had advanced. He reached the door of the church just as a flood of men came pouring out of it – the garrison of the building hastening to make good their retreat before they should be cut off and isolated. Hornblower tore his sword from its sheath, miraculously retaining his seat in the saddle.

'Come on!' he yelled, waving the weapon.

They did not understand his words, as they blinked at this vision in blue and gold before them, but anyone could understand his gestures. At the back of the group Hornblower caught a momentary glimpse of Clausewitz and Diebitch, who should have taken command here, but there was no time for argument, and racing through Hornblower's brain went the conviction at the same time that although they might be scientific soldiers they would be useless in a physical rough-and-tumble like this.

'Come on!' yelled Hornblower again, pointing with his sword at the flank of the assaulting column.

They turned to follow him – no one could have resisted the inspiration of his example and gestures. Column and line were still exchanging ragged volleys, the column still moving forward little by little, the line wavering and falling back.

'Form line!' yelled Hornblower, turning in his saddle, his spread arms and gesticulating fists telling the Russians what he wanted them to do. 'Load your muskets!'

They formed their line, marching up after him, hands busy with their ramrods – a couple of hundred men at most, jostling each other as they stumbled over the ruins of the cottages. Now they were right on the flank of the column; Hornblower saw faces turn towards them. He was even near enough to see surprise and dismay in the attitudes of the men who suddenly realised that a new force was about to assail their flank.

'Fire!' yelled Hornblower, and some sort of volley crashed out from the ragged line he led.

He saw two ramrods sail forward in soaring arcs, fired out of their muskets by excited men who had been caught in the act of loading by his order, and who had incontinently put their weapons to their shoulders and pulled their triggers. One ramrod buried itself like an arrow in the body of a French soldier. The column wavered and staggered – not one man in a hundred there had expected this attack on the flank; all their attention had been taken up by Essen's line in front of them.

'Charge!' yelled Hornblower, waving his sword and urging his horse forward.

The Russians followed him with a cheer; the whole column of the enemy, Hornblower saw, was wavering and melting away, the disordered ranks crumbling. They were turning their backs, and the memory streaked through his excited mind of a saying he had heard somewhere to the effect that the knapsacks of the enemy were the most cheering sight a soldier could behold. Then he saw one of the enemy swing back again and level his musket at him. As the smoke gushed from the barrel his horse gave a convulsive leap and then put his nose to the ground and somersaulted; for a moment Hornblower felt himself flying through the air; he was too excited and exalted to feel any fear, so that the crash with which he hit the earth came as a startling surprise to him. But even though the breath was dashed from his body and the jar shook every bone in it, his fantastic mind still thought clearly, and he heard and felt the flank attack which he had led sweep cheering over him. Only when he rose to his feet did he come to the sudden realisation that he was bruised and weak, so that it was hard to balance on his legs – they nearly gave way under him as he hobbled forward to pick up his sword which lay shining on the dusty earth between two dead men.

He felt suddenly alone, but the feeling had hardly time to take hold of him when he was engulfed in a wave of humanity, Essen and his staff roaring with exaltation and delight. He stood there, bruised and torn, his sword dangling from his hand, as they overwhelmed him with incomprehensible congratulations. One of the officers leaped down from his horse, and Hornblower was hauled and pushed up into the saddle, and they cantered forward, the horses picking their way delicately over the dead and wounded, over the tortured ground, towards the ramparts. The last remnants of the assaulting forces were being driven back through the breach to the accompaniment of a straggling musketry fire. As the neared the fortifications the guns of the foiled besiegers reopened fire, and a shot or two came howling overhead. Essen reined up, like a sensible man, and then walked his horse out of the line of fire.

'That was a moment to remember,' he said, looking round at the area where the clash had occurred.

Hornblower's head was still clear. He realised what a bitter blow this reverse must be to the besiegers. After all the fierce preliminary fighting they had sapped up to the ramparts, made their breach, and launched the assault which should have captured the place, only to be flung back when the breach was in their hands. He knew that Macdonald would have the greatest difficulty in inducing his men to assault again – a bloody failure like this would make them sulky and grudging of their lives. Certainly Macdonald would have to allow a considerable time to elapse, and would have to continue his battering for several more days, and multiply his approaches and parallels, before he could risk another assault. Maybe the town would hold. Maybe that attack would be the last. Hornblower felt prophetic, inspired. He remembered how he had heard the news of Masséna's retreat from before Lisbon – that had been the first of the ebb of the Empire in the South, and now Wellington was in Madrid and threatening France. Maybe Riga would mark the limits of the Empire in the North. Maybe that penetration through the breach would be remembered as the farthest north Bonaparte's men would ever attain. At that rate – Hornblower's pulse beat quicker – the flank attack he had led, that unforeseen charge of a couple of hundred men hurriedly gathered up in the tumult, had been the blow which had thwarted Bonaparte's schemes to conquer the world. That was what he had done. And it would look extraordinarily well in *The Times* that 'Commodore Sir Horatio Hornblower, K.B., had his horse killed under him while leading a charge.' Barbara would be pleased.

Exultation and inspiration ended abruptly, and Hornblower felt suddenly weak and ill. He knew that if he did not dismount quickly he would fall from his saddle. He took hold of the pommel and kicked his right foot clear of the stirrup, swung his leg over, and then as his feet touched ground the ground came up to meet him. He only recovered some indefinite number of minutes later, to find himself seated on the ground, his stock unbuckled, and his face clammy with cold sweat. Essen was bending anxiously over him, and someone, apparently a surgeon, was kneeling at his side. His sleeve was rolled up above the elbow, and the surgeon, lancet in hand, was about to open a vein to bleed him. Hornblower withdrew his arm abruptly, for he did not want to be touched by that thing, nor by those hands which were black with other men's blood.

The assembled staff raised their voices in protest, but Hornblower disregarded them with the sublime abstraction of a sick man. Then Brown appeared, cutlass at his side and pistols in his belt, followed by other members of the barge's crew. Apparently he had seen his captain ride over the bridge, and, like the good subordinate he was, had brought the boat across after him. Brown's face was contorted with anxiety, and he threw himself, too, on his knees beside Hornblower.

'Wounded, sir? Where is it? Can I—'

'No no no,' said Hornblower pettishly, pushing Brown away and getting to his feet, swaying. 'It's nothing.'

It was extraordinarily maddening to see a look of admiration come over Brown's face. Anyone would think he was being heroic instead of merely sensible. Not far away – at the foot of the breach, apparently – a trumpet was pealing, high challenging notes, and this served to distract the crowd from their solicitude. Everyone looked in the direction of the sound, and presently a group of Russian officers approached them, leading a blindfold figure dressed in the blue trimmed with grey astrakhan of the French Imperial Staff. A word from Essen removed the bandage, and the officer – he wore a grey Hussar moustache – saluted with dignity.

'The chef d'escadron Verrier,' he said, 'aide-de-camp to Marshal the Duke of Tarentum. I am ordered by the Marshal to suggest a suspension of hostilities for two hours. The breach is covered with the wounded

of both sides, and it would be only humane to remove them. Each side
can remove its own.'

'There are more French and German wounded than Russian, I am
sure,' said Essen, in his horrible French.

'French or Russian, sir,' said the parlementaire, 'they will die unless
they receive speedy aid.'

Hornblower's mind was beginning to work again. Ideas were leaping
to the surface like wreckage from a sunken ship. He caught Essen's eye
and nodded meaningly, and Essen, like a good diplomatist, gave no sign
of having received the hint as he shifted his glance back to Verrier.

'The request is granted, sir,' he said, 'in the name of humanity.'

'I thank Your Excellency, in the name of humanity,' said Verrier,
saluting, and then looking round for someone to blindfold him again
and lead him through the breach.

The moment he was gone Hornblower turned to Brown.

'Take the barge back to the ship,' he ordered. 'Hurry. My compliments to Captain Bush, and I would like you to bring back Lieutenant
von Bulow to me. One of the lieutenants of equal rank will have to
accompany him. Hurry!'

'Aye aye, sir.'

That was all that was necessary with Brown or Bush, thank God. A
simple order brought simple yet intelligent obedience. Hornblower
saluted Essen.

'Would it be possible, Your Excellency,' he asked, 'to bring the
Spanish troops over to this side of the river? I have a German prisoner
whom I am going to return to the enemy, and I should like him to see
the Spaniards with his own eyes first.'

Essen grinned with blubber lips.

'I do my best not merely to comply with every one of your wishes, sir,
but even to anticipate them. The last order I gave on the other side of
the river was for the Spaniards to be brought over – they were the nearest
formed troops and I intended to use them as garrison for the warehouses
on the quay. I have no doubt they are there already. You would like
them marched in this direction?'

'If you would be so kind, sir.'

Hornblower was casually waiting for nothing in particular at the
jetty when the boat touched at it, and Lieutenant von Bulow, of the
Fifty-first Regiment of Prussian Infantry, stepped ashore under the
escort of Mr Tooth and Brown and his men.

'Ah, Lieutenant,' said Hornblower.

Bulow saluted him stiffly, clearly puzzled at this new development,
which had snatched him from his confinement aboard ship and dumped
him at a moment's notice in the ruined village.

'There is an armistice at the moment,' explained Hornblower, 'between your army and ours. No, it is not peace – merely to clear the wounded from the breach. But I was going to take this opportunity of returning you to your friends.'

Bulow looked questions at him.

'It will save much formality with cartels and flags of truce,' explained Hornblower. 'At this moment you have merely to walk down the breach and join the men of your army. Naturally, you have not been properly exchanged, but you can, if you wish, give me your word that you will not serve against His Britannic Majesty nor against His Imperial Russian Majesty until an exchange has been effected.'

'I give you my word,' said Bulow, after a moment's thought.

'Excellent! Then perhaps I might give myself the pleasure of walking with you as far as the breach?'

As they left the jetty and began the brief walk through the ruins of the village Bulow was darting the quick glances of a professional soldier about him; he was perfectly entitled, under any military code, to take every advantage of carelessness on his enemy's part. His professional curiosity would have led him to stare about him in any case. Hornblower made polite conversation as they strolled.

'Your assault this morning – I daresay you heard the hubbub even on board? – was made by picked grenadiers, as far as I could judge by the uniforms. Most excellent troops – it is indeed a pity they suffered such loss of life. I trust that when you rejoin your friends you will convey to them my deepest condolences. But they had not a chance, of course.'

At the foot of the church tower there was a Spanish regiment, the men lying down in their ranks. At the sight of Hornblower the colonel called his men to their feet and saluted. Hornblower returned the salute, conscious as he did so that Bulow at his side had suddenly changed his gait; stealing a glance out of the tail of his eye he saw that Bulow was ponderously goose-stepping as long as the salutes were being exchanged. Yet it was very noticeable that even though Bulow's formal training forced him into a goose-step at a moment of military courtesy, he had not failed to notice the troops. His eyes were bulging with unasked questions.

'Spanish troops,' said Hornblower, casually. 'A division of Spaniards and Portuguese joined us from Bonaparte's main army a little while ago. They fight well – in fact they were responsible for the final repulse of the last assault. It is interesting to notice how Bonaparte's dupes are falling away from him now that the hollowness of his power is revealed.'

Bulow's astonished reply must either have been inarticulate or in German, for Hornblower could not understand it, but his tone conveyed his meaning well enough.

'It goes without saying,' said Hornblower casually, 'that I would like

to see the magnificent Prussian Army ranged among Bonaparte's enemies and England's allies, too. But naturally your King knows his own
policy best – unless, of course, surrounded as he is by Bonaparte's men,
he is not free to choose.'

Bulow stared at him in amazement; Hornblower was putting forward
a viewpoint which was quite new to him, but Hornblower still made
himself talk with the utmost casualness, as if he were doing no more
than making polite conversation.

'That's high politics,' he said with a laugh and a wave of his hand.
'But one day in the future we might look back on this conversation as
prophetic. One cannot tell, can one? Some time when we meet as pleni-
potentiaries I will be able to remind you of this talk. And here we are at
the breach. It irks me to have to say goodbye, at the same moment as it
gives me pleasure to restore you to your friends. My heartiest good
wishes, sir, for you for the future.'

Bulow saluted stiffly again, and then, as Hornblower held out his
hand, shook hands with him. To the Prussian it was a remarkable
occurrence, for a Commodore to condescend to shake hands with a mere
subaltern. He picked his way down the breach, over the tortured earth
where the stretcher-bearers still swarmed, like disturbed ants, gathering
in the wounded. Hornblower watched him until he reached his own men,
and then turned away. He was dreadfully tired, quite weak with fatigue,
in fact, and he was angry at himself for his weakness. It was all he could
do to walk back with dignity to the jetty, and he swayed as he sat in the
sternsheets of his barge.

'Are you all right, sir?' asked Brown, solicitously.

'Of course I am,' snapped Hornblower, amazed at the man's impertinence.

The question irritated him, and the irritation made him mount the
ship's side as fast as he could, and acknowledge merely coldly the
salutes he received on the quarterdeck; down in his cabin his irritation
persisted, and prevented him from obeying his first impulses to throw
himself across his cot and relax. He paced about for a moment. For
something to do he peered into the mirror. There was some excuse for
Brown after all, and his foolish questions. The face he looked at was
grimy with dust caked upon sweat, and there was a smear of blood over
one cheekbone from a slight scratch. His uniform was filthy, with one
epaulette awry. He looked like someone who had just emerged from the
fury of a battle to the death.

He peered more closely. That face was lined and drawn, the eyes red-
rimmed; with a sudden increase of attention he looked again, turning
his head. On his temples his hair was quite white. Not merely did he
look like someone fresh from battle; he looked like someone who had
been under frightful strain for a long time. So he had, indeed, he realised,

half wondering at himself. He had been bearing the burden of this horrible siege for months now. It had never occurred to him that his face, Hornblower's face, would tell tales about him as other men's faces told tales about them. He had striven all his life to restrain his features from revealing his feelings. There was something ironic and interesting about the fact that he could not prevent his hair from greying nor the grim lines from deepening about his mouth.

The desk under his feet was swaying, as if the ship were in the open sea, and yet even his veteran sea-legs had difficulty in keeping him upright, so that he had to hold on to the bracket before him. Only with extreme care could he let go his hold and pick his way to his cot, and fall across it, face downward.

XXIII

The new problem which Hornblower was debating as he walked his quarterdeck, while H.M.S. *Nonsuch* swung at anchor in Riga Bay, was one which he had long foreseen, but which lost none of its urgency for all that. Here was winter coming; there had been heavy frosts at night for as far back as he could remember, and the last two days had brought flurries of snow, which had temporarily whitened the landscape and had left a few drifts which even now showed as white streaks on the northern faces of the dykes. The days were growing short and the nights long, and the brackish water of Riga Bay was covered with a thin scum of ice. If he stayed much longer his ships would be frozen in. Essen had assured him that for at least two more weeks he would be able to make his exit along a channel sawn in the ice by labourers whom Essen would supply, but Hornblower was not so sure. A northerly gale – and one might arise at any moment – could keep him windbound while at the same time it would freeze everything up and jam the narrow exit to the Bay, between Oesel and the mainland, with piled-up drift ice that neither saws nor even explosives could pierce. A squadron frozen in was a squadron immobilised until next spring; and a squadron frozen in was one which was a certain prey to the French if Riga should fall. Twenty years ago a Dutch squadron at Amsterdam had been captured by French hussars charging over the ice. What a thundering bulletin of triumph Bonaparte would make of it if a British squadron, under the notorious Commodore Hornblower, should fall into his hands in the same way! Hornblower turned in his stride a yard before he had reached the limit of his walk. Prudence dictated an immediate withdrawal.

The breeching of that carronade were frayed. When Bush noticed it someone was in for a bad quarter of an hour. And yet he could not withdraw. When he had mentioned the possibility Essen had shown positive dismay. If his men were to see the British ships go away they would be quite sure the place was doomed. They would lose heart completely. The British naval officer who had led the final charge at Daugavgriva had grown into a legendary figure in their minds, a mascot, a symbol of good luck. If he were to leave them that would be a proof, in the men's minds, that he had lost hope. He could not possibly withdraw. He might compromise; he might send most of the squadron out and retain only a sloop and a gunboat; he might send everything out and remain himself, but to separate himself from his command was in direct violation of the Articles of War.

Here was a fool of a midshipman in his way dodging about in front of him as though bent on distracting him from his train of thought. It would be the masthead for him; God knew the commission had lasted long enough for every single person on board to have learned that the Commodore must not be distracted when he was walking the deck.

'What the hell—?' he bellowed at the blanching midshipman.

'B-b-boat approaching, sir,' stammered the youth. 'M-Mr Hurst told me to tell you. He thinks the Governor's on board.'

'Why wasn't I told before?' said Hornblower. 'Have you sent for Captain Bush, Mr Hurst? Call the guard!'

'Aye aye, sir!' said Hurst, and Hornblower saw Bush appear on the quarterdeck as the words left Hurst's lips, and the marine guard was already forming up abaft the mizzen-mast.

Of course Hurst had done all these things without waiting for orders; roused abruptly from his reverie Hornblower had not had the sense to realise it. He strode to the side. The Governor was approaching in a big pulling-boat, which was steering towards them along the clear channel through the thin ice which the last eddies of the Dwina river still kept clear before they lost themselves in the Bay. As the Governor caught sight of him he sprang up into the sternsheets waving his cocked hat, he even tried to dance, precariously, both arms extended over his head, at imminent risk of falling overboard.

'Something's up, sir,' said Bush at Hornblower's side.

'That looks like good news,' said Hornblower.

The Governor arrived on the quarterdeck, hat still in hand. He flung his arms round Hornblower and hugged him, swinging his lean body up into the air so that his feet left the deck. Hornblower could imagine the grins that were being exchanged around him as he kicked in the air like a baby. The Governor put him down, clapped his hat on his head, and then seized first Hornblower's hand and then Bush's, and tried to dance a sort of ring-a-ring-of-roses with the two Englishmen. There was no more controlling him than one could control a bear.

'What is the news, Your Excellency?' asked Hornblower; Essen's grip on his hand was painful.

'Oh,' said Essen, flinging the Englishman's hands away so as to spread his arms again. 'Bonaparte has started to retreat.'

'Has he, by God!' said Hornblower.

'What does he say, sir?' asked Bush, quite incapable of understanding Essen's French, but Hornblower had no time for Bush, because the Governor was pouring out his news in a torrent of gutturals, drawing upon the vocabularies of half Europe for his words so that even Hornblower could hardly understand what he was saying.

'He left Moscow five days back,' roared Essen. 'We beat him at Malo-Jaroslavetz. Beat him in a pitched battle, and now he's running as hard as he can for Smolensk and Warsaw. And he won't get there before the snows! He'll be lucky if he gets there at all! Chichagov is marching hard to cut off his retreat at the Beresina. He's ruined. They're dying in thousands every night already! Nothing to eat, and winter's here!'

Essen stamped grotesquely about the deck, more like a dancing bear than ever.

'Please, sir, *please*. What does he say?' asked Bush pathetically.

Hornblower translated to the best of his ability, the other quarter-deck officers eavesdropping shamelessly. As the wonderful nature of the good news dawned upon them they began to cheer; down on the main-deck they caught the infection, and all through the ship men were cheering and tossing their hats in the air, even though they hardly knew what they were cheering about, save for the hurried words that flew from lip to lip – 'Boney's beaten!'

'We can get out of this bay before the ice comes, by God!' said Bush, snapping his fingers; it was obvious that if he had not a wooden leg he would be dancing too.

Hornblower looked across at the mainland.

'Macdonald's shown no sign of retreating yet,' he said. 'If he had the Governor would have mentioned it.'

'But don't you think he'll have to, sir?' Bush's expressive face showed anxiety now instead of joy. A moment before anything delightful had been possible – escape from Riga Bay, possibly even escape from this landlocked Baltic altogether, maybe even a return to England, but now Bush was back again to the cold reality that the siege of Riga was still going on.

'He may have to retreat,' said Hornblower, 'but until then we stay here, unless I receive orders to the contrary.'

Essen caught sight of their sober faces and turned on them again. He slapped Bush on the back so that he staggered with the force of the blow; he snapped his fingers under Hornblower's nose, and pirouetted with the grace of a performing seal. It was absurd that with all this going on, with Bush asking questions regarding the future, with Essen acting like a lunatic, and with the whole ship forgetting discipline in a mad outburst of cheering, Hornblower's brain should be planning and thinking still, with that swift clarity and that fevered rapidity which he knew by now portended some new development. Bonaparte in retreat, Bonaparte beaten, meant a tremendous revulsion of feeling throughout Europe. All the world knew that Wellington was threatening France from the south; and now the Empire was in peril from the east. It would hardly be possible for Bonaparte's shattered army to hold on to Poland once it had begun its retreat; the next campaign would see the allies on the frontiers of Prussia and Austria, and it was likely that both Prussia and Austria would in that case be glad to change sides. The King of Prussia was practically a prisoner in French hands, but the Prussian army – the greater part of the force now besieging Riga – could act as a free agent if it wished. The desertion of the Spaniards had shown them the way, and the pamphlets which he had had printed in Riga and distributed among the besiegers by Russian pedlars would not let them forget the lesson. Bulow would be able to bear witness to the truth of his assertions – Hornblower was glad he had set him free.

'I am sending Diebitch out to beat up the besiegers' lines with a sally,' Essen was saying. 'I must see how *they* take this news. Would you care to accompany me, sir?'

'Of course,' said Hornblower, coming out abruptly from his dreaming. What with fatigue – he was always weary now – and rapid thinking and excitement he was still a little 'mazy', as they said of fuddled men in the village when he was a boy. He announced his departure to Bush.

'You're worn out, sir,' protested Bush. 'You're no more than a shadow. Send someone else, sir. Send me. Send Duncan. You've done all that's necessary, sir.'

'I haven't yet,' said Hornblower, but he stooped so far as to risk delay by offering Essen refreshment, with the suggestion that they should drink a toast to celebrate this glorious news.

'Thank you, no,' said Essen, to Hornblower's relief. 'Diebitch will attack at dusk, and the days are short now.'

'You'll take your barge, sir, won't you?' persisted Bush. 'Take Brown.'

Bush was like a fussy parent with a venturesome child – like a hen with one chick. He was always nervous about entrusting his precious Hornblower to these unpredictable Russians; Hornblower grinned at Bush's solicitude.

'Anything to keep you happy,' he said.

Hornblower's barge followed the Governor's pulling-boat along the channel through the ice; Hornblower sat with the Governor in the stern of the Russian boat. There was a chill wind blowing, and the skies were grey.

'We shall have more snow,' said Essen, looking up at the clouds. 'God help the French.'

In the absence of any sunshine there was a mortal chill in the air. Hornblower thought of the French marching over the desolate plains of Russia, and was sorry for them. And the snow came indeed, that afternoon, sweeping over river and village, making white innocuous mounds of the battered parapets and the shattered guns and the graves which were scattered through the village. It was already prematurely dark when the ever-patient Russian grenadiers lined the trenches and then sallied forth upon the enemy's lines. They were not more than half-way across no-man's-land before the guns began to fire upon them, stabbing the falling snow with their bright orange flashes.

'No sign of any retreat there,' was Clausewitz's comment as he watched the fierce struggle from the gallery of the church beside Essen and Hornblower.

And if confirmation was needed the attacking party could supply it when it came drifting back in the darkness, decimated. The besiegers had met their sally with spirit; they had had patrols out in no-man's-land, and the trenches were adequately guarded. In retaliation, the besiegers opened fire with their breaching batteries; the ground shook to the rumble of the discharges, and the black night was stabbed again by the flames of the guns. It was impossible to maintain good aim or elevation in the darkness; it was only a short time before the shots were flying wild, all over the village, so that the defenders as far back as the Dwina river had to keep low in their trenches. Shells were coming over, too, curving in high arcs from the mortar batteries which the besiegers had established in their second parallel. They fell and burst here, there, and everywhere, one every two or three minutes, in fountains of fragments and flame, save when chance guided them into deeper snow which extinguished the fuses.

'They have plenty of ammunition to waste,' grumbled Essen, shivering in his cloak.

'Perhaps they plan a counter-assault in the darkness,' said Clausewitz. 'I have kept the trenches fully manned in case they try it.'

Immediately under Hornblower's gaze there was a battery of four heavy pieces, firing regular salvoes at short intervals. He noted the four bursts of flame over and over again, so that when there was a longer interval he was surprised first by the absence of sound and then by its unexpected coming. The flashes endured their brief moment, to be succeeded again by night, but Hornblower found himself wondering what difference there had been between this salvo and the last, apart from the longer interval which had preceded it. One flash – the right-hand one – had not been as distinct as the other three, longer and yet intense. Some error in loading, perhaps. Then came the next salvo, and only three flashes; the right-hand gun had not fired. Maybe it had 'unbushed' itself – blown out its vent fitting, as guns sometimes did. Another long interval, and then another salvo – two sharp flashes, and one longer one. The next salvo only two guns fired, and Hornblower realised what had been going on. He plucked at Essen's sleeve.

'They are destroying their guns over there,' he said. 'They are firing some shots at us while at each salvo they fire a shot against the trunnions of one of the guns. There were four guns over there, Your Excellency. Now – see – there are only two.'

'Possibly,' admitted Essen, staring into the darkness.

'The firing is dying away,' agreed Clausewitz, 'but perhaps they are only growing tired of wasting ammunition.'

There was only one flash from the battery next time, and there was something clearly odd about it.

'The last gun in the battery,' commented Essen. 'Probably they have burst it by overloading.'

He trained his telescope in the darkness.

'Look over there at their main camps,' he added. 'Watch those fires. They seem to be burning brightly, but—'

Hornblower directed his gaze to the distant rows of camp-fires, sparkling very dimly in the thick night. He looked backwards and forwards along one of the rows, trying to keep track of them all. He thought he saw one fire wink and go out, but he could not be sure. His eyes were watering with the cold and with the strain, and as he rubbed them Essen shut his telescope with a snap.

'They are dying down,' he said. 'I'm sure of it, and no troops would allow their camp-fires to die down on a night like this. Clausewitz, get your men ready to attack again. Diebitch—'

The Governor began rapping out orders. Hornblower had a momentary feeling of pity for the Russian soldiers, huddled in their freezing trenches, dispirited by their recent repulse and losses, now ordered to go out again to what would seem to them to be certain disaster in the night. The wind suddenly shrieked down upon them, piercing him to the bone, despite the cloak he clutched round himself.

''Ere you are, sir,' said Brown's voice unexpectedly in his ear. 'I've brought you up a blanket. Let's put it round you under your cloak. And 'ere's your gloves, sir.'

Deftly in the darkness Brown draped the blanket over him, so that his cloak held it down over his shoulders. It would look fantastic in daylight, but fortunately it was still dark. Hornblower was shivering, and he stamped his frozen feet in an endeavour to warm them.

'Aren't those men of yours *ever* going to attack, Clausewitz?' grumbled Essen. 'What's the time? One o'clock? Send down to your brigadier and tell him I'll have him cashiered if he does not pull his men together for an immediate advance.'

There was a long freezing interval, before the darkness before them was pricked by a few little pin-points of flame – musket-shots in the second parallel.

'Ha!' said Essen.

There was another long wait before the message came back. The sortie had found the advanced trenches abandoned save for a few posts. They were pushing forward now through the snow and the darkness towards the main camp.

'They're going, then,' said Essen. 'Have the cavalry paraded two hours before dawn. I'll catch their rear-guard at daylight. I want all troops across the river then. And now a glass of tea, for the love of God.'

Warming himself at the fire burning on the flagged floor of the church, drinking hot tea through his chattering teeth, Hornblower looked round at these men of iron who showed no sign of fatigue and hardly any of cold. He himself was too chilled, and, oddly, too fatigued, to gain much benefit from the chance of resting for a couple of hours on the trusses of straw laid out beside the high altar, but Essen snored volcanically until the moment when his aide-de-camp shook him awake. Outside it was still dark, and colder than ever, when the horses were brought up to the church door for them to mount.

'I better come with you, sir,' said Brown. 'I got myself a 'orse.'

How Brown had done that Hornblower could not imagine, seeing the difficulties of language. Hornblower supposed Brown had learned to ride in those incredibly distant days at Smallbridge. The cavalcade moved slowly in the darkness towards the Mitau suburb, the horses slipping and stumbling in the snow; Hornblower found himself wishing he had been able to retain his blanket when he mounted, for it was colder than ever in the faint grey light. Suddenly from far ahead of them came a sullen flat thud, and another, and another – field-guns firing a long way off.

'Diebitch is up to their rear-guard,' said Essen. 'Good!'

There was enough light now to reveal the desolation of their sur-roundings as they approached the deserted siege-works. They could look down into the littered trenches; there were the batteries, with the shattered siege-guns standing drunkenly at the embrasures, and here was a dead horse, lying on its back, its belly shrouded with snow, out of which its legs pointed stiffly at the grey sky. And here was the main camp, rows and rows of little huts; mostly only two or three feet high, with the dead remains of camp-fires already buried in snow. Outside one hut, larger than the others, lay a soldier swathed in the grey capote of the French Army. He was face downwards and not dead, for they saw his feet move.

'Have they been fighting here?' conjectured Essen, puzzled; there was no sign of blood.

Someone dismounted and turned him over; his face was mottled with mulberry-coloured marks, and his eyes, though open, were unseeing.

'Keep away!' shouted one of the aides-de-camp suddenly. 'That is the plague!'

Everyone drew away from the dying man, and then they realised that the plague was all around them. One of the huts was full of dead, another was full of the dying. Essen shook his horse into a trot, and the party jingled away.

'It is in our ranks already,' said Essen to Hornblower. 'Kladoff had ten cases in his division two days ago.'

This, the first march in retreat of the invading army, was already finding out the weaklings. There were dead men, sick men, dying men alongside the track they were following, despite the fact that no fighting had taken place along it – Diebitch at the head of the pursuing force was on the Mitau road away on the left front, where the guns were still firing occasionally. When at last they reached the point where the track joined the high road the signs of real fighting began; dead and wounded soldiers, Russian, French, and German, where the Russian advance-guard had clashed with the rear-guard. Then they caught up with the Russian columns plodding sturdily up the road, and trotted past their interminable length, one division and then another; the men were silent with the exertion of stepping out as fast as their legs would carry them under their heavy knapsacks, and this ten miles of fast marching had greatly modified the first jubilation of pursuit.

'Macdonald has made a good retreat,' said Clausewitz 'at the cost of leaving his sick and his guns behind. I wonder how long he will be able to keep this pace up?'

Hornblower did not trouble to enter into the discussion. Saddle sore-ness was making him abstracted, apart from his fatigue and his general feeling of malaise. But he had to be able to report to his government that he had followed up the retreating army for at least one march on its way back to Germany; it would be better if it were two or three. And there was something else. He wanted to catch up with the Prussians, even if it were the last thing he did – and it was odd that he had this feeling that it was the last thing he was ever going to do. His head was whirling, and there was something comforting about the knowledge that Brown was just back there with the mounted orderlies.

A messenger brought back news from the advance-guard, and Horn-blower heard Clausewitz's explanation as if in a dream.

'The Prussians are making a stand at the fork in the roads ahead,' he said. 'They are covering the retreat while the other two army corps get away by the two roads.'

It was strange that this was just what he was expecting, as if it were a story he had already heard being retold.

'The Prussians!' he said, and without willing it he pressed his legs against his horse's sides to urge it to a faster pace towards where the flat reports of the guns showed where the Prussians were holding back the advance-guard. The headquarters party was clear of the main body now, trotting along the deeply rutted road, hemmed in here by a dense wood of coniferous trees. Beyond the wood the desolate landscape opened up to reveal a low ridge up which the road mounted ahead of them. On either side of the road here a brigade of the Russian advance-guard was halted, a battery of artillery was in action, and up on the ridge could be seen the Prussian infantry columns, black blocks against grey fields. Over on the right a grey-clad Russian column was plodding across country to turn the flank of the position, while between the two forces Russian horsemen – Cossacks – trotted in ones and twos on their shaggy ponies, their long lances vertical at their sides. A watery sun broke through the clouds at this moment, seeming merely to accentuate the gloominess of the landscape. A general came up to salute Essen, but Hornblower did not want to listen to what he had to say. He wanted to press forward towards the Prussians, and as the horses of the party followed the example of his own they moved steadily up the road, Essen half unconscious of the movements of his horse as he listened to the general's report. He was only recalled to his surroundings by the howl of a cannon-shot which pitched at the roadside near him, throwing snow and earth in all directions.

'What do we think we're doing?' he asked. 'We'll be getting ourselves shot in a moment.'

Hornblower was staring forward at the Prussian army, at the glitter of bayonets and the flags black against the snow.

'I want to go up to the Prussians,' he said.

The discharge of the battery close at hand drowned the words Essen said in reply, but what he meant to say was plain enough.

'I am going,' said Hornblower stubbornly. He looked round and caught Clausewitz's eye. 'Are you coming too, Colonel?'

'Of course he cannot,' expostulated Essen. 'He cannot risk being taken.'

As a renegade, a man fighting against his own country, Clausewitz was likely to be hanged if ever the Prussians laid hands on him.

'It would be better if he came,' said Hornblower, woodenly. This was a strange feeling of simultaneous clairvoyance and illness.

'I'll go with the Commodore,' said Clausewitz suddenly, making what was probably the bravest decision of his life. Perhaps he was carried away by Hornblower's automaton-like recklessness.

Essen shrugged his shoulders at this madness which had descended upon them.

'Go, then,' he said. 'Perhaps I may be able to capture enough generals to exchange for you.'

They trotted forward up the road; Hornblower heard Essen bellow an order to the battery commander to cease fire. He looked back; Brown was trotting after them, a respectful five lengths behind. They passed close to some of the Cossack light horse, who looked at them curiously, and then they were in among Prussian skirmishers, who, from the shelter of bushes and inequalities in the ground, were taking long shots at the Cossacks. No one fired at them as they rode boldly through. A Prussian captain beside the road saluted them, and Clausewitz returned the salute. Just beyond the skirmishing line was the first formed infantry, a Prussian regiment in battalion columns of companies, two on one side of the road and one on the other. The colonel and his staff were standing in the road staring at the odd trio approaching them – the British naval officer in his blue and gold, Clausewitz in his Russian uniform with the row of medals, and the British seaman with cutlass and pistols at his belt. The colonel asked a question in a loud dry tone as they approached, and Clausewitz answered it, reining in.

'Tell them we must see the general,' said Hornblower in French to Clausewitz.

There was a rapid exchange of dialogue between Clausewitz and the colonel, ending in the latter calling up two or three mounted officers – his adjutant and majors, perhaps – to accompany them up the road. Here they saw a larger infantry force formed up, and a line of guns, and here was a party on horseback, the feathers and braid and medals and mounted orderlies indicating the presence of a general's staff. This must be the general – Yorck, Hornblower remembered his name to be. He recognised Clausewitz at once, and addressed him abruptly in German. A few words on each side seemed only to add to the tension of the situation, and there was a short pause.

'He speaks French,' said Clausewitz to Hornblower, and they both turned and waited for him to speak.

'General,' said Hornblower; he was in a dream, but he made himself speak in his dream. 'I represent the King of England, and Colonel Clausewitz represents the Emperor of Russia. We are fighting to free Europe from Bonaparte. Are you fighting to maintain him as a tyrant?'

It was a rhetorical question to which no answer was possible. Silent perforce, Yorck could only await the rest of what Hornblower had to say.

'Bonaparte is beaten. He is retreating from Moscow, and not ten thousand of his army will reach Germany. The Spaniards have deserted him, as you know. So have the Portuguese. All Europe is turning upon him, having found out how little his promises mean. You know of his treatment of Germany – I need not tell you about that. If you fight for him you may keep him on his tottering throne for a few days longer. You may drag out Germany's agony by that length of time. But your duty is to your enslaved country, to your King who is a prisoner. You can free them. You can end the useless pouring-out of the blood of your men now, at this moment.'

Yorck looked away from him, over the bleak countryside, at the Russian army slowly deploying, before he replied.

'What do you suggest?' he said.

That was all Hornblower wanted to hear. If Yorck was willing to ask questions, instead of immediately making prisoners of them, the matter was as good as settled. He could leave the discussion to Clausewitz, and sink back into the weariness which was rising round him like a tide. He brought Clausewitz into the conversation with a glance.

'An armistice,' said Clausewitz. 'An immediate suspension of hostilities. The definitive terms can be settled easily enough at leisure.'

Yorck still hesitated for a moment. Hornblower, despite his weariness and illness, could study him with a renewed flicker of interest; the hard face, sunburned to mahogany, the white hair and moustache in strange contrast. Yorck was on the edge of his fate. At present he was a loyal subject of the King of Prussia, a comparatively undistinguished general. He had only to say two words, and they would make him a traitor now and conceivably an historic figure in the future. Prussia's defection – at any rate, the defection of the Prussian army – would reveal the hollowness of the Napoleonic Empire in a way nothing else could do. It rested with Yorck.

'I agree,' said Yorck.

That was all Hornblower wanted to hear. He could lapse into his dream – his nightmare – now, let the rest of the discussion take whatever course it would. When Clausewitz turned back down the road Hornblower's horse followed him without any guidance from Hornblower. Brown appeared, just his face; there was nothing else that Hornblower could see.

'Are you all right, sir?'

'Of course I am,' said Hornblower automatically.

The earth that Hornblower found himself treading was soft, as though he were walking on feather beds or on a loosely stretched bit of sailcloth. It might be better to lie down. And Hornblower was suddenly conscious that there was something beautiful about music after all. He had gone all his life thinking that it was only an irritating muddle of noises, but revelation had come to him at last. It was lovely, ecstatic, this music that he heard, peals and peals of it, great soaring melodies. He had to raise up his voice to join in with it, to sing and sing and sing. And then the music ended in a final crashing chord, leaving a silence in which his voice sounded hoarse, like a crow's. He stopped, feeling rather embarrassed. It was as well that somebody else was available to take up the song. The boatman was singing as he pulled at his sculls.

'Row, row, row you together to Hampton Court—'

A delightful tenor voice; on account of it Hornblower was ready to excuse the wherryman for such an impertinence as singing while he rowed up the river.

'Rowing in sunshiny weather—'

Barbara beside him was laughing deliciously. The sunshine was beautiful and so were the green lawns on the river banks. He had to laugh too, laugh and laugh. And here was little Richard climbing over his knees. What the devil was Brown doing, staring at him like this?

Lord
Hornblower

I

The chapel stall of carved oak on which Sir Horatio Hornblower was sitting was most uncomfortable, and the sermon which the Dean of Westminster was preaching was deadly dull. Hornblower fidgeted like a child, and like a child he peered round the chapel and at the congregation to distract his mind from his physical troubles. Over his head soared the exquisite fan tracery of what Hornblower soberly decided was the most beautiful building in the world; there was something mathematically satisfactory in the way the spreading patterns met and re-met, a sort of inspired logic. The nameless workmen who had done that carving must have been far-sighted, creative men.

The sermon was still going on, and Hornblower feared that when it was finished there would be some more singing, more of those high-pitched noises from the surpliced choirboys which would distress him painfully again, more painfully than the sermon or the oaken stall. This was the price he had to pay for having a ribbon and star to wear, for being a Knight of the Most Honourable Order of the Bath; as he was known to be on sick leave in England – and fully convalescent – he could not possibly evade attendance at this, the most important ceremonial of the Order. Certainly the chapel looked effective enough, the dull sunshine which made its way through the windows being reflected and multiplied into a soul-stirring glow by the knights' crimson mantles and flashing orders. There was at least this to be said for this pomp and vanity; it was certainly beautiful in a strange, effective way, even without regard to historical associations. Maybe the stall on which he sat had in earlier years caused the same discomfort to Hawke or Anson; maybe Marlborough, in crimson and white similar to his own, had fidgeted and fretted through a similar sermon.

The important-looking person over there with a silver-gilt crown on his head and velvet tabard embroidered in the royal arms was merely Bath King-at-Arms, some well-connected fellow who had this well-paid sinecure and could doubtless comfort himself, while sitting through the sermon, with the thought that he was earning his living by doing so once a year. Beside him was the Prince Regent, the Sovereign of the Order, his scarlet face at odds with the crimson of his mantle. And there were soldiers, generals and colonels, with whose faces he was unfamiliar.

But elsewhere in the chapel there were men with whom he was proud to share the brotherhood of the Order – Lord St Vincent, huge and grim, the man who took his fleet down into the heart of a Spanish squadron twice its strength; Duncan, who destroyed the Dutch Navy at Camperdown; and a dozen more of admirals and captains, some of them even junior to him in the Navy List – Lydiard, who captured the *Pomona* off Havannah; Samuel Hood, who commanded the *Zealous* at the Nile; and Yeo, who stormed the fort at El Muro. There was something pleasant and heartwarming at being a member of the same chivalrous Order as men like these – ridiculous, but true. And there were three times as many heroes as these, brother-knights also still at sea (for the ones present here were only those with shore appointments or on leave) making the final desperate effort to tear down the Napoleonic Empire. Hornblower felt a surge of patriotic emotion within him; his spirit soared, and then he incontinently began to analyse this wave of emotion and to wonder how much of it was due to the romantic beauty of his surroundings.

A uniformed naval lieutenant had made his way into the chapel, and stood hesitating for a moment before discovering Lord St Vincent and hastening to him, offering him the large despatch (whose seals were already broken) which he held in his hand. No one was paying any attention to the sermon now – the cream of the Royal Navy were all craning round, peering at St Vincent as he read the despatch, which had clearly arrived from the Admiralty at the other end of Whitehall. The Dean's voice wavered, and then he rallied gamely, droning on to deaf ears, and ears which remained deaf for a long time, for St Vincent, having read the despatch through once without any change of expression in his craggy face, immediately turned back to the beginning and read it through again. St Vincent who had so boldly risked the fate of England on a single prompt decision at the battle which gave him his title was nevertheless not a man to plunge hastily into action where there was time to think.

He finished his second reading, folded the despatch, and then swept his gaze round the chapel. Two score Knights of the Bath stiffened with excitement and hoped to catch his eye. St Vincent rose to his feet and clasped his crimson cloak about him; he threw a word to the waiting lieutenant, and then, seizing his plumed hat, proceeded to hobble stiffly out of the chapel. Attention immediately transferred itself to the lieutenant, who was watched by every eye as he walked across the transept, and Hornblower stirred uncomfortably, his heart beating fast, as he realised that the lieutenant was heading straight for him.

'His Lordship's compliments, sir,' said the lieutenant, 'and he would like a word with you immediately.'

Now it was Hornblower's turn to fasten his mantle and to remember to pick up his plumed hat. He must at all costs appear nonchalant, and give to the assembled Knights no chance to smile at him for appearing flustered at this summons from the First Lord. He must look as if he was accustomed to this sort of thing every day. He stepped negligently out of his stall; his sword made its way between his legs and only by the mercy of Providence was he saved from tumbling headlong. He recovered himself with a clatter of spurs and scabbard, and set himself to stalk with slow dignity down the aisle. Every eye was on him; the Army officers present must be feeling merely a disinterested curiosity, but the Navy – Lydiard and the others – must be wondering what new fantastic turn the naval war had taken, and envying him the adventures and distinction which must await him. At the back of the chapel, in the seats reserved for the privileged public, Hornblower caught sight of Barbara making her way out of her pew to meet him. He smiled nervously at her – he could not trust himself to speak with all those eyes on him – and gave her his arm. He felt the firm touch of her hand upon it, and heard her clear, incisive voice; of course Barbara would not be awed by the fact that everyone was watching them.

'Further trouble, I suppose, dear?' said Barbara.

'I suppose so,' mumbled Hornblower.

Beyond the door St Vincent was awaiting them, the little wind tossing the ostrich feathers of his hat and ruffling the crimson cloak of silk. His massive legs bulged the white silk trunk hose; and he was pacing up and down on huge, gouty, deformed feet that distorted the white silk shoes. But the fantastic costume in no way detracted from the grim dignity of the man. Barbara slipped her arm out of Hornblower's and discreetly dropped back to allow the two men to converse in private.

'Sir?' said Hornblower, and then, remembering – he was not used yet to dealings with the peerage – 'My lord?'

'You're ready for active service now, Hornblower?'

'Yes, my lord.'

'You'll have to start tonight.'

'Aye aye, sir – my lord.'

'When they bring my damned coach up I'll take you to the Admiralty and give you your orders.' St Vincent lifted his voice in a bellow that had hailed the maintop in West Indian hurricanes. 'Haven't they got those damned horses in *yet*, Johnson?'

St Vincent caught sight of Barbara over Hornblower's shoulder.

'Your servant, ma'am,' he said; he took off the plumed hat and held it across his breast as he bowed; age and gout and a lifetime at sea had not deprived him of the courtly graces, but the business of the country still had first call upon his attention, and he turned back immediately to Hornblower.

'What is the service, my lord?' asked the latter.

'Suppression of mutiny,' said St Vincent grimly. 'Damned bloody mutiny. It might be '94 over again. Did you ever know Chadwick – Lieutenant Augustine Chadwick?'

'Midshipman with me under Pellew, my lord.'

'Well, he's – ah, here's my damned coach at last. What about Lady Barbara?'

'I'll take my own carriage back to Bond Street,' said Barbara, 'and I'll send it back for Horatio at the Admiralty. Here it comes now.'

The carriage, with Brown and the coachman on the box, drew up behind St Vincent's coach, and Brown sprang down.

'Very good, then. Come on, Hornblower. Your servant, ma'am, again.'

St Vincent climbed in heavily, with Hornblower beside him, and the horses' hoofs clashed on the cobbles as the heavy vehicle crawled forward. The pale sunlight flickered through the windows on St Vincent's craggy face as he sat stoop-shouldered on the leather seat; some urchins in the street caught sight of the gaily attired individuals in the coach and yelled 'Hooray', waving their tattered caps.

'Chadwick had *Flame*, eighteen-gun brig,' said St Vincent. 'The crew's mutinied in the Bay of the Seine and are holding him and the other officers hostage. They turned a master's mate and four loyal hands hands adrift in the gig with an ultimatum addressed to the Admiralty. The gig made Bembridge last night, and the papers have just reached me – here they are.'

St Vincent shook in his gnarled hand the despatch and the enclosures which he had clasped since he received them in Westminster Abbey.

'What's the ultimatum, my lord?'

'Amnesty – oblivion. And hang Chadwick. Otherwise they turn the brig over to the French.'

'The crazy fools!' said Hornblower.

He could remember Chadwick in the *Indefatigable*; old for a midshipman then, twenty years ago. He must be in his fifties now, and only a lieutenant. He had been a vile-tempered midshipman; after being passed over continually for promotion he must be a worse-tempered lieutenant. He could make a little vessel like the *Flame*, in which probably he was the only commissioned officer, a perfect hell if he wanted to. That might be the basis of the mutiny. After the terrible lessons of Spithead and the Nore, after Pigott had been murdered in the *Hermione*, some of the worst characteristics of the naval service had been eliminated. It was still a hard, cruel life, but not one to drive men into the suicidal madness of mutiny unless there were some special circumstances involved. A captain both cruel and unjust, a determined and intelligent leader among the men – that combination might make a mutiny. But whatever the cause, mutiny must be suppressed instantly, visited with extreme punishment. Smallpox or the plague were no more infectious and no more fatal than mutiny in a fighting service. Allow one mutineer to escape punishment, and he would be remembered by every next man with a grievance, and his example followed.

And England was at the very climax of her struggle with the French despotism. Five hundred ships of war at sea – two hundred of them ships of the line – were striving to keep the seas clear of enemies. A hundred thousand men under Wellington were bursting over the Pyrenees into southern France. And all the motley armies of eastern Europe, Russians and Prussians, Austrians and Swedes, Croats and Hungarians and Dutch, were being clothed and fed and armed by England's exertions. It seemed as if England could not put forth one single further effort in the struggle; even as if she must falter and break down under the dreadful strain. Bonaparte was fighting for his life, with all the cunning and ferocity one might expect of him. A few more months of constancy, a few more months of fierce exertion, might bring him crashing down and restore peace to a mad world; a moment's wavering, a breath of doubt, and tyranny might be clamped upon mankind for another generation, for uncounted generations to come.

The coach was wheeling into the Admiralty yard, and two wooden-legged naval pensioners were stumping out to open the doors. St Vincent climbed out, and he and Hornblower, in their brilliant crimson and white silk, walked through to the First Lord's room.

'There's their ultimatum,' said St Vincent, throwing a paper upon the desk.

Written in a poor hand, was Hornblower's first mental note – not the work of some bankrupt tradesman or lawyer's clerk caught by the press-gang.

> On board H.M.S. *Flame* off Havre.
> 7th October, 1813.
>
> We are all loyal hearts and true here, but Lieutenant Augustine Chadwick has flogged us and starved us, and has turned up all hands twice a watch for a month. Yesterday he said that today he would flog every third man of us and the rest of us as soon as the others was healed. So we have him under lock and key in his cabin, and there's a whip rove at the fore yardarm waiting for him for he ought to be strung up after what he did to the boy James Jones, he killed him and we think he said in his report that he died of fever. We want their Lordships at the Admiralty to promise us to try him for his crimes and give us new officers and let bygones be bygones. We want to fight on for England's liberties for we are loyal hearts and true like we said but France is under our lee and we are all in this together and we are not going to be hanged as mutineers and if you try to take

this vessel we shall run him up the yardarm and go in to the French. We are all signing this.

Humbly and respectfully yours,

All round the margin of the letter were the signatures, seven of them, and several score of crosses, with a note against each cross – 'Henry Wilson, his mark'; 'William Owen, his mark', and so on; they indicated the usual proportion of literates and illiterates in an average ship's company. Hornblower looked up at St Vincent when he finished examining the letters.

'Mutinous dogs,' said St Vincent.

Maybe they were, thought Hornblower. But they had a right to be, he also thought. He could imagine perfectly well the sort of treatment to which they had been subjected, the unending wanton cruelty added to the normal hardship of life in a ship on blockading service; miseries which only death or mutiny could bring to an end – no other way out at all.

Faced with the certainty of a flogging in the immediate future, they had risen in mutiny, and he could not blame them. He had seen enough backs cut to ribbons; he knew that he himself would do anything, literally anything, to avoid such torture for himself if he were faced with the prospect of it. His flesh crept as he made himself seriously consider how he would feel if he knew he were to be flogged next week. The men had moral right on their side; it was not a matter of justice, but one of expediency, that they should be punished for their justifiable crime. The national existence of the country depended greatly on seizing the mutineers, hanging the ringleaders, flogging the rest; cauterising before the disease could spread farther this new plague spot which had appeared in England's right arm. They must be hanged, morally innocent or not – it was a part of war, like the killing of Frenchmen who were possibly admirable husbands and fathers. But it would be as well not to let St Vincent guess at his sentiments – the First Lord obviously hated mutineers just as mutineers, without troubling to think more deeply about their case.

'What orders do you have for me, my lord?' asked Hornblower.

'I'll give you *carte blanche*,' replied St Vincent. 'A free hand. Bring *Flame* back safe and sound, and the mutineers along with her, and you can set about it any way you choose.'

'You will give me full powers – to negotiate, for instance, my lord?'

'I didn't mean that, damn it,' replied St Vincent. 'I meant you could have any force you asked for. I could spare you three ships of the line, if you want them. A couple of frigates. Bomb-vessels. There's even a rocket-vessel if you think you could use it – this fellow Congreve wants to see his rockets in action again.'

'It doesn't appear to be the kind of situation in which great force would be of much use, my lord. Ships of the line would seem to be superfluous.'

'I know that too, damn it.' The struggle in St Vincent's mind was evident in his massive face. 'Those insolent rascals can slip into the Seine's mouth in two shakes of a duck's tail at the first sign of danger to themselves. It's brains that are needed here, I know. That's why I sent for *you*, Hornblower.'

A nice compliment. Hornblower preened himself a little; he was talking here on terms almost of equality to one of the greatest admirals who had ever hoisted his flag, and the sensation was extraordinarily pleasant. And the internal pressure which was mounting inside the First Lord suddenly forced out of him a yet more astonishing statement.

'And the men like you, Hornblower,' exploded St Vincent. 'Damn it, I don't know a man who doesn't. They'll follow you and listen to you. You're one of the officers the men talk about among themselves. They trust you and expect things of you – so do I, damn it, as you can see.'

'But if I talk to the men it will imply that I am negotiating with them, my lord.'

'No negotiations with mutineers!' blared St Vincent, striking the desk with a fist like a leg of mutton. 'We had enough of that in '94.'

'Then the *carte blanche* that you give me is no more than the usual naval officer's orders, my lord,' said Hornblower.

This was a serious matter; he was being sent out on an extremely difficult task, and would have to bear all the odium of failure should he be unsuccessful. He had never imagined himself bandying arguments with a First Lord, yet here he was actually doing so, impelled by sheer necessity. He realised in a moment of clairvoyance that he was not arguing on behalf of himself, after all; he was not trying to safeguard his own interests. He was debating purely impersonally; the officer who was to be sent out to recapture *Flame* and whose future might depend upon the powers given him was not the Hornblower sitting in this carved chair, dressed in crimson and white silk, but some poor devil he was sorry for and whose interests he had at heart because they represented the national interests. Then the two beings merged together again, and it was he, Barbara's husband, the man who had been at Lord Liverpool's dinner-party last night and had a slight ache in the centre of his forehead today in consequence, who was to go out on this unpleasant task, where not a ha'porth of glory or distinction was to be won and the gravest risk was to be run of a fiasco which might make him the laughing-stock of the Navy and an object of derision through the country.

He studied St Vincent's expression again attentively; St Vincent was no fool and there was a thinking brain behind that craggy brow – he was fighting against his prejudices, preparing to dispense with them in the course of his duty.

'Very well then, Hornblower,' said the First Lord at length. 'I'll give you full powers. I'll have your orders drawn up to that effect. You will hold your appointment as Commodore, of course.'

'Thank you, my lord,' said Hornblower.

'Here's a list of the ship's company,' went on St. Vincent. 'We have nothing here against any of them. Nathaniel Sweet, bos'un's mate – here's his signature – was first mate of a Newcastle collier brig once – dismissed for drinking. Maybe he's the ringleader. But it may be any of 'em.'

'Is the news of the mutiny public?'

'*No*. And please God it won't be until the court-martial flag is hoisted. Holden at Bembridge had the sense to keep his mouth shut. He put the master's mate and the hands under lock and key the moment he heard their news. *Dart*'s sailing for Calcutta next week – I'll ship 'em out in her. It'll be months before the story leaks out.'

Mutiny was an infection, carried by words. The plague spot must be isolated until it could be cauterised.

St Vincent drew a sheaf of papers to himself and took up his pen – a handsome turkey-feather with one of the new-fangled gold nibs.

'What force do you require?'

'Something handy and small,' said Hornblower.

He had not the remotest idea how he was going to deal with this problem of recovering a vessel which had only to drop two miles to leeward to be irrecoverable, but his pride made him assume an appearance of self-confidence. He caught himself wondering if all men were like himself, putting on a brave show of moral courage when actually they felt weak and helpless – he remembered Suetonius' remark about Nero, who believed all men to be privately as polluted as himself although they did not admit it publicly.

'There's *Porta Coeli*,' said St Vincent, raising his white eyebrows. 'Eighteen-gun brig – sister to *Flame*, in fact. She's at Spithead, ready to sail. Freeman's in command – he had the cutter *Clam* under your command in the Baltic. He brought you home, didn't he?'

'Yes, my lord.'

'Would she serve?'

'I think so, my lord.'

'Pellew's commanding the mid-Channel squadron. I'll send him orders to let you have any help you may request.'

'Thank you, my lord.'

Here he was, committing himself to a difficult – maybe an impossible – enterprise without any attempt to leave himself an avenue of retreat, neglecting utterly to sow any seed of future excuses which might be reaped to advantage in case of failure. It was utterly reckless of him, but that ridiculous pride of his, he knew, was preventing him. He could not use 'ifs' or 'buts' to men like St Vincent or to any man at all, for that matter. He wondered if it was because the First Lord's recent compliments had gone to his head, or maybe it was because of the casual remark that he could 'request' help of Pellew, a Commander-in-Chief, who had been his captain twenty years ago when he was a midshipman. He decided it was not either of these reasons. Just his nonsensical pride.

'Wind's nor'westerly and steady,' said St Vincent, glancing up at the dial which repeated the indications of the weather-vane on the Admiralty roof. 'Glass is dropping, though. The sooner you're off the better. I'll send your orders after you to your lodgings – take this chance to say goodbye to your wife. Where's your kit?'

'At Smallbridge, my lord. Almost on the road to Portsmouth.'

'Good. Noon now. If you leave at three; po'chaise to Portsmouth – you can't ride post with your sea-chest. Eight hours – seven hours, the roads aren't poached yet at this time o' year – you can be under way at midnight. I'll send Freeman his orders by post this minute. I wish you luck, Hornblower.'

'Thank you, my lord.'

Hornblower gathered his cloak round him, hitched up his sword, and took his leave. Before he had quitted the room a clerk had entered at the summons of St Vincent's jangling bell to take dictation of his order. Outside the northwesterly wind of which St Vincent had spoken blew freshly, and he felt chilled and forlorn in his gay crimson and white silk. But the carriage was there waiting for him, as Barbara had promised.

II

She was waiting for him when he arrived at Bond Street, steady of eye and composed of feature, as was to be expected of one of a fighting race. But she could only trust herself to say a single word.

'Orders?' she asked.

'Yes,' answered Hornblower, and then gave vent to some of the powerful mixed emotions within him. 'Yes, dear.'

'When?'

'I sail tonight from Spithead. They're writing my orders now – I must leave as soon as they reach me here.'

'I thought it would be like that, from the look on St Vincent's face. So I sent off Brown to Smallbridge to pack your kit. It'll be ready for you when we get there.'

Capable, farsighted, level-headed Barbara! Yet 'Thank you, dear,' was
all he could say. There were often these difficult moments even now,
after all this time with Barbara; moments when he was overflowing with
emotion (maybe that was the reason) and yet could not find words.

'May I ask where you are going, dear?'

'I cannot tell you if you do,' said Hornblower, forcing a smile. 'I'm
sorry, dear.'

Barbara would say no word to anyone, nor convey by any hint or
sign upon what kind of mission he was setting out, but, all the same, he
could tell her nothing. Then if news of the mutiny leaked out Barbara
could not be held responsible; but that was not the real reason. It was
his duty to keep silent, and duty allowed of no exceptions. Barbara
smiled back at him with the brightness that duty demanded. She turned
her attention to his silken cloak, and draped it more gracefully over his
shoulders.

'A pity,' she said, 'that in these modern days there are so few
opportunities for men to dress beautifully. Crimson and white sets off
your good looks, dear. You are a very handsome man – did you know
that?'

Then the brittle artificial barrier between them broke and vanished as
utterly as a punctured soap bubble. His was a temperament that longed
for affection, for the proofs of love; but a lifetime of self-discipline in an
unrelenting world had made it difficult, almost impossible, for him to
let the fact appear. Within him there was always the lurking fear of a
rebuff, something too horrible to risk. He always was guarded with
himself, guarded with the world. And she; she knew those moods of his,
knew them even while her pride resented them. Her stoic English upbringing had schooled her into distrusting emotion and into contempt
for any exhibition of emotion. She was as proud as he was; she could
resent being dependent on him for her life's fulfilment just as he could
resent feeling incomplete without her love. They were two proud people
who had made, for one reason or another, self-centred self-sufficiency a
standard of perfection to abandon which called for more sacrifice than
they were often prepared to make.

But in these moments, with the shadow of separation looming over
them, pride and resentment vanished, and they could be blessedly
natural, each stripped of the numbing armour the years had built about
them. She was in his arms, and her hands under his cloak could feel the
warmth of his body through the thin silk of his doublet. She pressed
herself against him as avidly as he grasped at her. In that uncorseted age
she was wearing only the slightest whalebone stiffening at the waist of
her gown; in his arms he could feel her beautiful body limp and yielding
despite the fine muscles (the product of hard riding and long walking)
which he had at last educated himself to accept as desirable in woman,

whom he had once thought should be soft and feeble. Warm lips were against warm lips, and then eyes smiled into eyes.

'My darling! My sweet!' she said, and then lip to lip again she murmured the endearment of the childless woman to her lover, 'My baby. My dear baby!'

The dearest thing she could say to him. When he yielded to her, when he put off his protective armour, he wanted to be her child as well as her husband; unconsciously he wanted the reassurance that, exposed and naked as he was, she would be true and loyal to him like a mother to her child, taking no advantage of his defenceless condition. The last reserve melted; they blended one into the other in that extremity of passion which they could seldom attain. Nothing could mar it now. Hornblower's powerful fingers tore loose the silken cord that clasped his cloak; the unfamiliar fastenings of his doublet, the ridiculous strings of his trunk hose – it did not break into his mood to have to deal with them. Some time Barbara found herself kissing his hands, the long beautiful fingers whose memory sometimes haunted her nights when they were separated, and it was a gesture of the purest passion without symbolism. They were free for each other, untrammelled, unhindered, in love. They were marvellously one, and one even when it was all over; they were complete and yet not sated. They were one even when he left her lying there, when he glanced into the mirror and saw his scanty hair madly tousled.

His uniform hung on the dressing-room door; Barbara had thought of everything during the time he had been with St Vincent. He washed himself in the hand-basin, sponging his heated body, and there was no thought of washing away impurity – the act was one of simple pleasure. When the butler knocked at the door he put his dressing-gown over his shirt and trousers and came out. It was his orders; he signed the receipt for them, broke the seal, and sat down to read them through to make sure there were no misunderstanding which ought to be cleared up before he left London. The old, old formulas – 'You are hereby requested and required'; 'You are therefore strictly charged' – the same ones under whose authority Nelson had gone into action at Trafalgar and Blake at Tenerife. The purport of the orders was plain, and the delegation of power unequivocating. If read aloud to a ship's company – or to a court martial – they would be readily understood. Would he ever have to read them aloud? That would mean he had opened negotiations with mutineers. He was entitled to do so, but it would be a sign of weakness, something that would mean lifted eyebrows throughout the Navy, and which would cast a shadow of disappointment over St Vincent's craggy face. Somehow or other he had to fool and trick a hundred English seamen into his power, so that they could be hanged and flogged for doing something he knew very well he would have done himself in the same circumstances. He had a duty to do; sometimes it was his duty to kill Frenchmen, and sometimes it might be another duty. He would prefer to have to kill Frenchmen if someone had to be killed. And how in Heaven's name was he to set about this present task?

The door to the bedroom opened and Barbara came in, radiant and smiling. Their spirits rushed together as their eyes met; the imminence of physical separation, and Hornblower's contemplation of his new distasteful duty, were not sufficient to disrupt the mental accord between them. They were more united than they had ever been before, and they knew it, the fortunate pair. Hornblower rose to his feet.

'I shall be ready to leave in ten minutes,' he said. 'Will you come with me as far as Smallbridge?'

'I was hoping you would ask me to do so,' said Barbara.

III

It was the blackest imaginable night, and the wind, backing westerly, was blowing half a gale and promised to blow harder. It blew round Hornblower, flapping his trouser-legs about his knees above his sea-boots and tugging at his coat, while all round and above him in the blackness the rigging shrieked in an insane chorus, as though protesting at the madness of mankind in exposing frail man-made equipment to the violence of the world's forces. Even here, in the lee of the Isle of Wight, the little brig was moving in lively fashion under Hornblower's feet as he stood on the tiny quarterdeck. Somewhere to windward of Hornblower someone – a petty officer, presumably – was cursing a seaman for some unknown error; the filthy words reached Hornblower's ears in gusts.

A lunatic, thought Hornblower, must know these mad contrasts, these sudden changes of mood, these violent alterations in the world about him; in the one case it was the lunatic who changed, but in his own case it was his surroundings. This morning, hardly more than twelve hours ago, he had been sitting in Westminster Abbey with the Knights of the Bath, all dressed in crimson and white silk; he had dined with the Prime Minister the night before. He had been in Barbara's arms; he had been living in Bond Street luxury, with every whim that might arise ready to be satisfied at the mere pulling of a bell-cord. It was a life of self-indulgent ease; a score of servants would be genuinely shocked and upset if the slightest thing occurred to disturb the even way of the life of Sir Horatio – they ran those two words together, of course, making a curious bastard word like Surroratio out of them. Barbara had watched over him all through the summer, to make sure that the last seeds of the

Russian typhus which had brought him home sick were eradicated. He had wandered in the sunshine through the gardens at Smallbridge hand in hand with little Richard, with the gardeners backing respectfully away and pulling at their hats. There had been that golden afternoon when he and Richard had lain side by side on their bellies beside the fishpond, trying to catch golden carp with their hands; returning to the house with the sunset glowing all about them, muddy and wet and gloriously happy, he and his little child, as close together as he had been with Barbara that morning. A happy life; too happy.

At Smallbridge this afternoon, while Brown and the post-boy were carrying out his sea-chest to the chaise, he had said goodbye to Richard, taking hold of his hand to shake it as man to man.

'Are you going back to fight, Father?' Richard asked.

He said one more goodbye to Barbara; it was not easy. If he had good fortune, he might be home again in a week, but he could not tell her that, for it might reveal too much about the nature of his mission. That little bit of deception helped to shatter the mood of unity and union; it made him a little cold and formal again. Hornblower had had a strange feeling as he turned away from her of something lost for ever. Then he had climbed into the chaise with Brown beside him and rolled away, skirting the autumnal Downs to Guildford in the gathering evening, and then down the Portsmouth Road – the road along which he had driven on so many momentous occasions – through the night. The transition was brief from luxury to hardship. At midnight he set foot in the *Porta Coeli*, welcomed by Freeman, square, stocky, and swarthy as ever, with black hair hanging to his cheeks, gipsy-fashion; one noted almost with surprise that there were no rings in his ears. Not more than ten minutes was necessary to tell Freeman, under seal of secrecy, the mission upon with the *Porta Coeli* was to be dispatched; in obedience to his orders received four hours earlier Freeman already had the brig ready for sea, and at the end of that ten minutes the hands were at the capstan getting in the anchor.

'It's going to be a dirty night, sir,' said Freeman out of the darkness beside him. 'Glass is still dropping.'

'I expect it will be, Mr Freeman.'

Freeman suddenly raised his voice to one of the loudest bellows that Hornblower had ever heard – that barrel-shaped chest could produce a surprising volume of sound.

'Mr Carlow! Have all hands shorten sail. Get that maintopmast stays'l in! Another reef in the tops'ls! S'uth-east by south, quartermaster.'

'South-east by south, sir.'

The deck under Hornblower's feet vibrated a little with the rush of the hands over the planking; otherwise there was nothing to show him in the darkness that Freeman's orders were being obeyed; the squeal of the sheave-pulleys in the blocks was swept away in the wind or drowned in the howling of the cordage, and he could see nothing of the rush of the men up the rigging to reef the topsails. He was cold and tired after a day which had begun – unbelievably, it seemed now – with the arrival of the tailor to dress him in the ceremonial costume of a Knight of the Bath.

'I'm going below, Mr Freeman,' he said. 'Call me if necessary.'

'Aye aye, sir.'

Freeman slid back the sliding hatch that covered the companion-way – *Porta Coeli* was flush-decked – and a faint light emerged, revealing the stair; a faint light, but dazzling after the intense blackness of the night. Hornblower descended, bowing almost double under the deck-beams. The door to his right opened into his cabin, six feet square and four feet ten high; Hornblower had to crouch down on his haunches to survey it by the wavering light of the lantern swinging from the deck above. The crampedness of these, the finest quarters in the brig, was nothing compared with the conditions in which the other officers lived, he knew, and twenty times nothing compared with the conditions in which the hands lived. Forward the height between decks was just the same as this – four feet ten – and there the men slept in two banks of hammocks, one suspended above the other, with the noses of the men of the upper tier scraping the deck above and the tails of the men in the lower tier bumping the deck below, and noses meeting tails in the middle. The *Porta Coeli* was the best fighting machine of her tonnage that could sail the seas; she carried guns that could smash any opponent of her own size; she had magazines that could supply those guns during hours or days of fighting; she carried provisions enough to enable her to keep the sea for months without touching land; she was staunch and stout enough to face any weather that blew; the only thing that was wrong with her was that to achieve these results in 190 tons the human beings who lived in her had to be content with living conditions to which no careful farmer would ever subject his livestock. It was at the cost of human flesh and blood that England maintained the countless small vessels which kept the seas safe for her under the protecting shield of the ponderous ships of the line.

The cabin, small though it was, housed a prodigious stink. The first thing the nostrils noticed was the sooty, stuffy smell of the lamp, but they immediately became aware of a whole gamut of supplementary odours. There was the flat bilge smell, tolerable, in fact almost unnoticed by Hornblower who had smelt bilge for twenty years. There was a penetrating smell of cheese, and as if to set that off there was a perceptible smell of rats. There was a smell of wet clothing, and finally there was a mixture of human odours, the long-confined body-odour of unwashed men predominating.

And all this mixture of smells was balanced by a battery of noises. Every timber resonated the shrieking of the rigging; to be inside the cabin was to be like a mouse inside a violin while it was being played. Overhead the continual footfalls on the quarterdeck and the clatter of ropes being thrown down made it seem – to continue the analogy – as if someone else were tapping the body of the violin at the same time with small mallets. The wooden sheathing of the brig creaked and crackled with the vessel's motion in the water like a giant's knuckles rapping on the exterior; and the shot in the racks rolled just a trifle with each movement, too, thumping solemnly and unexpectedly just at the end of the roll as they fetched up.

Hornblower had hardly entered his cabin when the *Porta Coeli* suddenly heeled over unexpectedly far; apparently as she was just emerging into the open Channel the full force of the westerly breeze caught her and laid her. Hornblower was taken by surprise – it always was a slow process recovering his sea-legs after a long stay ashore – and was precipitated forward, fortunately towards the cot, on which he was thrown face downward, and as he lay spreadeagled upon the cot his ears caught the assorted noises as the various loose objects, always not properly secured at the outset of a voyage, cascaded to the decks at this, the first big roll. Hornblower squirmed round on to the cot, bumped his head on the deck-beams above as another roll took him by surprise again, and fell back on to the coarse pillow, sweating in the wet stuffiness of the cabin both as a result of his exertions and with the beginnings of sea-sickness. He was cursing feebly and yet with all his heart; an intense hatred for this war, the more bitter for being completely hopeless, surged up inside him. What peace might be like he could hardly imagine – he had been a mere child when last the world was at peace – but he longed with uncontrollable yearning for peace as a cessation from war. He was weary of war, overweary of it, and his weariness was accentuated and embittered by the experiences of the last year. The news of the complete destruction of Bonaparte's army in Russia had early roused hopes of immediate peace; but France had shown no signs of wavering, had raised new armies, and had stemmed the torrent of the Russian counter-attack far from any vital point of the Empire. The wiseacres had pointed to the severity and all-embracing nature of Bonaparte's conscription, to the harshness of the taxation he exacted, and predicted an early upheaval in the interior of the Empire, backed maybe by a revolt of the generals. Ten months had elapsed since those predictions began generally to be made, and there was not a sign as yet of their coming true. When Austria and Sweden joined the ranks of Bonaparte's enemies, men looked again for immediate victory. They hoped that when Bonaparte's unwilling allies – Denmark, Holland, and the rest – fell away from their allegiance this presaged a prompt breaking-up of the Empire, and they were disappointed each time. For long it had been predicted by thoughtful men that when the tide of war washed back into the Empire itself, when Bonaparte should be compelled to make war support war on the soil of his subjects and not on that of his enemies or tributaries, the struggle would end almost automatically. Yet three months had elapsed since Wellington with a hundred thousand men had swept over the Pyrenees within the sacred frontiers, and still he was locked in a death grapple in the far south, still seven hundred miles from Paris. There seemed to be no end to Bonaparte's resources or determination.

To Hornblower in his present despairing mood it seemed as if the struggle must continue until every last man in Europe was dead, until the whole of England's substance was irrevocably consumed; and for himself that until old age should set him free he would be condemned, on account of the mad determination of one single man, to the loss of his liberty, to spending his days and his nights in hideous surroundings like the present, torn from his wife and his son, sea-sick and cold, depressed and unhappy. For almost the first time in his life he began to wish for a miracle, or for some unsought turn of good fortune – that a stray bullet should kill Bonaparte, or that some prodigious mistake would permit the gaining of an indisputable and decisive victory; that the people of Paris should rise successfully against the tyrant, that the French harvest should fail utterly, that the Marshals, to preserve their fortunes, should declare against the Emperor and succeed in inducing their soldiers to follow them. And none of these things, as he knew, was in the least likely; the struggle must go on and on, and he must remain a sea-sick prisoner in the chains of discipline until his hair turned white.

He opened his tightly closed eyes to find Brown standing over him.

'I knocked, sir, but you didn't hear me.'

'What is it?'

'Is there anything I can get for you, sir? They're just goin' to douse the galley fire. A cup o' coffee, sir? Tea? A hot grog?'

A good stiff dose of liquor might put him to sleep, would drown his morbid and gloomy thoughts, give him some respite from the black depression which was engulfing him. Hornblower found himself actually dallying with the temptation, and was genuinely shocked at himself. That he, who had not drunk to make himself drunk for nearly twenty years, who detested intoxication in himself even more than in other people, should give even a moment's favourable consideration to such a thought startled him in addition to appalling him. It was a new depravity that he had never known existed in him, made worse by the knowledge that he was on a secret mission of great importance, where a clear head and ready judgment would be vitally necessary. He spurned himself in bitter self-contempt.

'No,' he said. 'I shall go back on deck.'

He swung his legs down from the cot; the *Porta Coeli* was now well clear of the land, and was rolling and plunging like a mad thing in the choppy waters of the Channel. The wind on her quarter was laying her over so that as Hornblower rose to his feet he would have slid down to the opposite bulkhead if Brown had not put out a brawny hand and saved him. Brown never lost his sea-legs; Brown was never sick; Brown had the vast physical strength that Hornblower had always coveted. He stood on his straddled legs like a rock, quite unmoved by the antics of the brig, while Hornblower swayed uncertainly. He would have hit his head against the swinging lamp if Brown's firm hand on his shoulder had not deflected him.

'A dirty night, sir, an' it'll be a long sight worse afore it's better.'

Job had the same sort of comforters. Hornblower snarled sidelong at Brown in pettish bad temper, and the bad temper was only made worse by seeing Brown being philosophical about it. It was infuriating to be treated like a child in a tantrum.

'Best wear that scarf Her Ladyship made you, sir,' went on Brown, unmoved. ''Twill be mortal cold by morning.'

In a single movement he flipped open a drawer and produced the scarf. It was a square of priceless silk, light and warm, maybe the most costly thing Hornblower had ever owned, even taking into account his hundred-guinea sword. Barbara had embroidered upon it, with infinite pains – she detested fiddling with needle and thimble, and the fact that she had done so was the prettiest compliment she could pay him. Hornblower put it round his neck inside the collar of his pea-jacket, and was reassured by it, by its warmth and softness and by the memories of Barbara that it conjured up. He steadied himself, and then plunged for the door and up the five steps to the quarterdeck.

It was utterly dark up there, and Hornblower was blinded, emerging from even the miserable light of his cabin. All round him the wind roared hugely; he had to bend his head to meet it. The *Porta Coeli* was lying right over on her side, even though the wind was not abeam but over her quarter. She was both rolling and pitching. Spray and spindrift mixed with the rain that flew across her deck, stinging Hornblower's face as he clawed his way up to the weather bulwarks. Even when his eyes had grown accustomed to the darkness he could hardly make out the dim narrow rectangle of the reefed maintopsail. The little vessel leaped under his feet madly, like a horse; the sea was violent – even through the din of the gale Hornblower could hear the groan of the tiller-ropes as the quartermaster at the wheel fought to keep her from falling away into the trough.

Hornblower sensed the presence of Freeman somewhere near him, and ignored him. There was nothing to say, and even if there had been anything to say the violence of the wind would have made it difficult.

He hitched his elbow on the hammock-netting to steady himself and gazed into the darkness. Just overside the white top of each advancing wave was momentarily visible before the *Porta Coeli* lifted to it. Forward the hands were at work on the pumps; Hornblower's ear could catch the flat chatter of them at intervals. There was nothing surprising at that, because with the violent working of the vessel in the waves the seams must be gaping and closing like mouths. Somewhere in this black night ships would be sailing, worn down by the gale; somewhere ships would be driving ashore, and seamen would be dying in the surf with this pitiless wind howling over them. Anchors would be dragging and lines parting. And this wind would be blowing over the miserable bivouacs of embattled Europe, too. The million anonymous peasant soldiers huddled round the camp-fires which they could hardly keep alight would curse the wind and the rain as they lay sleepless and hungry awaiting tomorrow's battle. It was strange to think that upon them, upon these inconsiderable unknowns, depended, to a large part, his release from his present thraldom. He vomited excruciatingly into the scuppers as his sea-sickness reached a climax.

Freeman was speaking to him with unintelligible words. He could not understand them, and Freeman had to yell louder.

'It seems as if I shall have to heave-to, sir.'

Freeman had spoken in a moderate tone at first, a trifle embarrassed. It was a difficult position for Freeman; by the law and custom of the sea he was captain of this ship and Hornblower, although so far superior in rank, was no more than a passenger. Only an admiral could take command out of the hands of the officer appointed for that purpose, without a long and difficult process; a captain, even one who held Commodore's rank as did Hornblower, could not do so. Legally, and under the rulings of the Articles of War, Hornblower could only direct the *Porta Coeli*'s operations; Freeman was solely responsible for the manner in which Hornblower's orders were carried out. Legally it was entirely for Freeman to decide whether to heave-to or not; but no mere lieutenant commanding an eighteen-gun brig could happily disregard the wishes of a Commodore on board, especially when the Commodore happened to be Hornblower, with his reputation of impatience of delay and eagerness to set about the tasks before him – no lieutenant with a thought for his own future could do so, at any rate. Hornblower grinned to himself through his nausea at Freeman's dilemma.

'Heave-to if you wish, Mr Freeman,' he bellowed back, and as soon as he had said the words Freeman was shouting his orders through his speaking-trumpet.

'Heave-to! Get the foretops'l in! Set the maint'mast stays'l. Quarter-master, bring her to.'

'Bring her to, sir.'

The furling of the foretopsail eased her, and the staysail steadied her, and then she came to the wind. Until now she had fought against it; now she yielded to it, like a woman giving way at last to an importunate lover. She rose to an even keel, turning her starboard bow to the choppy seas, rising and falling to them with something of rhythm instead of her previous unpredictable plunges over the quartering waves. The starboard mainshrouds gave something of a lee to Hornblower where he stood against the starboard bulwark, so that even the force of the wind seemed to be a little moderated.

IV

Everything was much more comfortable, no doubt, much safer. There was no danger now of the *Porta Coeli* losing spars or canvas or working her seams considerably open. But it did not bring her any nearer to the *Flame* and her mutinous crew; on the contrary, it meant that every moment she was drifting farther away, and to leeward. To leeward! Hornblower's mind, like that of every sailor, was obsessed with the importance of keeping to windward of one's destination. He grudged bitterly every yard of leeway made, far more bitterly than any miser grudged paying out his pieces of gold. Here in the Channel in the late autumn, where westerly gales were to be expected daily, any drift to the eastward might have to be bought back at compound interest. Every hour of leeway would have to be regained when the wind moderated, by two or three hours of beating back to windward, unless the wind should come easterly, which one could not expect.

And every hour might count; no one could guess what might be the next mad action of the desperate men on board *Flame*. At any moment they might be led by panic to hand themselves over to the French; or the ringleaders might abandon the vessel and seek refuge in France, never to be regained for the hangman's rope. And at any moment the news might begin to seep through the Navy that a king's ship had successfully thrown off the bonds of discipline, that downtrodden seamen were negotiating, as one power with another, with the Lords of the Admiralty. Hornblower could guess only too well what might be the effect of that news. The sooner *Flame* was dealt with in exemplary fashion the better; but he was still without any idea as to how to deal with her. This present gale would hardly discommode her – she would be able to ride it out in the lee of the Normandy peninsula. A vessel of her tonnage could venture anywhere in the Bay of the Seine; on the one hand she could run for Le Havre, on the other to Caen river.

The batteries of the Cotentin coast would protect her; the chasse-marées and the Seine gunboats would be ready to come to her aid. Both at Cherbourg and at Le Havre there were French frigates and ships of the line, half manned and unready for sea, but always able at a pinch to push out a few miles from port and cover the escape of the *Flame*. At the approach of superior force she would certainly run; she might stand and fight an equal, such as this *Porta Coeli*, but Hornblower round himself hesitating at the prospect of meeting on equal terms a British ship manned by English sailors filled with the courage of despair. Victory would be dearly bought – what a triumphant clamour Bonaparte would raise through Europe at the news of a battle between two British ships! There would be many dead – what would be the effect on the Navy at the news of British sailors killing each other? What would be the results in Parliament? And the chances were certainly large that the two brigs would cripple each other so badly as to fall easy victims to the chasse-marées and gunboats. And worse than that, there was the chance of defeat. Equal ships, equal crews; a chance as arbitrary as the spin of a coin might decide the action. No, only as a last resort, perhaps not even then, would he fight a simple action against the *Flame*. But what the devil was he to *do*?

Hornblower shook himself into consciousness of the world about him, backing out of the blind alley of thought in which he had found himself. The wind was still shrieking round him, but it was no longer an avalanche of darkness. Before his eyes the lean rectangle of the reefed maintopsail was distinctly visible against the sky. There was a faint grey light about him; the white-flecked waves over which the brig was uneasily rising were plain to his sight. Morning was coming. Here he lay, hove-to in mid-Channel, out of sight of land. And it was still less than twenty-four hours since he had sat in silks amid the Knights of the Bath in Westminster Abbey, and much less than twenty-four hours since Barbara had – that was another line of thought from which he had hastily to shake himself free. It was raining again, the chill drops blowing into his face. He was cold through and through; as he moved he felt Barbara's scarf about his neck sopping wet with the water that had run down from his face. Freeman was beside him; the day-old beard that sprouted on Freeman's cheeks was an additional convincing touch in his gipsy appearance.

'The glass stays low, sir,' said Freeman. 'No sign of the weather moderating.'

'I can see none myself,' said Hornblower.

There was scanty material for conversation, even if Hornblower had wanted to enter into conversation with his subordinate. The grey sky and the grey sea, the shrieking wind, the chill that enveloped them, the pessimistic gloom which clouded Hornblower's thoughts, all these helped Hornblower to maintain the deliberate taciturnity which he had so long cultivated.

'Have me called at the first sign of a change, Mr Freeman,' he said.

He walked over to the hatchway; it was only with an effort that he could set one foot before the other, and he could hardly bend at all to get his hands on the hatch coaming as he descended. His joints groaned as he crept under the threatening deck-beams into his cabin. He was utterly numb with cold and fatigue and sea-sickness. He was just conscious, resentfully, that he must not fall, as he longed to do, fully clothed upon his cot – not for fear of rheumatism, but because there might be no chance for days of drying the cot's bedding if once he made it wet. And then here came Brown, materialising suddenly at his side – he must have been alert in the wardroom pantry on the watch for him.

'Let me take your coat, sir,' said Brown. 'You're cold sir. I'll untie that scarf. Those buttons, sir. Sit down now and I'll be able to get those boots off, sir.'

Brown was stripping him of his wet clothes as if he were a baby. He produced a towel as if by magic, and chafed Hornblower's ribs with it; Hornblower felt life returning through his veins at the touch of the coarse material. Brown slipped a flannel nightshirt over his head, and then knelt on the swaying deck to chafe his legs and feet. Through Hornblower's dazed mind there passed a momentary amazement at Brown's efficiency. Brown was good at everything to which he turned his hand; he could knot and splice, and he could drive a pair of horses; he could carve model ships for Richard, and be tutor and nursemaid to the boy as well; heave the lead, hand and reef, and wait at table; take a trick at the wheel or carve a goose; undress a weary man and – just as important – know when to cut off his flow of soothing remarks and lay him down in silence and pull the blankets over him, leaving him alone without any trite or irritating words about hoping he slept well. In Hornblower's last tumultuous thoughts before exhaustion plunged him into sleep he decided that Brown was a far more useful member of society than he himself was; that if in his boyhood Brown had been taught his letters and his figures, and if chance had brought him to the quarterdeck as a king's letter-boy instead of to the lower deck as a pressed man, he would probably be a captain by now. And, significantly, hardly a trace of envy tinged Hornblower's thoughts of Brown; he was mellow enough by now to admire without resentment. Brown would make some woman a fine husband, as long as there was no other woman within reach. Hornblower smiled at that, and went on smiling in his sleep, sea-sickness and the plunging of the *Porta Coeli* over the short seas notwithstanding.

He woke later feeling refreshed and hungry, listened benevolently to the tumult of the noisy ship about him, and then poked his head out of the blankets and shouted for Brown. The sentry outside the cabin door took up the cry, and Brown came in almost immediately.

'What's the time?'

'Two bells, sir.'

'In which watch?'

'Afternoon watch, sir.'

He might have known that without asking. He had been asleep for four hours, of course – nine years as a captain had not eradicated the habits acquired during a dozen years as a watchkeeping officer. The *Porta Coeli* stood up first on her tail and then on her nose as an unusually steep sea passed under her.

'The weather hasn't moderated?'

'Still blowin' a full gale, sir. West-sou'west. We're hove-to under maintopmast stays'l and maintops'l with three reefs. Out o' sight o' land, an' no sail visible neither, sir.'

This was an aspect of war to which he should have grown used; endless delay with peril just over the horizon. He felt marvellously fortified by his four hours' sleep; his depression and his yearning for the end of the war had disappeared, not eradicated but overlain by the regained fatalism of the veteran. He stretched luxuriously in his heaving cot. His stomach was decidedly squeamish still, but, rested and re-cumbent as he was, it was not in active rebellion, whatever it might promise should he become active. And there was no need to be active! There was nothing for him to do if he should rise and dress. He had no watch to keep; by law he was merely a passenger; and until this gale blew itself out, or until some unforeseen danger should develop, there was nothing about which he need trouble his head. He had still plenty of sleep to make up; probably there were anxious and sleepless nights ahead of him when he should come to tackle the duty to which he had been assigned. He might just as well make the most of his present languor.

'Very good, Brown,' he said, imparting to his voice the flat indifference after which he always strove. 'Call me when the weather moderates.'

'Breakfast, sir?' The surprise in Brown's voice was apparent and most pleasurable to Hornblower; this was the one reaction on his restless captain's part which Brown had not anticipated. 'A bite o' cold beef an' a glass o' wine, sir?'

'No,' said Hornblower. His stomach would not keep them down, he feared, in any case.

'Nothing, sir?'

Hornblower did not even deign to answer him. He had shown himself unpredictable, and that was really something gained. Brown might at any time grow too proprietorial and too pleased with himself. This incident would put him in his place again, make him not quite so sure of his acquaintance with all his captain's moods. Hornblower believed he could never be a hero to Brown; he could at least be quirky. He gazed placidly up at the deck-beams over his nose until the baffled Brown withdrew, and then he snuggled down again, controlling an expostulatory heave of his stomach. Contented with his lot, he was satisfied to lie and doze and daydream. At the back of the west wind a brig full of mutineers awaited him. Well, although he was drifting away from them at a rate of a mile or two in the hour, he yet was approaching them as fast as it was in his power to do so. And Barbara had been so sweet.

He was sleeping so lightly at the end of the watch that he was roused by the bos'un's calls turning out the watch below, a sound to which he should have been thoroughly used by now. He shouted for Brown and got out of bed, dressing hurriedly to catch the last of the daylight. Plunging out on deck, his eyes surveyed the same desolate scene as he had expected – an unbroken grey sky, a grey sea flecked with white, furrowed into the short steep rollers of the Channel. The wind still blew with gale force, the officers of the watch bending into it with their sou'westers pulled low over their eyes, and the watch crouching for shelter under the weather bulwarks forward.

Hornblower was aware, as he looked about him, of the commotion aroused by his appearance on deck. It was the first opportunity the ship's company of the *Porta Coeli* had had of seeing him in daylight. The midshipman of the watch, at a nudge from the master's mate, dived below, presumably to report his appearance to Freeman; there were other nudges observable among the hands forward. The huddle of dark tarpaulins showed a speckling of white as faces turned towards him. They were discussing him; Hornblower, who sank the *Natividad* in the Pacific, and fought the French fleet in Rosas Bay, and last year held Riga against all Boney's army.

Nowadays Hornblower could contemplate with a certain equanimity the possibility of being discussed by other people. There were undeniable achievements on his record, solid victories for which he had borne the responsibility and therefore deservedly wore the laurels. His weaknesses, his sea-sickness and his moodiness, could be smiled at now instead of being laughed at. The gilded laurels were only tarnished to his own knowledge, and not to that of others. They did not know of his doubts and his hesitations, not even of his actual mistakes – they did not know, as he did, that if he had only called off the bomb-vessels at Riga five minutes earlier – as he should have done – young Mound would be still alive and a distinguished naval officer. Hornblower's handling of his squadron in the Baltic had been described in Parliament as 'the most perfect example in recent years of the employment of a naval force against an army'; Hornblower knew of the imperfections, but apparently other people could be blind to them. He could face his brethren in the profession, just as he could face his social equals. Now he had a wife of beauty and lineage, a wife with taste and tact, a wife to be proud of and not a wife he could only gloweringly dare the world to criticise – poor Maria in her forgotten grave in Southsea.

Freeman came climbing out of the hatchway, still fastening his oil-skins; the two of them touched their hats to each other.

'The glass has begun to rise, sir,' shouted Freeman, his hands making a trumpet before his mouth. 'This'll blow itself out soon.'

Hornblower nodded, even while at that moment a bigger gust flogged his oilskins against his legs – the gustiness itself was a sign that the gale was nearing its end. The light was fast fading out of the grey sky; with sunset perhaps the wind would begin to moderate.

'Will you come round the ship with me?' yelled Hornblower, and this time it was Freeman's turn to nod. They walked forward, making their way with difficulty over the plunging, dripping decks, with Hornblower looking keenly about him. Two long guns forward – six-pounders; the rest of the armament twelve-pounder carronades. The breechings and preventer tackles were in good shape. Aloft, the rigging, both standing and running, was properly set up and cared for; but the best proof that the vessel was in good order lay in the fact that nothing had carried away during the weather of the last twenty-four hours. Freeman was a good captain; Hornblower knew that already. But it was not the guns, not even the vessel's weatherly qualities, which were of first importance in the present expedition. It was the human weapons that most mattered; Hornblower darted quick glances from side to side under his brows as he inspected the material of the brig – taking pains to observe the appearance and demeanour of the men. They seemed patient, not sullen, thank God. They were alert, seemingly ready for any duty. Hornblower dived down the fore hatchway into the unspeak-able din and stink of the battened-down 'tween-decks. There were sailors asleep in the fantastic fashion of the British tarpaulin – snoring heavily as they lay on the bare deck, despite the din about them. There were men huddled in gaming groups. He saw sleeves tugged and thumbs pointed as men caught sight of him – their first sight of the almost legendary Hornblower. An exchange of a nod and a wink. Hornblower, shrewdly estimating the feeling about him, guessed with pleasure that there was expectancy rather than resignation or reluctance.

It was an odd fact, but one whose existence could not be doubted, that men were pleased at the prospect of serving under him, Hornblower; the Hornblower, that is (qualified Hornblower), whom they thought existed, not the real actual Hornblower who wore the coat and trousers he was wearing. They hoped for victory, excitement, distinction, success; the poor fools. They did not stop to think that men died where Horn-blower took command. The clear-headedness resulting from sea-sickness and an empty stomach (Hornblower could not remember when last he had eaten) allowed free play to a whole conflict of emotions within him; pleasure at being so gladly followed, pity for the thoughtless victims; a thrill of excitement at the thought of future action, and a wave of doubt regarding his ability to pluck success this time from the jaws of chance; pleasure, reluctantly admitted, at finding himself at sea and in command again, and regret, bitter and soul-searching, for the life he had just left, for Barbara's love and little Richard's trusting affection. Hornblower, noting his inward turmoil, cursed himself for a sentimental fool at the very moment when his sharp eye picked out a seaman who was knuckling his forehead and bobbing and grinning with embarrassed pleasure.

'I know you,' said Hornblower, searching feverishly through his memory. 'Let me see now. It must have been in the old *Indefatigable*.'

'That's right, sir. We was shipmates then, sir. And you worn't more'n a nipper, then, sir, beggin' your pardon, sir. Midshipman of the foretop, you was, sir.'

The seaman wiped his hand on the leg of his trousers before gingerly accepting the hand which Hornblower held out to him.

'Harding's your name,' said Hornblower, his memory coming to his rescue, with a tremendous effort. 'You taught me long splicing while we were off Ushant.'

'That's right, sir. 'Deed you're right, sir. That were '92, or wore it '93?'

''Ninety-three. I'm glad to know you're on board, Harding.'

'Thank you kindly, sir, I'm sure. Thank you kindly.'

Why should the whole vessel buzz with pleasure because he had recognised an old shipmate of twenty years back? Why should it make a ha'porth of difference? But it did; Hornblower knew it and felt it. It was hard to say whether pity or affection for his weak fellow-men held first place in the new complex of emotions which the incident aroused. Bonaparte might be doing the same thing at that same moment, recognising in some German bivouac some old comrade in arms in the ranks of the Guard.

They had reached the after part of the brig now, and Hornblower turned to Freeman.

'I am going to dine, now, Mr Freeman,' he said. 'Perhaps after that we may be able to make some sail on the brig. I shall come on deck to see, in any case.'

'Aye aye, sir.'

Dinner; eaten seated on the small locker against the bulkhead. Cold salt beef – quite a good cut, tasty to a palate long accustomed to it and yet deprived of it for the last eleven months. 'Rexam's Superfine Ships' Biscuits' from a lead-lined box discovered and provided by Barbara –

the best ships' bread which Hornblower had ever tasted, costing maybe twenty times as much as the weevily stuff he had eaten often enough before. A bite of red cheese, tangy and seasoned, admirably suited to accompany the second glass of claret. It was quite absurd that he should feel any satisfaction at having to lead this sort of life again, and yet he did. Undeniably, he did.

He wiped his mouth on his napkin, climbed into his oilskins, and went up on deck.

'The wind's dropped a little, Mr Freeman, I fancy.'

'I fancy it has, sir.'

In the darkness the *Porta Coeli* was riding to the wind almost easily, with a graceful rise and swoop. The seas overside could not be nearly as steep as they had been, and this was rain, not spray, in his face, and the feel of the rain told him that the worst of the storm was over.

'With the jib and the boom-mains'l both reefed, we can put her on the wind, sir,' said Freeman, tentatively.

'Very well, Mr Freeman. Carry on.'

There was a special skill about sailing a brig, especially, of course, on a wind. Under jib and staysails and the boom-mainsail she could be handled like a fore-and-aft-rigged vessel; Hornblower knew it all theoretically, but he also knew that his practice would be decidedly rusty, especially in the dark and with a gale blowing. He was well content to remain in the background and let Freeman do what he would. Freeman bellowed his orders; with a mighty creaking of blocks the reefed boom-mainsail rose up the mast while men on the dizzy yard got in the maintopsail. The brig was hove-to on the starboard tack, and as the effect of the jib made itself felt she began to pay off a little.

'Mains'l sheets!' bellowed Freeman, and to the man at the wheel, 'Steady as you go!'

The rudder met and counteracted the tendency of the *Porta Coeli* to fall off, and the boom-mainsail caught the wind and forced her forward. In a moment the *Porta Coeli* changed from something quiescent and acquiescent into something fierce and desperate. She ceased to yield to wind and sea, ceased to let them hurtle past her; now she met them, she fought against them, battled with them. She was like some tigress previously content to evade the hunters by slinking from cover to cover, but now hurling herself on her tormentors mad with fighting fury. The wind laid her over, the spray burst in sheets across her bows. Her gentle rise and swoop were transformed into an illogical jerky motion as she met the steep waves with immovable resolution; she lurched and she shuddered as she battered her way through the waves. The forces of the world, the old primitive powers that had ruled earth and water since the creation, were being set at defiance by man, weak, mortal man, who by virtue of the brain inside his fragile skull was able not merely to face the forces of the world but to bend them to his will, compel them to serve him. Nature sent this brisk westerly gale up the Channel; subtly and insidiously the *Porta Coeli* was making use of it to claw her way westward – a slow, painful, difficult way, but westward all the same. Hornblower, standing by the wheel, felt a surge of exultation as the *Porta Coeli* thrashed forward. He was like Prometheus stealing fire from the gods; he was the successful rebel against the blind laws of nature; he could take pride in being a mere mortal man.

V

Freeman bent over the tallow that armed the bottom of the lead; a seaman held a lantern at his shoulder so as to let the light fall upon it. The master's mate and midshipman of the watch completed the group, a vignette of blackness and light in the massive darkness all around. Freeman was not hasty in reaching his decision; he peered at the sample brought up from the bottom of the sea first from one angle and then from another. He sniffed at it; he applied a forefinger to it and then carried the finger to his tongue.

'Sand and black shell,' he mused to himself.

Hornblower held back from the group; this was something Freeman could do better than he, although it would be nearly blasphemy to say so in public, seeing that he was a captain and Freeman a mere lieutenant.

'Maybe we're off Antifer,' said Freeman at length. He looked out of the light into the darkness towards where Hornblower was standing.

'Lay her on the other tack, if you please, Mr Freeman. And keep the lead going.'

Creeping about in the night off the treacherous Normandy coast was a nervous business, even though in the past twenty-four hours the wind had moderated to nothing more than a strong breeze. But Freeman knew what he was about; a dozen years spent in handling vessels in the soundings round the fringes of Europe had given him knowledge and insight obtainable in no other way. Hornblower had to trust Freeman's judgment; he himself with compass and lead and chart might do a good workmanlike job, but to rate himself above Freeman as a Channel pilot would be ridiculous. 'Maybe,' Freeman had said; but Hornblower could value that 'maybe' at its true worth. Freeman was confident about it. The *Porta Coeli* was off Cape Antifer, then, a trifle farther to leeward than he wished to be when dawn should come. He still had no plan in his head about how to deal with the *Flame* when he met her; there was no way round, as far as he could see, the simple geometrical difficulty that the mutineers, with Le Havre open to them on one side and Caen on the other, could not be cut off from taking refuge with the French if they wished to; for that matter, there were a dozen other inlets on the coast, all heavily protected by batteries, where the *Flame* could find a refuge. And any forcing of the matter might result easily enough in Chadwick being hoisted up to his yardarm, to dangle there as a dead man – the most horrible and dangerous incident in the history of the Navy since the murder of Pigott. But contact had to be made with the mutineers – that was clearly the first thing to do – and there was at least no harm in trying to make that contact at a point as advantageous as possible. Some miracle might happen; he must try and put himself across the course of wandering miracles. What was that Barbara had said to him once? 'The lucky man is he who knows how much to leave to chance.' Barbara had too good an opinion of him, even after all this time, but there was truth in what she said.

The *Porta Coeli* went smartly about, and reached to the north-westward, closehauled to the south-westerly wind.

'The tide starts to make about now, Sir Horatio,' said Freeman, beside him.

'Thank you.'

That was an additional bit of data in the problem of the morrow which was not yet fully revealed to him. War was as unlike spherical trigonometry as anything could be, thought Hornblower, grinning at the inconsequence of his thoughts. Often one approached a problem in war without knowing what it was one wanted to achieve, to prove, or construct, and without even knowing fully what means were available for doing it. War was generally a matter of slipshod, makeshift, hit-or-miss extemporisation. Even if it were not murderous and wasteful it would still be no trade for a man who enjoyed logic. Yet maybe he was taking too flattering a view of himself; maybe some other officer – Cochrane, say, or Lidyard – would, if in his position, already have a plan worked out for dealing with the mutineers, a plan that could not fail to bring satisfactory results.

Four bells rang out sharply; they had been over half an hour on this tack.

'Kindly go about on the other tack, Mr Freeman. I don't want to get too far from land.'

'Aye aye, sir.'

If it was not for the war, no captain in his senses would dream for a moment of plunging about in the darkness on this shoal coast, especially when he was extremely doubtful of his exact position – their present estimate was the sum of a series of guesses, guesses about the leeway made while hove-to, guesses at the effects of the tides, guesses at the correspondence between soundings taken overside and soundings marked on the chart.

'What do you think the mutineers will do, sir, when they sight us?' asked Freeman.

The fact that Hornblower had unbent enough to give an explanation of why he wanted to go about must have encouraged Freeman to this familiarity; Hornblower was irritated, but most of all because he had no thoughts on the matter.

'There's no profit in asking questions which time will surely answer, Mr Freeman,' he said, tartly.

'Yet speculation is a fascinating thing, Sir Horatio,' replied Freeman, so unabashed that Hornblower stared at him in the darkness. Bush, if Hornblower had spoken to him in that fashion, would have retired wounded into his shell.

'You may indulge yourself in it if you so desire, Mr Freeman. I have no intention of doing so.'

'Thank you, Sir Horatio.'

Now was there, or was there not, a hint of mockery behind the hint of subservience in that reply? Was it possible that Freeman could actually be smiling inwardly at his superior officer? If so, he was running a fearful risk; a suggestion of dissatisfaction in Hornblower's future report to the Admiralty would put Freeman on the beach for life. But Hornblower knew, the moment the thought came into his head, that he would do no such thing. He could never blast an able man's career just because that man had not treated him with slavish respect.

'Water's shoaling fast, sir,' said Freeman, suddenly – both he and Hornblower had subconsciously been listening to the cry of the leadsman in the chains. 'I should like to go about again.'

'Certainly, Mr Freeman,' said Hornblower, formally.

They were creeping round Cape de la Hève, the northerly point of the Seine estuary, just within which lies Le Havre. There was a chance, a tiny one, that they might find themselves at dawn both to leeward of the *Flame* and between her and France so that she would have no means of escape at all. And the night was wearing on; it would not be long now before daylight.

'You have a good man at the masthead, Mr Freeman?'

'Yes, Sir Horatio.'

He would have to tell the hands about the mission on which they had been sent, even though that meant violating the secrecy surrounding the mutiny. Normally there would be little enough need to confide in the hands; British seamen, fatalistic after twenty years of war, would fire into Frenchmen or Americans or Dutchmen without much thought about the rights or wrongs; but to ask them to fight against a sister-ship, to fire into a British vessel, which might, for all he knew, still be wearing her commissioning pendant and her White Ensign, might cause hesitation if he called upon them to do so without some preliminary warning. A careful officer would in ordinary circumstances never breathe the word 'mutiny' to his men; no lion-tamer would ever remind the lion that the lion was stronger than he. It was almost daylight.

'Would you be so good as to turn up the hands, Mr Freeman? I wish to address them.'

'Aye aye, sir.'

The pipes wailed through the brig, and the watch below came streaming up through the hatchway, pouring sleepily aft; the poor devils were losing an hour of sleep because of the inconsiderate way in which dawn did not correspond with the end of the watch. Hornblower looked round for some point of vantage from which he could address them; in a flush-decked vessel like the *Porta Coeli* he had not the advantage of speaking down into a waist from a quarterdeck. He swung himself up onto the weather bulwark, balancing himself with a hand on the main-backstay.

'Men,' he said, 'are you wondering what has sent you out here?'

Maybe they were, but the rather sleepy, apathetic, breakfastless lines before him showed little sign of it.

'Are you wondering what has sent me out to sea with you?'

By God, they *were* wondering that. There must have been speculation on the lower deck as to why a full commodore – and not only a commodore, but Hornblower of the legendary past – should have been sent to sea in a mere eighteen-gun brig. It was flattering to see a movement of interest in the lines, a lifting of heads, even while Hornblower cursed at fate for having to make use of rhetorical tricks, and more for having to exploit his own personal renown.

'There is villainy afloat,' said Hornblower. 'British seamen have disgraced themselves. They have mutinied in the very presence of the enemy.'

He had the men's interest now, without a doubt. He had said the word 'mutiny' to these slaves of the lash and the whistle. Mutiny, the remedy for all their ills, which would give them freedom from the hardship of their lives, the cruelty and the danger, the foul food and the severance from all the amenities of life. One crew had mutinied. Why should not they do so too? He would have to tell them about the *Flame*, remind them that close at hand lay the shores of France, where Bonaparte would gladly heap wealth and luxury upon any British seaman who brought a British ship of war over to him. Hornblower let a note of contempt creep into his voice.

'The crew of the *Flame*, our own sister-ship, has done this thing. Now they are sheltering here in this very bay of the Seine. Every man's hand is against them. The French have no use for mutineers, and it is our mission to dig these rats from their holes. They have betrayed England, forgotten their duty to King and Country. I expect most of them are honest but stupid, led astray by a few designing villains. It is those villains who must pay the price of their villainy, and we must see they have no chance of escape. If they are mad enough to offer fight, then we must fight them. If they surrender without bloodshed, that fact will be remembered in their favour when they are brought to trial. I want no bloodshed if I can help it – you know as well as I do that a cannon-shot will kill a man without stopping to ask whether he is a villain or just a fool. But if they want bloodshed, then we shall let them have it.'

Hornblower ended his speech, and looked over to Freeman to dismiss the men. It was a cheerless business making a speech to hungry men in a grey dawn, but Hornblower, darting glances at the men as they went about their business, saw that there was nothing to fear from the ship's company. They were buzzing with talk, of course, but news of mutiny would set any crew a-buzz, just as a village would be set a-buzz by news of a local murder. But it was only gossipy talk, he could see; the men were not making any deductions from the news. He had presented the case to them in such a way as to make it obvious to them that he expected them to obey his orders for dealing with the mutineers, and he had let no hint creep into his speech of his fear that they should be tempted to follow their example. That had not occurred to them yet – but it might, if they were allowed to ruminate over it. He must see that they were kept busy; the ordinary ship's routine was attending to that at the moment, for they were at work on the opening business of every naval day, washing down the decks before being piped to breakfast.

'Land!' yelled a voice from the masthead. 'Land on the port bow.'

It was rather thick weather, typical Channel weather for the end of the year, but in the growing light Hornblower could see the dark line against the grey. Freeman was scrutinising the coast through his glass.

'That's the south shore of the Bay,' said Freeman. 'There's the Cane river.'

Hornblower was only just beginning to realise that Freeman was anglicising the pronunciation of 'Caen' when Freeman trained his telescope round and gave a string of more surprising examples still of what an Englishman can do to French names.

'Yes, there's Cape dee lay Heave, and Harbour-Grace,' he said.

The growing light revealed the *Porta Coeli*'s position, over towards the southern shore of the estuary of the Seine.

'That was an excellent piece of navigation last night, Mr Freeman.'

'Thank you, Sir Horatio.'

Hornblower would have added more words of warmer praise, if it had not been for Freeman's rather chilling manner; he supposed Freeman was entitled to be short-tempered before breakfast if he wished. And any capable lieutenant was entitled to be jealous of a captain; in the opinion of every ambitious lieutenant a captain was just a lieutenant who had been lucky and who would continue to be lucky, drawing three times a lieutenant's pay and prize-money, reaping the harvest of the lieutenant's labours, and secure in the knowledge that time would make an admiral of him in the end while the lieutenant's promotion still depended on the whims of his superiors. Hornblower could remember feeling just the same when he was a lieutenant; for Freeman to show it was natural even though foolish.

The leadsman's cry in the chains indicated that the water was shoaling again; they had left the middle ground far behind them and had now crossed the southerly channel of the estuary. There was still plenty of water for the *Porta Coeli*; she had been expressly designed for this very purpose of penetrating into inlets and estuaries, carrying the war as close to Bonaparte's shores as might be. Bonaparte's dominion stopped short at the line which the shot from his shore batteries could reach, and beyond that line England ruled supreme and unchallenged.

'Sail on the lee bow!' yelled the lookout.

Freeman swung himself up to the lee main-shrouds with the agility of an ape; braced against the ratlines, he trained his glass forward.

'A brig, sir,' he hailed down to Hornblower, and a few seconds later, 'That's *Flame* all right, sir.'

'Put the helm up and we'll bear down on her, Mr Freeman, if you please.'

Flame was exactly where one would expect to find her, close up under the lee of the land, sheltered from any gale from northwest round to east; and free to consult her own safety whether attacked by British or French. Soon Hornblower's own glass picked her out from the grey murk. A trim, beautiful little vessel, lying hove-to on the edge of the shoals. She showed no signs, at that distance at least, of any disorder on board. Hornblower wondered how many telescopes there were being trained upon the *Porta Coeli*, what anxious debate was being held on board by men recognising the new arrival as the first move on the part of their Lordships of the Admiralty in reply to their suicidal ultimatum. Those men had ropes round their necks.

'She's waiting for us to come down to her,' said Freeman.

'I wonder for how long,' answered Hornblower.

'What are you men standing chattering there for?' suddenly blared out Freeman, addressing a group of excited seamen lining the bulwark forward. 'Master-at-arms! Master-at-arms! Take those men's names and bring them to me at the end of the watch! You, bos'un's mate, there!

Collier! Keep those men of yours at work! This is a King's ship, not a blasted school for young ladies!'

A thin beam of watery sunshine broke through the greyness and lit up the *Flame* as she lay in the circle of Hornblower's glass. He suddenly saw her yards swing round; she put herself before the wind and began to move in the direction of Honfleur. Her foretopsail was conspicuously patched – a light cross against the darker material, as if she were some crusading ship.

'They won't stand and wait for us,' said Freeman.

'Sail ho!' yelled the lookout again. 'Sail on the lee quarter!'

Telescopes swung round as if all were actuated by a single machine. A big ship with all plain sail set to the royals had appeared out of the mist beyond the middle ground, on a course rapidly diverging from that of the *Porta Coeli*. Hornblower recognised her instantly for what she was, and did not need Freeman's identification.

'French West Indiaman,' said Freeman. 'With a clear run to Harbour-Grace.'

One of the rare ships to run the continental blockade, bearing an invaluable cargo of grain and sugar to ease Bonaparte's distress; she had taken advantage of the recent gale, which had blown the blockading squadrons from their stations, to dash up the Channel. A cargo delivered into the Seine, where centred the Imperial power, and whence diverged the whole road and canal systems, was worth two brought into some isolated inlet on the Biscay coast. The small British vessels of war, like the *Porta Coeli* and the *Flame*, had been constructed and stationed to prevent this very thing.

'There'll be no catching her before she reaches Harbour-Grace,' muttered Freeman.

'Let her go, Mr Freeman,' said Hornblower, loudly. 'Our duty's with *Flame* at present. There goes ten pounds a man prize-money.'

There were enough hands within earshot to hear that speech; they would repeat it to the rest of the crew. No one who thought of the lost prize-money would feel any better disposed towards the mutineers.

Hornblower turned his attention back to the *Flame*; she was standing steadily and without hesitation on a course which would take her into Honfleur. It would not be long before she was in French power, and it would be foolish to press matters to such an extreme, even though it was a bitter pill to swallow, to admit a check.

'Oh, heave-to, Mr Freeman, please. Let's see what she does then.'

The *Porta Coeli* came up into the wind in response to sail and helm, Hornblower training round his glass to keep *Flame* under observation. The moment the *Porta Coeli*'s manoeuvre became apparent, the *Flame* imitated it, coming up into the wind and lying motionless, the white cross conspicuous on her foretopsail.

'Try bearing down on them again, Mr Freeman.'

Flame turned away instantly towards France.

'A wink's as good as a nod, Mr Freeman. Heave-to again.'

Clearly the mutineers had no intention of allowing the *Porta Coeli* to come any nearer than she was at present, well beyond cannon-shot. She would hand herself over to the French sooner than permit any closer approach.

'Mr Freeman, will you be so good as to have a boat hoisted out for me? I'll go and parley with the villains.'

That would be a sign of weakness, but the mutineers could be in no doubt about the weakness of his position and the corresponding strength of their own. It would be telling them nothing that they did not know already, that they held Hornblower and the Lords of the Admiralty and the British Empire itself in a cleft stick. Freeman showed no signs of his doubts regarding the advisability of a valuable captain putting himself in the power of mutineers. Hornblower went below to pocket his orders; it might even be necessary to show the mutineers the full powers with which he had been entrusted – but it would be only in the last resort that he would do so; that would be letting the mutineers too much into their Lordships' confidence. The boat was overside with Brown at the tiller when Hornblower came on deck again; Hornblower went down the side and settled himself into the sternsheets.

'Give way!' ordered Brown; the oars bit the water and the boat began to crawl towards the *Flame*, dancing over the little waves of the estuary,

Hornblower watched the brig as they approached; she lay hove-to. but Hornblower could see that her guns were run out and her boarding-nettings rigged, and she had clearly no intention of being taken by surprise. The hands were at their guns, there were lookouts aloft, a warrant officer aft with a telescope under his arm – not a sign in the world of mutiny on board.

'Boat ahoy!' came the hail across the water.

Brown held up his four fingers, the universal signal that there was a captain in the boat – four fingers for the four side-boys demanded by ceremonial.

'Who are ye?' hailed the voice.

Brown looked round at Hornblower, received a nod from him, and hailed back.

'Commodore Sir Horatio Hornblower, K.B.'

'We'll allow Commodore Hornblower on board, but no one else. Come alongside, and we've cold shot here to drop into you if you play any tricks.'

Hornblower reached for the main-chains and swung himself up into them; a seaman raised the boarding-nettings so that he could struggle under them to the deck.

'Kindly tell your boats to sheer off, Commodore. We're taking no risks,' said a voice.

It was a white-haired old man who addressed him, the telescope under his arm marking him out as officer of the watch. White hair fluttered about his ears; sharp blue eyes in a wrinkled face looked at Hornblower from under white brows. The only thing in the least bizarre about his appearance was a pistol stuck in his belt. Hornblower turned and gave the required order.

'And now may I ask your business here, Commodore?' asked the old man.

'I wish to speak to the leader of the mutineers.'

'I am captain of this ship. You can address yourself to me, Nathaniel Sweet, sir.'

'I have addressed myself to you as far as I desire, unless you are also the leader of the mutineers.'

'Then if you have done so, you can call back your boat and leave us, sir.'

An impasse already. Hornblower kept his eyes on the blue ones of the old man. There were several other men within earshot, but he could sense no wavering or doubt among them; they were prepared to support their captain. Yet it might be worth while speaking to them.

'Men!' said Hornblower, raising his voice.

'Belay that!' rapped out the old man. He whipped the pistol out of his belt and pointed it at Hornblower's stomach. 'One more word out of turn and you'll get an ounce of lead through you.'

Hornblower looked steadily back at him and his weapon; he was curiously unafraid, feeling as if he were watching move and counter-move in some chess game, without remembering that he himself was one of the pawns in it with his life at stake.

'Kill me,' he said with a grim smile, 'and England won't rest until you're swinging on a gallows.'

'England has sent you here to swing me on a gallows as it is,' said Sweet, bleakly.

'No,' said Hornblower. 'I am here to recall you to your duty to King and Country.'

'Letting bygones be bygones?'

'You will have to stand a fair trial, you and your confederates.'

'That means the gallows, as I said,' replied Sweet. 'The gallows for me, and I should be fortunate compared with some of these others.'

'A fair and honest trial,' said Hornblower, 'with every mitigating circumstance taken into consideration.'

'The only trial I would attend,' replied the old man, 'would be to bear witness against Chadwick. Full pardon for us – a fair trial for Chadwick. Those are our terms, sir.'

'You are foolish,' said Hornblower. 'You are throwing away your last chance. Surrender now, with Mr Chadwick unbound and the ship in good order, and those circumstances will weigh heavily in your favour at your trial. Refuse, and what have you to look for? Death. That is all. Death. What can save you from our country's vengeance? Nothing.'

'Begging your pardon, Captain, but Boney can,' interposed the old man, dryly.

'You trust Bonaparte's word?' said Hornblower, rallying desperately before this unexpected counter-attack. 'He'd like to have this ship, no doubt. But you and your gang? Bonaparte won't encourage mutiny – his power rests too much on his own army. He'll hand you back for us to make an example of you.'

It was a wild shot in the dark, and it missed its bull's-eye by an unmeasurable distance. Sweet stuck his pistol back into his belt and produced three letters from his pocket, waving them tauntingly in front of Hornblower.

'Here's a letter from the Military Governor of Harbour-Grace,' he said. 'That only promises us welcome. And here's a letter from the Prefect of the Department of the Inferior Seine. That promises us provisions and water should we need them. And here's a letter from Paris, sent down to us by post. It promises us immunity from arrest, civil rights in France, and a pension for every man from the age of sixty. That is signed "Marie Louise, Empress, Queen, and Regent". Boney won't go back on his wife's word, sir.'

'You've been in communication with the shore?' gasped Hornblower. It was quite impossible for him to make any pretence at composure.

'We have,' said the old man. 'And if *you* had the chance before you, Captain, of being flogged round the fleet, you would have done the same.'

It was hopeless to continue the present discussion. At least at the moment, the mutineers were unassailable. The only terms to which they would listen would be their own. There was no sign of doubt or dissension on board. But maybe if they were allowed more time to think about it, maybe if they had a few hours in which to consider the fact that Hornblower himself was on their trail, doubt might creep in. A party might form determined to save their necks by recapturing the ship; they might get at the liquor – Hornblower was completely puzzled by the fact that a mutinous British crew was not all roaring drunk – *something* might happen. But he must make a fighting retreat, not ignominiously crawl overside with his tail between his legs.

'So you are traitors as well as mutineers?' he blared. 'I might have expected it. I might have guessed what kind of curs you are. I won't foul my lungs by breathing the same air as you.'

He turned to the side and hailed for his boat.

'We're the kind of curs,' said the old man, 'who will let you go when we could clap you down below in the orlop with Chadwick. We could give you a taste of the cat, Commodore Sir Horatio Hornblower. How would you like *that*, sir? Remember, tomorrow, that the flesh is still on your ribs because *we* spared you. Good morning to you, Captain.'

There was sting and venom in those last words; they called up pictures in Hornblower's imagination that made his flesh creep. He did not feel in the least dignified as he wriggled under the boarding-netting.

The *Flame* still rode peacefully to the wind as the boat danced back over the waves. Hornblower gazed from the *Flame* to the *Porta Coeli*, the two sister-ships, identical in appearance save for the white cross-shaped patch on the *Flame*'s foretopsail. It was ironical that not even a trained eye could see any difference in appearance between the brig that was loyal to the King and the brig that was in open rebellion against him. The thought increased his bitterness; he had failed, utterly and completely, in his first attempt to win over the mutineers. He did not think there was the least possibility of their abating their terms; he would have to choose between agreeing to them, between promising the mutineers a free pardon and driving them into the hands of Bonaparte. In either case he would have failed in his mission; the merest least experienced midshipman in the Navy could have done as much. There was still some time to spare, for there was still little chance of news of the mutiny leaking out, but unless time brought dissension among the mutineers – and he saw no chance of that – it would be merely wasted time as far as he could see.

The boat was now half-way between the two brigs; with those two vessels under his command he could wage a lively war against the Normandy coast; he felt in his bones that he could set the whole Seine estuary in an uproar. His bitterness surged up stronger still, and then abruptly checked itself. An idea had come to him, and with the idea all the well-known old symptoms, the dryness in his throat, the tingling in his legs, the accelerated heartbeat. He swept his glance back and forth between the two brigs, excitement welling up inside him; calculations of wind and tide and daylight already formulating themselves, unsummoned, in his mind.

'Pull harder you men,' he said to the boat's crew, and they obeyed him, but the gig could not possibly travel fast enough to satisfy him in his new mood.

Brown was looking at him sidelong, wondering what plan was evoking itself in his captain's brain; Brown himself – as well aware of the circumstances as Hornblower was – could see no possible way out of the situation. All he knew was that his captain looked back over his shoulder time and time again at the mutinous brig.

'Oars!' growled Brown to the boat's crew, as the officer of the watch gave the signal to the boat to come alongside; the bowman hooked on to the chains, and Hornblower went up the brig's side with a clumsy impetuosity that he could not restrain. Freeman was waiting for him on the quarterdeck, and Hornblower's hand was still at his hat when he gave his first order.

'Will you pass the word for the sailmaker, Mr Freeman? And I shall want his mates, and every hand who can use a needle and palm.'

'Aye aye, sir.'

Orders were orders, even when they dealt with such extraneous matters as making sails while negotiating with a mutinous crew. Hornblower stared over at the *Flame*, still lying hove-to out of gunshot. The mutineers held a strong, an unassailable position, one which no frontal attack could break, and whose flanks were impregnable. It would be a very roundabout route that could turn such a position; maybe he had thought of one. There were some odd circumstances in his favour, fortunate coincidences. It was his business to seize upon those, exploit them to the utmost. He would have to take reckless chances, but he would do everything in his power to reduce the chances against him. The lucky man is he who knows how much to leave to chance.

A stoop-shouldered seaman was awaiting his attention, Freeman at his side.

'Swenson, sailmaker's mate, sir.'

'Thank you, Mr Freeman. You see that patched foretops'l? Swenson, look at it well through this glass.'

The Swedish sailmaker took the telescope in his gnarled hands and levelled it to his eye.

'Mr Freeman, I want *Porta Coeli* to have a foretops'l just like that, so that no eye can see any difference between the two. Can that be done?'

Freeman looked at Swenson.

'Aye aye, sir, I can do that,' said Swenson, glancing from Freeman to Hornblower and back again. 'There's a bolt o' white duck canvas, an' with the old foretops'l – I can do it, sir.'

'I want it finished and ready to bend by four bells in the afternoon watch. Start work on it now.'

A little group had formed behind Swenson, those members of the crew whom inquiry had ascertained to have sailmaking experience. There were broad grins on some of their faces; Hornblower seemed to be conscious of a little wave of excitement and anticipation spreading through the crew like a ripple over a pond set up by the stone dropped into it in the form of Hornblower's unusual request. No one could see clearly as yet what was in Hornblower's mind, but they knew that he intended some devilment. The knowledge was a better tonic to discipline and the happiness of the ship than any ordinary ship's routine.

'Now see here, Mr Freeman,' said Hornblower, moving towards the rail. 'What I propose is this – *Flame* and *Porta Coeli* are as like as two peas and they'll be liker yet as soon as we have that foretops'l set. The mutineers have been in communication with the shore; they told me so, and, what's more, Mr Freeman, the place they've had dealings with is Le Havre – Harbour-Grace, Mr Freeman. Boney and the governor have promised them money and immunity to bring the *Flame* in. We'll go in instead. There's that West Indiaman we saw come in this morning.'

'We'll bring her out, sir!'

'Maybe we will. God knows what we'll find inside, but we'll go in ready for anything. Pick twenty men and an officer, men you can rely on. Give each one his orders about what he is to do if we have a chance to take a prize – heads'ls, tops'ls, wheel, cutting the cable. You know about all that as well as I do. It'll be just at dusk that we stand in, if the wind doesn't change, and I don't think it will. It'll be strange if in the dark we don't contrive something to annoy the Frogs.'

'By God, sir, an' they'll think it's the mutineers! They'll think the mutiny was just a sham! They'll—'

'I hope they will, Mr Freeman.'

VI

It was late afternoon when the *Porta Coeli*, apparently unable to reach any decision, stood away from the *Flame* and crossed the broad estuary with the wind blowing briskly on her port beam. The thick weather still persisted; she was far enough both from *Flame* and from Le Havre for the details to be quite obscure when she took in her foretopsail and substituted for it the patched one which an enthusiastic gang of toilers had made ready on deck abaft the foremast. Hurried work with paintbrush and paint erased one name and substituted the other; Hornblower and Freeman wore their plain pea-jackets over their uniforms, concealing their rank. Freeman kept his glass trained on the harbour as they stood in.

'That's the Indiaman, sir. At anchor. And there's a lighter beside her. O' course, they wouldn't unload her at the quay. Not here, sir. They'd put her cargo into lighters an' barges, and send 'em up the river, to Rouen and Paris. O' course they would. I ought to ha' thought o' that before.' Hornblower had already thought of it. His glass was sweeping the defences of the town; the forts of Ste Adresse and Tourneville on the steep cliff above the town; the twin lighthouses on Cape de la Hève – which for a dozen years had not shown a light – the batteries on the low ground beside the old jetty. These last would be the great danger to the enterprise; he hoped that the big forts above would not know of what was going on down below in time to open fire.

'There's a lot of shipping farther in, sir,' went on Freeman. 'Might even be ships of the line. They haven't their yards crossed. I've never been in as close as this before.'

Hornblower turned to look at the western sky. Night was fast falling, and the thick weather on the horizon showed no signs of clearing. He wanted light enough to find his way, and darkness enough to cover him on his way out.

'Here's the pilot lugger standing out, sir,' said Freeman. 'They'll think we're *Flame* all right.'

'Very good, Mr Freeman. Set the men to cheering at the ship's side. Secure the pilot when he comes on board. I'll con her in.'

'Aye aye, sir.'

It was just the sort of order to suit the temperament of British seamen. They entered wholeheartedly into the spirit of the thing, yelling like lunatics along the bulwarks, waving their hats, dancing exuberantly, just as one would expect of a horde of mutineers. The *Porta Coeli* backed her maintopsail, the lugger surged alongside, and the pilot swung himself into the mainchains.

'Lee braces!' roared Hornblower, the maintopsail caught the wind again, the wheel went over, and the *Porta Coeli* stood into the harbour, while Freeman put his shoulder between the pilot's shoulder blades and shot him neatly down the hatchway where two men were waiting to seize and pinion him.

'Pilot secured, sir,' he reported.

He, too, was obviously carried away by the excitement of the moment, infected by the din the hands were making; his pose of amused irony had completely disappeared.

'Starboard a little,' said Hornblower to the helmsman. 'Meet her! Steady as you go!'

It would be the last word in ignominy if all their high hopes were to come to an end on the sandbanks guarding the entrance. Hornblower wondered if he would ever feel cool again.

'A cutter standing out to us, sir,' reported Freeman.

That might be a committee of welcome, or orders telling them where to berth – both at once, probably.

'Set the hands to cheering again,' ordered Hornblower. 'Have the boarding-party secured as they come on board.'

'Aye aye, sir.'

They were nearing the big Indiaman; she lay, her sails loose, swinging to a single anchor. There was a lighter beside her, but obviously little enough had been done so far towards unloading her. In the fading light Hornblower could just make out a dozen of her seamen standing at the ship's side gazing curiously at them. Hornblower backed the main-topsail again, and the cutter came alongside, and half a dozen officials climbed on to the *Porta Coeli*'s deck. Their uniforms proclaimed their connection with the navy, the army, and the customs service, and they advanced slowly towards Hornblower, looking curiously about them as they did so. Hornblower was giving the orders that got the *Porta Coeli* under way again, and as she drew away from the cutter in the gathering darkness he wore her round and headed her for the Indiaman. Cutlasses suddenly gleamed about the new arrivals.

'Make a sound and you're dead men,' said Freeman.

Somebody made a sound, beginning to protest volubly. A seaman brought a pistol butt down on his head and the protests ended abruptly as the protester clattered on the deck. The others were hustled down the hatchway, too dazed and startled to speak.

'Very well, Mr Freeman,' said Hornblower, drawling the words so as to convey the impression that he felt perfectly at home here in the middle of a hostile harbour. 'You may hoist out the boats. Maintops'l aback!'

The shore authorities would be watching the brig's movements by what little light was left. If the *Porta Coeli* did anything unexpected, they would wonder idly what unknown condition on board had caused the harbourmaster's representative – now gagged and bound under hatches – to change his plans. The *Porta Coeli*'s motion died away; the sheaves squealed as the boats dropped into the water, and the picked crews tumbled down into them. Hornblower leaned over the side.

'Remember men, don't fire a shot!'

The oars splashed as the boats pulled over to the Indiaman. It was practically dark by now; Hornblower could hardly follow the boats to the Indiaman's side fifty yards away, and he could see nothing of the men as they swarmed up her side. Faintly he heard some startled exclamations, and then one loud cry; that might puzzle the people on shore, but would not put them on their guard. Here were the boats returning, each pulled by the two men detailed for the work. The tackles were hooked on and the boats swayed up; as the sheaves squealed again Hornblower heard a crunching sound from the Indiaman, and a dull thump or two – the hand detailed to cut the cable was doing his work, and had actually remembered to carry the axe with him when he went up the ship's side. Hornblower felt the satisfaction of a job well done; his careful instruction of the boarding-party in the afternoon, his methodical allocation of duties to each individual man, and his reiteration of his orders until everyone thoroughly understood the part he had to play were bearing fruit.

Against the misty sky he saw the Indiaman's topsails changing shape; the men allotted to the task were sheeting them home. Thank God for a few prime seamen who, arriving in darkness in a strange ship, could find their way to the right places and lay their hands on the right lines without confusion. Hornblower saw the Indiaman's yards come round; in the darkness he could just see a black blur detach itself from her side, the lighter, cut adrift and floating away.

'You can square away, Mr Freeman, if you please,' he said. 'The Indiaman will follow us out.'

The *Porta Coeli* gathered way and headed for the south-eastern exit of the harbour, the Indiaman close at her stern. For several long seconds there was no sign of any interest being taken in these movements. Then came a hail, apparently from the cutter which had brought the officials aboard. It was so long since Hornblower had heard or spoken French that he could not understand the words used.

'*Comment*' he yelled back through the speaking-trumpet.

An irascible voice asked him again what in the name of the devil he thought he was doing.

'Anchorage – mumble – current – mumble – tide,' yelled Hornblower in reply.

This time the unknown in the cutter invoked the name of God instead of that of the devil.

'Who in God's name is that?'

'Mumble mumble mumble,' bellowed Hornblower back again, and quietly to the helmsman, 'Bring her slowly round to port.'

Carrying on a conversation with the French authorities while taking a vessel down an involved channel – however well he had memorised the latter on the chart – taxed his resources.

'Heave-to!' yelled the voice.

'Pardon, Captain,' yelled Hornblower back. 'Mumble – anchor-cable – mumble – impossible.'

Another loud hail from the cutter, full of menace.

'Steady as you go,' cried Hornblower to the helmsman. 'Mr Freeman, a hand at the lead, if you please.'

He knew there was no chance of gaining any more precious seconds; by the time the leadsman was calling the depths and revealing the brig's design of evasion the shore authorities would be fully alert. A pinpoint of light stabbed the thin mist and the sound of a musket-shot came over the water; the cutter was taking the quickest method of attracting the attention of the shore batteries.

'Stand by to go about!' rasped Hornblower; this was the most ticklish moment of the outward passage.

The brig's canvas volleyed as she came round, and simultaneously there was a bigger tongue of red flame in the darkness and the sound of the cutter's six-pounder bow chaser, cleared away and loaded at last. Hornblower heard no sound of the ball. He was busy looking back at the

Indiaman, dimly showing in the minute light of the brig's wake. She was coming about neatly. That master's mate – Calverly – whom Freeman had recommended for the command of the boarding-party was a capable officer, and must be highly praised when the time should come to send in a report.

And then from the jetty came a succession of flashes and a rolling roar; the big thirty-two-pounders there had opened fire at last. The sound of the last shot was instantly followed by the noise of a ball passing close by; Hornblower had time somehow to note how much he hated that noise. They were having to round the jetty, and would be within range for several minutes. There was no sign of damage either to the brig or the Indiaman as yet – and there was nothing in favour of returning the fire, for the brig's little six-pounders would make no impression on the solid battery, while the flashes would reveal the vessel's position. He took note of the cry of the leadsman; it would be some minutes before he could tack again and stand directly away from the jetty. It was a long time, on the other hand, before the battery fired again. Bonaparte must have stripped his shore defences of seasoned gunners in order to man the artillery of his army in Germany; untrained recruits, called upon suddenly to man their guns, and working in darkness, would naturally be unhandy. Here it came, the flash and the roar, but this time there was no sound of any shot passing – maybe the gunners had lost all sense of direction and elevation, which was easy enough in the darkness. And the flashes from the guns were convenient in enabling Hornblower to check his position.

A yell came from the lookout in the bows, and Hornblower, looking forward, could just make out the dark square of the top of the pilot-lugger's mainsail, close in on their starboard bow. They were making an effort to impede the brig's escape.

'Steady!' said Hornblower to the helmsman.

Let the weakest go to the wall; there was a shattering crash as brig and lugger met, starboard bow to starboard bow. The brig shuddered and lurched and drove on, the lugger rasping down her side. Something caught and tore loose again, and there came, as the vessels parted, a thin despairing yell from the lugger. The little vessel's bows must have been smashed in like an eggshell by that shock, and the water must be pouring in. The cries died away; Hornblower distinctly heard one wailing voice abruptly cut short, as if water was pouring into the mouth of the despairing swimmer. The Indiaman was still holding her course in the brig's wake.

'By the mark eight!' called the leadsman.

He could lay her on the other tack now, and as he gave the order the battery at the jetty again roared harmlessly. They would be out of range by the time the gunners could reload.

'A very good piece of work, Mr Freeman,' said Hornblower, loudly. 'All hands did their duty admirably.'

Somebody in the darkness began to cheer, and the cry was taken up throughout the brig. The men were yelling like madmen.

'Horny! Good old Horny!' yelled somebody, and the cheering redoubled.

Even from astern they could hear the exiguous prize crew of the Indiaman joining in; Hornblower felt a sudden smarting of the eyes, and then experienced a new revulsion of feeling. He felt a little twinge of shame at being fond of these simpletons. Besides—

'Mr Freeman,' he said, harshly, 'kindly keep the hands quiet.'

The risk he had run had been enormous. Not merely the physical danger, but the danger to his reputation. Had he failed, had the *Porta Coeli* been disabled and captured, men would not have stopped to think about his real motive, which was to make the French authorities believe that the *Flame*'s mutiny was merely a ruse to enable the brig to enter the harbour. No; men would have said that Hornblower had tried to take advantage of the mutiny to feather his own nest, had thrown away the *Porta Coeli* and had left the mutineers unmolested merely to grab at an opportunity to acquire prize-money. That was what they would have said – and all the appearances would have borne out the assumption – and Hornblower's reputation would have been eternally tarnished. He had risked his honour as well as his life and liberty. He had gambled everything in hare-brained fashion, thrown colossal stakes on the board for a meagre prize, like the fool he was.

Then the wave of black reaction ebbed away. He had taken a calculated risk, and his calculation had proved exact. It would be a long time before the mutineers could clear up their misunderstanding with the French authorities – Hornblower could imagine the messengers hurrying at this moment to warn the coastal defences at Honfleur and Caen – even if eventually they should succeed in doing so. He had turned the mutineers' position, cut off their retreat. He had bearded Bonaparte under the batteries of his own capital river. And there was the prize he had taken; at least a thousand pounds, his share would be, when the prize-money came to be reckoned up, and a thousand pounds was a welcome sum of money, a gratifying sum. Barbara and he would find it useful.

Emotion and excitement had left him tired. He was about to tell Freeman that he was going below, and then he checked himself. It would be an unnecessary speech; if Freeman could not find him on deck he would know perfectly well that he was in his cabin. He dragged himself wearily down to his cot.

VII

'Mr Freeman's respects, sir,' said Brown, 'an' he said to tell you that day's just breaking, fairly clear, sir. Wind's backed to sou'-by-west, sir, during the night, blowin' moderate. We're hove-to, us an' the prize, an' it's the last of the floodtide now, sir.'

'Very good,' said Hornblower, rolling out of his cot. He was still heavy with sleep, and the tiny cabin seemed stuffy, as well as chilly, although the stern window was open.

'I'll have my bath,' said Hornblower, reaching a sudden decision. 'Go and get the wash-deck pump rigged.'

He felt unclean; although this was November in the Channel he could not live through another day without a bath. His ear caught some surprised and jocular comments from the hands rigging the pump as he came up through the hatchway, but he paid them no attention. He threw off his dressing-gown, and a puzzled and nervous seaman, in the half-light, turned the jet of the canvas hose upon him while another worked the pump. The bitterly cold sea-water stung as it hit his naked skin, and he leaped and danced and turned about grotesquely, gasping. The seamen did not realise it when he wanted the jet stopped, and when he tried to escape from it they followed him up across the deck.

'Avast, there!' he yelled in desperation, half frozen and half drowned, and the merciless stream stopped.

Brown threw the big towel round him, and he scrubbed his tingling skin, while he jumped and shivered with the stimulus of the cold.

'I'd be frozen for a week if I tried that, sir,' said Freeman, who had been an interested spectator.

'Yes,' said Hornblower, discouraging conversation.

His skin glowed delightfully as he put on his clothes in his cabin with the window shut, and his shivering ceased. He drank thirstily of the steaming coffee which Brown brought him, revelling in the pleasant and unexpected feeling of well-being that filled him. He ran lightheartedly on deck again. The morning was already brighter; the captured Indiaman could now be made out, hove-to half a gunshot to leeward.

'Orders, Sir Horatio?' said Freeman, touching his hat.

Hornblower swept his glance round, playing for time. He had been culpably negligent of business; he had given no thought to his duty since he woke – since he went below to sleep, for that matter. He should order the prize back to England at once, but he could not do that without taking the opportunity of sending a written report back with her, and at this moment he simply hated the thought of labouring over a report.

'The prisoners, sir,' prompted Freeman.

Oh God, he had forgotten the prisoners. They would have to be interrogated and note made of what they had to say. Hornblower felt bone-lazy as well as full of well-being – an odd combination.

'They might have plenty to say, sir,' went on Freeman, remorselessly. 'The pilot talks some English, and we had him in the wardroom last night. He says Boney's been licked again. At a place called Leipzig, or some name like that. He says the Russians'll be over the Rhine in a week. Boney's back in Paris already. Maybe it's the end of the war.'

Hornblower and Freeman exchanged glances; it was a full year since the world had begun to look for the end of the war, and many hopes had blossomed and wilted during that year. But the Russians on the Rhine! Even though the English army's entrance upon the soil of France in the south had not shaken down the Empire, this new invasion might bring that about. Yet there had been plenty of forecasts – Hornblower had made some – to the effect that the first defeat of Bonaparte in the open field would bring to an end at the same time both his reputation for invincibility and his reign. These forecasts about the invasion of the Empire might be as inaccurate.

'Sail-ho!' yelled the lookout, and in the same breath, 'She's the *Flame*, sir.'

There she was, as before; the parting mist revealed her for only a moment before closing round her again, and then a fresh breath of wind shredded the mist and left her in plain sight. Hornblower reached the decision he had so far been unable to make.

'Clear the ship for action, Mr Freeman, if you please. We're going to fetch her out.'

Of course, it was the only thing to do. During the night, within an hour of the cutting-out of the French Indiaman, the word would be sent flying round warning all French ports in the neighbourhood that the British brig with the white cross on her foretopsail was playing a double game, and only masquerading as a mutinous vessel. The news must have reached this side of the estuary by midnight – the courier could cross on the ferry at Quillebœuf or elsewhere. Everyone would be on the watch for the brig to attempt another coup, and this bank of the river would be the obvious place. Any delay would give the mutineers a chance to reopen communication with the shore and to clear up the situation; if the authorities on shore were once to discover that there were two brigs, sister-ships, in the Bay of the Seine the mutineers might be saved that trouble. Not an hour ought to be lost.

It was all very clear and logical, yet Hornblower found himself gulping nervously as he stood on the quarterdeck. It could only mean a hammer-and-tongs battle – he would be in the thick of it in an hour. This deck which he trod would be swept by the grapeshot of the *Flame*'s carronades; within the hour he might be dead; within the hour he might be shrieking under the surgeon's knife. Last night he had faced disaster, but this morning he was facing death. That warm glow which his bath had induced in him had vanished completely, so that he found himself on the point of shivering in the chill of the morning. He scowled at himself in frantic self-contempt, and forced himself to pace brightly and jerkily up and down the tiny quarterdeck. His memories were unmanning him, he told himself. The memory of Richard trotting beside him in the sunset, holding his finger in an unbreakable clutch; the memory of Barbara; the memory even of Smallbridge or of Bond Street – he did not want to be separated from these things, to 'leave the warm precincts of the cheerful day'. He wanted to live, and soon he might die.

Flame had set more sail – boom-mainsail and jibs; closehauled she could fetch Honfleur without ever coming within range of the *Porta Coeli*'s guns. Hornblower's fears withdrew into the background as his restless mind, despite itself, interested itself in the tactical aspects of the problem before it.

'See that the hands have some breakfast, if you please, Mr Freeman,' he said. 'And it would be best if the guns were not run out yet.'

'Aye aye, sir.'

It might be a long, hard battle, and the men should have their breakfast first. And running out the guns would tell the people in *Flame* that the *Porta Coeli* expected a fight, and that would warn them that maybe their escape into French protection might not be easy. The more perfect the surprise, the greater the chance of an easy victory. Hornblower glowered at the *Flame* through his glass. He felt a dull, sullen rage against the mutineers who had caused all this trouble, whose mad action was imperilling his life. The sympathy he had felt towards them when he was seated in the safety of the Admiralty was replaced now by a fierce resentment. The villains deserved hanging – the thought changed his mood so that he could smile as he met Freeman's eyes when the latter reported the brig cleared for action.

'Very good, Mr Freeman.'

His eyes were dancing with excitement; he looked over at *Flame* again just as a fresh hail came from the masthead.

'Deck, there! There's a whole lot of small craft putting out from the beach, sir. Headin' for *Flame* it looks like, sir.'

The mutineers' brig was going through the same performance as yesterday, heading towards the French coast just out of gunshot of the *Porta Coeli*, ready to take refuge sooner than fight; the mutineers must think the small craft a welcoming deputation, coming to escort them in. And there was thick weather liable to close in on them again at any moment. *Flame* was spilling the wind from her mainsail, her every action denoting increasing hesitation. Probably on her quarterdeck there was a heated argument going on, one party insisting on keeping out of range of the *Porta Coeli* while another hesitated before such an irrevocable action as going over to the French. Maybe there was another party clamouring to turn and fight – that was quite likely; and maybe even there was a party of the most timid or the least culpable who wished to surrender and trust to the mercy of a court martial. Certainly counsel would be divided. She was hauling on her sheet again now, on a straight course for Honfleur and the approaching gunboats; two miles of clear water separated her from the *Porta Coeli*.

'Those gunboats are closing in on her, sir,' said Freeman, glass to eye. 'And that chasse-marée lugger's full of men. Christ! There's a gun.'

Someone in the *Flame* had fired a warning shot, perhaps to tell the French vessels to keep their distance until the debate on her deck had reached a conclusion. Then she wore round, as if suddenly realising the hostile intent of the French, and as she wore the small craft closed in on her, like hounds upon a deer. Half a dozen shots were fired, too ragged to be called a broadside. The gunboats were heading straight at her, their sweeps out, six a side, giving them additional speed and handiness. Smoke spouted from their bows, and over the water came the deep-toned heavy boom of the twenty-four-pounders they mounted – a sound quite different from the higher-pitched, sharper bang of the *Flame*'s carronades. The lugger ran alongside her, and through his glass Hornblower could see the boarders pouring on to the *Flame*'s deck.

'I'll have the guns run out, Mr Freeman, if you please,' he said.

The situation was developing with bewildering rapidity – he had foreseen nothing like this. There was desperate fighting ahead, but at least it would be against Frenchmen and not against Englishmen. He could see puffs of smoke on the *Flame*'s deck – some, at least, of the crew were offering resistance.

He walked forward a few yards, and addressed himself to the gunners.

'Listen to me, you men. Those gunboats must be sunk when we get in among 'em. One broadside for each will do that business for 'em if you make your shots tell. Aim true, at the base of their masts. Don't fire until you're sure you'll hit.'

'Aye aye, sir,' came a few voices in reply.

Hornblower found Brown beside him.

'Your pistols, sir. I loaded 'em afresh, an' primed 'em with new caps.'

'Thank you,' said Hornblower. He stuck the weapons into his belt, one on each side, where either hand could grasp them as necessary. It was like a boy playing at pirates, but his life might depend on those pistols in five minutes' time. He half drew his sword to see that it was free in its sheath, and he was already hastening back to take his stand by the wheel as he thrust it in again.

'Luff a little,' he said. 'Steady!'

Flame had flown up into the wind and lay all aback – apparently there was no one at the helm at the moment. The lugger was still alongside her, and the four gunboats, having taken in their sails, were resting on their oars, interposing between the *Porta Coeli* and the pair of ships. Hornblower could see the guns' crews bending over the twenty-four-pounders in their bows.

'Hands to the sheets, Mr Freeman, please. I'm going between them – there. Stand to your guns, men! Now, hard down!'

The wheel went over, and the *Porta Coeli* came about on the other tack, handily as anyone could desire. Hornblower heard the thunder of a shot close under her bows, and then the deck erupted in a flying shower of splinters from a jagged hole close to the mainmast bitts – a twenty-four-pound shot, fired upwards at close elevation, had pierced the brig's frail timbers, and, continuing its flight, had burst through the deck.

'Ready about! Hard over!' yelled Hornblower, and the *Porta Coeli* tacked again into the narrow gap between two gunboats. Her carronades went off in rapid succession on both sides. Looking to starboard, Hornblower had one gunboat under his eye. He saw her there, half a dozen men standing by the tiller aft, two men at each sweep amidships tugging wildly to swing her round, a dozen men at the gun forward. A man with a red handkerchief round his head stood by the mast, resting his hand against it – Hornblower could even see his open mouth as his jaw dropped and he saw death upon him. Then the shots came smashing in. The man with the red handkerchief disappeared – maybe he was dashed overboard, but most likely he was smashed into pulp. The frail frame of the gunboat – nothing more than a big rowing-boat strengthened forward for a gun – disintegrated; her side caved in under the shots as though under the blows of some vast hammer. The sea poured in even as Hornblower looked; the shots, fired with extreme depression, must have gone on through the gunboat's bottom after piercing her side. The dead weight of the gun in her bows took charge as her stability vanished, and her bows surged under while her stern was still above water. Then the gun slid out, relieving her of its weight, and the wreck righted itself for an instant before capsizing. A few men swam among the wreckage. Hornblower looked over to port; the other gunboat had been as hard hit, lying at that moment just at the surface with the remains of her crew swimming by her. Whoever had been in command of those gunboats had been a reckless fool to expose the frail vessels to the fire of a real vessel of war – even one as tiny as the *Porta Coeli* – as long as the latter was under proper command. Gunboats were only of use to batter into submission ships helplessly aground or dismasted.

The chasse-marée and the *Flame*, still alongside each other, were close ahead.

'Mr Freeman, load with canister, if you please. We'll run alongside the Frenchman. One broadside, and we'll board her in the smoke.'

'Aye aye, sir.'

Freeman turned to bellow orders to his crew.

'Mr Freeman, I shall want every available hand in the boarding-party. You'll stay here—'

'Sir!'

'You'll stay here. Pick six good seamen to stay with you to work the brig out again if we don't come back. Is that clear, Mr Freeman?'

'Yes, Sir Horatio.'

There was still time for Freeman to make the arrangements as the *Porta Coeli* surged up towards the Frenchman. There was still time for Hornblower to realise with surprise that what he had said about not coming back was sincere, and no mere bombast to stimulate the men. He was most oddly determined to conquer or die, he, the man who was afraid of shadows. The men were yelling madly as the *Porta Coeli* drew up to the Frenchman, whose name – the *Bonne Celestine* of Honfleur – was now visible on her stern. Blue uniforms and white breeches could be seen aboard her; soldiers – it was true, then, that Bonaparte's need for trained artillerymen had forced him to conscript his seamen, replacing them with raw conscript soldiers. A pity the action was not taking place out at sea, for then they would most of them be seasick.

'Lay us alongside,' said Hornblower to the helmsman. There was confusion on the decks of the *Bonne Celestine*; Hornblower could see men running to the guns on her disengaged port side.

'Quiet, you men!' bellowed Hornblower. 'Quiet!'

Silence fell on the brig; Hornblower had hardly to raise his voice to make himself heard on the tiny deck.

'See that every shot tell, you gunners,' said Hornblower. 'Boarders, are you ready to come with me?'

Another yell answered him. Thirty men were crouching by the bulwarks with pikes and cutlasses; the firing of the broadside and the dropping of the mainsail would set free thirty more, a small enough force unless the broadside should do great execution and the untrained landsmen in the *Bonne Celestine* should flinch. Hornblower stole a glance at the helmsman, a grey-bearded seaman, who was coolly gauging the distance between the two vessels while at the same time watching the mainsail as it shivered as the *Porta Coeli* came to the wind. A good seaman, that – Hornblower made a mental note to remember him for commendation. The helmsman whirled the wheel over.

'Down mains'l,' roared Freeman.

The *Bonne Celestine*'s guns bellowed deafeningly, and Hornblower felt powder grains strike his face as the smoke eddied round him. He drew his sword as the *Porta Coeli*'s carronades crashed out, and the two vessels came together with a squealing of timber. He sprang upon the bulwark in the smoke, sword in hand; at the same moment a figure beside him cleared the bulwark in a single motion and dropped upon the *Bonne Celestine*'s deck – Brown, waving a cutlass. Hornblower leaped after him, but Brown stayed in front of him, striking to left and right at the shadowy figures looming in the smoke. Here there was a pile of dead and wounded men, caught in the blast of canister from one of the *Porta Coeli*'s carronades. Hornblower stumbled over a limb, and recovered himself in time to see a bayonet on the end of a musket lunging at him. A violent twisting of his body evaded the thrust. There was a pistol in his left hand, and he fired with the muzzle almost against the Frenchman's breast. Now the wind had blown the cannon-smoke clear. Forward some of the boarders were fighting with a group of the enemy cornered in the bow – the clash of the blades came clearly to Hornblower's ears – but aft there was not a Frenchman to be seen. Gibbons, master's mate, was at the halliards running down the tricolour from the masthead. At the starboard side lay the *Flame*, and over her bulwarks were visible French infantry shakoes; Hornblower saw a man's head and shoulders appear, saw a musket being pointed. It shifted its aim from Gibbons to Hornblower, and in that instant Hornblower fired the other barrel of his pistol, and the Frenchman fell down below the bulwarks, just as a fresh wave of boarders came pouring on board from the *Porta Coeli*.

'Come on!' yelled Hornblower – it was desperately important to make sure of the *Flame* before a defence could be organised.

The brigs stood higher out of the water than did the chasse-marée; this time they had to climb upward. He got his left elbow over the bulwark, and tried to swing himself up, but his sword hampered him.

'Help me, damn you!' he snarled over his shoulder, and a seaman put his shoulder under Hornblower's stern and heaved him up with such surprising goodwill that he shot over the bulwarks and fell on his face in the scuppers on the other side, his sword slithering over the deck. He started to crawl forward towards it, but a sixth sense warned him of danger, and he flung himself down and forward inside the sweep of a cutlass, and cannoned against the shins of the man who wielded it. Then a wave of men burst over him, and he was kicked and trodden on and then crushed beneath a writhing body with which he grappled with desperate strength. He could hear Brown's voice roaring over him, pistols banging, sword-blades clashing before sudden silence fell round him. The man with whom he was struggling went suddenly limp and inert, and then was dragged off him. He rose to his feet.

'Are you wounded, sir?' asked Brown.

'No,' he answered. Three or four dead men lay on the deck; aft a group of French soldiers with a French seaman or two among them stood by the wheel, disarmed, while two British sailors, pistol in hand, stood guard over them. A French officer, blood dripping from his right sleeve, and with tears on his cheeks – he was no more than a boy – was sitting on the deck, and Hornblower was about to address him when his attention was suddenly distracted.

'Sir! Sir!'

It was an English seaman he did not recognise, in a striped shirt of white and red, his pigtail shaking from side to side as he gesticulated with the violence of his emotion.

'Sir! I was fightin' against the Frogs. Your men saw me. Me an' these other lads here.'

He motioned behind him to an anxious little group of seamen who had heretofore hung back, but now came forward, some of them bursting into speech, all of them nodding their heads in agreement.

'Mutineers?' asked Hornblower. In the heat of battle he had forgotten about the mutiny.

'I'm no mutineer, sir. I did what I had to or they'd 'a killed me. Ain't that so, mates?'

'Stand back, there!' blared Brown; there was blood on the blade of his cutlass.

A vivid prophetic picture suddenly leaped into Hornblower's mind's eye – the court martial, the semicircle of judges in glittering full dress, the tormented prisoners, tongue-tied, watching, only half understanding, the proceedings which would determine their lives or deaths, and he himself giving his evidence, trying conscientiously to remember every word spoken on both sides; one word remembered might make the difference between the lash and the rope.

'Arrest those men!' he snapped. 'Put them under confinement.'

'Sir! Sir!'

'None o' that!' growled Brown.

Remorseless hands dragged the protesting men away.

'Where are the other mutineers?' demanded Hornblower.

'Down below, sir, I fancies,' said Brown. 'Some o' the Frenchies is down there, too.'

Odd how a beaten crew so often scuttled below. Hornblower honestly believed that he would rather face the fighting madness of the victors on deck than surrender ignominiously in the dark confines of the 'tween-decks.

A loud hail from the *Porta Coeli* came to his ears.

'Sir Horatio!' hailed Freeman's voice. 'We'll be all aground if we don't get way on the ships soon. I request permission to cast off and make sail.'

'Wait!' replied Hornblower.

He looked together round him; the three ships locked together, prisoners under guard here, there, and everywhere. Below decks, both in the *Bonne Celestine* and in the *Flame*, there were enemies still unsecured, probably many more in total than he had men under his orders. A shattering crash below him, followed by screams and cries; the *Flame* shook under a violent blow. Hornblower remembered the sound of a cannon-shot striking on his inattentive ears a second before; he looked round. The two surviving gunboats were resting on their oars a couple of cables' lengths away, their bows pointing at the group of ships. Hornblower could guess they were in shoal water, almost immune from attack. A jet of smoke from one of the gunboats, and another frightful crash below, and more screams. Those twenty-four-pounder balls were probably smashing through the whole frail length of the brig, whose timbers could resist their impact hardly better than paper. Hornblower plunged into the urgency of the business before him like a man into a raging torrent which he had to swim.

'Get those hatches battened down, Brown!' he ordered. 'Put a sentry over each. Mr Gibbons!'

'Sir?'

'Secure your hatches. Get ready to make sail.'

'Aye aye, sir.'

'What topmen are there here? Man the halliards. Who can take the wheel? Wheel none of you? Mr Gibbons! Have you a quartermaster to spare? Send one here immediately. Mr Freeman! You can cast off and make sail. Rendezvous at the other prize.'

Another shot from those accursed gunboats crashed into the *Flame*'s stern below him. Thank God the wind was off shore and he could get clear of them. The *Porta Coeli* had set her boom-mainsail again and had got clear of the *Bonne Celestine*; Gibbons was supervising the setting of the latter's lug-mainsail while half a dozen hands boomed her off from the *Flame*.

'Hoist away!' ordered Hornblower as the vessels separated. 'Hard a-starboard, Quartermaster.'

A sound overside attracted his attention. Men – mutineers or Frenchmen – were scrambling out through the shot-holes and hurling themselves into the sea, swimming towards the gunboats. Hornblower saw the white hair of Nathaniel Sweet trailing on the surface of the water as he struck out, twenty feet away from him. Of all the mutineers he was the one who most certainly must not be allowed to escape. For the sake of England, for the sake of the service, he must die. The seaman acting as sentry at the after hatchway did not look as if he were a capable marksman.

'Give me your musket,' said Hornblower, snatching it.

He looked at priming and flint as he hurried back to the taffrail. He trained the weapon on the white head, and pulled the trigger. The smoke blew back into his face, obscuring his view only for a moment. The long white hair was visible for a second at the surface when he looked again, and then it sank, slowly, out of sight. Sweet was dead. Maybe there was an old widow who would bewail him, but it was better that Sweet was dead. Hornblower turned back to the business of navigating the *Flame* back to the rendezvous.

VIII

This fellow Lebrun was an infernal nuisance, demanding a private interview in this fashion. Hornblower had quite enough to do as it was; the gaping shot-holes in *Flame*'s side had to be patched sufficiently well to enable her to recross the Channel; the exiguous crew of the *Porta Coeli* – not all of them seamen by any means – had to be distributed through no fewer than four vessels (the two brigs, the Indiaman, and the chasse-marée), while at the same time an adequate guard must be maintained over more than a hundred prisoners of one nationality or another; the mutineers must be supervised so that nothing could happen to prejudice their trial; worst of all, there was a long report to be made out. Some people would think this last an easy task, seeing that there was a long string of successes to report, two prizes taken, the *Flame* recaptured, most of the mutineers in irons below decks and their ring-leader slain by Hornblower's own hand. But there was the physical labour of writing it out, and Hornblower was very weary. Moreover, the composition of it would be difficult, for Hornblower could foresee having to steer a ticklish course between the Scylla of open boastfulness and the Charybdis of mock-modesty – how often had his lips wrinkled in distaste when reading the literary efforts of other officers! And the killing of Nathaniel Sweet by the terrible Commodore Hornblower, although it would look well in a naval history, and although, from the point of view of the discipline of the service, it was the best way in which the affair could have ended, might not appear so well in Barbara's eyes. He himself did not relish the memory of that white head sinking beneath the waves, and he felt that Barbara, with her attention forcibly called to the fact that he had shed blood, had taken a human life, with his own hands (those hands which she said she loved, which she had some-times kissed), might feel a repulsion, a distaste.

Hornblower shook himself free from a clinging tangle of thoughts and memories, of Barbara and Nathaniel Sweet, to find himself still staring abstractedly at the young seaman who had brought to him Freeman's message regarding Lebrun's request.

'My compliments to Mr Freeman, and he can send this fellow in to me,' he said.

'Aye aye, sir,' said the seaman, his knuckles to his forehead, turning away with intense relief. The Commodore had been looking through and through him for three minutes at least – three hours, it seemed like, to the seaman.

An armed guard brought Lebrun into the cabin, and Hornblower looked him keenly over. He was one of the half-dozen prisoners taken when the *Porta Coeli* came into Le Havre, one of the deputation which had mounted her deck to welcome her under the impression that she was the *Flame* coming in to surrender.

'Monsieur speaks French?' said Lebrun.

'A little.'

'More than a little, if all the tales about Captain Hornblower are true,' replied Lebrun.

'What is your business?' snapped Hornblower, cutting short this continental floweriness. Lebrun was a youngish man, of olive complexion, with glistening white teeth, who conveyed a general impression of oiliness.

'I am *adjoint* to Baron Momas, Mayor of Le Havre.'

'Yes?' Hornblower tried to show no sign of interest, but he knew that under the Imperial régime the mayor of a large town like Le Havre was a most important person, and that his *adjoint* – his assistant, or deputy – was a very important permanent official.

'The firm of Momas Frères is one you must have heard of. It has traded with the Americas for generations – the history of its rise is identical with the history of the development of Le Havre itself.'

'Yes?'

'Similarly, the war and the blockade have had a most disastrous effect upon the fortunes both of the firm of Momas and upon the city of Le Havre.'

'Yes?'

'The *Caryatide*, the vessel that you so ingeniously captured two days ago, monsieur, might have restored the fortunes of us all – a single vessel running the blockade, as you will readily understand, is worth ten vessels arriving in peacetime.'

'Yes?'

'M. le Baron and the city of Le Havre will be desperate, I have no doubt, as the result of her capture before her cargo could be taken out.'

'Yes?'

The two men eyed each other, like duellists during a pause,

Hornblower determined to betray none of the curiosity and interest that he felt, and Lebrun hesitating before finally committing himself.

'I take it, monsieur, that anything further I have to say will be treated as entirely confidential.'

'I promise nothing. In fact, I can only say that it will be my duty to report anything you say to the Government of His Majesty of Great Britain.'

'They will be discreet for their own sake, I expect,' ruminated Lebrun.

'His Majesty's ministers can make their own decisions,' said Hornblower.

'You are aware, monsieur,' said Lebrun, obviously taking the plunge, 'that Bonaparte has been defeated in a great battle at Leipzig?'

'Yes.'

'The Russians are on the Rhine.'

'That is so.'

'The Russians are on the Rhine!' repeated Lebrun, marvelling. The whole world, pro-Bonaparte or anti-Bonaparte, was marvelling that the massive Empire should have receded half across Europe in those few short months.

'And Wellington is marching on Toulouse,' added Hornblower – there was no harm in reminding Lebrun of the British threat in the south.

'That is so. The Empire cannot much longer endure.'

'I am glad to hear your opinion in the matter.'

'And when the Empire falls there will be peace, and when peace comes trade will recommence.'

'Without a doubt,' said Hornblower, still a little mystified.

'Profits will be enormous during the first few months. All Europe has for years been deprived of foreign produce. At this moment genuine coffee commands a price of over a hundred francs a pound.'

Now Lebrun was showing his hand, more involuntarily than voluntarily. There was a look of avarice in his face which told Hornblower much.

'All this is obvious, monsieur,' said Hornblower, non-committally.

'A firm which was prepared for the moment of peace, with its warehouses gorged with colonial produce ready to distribute, would greatly benefit. It would be far ahead of its competitors. There would be millions to be made. Millions.' Lebrun was obviously dreaming of the possibility of finding some of those millions in his own pocket.

'I have a great deal of business to attend to, monsieur,' said Hornblower. 'Have the goodness to come to the point.'

'His Majesty of Great Britain might well allow his friends to make those preparations in advance,' said Lebrun, the words coming slowly; well they might, for they could take him to the guillotine if Bonaparte ever heard of them. Lebrun was offering to betray the Empire in exchange for commercial advantages.

'His Majesty would first need undeniable proof that his friends *were* his friends,' said Hornblower.

'A *quid pro quo*,' said Lebrun, thereby for the first time during the conversation putting Hornblower at a loss – the Frenchman's pronunciation of Latin being quite unlike anything he was accustomed to, so that he had to grope about in his mind wondering what unaccustomed word Lebrun was using before at length he understood.

'You may tell me the nature of your offer, monsieur,' said Hornblower with solemn dignity, 'but I can make no promises of any sort in return. His Majesty's Government will probably refuse to bind themselves in any way whatsoever.'

It was curious how he found himself aping the ministerial manner and diction – it might have been his solemn brother-in-law, Wellesley, speaking. Maybe high politics had that effect on everyone; it was useful in this particular case, because it helped him to conceal his eagerness.

'A *quid pro quo*,' said Lebrun, again, thoughtfully. 'Supposing the city of Le Havre declared itself against the Empire, declared itself for Louis XVIII?'

The possibility had occurred to Hornblower, but he had put it aside as being potentially too good to be true.

'Supposing it did?' he said cautiously.

'It might be the example for which the Empire is waiting. It might be infectious. Bonaparte could not survive such a blow.'

'He has survived many blows.'

'But none of this sort. And if Le Havre declared for the King the city would be in alliance with Great Britain. The blockade could not continue to apply. Or if it did a licence to import could be granted to the house of Momas Frères, could it not?'

'Possibly. Remember, I make no promises.'

'And when Louis XVIII was restored to the throne of his fathers he would look with kindness upon those who first declared for him,' said Lebrun. 'The *adjoint* to Baron Momas might expect to find a great career open to him.'

'No doubt of that,' agreed Hornblower. 'But – you have spoken of your own sentiments. Can you be sure of those of M. le Baron? And whatever may be M. le Baron's sentiments, how can he be sure that the city would follow him should he declare himself?'

'I can answer for the Baron, I assure you, sir. I know – I have certain knowledge of his thoughts.'

Probably Lebrun had been spying on his master on behalf of the Imperial Government, and had no objection to applying his knowledge in another and more profitable cause.

'But the city? The other authorities?'

'The day you took me prisoner, sir,' said Lebrun, 'there arrived from Paris some sample proclamations and advance notice of some Imperial decrees. The proclamations were to be printed – my last official act was to give the order – and next Monday the proclamations were to be posted and the decrees made public.'

'Yes?'

'They are the most drastic in the drastic history of the Empire. Conscription – the last of the class of 1815 is to be called, and the classes all the way back to that of 1802 are to be revised. Boys of seventeen, cripples, invalids, fathers of families, even those who have purchased exemption; they are all to be called.'

'France must have grown used to conscription.'

'France has grown weary of it, rather, sir. I have official knowledge of the number of deserters and the severity of the measures directed against them. But it's not merely the conscription, sir. The other decrees are more drastic still. The taxes! The direct imposts, the indirect imposts, the *droits réunis*, and the others! Those of us who survive the war will be left beggars.'

'And you think publication of these decrees will rouse sufficient discontent to cause rebellion?'

'Perhaps not. But it would constitute an admirable starting-point for a determined leader.'

Lebrun was shrewd enough – this last remark was acute and might be true.

'But the other authorities in the town? The military governor? The Prefect of the Department?'

'Some of them would be safe. I know their sentiments as well as I know Baron Momas'. The others – a dozen well-timed arrests, carried out simultaneously, an appeal to the troops in the barracks, the arrival of British forces (*your* forces, sir), a heartening proclamation to the people, the declaration of a state of siege, the closing of the gates, and it would be all over. Le Havre is well fortified, as you know, sir. Only an army and a battering train could retake it, and Bonaparte has neither to spare. The news would spread like wildfire through the Empire, however Bonaparte tried to stop it.'

This man Lebrun had ideas and vision, whatever might be thought of his morals. That was a neat thumbnail sketch he had drawn of a typical *coup d'état*. If the attempt were successful the results would be profound. Even if it were to fail, loyalty throughout the Empire would be shaken. Treason was infectious, as Lebrun had said. Rats in a sinking ship were notoriously quick in following an example in leaving it. There would be little enough to risk losing in supporting Lebrun's notions, and the gains might be immense.

'Monsieur,' said Hornblower, 'so far I have been patient. But in all this time you have made me no concrete proposal. Words – nebulous ideas – hopes – wishes, that is all, and I am a busy man, as I told you. Please be specific. And speedy, if that is not too much trouble to you.'

'I shall be specific, then. Set me on shore – as an excuse I could be sent to arrange a cartel for the exchange of prisoners. Let me be able to assure M. le Baron of your instant support. In the three days before next Monday I can complete the arrangements. Meanwhile, you remain close in the vicinity with all the force you can muster. The moment we secure the citadel we shall send up the white flag, and the moment you see that you enter the harbour and overawe any possible dissentients. In return for this – a licence to Momas Frères to import colonial produce, and your word of honour as a gentleman that you will inform King Louis that it was I, Hercule Lebrun, who first suggested the scheme to you.'

'Ha – h'm,' said Hornblower. He hardly ever made use of that sound now, after his wife had teased him about it, but it escaped from him at this moment of crisis. He had to think. He had to have time to think. The long conversation in the French which he was not accustomed to using had been exhausting. He lifted his voice in a bellow to the sentry outside the door.

'Pass the word for the armed guard to take this prisoner away.'

'Sir!' protested Lebrun.

'I will give you my decision in an hour,' said Hornblower. 'Meanwhile for appearance's sake you must be treated harshly.'

'Sir! Remember to be secret! Remember not to utter a word! For God's sake—!'

Lebrun had a very proper sense of the necessity for secrecy in planning a rebellion against such a potentate as Bonaparte. Hornblower took that into consideration as he went up on deck, there to pace up and down, thrusting the minor administrative problems out of his mind as he debated this, the greatest problem of all.

IX

The tricolour was still flying over the citadel – the fortress of Ste Adresse – of Le Havre; Hornblower could see it through his glass as he stood on the deck of the *Flame*, which was creeping along under easy sail, just out of range of the shore batteries. He had decided, inevitably, to assist Lebrun in his scheme. He was telling himself again, at that very moment, and for the thousandth time, that there was much to gain whatever the result, and little enough to lose. Only Lebrun's life, and perhaps Hornblower's reputation. Heaven only knew what Whitehall and Downing Street would say when they heard of what he had been doing. No one had decided yet what to do about the government of France when Bonaparte should fall; certainly there was no unanimity of opinion regarding the restoration of the Bourbons. The Government could refuse to honour the promises he had made regarding import licences; they could come out with a bold announcement that they had no intention of recognising Louis XVIII's pretensions; they could rap him over the knuckles very sharply indeed for most of his actions since recapture of the *Flame*.

He had used his powers to pardon forty mutineers, all the seamen and boys, in fact, that were in the crew of the latter vessel. He could plead sheer necessity as a defence for that decision; to keep the mutineers as well as the prisoners under guard, and to provide prize crews for the two prizes, would have called for the services of every man at his disposal. He would hardly have had enough to handle the vessels, and certainly he could have attempted nothing further. As it was, he had relieved himself of all these difficulties by a few simple decisions. Every Frenchman had been sent on shore in the *Bonne Celestine* under flag of truce, with Lebrun ostensibly to arrange for their exchange; the Indiaman had been manned by a minimum crew and sent with despatches to Pellew and the Mid-Channel Squadron, and he had been able to retain the two brigs, each at last sufficiently manned, under his own command. That had been a convenient way of getting rid of Chadwick, too – he had been entrusted with the despatches and the command of the Indiaman. Chadwick had been pale, as a result of two weeks' confinement in the Black Hole, and two weeks' imminent danger of hanging. There had been no evident pleasure in his red-rimmed eyes when he realised that his rescuer had been young Hornblower, once his junior in the gunroom of the *Indefatigable* and now his immeasurable superior. Chadwick had snarled a little on receiving his orders – only a little. He had weighed the despatches in his hand, presumably wondering what was said in them about himself, but discretion or long habit had their way, and he said, 'Aye aye, sir,' and turned away.

By now those despatches should have passed through Pellew's hands, and, their contents noted, might even be on their way to Whitehall. The wind had been fair for the Indiaman to have fetched the Mid-Channel Squadron off the Start – fair, too, for the reinforcements Hornblower had asked for to make their way to him. Pellew would send them, he knew. It was fifteen years since they had last met; nearly twenty years since Pellew had promoted him to a lieutenancy in the *Indefatigable*. Now Pellew was an admiral and a commander-in-chief, and he was a commodore, but Pellew would be the loyal friend and the helpful colleague he had always been.

Hornblower glanced out to seaward, where, dim on the horizon, the *Porta Coeli* patrolled in the mist. She would halt the reinforcements before they could be sighted from the shore, for there was no reason why the authorities in Le Havre should be given the least chance to think that anything unusual portended, although it was not a vital matter. England had always flaunted her naval might in sight of the enemy, making the hostile coast her sea frontier – the *Flame*, here, wearing the White Ensign under the noses of the citizens of Le Havre, was no unusual sight to them. That was why he did not hesitate to stay here, with the tricolour on the citadel within range of his telescope.

'Keep a sharp lookout for any signal from the *Porta Coeli*,' he said sharply to the midshipman of the watch.

'Aye aye, sir.'

Porta Coeli, the Gate of Heaven; the Silly Porter was what the men called her. Hornblower had a vague memory of reading about the action which resulted in the strange name appearing in the Navy List. The first *Porta Coeli* had been a Spanish privateer – half pirate, probably – captured off Havannah. She had put up so fierce a resistance that the action had been commemorated by naming an English ship after her. The *Tonnant*, the *Temeraire*, most of the foreign names in the Navy List came there as a result of similar actions – if the war were to go on long enough there would be more ships in the Navy with foreign names than with English ones, and among the rival navies the converse might eventually become true. The French Navy boasted a *Swiftsure*; maybe the Americans would have a *Macedonian* on their Navy List in future years. He had not heard yet of a French *Sutherland*; Hornblower felt a sudden twinge of strange regret. He snapped his telescope shut and turned abruptly on his heel, walking fast as though to shake off the memories that assailed him. He did not like to think about surrendering the *Sutherland*, even though the court martial had so honourably acquitted him; and, strangely enough, the passage of time made his feelings of shame about the incident more acute instead of less. And his regrets about the *Sutherland* brought with them inevitably, memories of Maria, now nearly three years in her grave. Memories of poverty and despair, of pinchbeck shoebuckles; of the pity and sympathy he had felt for Maria – a poor substitute for love, and yet the memory of it hurt intensely. The past was coming to life again in his mind, a resurrection as horrible as any other resurrection would be. He remembered Maria, snoring softly in her sleep beside him, and he remembered the sour smell of her hair; Maria, tactless and stupid, of whom he had been fond as one is fond of a child, although not nearly as fond as he was now of Richard. He was almost shaking with the memory when it abruptly faded out and was replaced by the memory of Marie de Graçay – why the devil was he thinking about *her*? The unreserved love that she gave him, her warmth and tenderness, the quickness of perception with which she understood his moods; it was insane that he should find himself hungering at this day for Marie de Graçay, and yet he was, even though it was hardly a week since he had left the arms of a loyal and understanding wife. He tried to think about Barbara, and yet the mental images he conjured up were instantly thrust again into the background by pictures of Marie. It would be better even to think about surrendering the *Sutherland*. Hornblower walked the deck of the *Flame* with ghosts at his side in the chill, bleak wintry day. Men saw his face and shrank from crossing his path with greater care even than usual. Yet most of them thought Hornblower was only planning some further deviltry against the French.

It was late afternoon before the expected interruption came.

'Signal from *Porta Coeli*, sir! Eighteen – fifty-one – ten. That's friendly ships in sight, bearing nor'west.'

'Very good. Ask their numbers.'

This must be the reinforcements sent by Pellew. The signal hands bent on the flags and hauled away at the halliards; it was several minutes before the midshipman noted the reply and translated it by reference to the list.

'*Nonsuch*, 74, Captain Bush, sir.'

'Bush, by God!'

The exclamation leaped uncontrolled from Hornblower's lips; the devils that surrounded him were chased away as though by holy water at the thought of his old staunch matter-of-fact friend being only just over the horizon. Of course Pellew would send Bush if he were available, knowing the friendship that had so long existed between him and Hornblower.

'*Camilla*, 36, Captain Howard, sir.'

He knew nothing about Howard whatever. He looked at the list – a captain of less than two years' seniority. Presumably Pellew had selected him as junior to Bush.

'Very good. Reply – "Commodore to—"'

'*Porta*'s still signalling, begging your pardon, sir. "*Nonsuch* to Commodore. Have – on board – three hundred – marines – above – complement".'

Good for Pellew. He had stripped his squadron to give Hornblower a landing force that could make itself felt. Three hundred marines, and the *Nonsuch*'s detachment as well, and a body of seamen. He could march five hundred men into Le Havre should the opportunity arise.

'Very good. Make "Commodore to *Nonsuch* and *Camilla*. Delighted to have you under my command".'

Hornblower looked again over at Le Havre. He looked up at the sky, he gauged the strength of the wind, remembered the state of the tide, calculated the approach of night. Over there Lebrun must be bringing his plans to fruition, tonight if at all. He must be ready to strike his blow.

'Make "Commodore to all vessels. Join me here after dark. Night signal two lanterns horizontally at fore yardarms".'

'– fore yardarms. Aye aye, sir,' echoed the midshipman, scribbling on his slate.

It was good to see Bush again, to shake his hand in welcome as he hoisted himself in the darkness on to the *Flame*'s deck. It was good to sit in the stuffy little cabin with Bush and Howard and Freeman as he told them about his plans for the morrow. It was wonderful to be planning action after that day of horrible introspection. Bush looked at him closely with his deep-set eyes.

'You've been busy, sir, since you came to sea again.'

'Of course,' said Hornblower.

The last few days and nights had been a turmoil; even after the recapture of the *Flame* the business of reorganisation, the sessions with Lebrun, the writing of the despatches had all been exhausting.

'Too busy, if you'll pardon me, sir,' went on Bush. 'It was too soon for you to resume duty.'

'Nonsense,' protested Hornblower. 'I had almost a year's leave.'

'Sick leave, sir. After typhus. And since then—'

'Since then,' interjected Howard, a handsome, dark, young-looking man, 'a cutting-out action. A battle. Three prizes taken. Two vessels sunk. An invasion planned. A midnight council of war.'

Hornblower felt suddenly irritated.

'Are you gentlemen trying to tell me,' he demanded, glowering round at them, 'that I'm unfit for service?'

They quailed before his anger.

'No, sir,' said Bush.

'Then be so good as to keep your opinions to yourselves.'

It was hard luck on Bush, who, after all, was only making a kindly inquiry about his friend's health. Hornblower knew it, and he knew how desperately unfair it was to make Bush pay for the miseries Hornblower had suffered that day. Yet he could not resist the temptation for the moment. He swept his glance round them again, forcing them to drop their gaze to the deck, and he had no sooner done it, no sooner obtained for himself this pitiful bit of self-gratification, than he regretted it and sought to make amends.

'Gentlemen,' he said, 'I spoke in haste. We must all have the most complete confidence in each other when we go into action tomorrow. Will you forgive me?'

They mumbled back at him, Bush profoundly embarrassed at receiving an apology from a man who, in his opinion, was free to say what he liked to anyone.

'You all understand what I want done tomorrow – if tomorrow is the day?' Hornblower went on.

They nodded, turning their eyes to the chart spread out in front of them.

'No questions?'

'No, sir.'

'I know this is only the sketchiest plan. There will be contingencies, emergencies. No one can possibly foresee what will happen. But of one thing I am certain, and that is that the ships of this squadron will be commanded in a way that will bring credit to the service. Captain Bush and Mr Freeman have acted with bravery and decision under my own eyes too often, and I know Captain Howard too well by reputation for me to have any doubt about that. When we attack Havre, gentlemen, we shall be turning a page, we shall be writing the end of a chapter in the history of tyranny.'

They were pleased with what he said, and they could have no doubt regarding his sincerity, because he spoke from his heart. They smiled as he met their eyes. Maria, when she was alive, had sometimes made use of a strange expression about polite phrases uttered in order to get the recipient into a good humour. She referred to them as 'a little bit of sugar for the bird'. That was what this final speech of his had been, a little bit of sugar for the bird – and yet he had meant every word of it. No, not quite – he was still almost ignorant of Howard's achievements. To that extent the speech was formal. But it had served its purpose.

'Then we have finished with business, gentlemen. What can I offer you by way of entertainment? Captain Bush can remember games of whist played on the nights before going into action. But he is by no means an enthusiastic whist player.'

That was understating the case – Bush was the most reluctant whist player in the world, and he grinned sheepishly in acknowledgement of Hornblower's gentle gibe; but it was pathetic to see him pleased at Hornblower's remembering this about him.

'You should have a night's rest, sir,' he said, speaking, as the senior, for the other two, who looked to him for guidance.

'I should get back to my ship, sir,' echoed Howard.

'So should I, sir,' said Freeman.

'I don't want to see you go,' protested Hornblower.

Freeman caught sight of the playing-cards on the shelf against the bulkhead.

'I'll tell your fortunes before we leave,' he volunteered. 'Perhaps I can remember what my gipsy grandmother taught me, sir.'

So there really was gipsy blood in Freeman's veins; Hornblower had often wondered about it, noticing his swarthy skin and dark eyes. Hornblower was a little surprised at the carelessness with which Freeman admitted it.

'Tell Sir Horatio's,' said Bush.

Freeman was shuffling the pack with expert fingers; he laid it on the table, and took Hornblower's hand and placed it on the pack.

'Cut three times, sir.'

Hornblower went through the mumbo-jumbo tolerantly, cutting and cutting again as Freeman shuffled. Finally Freeman caught up the pack and began to deal it face upward on the table.

'On this side is the past,' he announced, scanning the complicated pattern, 'on that side is the future. Here in the past there is much to read. I see money, gold. I see danger. Danger, danger, danger.. I see prison – prison twice, sir. I see a dark woman. And a fair woman. You have journeyed over sea.'

He poured out his patter professionally enough, reeling it off without stopping to take breath. He made a neat résumé of Hornblower's career, and Hornblower listened with some amusement and a good deal of admiration for Freeman's glibness. What Freeman was saying could be said by anyone with an ordinary knowledge of Hornblower's past. Hornblower's eyebrows came together in momentary irritation at the brief allusion to the dead Maria, but he smiled again when Freeman passed rapidly on, telling of Hornblower's experiences in the Baltic, translating the phrases of ordinary speech into the gipsy clichés with a deftness that could not but amuse.

'And there's an illness, sir,' he concluded, 'a very serious illness, ending only a short time back.'

'Amazing!' said Hornblower, in mock admiration. The glow of anticipated action always brought out his best qualities; he was cordial and human towards this junior officer in a way that would be impossible to him at any other time.

'Amazing's the word, sir,' said Bush.

Hornblower was astonished to see that Bush was actually impressed; the fact that he was taken in by Freeman's adroit use of his knowledge of the past would go far towards explaining the success of the charlatans of this world.

'What about the future, Freeman?' asked Howard. It was a relief to see that Howard was only tolerantly interested.

'The future,' said Freeman, drumming with his fingers on the table as he turned to the other half of the arrangement. 'The future is always more mysterious. I see a crown. A golden crown.'

He rearranged the pattern.

'A crown it is, sir, try it any way you will.'

'Horatio the First, King of the Cannibal Isles,' laughed Hornblower. The clearest proof of his present mellowness was this joke about his name – a sore subject usually with him.

'And here there is more danger. Danger and a fair woman. The two go together. Danger because of a fair woman – danger *with* a fair woman. There's all kinds of danger here, sir. I'd advise you to beware of fair women.'

'No need to read cards to give that advice,' said Hornblower.

'Sometimes the cards speak truth,' replied Freeman, looking up at him with a peculiar intensity in his glittering eyes.

'A crown, a fair woman, danger,' repeated Hornblower. 'What else?'

'That's all that I can read, sir,' said Freeman, sweeping the cards together.

Howard was looking at the big silver watch that he pulled from his pocket.

'If Freeman could have told us whether or no we will see a white flag over the citadel tomorrow,' he said, 'it might help us to decide to prolong this pleasant evening. As it is, sir, I have my orders to give.'

Hornblower was genuinely sorry to see them go. He stood on the deck of the *Flame* and watched their gigs creep away in the black winter night, while the pipe of the bo'sun's mate was calling the hands for the middle watch. It was piercing cold, especially after the warm stuffiness of the cabin, and he felt suddenly even more lonely than usual, maybe as a result. Here in the *Flame* he had only two watch-keeping officers, borrowed from the *Porta Coeli*; tomorrow he would borrow another from the *Nonsuch* or the *Camilla*. Tomorrow? That was today. And today perhaps Lebrun's attempt to gain control of Le Havre might be successful. Today he might be dead.

X

It was as misty as might be expected of that season and place when day broke, or rather when the grey light crept almost unnoticed into one's consciousness. The *Porta Coeli* was dimly visible, an almost unnoticeable denser nucleus in the fog. Hailing her at the top of his lungs, Hornblower received the faint reply that *Nonsuch* was in sight astern of her, and a few seconds later the additional information that *Camilla* was in sight of *Nonsuch*. He had his squadron in hand, then, and there was nothing to do but wait, and to ponder for the hundredth time over the question as to how the hands, barefooted with the icy water surging round their feet, could possibly bear their morning duty of washing down the decks.

But they were laughing and skylarking as they did it; the British seaman was of tough material. Presumably the lower deck guessed that there was something in the wind, that this concentration of force portended fresh action, and they found the prospect exhilarating. Partly, Hornblower knew, it was because they felt assured of success in the unknown enterprise before them. It must be amazingly pleasant to be able to put one's trust in a man and have no further doubts. Hornblower watched the men at work with envy as well as pity.

He himself was in a fever of anxiety, turning over in his mind the arrangements he had finally made with Lebrun before sending him ashore. They were simple enough; absurdly simple, it seemed to him now. The whole plan seemed a feeble thing with which to overturn an Empire that dominated Europe. Yet a conspiracy should be simple – the more elaborate the machinery the greater the chance of its breaking down. That was one reason why he had insisted on daylight for his part of the business. He had dreaded the possible mishaps if he had plunged ashore in darkness into an unknown town with his little army. Daylight doubled the chances of success while it doubled at least the possible loss in case of failure.

Hornblower looked at his watch – for the last ten minutes he had been fighting down the urge to look at it.

'Mr Crawley,' he said, to the master's mate who was his new first lieutenant in the *Flame*. 'Beat to quarters and clear the brig for action.'

The wind was a light air from the east, as he had expected. Fetching into Le Havre would be a ticklish business, and he was glad that he had resolved to lead in the small and hardy *Flame* so as to show the way to the ponderous old *Nonsuch*.

'Ship cleared for action, sir,' reported Crawley.

'Very good.'

Hornblower looked at his watch – it was fully a quarter-hour yet before he should move in. A hail to the *Porta Coeli* astern brought him the information that all the other vessels had cleared for action, and he smiled to himself. Freeman and Bush and Howard had no more been able to wait the time out than he had been.

'Remember, Mr Crawley,' he said, 'if I am killed as we go in, the *Flame* is to be laid alongside the quay. Captain Bush is to be informed as soon as possible, but the *Flame* is to go on.'

'Aye aye, sir,' said Crawley. 'I'll remember.'

Damn his eyes, he need not be so infernally ordinary about it. From the tone of Crawley's voice one might almost assume that he expected Hornblower to be killed. Hornblower turned away from him and walked the deck briskly to shake off the penetrating cold. He looked along at the men at their stations.

'Skylark, you men,' he ordered. 'Let's see how you can jump.'

There was no use going into action with men chilled to numbness. The men at the guns and waiting at the sheets began to caper at their posts.

'Jump, you men, jump!'

Hornblower leaped grotesquely up and down to set them an example; he wanted them thoroughly warmed up. He flapped his arms against his sides as he leaped, the epaulettes of the full-dress uniform he was wearing pounded on his shoulders.

'Higher than that! Higher!'

His legs were beginning to ache, and his breath came with difficulty, but he would not stop before the men did, although he soon came to regret the impulse which had made him start.

'Still!' he shouted at last, the monosyllable taking almost the last breath from his body. He stood panting, the men grinning.

'Horny for ever!' yelled an unidentifiable voice forward, and a ragged cheer came from the men.

'Silence!'

Brown was beside him with his pistols, a twinkle in his eye.

'Take that grin off your face!' snapped Hornblower.

There would be another Hornblower legend growing up in the Navy, similar to the one about the hornpipe danced on the deck of the *Lydia* during the pursuit of the *Natividad*. Hornblower pulled out his watch, and when he had replaced it took up his speaking-trumpet.

'Mr Freeman! I am going about on the other tack. Hail the squadron to tack in succession. Mr Crawley!'

'Sir!'

'Two hands at the lead, if you please.'

One man might be killed, and Hornblower wanted no possible cessation in the calling of soundings.

'Headsail sheets! Mains'l sheets!'

The *Flame* went about on the starboard tack, making about three knots under fore-and-aft sail in the light breeze. Hornblower saw the shadowy *Porta Coeli* follow the *Flame*'s example. Behind her, and invisible, was the old *Nonsuch* – Hornblower had still to set eyes on her since her arrival. He had not seen her, for that matter, since he quitted her to catch the typhus in Riga. Good old Bush. It gave Hornblower some comfort to think that he would be supported today by the *Nonsuch*'s thundering broadsides and Bush's stolid loyalty.

The leadsmen were already chanting the depths as the *Flame* felt her way up the fairway towards Le Havre. Hornblower wondered what was going on in the city, and then petulantly told himself that he would know soon enough. It seemed to him as if he could remember every single word of the long discussion he had had with Lebrun, when between them they had settled the details of Lebrun's harebrained scheme. They had taken into account the possibility of fog – any seaman would be a fool who did not do so in the Bay of the Seine in winter.

'Buoy on the starboard bow, sir,' reported Crawley.

That would mark the middle ground – it was the only buoy the French had left on the approaches to Le Havre. Hornblower watched it pass close alongside and then astern; the flowing tide was heeling it a little and piling up against the seaward side of it. They were nearing the entrance.

'Listen to me, you men,' said Hornblower, loudly. 'Not a shot is to be fired without my orders. The man who fires a gun, for no matter what reason, unless I tell him to, I will not merely flog. I'll hang him. Before sunset today he'll be at the yardarm. D'you hear me?'

Hornblower had every intention of executing his threat – at least at that moment – and as he looked round him his expression showed it. A few muttered Aye aye, sir's showed him he had been understood.

'*Qui va là?*' screamed a voice through the fog from close overside; Hornblower could just see the French boat which habitually rowed guard over the entrance in thick weather. The guard-boat, as Hornblower and Lebrun had agreed, would not be easily diverted from its duty.

'Despatches for M. le Baron Momas,' hailed Hornblower in return.

The confident voice, the fluent French, the use of Momas' name, might all gain time for the squadron to enter.

'What ship?'

It was inconceivable that the seamen in the guard-boat did not recognise the *Flame* – the question must be a merely rhetorical one asked while the puzzled officer in command collected his thoughts.

'British brig *Flame*,' called Hornblower; he had the helm put over at that moment to make the turn past the point.

'Heave-to, or I will fire into you!'

'If you fire, you will have the responsibility,' replied Hornblower. 'We bear despatches for Baron Momas.'

It was a fair wind now for the quay. The turn had brought the guard-boat alongside; Hornblower could see the officer standing up in the bows beside the bow-gun, a seaman at his shoulder with a glowing linstock in his hand. Hornblower's own full-dress uniform must be visible and cause some delay, too, for men expecting to fight would not be expected to wear full dress. He saw the officer give a violent start, having caught sight of the *Porta Coeli* looming up in the mist astern of the *Flame*. He saw the order given, saw the spark thrust on the touchhole. The three-pounder roared, and the shot crashed into the *Flame*'s side. That would give the alarm to the batteries at the point and above the quay.

'We do not fire back,' he hailed – maybe he could gain a little more time, and maybe that time would be of use, although he doubted it.

Here inside the harbour the mist was not so thick. He could see the shadowy shape of the quay rapidly defining itself. In the next few seconds he would know if this were a trap or not, if the batteries should open in a tempest of flame. One part of his mind raced through the data, while another part was working out how to approach the quay. He could not believe that Lebrun was playing a double game, but if it were so only he and the *Flame* would be lost – the other vessels would have a chance to get clear.

'Luff!' he said to the helmsman. There were a few busy seconds as he applied himself to the business of bringing the *Flame* alongside the quay as speedily as possible and yet without damaging her too severely. She came alongside with a creak and a clatter, the fenders groaning as if in agony. Hornblower sprang onto the bulwark and from there to the quay, sword, cocked hat, epaulettes and all. He could not spare time to look round, but he had no doubt that the *Porta Coeli* had anchored, ready to give assistance where necessary, and that the *Nonsuch* in her turn was nearing the quay, her marines drawn up ready for instant landing. He strode up the quay, his heart pounding. There was the first battery, the guns glaring through the embrasures. He could see movement behind the guns, and more men running to the battery from the guardhouse in the rear. Now he had reached the edge of the moat, his left hand held up in a gesture to restrain the men at the guns.

'Where is your officer?' he shouted.

There was a momentary delay, and then a young man in blue and red artillery uniform sprang upon the parapet.

'What do you want?' he asked.

'Tell your men not to fire,' said Hornblower. 'Have you not received your new orders?'

The full dress, the confident bearing, the extraordinary circumstances puzzled the young artillery officer.

'New orders?' he asked feebly.

Hornblower simulated exasperation.

'Get your men away from those guns,' he said. 'Otherwise there may be a deplorable accident.'

'But, monsieur—' The artillery lieutenant pointed down to the quay, and Hornblower now could spare the time to glance back, following the gesture. What he saw made his pounding heart pound harder yet for sheer pleasure. There was the *Nonsuch* against the quay, there was the *Camilla* just coming alongside; but more important yet, there was a big solid block of red coats forming up on the quay. One section with an officer at its head was already heading towards them at a quick step, muskets sloped.

'Send a messenger instantly to the other battery,' said Hornblower, 'to make sure the officer in command there understands.'

'But, monsieur—'

Hornblower stamped his foot with impatience. He could hear the rhythmic tread of the marines behind him, and he gesticulated to them with his hand behind his back. They marched along past him.

'Eyes left!' ordered the subaltern in command, with a smart salute to the French officer. The courtesy took what little wind was left out of the sails of the Frenchman, so that his new protest died on his lips. The marine detachment wheeled to its left round the flank of the battery on the very verge of its dry ditch. Hornblower did not dare take his eyes from the young Frenchman on the parapet, but he sensed what was going on in the rear of the battery. The sally-port there was open, and the marines marched in, still in column of fours, still with their muskets sloped. Now they were in among the guns, pushing the gunners away from their pieces, knocking the smouldering linstocks out of their hands. The young officer was wringing his hands with anxiety.

'All's well that ends well, monsieur,' said Hornblower. 'There might have been a most unpleasant incident.'

Now he could spare a moment to look round. Another marine detachment was off at the quickstep, marching for the other battery. Other parties, seamen and marines, were heading for the other strategic points he had listed in his orders. Brown was coming panting up the slope to be at his side.

The clatter of a horse's hoofs made him turn back again; a mounted French officer was galloping towards them, and reined up amid a shower of flying gravel.

'What is all this?' he demanded. 'What is happening?'

'The news apparently has been delayed in reaching you, monsieur,' said Hornblower. 'The greatest news France has known for twenty years.'

'What is it?'

'Bonaparte rules no more,' said Hornblower. 'Long live the King!'

Those were magic words; words like those of some old-time spell or incantation. No one in the length and breadth of the Empire had dared to say '*Vive le Roi!*' since 1792. The mounted officer's jaw dropped for a moment.

'It is false!' he cried, recovering himself. 'The Emperor reigns.'

He looked about him, gathering his reins into his hands, about to ride off.

'Stop him, Brown!' said Hornblower.

Brown took a stride forward, seized the officer's leg in his huge hands, and with a single heave threw him out of the saddle, Hornblower grabbing the bridle in time to prevent the horse from bolting. Brown ran round and extricated the fallen officer's feet from the stirrups.

'I have need of your horse, sir,' said Hornblower.

He got his foot into the stirrup and swung himself awkwardly up into the saddle. The excited brute plunged and almost threw him, but he squirmed back into the saddle, tugged the horse's head round, and then let him go in a wild gallop towards the other battery. His cocked hat flew from his head, his sword and his epaulettes jerked and pounded as he struggled to keep his seat. He tore past the other marine detachment, and heard them cheer him, and then he managed to rein in the frantic horse on the edge of the ditch. Struck with a new idea, he trotted round to the rear of the battery to the main gate.

'Open,' he shouted, 'in the name of the King!'

That was the word of power. There was a clatter of bolts and the upper half of the huge oaken door opened and a couple of startled faces looked out at him. Behind them he saw a musket levelled at him – someone who was a fanatical Bonapartist, probably, or someone too stolid to be taken in by appearances.

'Take that imbecile's musket away from him!' ordered Hornblower. The pressing need of the moment gave an edge to his tone, so that he was obeyed on the instant. 'Now, open the gate.'

He could hear the marines marching up towards him.

'Open the gate!' he roared.

They opened it, and Hornblower walked his horse forward into the battery.

There were twelve vast twenty-four-pounders mounted inside, pointing out through the embrasures down into the harbour. At the back stood the furnace for heating shot with a pyramid of balls beside it. If the two batteries had opened fire nothing hostile could have endured long on the water, and not merely the water but the quay and the waterfront could have been swept clean. And those batteries, with their parapets five feet thick and eight feet high, and their dry ditches, ten feet deep, cut square in the solid rock, could never have been stormed without regular siege methods. The bewildered gunners stared at him, and at the red-coated marines who came marching in behind him. A callow subaltern approached him.

'I do not understand this, sir,' he said. 'Who are you, and why did you say what you did?'

The subaltern could not bring himself to utter the word 'King'; it was a word that was taboo – he was like some old maid posing a delicate question to a doctor. Hornblower smiled at him, using all his self-control to conceal his exultation, for it would never do to triumph too openly.

'This is the beginning of a new age for France,' he said.

The sound of music came to his ears. Hornblower dismounted and left his horse free, and ran up the steps cut in the back of the parapet, the subaltern following. Standing on the top of the parapet with the vast arms of the semaphore over their heads, the whole panorama of the port was open to them; the squadron lying against the quay, the detachments of the landing party, red-coated or white-shirted, on the march hither and thither, and, on the quay itself, the marine band striding up towards the town, the drums thundering and the bugles braying, the red coats and the white crossbelts and the glittering instruments making a brave spectacle. That had been Hornblower's crowning idea; nothing would be more likely to convince a wavering garrison that he came in peace than a band calmly playing selections as it marched in.

The harbour defences were secured now; he had carried out his part of the scheme. Whatever had happened to Lebrun, the squadron was not in serious danger; if the main garrison had refused to be seduced, and turned against him, he could spike the batteries' guns, blow up the magazines, and warp his ships out almost at leisure, taking with him whatever prisoners and booty he could lay his hands on. The awkward moment had been when the guard-boat had fired its gun – firing is infectious. But the fact of only one shot being fired, the delay, the mist, had made the inexperienced officer in command at the batteries wait for orders, giving him time to use his personal influence. It was evident already that part of Lebrun's scheme, at least, had been successful. Lebrun had not made up his mind, at the time of his leaving the *Flame*, whether it would be a banquet or a council of war to which he would summon the senior officers, but whichever it was he had clearly succeeded in depriving the harbour defences of all direction. Apparently, too, Lebrun's story that a blockade runner was expected to arrive during the night and his request that the harbour defences should hold their fire until certain as to the identity of any ship entering the port, had had their effect as well – Lebrun had told Hornblower of his intention of making much of the fact that the *Flame*, on her way in to surrender, had actually been attacked so as to give the English the opportunity to recapture her.

'I will have no more muddles of that sort,' Lebrun had said, with a grin. 'Order, counter-order, disorder.'

One way and another he had certainly contrived to create such disorder and such an atmosphere of uncertainty in the batteries as to give Hornblower every chance – the man was a born intriguer; but Hornblower still did not know whether the rest of his *coup d'état* had succeeded. This was no time for delay; there were too many examples in history of promising enterprises brought to naught after a good beginning solely because someone did not push on at the psychological moment.

'Where is my horse?' said Hornblower, leaving the subaltern's

desire for information unsatisfied except by the vague statement that
a new age was beginning for France.

He climbed down from the parapet again, to find that an intelligent
marine was holding the horse's head. The redcoats were making a
ludicrous attempt to fraternise with the puzzled French recruits. Hornblower climbed up into the saddle, and trotted out into the open. He
wanted to make a bold push, but at the same time he felt nervous about
involving his landing party in the narrow streets of the town without
some assurance of a friendly reception there. Here came Howard,
riding gracefully; apparently he, too, had been able to procure himself
a horse.

'Any orders, sir?' Howard asked. Two midshipmen and Brown were
running beside him, the midshipmen presumably to act as messengers.

'Not yet,' answered Hornblower, fuming inwardly with anxiety while
trying to appear calm.

'Your hat, sir,' said the admirable Brown, who had picked the thing
up while on his way from the other battery.

Here came a horseman at a gallop, a white band on his arm, a white
handkerchief fluttering in his hand. He reined in when he saw Hornblower's gold lace.

'You are Monsieur – Monsieur—' he began.

'Hornblower.' No Frenchman had ever been able to pronounce that
name.

'From Baron Momas, sir. The citadel is secure. He is about to descend into the main square.'

'The soldiers in the barracks?'

'They are tranquil.'

'The main guard at the gate?'

'I do not know, sir.'

'Howard, take your reserve. March for the gate as hard as you can.
This man will go with you to explain to the guard. If they will not come
over, let them desert. They can march out into the open country – it
will not matter. No bloodshed if you can help it, but make sure of the
gate.'

'Aye aye, sir.'

Hornblower explained to the Frenchman what he had said.

'Brown, come with me. I shall be in the main square if needed,
Howard.'

It was not much of a procession Howard was able to form, two score
marines and seamen, but the band blared out as best it could as Hornblower marched triumphantly up the street. The people on the route
looked at them, curious or sullen or merely indifferent, but there was no
sign of active resentment. In the Place de l'Hôtel de Ville there was far
more bustle and life. Numerous men sat their horses there; a detach-

ment of police, drawn up in line, gave an appearance of respectability to the proceedings. But what caught the eye was the multitude of white emblems. There were white cockades in the hats of the gendarmes, and the mounted officials wore white scarves or armbands. White flags – bed sheets, apparently – hung from most of the windows. For the first time in more than twenty years the Bourbon white was being flaunted on the soil of France. A fat man on foot, a white sash round his belly where (Hornblower guessed) yesterday he had worn the tricolour, hurried towards him as he rode in. Hornblower signalled frantically to the band to stop, and scrambled down from the saddle, handing the reins to Brown as he advanced towards the man he guessed to be Momas.

'Our friend!' said Momas, his arms outspread. 'Our ally!'

Hornblower allowed himself to be embraced – even at that moment he wondered at what the leathernecks behind him would think about the sight of a commodore being kissed by a fat Frenchman – and then saluted the rest of the Mayor's staff as they came to greet him. Lebrun was at their head, grinning.

'A great moment, sir,' said the Mayor.

'A great moment indeed, Monsieur le Baron.'

The Mayor waved his hand towards the flagstaff that stood outside the Mairie.

'The ceremony is about to take place,' he said.

Lebrun was at his side with a paper, and Momas took it and mounted the steps at the foot of the flagstaff. He inflated his lungs and began to read at the top of his voice. It was curious how the French love of legal forms and appearances showed itself even here, at this moment of treason; the proclamation was studded with archaisms and seemed interminable in its prolixity. It mentioned the misdeeds of the usurper, Napoleon Bonaparte, it denounced all his pretensions to sovereignty, it disclaimed all allegiance to him. Instead it declared that all Frenchmen voluntarily recognised the unbroken reign of His Most Christian Majesty, Louis XVIII, King of France and Navarre. At those resounding words the men at the foot of the flagstaff hauled busily at the halliards, and the white standard of the Bourbons soared up the mast. It was time for a gesture on the part of the British. Hornblower turned to his men.

'Three cheers for the King!' he yelled.

He waved his cocked hat over his head.

'Hip – hip – hip—' he called.

'Hooray!' yelled the marines.

The cheer rang hollowly round the square; probably not one marine in ten had any idea as to which king he was cheering, but that did not matter.

'Hip – hip – hip—'

'Hooray!'

'Hip – hip – hip—'
'Hooray!'
Hornblower replaced his hat and stiffly saluted the white flag. Now it was time, and high time, to start organising the defence of the town against Bonaparte's wrath.

XI

'Your Excellency,' said Lebrun, sidling into the room where Hornblower sat at his desk, 'a fishermen's deputation has asked for an audience.'

'Yes?' said Hornblower. With Lebrun he was careful not to commit himself prematurely.

'I have endeavoured to discover what it is they seek, Your Excellency.'

Anyone could be quite sure that Lebrun would try to find things out. And so far Hornblower had carefully left Lebrun under the not unnatural illusion that he liked being addressed as 'Your Excellency' in every other sentence, and would be more malleable in consequence.

'Yes?'

'It is a question of one of their vessels being taken as a prize.'

'Yes?'

'It carried one of your certificates to the effect that the vessel was sailing from the free port of Le Havre, and yet an English ship of war took possession of her.'

'Indeed?'

What Lebrun did not know was that lying on the desk before him Hornblower had the report of the captain of the English brig which had made the capture. The captain was convinced that the vessel, before he took her, had just slipped out from Honfleur, across the estuary, having sold her catch there. Honfleur, being still under Bonaparte's rule, and under blockade in consequence, would pay three times as much for fish as could be obtained in liberated Le Havre. It was a question of trading with the enemy, and the Prize Court could be relied upon to adjudicate on the matter.

'We wish to retain the goodwill of the people, Your Excellency, especially of the maritime population. Could you not assure the deputation that the boat will be returned to its owners?'

Hornblower wondered how much the fishing-boat owners of the city had paid Lebrun to exert his influence on their behalf. Lebrun must be making the fortune he craved as much as he craved power.

'Bring the deputation in,' said Hornblower; he had a few seconds in which to compose his speech to them – that was always as well, because his French was deficient enough to make circumlocutions necessary when a word or a grammatical construction evaded him.

The deputation, three grey-haired Norman fishermen with an intense air of respectability and in their Sunday best, came in as near smiles as was possible to their solemn natures; Lebrun must have assured them in the anteroom of the certainty of their request being granted. They were quite taken aback when Hornblower addressed them on the subjects of trading with the enemy and its consequences. Hornblower pointed out that Le Havre was at war with Bonaparte, war to the death. Heads would fall in hundreds if Bonaparte should emerge victorious from this war and recapture Le Havre. The scenes of horror that had been witnessed when Toulon fell twenty years before would be reproduced a thousandfold in Le Havre. A united effort was still necessary to pull the tyrant down. Let them attend to that, and make no further attempt to increase their personal fortunes. Hornblower wound up by announcing not merely his intention of allowing the fishing-boat to come under the adjudication of the British Prize Court, but also his fixed determination, in the case of any repetition of the offence, to send officers and crew before a court martial whose sentence undoubtedly would be death.

Lebrun ushered the deputation out again. For a moment Hornblower wondered how Lebrun would explain the failure, but he had no time to wonder for more than a moment. The demands upon the time and energy of the Governor of Le Havre were enormous; Hornblower sighed as he looked at the papers stacked on his desk. There was so much to do; Saxton, the engineer officer just arrived from England, was clamouring to build a new battery, a demi-lune or a redan in his barbarous sapper vocabulary – to cover the defences of the Rouen Gate. All very well, but he would have to exact forced labour from the citizens to construct it. There was a mass of papers from Whitehall, mostly reports of spies regarding Bonaparte's strength and movements; he had skimmed through them, but one or two of them needed closer reading. There was the question of unloading the food ships which Whitehall had sent him – Le Havre should undoubtedly be well stocked with food in case of a close siege, but it was left to him to plan the warehousing of a thousand barrels of salt beef. There was the question of policing the streets. Old personal scores had been wiped out, Hornblower guessed, in the one or two murders of prominent Bonapartists – he even suspected Lebrun of having a hand in one of them – and there had already been some attempt at reprisal by secret assassination. He could run no risk, now that the city was under control, of allowing it to be divided against itself. The court martial was in progress of those mutineers of the *Flame* whom he had not pardoned. In every case the sentence would be death, inevitably, and there was food for thought in that. He was Commodore of the British Squadron as well as Governor of Le Havre, and there was all the manifold business of the squadron to be attended to. He must decide about—

Hornblower was already walking up and down. This vast room in the Hôtel de Ville was far better adapted for walking in than was any quarterdeck. He had had two weeks now to adapt himself to the absence of fresh air and wide horizons; his head was bent on his breast and his hands were clasped behind him as he paced, forming the decisions that were demanded of him. This was the reward of success; confinement in an office, chained to a desk; parcelling out his time among a dozen heads of departments and innumerable persons seeking favours. He might as well be a harassed City merchant instead of a naval officer, with the exception that as a naval officer he had the additional labour and responsibility of sending long daily reports to Whitehall. It may have been a great honour to be entrusted with the governorship of Le Havre, to head the attack upon Bonaparte, but it was onerous.

Here came another interruption; an elderly officer in a dark-green uniform waving a paper in his hand. This was – what was his name again? – Hau, a captain in the 60th Rifles. Nobody knew quite what his nationality was by this time; maybe he did not know himself. The 60th, since it had lost its title of Royal Americans, had become rather a depository for aliens in the service of the Crown. He apparently, before the French Revolution, had been a Court official of one of the innumerable little states on the French side of the Rhine. His master had been an exile for twenty years, his master's subjects had been Frenchmen for twenty years, and he himself had been for twenty years employed in odd duties by the British Government.

'The Foreign Office bag is in, sir,' said Hau, 'and this despatch was marked "urgent".'

Hornblower took his mind from the problem of nominating a new *juge de paix* (to take the place of the recent incumbent, who had apparently escaped to Bonapartist territory) to deal with the new problem.

'They're sending us a prince,' said Hornblower, having read the letter.

'Which one, sir?' asked Hau, with keen and immediate interest.

'The Duc d'Angoulême.'

'Eventual heir of the Bourbon line,' said Hau, judiciously. 'Eldest son of the Comte d'Artois, Louis' brother. By his mother he descends from the House of Savoy. And he married Marie Thérèse, the Prisoner of the Temple, daughter of the martyred Louis XVI. A good choice. He must be aged about forty now.'

Hornblower wondered vaguely what use a royal prince would be to him. It might sometimes be a convenience to have a figurehead, but he could foresee – Hornblower was labouring under all the burden of disillusionment – that the Duke's presence would much more often involve him in additional and unprofitable labours.

'He will arrive tomorrow if the wind is fair,' said Hau.

'And it is,' said Hornblower, looking out of the window at the flagstaff, where fluttered, side by side, the Union flag of England and the white flag of the Bourbons.

'He must be received with all the solemnity the occasion demands,' said Hau, dropping unconsciously into French through a fairly obvious association of ideas. 'A Bourbon prince setting foot on French soil for the first time in twenty years. At the quay he must be greeted by all the authorities. A royal salute. A procession to the church. Te Deum to be sung there. A procession to the Hôtel de Ville, and there a grand reception.'

'That is all your business,' said Hornblower.

The bitter cold of winter still persisted unbroken. Down on the quay, where Hornblower waited while the frigate bearing the Duke was being warped in, a cutting north-easterly wind was blowing, which pierced through the heavy cloak he was wearing. Hornblower was sorry for the seamen and the troops drawn up in line, and for the other seamen who manned the yards of the men-of-war in the harbour. He himself had only just come down from the Hôtel de Ville, staying there until the last moment when a messenger brought him the information that the Duke was about to land, but the dignitaries and minor officials grouped behind him had been assembled some time. It seemed to Hornblower that where he stood he could hear teeth chattering in unison.

He watched with professional interest the warping in of the frigate; he heard the clanking of the windlass and the sharp orders of the officers. Slowly she drew up to the quay. The side-boys and the bosun's mates came running up the gangway, followed by the officers in full dress. The marine guard of honour formed up. A brow was thrown from the gangway to the quay, and here came the Duke, a tall, stiff man in a Hussar uniform, a blue ribbon across his chest. In the ship the pipes of the bosun's mates twittered in a long call, the marines presented arms, the officers saluted.

'Step forward to greet His Royal Highness, sir,' prompted Hau at Hornblower's elbow.

There was a magic mid-point in the brow over which the Duke was walking; as he passed it he crossed from the British ship to the soil of France. Down came the French royal standard from the frigate's masthead. The pipes died away in one last ecstatic wail. The massed bands burst out in a triumphal march, the salutes began to roar, seamen and soldiers of the guard of honour presented arms after the fashion of two services and two nations. Hornblower found himself stepping forward, laying his cocked hat across his breast in the gesture he had painfully rehearsed under Hau's guidance that morning, and bowing to the representative of His Most Christian Majesty.

'Sir 'Oratio,' said the Duke cordially – for all his lifetime in exile apparently he still had a Frenchman's difficulty in dealing with aspirates. He looked round him. 'France, beautiful France.'

Anything less beautiful than the waterfront of Le Havre with a nor'easter blowing Hornblower could not imagine, but perhaps the Duke meant it, and, anyway, the words would sound well to posterity. Probably the Duke had been coached beforehand to say them, by the grave and uniformed dignitaries who followed him down the brow. One of these the Duke indicated as Monsieur – Hornblower did not catch the name – the *chevalier d'honneur*, and this gentleman in turn presented the equerry and the military secretary.

Out of the tail of his eye Hornblower saw the massed dignitaries behind him straightening themselves up from their concerted bow, their hats still across their stomachs.

'Cover yourselves, gentlemen, I beg of you,' said the Duke, and the grey hairs and the bald heads disappeared as the dignitaries gratefully shielded themselves from the wintry wind.

The Duke's teeth, too, apparently were chattering with cold. Hornblower darted a glance at Hau and at Lebrun, who were, with imperturbable politeness, elbowing each other to be nearest him and the Duke, and decided on the spot to cut down the further presentations to a bare minimum, ignoring the elaborate programme with which Hau and Lebrun had provided him. There would be no use in having a Bourbon prince sent him if he let him die of pneumonia. He had to present Momas, of course – the Baron's name would go down through history; and Bush, the senior naval officer – one of each country to mark the alliance between them, which was convenient, for Bush loved a lord, and royalty he adored. The Duke would be an important name on the list in Bush's memory headed by the Tsar of All the Russias. Hornblower turned and beckoned for the horses to be led up; the equerry hastened to hold the stirrup, and the Duke swung himself into the saddle, a born horseman like all his family. Hornblower mounted the quiet horse he had reserved for himself, and the others followed his example, a few of the civilians a little hampered by their unaccustomed swords. It was only a scant quarter of a mile to the church of Our Lady, and Lebrun had seen to it that every yard of it proclaimed a welcome to the Bourbons – there were white banners in every window, and a triumphal arch in fleurs-de-lis over the approach to the west portal of the church. But the cheers of the people in the street sounded thin in the cutting wind, and the procession could not have been very inspiring, with everybody hunched forward in self-protection.

The church offered them grateful shelter – like the figurative shelter she had to offer to all sinners, thought Hornblower, in a moment before he was engulfed in affairs again. He took his seat behind the Duke; in the tail of his eye he could see Lebrun, who was intentionally stationed there for Hornblower's benefit. By watching him Hornblower could see what had to be done, when to stand and when to kneel, for this was the first time he had ever been in a Catholic church or attended a Catholic ceremony. He was a little sorry that the activity of his mind prevented him from observing everything as closely as he would have liked. The vestments, the age-old ceremonial, might have appealed to him, but he was distracted by thoughts about what sort of pressure Lebrun had put on the officiating priests to get them to risk Bonaparte's wrath in this fashion, and by his wonderings about how much this scion of the Bourbons would wish to take a real part in the campaign, and about what was the exact significance of the reports which had begun to dribble in to the effect that at last Imperial troops were moving on Le Havre.

The incense and the warmth and his fatigue and the inconsequence of his thoughts made him drowsy; he was on the point of nodding off when he was roused by Lebrun's rising to his feet. He hastened to do the same, and the procession filed out of the church again.

From Notre Dame they rode up the Rue de Paris, scourged by the wind, and all round the grand square before dismounting again outside the Hôtel de Ville. The cheers of the people seemed thin and spiritless, and the wave of the hand or the lifting of the hat with which the Duke acknowledged them seemed wooden and mechanical. His Royal Highness possessed much of that stoical power to endure hardship in public without flinching which royalty must always display, but seemingly it had been acquired at the cost of making him silent and reserved. Hornblower wondered whether anything could be made of him, for under the Duke's nominal leadership Frenchmen would soon be shedding the blood of Frenchmen, or would be the moment Hornblower could be sure that he could trust the Bourbon partisans in action against the Bonapartists.

Hornblower watched him down the length of the great hall in the Hôtel de Ville – freezing cold, too, despite the fires which blazed at either end – as he greeted in turn the local dignitaries and their wives who were led up to him. The mechanical smile, the apt but formal phrase of greeting, the carefully graded courtesies, from the inclination of the head to the slight bow; all these indicated the care taken in his schooling. And clustered behind him and at his side were his advisers, the *émigré* nobles he had brought with him, Momas and Lebrun representing France since the revolution, Hau watching over British interests. No wonder the man acted like a wooden puppet, with all these people pulling the strings.

Hornblower saw the red noses and, above their gloves, the red elbows of the women shivering in the extreme *décolleté* of their Court gowns. Tradesmen's wives, petty officials' wives, badly dressed in clothes hurriedly run up that very day at the news that they were invited to the reception; some of the fat ones panted in corsets pulled tight, and some of the more slender ones tried to display the languorous uncorseted grace which had been fashionable ten years ago. They seethed with excitement at the prospect of meeting royalty. Their husbands caught some of the infection, and bustled about from group to group, but Hornblower knew of the anxiety that gnawed at them, the fear lest the monstrous power of Bonaparte should not be destroyed, lest a few days should find them stripped of their petty fortunes or their prospects of pensions, penniless exiles or victims of the guillotine. One reason why the Duke had come was to force these people to declare themselves openly for the Bourbon cause, and doubtless private hints from Lebrun had much to do with their appearance here. The doubts and the heart-aches were concealed – history later would only tell of the brilliant reception which signalled the arrival of a Bourbon prince on French soil. The Young Pretender's reception at Holyrood must have been full of similar undercurrents, Hornblower realised suddenly, whatever popular legend made of it nowadays. But, on the other hand, the Pretender's reception had not been graced by the scarlet of the marines and the blue and gold of the Navy.

Someone was twitching at his sleeve; there seemed to be warning in the touch, and Hornblower turned slowly to find Brown, soberly dressed in his best clothes, at his elbow.

'Colonel Dobbs sent me in to you, sir,' said Brown.

He spoke quietly, without looking directly at his captain, and without moving his lips more than was absolutely necessary. He neither wanted to call the attention of the company to his presence nor to give anyone an opportunity of hearing what he said.

'Well?' asked Hornblower.

'Despatch come in, sir, and Colonel Dobbs says he'd like you to see it, sir.'

'I'll come in a moment,' said Hornblower.

'Aye aye, sir.'

Brown sidled away; despite his bulk and height, he could be very unobtrusive when he wished. Hornblower waited long enough to make it appear unlikely that his own departure was connected with Brown's message, and then made his way out past the sentries at the door. He strode up the stairs two at a time to his office, where the red-coated marine colonel stood waiting for him.

'They're on their way at last, sir,' said Dobbs, handing over the message for Hornblower to read.

It was a long, narrow strip of paper, yet narrow as it was, it had been longitudinally folded as well as crossways; such a peculiar letter that Hornblower looked a question at Dobbs before reading it.

'It was folded up in a button on the messenger's coat, sir,' explained Dobbs. 'From an agent in Paris.'

Plenty of people in high position, Hornblower knew, were betraying their Imperial master, selling military and political secrets either for present gain or for future advancement. This letter must have been sent by someone of that sort.

'The messenger left Paris yesterday,' said Dobbs. 'He rode post to Honfleur, and crossed the river after dark today.'

The message was written by someone who knew his business.

'This morning,' it said, 'siege artillery left the artillery park at Sablons by river, going downstream. It included the 107th Regiment of Artillery. The guns were 24-pounders, and I believe there were 24 of them. Three companies of sappers and a company of miners were attached. It is said that General Quiot will command. I do not know what other forces he will have.'

There was no signature, and the handwriting was disguised.

'Is this genuine?' asked Hornblower.

'Yes, sir. Harrison says so. And it agrees with those other reports we've been receiving from Rouen.'

So Bonaparte, locked in a death struggle in eastern France with the Russians and the Prussians and the Austrians, fighting for his life in the south against Wellington, had yet contrived to scrape together a force to counter the new menace in the north. There could be no doubt against whom the siege artillery was destined to be used. Down the Seine from Paris his only enemies were the rebels in Le Havre; the presence of sappers and miners was a clear proof that a siege was intended, and that the guns were not merely intended to strengthen some land fortification. And Quiot had some two divisions mustering in Rouen.

The Seine offered Bonaparte every convenience for striking a blow at Le Havre. By water the heavy guns could be moved far more quickly than by road, especially by winter roads; even the troops, packed into barges, would travel faster than on their own feet. Night and day those barges would be towed downstream – by now they must already be nearing Rouen. It could be no more than a matter of a few days before Quiot closed in on the city. Hornblower went back in his mind to the last siege he had witnessed, that of Riga. He remembered the relentless way the approaches crept forward, the steady advance with gabion and fascine; within a few days it would be his responsibility to counter that deadly menace.

He felt a sudden gust of resentment against London for having left him so poorly supported; during the two weeks that Le Havre had been in British hands much might have been done. He had written as strongly as he dared on the inadvisability of an inactive policy – those were the very words he had used, he remembered – but England, with her whole army engaged under Wellington in the south, her lifeblood drained by twenty years of warfare, had little enough to spare for him. The rebellion he had instigated had been forced to remain a rebellion on the defensive, and as such only a minor military factor in the tremendous crisis. Politically and morally the effect of his action had been enormous, so they assured him, flatteringly, but the means were utterly wanting to reap any military harvest. Bonaparte, whose Empire was supposed to be tottering, who was fighting for his life on the snow-covered fields of Champagne, could still find two divisions and a siege-train to recapture Le Havre. Was it possible that man could ever be beaten?

Hornblower had forgotten the presence of the marine colonel; he looked past him into vacancy. It was time for the rebellion to cease the defensive, and to take the offensive, however limited its means, however powerful the enemy. Something must be done, something must be dared. He could not bear the thought of cowering behind the fortifications of Le Havre, like a rabbit in its burrow, waiting for Quiot and his sappers to come and ferret him out.

'Let me see that map again,' he said to Dobbs. 'How are the tides now? You don't know? Then find out, man, immediately. And I want a report on the roads between here and Rouen. Brown! Go and get Captain Bush out of the reception.'

He was still making plans and giving provisional orders, when Hau came into the room.

'The reception is ending, sir,' said Hau. 'His Royal Highness is about to retire.'

Hornblower cast one more look at the map of the lower Seine spread before him; his brain was seething, with calculations regarding tides and road distances.

'Oh, very well,' he said. 'I'll come for five minutes.'

He was smiling as he walked in – many eyes turned towards him and noticed it. It was a little ironical that the good people at the reception should feel reassured just because Hornblower had received news of the developing threat to their city.

XII

The murky winter day was giving place to murky night. There was little of the grey winter afternoon left as Hornblower stood on the quay watching the boats make ready. It was already dark enough and misty enough for the preparations to be invisible to anyone outside the town, whatever point of vantage he might have chosen for himself. So it was safe for the seamen and the marines to begin to man the boats; it was only an hour before the flood tide should begin, and no moment of the tide ought to be wasted.

This was another of the penalties of success; that he should have to stand here and watch others set off on an expedition that he would have loved to head. But the Governor of Le Havre, the Commodore, could not possibly risk his life and liberty with a petty sortie; the force he was sending out, crammed into half a dozen ships' longboats, was so small that he was hardly justified in putting a post captain in command.

Bush came stumping up to him, the thump of his wooden leg on the cobbles alternating with the flatter sound of his one shoe.

'No further orders, sir?' asked Bush.

'No, none. I only have to wish you the best of good fortune now,' said Hornblower.

He put out his hand, and Bush took it – amazing how Bush's hand remained hard and horny as if he still had to haul on braces and halliards. Bush's frank blue eyes looked into his.

'Thank you, sir,' said Bush, and then, after a moment's hesitation, 'Don't you go worrying about us, sir.'

'I won't worry with you in command, Bush.'

There was some truth in that. In all these years of close association Bush had learned his methods, and could be relied upon to execute a plan intelligently. Bush knew as well as he did now the value of surprise, the importance of striking swiftly and suddenly and unexpectedly, the necessity for close co-operation between all parts of the force.

The *Nonsuch*'s longboat was against the quay, and a detachment of marines was marching down into it. They sat stiff and awkward on the thwarts, their muskets pointing skywards between their knees, while the seamen held the boat off.

'All ready, sir?' piped up a voice from the sternsheets.

'Goodbye, Bush,' said Hornblower.

'Goodbye, sir.'

Bush's powerful arms swung him down into the longboat with no difficulty despite his wooden leg.

'Shove off.'

The boat pushed out from the quay; two other boats left the quay as well. There was still just enough light to see the rest of the flotilla pull away from the sides of the ships moored in the harbour. The sound of the orders came to Hornblower's ears across the water.

'Give way.'

Bush's boat swung round and headed the procession out into the river, and the night swallowed it. Yet Hornblower stood looking after them into the blackness for some time before he turned away. There could be no doubt at all, having regard to the state of the roads, and the reports of the spies, that Quiot would bring his siege-train as far as Caudebec by water – barges would carry his vast twenty-four-pounders fifty miles in a day, while over those muddy surfaces they would hardly move fifty miles in a week. At Caudebec there was an *estacade* with facilities for dealing with large cargoes. Quiot's advanced guards at Lillebonne and Bolbec would cover the unloading – so he would think. There was a good chance that boats, coming up the river in the darkness swiftly with the tide, might arrive unobserved at the *estacade*. The landing party could burn and destroy to their hearts' content in that case. Most likely Bonaparte's troops, which had conquered the land world, would not think of the possibility of an amphibious expedition striking by water round their flank; and even if they did think of it there was more than a chance that the expedition, moving rapidly on the tide, would break through the defence in the darkness as far as the barges. But though it was easy enough to form these comforting conclusions, it was not so easy to see them go off in the darkness like this. Hornblower turned away from the quay and began to walk up the dark Rue de Paris to the Hôtel de Ville. Half a dozen dimly perceived figures detached themselves from street corners and walked along a few yards in front and behind him; these were the bodyguards that Hau and Lebrun had detailed for him. They had both of them raised hands and eyes in horror at the thought that he should go about the town unescorted – on foot to make it worse – and when he had refused utterly to have a military guard permanently about him they had made this other arrangement. Hornblower aroused himself by walking as fast as his long thin legs would carry him. The exercise was pleasurable, and it made him smile to himself to hear the pattering of feet as his escort strove to keep pace with him; it was curious that nearly all of them were short-legged men.

In his bedroom there was a privacy to be obtained which he could not hope for elsewhere. He dismissed Brown as soon as the latter had lighted the candles in the stick on the night table at the bedhead, and with a grateful sigh he stretched himself out on the bed, careless of his uniform. He rose again to get his boat-cloak and spread it over himself, for the room was dank and cold despite the fire in the grate. Then at last he could take the newspaper from the top of the pile at the bedhead, and set himself to read seriously the marked passages at which previously he had merely glanced – Barbara had sent him those newspapers; her letter, read and reread, was in his pocket, but all through the day he had not found leisure for the papers.

If the Press was, as it claimed to be, the voice of the people, then the British public most strongly approved of him and his recent actions. It was strangely difficult for Hornblower to recapture the mood of only a few weeks back; the manifold distractions of his duties as Governor of Le Havre made the events preceding the capture of the city very blurred and indistinct in his memory. But here was *The Times* running over with praise for his handling of the situation in the Bay of the Seine. The measures he had taken to make it impossible for the mutineers to take the *Flame* in to the French authorities were described as 'a masterpiece of the ingenuity and skill which we have come to expect of this brilliant officer'. The pontifical manner of the article left Hornblower with the impression that it would have been more appropriate if the 'we' had been spelt with a capital W.

Here was the *Morning Chronicle* expiating on his capture of the *Flame* across the decks of the *Bonne Celestine*. There was only one example in history of a similar feat – Nelson's capture of the *San Josef* at Cape St Vincent. Hornblower's eyebrows rose as he read. The comparison was quite absurd. There had been nothing else for him to do; he had had only to fight the *Bonne Celestine*'s crew, for hardly a man in the *Flame*'s company had raised a hand to prevent the vessel's recapture. And it was nonsense to compare him with Nelson. Nelson had been brilliant, a man of lightning thought, the inspiration of all who came in contact with him. He himself was only a fortunate plodder by comparison. Extraordinary good fortune was the root of all his success; good fortune, and long thought, and the devotion of his subordinates. It was perfectly horrible that he should be compared with Nelson; horrible and indecent. As Hornblower read on he felt a disquieting sensation in his stomach, exactly as he felt during his first hours at sea after a spell on land, when the ship he was in slid down a wave. Now that this comparison with Nelson had been made the public and the service would judge his future actions by the same standard, and would turn and rend him in their disappointment should he fail. He had climbed high, and as a natural result there was a precipice at his feet. Hornblower remembered how he had felt as a king's letter-boy, when he had first climbed to the main-truck of the *Indefatigable*. The climbing had not been so difficult, not even the futtock-shrouds, but when at the masthead he had looked down he felt dizzy and nauseated, appalled at the distance below him – just as he felt now.

He flung the *Morning Chronicle* aside and took up the *Anti-Gallican*. The writer here gloated over the fate of the mutineers. He exulted over the death of Nathaniel Sweet, laying special stress on the fact that he had died at Hornblower's own hands. He went on to hope that Sweet's accessories in the horrible crime of mutiny would shortly meet the fate they deserved, and he hoped that the happy issue of Hornblower's recapture of the *Flame* would not be allowed to serve as an excuse for mercy or sentimental considerations. Hornblower, with twenty sentences of death awaiting his signature, felt his nausea renewed. This writer in the *Anti-Gallican* did not know what death was. Before Hornblower's eyes floated once more the memory of Sweet's white hair in the water as the smoke from the musket-shot drifted away. That old man – Chadwick had sworn to disrate him and then flog him. Hornblower decided for the twentieth time that he would have mutinied, too, if confronted with the certainty of a flogging. This writer knew nothing of the sickening crack of the cat-o'-nine-tails as it fell on a naked back. He could never have heard the yell of agony of a grown man under torment.

A later number of *The Times* discussed the capture of Le Havre. There were the words he had been dreading to read, but in Latin, as one might expect of *The Times*. *Initium finis* – the beginning of the end. *The Times* expected Bonaparte's dominion, which had endured all these years, to melt away in the next few days. The crossing of the Rhine, the fall of Le Havre, the declaration of Bordeaux in favour of the Bourbons, made the writer certain that Bonaparte would be dethroned immediately. Yet Bonaparte with a solid army was still striking back at his enemies today. The last reports told of his victories over the Prussians and the Austrians; Wellington in the south was making only the slowest progress against Soult. No one could foresee an immediate end to the war save this inky scribbler safe in some dusty office in Printing House Square.

But there was a morbid fascination about reading these newspapers. Hornblower put down this copy and reached for another, knowing as he did so that it would only disgust him or frighten him. It was as hard to resist as opium was to an addict. Hornblower read on and on through the marked passages, which dealt mainly with his own achievements, in much the same way that an old maid, by chance alone in her house on a wintry night, might go on reading one of Monk Lewis's terrifying novels, too frightened to stop, and yet knowing that every word she read would only make the stopping more frightening still.

He had hardly finished the pile of newspapers when he noticed the bed jar slightly under him and the candle-flames flicker for a moment. He paid almost no attention to the phenomenon – it might have been a heavy gun being fired, although he had not heard the explosion – but a few seconds later he heard the bedroom door stealthily opened. He looked up to see Brown peering round the corner at him to see if he were asleep.

'What do you want?' he snapped. His ill-temper was so obvious that even Brown hesitated to speak.

'Out with it,' snarled Hornblower. 'Why am I being disturbed contrary to my orders?'

Howard and Dobbs made their appearance behind Brown; it was to their credit that they were willing not merely to take the responsibility but to receive the first impact of the wrath of the Commodore.

'There's been an explosion, sir,' said Howard. 'We saw the flash of it in the sky, east by north of here – I took the bearing. That could be at Caudebec.'

'We felt the jar, sir,' said Dobbs. 'But there was no sound – too far away. A big explosion to shake us here and yet be unheard.'

That meant, almost for certain, that Bush had been successful. He must have captured the French powder-barges and blown them up. A thousand rounds for each of twenty-four twenty-four-pounders – the minimum for a siege; eight pounds of powder for each round. That would be eight times twenty-four thousand. That would be nearly two hundred thousand pounds. That would be almost a hundred tons. A hundred tons of gunpowder would make a fair explosion. Having computed his calculation, Hornblower refocused his eyes on Dobbs and Howard; until then he had looked at them without seeing them. Brown had tactfully slipped out from this council of his betters.

'Well?' said Hornblower.

'We thought you would like to know about it, sir,' said Dobbs, lamely.

'Quite right,' said Hornblower, and held up his newspaper between them again. Then he pulled it down again just long enough to say, 'Thank you.'

From behind his newspaper Hornblower heard his two staff officers creep out of the room and shut the door gently behind them. He was pleased with his performance; that final 'thank you' had been a masterly touch, conveying the impression that, even though he was loftily above such trifles as the mere destruction of a siege-train, he could yet remember his manners before his inferiors. Yet it was only a moment before he was sneering at himself for relishing such a petty triumph. He felt a sudden self-contempt, which even when it passed left him depressed and unhappy. The unhappiness had a special quality; Hornblower, laying aside his newspaper to look up at the play of shadows on the bedtester, suddenly realised he was lonely. He wanted company. He wanted friendship. Much more than that, he wanted comforting, he wanted affection, he wanted just what he could not have as Governor of this bleak, beleaguered city. He bore all the vast weight of responsibility, and he had no one to share his fears and hopes. Hornblower pulled himself up on the verge of an abyss of self-pity, his self-contempt greatly increased by the discovery. He had always been too self-analytical and too conscious of his own faults to be sorry for himself. His present loneliness was of his own making. He need not have been so gratuitously reserved with Dobbs and Howard; a sensible man would have shared their pleasure, would have sent for a bottle of champagne to celebrate the success, would have passed a pleasant hour or two with them – and would certainly have increased their pleasure and their loyalty by hinting that the success was largely due to their contributions to the plan, even though it was not true. For the ephemeral and extremely doubtful pleasure of showing himself to be what he was not, a man untouched by human emotions, he was now having to pay the present price of loneliness. Well, decided Hornblower, swallowing a decidedly bitter truth, it served him right.

He pulled out his watch; half an hour since the explosion, and the ebb tide had been running here at the river's mouth for a full hour longer than that. It must have turned some time ago at Caudebec; it was to be hoped that Bush and his flotilla were running down with it, exulting in their victory. Fully twenty-five miles by road, thirty at least by river, from their nearest enemies at Le Havre, the soldiers of the French siege-train must have thought themselves perfectly secure with an army of nearly twenty thousand men to protect them from an enemy who so far had shown no sign of taking the offensive. Yet in less than six hours, even in darkness, well-manned boats with the racing Seine tide behind them could span the interval that infantry would take two days – the daylight hours of two days – to cross. Boats could strike and escape again in the course of a single night up the broad and bridgeless river; and the fact that the river was broad and bridgeless would encourage Quiot's army to look upon the Seine as a protection to their flank and so to forget its potentialities as a highway for their enemies. Quiot had until recently commanded a division in the Imperial Guard, and never, in its ten victorious years, had the Imperial Guard taken part in an amphibious campaign.

Hornblower realised that he had been through all this train of thought before, many times over. He snuffed the guttered candles, looked at his watch again, and stretched his legs restlessly under his cloak. His hand fluttered tentatively towards the tumbled newspapers and was withdrawn immediately. Rather the unpalatable company of his own thoughts than that of *The Times* and the *Morning Chronicle*. Rather than either – humble pie, especially as it would be made a little more appetising by the knowledge that he would be doing his duty. He flung the cloak off his legs and rose to his feet. He went to some trouble to pull his coat into position, and he combed his hair with some care before sauntering out of his bedroom. The sentry at the door came to attention with a jerk – Hornblower guessed that he had been sleeping on his feet –

while Hornblower crossed the hall to the room beyond. He opened the
door into warm stuffiness. A single shaded candle hardly illuminated
the room enough for him to see. Dobbs was asleep in a chair at a table,
his head resting on his folded forearms; beyond the table lay Howard on
a cot. The shadow there was so dense that Hornblower could not see
his face, but he could hear his low, measured snores.

So nobody wanted his company after all. Hornblower withdrew and
shut the door quietly. Brown presumably was asleep in some cubbyhole
of his own; Hornblower toyed with the idea of sending for him and
having him make him a cup of coffee, but decided against it out of pure
humanity. He climbed back on to his own bed and dragged the cloak
over him. A whistling draught decided him to draw the curtains round
the bed, and he did so after extinguishing the candles. It occurred to
him that he would have been much more comfortable had he undressed
and got into the bed, but he could not face the effort – it suddenly became plain to him that he was very weary. His eyelids closed before the
solid darkness within the curtains, and he slept, fully dressed.

XIII

The fact that he had not taken off his clothes told Brown and Dobbs and
Howard at dawn that Hornblower had not been as composed and self-
confident as he had tried to appear, but not one of them was foolish
enough to comment on the fact. Brown merely opened the curtain and
made his report.

'Day just breaking, sir. Cold morning with a bit o' fog. The last o'
the ebb, sir, and no news as yet of Captain Bush an' the flotilla.'

'Right,' said Hornblower, getting stiffly to his feet. He yawned and
felt his bristling cheeks. He wished he knew how Bush had succeeded.
He wished he did not feel so unwashed and unclean. He wanted his
breakfast, but he wanted news of Bush even more. He was still deadly
tired despite his hours of unbroken sleep. Then he fought down his
weariness in a direct personal struggle like that of Christian with
Apollyon.

'Get me a bath, Brown. Make it ready while I shave.'

'Aye aye, sir.'

Hornblower stripped off his clothes and proceeded to shave himself
at the wash-hand-stand in the corner of the room. He kept his eyes from
his naked body reflected in the mirror, from his skinny, hairy legs and
slightly protuberant belly, as resolutely as he kept his mind from his

fatigue and from his anxiety about Bush. Brown and a marine private came in carrying the bath and put it on the floor near him; Hornblower, shaving carefully round the corners of his lips, heard the hot water being poured into it from buckets. It took a little while to compound the mixture in the right proportion so as to get the temperature suitable; Hornblower stepped into it and sank down with a sigh of satisfaction – an immense amount of water poured over the sides, displaced by his body, but he did not care. He thought about soaping himself, but flinched from the effort and the physical contortions necessary, and instead he lay back and allowed himself to soak and relax. He closed his eyes.

'Sir!'

Howard's voice caused him to reopen them.

'Two boats are in sight coming down the estuary, sir. Only two.'

Bush had taken seven boats with him to Caudebec. Hornblower could only wait for Howard to finish his report.

'One of 'em's *Camilla*'s launch, sir. I can recognise her through the glass. I don't think the other is from *Nonsuch*, but I can't be sure.'

'Very good, Captain. I'll join you in a moment.'

Ruin and destruction; five boats lost out of seven – and Bush lost too, seemingly. The destruction of the French siege-train – if it were destroyed – would be well worth the loss of the whole flotilla, to someone who could coldly balance profit and loss. But Bush gone! Hornblower could not bear the thought of it. He sprang from his bath and looked round for a towel. He saw none, and with exasperation tore a sheet from the bed on which to dry himself. Only when he was dry and seeking his clean shirt did he find the towels by the dressing-table where they should have been. He dressed hurriedly, and at every moment his fears and his sorrow on account of Bush increased – the first shock had not been nearly as severe as this growing realisation of his bereavement. He came out into the ante-room.

'One boat's coming into the quay, sir. I'll have the officer reporting here in fifteen minutes,' said Howard.

Brown was across the room at the far door. Now, if ever, Hornblower had the opportunity – his unaccountable brain recognised it at this moment – to show himself a man of iron. All he had to do was to say, 'My breakfast, Brown,' and sit down and eat it. But he could not pose, faced as he was by the possibility of Bush's death. It was all very well to do those things when it was merely a battle that lay before him, but this was the loss of his dearest friend. Brown must have read the expression on his face, for he withdrew without making any suggestion about breakfast. Hornblower stood undecided.

'I have the court-martial verdicts here for confirmation, sir,' said Howard, calling his attention to a mass of papers.

Hornblower sat down and picked one up, looked at it unseeing, and put it down again.

'I'll deal with later on,' he said.

'Cider's begun coming into the city from the country in great quantity, sir, now that the farmers have found it's a good market,' said Dobbs. 'Drunkenness among the men's increasing. Can we—?'

'I'll leave it to your judgment,' said Hornblower. 'Now. What is it you want to do?'

'I would submit, sir, that—'

The discussion lasted a few minutes. It led naturally to the vexed question of an established rate of exchange for British and French currency. But it could not dull the gnawing anxiety about Bush.

'Where the hell's that officer?' said Howard, petulantly pushing back his chair and going out of the room. He was back almost immediately.

'Mr Livingstone, sir,' he said. 'Third of *Camilla*.'

A middle-aged lieutenant, steady and reliable enough to outward appearance; Hornblower looked him over carefully as he came into the room.

'Make your report, please.'

'We went up the river without incident, sir. *Flame*'s boat went aground but was refloated directly. We could see the lights of Caudebec before we were challenged from the bank – we were just rounding the bend, then. Cap'n Bush's longboat was leading, sir.'

'Where was your boat?'

'Last in the line, sir. We went on without replying, as our orders said. I could see two barges anchored in midstream, an' clusters of others against the bank. I put the tiller over and ran beside the one farthest downstream, as my orders said, sir. There was a lot of musketry fire higher up, but only a few Frenchies where we were, an' we chased 'em away. On the bank where we were there were two twenty-four-pounders on travelling carriages. I had 'em spiked, and then we levered them off the bank into the river. One fell on to the barge underneath an' went through it, sir. It sank alongside my launch, deck just level with the water; just before the turn of the tide, that was. Don't know what she carried, sir, but I think she was light, judging by the height she rode out of the water when I boarded her. Her hatches were open.'

'Yes?'

'Then I led my party along the bank as ordered, sir. There was a lot of shot there, just landed from the next barge. The barge was only half unloaded. So I left a party to scuttle the barge and roll the shot into the river, an' went on myself with about fifteen men, sir. *Flame*'s boat's crew was there, an' the party they were fighting against ran away when we came on their flank. There were guns on shore and guns still in the barges, sir. We spiked 'em all, threw the ones that had been landed into the river, and scuttled the barges. There was no powder, sir. My orders were to blow the trunnions off the guns if I could, but I couldn't.'

'I understand.'

Guns spiked and pitched into the slime at the bottom of a rapid tidal river would be out of action for some time, even though it would have been better to blow off their trunnions and disable them permanently. And the shot at the bottom of the river would be difficult to recover. Hornblower could picture so well in his mind the fierce and bloody little struggle in the dark on the river bank.

'Just then we heard drums beating, sir, and a whole lot of soldiers came bearing down on us. A battalion of infantry, I should think it was – I think we had only been engaged up to then with the gunners an' sappers. My orders were to withdraw if opposed in force, so we ran back to the boats. We'd just shoved off and the soldiers were firing at us from the banks when the explosion came.'

Livingstone paused. His unshaven face was grey with fatigue, and when he mentioned the explosion his expression changed to one of helplessness.

'It was the powder-barges higher up the river, sir. I don't know who set them off. Maybe it was a shot from the shore. Maybe Cap'n Bush, sir—'

'You had not been in touch with Captain Bush since the attack began?'

'No, sir. He was at the other end of the line to me, and the barges were in two groups against the bank. I attacked one, an' Cap'n Bush attacked the other.'

'I understand. Go on about the explosion.'

'It was a big one, sir. It threw us all down. A big wave came an' swamped us, filled us to the gunnels, sir. I think we touched the bottom of the river, sir, after that wave went by. A bit of flying wreckage hit *Flame*'s boat. Gibbons, master's mate, was killed an' the boat smashed. We picked up the survivors while we bailed out. Nobody was firing at us from the bank any more, so I waited. It was just the top of the tide, sir. Presently two boats came down to us, *Camilla*'s second launch and the fishing-boat that the marines manned. We waited, but we could not see anything of *Nonsuch*'s boats. Mr Hake of the marines told me that Cap'n Bush an' the other three boats were all alongside the powder-barges when the explosion happened. Perhaps a shot went into the cargo, sir. Then they began to open fire on us from the bank again, and as senior officer I gave the order to retire.'

'Most likely you did right, Mr Livingstone. And then?'

'At the next bend they opened fire on us with field-pieces, sir. Their practice was bad in the dark, sir, but they hit and sank our second launch with almost their last shot, and we lost several more men – the current was running fast by tnen.'

That was clearly the end of Livingstone's story, but Hornblower could not dismiss him without one more word.

'But Captain Bush, Mr Livingstone? Can't you tell me any more about him?'

'No, sir. I'm sorry, sir. We didn't pick up a single survivor from the *Nonsuch*'s boats. Not one.'

'Oh, very well then, Mr Livingstone. You had better go and get some rest. I think you did very well.'

'Let me have your report in writing and list of casualties before the end of the day, Mr Livingstone,' interposed Dobbs – as Assistant-Adjutant-General he lived in an atmosphere of reports and lists of casualties.

'Aye aye, sir.'

Livingstone withdrew, and the door had hardly closed upon him before Hornblower regretted having let him go with such chary words of commendation. The operation had been brilliantly successful. Deprived of his siege-train and munitions, Quiot would not be able to besiege Le Havre, and it would probably be a long time before Bona-parte's War Ministry in Paris could scrape together another train. But the loss of Bush coloured all Hornblower's thoughts. He found himself wishing that he had never conceived the plan – he would rather have stood a siege here in Le Havre and have Bush alive at his side. It was hard to think of a world without Bush in it, of a future where he would never, never see Bush again. People would think the loss of a captain and a hundred and fifty men a small price to pay for robbing Quiot of all his offensive power, but people did not understand.

Dobbs and Howard were sitting glum and silent when he glanced at them; they respected his sorrow. But the sight of their deferential gloom roused Hornblower's contrariness. If they expected him to be upset and unable to work, he would show them how mistaken they were.

'I'll see those court-martial reports now, Captain Howard, if you please.'

The busy day's work began; it was possible to think clearly, to make decisions, to work as if nothing had happened, despite the feeling of of being drained dry by unhappiness. Not merely that; it was even possible to think of new plans.

'Go and find Hau,' he said to Howard. 'Tell him I'd like to see the Duke for a moment.'

'Aye aye, sir.' Howard rose to his feet. He allowed himself a grin and a twinkle as he pompously reworded Hornblower's language.

'Sir Horatio solicits the favour of a short audience with His Royal

Highness if His Royal Highness will be so kind as to condescend to receive him.'

'That's right,' said Hornblower, smiling in spite of himself. It was even possible to smile.

The Duke received him standing, warming the royal back before a cheerful fire.

'I do not know,' began Hornblower, 'if Your Royal Highness is acquainted with the circumstances which first brought me to the waters on this part of the coast.'

'Tell me about them,' said the Duke. Maybe it was not etiquette for royalty to admit ignorance on any subject. The Duke's attitude did not seem to convey a feeling of much interest in any case.

'There was a mutiny in one of His Majesty's – one of His Britannic Majesty's – ships of war.'

'Indeed?'

'I was sent to deal with it, and I succeeded in capturing the vessel and most of the mutineers, Your Royal Highness.'

'Excellent, excellent.'

'Some twenty of them were tried, convicted, and have now been sentenced to death.'

'Excellent.'

'I would be glad not to carry those sentences out, Your Royal Highness.'

'Indeed?' His Royal Highness was not apparently interested – a yawn seemed to be hesitating only just inside the royal lips.

'As far as my service is concerned, it is impossible for me to pardon the men without the gravest prejudice to discipline, Your Royal Highness.'

'Quite so. Quite so.'

'But if Your Royal Highness were to intervene on behalf of the men, I might then be able to pardon them without prejudice to discipline, being in a position where I can deny Your Royal Highness nothing.'

'And why should I intervene, Sir 'Oratio?'

Hornblower sidestepped the question for the moment.

'Your Royal Highness could take the stand that it would be unfitting that the opening days of the return of the Dynasty to France should be marred by the shedding of the blood of Englishmen, however guilty. It would then be possible for me to pardon them, with a great show of reluctance. Men tempted to mutiny in the future would not have their temptation greatly increased by the hope of a similar event saving them from the consequences of their actions – the world will never again be so fortunate as to see a return of Your Royal Highness's family to its legitimate position.'

This last was a clumsy compliment, clumsily worded and susceptible to misunderstanding, but luckily the Duke took it in the spirit in which it was ostensibly meant. Nevertheless, he hardly seemed enthusiastic; he went back to his original point with Bourbon stubbornness.

'But why *should* I do this, Sir 'Oratio?'

'In the name of common humanity, Your Royal Highness. There are twenty lives to be saved, the lives of useful men.'

'Useful men? Mutineers? Presumably Jacobins, revolutionaries, equalitarians – even Socialists!'

'They are men who lie in irons today and expect to be hanged tomorrow, Your Royal Highness.'

'As I have no doubt whatever, they deserve, Sir 'Oratio. It would be a fine beginning to the Regency with which His Most Christian Majesty has entrusted me if my first public act should be to solicit the lives of a parcel of revolutionaries. His Most Christian Majesty has not spent the past twenty-one years combating the spirit of revolution for that. The eyes of the world are upon me.'

'I have never yet known the world offended by an act of clemency, Your Royal Highness.'

'You have strange ideas of clemency, sir. It appears to me as if this remarkable suggestion of yours has some purpose other than is apparent. Perhaps you are a Liberal yourself, one of these dangerous men who consider themselves thinkers. It would be a good stroke of policy for you to induce my family to brand itself by its first act as willing to condone revolution.'

The monstrous imputation took Hornblower completely aback.

'Sir!' he spluttered. 'Your Royal Highness—'

Even if he had been speaking in English words would have failed him. In French he was utterly helpless. It was not merely the insult, but it was the revelation of the Bourbon narrow-mindedness and suspicious cunning that helped to strike him dumb.

'I do not see fit to accede to your request, sir,' said the Duke, his hand on the bellrope.

Outside the audience chamber Hornblower strode past courtiers and sentries, his cheeks burning. He was blind with fury – it was very rarely that he was as angry as this; nearly always his tendency to look at both sides of a question kept him equable and easy-going; weak, he phrased it to himself in moment of self-contempt. He stamped into his office, flung himself into his chair and sprang up from it again a second later, walked round the room and sat down again. Dobbs and Howard looked with astonishment at the thundercloud on his brow, and after their first glance bent their gaze studiously upon the papers before them. Hornblower tore open his neckcloth. He ripped open the buttons of his waistcoat, and the dangerous pressure within began to subside. His mind was in a maelstrom of activity, but over the waves of thought, like a beam of sunshine through a squall at sea, came a gleam of amusement at his own fury. With no softening of his resolution his mischievous sense of humour began to assert itself; it only took a few minutes for him to decide on his next action.

'I want those French fellows brought in here who came with the Duke,' he announced. 'The equerry, and the *chevalier d'honneur*, and the almoner. Colonel Dobbs, I'll trouble you to make ready to write from my dictation.'

The *émigré* advisers of the Duke filed into the room a little puzzled and apprehensive; Hornblower received them still sitting, in fact almost lounging back in his chair.

'Good morning, gentlemen,' he said, cheerfully. 'I have asked you to come to hear the letter I am about to dictate to the Prime Minister. I think you understand English well enough to get the gist of the letter. Are you ready, Colonel?

"To the Right Honourable Lord Liverpoool.

My Lord, I find I am compelled to send back to England His Royal Highness the Duc d'Angoulême".'

'Sir!' said the astonished equerry, breaking in, but Hornblower waved him impatiently to silence.

'Go on, Colonel, please.

"I regret to have to inform Your Lordship that His Royal Highness has not displayed the helpful spirit the British nation is entitled to look for in an ally".'

The equerry and the *chevalier d'honneur* and the almoner were on their feet by now. Howard was goggling at him across the room; Dobbs' face was invisible as he bent over his pen, but the back of his neck was a warm purple which clashed with the scarlet of his tunic.

'Please go on, Colonel.

"During the few days in which I have had the honour of working with His Royal Highness, it has been made plain to me that His Royal Highness has neither the tact nor the administrative ability desirable in one in so high a station".'

'Sir!' said the equerry. 'You cannot send that letter.'

He spoke first in French and then in English; the *chevalier d'honneur* and the almoner made bilingual noises of agreement.

'No?' said Hornblower.

'And you cannot send His Royal Highness back to England. You cannot! You cannot!'

'No?' said Hornblower again, leaning back in his chair.

The protests died away on the lips of the three Frenchmen. They knew as well as Hornblower, as soon as they were forced to realise the unpalatable truth, who it was that held the power in Le Havre. It was the man who had under his command the only disciplined and reliable military force, the man who had only to give the word to abandon the city to the wrath of Bonaparte, the man at whose word the ships came in and went out again.

'Don't tell me,' said Hornblower with elaborate concern, 'that His Royal Highness would physically oppose an order from me consigning him on board a ship? Have you gentlemen ever witnessed a deserter being brought in? The frog-march is a most undignified method of progression. Painful, too, I am informed.'

'But that letter,' said the equerry, 'would discredit His Royal Highness in the eyes of the world. It would be a most serious blow to the cause of the Family. It might endanger the succession.'

'I was aware of that when I invited you gentlemen to hear me dictate it.'

'You would never send it,' said the equerry with a momentary doubt regarding Hornblower's strength of will.

'I can only assure you gentlemen that I both can and will.'

Eyes met eyes across the room, and the equerry's doubt vanished. Hornblower's mind was entirely made up.

'Perhaps, sir,' said the equerry, clearing his throat and looking sidelong at his colleagues for their approval, 'there has been some misunderstanding. If His Royal Highness has refused some request of Your Excellency's, as I gather has been the case, it must have been because His Royal Highness did not know how much importance Your Excellency attached to the matter. If Your Excellency would allow us to make further representations to His Royal Highness—'

Hornblower was looking at Howard, who very intelligently recognised his cue.

'Yes, sir,' said Howard. 'I'm sure His Royal Highness will understand.'

Dobbs looked up from his paper and made corroborative sounds. But it took several minutes before Hornblower could be persuaded to postpone putting his decision into instant effect. It was only with the greatest reluctance that he yielded to the pleadings of his own staff and the Duke's. After the equerry had led his colleagues from the room to seek the Duke, Hornblower sat back with a real relaxation replacing the one he had simulated. He was tingling and glowing both with the after effects of excitement and with his diplomatic victory.

'His Royal Highness will see reason,' said Dobbs.

'No doubt about it,' agreed Howard, judiciously.

Hornblower thought of the twenty seamen chained in the hold of the *Nonsuch* expecting to be hanged tomorrow.

'An idea has struck me, sir,' said Howard. 'I can send a flag of truce out to the French forces. A *parlementaire* – a mounted officer with a white flag and a trumpeter. He can carry a letter from you to General Quiot, asking for news about Captain Bush. If Quiot knows anything at all I'm sure he'll have the courtesy to inform you, sir.'

Bush! In the excitement of the last hour Hornblower had forgotten about Bush. His pleasurable excitement escaped from him like grain from a ripped sack. Depression closed in upon him again. The others saw the change that came over him; as an example of the affection for him which he had inspired in this short time of contact it is worthy of mention that they would rather have seen the black thundercloud of rage on his brow than this wounded unhappiness.

XIV

It was the day that the *parlementaire* returned; Hornblower would always remember it for that reason. Quiot's courteous letter left no ground for hope whatever; the gruesome details which it included told the whole story. A few rags and tatters of men had been found and had been buried, but nothing that could be identified as any individual. Bush was dead; that burly body of his had been torn into shreds by the explosion. Hornblower was angry with himself for allowing the fact that Bush's grave would never be marked, that his remains were utterly destroyed, to increase his sadness. If Bush had been given a choice, he presumably would have chosen to die at sea, struck down by a shot in the moment of victory at the climax of a ship-to-ship action; he would have wished to have been buried in his hammock, round-shot at his feet and head, with seamen weeping as the grating tilted and the hammock slid from under the flag into the sea and the ship rocked on the waves, hove-to with backed topsails. It was a horrid irony that he should have met his end in a minor skirmish on a river bank, blown into bloody unidentifiable rags.

And yet what did it matter how he died? One moment he had been alive and the next dead, and in that he had been fortunate. It was a far greater irony that he should have been killed now, after surviving twenty years of desperate warfare. Peace was only just over the horizon, with the allied armies closing in on Paris, with France fast bleeding to death, with the allied Governments already assembling to decide on the peace terms. Had Bush survived this one last skirmish, he would have been able to enjoy the blessings of peace for many years, secure in his captain's rank, in his pension, in the devotion of his sisters. Bush would have enjoyed all that, if only because he knew that all sensible men enjoyed peace and security. The thought of that only increased Hornblower's feeling of bitter personal loss. He had never thought he could mourn for anyone as he mourned for Bush.

The *parlementaire* had only just returned with Quiot's letter; Dobbs was still eagerly questioning him about what he had been able to observe of the condition of the French forces, when Howard came rapidly in.

'*Gazelle*, sloop of war, just entering the harbour, sir. She is wearing the Bourbon flag at the main and makes this signal, sir. "Have on board Duchess of Angoulême".'

'She has?' said Hornblower. His spirit climbed wearily out of its miserable lethargy. 'Tell the Duke. Let Hau know and tell him to arrange about salutes. I must meet her on the quay along with the Duke. Brown! Brown! My dress coat and my sword.'

It was a watery day with a promise of early spring. The *Gazelle* came warping against the quay, and the salutes rolled round the harbour just as they had done when His Royal Highness arrived. The Duke and his entourage stood in almost military formation on the quay; upon the deck of the *Gazelle* was gathered a group of women in cloaks awaiting the casting of the brow across to the quay. Bourbon court etiquette seemed to dictate a rigid absence of any appearance of excitement; Hornblower, standing with his staff a little to the rear and to the side of the Duke's party, noted how the women on deck and the men on the quay made no signal of welcome to each other. Except for one woman, who was standing by the mizzenmast waving a handkerchief. It was something of a comfort to see that there was at least one person who refused to be bound by stoical etiquette; Hornblower supposed that it must be some serving-woman or lady's maid who had caught sight of her lover in the ranks on the quay.

Over the brow came the Duchess and her suite; the Duke took the regulation steps forward to greet her. She went down in the regulation curtsy, and he lifted her up with the regulation condescension, and they put cheek to cheek in the regulation embrace. Now Hornblower had to come forward to be presented, and now he was bowing to kiss the gloved hand laid upon his levelled forearm.

'Sir 'Oratio! Sir 'Oratio!' said the Duchess.

Hornblower looked up to meet the blue Bourbon eyes. The Duchess was a beautiful woman of some thirty years of age. She had something urgent to say, obviously. As if tongue-tied, she was unable to say it, the rules of etiquette making no allowance for this situation. Finally she made a frantic gesture, and looked round her to call Hornblower's attention to someone behind her. A woman stood there, standing alone, separated a little from the group of ladies-in-waiting and *dames d'honneur*. It was Barbara – Hornblower had to look twice before he could believe his eyes. She stepped towards him, smiling. Hornblower took two strides towards her – in the midst of them he thought briefly of the necessity of not turning his back upon royalty, but threw discretion to the winds – and she was in his arms. There was a tumult of thoughts in his mind as she put her lips, icy cold from the sea air, against his. It was sensible enough that she had come, he supposed, although he had always strongly disapproved of captains and admirals who had their wives with them on active service. As the Duchess had come it would be quite desirable to have Barbara here as well. All this in a flash, before more human feelings became apparent. A warning cough from Hau behind him told him that he was holding up the proceedings, and he hastily took his hands from Barbara's shoulders and stepped back a little sheepishly. The carriages were waiting.

'You go with the royal pair, sir,' whispered Hau, hoarsely.

The carriages requisitioned in Le Havre were not striking examples of coach-building, but they served. The Duke and Duchess were seated, and Hornblower handed Barbara in and took his seat beside her, his back and hers to the horses. With a clatter of hoofs and a generous squeaking they set off up the Rue de Paris.

'Was that not a pleasant surprise, Sir 'Oratio?' asked the Duchess.

'Your Royal Highness was far too kind,' said Hornblower.

The Duchess leaned forward and put her hand on Barbara's knee.

'You have a most beautiful and most accomplished wife,' she said.

The Duke beside her uncrossed his knees and coughed uncomfortably, for the Duchess was acting with a condescension a trifle excessive in a king's daughter, a future queen of France.

'I trust you had a comfortable voyage,' said the Duke, addressing himself to his wife; a mischievous curiosity prompted Hornblower to wonder if there was ever a moment when he did not use a tone of such rigid formality towards her.

'We will pass over the memory of it,' said the Duchess with a laugh.

She was a high-spirited and lovely creature, and running over with excitement at his new adventure. Hornblower watched her curiously. Her infancy had been passed as a princess in the most splendid Court of Europe; her childhood as a prisoner of the revolutionaries. Her father and mother, the king and queen, had died under the guillotine; her brother had died in prison. She herself had been exchanged for a parcel of captive generals, and married to her cousin, had wandered through Europe as the wife of the heir to a penniless but haughty Pretender. Her experiences had left her human – or was it that formalities of shabby-genteel royalty had not succeeded in dehumanising her? She was the only living child of Marie Antoinette, whose charm and vivacity and indiscretion had been proverbial. That might explain it.

Here they were, climbing out of the carriage at the Hôtel de Ville; a naval cocked hat was a clumsy thing to keep under the arm while handing ladies out. There was to be a reception later, but time must be allowed for the Duchess's trunks to be swayed up out of the *Gazelle*'s hold, and for the Duchess to change her dress. Hornblower found himself leading Barbara to the wing which constituted his headquarters. In the lobby orderlies and sentries came to attention; in the main office Dobbs and Howard gaped at the spectacle of the Governor ushering in a lady. They scrambled to their feet and Hornblower made the presentations. They bowed and scraped to her; they knew of her, of course – everyone had heard about Lady Barbara Hornblower, the Duke of Wellington's sister.

Glancing automatically at his desk, Hornblower caught sight of Quiot's letter lying there where he had left it, with its beautiful handwriting and elaborate signature and paraph. It reminded him once more that Bush was dead. *That* sorrow was real, acute, actual; Barbara's coming had been so unexpected that it was not real to him yet. That fantastic mind of his refused to dwell on the central point that Barbara was once more with him, but flew off at ridiculous tangents. It liked its details well ordered, and insisted on them; it would not let him sink into simple luxurious happiness, but rather chose to work on the practical details – never thought of until that time – of the arrangement of the life of an officer on active service, who, while locked in a death grapple with an Emperor, yet had a wife to think about. Many-sided Hornblower may have been, but the mainspring of his life was his professional duty. For more than twenty years, for all his adult life, he had been accustomed to sacrifice himself for that, to such an extent and for so long that the sacrifice now was automatic and usually ungrudging. He was so set on his struggle with Bonaparte and had been plunged so deep into it during the last months that he was inclined to resent distractions.

'This way, dear,' he said, at length, a little hoarsely – he was about to clear his throat when he checked himself. The need for throat-clearing was a sure symptom of nervousness and shyness. Barbara had lightly teased him out of it years ago, and he would not clear his throat now, not in front of Barbara, not in front of himself.

They crossed the little ante-room and Hornblower threw open the door into the bedroom, standing aside for Barbara to pass through, and then he entered after her and shut the door. Barbara was standing in the centre of the floor, her back to the foot of the big bed. There was a smile on one side of her mouth; one eyebrow was raised above the other. She raised one hand to unfasten the clasp of her cloak, but let it drop again, its work uncompleted. She did not know whether to laugh or to cry over this incalculable husband of hers; but she was a Wellesley, and pride forbade her to weep. She stiffened herself just one second before Hornblower came forward to her one second too late.

'Dear,' he said, and took her cold hands.

She smiled at him in return, but there could have been more tenderness in her smile, light and playful though it was.

'You are pleased to see me?' she asked; she kept her tone light, and kept her anxiety out of it.

'Of course. Of course, dear.' Hornblower tried to make himself human, fighting down the instinctive impulse to withdraw into himself that was roused when his telepathic sensitivity warned him of danger. 'I can hardly believe yet that you *are* here, dear.'

That was the truth, heartfelt, and to say it was a relief, easing some of his tension. He took her into his arms and they kissed; tears were stinging her eyes when their lips parted again.

'Castlereagh decided the Duchess should come here, just before he left for Allied Headquarters,' she explained. 'So I asked if I could come too.'

'I'm glad you did,' said Hornblower.

'Castlereagh calls her the only man in the whole Bourbon family.'

'I shouldn't be surprised if that were true.'

They were warming to each other now; two proud people, learning anew the sacrifice each had to make to admit to the other their mutual need of each other. They kissed again, and Hornblower felt her body relaxing under his hands. Then came a knocking at the door, and they drew apart. It was Brown, supervising the work of a half-dozen seamen dragging in Barbara's trunks. Hebe, Barbara's little Negro maid, hovered on the threshold before coming in with the baggage. Barbara walked over to the mirror and began to take off her hat and cloak before it.

'Little Richard,' she said, in a conversational tone, 'is very well and happy. He talks unceasingly, and he still digs. His particular corner of the shrubbery looks as if an army of badgers had been at work. In that trunk I have some drawings of his that I kept for you – although one can hardly say they display any noticeably artistic ability.'

'I'd be astonished if they did,' said Hornblower, sitting down.

'Easy with that there portmanteau,' said Brown to one of the seamen. 'That's no barrel o' beef you're handling. Handsomely, now. Where shall we put her ladyship's trunk, sir?'

'Leave it against the wall there, Brown, if you please,' said Barbara. 'Here are the keys, Hebe.'

It seemed quite fantastic and unnatural to be sitting here watching Barbara at the mirror, watching Hebe unpack the baggage, here in a city of which he was military governor. Hornblower's masculine narrow-mindedness was disquieted by the situation. Twenty years of life at sea had made his lines of thought a little rigid. There should be a time and a place for everything.

A little squeal came from Hebe, instantly suppressed; Hornblower,

looking round, caught a rapid interchange of glances between Brown
and the seaman – the latter, seemingly, had no such views about time
and place and had taken a sly pinch at Hebe. Brown could be trusted to
deal with the seaman; it was not a matter in which it was consonant with
the dignity of a commodore and a governor to interfere. And Brown had
hardly taken his working party away when a succession of knocks at the
door heralded a procession of callers. An equerry came in, bearing the
royal command that at dinner tonight the company should be in full
dress with powder. Hornblower stamped with rage at that; he had not
floured his head more than three times in his life, and he felt ridiculous
when he did. Immediately afterwards came Hau, his mind beset with
the same problems, in a different guise, as were disturbing Hornblower.
Under what authority should he issue rations to Lady Barbara and
Lady Barbara's maid? Where should the latter be quartered? Hornblower
drove him forth with orders to read the regulations for himself and discover his own legal formulas; Barbara, coolly straightening her ostrich
feathers, told him that Hebe would sleep in the dressing-room opening
from this bedroom. Next came Dobbs; he had read through the despatches brought by *Gazelle*, and there were some which Hornblower
should see. Moreover, there were certain papers which needed the
Governor's attention. A packet was sailing tonight. And the night orders
certainly needed the Governor's signature. And—'

'All right, I'll come,' said Hornblower. 'Forgive me, my dear.'

'Boney's been beaten again,' said Dobbs, gleefully, the moment they
were out of the bedroom. 'The Prussians have taken Soissons and cut
up two of Boney's army corps. But that's not all.'

By now they were in the office and Dobbs produced another despatch
for Hornblower's perusal.

'London's going to put some force at our disposal at last, sir,' explained Dobbs. 'The militia have begun to volunteer for foreign service
– now that the war's nearly over – and we can have as many battalions
as we want. This should be answered by tonight's packet, sir.'

Hornblower tried to shake from his mind thoughts about hair powder,
about Hebe's amorous proclivities, to deal with this new problem regarding the launching of a campaign up the Seine valley against Paris.
What did he know about the military capacity of the militia? He would
have to have a general to command them, who would certainly be senior
in rank to himself. What was the law regarding seniority as between a
governor appointed by letters-patent and officers commanding troops?
He ought to know, but it was not easy to remember the wording. He
read the despatch through once without comprehending a word of it
and had to apply himself to it again seriously from the beginning. He
put aside the temptation that momentarily assailed him, to throw the
despatch down and tell Dobbs to act according to his own judgment;

mastering himself, he began soberly to dictate his reply. As he warmed to his work he had to restrain himself so as to give Dobbs' flying pen a chance to keep up with him.

When it was all done, and he had dashed off his signature on a dozen documents, he went back to the bedroom. Barbara was before the mirror, looking herself over in a white brocade gown, feathers in her hair and jewels at her throat and ears; Hebe was standing by her with the train ready to attach. Hornblower stopped short at sight of Barbara, lovely and dignified, but it was not only her distinguished appearance that checked him. It was also the sudden realisation that he could not have Brown in to help him dress, not here. He could not exchange his trousers for breeches and stockings with Barbara and Hebe and Brown all present. He made his apologies, for Brown, aware by his usual sixth sense that Hornblower had finished his office work, was already tapping at the door. They gathered up whatever they thought they might need and went into the dressing-room – even here women's perfumes were instantly noticeable – and Hornblower began hurriedly to dress. The breeches and stockings, the gold-embroidered sword-belt. Brown had already, as might have been expected, found a woman in the town who could starch neckcloths admirably, stiff enough to retain their curves when folded, and yet soft enough not to snap in the bending. Brown hung a dressing-gown over Hornblower's shoulders, and Hornblower sat with his head lowered while Brown plied the flour-dredger and comb. When he straightened up and looked in the mirror he felt a sneaking pleasure at the result. He had allowed what was left of his curls to grow long lately, simply because he had been too busy to have his hair cropped, and Brown had combed the snow-white mop to the best advantage so that no trace of bare scalp was visible. The powdered hair set off his weather-beaten face and brown eyes admirably. The cheeks were a little hollow and the eyes a little melancholy, but it was by no means the face of an old man, so that the white hair made a most effective contrast, giving him the youthful appearance and calling that attention to his personality which presumably the fashion had in mind when it began. The blue and gold of the uniform, the white of neckcloth and powder, the ribbon of the Bath and the glittering star set him off as a very personable figure. He could wish he had more calf inside the stockings; that was the only fault he could find with his appearance. He made sure that his belt and sword were properly adjusted, put his hat under his arm, picked up his gloves, and went back into the bedroom, remembering in the nick of time to pound on the door before he turned the handle.

Barbara was ready; stately, almost like a statue, in her white brocade. The likeness to a statue was something more than what a casual simile implied; Hornblower remembered a statue of Diana that he had seen somewhere – was it Diana? – with the end of her robe caught up over her left arm exactly the way Barbara was carrying her train. Her powdered hair made her face seem a little cold in its expression, for the style did not suit her colouring and features. A glance at it reminded Hornblower of Diana again. She smiled when she saw him.

'The handsomest man in the British Navy,' she said.

He gave her a clumsy bow in return.

'I only wish I were worthy of my lady,' he said.

She took his arm and stood beside him in front of the mirror. Because of her height her feathers overtopped him; she flicked open her fan with an effective gesture.

'How do you think we look?' she asked.

'As I said,' repeated Hornblower, 'I only wish I were worthy of you.'

Brown and Hebe were gaping at them behind them, as he could see in the mirror, and Barbara's reflection smiled at him.

'We must go,' she said, with a pressure upon his arm. 'It would never do to keep Monseigneur waiting.'

They had to walk from one end of the Hôtel de Ville to the other, through corridors and ante-rooms filled with a multitude dressed in every type of uniform – it was a curious chance that had made this not very distinguished building a seat of government, the palace of a regent, the headquarters of an invading army, and the flagship of a squadron, too, for that matter, all at the same time. People saluted and drew aside respectfully against the walls as they went by – Hornblower had a clear notion of what it felt like to be royalty as he acknowledged the compliments on either side. There was noticeable an obsequiousness and a subservience very unlike the disciplined respect he was accustomed to receive in a ship. Barbara sailed along beside him; the glances that Hornblower stole at her sidelong showed her to him as struggling conscientiously against the artificiality of her smile.

A silly wave of feeling came over him; he wished he were some simple-minded fellow who could rejoice naturally and artlessly in the unexpected arrival of his wife, who could take lusty pleasure of her without self-consciousness. He knew himself to be absurdly sensitive to minute influences, even influences that did not exist except in his own ridiculous imagination but which were none the less powerful. His mind was like a bad ship's-compass, not sufficiently deadbeat, wavering uncertainly and swinging to every little variation of course, swinging more widely in response to the correction, until at the hands of a poor helmsman the ship would find herself chasing her tail or taken all aback. He felt as if he were chasing his tail at the present moment; it made no difference to the complexity of his relations with his wife to know that it was all his fault, that her emotions towards him would be simple and straightforward did they not reflect his own tangled feelings – on the contrary, thinking about that made confusion worse confounded.

He tried to fling off his melancholy, to cling to some simple fact or other to steady himself, and with frightful clarity one of the central facts in his consciousness made its appearance in his mind, horribly real – like the memory of a man he had once seen hanged, writhing with hand-kerchief-covered face at the end of a rope. He had not yet told Barbara about it.

'Dear,' he said, 'you didn't know. Bush is dead.'

He felt Barbara's hand twitch on his arm, but her face still looked like that of a smiling statue.

'He was killed, four days back,' babbled on Hornblower with the madness of those whom the gods wish to destroy.

It was an insane thing to say to a woman about to walk into a royal reception, on the very point of setting her foot across the threshold, but Hornblower was sublimely unconscious of his offence. Yet he had at that last moment the perspicacity to realise – what he had not realised before – that this was one of the great moments of Barbara's life; that when she had been dressing, when she had smiled at him in the mirror, her heart had been singing with anticipation. It had not occurred to his stupidity that she could enjoy this sort of function, that it could give her pleasure to sail into a glittering room on the arm of Sir Horatio Hornblower, the man of the hour. He had been taking it for granted that she would extend to these ceremonies the same sort of strained tolerance that he felt.

'Their Excellencies the Governor and Milady Barbara 'Ornblor,' blared the major-domo at the door.

Every eye turned towards them as they entered. The last thing that Hornblower was conscious of, before he plunged into the imbecilities of a social function, was that he had somehow spoiled his wife's evening, and there was some angry resentment in his heart; against her, not against himself.

XV

The militia had arrived, pouring, still green with seasickness, from the close-packed transports. They were something better than a rabble in their scarlet uniforms; they could form line and column, and could march off smartly enough behind the regimental bands, even though they could not help gaping at the strangeness of this foreign town. But they drank themselves into madness or stupor at every opportunity, they insulted the women either innocently or criminally, they were guilty of theft and of wanton damage and of all the other crimes of imperfectly disciplined troops. The officers – one battalion was commanded by an earl, another by a baronet – were not sufficiently experienced to keep their men in hand. Hornblower, facing the indignant protests of the Mayor and the civil authorities, was glad when the horse-transports came in bringing the two regiments of yeomanry that had been promised him. They provided the cavalry he needed for an advanced guard, so that now he could send his little army out in its push towards Rouen, towards Paris itself.

He was at breakfast with Barbara when the news arrived; Barbara in a grey-blue informal garment with the silver coffee-pot before her, pouring his coffee, and being helped by him to bacon and eggs – a domesticity that was still unreal to him. He had been hard at work for three hours before he had come in to breakfast, and he was still too set in his ways to make the change easily from a military atmosphere to one of connubial intimacy.

'Thank you, dear,' said Barbara, accepting the plate from him.

A thump at the door.

'Come in!' yelled Hornblower.

It was Dobbs, one of the few people privileged to knock at that door when Sir Horatio was at breakfast with his wife.

'Despatch from the army, sir. The Frogs have gone.'

'Gone?'

'Up-stick and away, sir. Quiot marched for Paris last night. There's not a French soldier in Rouen.'

The report that Hornblower took from Dobbs' hand merely repeated in more formal language what Dobbs had said. Bonaparte must be desperate for troops to defend his capital; by recalling Quiot he had left all Normandy exposed to the invader.

'We must follow him up,' said Hornblower to himself, and then to Dobbs, 'Tell Howard – no I'll come myself. Excuse me, my dear.'

'Is there not even time,' said Barbara to him, sternly, 'to drink your coffee and eat your breakfast?'

The struggle on Hornblower's face was so apparent that she laughed outright at him.

'Drake,' she went on, 'had time to finish the game and beat the Spaniards too. I was taught that in the schoolroom.'

'You're quite right, my dear,' said Hornblower. 'Dobbs, I'll be with you in ten minutes.'

Hornblower applied himself to bacon and eggs. Maybe it would be good for discipline, in the best sense of the term, if it became known that the legendary Hornblower, the man of so many exploits, was human enough to listen sometimes to his wife's protests.

'This is victory,' he said, looking at Barbara across the table. 'This is the end.'

He knew it in his soul now; he had arrived at this conclusion by no mere intellectual process. The tyrant of Europe, the man who had bathed the world in blood, was about to fall. Barbara met his eyes, and their emotion admitted of no words. The world which had been at war since their childhood was about to know peace, and peace had something of the unknown about it.

'Peace,' said Barbara.

Hornblower felt a little unsteady. It was impossible for him to analyse his feelings, for he had no data from which to begin his deductions. He had joined the Navy as a boy, and he had known war ever since; he could know nothing of the Hornblower, the purely hypothetical Hornblower, who would have existed had there been no war. Twenty-one years of frightful strain, of peril and hardship, had made a very different man of him from what he would have become otherwise. Hornblower was no born fighting man; he was a talented and sensitive individual whom chance had forced into fighting, and his talents had brought him success as a fighter just as they would have brought him success in other walks of life, but he had had to pay a higher price. His morbid sensitiveness, his touchy pride, the quirks and weaknesses of his character might well be the result of the strains and sorrows he had had to endure. There was a coldness between him and his wife at the moment (a coldness masked by camaraderie; the passion to which both of them had given free rein had done nothing to dispel it) which might in large part be attributed to the defects of his character – a small part of it was Barbara's fault, but most of it was his.

Hornblower wiped his mouth and stood up.

'I really should go, dear,' he said. 'Please forgive me.'

'Of course you must go if you have your duty to do,' she answered, and held up her lips to him.

He kissed her and hurried from the room. Even with the kiss on his lips he knew that it was a mistake for a man to have his wife with him on active service; it was liable to soften him, to say nothing of the practical inconveniences, like the occasion two nights ago when an urgent message had to be brought in to him when he was in bed with Barbara.

In the office he read the reconnaissance report again. It stated unequivocally that no contact could be made with any Imperial troops whatever, and that prominent citizens of Rouen, escaping from the town, assured the outposts that not a Bonapartist soldier remained there. Rouen was his for the taking, and obviously the tendency to desert Bonaparte and join the Bourbons was becoming more and more marked. Every day the number of people who came into Le Havre by road or by boat to make their submission to the Duke grew larger and larger.

'*Vive le Roi!*' was what they called out as they neared the sentries. 'Long live the King!'

That was the password which marked the Bourbonist – no Bona-partist, no Jacobin, no republican would soil his lips with those words. And the number of deserters and refractory conscripts who came pouring in was growing enormous. The ranks of Bonaparte's army were leaking like a sieve, and Bonaparte would find it difficult to replace the missing ones, when his conscripts were taking to the woods or fleeing to English protection to avoid service. It might be thought possible that a Bourbonist army could be built up from this material, but the attempt was a failure from the start. Those runaways objected not merely to fighting for Bonaparte, but to fighting at all. The Royalist army which Angoulême had been sent here to organise still numbered less than a thousand men, and of these thousand more than half were officers, old *émigrés* sent here after serving in the armies of the enemies of France.

But Rouen awaited a conqueror, nevertheless. His militia brigade could tramp the miry roads to the city, and he and Angoulême could get into carriages and drive after them. He would have to make the entrance as spectacular as possible; the capital of Normandy was no mean city, and beyond it lay Paris, quivering and sensitive. A fresh idea struck him. In eastern France the allied monarchs were riding every few days into some new captured town. It was in his power to escort Angoulême into Rouen in more spectacular fashion, demonstrating at the same time the long arm of England's sea-power, and rubbing in the lesson that it was England's naval strength which had turned the balance of the war. The wind was westerly; he was a little vague about the state of the tide, but he could wait until it should serve.

'Captain Howard,' he said, looking up, 'warn *Flame* and *Porta Coeli* to be ready to get under way. I shall take the Duke and Duchess up to Rouen by water. And their whole suite – yes, I'll take Lady Barbara too. Warn the captains to make preparations for their reception and accom-modation. Send me Hau to settle the details. Colonel Dobbs, would you be interested in a little yachting trip?'

It seemed indeed like a yachting trip next morning, when they gathered on the quarterdeck of the *Porta Coeli*, a group of men in brilliant uniforms and women in gay dresses. *Porta Coeli* had already warped away from the quay, from which they rowed out to her, and Freeman, at a nod from Hornblower, had only to bellow the orders for sail to be set and the anchor hove in for them to start up the broad estuary. The sun was shining with the full promise of spring, the wavelets gleamed and danced. Down below decks, Hornblower could guess from the sounds, there was trouble and toil, while they were still trying to rig accommodation for the royal party, but here by the taffrail all was laughter and expectancy. And it was heavenly to tread a deck again, to feel the wind on his cheeks, to look aft and see *Flame* under all fore-and-aft sail in her station astern, to have the white ensign overhead and his broad pendant hoisted, even though the Bourbon white and gold flew beside it.

He met Barbara's eye and smiled at her; the Duke and Duchess condescended to step to his side and engage him in conversation. The fairway led close by the northern shore of the estuary; they passed Harfleur, and the battery there exchanged salutes with them. They were bowling up the channel at a full eight knots, faster than if they had gone in carriages, but of course when the river began to narrow and to wind it might be a different story. The southern shore came northward to meet them, the flat green shore becoming more and more defined, until in a flash, as it seemed, they were out of the estuary and between the banks of the river, leaving Quillebœuf behind and opening up the long reach that led to Caudebec, the left bank green pasture-land studded with fat farms, the right bank lofty and wooded. Over went the helm, the sheets were hauled in. But with the wind tending to funnel up the valley it was still well over their quarter, and with the racing tide behind them they fairly tore along the river. Luncheon was announced, and the party trooped below, the women squealing at the lowness of the decks and the difficulty of the companion. Bulkheads had been ripped out and replaced to make ample room for royalty – Hornblower guessed that half the crew would be sleeping on deck in consequence of the presence of the Duke and Duchess. The royal servants, assisted by the wardroom stewards – the former as embarrassed by their surroundings as the latter by the company on whom they had to wait – began to serve the food, but luncheon had hardly begun when Freeman came in to whisper to Hornblower as he sat between the Duchess and the *dame d'honneur*.

'Caudebec in sight, sir,' whispered Freeman; Hornblower had left orders to be told when this happened.

With an apology to the Duchess and a bow to the Duke, Hornblower slipped unobtrusively out of the room; the etiquette of royalty even covered events on shipboard, and sailors could come and go with little ceremony if the management of the vessel demanded it. Caudebec was in sight at the top of the reach, and they were approaching it fast, so that it was only a matter of minutes before there was no need for the glass that Hornblower trained on the little town. The damage caused by the explosion which had cost Bush's life was very obvious. Every house had been cut off short six or eight feet from the ground; the massive church had withstood the shock save that most of its roof had been stripped off and its windows blown in. The long wooden quay was in ruins, and a few stumps of blackened wrecks showed above water-level beside it. A single cannon – a twenty-four-pounder on a travelling carriage – stood on the river bank above the quay, all that remained of Quiot's siege-train. A few people were to be seen; they stood staring at the two men-o'-war brigs sailing along the river past them.

'A nasty sight, sir,' said Freeman beside him.

'Yes,' said Hornblower.

This was where Bush died; Hornblower stood silent in tribute to his friend. When the war was over he would erect a little monument on the river bank there above the quay. He could wish that the ruined town would never be rebuilt; that would be the most striking monument to his friend's memory – that or a pyramid of skulls.

'Mains'l sheets! Jib sheets!' roared Freeman.

They had come to the head of the reach, and were beginning the long turn to starboard. Jibing a big brig in a narrow river was no child's play. The flattened sails roared like thunder as they caught the back-lash of the wind from the heights. The brig's way carried her forward, and she rounded to, slowly, round the bend. Letting out the mainsail sheet gave them the needed push and steerage way; the farther she came round the flatter the sails were hauled, until at last she was closehauled on a course almost opposite to the one by which she had approached Caudebec, sailing closehauled up the new reach which presented itself to their gaze.

Here was Hau beside him now.

'Monseigneur wishes to know,' he said, 'whether your business on deck is very urgent. His Royal Highness has a toast to propose, and wishes that you could join in it.'

'I'll come,' said Hornblower.

He took a last glance aft at Caudebec, vanishing round the bend, and hurried below. The big extemporised cabin was parti-coloured with sunlight coming in through the open ports. Angoulême caught sight of him as he entered, and rose to his feet, crouching under the low deck-beams.

'To His Royal Highness the Prince Regent!' he said, lifting his glass. The toast was drunk, and everyone looked to Hornblower for the proper response.

'His Most Christian Majesty!' said Hornblower, and when the ceremony was completed raised his glass again.

'His Most Christian Majesty's Regent in Normandy, Monseigneur His Royal Highness the Duc d'Angoulême!'

The toast was drunk amid a roar of acclamation. There was something dramatic and painful about being down here below decks drinking toasts while an Empire was falling in ruins outside. The *Porta Coeli* was sailing as close to the wind as she could lie, so Hornblower guessed from the feel of the vessel under his feet and the sound of her passage through the water. Freeman on deck would have difficulty in weathering the next bend – he had noticed before he came down that the reach they had entered trended a little into the wind. Hornblower heard Freeman roar a fresh order on deck, and was consumed with restlessness. Down here it was like being with a nursery party of children, enjoying themselves while the adults attended to the management of the world. He made his apologetic bow again and slipped out to go on deck.

It was as he thought; the *Porta Coeli* was as closehauled as she would lie, almost closer. Her sails were shivering and her motion sluggish, and the bend in the river that would give her relief was a full half-mile farther ahead. Freeman looked up at the flapping sails and shook his head.

'You'll have to clubhaul her, Mr Freeman,' said Hornblower. To tack in that narrow channel, even with the tide behind them, would be too tricky an operation altogether.

'Aye aye, sir,' said Freeman.

He stood for a second judging his distances; the hands at the sheets, in no doubt about the delicacy of the ensuing manoeuvres, waiting keyed up for the rapid succession of orders that would follow. Filling the sails for a moment gave them plenty of way again, although it brought them perilously close to the leeward shore. Then in came the sheets, over went the helm, and the *Porta Coeli* snatched a few yards into the wind, losing most of her way in the process. Then out went the sheets, up came the helm a trifle, and she gathered way again, closehauled yet edging down perceptibly towards the lee shore.

'Well done,' said Hornblower. He wanted to add a word of advice to the effect that it would be as well not to leave it so late next time, but he glanced at Freeman sizing up the distances and decided it was unnecessary. Freeman wanted none of the brig's way lost this time. The moment the sails flapped he threw them back, put his helm over, and this time gained the full width of the river into the wind. Looking aft, Hornblower saw that the *Flame* was following her consort's example. The lee shore seemed to come to meet them; it seemed a very short time before the manoeuvre would have to be repeated, and Hornblower was relieved to see that the bend was appreciably nearer.

It was at that moment that the Duke's head appeared above the coaming as he climbed the little companion, and the royal party began to swarm on deck again. Freeman looked with despair at Hornblower, who took the necessary decision. He fixed the nearest courtier – the equerry, it happened to be – with a look that cut short the laughing speech he was addressing to the lady at his side.

'It is not convenient for His Royal Highness and his suite to be on deck at present,' Hornblower said loudly.

The gay chatter stopped as if cut off with a knife; Hornblower looked at the crestfallen faces and was reminded of children again, spoiled children deprived of some minor pleasure.

'The management of the ship calls for too much attention,' went on Hornblower, to make his point quite clear. Freeman was already bellowing at the hands at the sheets.

'Very well, Sir 'Oratio,' said the Duke. 'Come, ladies. Come, gentlemen.'

He beat as dignified a retreat as possible, but the last courtier down the companion was sadly hustled by the rush of the hands across the deck.

'Up helm!' said Freeman to the steersman, and then, in the breathing space while they gathered way closehauled, 'Shall I batten down, sir?'

The outrageous suggestion was made with a grin.

'No,' snapped Hornblower, in no mood for joking.

On the next tack *Porta Coeli* succeeded in weathering the point. Round she came and round; Freeman jibed her neatly, and once more with the wind on her quarter the brig was running free up the next reach, wooded hills on one side, fat meadow-land on the other. Hornblower thought for a moment of sending a message down that the royal party could come on deck for the next quarter of an hour, but thought better of it. Let 'em stay below, Barbara and all. He took his glass and laboriously climbed the main-shrouds; from the main-crosstrees his view over the countryside was greatly extended. It was oddly pleasant to sit up here and look over this green and lovely land of France like some sightseeing traveller. The peasants were at work in the fields, hardly looking up as the two beautiful vessels sailed past them. There was no sign of war or desolation here; Normandy beyond Caudebec was untouched as yet by invading armies. Then, for one moment, as the brig neared the next bend and preparations were being made for jibing her round, Hornblower caught a glimpse of Rouen far away across the country, cathedral towers and steeples. It gave him a queer thrill, but immediately the wooded heights as the brig came round cut off his view, and he snapped his glass shut and descended again.

'Not much of the tide left, sir,' said Freeman.

'No. We'll anchor in the next reach, if you please, Mr Freeman. Anchor bow and stern, and make a signal to *Flame* to the same effect.'

'Aye aye, sir.'

Natural phenomena, like nightfall and tides, were far more satisfactory things to deal with than human beings and their whims, than princes – and wives. The two brigs anchored in the stream to ride out the ebb tide and the hours of darkness to follow. Hornblower took the natural precautions against attack and surprise, rigging the boarding-nettings and keeping a couple of boats rowing guard during the night, but he knew there was little to fear from that exhausted and apathetic countryside. If there had been any of the army left within striking distance, if Bonaparte had been operating west of Paris instead of east, it would be a different story. But save for Bonaparte and the armed forces which he compelled to fight for him there was no resistance left in France; she lay helpless, the inert prize of the first conqueror to arrive.

The party on board the *Porta Coeli* went on being gay. It was a nuisance that the Duke and Duchess and their suite continually discovered that servants or pieces of baggage needed in *Porta Coeli* were in *Flame,* and vice versa, so that there was a continual need for boats between the two vessels, but presumably that was only to be expected from these people. They made surprisingly little complaint about the crowding in the sleeping accommodations. Barbara went off philosophically to bed in Freeman's cabin along with four other women – Freeman's cabin would be uncomfortable quarters for two. The royal servants slung hammocks for themselves under the amused tuition of the hands with no demur at all; it seemed as if during twenty years of exile, of wandering through Europe, they had learned in adversity some lessons which they had not forgotten as yet. No one seemed likely to sleep – but in the prevailing excitement and pleasurable anticipation they would probably not have slept even in downy beds in palaces.

Certainly Hornblower, after trying to compose himself for an hour or two in the hammock slung for him on deck (he had not slept in a hammock since the time when he refitted the *Lydia* at the island of Coiba), gave up the attempt, and lay looking up at the night sky, save when a couple of sharp showers drove him to cover himself over, head and all, with the tarpaulin provided for him. Staying awake did at least keep him assured that the westerly wind was still blowing, as might be expected at that time of year. If it had dropped or changed he was prepared to push on for Rouen in the ships' boats. There was no need; dawn and an increase in the westerly breeze came together, along with more rain, and two hours after the first daylight the flood set in and Hornblower could give the word to up anchor.

At the next bend Rouen's cathedral towers were plain to the sight; at the one after that only a comparatively narrow neck of land separated them from the city, although there was still a long and beautiful curve of the river to navigate. It was still early afternoon when they rounded the last bend and saw the whole city stretched before them, the island with its bridges, its wharves cluttered with river boats, the market hall across the quay, and the soaring Gothic towers which had looked down upon the burning of Joan of Arc. It was a tricky business anchoring there just below the town with the last of the flood still running; Hornblower had to take advantage of a minor bend in the stream to throw all aback and anchor by the stern, two cables' lengths farther from the city than he would have chosen in other circumstances. He scanned the city through his glass for signs of a deputation coming to greet them, and the Duke stood beside him, inclined to chafe at any delay.

'I'll have a boat, if you please, Mr Freeman,' Hornblower said at length. 'Will you pass the word for my coxswain?'

Crowds were already gathering on the quays to stare at the English ships, at the White Ensign and at the Bourbon lilies; it was twenty years since either had been seen there. There was quite a mass of people assembled when Brown laid the boat alongside the quay just below the bridge. Hornblower walked up the steps, eyed by the crowd. They were apathetic and silent, not like any French crowd he had seen or heard before. He caught sight of a man in uniform, a sergeant of *douaniers*.

'I wish to visit the Mayor,' he said.

'Yes, sir,' said the *douanier* respectfully.

'Call a carriage for me,' said Hornblower.

There was a little hesitation; the *douanier* looked about him doubtfully, but soon voices from the crowd began to make suggestions, and it was not long before a rattling hackney coach made its appearance. Hornblower climbed in, and they clattered off. The Mayor received him on the threshold of the Hôtel de Ville, having hastened there to meet him from his desk as soon as he heard of his arrival.

'Where is the reception for His Royal Highness?' demanded Hornblower. 'Why have no salutes been fired? Why are the church bells not ringing?'

'Monsieur – Your Excellency—' The Mayor knew not quite what Hornblower's uniform and ribbon implied and wanted to be on the safe side. 'We did not know – we were not certain—'

'You saw the royal standard,' said Hornblower. 'You knew that His Royal Highness was on his way here from Le Havre.'

'There had been rumours, yes,' said the Mayor reluctantly. 'But—'

What the Mayor wanted to say was that he hoped the Duke would arrive not only with overpowering force but also would make an unassuming entrance so that nobody would have to commit themselves too definitely on the Bourbon side according him a welcome. And that was exactly what Hornblower had come to force him to do.

'His Royal Highness,' said Hornblower, 'is seriously annoyed. If you wish to regain his favour, and that of His Majesty the King who will follow him, you will make all the amends in your power. A deputation – you, all your councillors, all the notables, the Prefect and the Subprefect if they are still here, every person of position, in fact, must be on hand two hours from now to welcome Monseigneur when he lands.'

'Monsieur—'

'Note will be taken of who is present. And of who is absent,' said Hornblower. 'The church bells can begin to ring immediately.'

The Mayor tried to meet Hornblower's eyes. He was still in fear of Bonaparte, still terrified in case some reversal of fortune should leave

him at Bonaparte's mercy, called to account for his actions in receiving
the Bourbon. And, on the other hand, Hornblower knew well enough
that if he could persuade the city to offer an open welcome, Rouen
would think twice about changing sides again. He was determined upon
winning allies for his cause.

'Two hours,' said Hornblower, 'will be ample for all preparations to
be made, for the deputation to assemble, for the streets to be decorated,
for quarters to be prepared for His Royal Highness and his suite.'

'Monsieur, you do not understand all that this implies,' protested the
Mayor. 'It means—'

'It means that you are having to decide whether to enjoy the King's
favour or not,' said Hornblower. 'That is the choice before you.'

Hornblower ignored the point that the Mayor was also having to
decide whether or not to risk the guillotine at Bonaparte's hands.

'A wise man,' said Hornblower, meaningfully, 'will not hesitate a
moment.'

So hesitant was the Mayor that Hornblower began to fear that he
would have to use threats. He could threaten dire vengeance tomorrow or
the next day when the advancing army should arrive; more effectively,
he could threaten to knock the town to pieces immediately with his
ships' guns, but that was not a threat he wanted to put into execution at
all; it would be far from establishing the impression he wished to convey
of a people receiving its rulers with acclamation after years of suffering
under a tyrant.

'Time presses,' said Hornblower, looking at his watch.

'Very well,' said the Mayor, taking the decision which might mean
life or death to him. 'I'll do it. What does Your Excellency suggest?'

It took only a matter of minutes to settle the details; Hornblower had
learned from Hau much about arranging the public appearances of
royalty. Then he took his leave, and drove back again to the quay
through the silent crowds, to where the boat lay with Brown growing
anxious about him. They had hardly pushed off into the stream when
Brown cocked his ear. A church carillon had begun its chimes, and
within a minute another had joined in. On the deck of the *Porta Coeli*
the Duke listened to what Hornblower had to tell him. The city was
making ready to welcome him.

And when they landed on the quay there was the assembly of notables,
as promised; there were the carriages and the horses; there were the
white banners in the streets. And there were the apathetic crowds,
numbed with disaster. But it meant that even if Rouen was quiet during
their stay there, the reception could at least have an appearance of
gaiety, so that Barbara and Hornblower went to bed each night worn out.

Hornblower turned his head on the pillow as the thumping on the
door penetrated at last into his consciousness.

'Come in!' he roared; Barbara beside him moved fretfully as he reached out, still half alseep, and pulled open the curtains.

It was Dobbs, slippered and in his shirtsleeves, his braces hanging by his thighs, his hair in a mop. He held a candle in one hand and a despatch in the other.

'It's over!' he said. 'Boney's abdicated! Blucher's in Paris!'

So there it was. Victory; the end of twenty years of war. Hornblower sat up and blinked at the candle.

'The Duke must be told,' he said. He was gathering his thoughts. 'Is the King still in England? What does that despatch say?'

He got himself out of bed in his nightshirt, while Barbara sat up with her hair in disorder.

'All right, Dobbs,' said Hornblower. 'I'll be with you in five minutes. Send to wake the Duke and warn him that I am about to come to him.'

He reached for his trousers as Dobbs left him, and, balancing on one leg, he met Barbara's sleepy gaze.

'It's peace,' he said. 'No more war.'

Even when roused out in this fashion Hornblower dressed, as he did all that came his way, extraordinarily quickly. He was tucking his nightshirt into his trousers – the long skirts of the warm and bulky garment packed the latter uncomfortably full – before Barbara replied.

'We knew it would come,' she said, a little fretfully. During recent events Barbara had had small time to sleep.

'The Duke must be told immediately, all the same,' said Hornblower, thrusting his feet into his shoes. 'I expect he'll start for Paris at dawn.'

'At dawn? What time is it now?'

'Six bells, I should fancy – three o'clock.'

'Oh!' said Barbara, sinking back on her pillow.

Hornblower pulled on his coat and stopped to kiss her, but she kissed him back only perfunctorily.

The Duke kept him waiting fifteen minutes in the drawing-room of the residence of the departed Prefect where he had been installed. He heard the news with his council round him, and with royal stoicism showed no sign of emotion.

'What about the usurper?' was his first question after hearing what Hornblower had to say.

'His future is partially decided, Your Royal Highness. He has been promised a minor sovereignty,' said Hornblower. It sounded absurd to him as he said it.

'And His Majesty, my uncle?'

'The despatch does not say, Your Royal Highness. Doubtless His Majesty will leave England now. Perhaps he is already on his way.'

'We must be at the Tuileries to receive him.'

XVI

Hornblower sat in his sitting-room in the Hôtel Meurice in Paris re-reading the crackling parchment document that had arrived for him the previous day. The wording of it might be called as gratifying as the pur-port of it, to one who cared for such things.

'As the grandeur and stability of the British Empire depend chiefly upon knowledge and experience in maritime affairs, We esteem those worthy of the highest honours who, acting under Our influence, exert themselves in maintaining Our dominion over the sea. It is for this reason that We have determined to advance to the degree of Peerage Our trusty and well beloved Sir Horatio Hornblower, Knight of the Most Honourable Order of the Bath, who, being descended from an ancient family in Kent, and educated from his youth in the sea service, hath through several posts arrived to high station and com-mand in Our navy, by the strength of his own abilities, and a merit distinguished by Us, in the many important services, which he has performed with remarkable fidelity, courage and success. In the late vigorous wars, which raged so many years in Europe; wars fruitful of naval combats and expeditions; there was scarce any action of conse-quence wherein he did not bear a principal part, nor were any dangers or difficulties too great, but he surmounted them by his exquisite conduct, and a good fortune that never failed him.

'It is just, therefore, that We should distinguish with higher titles a subject who has so eminently served Us and his country, both as monuments of his own merit, and to influence others into a love and pursuit of virtue.'

So now he was a Peer of the Realm, a Baron of the United Kingdom, Lord Hornblower of Smallbridge, County of Kent. There were only two or three other examples in history of a naval officer being raised to the peerage before attaining flag rank. Lord Hornblower of Smallbridge; of course he had decided to retain his own name in his title. There might be something grotesque about the name of Hornblower, and yet he was fond of it, and he had no desire to lose it in the almost anonymity of Lord Smallbridge or Lord Something-else. Pellew, he had heard, had elected to become Lord Exmouth. That might suit Pellew, but it would not suit him. His brother-in-law, when he received a step in the peerage, had actually reverted from a territorial to a personal title, becoming Marquis Wellesley instead of Earl of Mornington. Another brother-in-law, unable to use the Wellesley name in consequence of his brother's pre-emption of it, had become Wellington, apparently in an effort to retain as much of the family name as possible. He was a Duke now, far above a mere Baron, and yet they were all three Peers together. Lords, hereditary legislators. Little Richard was now the Honourable Richard Hornblower, and some time would be Lord Hornblower in succession to his father. All the formalities regarding titles were a little amusing. Barbara, for instance; as the daughter of an earl – it was her father's rank that mattered, not the fact that one brother was now a marquis and one a duke – she had had higher precedence than as the wife of a Knight of the Bath. She had been Lady Barbara Hornblower up to yesterday. But now as a result of her husband's peerage she would be Lady Hornblower. Lord and Lady Hornblower. It sounded well. It was a great honour and distinction, the coping-stone of his professional career. Oh, to be truthful about it, it was the sheerest lot of tommy-nonsense. Robes and a coronet. Hornblower stiffened in his chair as a thought struck him. Freeman's ridiculous prophecy over the cards in the cabin of the *Flame* about a golden crown had this much confirmation now. It was an amazingly shrewd guess on the part of Freeman; it had never occurred to him himself for one moment that he might become a peer. But the rest of Freeman's prophecy had fallen to the ground. Danger and a fair woman, Freeman had foreseen. And now the danger was all over with the coming of peace, and there was no fair woman in his life, unless Barbara, with her blue eyes and light-brown hair, could be called fair.

He rose to his feet in his irritation, and perhaps was going to stamp round the room, but Barbara came in at that moment from her bedroom, ready for the Ambassador's party. She was all in unrelieved white, for the party had been planned as a culminating demonstration of loyalty to the Bourbons, and the women were to wear white regardless as to whether or not their complexions could stand it; maybe that was the most convincing proof of loyalty to the newly restored dynasty that could be offered. Hornblower picked up his hat and cloak in readiness to escort her; it was the fortieth time in forty nights, he fancied, that he had done just the same thing.

'We won't stay at Arthur's late,' said Barbara.

Arthur was her brother the Duke of Wellington, lately and strangely transferred from commanding the army fighting France to His Britannic Majesty's Embassy to His Most Christian Majesty. Hornblower looked his surprise.

'We shall go on to the Polignacs' ' explained Barbara. 'To meet M. le Prince.'

'Very well, dear,' said Hornblower. He thought he kept the resignation out of his voice perfectly convincingly.

M. le Prince; that was the Prince of Condé, of a younger Bourbon line. Hornblower had begun to learn his way through the complexities of French society – the complexities of the last century transported bodily back into this. He wondered if he were the only man who thought of them as outmoded anachronisms. M. le Prince; M. le Duc – that was the Duc de Bourbon, wasn't it? Monsieur – plain Monsieur, with no honorifics at all – was the Comte d'Artois, the King's brother and heir. Monseigneur, on the other hand, was the Duc d'Angoulême, Monsieur's son, who would one of these days be Dauphin if his father survived his uncle. The very name of Dauphin was anachronistic, smacking of the Dark Ages. And the future Dauphin, as Hornblower well knew, was a man of convinced stupidity whose characteristic most easily remembered was a high-pitched mirthless laugh something like the cackling of a hen.

They had descended the stairs by now and Brown was waiting to hand them into the waiting carriage.

'The British Embassy, Brown,' said Hornblower.

'Yes, my lord.'

Brown had not stumbled over the new title once in the twenty-four hours he had borne it; Hornblower felt in his exasperation that he would have given anything for Brown to slip into 'Aye aye, sir'. But Brown was too clear-headed and quick-thinking a person to make any such blunder; it was surprising that Brown should have elected to stay on in his service. He might well have made a career for himself.

'You're not listening to a word I'm saying,' said Barbara.

'Please forgive me, dear,' said Hornblower – there was no denying the accusation.

'It's very important indeed,' said Barbara. 'Arthur is going to Vienna to represent us at the Congress. Castlereagh has to come home to manage the House.'

'Arthur will give up the Embassy?' asked Hornblower, making polite conversation. The carriage roared over the cobbles; the occasional lights revealed through the windows the bustling multi-uniformed crowd of Paris in the whirl of peace.

'Of course. *This* is much more important. All the world will be in Vienna – every Court in the world will be represented.'

'I suppose so,' said Hornblower. The destinies of the world were to be decided at the Congress.

'That's what I was going to tell you about. Arthur will need a hostess there – there'll be constant entertaining, of course – and he has asked me to come and act for him.'

'My God!' Polite conversation had led straight to the brink of this abyss.

'Don't you think it's wonderful?' asked Barbara.

Hornblower was on the point of saying, 'Yes, dear,' when rebellion surged up within him. He had endured for his wife's sake uncounted martyrdoms already. And this would be one far more violent and prolonged. Barbara would be the lady of the house, hostess of the most important delegate to the most important Congress in the world. The seeds of diplomacy, Hornblower had already learned, were planted far more often in drawing-rooms than in Cabinets. Barbara's drawing-room would be a place of intrigue and double-dealing. She would be hostess, Wellington would be the man of the house, and he – what would he be; something even more unnecessary than he was at present. Hornblower saw stretching before him a three-months' vista of salons and balls and visits to the ballet, outside the inner circle, outside the outer circle too. No Cabinet secrets would be entrusted to him, and he did not want to have anything to do with the petty gossip and polite scandal of the great world. A fish out of water was what he would be – and not a bad metaphor, either, when applied to a naval officer in the salons of Vienna.

'You don't answer me?' said Barbara.

'I'm utterly damned if I'll do it!' said Hornblower – strange that, with all his tact and intuition, he always took a sledge-hammer in his rare arguments with Barbara, to kill flies with.

'You won't do it, dear?'

In the course of that brief sentence Barbara's tone changed from disappointment at the beginning to bitter hostility at the end.

'No!' said Hornblower, in a roar.

He had kept the lid on his feeling for so long and so tightly that the explosion was violent when it came.

'You'll deprive me of the greatest thing that has ever happened to me?' said Barbara, a hint of ice edging the words.

Hornblower fought down his feelings. It would be easier to give way – ever so easy. But no, he would not. Could not. Yet Barbara was quite right about its being a wonderful thing. To be hostess to a European Congress, to help mould the future of the world – and then, on the other hand, Hornblower had no wish whatever to be a member, and an unimportant member at that, of the Wellesley clan. He had been captain of a ship too long. He did not like politics, not even politics on a European scale. He did not want to kiss the hands of Hungarian countesses, and exchange inanities with Russian grand dukes. That had been fun in the old days when his professional reputation hinged on some such success, as it had done. But he needed more of a motive than the mere maintenance of his reputation as a beau.

Quarrels in a carriage always seemed to reach a climax just as the drive ended. The carriage had halted and porters in the Wellington livery were opening the door before Hornblower had had time either to explain or make amends. As they walked into the Embassy Hornblower's apprehensive side glances revealed that Barbara's colour was high and her eyes dangerously bright. So they remained during the whole of the reception; Hornblower looked across the room at her whenever he could, and every time she was clearly in high spirits, or laughing with the groups in conversation with her, tapping with her fan. Was she flirting? The red coats and the blue coats, the black coats and the green coats, that assembled round her bent their shoulders in obvious defer- ence to her. Every glance Hornblower took seemed to increase his resentment.

But he fought it down, determined to make amends.

'You had better go to Vienna, dear,' he said, as they were once more in the carriage on their way to the Polignacs'. 'Arthur needs you – it's your duty.'

'And you?' Barbara's tone was still chilly.

'You don't need me. The skeleton at the feast, dear. I'll go to Small- bridge.'

'That is very kind of you,' said Barbara. Proud as she was, she resented a little having to be beholden to anyone. To ask permission was bad enough; to receive grudging permission was dreadful.

Yet here they were at the Polignacs'.

'Milord and milady Hornblower,' roared the major-domo.

They paid their respects to the Prince, received their host's and hostess's greetings. What in the world—? What—? Hornblower's head was spinning. His heart was pounding, and there was a roaring in his ears like when he had battled for his life in the waters of the Loire. The whole glittering room was seemingly banked in fog, save for a single face. Marie was looking at him across the room, a troubled smile on her lips. Marie! Hornblower swept his hand over his face, forced himself to think clearly as he had sometimes had to do when exhausted in battle. Marie! Not so many months before his marriage to Barbara he had told Marie he loved her, and he had been on the verge of sincerity when he said it. And she had told him she loved him, and he had felt her tears on his face. Marie the tender, the devoted, the sincere. Marie, who had needed him, whose memory he had betrayed to marry Barbara.

He forced himself to cross the room to her, to kiss with simple for- mality the hand she offered. That troubled smile was still on her lips; she had looked like that when – when – when he had selfishly taken all she had to give, like some thoughtless child claiming a sacrifice from a loving mother. How could he meet her eyes again? And yet he did. They looked each other over with mock whimsicality. Hornblower had the impression of something vivid and vital. Marie was dressed in cloth of gold. Her eyes seemed to burn into him – that was no careless metaphor. Mentally he tried to cling to Barbara, like a shipwrecked sailor to a broken mast tossing in the surf. Barbara slim and elegant; and Marie warm and opulent. Barbara in white which did not do her justice, Marie in gold. Barbara's blue eyes, sparkling, and Marie's brown eyes, warm and tender. Barbara's hair fair and almost brown; Marie's, golden and almost auburn. It did not do to think about Barbara while looking at Marie.

Here was the Count, quizzically kindly, awaiting his attention – the kindliest man in all the world, whose three sons had died for France, and who had told Hornblower once that he felt towards him as towards a son. Hornblower clasped hands with him in an outpouring of affection. The introductions were not easy. It was not easy to introduce his wife and his mistress.

'Lady Hornblower – Mme la Vicomtesse de Graçay. Barbara, my dear – M. le Comte de Graçay.'

Were they sizing each other up, these two women? Were they measuring swords, his wife and his mistress, the woman whom he had publicly chosen and the one he had privately loved?

'It was M. le Comte,' said Hornblower, feverishly, 'and his daughter-in-law who helped me escape from France. They hid me until the pursuit was over.'

'I remember,' said Barbara. She turned to them and spoke in her shocking schoolroom French. 'I am eternally grateful to you for what you did for my husband.'

It was difficult. There was a puzzled look on the faces of Marie and the Count; this was nothing like the wife Hornblower had described to them four years ago when he had been a fugitive hidden in their house. They could hardly be expected to know that Maria was dead and that Hornblower had promptly married Barbara, who was as unlike her predecessor as she well could be.

'We would do as much again, madame,' said the Count. 'Fortunately there will never be any need.'

'And Lieutenant Bush?' asked Marie of Hornblower. 'I hope he is well?'

'He is dead, madame. He was killed in the last month of the war. He was a captain before he died.'

'Oh!'

It was silly to say he had been a captain. For anyone else it would not have been. A naval officer hungered and yearned so inexpressibly for that promotion that speaking of a casual acquaintance one could think his death requited by his captaincy. But not with Bush.

'I am sorry,' said the Count. He hesitated before he spoke again – now that they had emerged from the nightmare of war it was apprehensively that one asked about old friends who might have been killed. 'But Brown? That pillar of strength? He's well?'

'Perfectly well, M. le Comte. He is my confidential servant at this moment.'

'We read a little about your escape,' said Marie.

'In the usual garbled Bonaparte form,' added the Count. 'You took a ship – the – the—'

'The *Witch of Endor*, sir.'

Was all this too painful or too pleasant? Memories were crowding in on him, memories of the Château de Graçay, of the escape down the Loire, of the glorious return to England; memories of Bush; and memories – honey-sweet memories – of Marie. He met her eyes, and the kindness in them was unfathomable. God! This was unendurable.

'But we have not done what we should have done at the very first,' said the Count. 'We have not offered our felicitations, our congratulations, on the recognition your services have received from your country. You are an an English lord, and I well know how much that implies. My sincerest congratulations, milord. Nothing – nothing can ever give me greater pleasure.'

'Nor me,' said Marie.

'Thank you, thank you,' said Hornblower. He bowed shyly. It was for him, too, one of the greatest pleasures in his life to see the pride and affection beaming in the old Count's face.

Hornblower became aware that Barbara standing by had lost the thread of the conversation. He offered her a hurried English translation, and she nodded and smiled to the Count – but the translation was a false move. It would have been better to have let Barbara blunder along with French; once he started interpreting for her the barrier of language was raised far higher, and he was put into the position of intermediary between his wife and his friends, tending to keep her at a distance.

'You are enjoying life in Paris, madame?' asked Marie.

'Very much, thank you,' said Barbara.

It seemed to Hornblower as if the two women did not like each other. He plunged into a mention of the possibility of Barbara's going to Vienna; Marie listened apparently in rapture at Barbara's good fortune. Conversation became formal and stilted; Hornblower refused to allow himself to decide that this was a result of Barbara's entry into it, and yet the conclusion formed in his inner consciousness. He wanted to chatter free and unrestrained with Marie and the Count, and somehow it could not be done with Barbara standing by. Relief actually mingled with his regret when the surge of people round them and the approach of their host meant that their group would have to break up. They exchanged addresses; they promised to call on each other, if Barbara's probable departure for Vienna left her time enough. There was a soul-searing glimpse of sadness in Marie's eyes as he bowed to her.

In the carriage again, going back to their hotel, Hornblower felt a curious little glow of virtue over the fact that he had suggested that Barbara should go to Vienna without him before they had met the

Graçays. Why he should derive any comfort from that knowledge was more than he could possibly imagine, but he hugged the knowledge to him. He sat in his dressing-gown talking to Barbara while Hebe went through the elaborate process of undressing her and making her hair ready for the night.

'When you first told me about Arthur's suggestion, my dear,' he said, 'I hardly realised all that it implied. I am so delighted. You will be England's first lady. And very properly, too.'

'You do not wish to accompany me?' said Barbara.

'I think you would be happier without me,' said Hornblower with perfect honesty. Somehow he would spoil her pleasure, he knew, if he had to endure a succession of balls and ballets in Vienna.

'And you?' asked Barbara. 'You will be happy at Smallbridge, you think?'

'As happy as I ever can be without you, dear,' said Hornblower, and he meant it.

So far not a word about the Graçays had passed between them. Barbara was commendably free from the vulgar habit which had distressed him so much in his first wife of talking over the people they had just met. They were in bed together, her hands in his, before she mentioned them, and then it was suddenly, with no preliminary fencing, and very much not *à propos*.

'Your friends the Graçays are very charming,' she said.

'Are they not all that I told you about them?' said Hornblower, immensely relieved that in telling Barbara of his adventures he had made no attempt to skirt round that particular episode, even though he had not told her all – by no means all. Then a little clumsily he went on, 'The Count is one of the most delightful and sweetest-natured men who ever walked.'

'She is beautiful,' said Barbara, pursuing undeflected her own train of thought. 'Those eyes, that complexion, that hair. So often women with reddish hair and brown eyes have poor complexions.'

'Hers is perfect,' said Hornblower – it seemed the best thing to do to agree.

'Why has she not married again?' wondered Barbara. 'She must have been married very young, and she has been a widow for some years, you say?'

'Since Aspern,' he explained. 'In 1809. One son was killed at Austerlitz, one died in Spain, and her husband, Marcel, at Aspern.'

'Nearly six years ago,' said Barbara.

Hornblower tried to explain; how Marie was not of blue blood herself, how whatever fortune she had would certainly revert to the Graçays on her remarriage, how their retired life gave her small chance of meeting possible husbands.

'They will be moving much in good society now,' commented Barbara, thoughtfully. And some time afterwards, *à propos* of nothing, she added, 'Her mouth is too wide.'

Later that night, with Barbara breathing quietly beside him, Hornblower thought over what Barbara had said. He did not like to think about Marie's remarriage, which was perfectly ridiculous of him. He would almost certainly never see her again. He might call once, before he returned to England, but that would be all. Soon he would be back in Smallbridge, in his own house, with Richard, and with English servants to wait on him. Life in future might be dull and safe, but it would be happy. Barbara would not be in Vienna for always. With his wife and his son he would lead a sane, orderly, and useful life. That was a good resolution on which to close his eyes and compose himself to sleep.

XVII

Two months later saw Hornblower sitting in a chaise driving along through France towards Nevers and the Château of Graçay. The Congress of Vienna was still sitting, or dancing – someone had just made the remark that the Congress danced but made no progress – and Barbara was still entertaining. Little Richard spent his mornings in the schoolroom now, and there was nothing for an active man to do in Smallbridge except feel lonely. Temptation had crept up on him like an assassin. Six weeks of mooning round the house had been enough for him; six weeks of an English winter of rain and cloud, six weeks of being hovered over by butler and housekeeper and governess, six weeks of desultory riding through the lanes and of enduring the company of his bucolic neighbours. As a captain he had been a lonely man and yet a busy one, a very different thing from being a lonely man with nothing to do. Even going round to parties in Paris had been better than this.

He had caught himself talking to Brown, harking back to old experiences, reminiscing, and that would never do. He had his dignity still to consider; no strong man could be weak enough to yearn for activity and interest. And Brown had talked eagerly about France, about the Château of Graçay, about their escape down the Loire – maybe it was Brown's fault that Hornblower's thoughts had turned more and more towards Graçay. As a fugitive he had found a welcome there, a home, friendship, and love. He thought about the Count – it may have been because his conscience troubled him, but undoubtedly at first it was the Count whom he thought about rather than Marie – with his courtesy and kindliness and general lovableness. With Bush dead it was likely that the Count was the man of whom Hornblower was fondest in all the world. The spiritual tie of which Hornblower had been conscious years ago was still in existence. Under the surface of his thoughts there may have been a tumultuous undercurrent of thoughts about Marie, but it was not apparent to him. All he knew was that one morning the pressure of his restlessness had become overwhelming. He fingered in his pocket the Count's pleasant letter, received some days ago, telling him of his and his daughter-in-law's return to Graçay, and repeating his invitation to come and stay. Then he had shouted to Brown to pack clothes for both of them and to have horses put to the chaise.

Two nights ago they had slept at the Sign of the Siren in Montargis; last night at the post-house at Briare. Now here they were driving along a lonely road overlooking the Loire, which ran like a grey ocean at their right hand, wide and desolate, with forlorn willows keeping a desperate foothold waist deep in the flood. Lashing rain beat down upon the leather tilt of the chaise, thundering down upon the taut material with a noise that made conversation difficult. Hornblower had Brown beside him in the chaise; the unfortunate postilion, hat drawn down over his ears to meet the collar of his cape, riding the near-side horse in front of them. Brown sat with folded arms, the model gentleman's servant, ready to converse politely if Hornblower showed any inclination to do so, keeping a discreet silence until addressed. He had managed every detail of the journey remarkably well – not that it would be difficult to manage any journey in France for an English milord. Every post-house keeper, however insolent in his office, was reduced to instant deference at the mention of Hornblower's rank.

Hornblower felt Brown stiffen beside him, and then peer forward through the driving rain.

'The Bec d'Allier,' said Brown, without being spoken to first.

Hornblower could see where the grey Allier joined the grey Loire at an acute angle – all this country was under moderate floods. There was something a little odd about having a coxswain who spoke French with the facility and good accent of Brown, who must have made (of course Hornblower knew he had) the best use of his months of living below stairs at Graçay when they had been escaped prisoners of war together – they and Bush. Hornblower could feel a mounting excitement in Brown, comparable with his own, and that was hard to explain in Brown's case. There was no reason for Brown to feel the same sort of homesickness for Graçay that Hornblower felt.

'Do you remember coming down here?' asked Hornblower.

'Aye, my lord, that I do,' said Brown.

It was down the Loire that they had made their historic escape from France, a long, curiously happy voyage to Nantes, to England, and to fame. Graçay could only be a few miles ahead now; Brown was leaning

forward expectantly in the chaise. There it was, the grey pepper-pot
turrets only just visible in the distance against the grey sky through the
rain. A flag flying from the flagstaff made a tiny darker spot above the
château. The Count was there. Marie was there. The postilion shook
up his depressed horses into a smarter trot, and the château came
nearer and nearer; the unbelievable moment was at hand. All the way
from Smallbridge, from the time when Hornblower had decided to
start, it had seemed as if it was quite impossible that they were going to
Graçay. Hornblower had seemed to himself like a child crying for the
moon, for their goal was so desirable as to seem necessarily unattainable.
Yet here they were, reining up at the gates, and here the gates were
opening and they were trotting forward into the so-well-remembered
courtyard. Here was old Felix the butler hurrying out into the rain to
welcome them, and over there by the kitchens stood a group of serving-
women, fat Jeanne the cook among them. And here, beside the chaise,
at the head of the far stone steps sheltered from the rain by the pro-
jecting roof overhead, were the Count and Marie. It was a homecoming.

Hornblower scrambled down awkwardly from the chaise. He stooped
to kiss Marie's hand; he went into the Count's arms and laid cheek to
cheek to the manner born. The Count was patting his shoulder.

'Welcome. Welcome.'

There was no pleasure on earth comparable with this sensation of
being looked for and of feeling that his arrival was causing pleasure.
Here was the well-remembered drawing-room with the old gilt Louis-
Seize chairs. The Count's wrinkled old face was mobile with delight,
and Marie was smiling. This man had broken her heart once, and she
was ready to let him break it all over again – she knew he would – because
she loved him. All Hornblower was conscious of was her smile, welcoming and – and – was it maternal? There was a proud sadness in that
smile, like that perhaps of a mother watching her son grown up now and
soon to be lost to her. It was only a fleeting feeling that Hornblower had;
his powers of observation were negatived immediately by his own wave
of personal feeling. He wanted to take Marie to him, to feel her rich
flesh in the circle of his arms, to forget his troubles and doubts and
disillusionments in the intoxication of her embrace; just as four years
ago he had found oblivion there, selfishly.

'A more cheerful arrival than your last, milord,' said the Count.

Hornblower's last arrival had been as a fugitive, carrying the wounded
Bush, and hunted by Bonaparte's gendarmes.

'Yes, indeed,' said Hornblower. Then he realised how formally the
Count had addressed him. 'Must I be "milord" to you, sir? It seems—'

They all smiled together.

'I shall call you 'Oratio, then, if you will permit me,' said the Count.
'I feel the greatness of the honour of such intimacy.'

Hornblower looked towards Marie.

"'Oratio,' she said. "'Oratio.'

She had called him that before in little broken tones when they had been alone together. Just to hear her say it again sent a wave of passionate emotion through Hornblower's body. He was filled with love – the sort of love of which he was capable. He was not conscious yet of any wickedness about his action in coming thus to torment Marie again. He had been overborne by his own wild longing – and perhaps in his excuse it could also be pleaded that his silly modesty made him incapable of realising how much a woman could love him. Here came Felix with wine; the Count raised his glass.

'To your happy return, 'Oratio,' he said.

The simple words called up a momentary pageant in Hornblower's memory, a sort of procession of returns, like the procession of kings in Macbeth's imagination. A sailor's life was a chain of departures and homecomings. Homecomings to Maria now dead and gone, homecomings to Barbara – and now this homecoming to Marie. It was not well to think of Barbara while he was with Marie; he had thought of Marie while he was with Barbara.

'I suppose Brown has made himself comfortable, Felix?' he asked. A good master always sees after the well-being of his servant – but this question was also intended to change his own train of thought.

'Yes, milord,' said Felix. 'Brown has made himself at home.'

Felix's face was devoid of expression, his voice devoid of tone. Were they too much so? Was there some subtle implication about Brown of which Hornblower should be aware? It was curious. Yet Brown was still the model servant when Hornblower found him in his room on withdrawing there to make ready for dinner. The portmanteaux and dressing-case were unpacked, the black dress-coat – London's latest fashion – was laid out with the shirt and cravat. A cheerful fire burned in the bedroom grate.

'Are you glad to be here again, Brown?'

'Very glad indeed, my lord.'

An accomplished linguist indeed was Brown – he could speak with fluency the language of the servant, the language of the lower deck, the language of the country lanes and of the London alleys, and French besides. It was faintly irritating that he never mixed them up, thought Hornblower, tying his cravat.

In the upper hall Hornblower met Marie, about to descend to dinner like himself. They both of them stood stock still for a moment, as though each of them was the last person in the world the other expected to see. Then Hornblower bowed and offered his arm, and Marie curtsied and took it. The hand she laid on his arm was trembling, and the touch of it sent a wave of warmth against him as though he were passing by an open furnace foor.

'My darling! My love!' whispered Hornblower, driven almost beyond his self-control.

The hand on his arm fluttered, but Marie continued unfaltering to walk on down the stair.

Dinner was a cheerful function, for fat Jeanne the cook had surpassed herself, and the Count was in his best form, droll and serious in turns, witty and well informed. They discussed the policy of the Bourbon Government, wondered about the decisions being reached at the Congress of Vienna, and spared a few passing thoughts for Bonaparte in Elba.

'Before we left Paris,' remarked the Count, 'there was talk that he was too dangerous a neighbour there. It was being suggested that he should be transferred to a safer place – your island of St Helena in the South Atlantic was named in that connection.'

'Perhaps that would be better,' agreed Hornblower.

'Europe will be in a ferment as long as that man can be the centre of intrigues,' said Marie. 'Why should he be allowed to unsettle us all?'

'The Tsar is sentimental, and was his friend,' explained the Count with a shrug. 'The Emperor of Austria is, after all, his father-in-law.'

'Should they indulge their preferences at the expense of France – of civilisation?' asked Marie, bitterly.

Women always seemed to be more hotly partisan than men.

'I don't think Bonaparte constitutes a very active danger,' said Hornbower, complacently.

As the Count sipped his coffee after dinner his eyes wandered longingly towards the card-table.

'Have you lost your old skill at whist, 'Oratio?' he asked. 'There are only the three of us, but I thought we might make use of a dummy. In some ways – heretical though the opinion may appear – I feel that the game with a dummy is the more scientific.'

Nobody mentioned how Bush used to play with them, but they all thought of him. They cut and shuffled and dealt, cut and shuffled and dealt. There was some truth in what the Count said about whist with a dummy being more scientific; certainly it allowed for a closer calculation of chances. The Count played with all his old verve, Marie seemingly with all her old solid skill, and Hornblower sought to display his usual scientific precision. Yet something was not quite right. Dummy whist was somehow unsettling – perhaps it was because the need for changing seats as the deal passed broke the continuity of the play. There was no question of simply losing oneself in the game, as Hornblower usually could do. He was vastly conscious of Marie, now beside him, now opposite him, and twice he made minor slips in play. At the end of the second rubber Marie folded her hands on her lap.

'I think I have played all I can this evening,' she said. 'I am sure 'Oratio is as much a master of piquet as he is of whist. Perhaps you can entertain each other with that while I go to bed.'

The Count was on his feet with his usual deferential politeness, asking if she felt quite well, and, when she assured him that she was merely tired, escorting her to the door exactly as he would have escorted a queen.

'Good night, 'Oratio,' said Marie.

'Good night, madame,' said Horatio, standing by the card-table.

One glance passed between them – one glance, enduring less than one-tenth of a second, but long enough for each to tell the other all.

'I trust Marie was correct in her assumption that you are a master of piquet, 'Oratio,' said the Count, returning from the door. 'She and I have played much together in default of whist. But I am taking it for granted that you wish to play? How inconsiderate of me! Please—'

Hornblower hastened to assure the Count that he would like nothing better.

'That is delightful,' said the Count, shuffling the cards with his slender white fingers. 'I am a fortunate man.'

He was fortunate at least in his play that night, taking his usual bold risks and being rewarded by unpredictable good luck in his discards. His minor seizièmes outranked Hornblower's major quints, a quatorze of knaves saved him when Hornblower had three aces, three kings and three queens, and twice carte blanche rescued him from disaster in face of Hornblower's overwhelming hands. When Hornblower was strong, the Count was lucky; and when Hornblower was weak the Count was overpoweringly strong. At the conclusion of the third *partie* Hornblower gazed helplessly across at him.

'I fear this has not been very interesting for you,' said the Count remorsefully. 'This is a discourteous way to treat a guest.'

'I would rather lose in this house,' said Hornblower, perfectly truthfully, 'than win in any other.'

The Count smiled with pleasure.

'That is too high a compliment,' he said. 'And yet I can only say in reply that with you in this house I care not whether I win or lose. I trust that I shall have the further good fortune of your making a long stay here?'

'Like the fate of Europe,' said Hornblower, 'that depends on the Congress of Vienna.'

'You know this house is yours,' said the Count, earnestly. 'Marie and I both wish you to look on it as your own.'

'You are too good, sir,' said Hornblower. 'May I ring for my candle?'

'Allow me,' said the Count, hastening to the bell-cord. 'I trust you are not overtired after your journey? Felix, milord is retiring.'

Up the oaken stairs with their carved panelling, Felix hobbling goutily ahead with the candle. A sleepy Brown was waiting for him in the sitting-room of the little suite, to be dismissed at once when Hornblower announced his intention of putting himself to bed. That door there, inconspicuous in the corner, led to the hall outside Marie's suite in the turret – how well Hornblower remembered it. Generations of the Ladons, Count of Graçay, had conducted intrigues in the château; perhaps kings and princes had passed through that door on the way to their lights-of-love.

Marie was waiting for him, weighted down with longing, heavy with love, tender and sweet. To sink into her arms was to sink into peace and happiness, illimitable peace, like that of a sunset-lit sea. The rich bosom on which he could pillow his head made him welcome; its fragrance comforted while it intoxicated. She held him, she loved him, she wept with happiness. She had no more than half his heart, she knew. He was cruel, unthinking, selfish, and yet this bony, slender body that lay in her arms was everything in the world to her. It was monstrous that he should come back to claim her like this. He had made her suffer before, and she knew her suffering in the past would be nothing compared with her suffering that lay in the future. Yet that was his way. That was how she loved him. Time went so fast; she had only this little moment before a lifetime of unhappiness to come. Oh, it was so urgent! She caught him to her madly, crying out with passion, crying out to time to stand still. It seemed to do so at that moment. Time stood still while the world whirled round her.

XVIII

'May I speak to you, my lord?' asked Brown.

He had put the breakfast tray by the bed, and had drawn aside the window curtains. Spring sunshine was gleaming on the distant Loire. Brown had waited respectfully until Hornblower had drunk his first cup of coffee and was coming slowly back to the world.

'What is it?' asked Hornblower, blinking over at him where he stood against the wall. Brown's attitude was not a usual one. Some of the deferential bearing of the gentleman's servant had been replaced by the disciplined erectness of the old days, when a self-respecting sailor held his head up and his shoulders back whether he was being condemned to the cat or commended for gallantry.

'What is it?' asked Hornblower again, consumed with curiosity.

He had had one moment of wild misgiving, wondering if Brown were going to be such a frantic fool as to say something about his relations with Marie, but the misgiving vanished as he realised the absurdity and impossibility of such a thing. Yet Brown was acting strangely – one might almost think he was feeling shy.

'Well, sir – I mean my lord' (that was the first time Brown had slipped over Hornblower's title since the peerage was conferred), 'I don't know rightly if it's anything your lordship would wish to know about. I don't want to presume, sir – my lord.'

'Oh, spit it out, man,' said Hornblower testily. 'And call me "sir", if it's any comfort to you.'

'It's this way, my lord. I'm wanting to get married.'

'Good God!' said Hornblower. He had a vague idea that Brown had been a terror for women, and the possibility of his marrying had never crossed his mind. He hastened to say what he thought would be appropriate. 'Who's the lucky woman?'

'Annette, my lord. Jeanne and Bertrand's daughter. And I am the lucky one, my lord.'

'Jeanne's daughter? Of, of course. The pretty one with the dark hair.'

Hornblower thought about a lively French girl marrying a sturdy Englishman like Brown, and for the life of him he could see no reason against it at all. Brown would be a better husband than most – it certainly would be a lucky woman who got him.

'You're a man of sense, Brown,' he said. 'You needn't ask me about these things. I'm sure you've made a wise choice, and you have all my best wishes for your happiness and joy.'

'Thank you, my lord.'

'If Annette can cook as well as her mother,' Hornblower went on meditatively, 'you're a lucky man indeed.'

'That was another thing I wanted to say to you, my lord. She's a cook second to none, young though she is. Jeanne says so herself, and if she says so—'

'We can be sure of it,' agreed Hornblower.

'I was thinking, my lord,' went on Brown, 'not wanting to presume, that if I was to continue in your service your lordship might consider engaging Annette as cook.'

'God bless my soul,' said Hornblower.

He mentally looked down a vista a lifetime long of dinners as good as Jeanne cooked. Dinners at Smallbridge had been almost good but most decidedly plain. Smallbridge and French cooking offered a most intriguing study in contrasts. Certainly Smallbridge would be more attractive with Annette as cook. And yet what was he thinking about? What had happened to those doubts and tentative notions about never seeing Smallbridge again? Some such ideas had certainly passed through his mind when he thought about Marie, and yet here he was thinking about Smallbridge and thinking about Annette heading his kitchen. He shook himself out of his reverie.

'Of course I can give no decision on the point myself,' he said, fencing for time. 'Her Ladyship will have to be consulted, as you understand, Brown. Have you any alternative in mind?'

'Plenty, my lord, as long as you are satisfied. I've thought of starting a small hotel – I have all my prize-money saved.'

'Where?'

'In London, perhaps, my lord. But maybe in Paris. Or in Rome. I have been discussing it with Felix and Bertrand and Annette.'

'My God!' said Hornblower again. Nothing like this had crossed his mind for a single moment, and yet— 'I have no doubt you would be successful, Brown.'

'Thank you, my lord.'

'Tell me, this seems to have been a lightning courtship. Is that so?'

'Not really, my lord. When I was here last Annette and I – you understand, my lord.'

'I do now,' said Hornblower.

It was fantastic that Brown, the man who hove the line that saved the *Pluto*, the man who silenced Colonel Caillard with a single blow of his fist, should be talking calmly about the possibility of opening an hotel in Rome. Actually it was no more fantastic than that he himself should have seriously debated with himself the possibility of becoming a French *seigneur*, and turning his back on England. He had done that no later than last night; love for Marie had grown during the last five days even while his passion was indulged – and Hornblower was not the sort of fool to be ignorant of how much that implied.

'When are you thinking of marrying, Brown?' he asked.

'As soon as the law of this country allows, my lord.'

'I've no idea how long that means,' said Hornblower.

'I am finding out, my lord. Will that be all you need at present?'

'No. I'll get up at once – can't stay in bed after hearing all this exciting news, Brown. I'll come through with a handsome wedding-present.'

'Thank you, my lord. I'll fetch your hot water, then.'

Marie was waiting for him in her boudoir when he was dressed. She kissed him good morning, passed a hand over his smoothly shaven cheeks, and, with her arm over his shoulder, led him to her turret window to show him that the apple trees in the orchard below were showing their first blossoms. It was spring; and it was good to be in love and to be loved in this green and lovely land. He took her white hands in his, and he kissed every finger on them, with a surge of reverent passion. As each day passed he had come to admire her the more, her sweetness of character and the unselfishness of her love. For Hornblower respect and love made a heady mixture – he felt he could kneel to her as to a saint. She was conscious of the passion that was carrying him away, as she was conscious of everything about him.

''Oratio,' she said – why should it stir him so frightfully to hear that ridiculous name of his pronounced in that fashion?

He clung to her, and she held him and comforted him as she always did. She had no thought for the future now. In the future lay tragedy for her, she knew; but this was the present, and during the present Hornblower had need of her. They came out of their paroxysm of passion smiling as they always did.

'You heard the news about Brown?' he asked.

'He is going to marry Annette. That is very proper.'

'It does not seem to be news to you?'

'I knew it before Brown did,' said Marie. There was a dimple that came and went in her cheek, and a little light of mischief could sparkle in her eyes. She was wholly and utterly desirable.

'They should make a good pair,' said Hornblower.

'Her chest of linens is all ready,' said Marie, 'and Bertrand has a *dot* for her.'

They went downstairs to tell the Count the news, and he heard it with pleasure.

'I can perform the civil ceremony myself,' he said. 'Do you remember that I am the *maire* here, 'Oratio? A position that is almost a sinecure, thanks to the efficiency of my *adjoint*, and yet I can make use of my powers should the whim ever overtake me.'

Fortunately, as regards the saving of time, Brown was able – as they found out on calling him in to ask him – to declare himself an orphan and head of his family, thus obviating the need for parental permission on which French law insisted. And King Louis XVIII and the Chamber had not yet carried out their declared intention of making a religious ceremony a necessary part of the legal marriage. There would be a religious ceremony, all the same, and the blessing of the Church would be given to the union, with the safeguards always insisted on in a mixed marriage. Annette was never to cease to try to convert Brown, and the children were to be brought up in the Catholic faith. Brown nodded as this was explained to him; religious scruples apparently weighed lightly enough on his shoulders.

The village of Smallbridge had already been scandalised by the introduction into its midst of Barbara's negro maid; it had shaken disapproving heads over Hornblower's and Barbara's heathen habit of a daily bath; what it would say in the future about the presence of a popish female and a popish family Hornblower could hardly imagine.

There he was, thinking about Smallbridge again. This was a double life in very truth. He looked uneasily across at the Count whose hospitality he was abusing. It was hard to think of guilty love in connection with Marie – there was no guilt in her. And in himself? Could he be held guilty for something he could do nothing to resist? Was he guilty when the current whirled him away in the Loire, not a mile from where he was standing at present? He shifted his glance to Marie, and felt his passion surge up as strongly as ever, so that he started nervously when it penetrated his consciousness that the Count was addressing him in his gentle voice.

"Oratio,' said the Count, 'shall we dance at the wedding?'

They made quite a gala occasion óf it, a little to the surprise of Hornblower, who had vague and incorrect ideas about the attitude of French *seigneurs* of the old régime towards their dependants. The barrels of wine were set up in the back courtyard of the château, and quite an orchestra was assembled, of fiddlers, and of pipers from the Auvergne who played instruments something like Scottish bagpipes that afflicted Hornblower's tone-deaf ear atrociously. The Count led out fat Jeanne in the dance, and the bride's father led out Marie. There was wine, there were great masses of food, there were bawdy jokes and highfalutin speeches. The countryside seemed to show astonishing tolerance towards this marriage of a local girl to an heretical foreigner – local peasant farmers clapped Brown on the back and their wives kissed his weather-beaten cheeks amidst screams of mirth. But then, Brown was universally popular, and seemed to know the dances by instinct.

Hornblower, unable to tell one note of music from another, was constrained to listen intently to the rhythm, and, intently watching the actions of the other, he was able to scramble grotesquely through the movements of the dances, handed on from one apple-cheeked woman to another. At one moment he sat gorged and bloated with food at a trestle table, at another he was skipping madly over the courtyard cobbles between two buxom maidens, hand in hand with them and laughing unrestrainedly. It was extraordinary to him – even here he still had moments of self-analysis – that he could ever enjoy himself so much. Marie smiled at him from under level brows.

He was amazingly weary and yet amazingly happy when he found himself back again in the salon of the château, his legs stretched out in inelegant ease while Felix, transformed again into the perfect major-domo, took the orders of him and the Count.

'There is an odd rumour prevalent,' said the Count, sitting upright in his chair apparently as unwearied and as dapper as ever. 'I did not wish to disturb the fête by discussing it there. People are saying that Bonaparte has escaped from Elba and has landed in France.'

'That is indeed odd,' agreed Hornblower lazily, the import of the news taking some time to penetrate his befogged brain. 'What can he intend to do?'

'He claims the throne of France again,' said the Count, seriously.

'It is less than a year since the people abandoned him.'

'That is true. Perhaps Bonaparte will solve the problem for us that we were discussing a few nights ago. There is no doubt that the King will have him shot if he can lay hands on him, and that will be an end of all possibility of intrigue and disturbance.'

'Quite so.'

'But I wish – foolishly perhaps – that we had heard of Bonaparte's death at the same time as we heard of his landing.'

The Count appeared grave, and Hornblower felt a little disturbed. He knew his host to be an acute political observer.

'What is it you fear, sir?' asked Hornblower, gradually gathering his wits about him.

'I fear lest he gain some unexpected success. You know the power of his name, and the King – the King or his advisers – has not acted as temperately as he might have done since his restoration.'

The entrance of Marie, smiling and happy, interrupted the conversation, nor was it restarted when they resumed their seats. There were moments during the next two days when Hornblower felt some slight misgivings, even though the only news that came in was a mere confirmation of the rumour of the landing with no amplification. It was a shadow across his happiness, but so great and so intense was the latter that it took more than a slight shadow to chill it. Those lovely spring days, wandering under the orchard blossoms, and beside the rushing Loire; riding – how was it that riding was a pleasure now when always before he had detested it? – through the forest; even driving into Nevers on the one or two ceremonial calls his position demanded of him; those moments were golden, every one of them. Fear of Bonaparte's activity could not cloud them – not even fear of what would be said to him in a letter that must inevitably soon come from Vienna could do that. On the surface Barbara had nothing to complain about; she had gone to Vienna, and during her absence Hornblower was visiting old friends. But Barbara would know. Probably she would say nothing, but she would know.

And great as was Hornblower's happiness it was not untrammelled, as Brown's happiness was untrammelled – Hornblower found himself envying Brown and the public way in which Brown could claim his love. Hornblower and Marie had to be a little furtive, a little guarded, and his conscience troubled him a little over the Count. Yet even so, he was happy, happier than he had ever been in his tormented life. For once self-analysis brought him no pangs. He had doubts neither about himself nor about Marie, and the novelty of that experience completely overlaid all his fears and misgivings about the future. He could live in peace until trouble should overtake him – if a spice to his happiness were necessary (and it was not), it was the knowledge that trouble lay ahead and that he could ignore it. All that guilt and uncertainty could do was to drive him more madly still into Marie's arms, not consciously to forget, but merely because of the added urgency they brought.

This was love, unalloyed and without reservations. There was an ecstasy in giving, and no amazement in receiving. It had come to him at last, after all these years and tribulations. Cynically it might be thought that it was merely one more example of Hornblower's yearning for the thing he could not have, but if that was the case Hornblower for once was not conscious of it. There was some line from the prayer-book that ran in Hornblower's head during those days – 'Whose service is perfect freedom'. That described his servitude to Marie.

The Loire was still in flood; the cataract where once he had nearly drowned – the cataract which was the cause of his first meeting with Marie – was a rushing slope of green water, foam-bordered. Hornblower could hear the sound of it as he lay in Marie's arms in her room in the turret; often they walked beside it, and Hornblower could contemplate it without a tremor or a thrill. That was all over. His reason told him that he was the same man as boarded the *Castilla*, the same man who faced El Supremo's wrath, the man who fought to the death at Rosas Bay, the man who had walked decks awash with blood, and yet oddly he felt as if those things had happened to someone else. Now he was a man of peace, a man of indolence, and the cataract was not a thing that had nearly killed him.

It seemed perfectly natural when the Count came in with good news.

'The Count d'Artois has defeated Bonaparte in a battle in the south,' he said. 'Bonaparte is a fugitive, and will soon be a prisoner. The news is from Paris.'

That was as it should be; the wars were over.

'I think we can light a bonfire tonight,' said the Count, and the bonfire blazed and toasts were drunk to the King.

But it was no later than next morning that Brown, as he put the breakfast tray beside Hornblower's bed, announced that the Count wished to speak to him as early as convenient, and he had hardly uttered the words when the Count came in, haggard and dishevelled in his dressing-gown.

'Pardon this intrusion,' said the Count – even at that moment he could not forget his good manners – 'but I could not wait. There is bad news. The very worst.'

Hornblower could only stare and wait, while the Count gathered his strength to tell his news. It took an effort to say the words.

'Bonaparte is in Paris,' said the Count. 'The King has fled and Bonaparte is Emperor again. All France has fallen to him.'

'But the battle he had lost?'

'Rumour – lies – all lies. Bonaparte is Emperor again.'

It took time to understand all that this implied. It meant war again, that was certain. Whatever the other Great Powers might do, England could never tolerate the presence of that treacherous and mighty enemy across the Channel. England and France would be at each other's throats once more. Twenty-two years ago the wars had started; it seemed likely that it would be another twenty-two years before Bonaparte could be pulled from his throne again. There would be another twenty-two years of misery and slaughter. The prospect was utterly hideous.

'How did it happen?' asked Hornblower, more to gain time than because he wanted to know.

The Count spread his delicate hands in a hopeless gesture.

'Not a shot was fired,' he said. 'The army went over to him *en masse*. Ney, Labédoyère, Soult – they all betrayed the King. In two weeks Bonaparte marched from the Mediterranean to Paris. That would be fast travelling in a coach and six.'

'But the people do not want him,' protested Hornblower. 'We all know that.'

'The people's wishes do not weigh against the army's,' said the Count. 'The news has come with the usurper's first decrees. The classes of 1815 and 1816 are to be called out. The Household troops are disbanded, the Imperial Guard is to be reconstituted. Bonaparte is ready to fight Europe again.'

Hornblower vaguely saw himself once more on the deck of a ship, weighed down with responsibility, encompassed by danger, isolated and friendless. It was a bleak prospect.

A tap on the door heralded Marie's entrance, in her dressing-gown, with her magnificent hair over her shoulders.

'You have heard the news, my dear?' asked the Count. He made no comment either on her presence or on her appearance.

'Yes,' said Marie. 'We are in danger.'

'We are indeed,' said the Count. 'All of us.'

So appalling had been the news that Hornblower had not yet had leisure to contemplate its immediate personal implications. As an officer of the British Navy, he would be seized and imprisoned immediately. Not only that, but Bonaparte had intended years ago to try him and shoot him on charges of piracy. He would carry that intention into effect – tyrants have long memories. And the Count, and Marie?

'Bonaparte knows now that you helped me escape,' said Hornblower. 'He will never forgive that.'

'He will shoot me if he can catch me,' said the Count; he made no

reference to Marie, but he glanced towards her. Bonaparte would shoot
her too.

'We must get away,' said Hornblower. 'The country cannot be settled
under Bonaparte yet. With fast horses we can reach the coast—'

He took his bedclothes in his hand to cast them off, restraining himself in the nick of time out of deference to Marie's presence.

'I shall be dressed in ten minutes,' said Marie.

As the door closed behind her and the Count, Hornblower hurled
himself out of bed shouting for Brown. The transition from the sybarite
to the man of action took a few moments, but only a few. As he tore off
his nightshirt he conjured up before his mind's eye the map of France,
visualising the roads and ports. They could reach La Rochelle over the
mountains in two days of hard riding. He hauled up his trousers. The
Count had a great name – no one would venture to arrest him or his
party without direct orders from Paris; with bluff and self-confidence
they could get through. There were two hundred golden napoleons in
the secret compartment of his portmanteau – maybe the Count had
more. It was enough for bribery. They could bribe a fisherman to take
them out to sea – they could steal a boat, for that matter.

It was humiliating thus to run like rabbits at Bonaparte's first re-
appearance; it was hardly consonant with the dignity of a peer and a
commodore, but his first duty was to preserve his life and his usefulness.
A dull rage against Bonaparte, the wrecker of the peace, was growing
within him, but was still far from mastering him as yet. It was resentment as yet, rather than rage; and his sullen resignation regarding the
change in conditions was slowly giving way to tentative wonderings
regarding whether he could not play a more active part in the opening
of the struggle than merely running away to fight another day. Here he
was in France, in the heart of his enemy's country. Surely he could strike
a blow here that could be felt. As he hauled on his riding-boots he spoke
to Brown.

'What about your wife?' he asked.

'I hoped she could come with us, my lord,' said Brown, soberly.

If he left her behind he would not see her again until the end of the
war twenty years off; if he stayed with her he would be cast into prison.

'Can she ride?'

'She will, my lord.'

'Go and see that she gets ready. We can carry nothing more than
saddle-bags. She can attend Mme la Vicomtesse.'

'Thank you, my lord.'

Two hundred gold napoleons made a heavy mass to carry, but it was
essential to have them with him. Hornblower thumped down the stairs
in his riding-boots; Marie was already in the main hall wearing a black
habit and a saucy tricorne hat with a feather. He ran his eyes keenly over

her; there was nothing about her appearance to excite attention – she was merely a lady of fashion soberly dressed.

'Shall we take any of the men with us?' she asked.

'They are all old. It would be better not to. The Count, you, myself, Brown and Annette. We shall need five horses.'

'That is what I expected,' answered Marie. She was a fine woman in a crisis.

'We can cross the bridge at Nevers, and head for Bourges and La Rochelle. In the Vendée we shall have our best chance.'

'It might be better to make for a little fishing village rather than a great port,' commented Marie.

'That's very likely true. We can make up our minds about it, though, when we are near the coast.'

'Very well.'

She appreciated the importance of unity of command even though she was ready with advice.

'What about your valuables?' asked Hornblower.

'I have my diamonds in my saddle-bag here.'

As she spoke the Count came in, booted and spurred. He carried a small leather sack which clinked as he put it down.

'Two hundred napoleons,' he said.

'The same as I have. It will be ample.'

'It would be better if it did not clink, though,' said Marie. 'I'll pack it with a cloth.'

Felix entered with the Count's saddle-bags and the announcement that the horses were ready – Brown and Annette awaited them in the courtyard.

'Let us go,' said Hornblower.

It was a sorry business saying goodbye. There were tears from the women – Annette's pretty face was all beslobbered with grief – even though the men, trained in the stoical school of gentlemen's service, kept silence.

'Goodbye, my friend,' said the Count, holding out his hand to Felix. They were both old men, and the chances were that they would never meet again.

They rode out of the courtyard, and down to the road along the river; it was ironical that it should be a lovely spring day, with the fruit blossom raining down on them and the Loire sparkling joyously. At the first turn in the road the spires and towers of Nevers came into sight; at the next they could clearly see the ornate Gonzaga palace. Hornblower spared it a casual glance, blinked, and looked again. Marie was beside him and the Count beyond her, and he glanced at them for confirmation.

'That is a white flag,' said Marie.

'I thought so too,' wondered Hornblower.

'My eyes are such that I can see no flag at all,' said the Count ruefully. Hornblower turned in his saddle to Brown, riding along encouraging Annette.

'That's a white flag over the palace, my lord.'

'It hardly seems possible,' said the Count. 'My news this morning came from Nevers. Beauregard, the Prefect there, had declared at once for Bonaparte.'

It was certainly odd – even if the white flag had been hoisted inadvertently it was odd.

'We shall know soon enough,' said Hornblower, restraining his natural instinct to push his horse from a trot into a canter.

The white flag still flew as they approached. At the octroi gate stood half a dozen soldiers in smart grey uniforms, their grey horses tethered behind them.

'Those are Grey Musketeers of the Household,' said Marie. Hornblower recognised the uniforms. He had seen those troops in attendance on the King both at the Tuileries and at Versailles.

'Grey Musketeers cannot hurt us,' said the Count.

The sergeant of the picket looked at them keenly as they approached, and stepped into the road to ask them their names.

'Louis-Antoine-Hector-Savinien de Ladon, Comte de Graçay, and his suite,' said the Count.

'You may pass, M. le Comte,' said the sergeant. 'Her Royal Highness is at the Prefecture.'

'*Which* Royal Highness?' marvelled the Count.

In the Grand Square a score of troopers of the Grey Musketeers sat their horses. A few white banners flew here and there, and as they entered the square a man emerged from the Prefecture and began to stick up a printed poster. They rode up to look at it – the first word was easily read – 'Frenchmen!' it said.

'Her Royal Highness is the Duchess of Angoulême,' said the Count.

The proclamation called on all Frenchmen to fight against the usurping tyrant, to be loyal to the ancient House of Bourbon. According to the poster, the King was still in arms around Lille, the south had risen under the Duc d'Angoulême, and all Europe was marching armies to enchain the man-eating ogre and restore the Father of his People to the throne of his ancestors.

In the Prefecture the Duchess received them eagerly. Her beautiful face was drawn with fatigue, and she still wore a mud-splashed riding habit – she had ridden through the night with her squadron of musketeers, entering Nevers by another road on the heels of Bonaparte's proclamation.

'They changed sides quickly enough again,' said the Duchess.

Nevers was not a garrison town and contained no troops; her hundred disciplined musketeers made her mistress of the little place without a blow struck.

'I was about to send for you, M. le Comte,' went on the Duchess. 'I was not aware of our extraordinary good fortune in Lord 'Ornblower's being present here. I want to appoint you Lieutenant-General of the King in the Nivernais.'

'You think a rising can succeed, Your Royal Highness?' asked Hornblower.

'A rising?' said the Duchess, with the faintest of interrogative inflections.

To Hornblower that was the note of doom. The Duchess was the most intelligent and spirited of all the Bourbons, but not even she could think of the movement she was trying to head as a 'rising'. Bonaparte was the rebel; she was engaged in suppressing rebellion, even if Bonaparte reigned in the Tuileries and the army obeyed him. But this was war; this was life or death, and he was in no mood to quibble with amateurs.

'Let us not waste time over definitions, madame,' he said. 'Do you think there is in France strength enough to drive out Bonaparte?'

'He is the most hated man in this country.'

'But that does not answer the question,' persisted Hornblower.

'The Vendée will fight,' said the Duchess. 'Laroche-Jacquelin is there, and they will follow him. My husband is raising the Midi. The King and the Household are holding out in Lille. Gascony will resist the usurper – remember how Bordeaux cast off allegiance to him last year.'

The Vendée might rise; probably would. But Hornblower could not imagine the Duc d'Angoulême rousing much spirit of devotion in the south, nor the fat and gouty old King in the north. As for Bordeaux casting off her allegiance, Hornblower remembered Rouen and Le Havre, the apathetic citizens, the refractory conscripts whose sole wish was to fight no one at all. For a year they had now enjoyed the blessings of peace and liberal government, and they might perhaps fight for them. Perhaps.

'All France knows now that Bonaparte *can* be beaten and dethroned,' said the Duchess acutely. 'That makes a great difference.'

'A powder magazine of discontent and disunion,' said the Count. 'A spark may explode it.'

Hornblower had dreamed the same dream when he had entered Le Havre, and used the same metaphor to himself, which was unfortunate.

'Bonaparte has an army,' he said. 'It takes an army to defeat an army. Where is one to be found? The old soldiers are devoted to Bonaparte. Will the civilians fight, and if so, can they be armed and trained in time?'

'You are in a pessimistic mood, milord,' said the Duchess.

'Bonaparte is the most able, the most active, the fiercest and the most cunning soldier the world has ever seen,' said Hornblower. 'To parry his strokes I ask for a shield of steel, not a paper hoop from a circus.'

Hornblower looked round at the faces; the Duchess, the Count, Marie, the silent courtier-general who had stood behind the Duchess since the debate began. They were sombre, but they showed no signs of wavering.

'So you suggest that M. le Comte here, for example, should submit tamely to the usurper and wait until the armies of Europe reconquer France?' asked the Duchess with only faint irony. She could keep her temper better than most Bourbons.

'M. le Comte has to fly for his life on account of his late kindness to me,' said Hornblower, but that was begging the question, he knew.

Any movement against Bonaparte in the interior of France might be better than none, however easily suppressed and whatever blood it cost. It might succeed, although he had no hope of it. But at least it would embarrass Bonaparte in his claim to represent all France, at least it would hamper him in the inevitable clash on the north-eastern frontier by forcing him to keep troops here. Hornblower could not look for victory, but he supposed there was a chance, the faintest chance, of beginning a slight guerrilla war, maintained by a few partisans in forests and mountains, which might spread in the end. He was a servant of King George; if he could encompass the death of even one of Bonaparte's soldiers, even at the cost of a hundred peasant lives, it was his duty to do so. A momentary doubt flashed through his mind; was it mere humanitarian motives that had been influencing him? Or were his powers of decision becoming enfeebled? He had sent men on forlorn hopes before this; he had taken part in some himself; but this was, in his opinion, an utterly hopeless venture – and the Count would be involved in it.

'But still,' persisted the Duchess, 'you recommend supine acquiescence, milord?'

Hornblower felt like a man on a scaffold taking one last look at the sunlit world before being thrust off. The grim inevitabilities of war were all round him.

'No,' he said. 'I recommend resistance.'

The sombre faces round him brightened, and he knew now that peace or war had lain in his choice. Had he continued to argue against rebellion, he would have persuaded them against it. The knowledge increased his unhappiness, even though he tried to assure himself – which was the truth – that fate had put him in a position where he could argue no longer. The die was cast, and he hastened to speak again.

'Your Royal Highness,' he said, 'accused me of being pessimistic. So I am. This is a desperate adventure, but that does not mean it should not be undertaken. But we must enter upon it in no light-hearted spirit. We must look for no glorious or dramatic successes. It will be inglorious, long, and hard. It will mean shooting French soldiers from behind a tree and then running away. Crawling up in the night to knife a sentry. Burning a bridge, cutting the throats of a few draught horses – those will be our great victories.'

He wanted to say, 'those will be our Marengos and our Jenas', but he could not mention Bonaparte victories to a Bourbon gathering. He raked back in his memory for Bourbon victories.

'Those will be our Steinkerks and our Fontenoys,' he went on. To describe the technique of guerrilla warfare in a few sentences to people absolutely ignorant of the subject was not easy. 'The Lieutenant-General for the King in the Nivernais will be a hunted fugitive. He will sleep among rocks, eat his meat raw lest a fire should betray him. Only by being reconciled to measures of this sort can success be won in the end.'

'I am ready to do those things,' said the Count, 'to my last breath.'

The alternative was exile until his death, Hornblower knew.

'I never doubted that I could rely on the loyalty of the Ladons,' said the Duchess. 'Your commission will be ready immediately, M. le Comte. You will exercise all royal power in the Nivernais.'

'What does Your Royal Highness intend to do in person?' asked Hornblower.

'I must go on to Bordeaux, to rally Gascony.'

It was probably the best course of action – the wider spread the movement the greater Bonaparte's embarrassment. Marie could accompany the Duchess, too, and then if the enterprise ended in complete disaster escape would be possible by sea.

'And you, milord?' asked the Duchess.

All eyes were upon him, but for once he was not conscious of it. It was an entirely personal decision that he had to make. He was a distinguished naval officer; let him make his way to England and the command of a squadron of ships of the line was his for certain. The vast fleets would range the seas again, and he would play a major part in directing them; a few years of war would see him an admiral with a whole fleet, the man upon whom the welfare of England would depend. And if he stayed here the best he could hope for was the life of a hunted fugitive at the head of a ragged and starving brigand band; at worst a rope and a tree. Perhaps it was his duty to save himself and his talents for England, but England had able naval officers by the score, while he had the advantage of knowing much about France and the French, and even of being known to them. But all these arguments were beside the point. He would not – could not – start a little feeble squib of a rebellion here and then run away and leave his friends to bear the brunt of failure.

'I will stay with M. le Comte,' he said. 'Provided that Your Royal Highness and he approve of such a course. I hope I will be of assistance.'

'Certainly,' said the Duchess.

Hornblower caught Marie's eye, and a horrid doubt suddenly assailed him.

'Madame,' he said, addressing her, 'you will accompany Her Royal Highness, I presume?'

'No,' said Marie. 'You will need every man, and I am as useful as a man. I know every ford and bridle-path round here. I stay with M. le Comte too.'

'But Marie—' said the Count.

Hornblower made no protest at all. He knew he might as well protest about the fall of an elm-tree branch or a change in the direction of the wind. He seemed to recognise destiny – the utterly inevitable – in all this. And one glance at Marie's face silenced the Count's expostulations.

'Very well, said the Duchess.

She looked round at them; it was time for the rebellion to begin in earnest. Hornblower put aside his personal feelings. There was a war to be fought; war with all its problems of space and time and psychology. He set himself, almost without willing it, to pick up the tangled threads. Above the desk where the Prefect had sat to execute instructions from the Paris Government was a large-scale map of the Department. On the other walls hung even larger-scale maps of the sub-prefectures. He looked over at them. Roads, rivers, forests. Goodbye to England.

'The first important thing to know,' he began, 'is where the nearest regular troops are stationed.'

The campaign of the Upper Loire was begun.

XIX

The forest track which they were following met another at right angles. It was frightfully hot even here in the shade of the pines, thunderstorm weather. Hornblower's feet were badly blistered, and he was hobbling along with difficulty even on the soft pine-needle mould underfoot. There was no wind to call forth any sound from the trees; everything was silent. Even the hoofs of the horses made no sound – the three pack-horses that carried food and ammunition, the two horses carrying wounded men, and the one horse that carried His Excellency the King's Lieutenant-General for the Nivernais. Twenty men and two women were shuffling along the trail with Hornblower, the main body of His Most Christian Majesty's army. There was an advance guard of five under Brown out ahead, a rearguard of five far behind.

Where the tracks crossed a man was waiting for them, a connecting file that Brown, like a prudent officer, had left behind so as to leave the main body in no doubt about which track he was following; as they came up he turned and pointed to something hanging beside the trail – something grey and white. It was the dead body of a man, clothed in peasant's dress, hanging by his neck from a pine-tree limb; the white colour was a large placard fastened to his chest.

'Frenchmen of the Nivernais!' it said. 'With my arrival at the head of a large body of troops all foolish attempts to resist the Government of our august Emperor Napoleon must cease forthwith. It is gratifying to me to find that so poor a reception has been given to the Count de Graçay's insane attempt to oppose the Emperor, recalled to his throne by the supplication and suffrages of forty million of his loyal subjects. Yet some unfortunate people have been deluded into taking up arms.

'Know, therefore, I am instructed by the clemency of His Imperial Majesty to proclaim that any Frenchman, with the exceptions mentioned below, who hands in his arms and makes personal surrender to any troops under my command before fifteen days from the date of this proclamation will receive amnesty and pardon. He will be free to return to his farm, to his shop, to the bosom of his family.

'Anyone remaining in arms will receive sentence of death, to be carried out immediately.

'Any village offering shelter to the rebels will be burned to the ground, and its leading inhabitants shot.

'Any person giving assistance to the rebels, whether by acting as guide or by giving them information, will be shot.

'Exceptions to the amnesty. The above-named Count de Graçay. His daughter-in-law, known as the Vicomtesse de Graçay. With them are included the Englishman, known as Lord Hornblower, who is required to pay for a life of outrage and crime.

'Signed,

EMMANUEL CLAUSEN, *Count, General of Division.*

June 6th, 1815.'

The Count looked up at the blackened face of the corpse.

'Who is it?' he asked.

'Paul-Marie of the mill, sir,' said the man who had waited for them.

'Poor Paul-Marie!'

'So they have crossed this track already,' said Hornblower. 'We're round behind them.'

Somebody reached up a hand to the corpse, perhaps to tear off the placard.

'Stop!' said Hornblower, just in time. 'They must not know that we have come this way.'

'For the same reason we must leave the poor devil unburied,' said the Count.

'We must keep marching,' said Hornblower. 'Once over the ford and we shall have time to take breath.'

He looked round at his pitiful little army. Some of them, at the moment of halting, had sunk to the ground. Some were leaning on their muskets, and some were spelling out the placard that hung on the breast of the dead Paul-Marie. It was not the first copy of it they had seen.

'Come on, my children,' said the Count.

The old man's face was white with weariness, and he drooped in his saddle; the wretched horse he rode was hardly in better condition, moving forward reluctantly with hanging head at the prod of the spurs. Shambling, hungry, and ragged, the others followed him, most of them looking up at the dead Paul-Marie as they passed. Hornblower noticed some who lingered, and dropped back to be with them; he had pistols in his belt. Deserters, as well as being a loss of strength, would give information of their intention to cross the ford. Clausen had scored a distinct point with his offer of amnesty, for there were many in the band – Hornblower could list in his mind a number of them – who must already be wondering whether it was worth going on with the struggle. Men with nothing save certain death ahead of them fight far harder in a losing battle than those with a chance to surrender, and his followers must be thinking regretfully of the rapid passing of the fifteen days allowed them in the proclamation. This was June 18th – Sunday, June 18th, 1815. He had to keep his men together for three more days to make sure that they would fight on with their necks at stake.

His blistered feet were causing him agony, for the short pause beside Paul-Marie's hanging body had brought back the life into them, and he would have to walk on them for some distance farther before they would be numb again. He had to drive himself to quicken his stride to catch up Marie, walking in the middle of the group with a musket slung across her back and Annette beside her. Marie had cut off her masses of hair – sawed them off with a knife after her first night as a guerrilla soldier – and the ends hung irregularly round her face, which was wet with sweat and streaked with dirt. But both she and Annette were in far better physical condition than Hornblower, stepping out with un-blistered feet and still with a certain freedom of stride as compared with Hornblower's leg-weary stagger. They were ten and fifteen years younger than he.

'Why not leave Pierre behind and take his horse, 'Oratio?' asked Marie.

'No,' said Hornblower.

'He will die anyway,' argued Marie. 'That wound will gangrene.'

'Bad for the other men to leave him here to die alone in the forest,' said Hornblower. 'Besides, Clausen might find him before he died and find out from him what we intend to do.'

'Kill him and bury him, then,' said Marie.

Women when they go to war are fiercer than men and inclined to carry the logic of war to still greater logical extremes. This was the tender, gentle Marie, the kind and understanding, who had wept for love of him.

'No,' said Hornblower again. 'We'll capture some more horses soon.'

'Providing we do,' said Marie.

It was hard to keep horses alive in these conditions; they died or went lame while men still lived and marched. Only two weeks had passed since Clausen, marching down from Briare, had forced them to evacuate Nevers, and in the fierce man-hunts that had followed horses had died in dozens. Clausen must be an active and energetic officer; his columns had marched hotfoot after them in unceasing pursuit. Only night-march after night-march, stratagems and cunning, had kept them out of his clutches. Twice there had been fierce little rearguard actions; once they had ambushed a troop of pursuing Hussars – Hornblower remembered the gaily uniformed soldiers tumbling from their saddles as the volley blazed from the roadside – and now here they were with half their strength gone already, marching by day, having marched the night before, to cross the rear of one of Clausen's circling columns. Marie knew of a dangerous and little-known ford across the Loire ahead. Once over that they could rest for a day in the forest of Runes before showing themselves in the valley of the Allier and causing fresh turmoil there. Clausen would be after them at once, but that was far enough to look ahead; the next move would depend on the new circumstances.

Active and energetic Clausen certainly was – he must have learned about fighting guerrillas in Spain. But he had a considerable force to back him up; Hornblower knew of the 14th Leger and the 40th Ligne – the 14th Light Infantry and the 40th of the Line – and there was another regiment with which he had not yet come into contact, and at least one squadron of the 10th Hussars. Nine battalions or more – six or seven thousand men – all chasing his ragged thirty. He was doing his duty, for those seven thousand men could be better employed on the Belgian frontier, where undoubtedly some action was stirring. And if he could only keep up the struggle he could wear down even those seven thousand men, wear out their boots and wear down their spirits. He could! Hornblower gritted his teeth and marched on; his feet were numb again now and had ceased to pain him. Only the terrible weariness in his legs distressed him now.

He became aware of a low muttering roar in the distance.

'Guns?' he asked, a little puzzled.

'Thunder,' said Marie.

They had chattered so light-heartedly once; had walked carefree and gay, hand in hand. It hardly seemed as if it were they two who had walked like that, in that breathing space of peace before Bonaparte returned from Elba. Hornblower was too fatigued to love now. The thunder muttered again; the heat was more oppressive. Inside his clothes Hornblower could feel the prickliness of his sweat. He was thirsty, too, but his thirst was not as severe as his physical weariness. In the forest it was growing dark, not with the approach of evening, which was still far off, but with the massing of stormclouds overhead. Somebody close behind him groaned, and Hornblower made himself look round and grin.

'Who's that lowing like a cow?' he asked. 'Old Father Fermiac? Five years younger than me, and they call him Father Fermiac and he lows like a cow! Cheer up, Father. Maybe we'll find a bull for you the other side of the Loire.'

That raised a cackle of laughter – some of it pure hysteria, some of it amusement at his not-quite-perfect French, some of it roused by the incongruity of a great English lord cracking jokes with French peasants. The thunder crashed almost overhead, and they could hear the rain beginning to patter on the trees. A few drops found their way down on their sweating faces.

'Here comes the rain,' said someone.

'I've had water underfoot for the past two days,' said Hornblower. 'You ought to see my blisters. Even the good Jesus never walked on as much water as I have.'

The daring blasphemy raised another cackle, got the men along for another hundred yards. The heavens were opening overhead, and the rain was falling in cataracts. Hornblower dropped back to the pack-horses, to make sure that the leather covers were securely over the panniers. He had two thousand rounds of musket ammunition there which he did not want spoiled – it would be harder to replace than food or even shoe-leather. They plodded on, in the semi-darkness, their clothes growing heavier with the rain soaking into them. The earth beneath their feet grew spongy and soggy, while the storm showed no sign of diminishing. The thunder still roared and the lightning flashed, lighting up the dark spaces under the trees.

'How much farther?' asked Hornblower of Marie.

'Two leagues and a half, perhaps.'

Three hours more of marching; it would be almost dark, if not quite, by the time they arrived.

'This rain will deepen the ford,' said Marie, sounding the first note of a new anxiety.

'My God!' said Hornblower before he could check himself.

There were eighteen half-battalion columns scattered in pursuit of them, and he was threading his way through the midst of them. He was risking almost everything on being able to cross the river at this unexpected point, which would throw off pursuit for a time at least. Their danger would be extreme if they were unable to pass. This was a rocky country in general, with a shallow topsoil, among the headwaters of the great river, and rain would affect the level of the water after only a short interval. He turned on his weary legs to urge the men to lengthen their stride. That was something he had to do every few minutes during the rest of that dreadful march, as darkness closed in prematurely about them, as the rain roared down upon them incessantly, as the led horses stumbled and plunged and the two wounded men groaned in agony. The Count rode without a word, bowed forward in the saddle with the water streaming from him. He was in the last stages of exhaustion, Hornblower knew.

Someone ahead challenged through the rain and dark; it was a man sent back from Brown's advanced guard. Brown had reached the edge of the forest, and the river lay a short distance ahead across the rocky flood plain. They all halted together under the last of the trees while scouts moved cautiously forward to discover if this lonely stretch of river bank were patrolled – there could not be too many precautions taken, even though any self-respecting sentry would sneak away to find shelter on a night like this.

'The river sounds loud,' said Marie. They could hear it even through the noise of the rain where they lay in the wet mud, and Hornblower dared not think what that implied.

Brown's messenger came back; he had explored the river bank and found no sign of the enemy, as was to be expected. Clausen's division would be sufficiently dispersed guarding likely places, let alone the unlikely ones. They got to their feet, Hornblower feeling new agony as his weight came again on his blisters. He could hardly step at first, and his legs were stiff and weary as well and hardly obeyed his wishes. The Count was able to mount his horse, but the poor brute seemed as leg weary as Hornblower himself. It was a sorry party that limped and hobbled and stumbled forward in the gathering darkness. The thunder had long ceased, but the rain continued to fall steadily, with every promise of going on through the night.

The turbulent surface of the river gleamed in the half-light ahead of them.

'The ford begins down by those trees,' said Marie. 'It is a ledge under the surface that runs diagonally upstream from there to the middle of the river. That is how you cross the deep part.'

'Come on, then,' said Hornblower. In his pain and weariness he felt as if he would like to cover that last half-mile on his hands and knees.

They came to the water's edge; the rushing river boiled at their feet among the rocks.

'It is too deep already,' said Marie. She was only voicing the suspicion that had formed in every mind. There was no expression in her tone at all; her voice was flat and dead.

'I'll take a horse and try it,' she went on. 'Here, help Pierre down.'

'Let me try, madame,' said Brown, but Marie paid him no attention.

She climbed astride into the saddle, hitching up the skirts of her habit to permit her to do so. Then she urged the horse forward into the water. The animal balked, nearly lost its footing among unseen rocks, and went forward with the utmost reluctance under the urging of Marie's heels. The water was almost up to its belly before – as Hornblower guessed – it had reached the end of the ledge of rock that Marie had spoken about. There was another battle of wills between Marie and the horse, and it plunged forward again. Three strides and it was out of its depth, struggling madly over the irregular bottom, almost vanishing from sight, and whirling downstream at frightening speed before it regained its footing. Marie, flung from the saddle, somehow hung on to the pommel, avoiding the lashing hoofs as the horse headed for the shore, and found her footing as it came out from the shallows snorting in fear. Marie struggled on to the bank weighed down by her dripping clothing. No one had uttered a sound while the trial was being made, not even in the moment of Marie's greatest peril. It was plain now to everybody that the ford was impassable.

'We must all walk on water now besides milord,' said a voice. It might have been a joke, but anyone who heard it knew that it was not.

Hornblower made himself come out of his daze. He had to think and plan and lead.

'No,' he said. 'I'm the only one who can do that. And none of us care to swim. Do we? Then let us keep along the river bank until we find a boat. I'll exchange ten miracles for one boat.'

The suggestion was received in depressed silence. Hornblower wondered if the men were one-half as tired as he was. He forced himself to his feet, by a fierce effort of will ignoring the pain of the blisters.

'Come on,' he said. 'At least we cannot stay here.'

No guerrilla leader in his senses would camp for the night beside an unfordable river against which he could be hemmed in, and with the rain continuing it would be at least twenty-four hours before it would be passable again.

'Come on,' he repeated. 'Come on, Frenchmen.'

Then he knew he had failed. A few stirred reluctantly; more looked to see how their comrades acted, and then deliberately lay down again, some on their backs, some with their faces pillowed on their forearms, with the rain still dropping on them.

'An hour's rest,' pleaded one voice.

Someone – Hornblower guessed it was young Jean, not yet seventeen – was sobbing unashamedly and loudly. The men had reached breaking point. Someone else, someone with greater powers of inspiration, might have got them to move again, Hornblower told himself, but it was beyond him. Had the ford been practicable they would have crossed it, and staggered on a mile or two the other side, but in the face of this disappointment they were capable of nothing further tonight. And they knew, the same as he did, that there was nothing to go on for. The rebellion was at an end, whether they marched till they died or gave up now. The thunderstorm, the flooding of the ford, had balked it. The men were realists after this experience of guerrilla warfare, and knew that anything further they did would be only a gesture. They all knew of Clausen's proclamation offering amnesty, too. Brown was at his side, eloquent in his silence, a hand on the butt of a pistol in his belt. Brown, himself, Marie; the Count and Annette, for what they were worth. One or two more – old Fermiac for one – were all he could count on. It would be enough for the moment. He could shoot a couple of the most obstinate of the objectors, and the rest would get to their feet and march, sulkily. But he could hardly keep unwilling men together in a march in darkness. They could slip away too easily; nor would it be difficult for someone more discontented or desperate than the others to slip a knife into his back on the march or put the muzzle of his musket to his ribs and pull the trigger. He was prepared to face that risk, he was prepared to kill a couple of malcontents, but he could see no real benefit from such action. There was one thing left for him to do, the last resource of the hunted guerrilla leader, to disperse his band and hope for better days to come. It was a bitter pill to swallow, especially in view of the desperate danger to Marie and the Count, but it was not a matter of choosing the best of possible alternatives. He had to choose the least bad. But failure was a horrible thing.

'Very well,' he said. 'It is here that we say goodbye.'

Some of the men stirred at those words.

''Oratio!' said Marie, and then ceased abruptly. She had learned the lessons of discipline.

'Your lives are safe,' went on Hornblower. 'You have all read Clausen's proclamation. Tomorrow – tonight if you will – you can make

your way to the troops and surrender. You can go to your homes.
Madame and the Count and I go on, for go on we must. And we would
even if we need not.'

The men were stunned into silence by his words. No one stirred, no
one spoke in the darkness. The two weeks of toil and danger and hardship through which they had just passed seemed like a lifetime to most
of them, and it was hard to realise that a lifetime had come to an
end.

'We shall return,' continued Hornblower. 'Remember us when you
are in your homes. Think of us. We shall return with a fresh call to arms.
Then we shall all of us gather again in our strength to thrust down the
tyrant. Remember that. And now one last cheer for the King! *Vive le
Roi!*'

They cheered, feebly enough, but Hornblower had achieved what he
set out to do. He had sowed the seeds of a later rebellion; when Clausen's
division should move away it would be possible to set the Nivernais in a
turmoil once more should a leader arise – should he and the Count ever
succeed in making their way back into the province. It was a desperate,
slight hope, but it was all that remained.

'In the name of God!' said Fermiac. 'I come with you now.'

'I also,' said another voice in the darkness.

Perhaps with these Frenchmen it might be possible now to make an
hysterical appeal to them, carry them away on a wave of emotion, set
them marching once more. Hornblower felt the temptation, and he had
to balance the pros and cons coldly. That sort of hysteria would hardly
survive the shock of the men's feeling their leg weariness. Some of the
men simply could not march farther. It would not do; by dawn next
day he would not have six men with him, and time would have been
irretrievably lost.

'Thank you,' said Hornblower. 'I shall remember that in time to
come, Fermiac, my friend. But we must ride, and ride hard. Four of us
and six horses gives us the best chance. Go back to your wife, Fermiac,
and try not to beat her on Saturday nights.'

He even got a laugh by that, at this moment of all moments. It helped
to keep the parting on a sane level, the level he was aiming at with an
eye to the future. Yet he knew there was no future; he knew it in his
soul, in his bones, even while he gave the order for the pack-horses to
be stripped of their loads, even while he forced Brown in a bitter argument to leave Annette behind and make her life safe. He was going
to die; probably Brown was going to die. And Marie, dear Marie – while
his spirit tossed on wave after wave of emotion, of remorse and self-
condemnation, of fear and regret, uncertainty and despair, his love for
her endured and increased, so that her name was in his mind as a
constant accompaniment to his thoughts, so that her image was in his

mind's eye whatever else he was picturing. Dear Marie, sweet, beloved Marie.

She was leading a spare horse, and Brown was leading the other; the four of them were mounted on the best of the six. The animals slipped and plunged over the rough surface at the water's edge until they reached the path above the river. They walked dispiritedly through the darkness. Hornblower could hardly sit in his saddle with his weariness; he felt giddy and sick, so that he had to hold on to the pommel of the saddle in front of him. He closed his eyes for a moment and instantly seemed to be swept over some vast smooth declivity, like the boat going over the cataract of the Loire four years before; he was almost out of his saddle before he recovered himself, jerking himself upright and clinging to the pommel like a drowning man. Yet at the foot of the declivity he had known that Marie was waiting for him with the brooding love in her eyes.

He shook off delirium. He had to make plans, to think how they could escape. He called up before his mind's eye the map of the country, and marked on it what he knew of the situation of Clausen's flying columns. They constituted a semicircular cordon, whose diameter was the river, and at whose centre he found himself at present. So far he had buoyed himself up in this danger with the hope of passing the river by Marie's ford. Hard on their heels, he knew, was marching a half-battalion of the 14th Leger, which had apparently been given the duty of direct pursuit while the other columns headed him off. At nightfall that half-battalion was presumably six or seven miles behind, unless – as might easily be the case – its commanding officer forced his men to march on in the darkness. Should he try to pierce the cordon or try to pass the river?

The Count's horse in front of him fell with a crash and a clatter, and his own nearly threw him as it plunged to avoid treading on it.

'Are you hurt, sir?' came Brown's voice in the darkness; he must have slipped down instantly from the saddle despite the handicap of a led horse.

'No,' said the Count quietly. 'But I'm afraid the horse is.'

There was a chink of bridles as Brown and the Count felt about in the dark.

'Yes. He's slipped his shoulder, sir,' reported Brown at length. 'I'll change saddles to the other horse.'

'Are you sure you are not hurt, Father?' asked Marie, using the intimate form of address which was by no means the rule between them.

'Not in the least, dear,' answered the Count, in just the same tone as he would use in a drawing-room.

'If we turn this horse loose they'll find it when they come along, my lord,' said Brown.

'They' meant the pursuing troops, of course.

'Yes,' said Hornblower.

'I'll take him away from the path and shoot him, my lord.'

'You won't be able to lead him far,' said the Count.

'A few yards may be enough,' said Brown, 'if you'll be kind enough to hold these two horses, sir.'

They sat and stood while Brown persuaded the suffering creature to hobble away to his doom. Through the gentle noise of the rain they heard the click as the pistol misfired, waited while Brown reprimed, and then heard the crack of the weapon.

'Thank you, sir,' Hornblower heard Brown say, presumably as he took over the horse the Count had been holding, and then he added, 'Can I take over your led horse, madame?'

Hornblower made up his mind at that moment.

'We will keep along the river bank a little longer,' he said. 'Then we can rest until dawn, and try to make a crossing.'

XX

They all of them slept a little that night, an hour or so altogether perhaps, in fits and snatches. They were all of them wearing clothing completely saturated, and although in the dark they found a bit of grassy bank on which to lie, the rock was only just below the surface and made itself felt. But such was their fatigue and shortage of sleep that they lost consciousness now and then, forgot the cold and their aching joints. It was the most natural thing in the world that Hornblower and Marie should lie in each other's arms, with his wet cloak beneath them and hers above. It was warmer that way. Probably they would have slept in each other's arms if they had been nothing to each other; and in one way, as a result of their fatigue, they *were* nothing to each other. The great surge of love and tenderness which Hornblower experienced had nothing to do with the contact of his battered body against Marie's. He was too cold and too tired for passion to rouse itself at all. But Marie lay in the darkness with an arm over him; she was younger and less weary than he was, and maybe she loved more dearly. There was one blessed half-hour after the rain ceased, before the coming of light, when Hornblower slept tranquilly with his head on her shoulder, when he was all hers. War was behind them and death in front of them, and nothing could come between them at that moment. Maybe that was the happiest half-hour that Hornblower had ever given her.

Hornblower woke with the first beginning of light. A heavy mist had arisen from the river and the saturated fields, and through it he saw a faint object a few yards away, which with difficulty he recognised as the Count, sitting up enveloped in his cloak. Brown lay beside him snoring gently – apparently they two had slept together as well. It took Hornblower a moment or two to collect his faculties; the roar of the rapid river close at hand was the next thing he recognised. He sat up and Marie woke beside him. He stood up, to be sharply reminded of the pain in his blistered feet and the ache in every joint. The pain was hard to ignore, for every step was torture, as frightful as anything the Middle Ages ever devised, but he said no word about it.

Soon they were on their way, mounted on horses that seemed in no better condition than the night before. This was the life that killed horses. The day was clearing fast; Hornblower expected one of those typical summer days of central France, breezy and sunny together. He could expect the mist to vanish altogether in an hour or less. Beside them the river roared and sang; when the mist thinned they could see its wide grey surface streaked with white. Not far on their right hand was the great road to Briare and Paris; what they were following was the country path skirting the flood plain. With the river beside him Hornblower sketched rapidly what he intended to do to cross. That great expanse of water concealed shallows over much of its width, as they all knew. The main body of water and the main current was to be found in one channel, sometimes on this side, sometimes on that, sometimes in the middle – how well he remembered that phenomenon from the days when he had escaped down the river in a small boat! If they could get themselves across this channel, and swim the horses over, the shallows would hardly delay them. At Marie's ford they had relied on a ridge of rock which crossed the channel near enough to the surface to be passable at low water; as that ridge had failed them they must rely on other means. Even a little rowing-boat such as most riverside farms possessed would suffice. Marie's ford would have been far better, in that the pursuers would have no means of guessing that they had crossed, but anything was better than nothing. Across the river they could steal fresh horses for themselves and shake off pursuit. The Count snorted a little when Hornblower used the world 'steal'; but did not carry his protest into actual words.

The sun had broken through the mist now, and was shining at them almost level over the edge on their right hand; the river's surface still steamed a little. Certainly it was going to be a hot day. And then they saw what they were seeking, a small farm and outbuildings sheltering below the ridge and above the water's edge. It stood bold and black against the mist with the sun on it. The instinct of war made them wheel instantly into a low basin screened by willows, and dismount for concealment.

'Shall I go ahead, my lord?' asked Brown.

Perhaps it was his way of keeping himself sane, thus to speak formally and with the bearing of the good servant.

'Yes, go on,' said Hornblower.

Hornblower edged himself forward to a position of advantage whence he could watch Brown carefully worm his way towards the farm. If there were troops anywhere near, they would be quartered here. But then, on the other hand, at this time in the morning troops would be moving about round the outbuildings, and not a uniformed man was visible. A young woman made her appearance, and then an old man, while Hornblower watched. And then he saw something else, something which made him choke with anticipation and hope. Lying on the rocky bank of the river, at the water's edge below the farm, was a boat – the outline was unmistakable. The young woman was on her way towards the vineyard above the farm, when Brown, concealed in the ditch, attracted her attention. Hornblower saw the two in conversation, saw Brown rise to his feet, and walk towards the building. A minute later he appeared again and waved an arm to tell them all was well. They mounted, and with Marie leading Brown's horse and Hornblower leading the spare they trotted down to the farm. Brown awaited them, his pistol handy in his belt, and the old man stared at them as they dismounted. They were something to stare at, Hornblower realised, dirty and bedraggled and unshaven. Marie looked like a beggar's wench.

'The Frogs were here yesterday, my lord,' said Brown. 'Cavalry, the same Hussars as we beat last week, as far as I can make out. But they left early yesterday morning.'

'Very good,' said Hornblower. 'Let's get the boat launched.'

'The boat!' exclaimed the old man, staring at them. 'The boat!'

'Why do you say that?' asked Hornblower sharply, wondering with a pang what fresh blow Fate had to deal him.

'Look at the boat!' said the old man.

They walked down towards it. Someone with an axe had struck it four powerful blows; in four different places the bottom was smashed in.

'The Hussars did that,' piped the old man, dwelling on the horrid details with zest. ' "Smash that boat," said the officer, so they smashed it.'

The troops had been as fully aware, of course, as Hornblower had been of the importance of keeping the river barred. They had taken all the precautions they could think of to prevent unauthorised persons crossing. That was why Marie's ford would have been invaluable if they had been able to cross it yesterday.

It was a staggering blow; Hornblower looked out over the raging river and the fields and vineyards warm in the young day. Marie and the Count were waiting for a decision from him.

'We can make that boat float,' said Hornblower. 'The oars are still here. Two empty kegs fastened under the thwarts – there'll be kegs to be found here, seeing they make wine. We can patch a little, stuff the holes, and with the kegs to keep her afloat we'll cross all right. Brown, you and I had better get it done.'

'Aye aye, sir,' said Brown. 'There'll be tools in the wagon shed yonder.'

It was necessary to guard against surprise; the repair work on the boat would take some hours.

'Marie,' said Hornblower.

'Yes, 'Oratio?'

'Ride up above the vineyard there. Keep a watch on the high road. Remember to keep yourself and your horse hidden.'

'Yes, 'Oratio.'

Simply 'Yes, 'Oratio', as Hornblower realised a moment later. Any other woman would have made it clear by word or intonation that the last sentence of his instructions was superfluous to someone who had learned her job. As it was she mounted and rode off in simple obedience. Hornblower caught the Count's eye. He wanted to tell him to rest – the Count's face was as grey as the stubble that grew thick on his cheeks – but he refrained from brutally saying so. It was necessary to keep the Count in good spirits, and that was not the way to do so.

'We shall need your help, sir, soon,' he said. 'Can we call on you when it is needed?'

'Of course,' said the Count.

Brown appeared with barrel staves, hammer, and nails, some lengths of cord.

'Excellent!' said Hornblower.

Feverishly they went to work on the boat. In two places both strakes and frames were smashed. To patch the holes was a comparatively simple matter, but the broken frames presented a more difficult problem. To cross that fast current they would have to row vigorously, and the boat might buckle under the strain. The simplest way to stiffen it would be to strengthen the strakes with one or two diagonal thicknesses of new planking.

'When we turn her over we'll see how she looks,' said Hornblower.

The hammers rang out as they drove the nails home and clinched them. Hornblower thought of the lusty tugs on the oars necessary to drive the boat through those turbulent waters. Both longitudinally and transversely the strain on the fabric would be severe. They worked furiously. The old man hovered round them. He expected the Hussars back again at any moment, he said – they were constantly patrolling along the river bank. He told them this with that seeming delight in calamity that distinguished his type.

And he had hardly repeated his warning when the sound of hoofs caused them to look up from their work; it was Marie, pushing her horse down the slope as hard as it would move.

'Hussars!' she said briefly. 'Coming along the main road from the south. Twenty of them, I should think.'

It did not seem possible that Fate could be as unkind as she appeared to be. Another hour's work would see the boat ready to float.

'They'll come down here,' said the old man gloatingly. 'They always do.'

Once more it was matter for instant decision.

'We must ride off and hide,' said Hornblower. 'Nothing else for it. Come on.'

'But the repairs on the boat, sir? They'll see 'em,' said Brown.

'They were only a mile away,' said Marie. 'They'll be here in five minutes.'

'Come on,' said Hornblower. 'Count, please get on your horse.'

'Tell the Hussars if they come it was you who was making these repairs,' said Brown to the old man. Brown thrust his shaggy face close to the wrinkled one.

'Come along, Brown,' said Hornblower.

They rode back to the hollow place where they had hidden themselves before. They tethered the horses to the willows, and crawled back among the rocks to watch. They had hardly settled themselves when a murmur from Marie called their attention to the coming of the Hussars. It was only a small patrol – half a dozen troopers and a non-commissioned officer. The plumed busbies came in sight first, over the ridge, and then the grey jackets. They trotted down the cart-track beside the vineyard to the farm. The old man was waiting for them at the entrance to the courtyard, and the fugitives watched as they reined up and questioned him. There was a catch in Hornblower's breath as he watched the old man, his face raised to the mounted men, replying to the questions. Hornblower saw the non-commissioned officer lean out of his saddle and take the old man by the breast of his coat and shake him. He knew now they would get the truth out of him. Those threats in Clausen's proclamation were not empty ones. A single reminder would make the old man talk – he would only hesitate long enough to salve his conscience. The non-commissioned officer shook him again; a trooper apparently idly walked his horse towards the river and the boat and returned at once with the news of the repairs. Now the old man was talking; excitement was infecting the Hussars' horses, which were moving about restlessly. At a wave from the non-commissioned officer's hand a trooper set his horse up the slope, clearly to carry word to the remainder of the squadron. The old man was pointing in their direction; the Hussars wheeled their horses about, and, spreading out, began to trot towards them. This was the end.

Hornblower glanced at his companions, who looked back at him. In the flying seconds minds worked quickly. There was no purpose in trying to ride away – the fresh horses of the Hussars would overtake them in an instant. The Count had drawn his pistols and looked to the priming.

'I left my musket at the ford,' said Marie, in a choking tone, but she, too, had a pistol in her hand.

Brown was coolly looking about him at the tactical situation.

They were going to fight it out to the very end, then. All the feeling of finality, of inevitability, that had haunted Hornblower from the very beginning of the rebellion – since the interview with the Duchesse d'Angoulême – came over him with renewed force. This was indeed the end. To die among the rocks today, or before a firing party tomorrow. Neither of them very dignified ends, but perhaps this one was the better. Yet it did not seem right or fitting that he should die now. For the moment he could not accept his fate with the apparent indifference of his companions; he knew actual fear. Then it passed as suddenly as it came, and he was ready to fight, ready to play out the losing hand to the drop of the last card.

A trooper was riding towards them, not more than a few yards away now. Brown levelled his pistol and fired.

'Missed him, by God!' said Brown.

The Hussar reined his horse round and galloped out of range; the sound of the shot attracted the notice of all the rest of the patrol, which promptly sheered away out of musket-shot and began to circle, spreading out. The forlorn situation of the group in the rocky hollow must have become apparent to them immediately. Any attempt on the fugitives' part to escape must result in their being immediately ridden down, so that there was no need for hurry. The Hussars sat their horses and waited.

It was not more than half an hour before reinforcements arrived, two more troops under an officer whose aigrette and gold-laced dolman displayed the dandyism traditional in the Hussar regiments; the trumpeter beside him was nearly as resplendent. Hornblower watched as the sergeant's hand pointed out the tactical situation, and then he saw the officer's hand indicate the movements he wanted his men to make. The officer could see at a glance the ground was too broken for concerted mounted action; with disciplined rapidity the new arrivals dismounted, and the horses were led off by threes while the remainder of the two troops, carbine in hand, prepared to advance in skirmishing order against the hollow from two directions. For dismounted cavalry deployed as skirmishers, with their long boots and spurs and inaccurate carbines and lack of drill, Hornblower would nominally have felt nothing but contempt, but fifty of them advancing against three men and a woman armed only with pistols meant defeat and death.

'Make every shot tell, this time,' said Hornblower – the first words anyone had spoken for a long time.

Brown and the Count were lying in niches between rocks; Marie was crawling round so as to bring herself to face the flanking column. At a hundred yards the skirmishers grew more cautious, stealing forward trying to shelter themselves behind bushes and rocks, and obviously expecting the musket-shots that did not come. One or two of them fired their carbines, so wildly that Hornblower did not even hear the bullets; he could imagine the non-commissioned officers rating the men who were thus wasting ammunition. They were within possible range now of his own rifled pistols – Barbara's gift to him. He lay with his right arm extended, his forearm supported on the rock that sheltered him, and took prolonged and careful aim at the easiest mark before him – a Hussar walking towards him in the open, his carbine across his body. He pressed the trigger, and through the smoke saw the Hussar whirl round and fall, to rise to a sitting position a moment later with his hand to his wounded arm. Hot with a new battle fury, Hornblower fired the other barrel, and the Hussar fell back, limp and motionless; Hornblower cursed himself for wasting a shot and for killing a wounded man who would have been out of the battle in any event. A fierce yell went up from the ring of skirmishers, while Hornblower reloaded his empty pistols, restraining himself as his fever tempted him to hurry. He poured the charges into the barrels, wrapped the bullets and rammed them home, and carefully placed the caps upon the nipples. The sight of their comrade's fall had instilled extra caution into the skirmishers, despite their battle yell – no one wished to be the next inglorious victim. That was a sergeant, there, calling to his men to come on. Hornblower sighted again and fired, and the sergeant dropped. This was better. There was a savage satisfaction in killing when he was about to be killed. Carbines were firing from all round the ring; Hornblower would hear the bullets passing overhead.

At that moment a loud fanfare from the trumpet attracted the attention of everyone; it was repeated, and Hornblower looked round while the carbine-fire died away. The officer was walking his horse towards them, a white handkerchief waving from his hand, while the trumpeter rode close behind blowing for a parley in accordance with military etiquette.

'Shall I kill him sir?' asked Brown.

'No,' said Hornblower. It would be pleasant to take the officer with him to hell, but it would give Bonaparte too good an opportunity to sully his name and thus discredit the Bourbon movement. He knelt up behind his rock and shouted 'Come no farther!'

The officer reined up.

'Why not surrender?' he shouted back. 'You have nothing to gain by further resistance.'

'What terms do you offer?'

The officer with difficulty suppressed a shrug.

'A fair trial,' he shouted back. 'You can appeal to the mercy of the Emperor.'

The irony of those sentences could not have been greater if it had been deliberate.

'To hell with you!' yelled Hornblower. 'And to hell with the 10th Hussars! Run, or I fire!'

He raised his pistol, and the officer hastily wheeled his horse and trotted back without dignity. Why should it be that with death only half an hour away there should be any satisfaction in thus humiliating the man? He had only been doing his duty, trying to save the lives of his men; why this bitter personal animosity? This insane self-analysis coursed through Hornblower's mind even while he dropped on his stomach again and wriggled into a firing position. He had time to think scorn of himself before a bullet passing close above his head drove him to think about nothing save the business in hand. If the Hussars would only rise to their feet and charge in they might lose half a dozen lives but it would be over quickly. Marie's pistol cracked not far from his right hand, and he looked round at her.

At that moment it happened; Hornblower heard the impact of the bullet, saw the force of it half roll her over. He saw the puzzled look on her face, saw the puzzled look change to a grimace of agony, and without even knowing what he was doing he sprang to her and knelt beside her. A bullet had struck her on the thigh; Hornblower turned back the short skirt of her riding habit. One leg of her dark breeches was already soaked with blood, and while he was gathering himself to act he twice saw the blood pulsate redly – the great artery of the thigh was torn. A tourniquet – pressure – Hornblower's mind hastily recalled all it had ever learned about emergency treatment of the wounded. He thrust his fingers into her groin, unavailingly, the folds of the breeches balking his attempt to apply pressure to the artery. Yet every moment was precious. He felt for his penknife to rip open her breeches, and at the same time a shattering blow on his shoulder flung him on to the ground beside her. He had heard nothing of the Hussars' charge, nothing of the pistol-shots fired by Brown and the Count unavailingly to turn the charge back. Until the carbine-butt struck him down he had been ignorant of what was going on. Even as it was he struggled to his knees again with only the thought in his head of the urgent need to stop the artery. He vaguely heard a shout beside him as a sergeant stopped a trooper from striking him again, but he thought nothing of it. He opened his knife, but Marie's body was limp and lifeless under his hands. He glanced at her grimy face; it was white under the dirt and sunburn, her mouth hung open, and her eyes stared up at the sky as only the eyes of the dead stare. Hornblower knelt looking down on her, his open penknife still in his hand, completely numb. The penknife fell from his fingers, and he became aware of another face beside his own looking down on Marie.

'She is dead,' said a French voice. 'A pity.'

The officer rose again to his feet, while Hornblower knelt over the body.

'Come, you,' said a harsher voice, and Hornblower was roughly shaken by a hand on his shoulder. He stood up, still dazed, and looked round him. There was the Count, on his feet, between two Hussars; there was Brown sitting on the ground with his hand to his head slowly recovering from the blow which had struck him senseless, while over him stood a trooper with his carbine cocked.

'Madame's life would have been spared after trial,' said the officer, his voice coming from miles away. The bitterness of that remark helped to clear the fog from Hornblower's brain. He made a wild movement, and two men sprang forward and seized his arms, sending a wave of agony through his shoulder where the carbine-butt had struck him. There was a momentary pause.

'I shall take these men to headquarters,' announced the officer. 'Sergeant, take the bodies down to the farmhouse. I will send you orders later.'

A low moan came from the Count's lips like the cry of a hurt child.

'Very well, sir,' said the sergeant.

'Bring the horses up,' went on the officer. 'Is that man well enough to ride? Yes.'

Brown was looking dazedly around him, one side of his face swollen and bruised. It was all like a dream, with Marie lying there glaring at the sky.

'Come along,' said someone, and they dragged at Hornblower's arms to lead him out of the hollow. His legs were weak under him, his blistered feet resented the movement and he would have fallen if they had not helped him up and dragged him forward.

'Courage, coward,' said one of his guards.

No one – save himself – had ever called him that before. He tried to shake himself free, but they only held him the harder, his shoulder paining him excruciatingly. A third man put his hands on his back and all three ran him up out of the hollow without dignity. Here were the horses, a hundred of them, moving about restlessly still under the influence of the recent excitement. They shoved him up into the saddle of a horse, and divided the reins, a trooper mounting on each side and taking half the reins each. It added to Hornblower's feeling of helplessness to sit in a saddle with no reins to hold, and he was so exhausted that he could hardly sit upright. As the horse fidgeted under him he saw Brown and the Count made to mount as well, and then the cavalcade moved up to the road. There they broke into a rapid trot, which tossed him about in his saddle as he held on to the pommel. Once he came near to losing his balance, and the trooper beside him put an arm round him and hove him back into a vertical position.

'If you fell in a column like this,' said the trooper, not unkindly, 'that would be the end of your troubles.'

His troubles! Marie was dead back there, and it might just as well have been his own hand that killed her. She was dead – dead – dead. He had been mad to try to start this rebellion, madder still, infinitely madder, to allow Marie to take part in it. Why had he done it? And a man more skilful with his hands, more ready of resource, would have been able to compress that spouting artery. Hankey, the surgeon of the *Lydia*, had said once (as though licking his lips) that thirty seconds was as long as anyone ever lived after the femoral artery was cut. No matter. He had allowed Marie to die under his hands. He had had thirty seconds, and he had failed. Failed everywhere, failed in war, failed in love, failed with Barbara – God, why did he think of Barbara?

The pain in his shoulder may have saved him from madness, for the jolting of the horse was causing him agony of which he could no longer remain ignorant. He slipped his dangling hand between the buttons of his coat as a makeshift sling, which brought him a little relief, and a short while later he received further relief when a shouted order from the officer at the head of the column reduced the horses' pace to a walk. Exhaustion was overcoming him, too; although thoughts were whirling through his brains they were ceasing to be well-defined and logical thoughts – rather were they nightmare images, terrifying but blurred. He had sunk into a delirious stupor when a new order which sent the horses into a trot again roused him from it. Walk and trot, walk and trot; the cavalry was pushing along the road as fast as the horses could go, hurrying him to his doom.

The château guarded by half a battalion of soldiers was General Clausen's headquarters; the prisoners and their escorts rode into the courtyard and dismounted there. The Count was almost unrecognisable by reason of the grey stubble thick over his face; Brown, as well as being bearded, had one eye and cheek swollen purple with a bruise. There was no time to exchange more than a look, no time for a word, when a dapper dismounted officer came out to them.

'The General is waiting for you,' he said.

'Come along,' said the Hussar officer.

Two soldiers put their hands under Hornblower's arms to urge him forward, and once again his legs refused to function. There was not a voluntary contraction left in his muscles, and his blistered feet flinched from any contact with the earth. He tried to take a step, and his knees gave way under him. The Hussars held him up, and he tried again, but it was unavailing – his legs floundered like those of a leg-weary horse, and, indeed, for the same reason.

'Hurry up!' snapped the officer.

The Hussars supported him, and with his legs half trailing, half walking, they dragged him along, up a brief marble stair under a portico, and into a panelled room where behind a table sat General Clausen – a big Alsatian with bulging blue eyes and red cheeks and a bristling red moustache. The blue eyes bulged a little wider at the sight of the three wrecks of men dragged in before him. He looked from one to another with uncontrolled surprise; the dapper aide-de-camp who had slipped into a seat beside him, with paper and pens before him, made more effort to conceal his astonishment.

'Who are you?' asked the General.

After a moment the Count spoke first.

'Louis-Antoine-Hector-Savinien de Ladon, Comte de Graçay,' he said, with a lift of his chin.

The round blue eyes turned towards Brown.

'And you?'

'My name is Brown.'

'Ah, the servant who was one of the ringleaders. And you?'

'Horatio, Lord Hornblower.' Hornblower's voice cracked as he spoke; his throat was parched.

'Lord 'Ornblower. The Comte de Graçay,' said the General, looking from one to the other. He made no spoken comment – his mere glance was a commentary. The head of the oldest family in France, the most distinguished of the younger officers of the British Navy – these two exhausted tatterdemalions.

'The court martial which will try you will assemble this evening,' said the General. 'You have today in which to prepare your defence.'

He did not add 'if any'.

A thought came into Hornblower's mind. He made himself speak.

'This man Brown, monsieur. He is a prisoner of war.'

The arched sandy eyebrows arched higher yet.

'He is a sailor of His Britannic Majesty's Navy. He was doing his duty under my orders as his superior officer. He is not amenable to court martial in consequence. He is a legitimate combatant.'

'He fought with rebels.'

'That does not affect the case, sir. He is a member of the armed forces of the British Crown, with the grade of – of—'

For the life of him Hornblower could not remember the French equivalent of 'coxswain', and for the lack of anything better he used English word. The blue eyes suddenly narrowed.

'This is the same defence as you will be putting forward at your court martial,' said Clausen. 'It will not avail you.'

'I had not thought about my defence,' said Hornblower, so genuinely that his tone could not but carry conviction. 'I was only thinking about Brown. There is nothing of which you can accuse him. You are a soldier yourself, and must understand that.'

His interest in the present discussion made him forget his weariness, made him forget his own instant peril. The genuineness and sincerity of his anxiety about Brown's welfare had their effect on Clausen, who could not fail to be affected by these pleadings for a subordinate by a man who himself was about to lose his life. The blue eyes softened with a hint of admiration that was lost on Hornblower, keen-witted and sympathetic though the latter was. To him it was such an obvious thing to do to look after Brown that it did not cross his mind that it might be admirable as well.

'I will take the matter under consideration,' said Clausen, and then, addressing the escort, 'Take the prisoners away'.

The dapper aide-de-camp whispered hurriedly to him, and he nodded with Alsatian solemnity.

'Take what measures you think fit,' he said. 'I make you responsible.'

The aide-de-camp rose from his seat and accompanied them out of the hall as the soldiers helped Hornblower to walk. Once through the door the aide-de-camp issued his orders.

'Take that man,' – indicating Brown – 'to the guardhouse. That man,' – this was the Count – 'to the room there. Sergeant, you will have charge of him. Lieutenant, you will be personally responsible for this man 'Ornblower. You will keep two men with you, and you and they will never let him out of your sight. Not for a moment. There is a dungeon under the château here. Take him to it, and stay there with him, and I will come and inspect at intervals. This is the man who escaped four years ago from the Imperial gendarmerie, and who has already been condemned to death in his absence. He is desperate, and you can expect him to be cunning.'

'Very well, sir,' said the lieutenant.

A stone staircase led down to the dungeon, a relic of the not so distant days when the lord of the manor had the right of the high justice, the middle and the low. Now the dungeon showed every sign of long disuse when the clashing bars opened the door into it. It was not damp; on the contrary, it was thick with dust. Through the high barred window came a shaft of sunlight, just sufficient to illuminate the place. The lieutenant looked round at the bare walls; two iron chains stapled to the floor comprised the only furniture.

'Bring some chairs,' he said to one of the men with him, and, after a glance at his weary prisoner, 'And find a mattress and bring that too. A palliasse of straw at the least.'

It was chill in the dungeon, and yet Hornblower felt sweat upon his forehead. His weakness was growing with every second, his legs giving way under him even while he stood still, his head swimming. The mattress had hardly been laid upon the floor before he staggered to it and collapsed across it. Everything was forgotten in that moment, even his misery regarding Marie's death. There was no room for remorse, none for apprehension. He lay there face downward, not quite unconscious, not quite asleep, but oblivious; the throbbing in his legs, the roaring in his ears, the pain in his shoulder, the misery in his soul – all these were nothings at that moment of collapse.

When the bars at the door clashed to herald the entrance of the aide-de-camp Hornblower had recovered somewhat. He was still lying face downward, by now almost enjoying the lack of need to move or think, when the aide-de-camp came in.

'Has the prisoner spoken at all?' he heard the aide-de-camp ask.

'Not a single word,' said the lieutenant.

'The depths of despair,' commented the aide-de-camp with facile sententiousness.

The remark irritated Hornblower, and he was further annoyed at being caught in such an undignified attitude. He turned over and sat up on his palliasse and glared up at the aide-de-camp.

'You have no requests to make?' asked the latter. 'No letters you wish to write?'

He did not wish to write a letter upon which his gaolers would fall like vultures upon a corpse. Yet he had to be exigent, had to do something to remove that impression of being in despair. And with that he knew what he wanted and how desperately he wanted it.

'A bath,' he said. He put his hand to his hairy face. 'A shave. Clean clothes.'

'A bath?' repeated the aide-de-camp, a little startled. Then a look of suspicion came into his face. 'I cannot trust you with a razor. You would try to cheat the firing party.'

'Have one of your men shave me,' said Hornblower, and seeking for something to say to irritate he added, 'You can tie my hands while he does it. But first a bucket of hot water, soap, and a towel. And a clean shirt at least.'

The aide-de-camp yielded.

'Very well,' he said.

A queer mood of light-hearted exaltation came to Hornblower's rescue. It was nothing to strip himself naked under the eyes of four curious men, to wash the filth from his body and to towel himself dry, ignoring the pain in his injured shoulder. It was not the legendary and strange Englishman that they were interested in so much as in the man about to die. This man soaping himself was shortly to pass through the gates ahead of them all; this white body was soon to be torn asunder by musket bullets. Telepathically he felt his gaolers' morbid curiosity, and proudly and disdainfully he would indulge it. He dressed himself again while they watched his every movement. A trooper came in with his hands full of lather-bowls and razors.

'The regimental barber,' said the aide-de-camp. 'He will shave you.'

There was no suggestion now of tying his hands; as Hornblower sat with the razor rasping over his throat he thought of reaching suddenly up and grasping the blade. His jugular vein, his carotid artery were there; one deep cut at the side and he would be out of his torment, and there would be the additional satisfaction of having completely outwitted the supercilious aide-de-camp. The temptation was momentarily keen; he could visualise his corpse collapsing in the chair, blood pouring from his throat, to the consternation of the officers. So clear was the vision for the moment that he dallied with it, enjoying it. But the fate of a suicide would not arouse nearly as much resentment as a judicial murder. He must let Bonaparte kill him, he must make that one last sacrifice to his duty. And Barbara – he would not like Barbara to think of him as a suicide.

The barber held a mirror before him just in time to break this new chain of thought; the face he looked at was the same familiar one, deeply sunburned. The lines about his mouth were perhaps more noticeable. The eyes were perhaps more pathetic than ever, more appealing. Disgustingly the forehead was a little higher, the scalp more visible. He nodded his approval to the barber, and rose to his feet as the towel was taken from under his chin, making himself stand firm despite the pain of his blisters on the feet. He swept his glance imperiously round, abashing the curious stares. The aide-de-camp pulled out his watch, most likely to conceal some embarrassment.

'In an hour the court martial will assemble,' he said. 'Do you wish for food?'

'Certainly,' said Hornblower.

They brought him an omelette, bread, wine, cheese. There was no suggestion that anyone should eat with him; they sat and stared as he carried each mouthful to his lips. He had not eaten for a long time, and now that he felt clean he was ravenously hungry. Let them stare; he wanted to eat and drink. The wine was delicious, and he drank of it thirstily.

'The Emperor won two great victories last week,' said the aide-de-camp suddenly, breaking into Hornblower's mood. Hornblower paused in the act of wiping his mouth with his napkin to stare at him.

'Your Wellington,' went on the aide-de-camp, 'has met his destiny at last. Ney beat him thoroughly at a place south of Brussels called Les Quatre Bras, and on the same day His Majesty destroyed Blucher and the Prussians at Ligny, which is the old battlefield of Fleurus, according to the map. It was a pair of victories as decisive as Jena and Auerstadt.'

Hornblower forced himself to complete the wiping of his mouth apparently unmoved. He addressed himself to pouring himself out another glass of wine; he felt that the aide-de-camp, annoyed by his apparent indifference to his fate, was telling him this news in an endeavour to penetrate his armour. He tried to think of a riposte.

'How did this news reach you?' he asked, apparently all polite attention.

'The official bulletin reached us three days back. The Emperor was in full march for Brussels.'

'My felicitations, monsieur. For your sake I hope the news is true. But is there not a saying in your army about "to lie like a bulletin"?'

'This bulletin is from the Emperor's own headquarters,' said the aide-de-camp indignantly.

'Then there can be no doubt about it, of course. Let us hope that Ney informed the Emperor correctly of the facts, for his defeat of Wellington is a remarkable reversal of history. In Spain Wellington defeated Ney several times, as well as Masséna and Soult and Victor and Junot and all the others.'

The aide-de-camp's expression showed how much the speech nettled him.

'There can be no doubt of this victory,' he said, and he added viciously, 'Paris will hear the same day of the Emperor's entry into Brussels and of the final suppression of brigandage in the Nivernais.'

'Oh,' said Hornblower politely, with raised eyebrows. 'You have brigands in the Nivernais? I commiserate with you, sir – but I met none in my travels through the country.'

The aide-de-camp's mortification showed in his face more plainly than ever, and Hornblower sipped his wine and felt pleased with himself. What with the wine and his light-headed elation he could find little to fear in the prospect that soon he would be condemned to death. The aide-de-camp rose and clanked out of the cell, while Hornblower pushed back his chair and stretched his legs with an elaborate pose of well-being that was only partly assumed. They sat on in silence, himself and his three watchers, for some considerable time before the clash of the bars told of the door being opened afresh.

'The court is waiting. Come,' said the aide-de-camp.

No sense of well-being could disguise from Hornblower the soreness of his feet. He tried to walk with dignity, but he could only limp grotesquely – he remembered how only yesterday he had found that the first hundred yards after a halt were acutely painful until his feet grew numb. And today it was far less than a hundred yards to the great hall of the château. As Hornblower and his escort came up on to ground level they met the Count, walking between two Hussars, and the groups paused for a moment.

'My son, my son,' said the Count, 'forgive me for what I have done.'

There was nothing odd to Hornblower's mind in being addressed as 'son' by the Count. Quite automatically he made the equivalent reply.

'There is nothing for me to forgive, Father,' he said, 'but it is I who ask forgiveness.'

What compelling motive was it that made him drop on his knee and bow his head? And why did an old free-thinker and Voltairean like the Count extend his hand to him?

'Bless you, my son. God bless you,' he said.

Then he passed on, and when Hornblower looked back the grey head and spare figure turned the corner and disappeared.

'He is to be shot at dawn tomorrow,' explained the aide-de-camp, as he opened the door into the great hall.

Clausen at his table was now flanked by three officers on either side, and at each end of the table sat a junior officer with papers before them. Hornblower hobbled towards them, struggling and failing to walk with any dignity. When he reached the table the officer at one end rose.

'Your name?' he asked.

'Horatio, Lord Hornblower, Knight of the Most Honourable Order of the Bath, Commodore in His Britannic Majesty's Navy.'

The court exchanged glances; the officer at the other end of the table, who was apparently acting as secretary, scribbled furiously. The officer who had asked the question – clearly the prosecutor – turned to address the court.

'The prisoner has admitted his identity. And I understand that he has previously already done so, to General Count Clausen and to Captain Fleury. His appearance also corresponds with his published description. It is submitted, then, that his identity is proved.'

Clausen looked round at his fellow judges, who nodded.

'It only remains, then,' went on the prosecutor, 'to submit to the court the verdict of a court martial held on June 10th, 1811, wherein this said 'Oratio 'Ornblower was condemned to death, he having purposely absented himself, on charges of piracy and violation of the laws of war; that sentence being confirmed on June 14th of the same year by His Imperial and Royal Majesty the Emperor. The judges will find attested copies before them. I must request that the death sentence be enforced.'

Again Clausen looked at his fellow judges, and received a sixfold nod. Clausen looked down at the table before him, and drummed for a moment with his fingers before he looked up again. He was making himself meet Hornblower's eyes, and when he did Hornblower's strange clairvoyance told him of the repeated orders that had come from Bonapart to Clausen – 'this Hornblower is to be taken and shot wherever found', or something to that affect. There was a decided apology in Clausen's blue eyes.

'It is the order of this military commission,' said Clausen slowly, 'that the said 'Oratio 'Ornblower suffer death by shooting at dawn tomorrow, immediately after the execution of the rebel Graçay.'

'Pirates are hanged, Your Excellency,' said the prosecutor.

'It is the order of this commission that 'Ornblower be shot,' repeated Clausen. 'Remove the prisoner. The commission is terminated.'

There it was. Hornblower knew that every eye was on his back as he turned away and walked down the hall. He wished he could stride out, head up and shoulders back, but he could only hobble out, with halting steps and shoulders bent. He had had no opportunity to say a word in his own defence, and perhaps it was as well. He might have stammered and hesitated, tongue-tied, for he had made no speech ready. He hobbled down the steps. At least he was to be shot and not hanged – but would the impact of the bullets on his chest be any less agonising than the tightening of the rope round his throat? He stumbled into the cell, which was now quite dark. He found the mattress and sat down on it. This was final defeat – he had not looked upon it in that light before. Bonaparte had won the last round of the struggle he had waged against him for twenty years. There was no arguing with bullets.

They brought in three candles, which brightly lit the cell. Yes, this was defeat. With bitter self-contempt Hornblower remembered so recently preening himself on his silly verbal victories over the aide-de-camp. Fool that he was! The Count condemned to death, and Marie–oh, Marie, Marie! He found actual tears in his eyes, and he hurriedly shifted his position on the mattress so that the watchers should not see them. Marie had loved him, and his own folly had killed her. His own folly and Bonaparte's superior genius. God, if only he could have the chance to live the last three months over again. Marie, Marie. He was going to sink his head into his hands, and checked himself when he remembered there were three pairs of eyes stolidly watching him. He must not have it said of himself that he died like a coward. For little Richard's sake, for Barbara's sake, that must not be. Barbara would love and cherish Richard, he could be sure of that. What would she think of her late husband? She would know – she would guess – why he had come to France, and she would guess at his infidelity. She would be deeply hurt. She would be blameless if she held no allegiance to his memory. She would marry again. Still young, beautiful, wealthy, well connected; of course she would. Oh God, that added to the pain, to think of Barbara in another man's arms, laughing with the joy of it. And yet he had lain in Marie's. Oh, Marie.

His nails were hurting his palms, so tightly were his fists clenched. He glanced round to find the eyes still on him. He must show no weakness.

If that thunderstorm had not burst and flooded the Loire, he would still be at liberty, Marie would still be alive, the rebellion would still be active. It had called for the direct interposition of fate as well as Bonaparte's genius to defeat him. Those battles that had been fought in Belgium – maybe the bulletins had lied about Bonaparte's victories. Maybe they were not decisive. Maybe Clausen's division, kept inactive in the Nivernais, might have made them decisive had it been present. Maybe – what a fool he was to try to comfort himself with these vain delusions! He was going to die, he was going to solve the mystery that he had only sometimes allowed himself to think about. By this time tomorrow – in a few hours – he would have gone the road so many others had trodden before him.

They were lighting fresh candles; the old ones were burned to stubs. Was the night then passing so fast? Dawn would be here soon, soon – day breaks early in June. He met the eyes of one of the watchers, although the latter tried to evade his glance. He tried to force himself to smile, and knew instantly that the smile was lopsided and forced. A rattle outside the door. That could not be that they were coming for him already! Yes it was, the bars were clashing, the door was opening, the aide-de-camp was entering. Hornblower tried to rise to his feet, and to his horror found that his legs were too weak to support him. He made another effort to stand, unavailing again. He must sit and let them drag him out like a coward. He forced himself to raise his chin and look at the aide-de-camp, trying not to make it the fixed and glassy stare he knew it to be.

'It is not death,' said the aide-de-camp.

Hornblower looked; he tried to speak, but no word came from his open mouth. And the aide-de-camp was trying to force a smile too – an ingratiating smile.

'There is news from Belgium,' said the aide-de-camp. 'The Emperor has been defeated in a great battle. At a place called Waterloo. Already Wellington and Blucher are over the frontier and marching on Paris. The Emperor is there already and the Senate are demanding that he abdicate again.'

Hornblower's heart was pounding so hard that he was still incapable of speech.

'His Excellency the General,' went on the aide-de-camp 'has decided that in this case the executions are not to take place this morning.'

Hornblower found speech at last.

'I will not insist,' he said.

The aide-de-camp went on to say something about the restoration of His Most Christian Majesty, but Hornblower did not listen to him. He was wondering about Richard. And Barbara.

Hornblower

in the

West Indies

ST ELIZABETH OF HUNGARY

Rear-Admiral Lord Hornblower, for all his proud appointment as Commander-in-Chief of His Majesty's ships and vessels in the West Indies, paid his official visit to New Orleans in H.M. schooner *Crab*, only mounting two six-pounders and with a crew of no more than sixteen men, not counting supernumeraries.

His Britannic Majesty's Consul-General at New Orleans, Mr Cloudesley Sharpe, remarked on the fact.

'I hardly expected to see Your Lordship in so diminutive a craft,' he said, looking round him. He had driven down in his carriage to the pier against which *Crab* was lying, and has sent his liveried footman to the gangway to announce him, and it had been something of an anticlimax to be received by the trilling of the only two bosun's calls that *Crab* could muster, and to find on the quarterdeck to receive him, besides the Admiral and his flag-lieutenant, a mere lieutenant in command.

'The exigencies of the services, sir,' explained Hornblower. 'But if I may lead the way below I can offer you whatever hospitality this temporary flagship of mine affords.'

Mr Sharpe – surely there never was a name that accorded so ill with its possessor's figure, for he was a fat man, a mountain of puffy flesh – squeezed himself into a chair at the table in the pleasant little cabin, and replied to Hornblower's suggestion of breakfast with the statement that he had already broken his fast. He obviously had the gravest doubts as to the quality of any breakfast that could be served in this little ship. Gerard, the flag-lieutenant, made himself inconspicuous in a corner of the cabin, notebook and pencil on his knee, while Hornblower reopened the conversation.

'*Phoebe* was struck by lightning off Morant Cape,' said Hornblower. 'She was the ship I had planned to come in. *Clorinda* was already in dock, refitting. And *Roebuck*'s off Curaçao, keeping an eye on the Dutchmen – there's a brisk trade in arms with Venezuela at present.'

'Well I know that,' said Sharpe.

'Those are my three frigates,' said Hornblower. 'With the arrangements all made I judged it better to come in this schooner rather than not to come at all.'

'How are the mighty fallen!' was Mr Sharpe's comment. 'Your

Lordship, a commander-in-chief, with no more than three frigates and half a dozen sloops and schooners.'

'Fourteen sloops and schooners, sir,' corrected Hornblower. 'They are very desirable craft for the duties I have to perform.'

'No doubt, My Lord,' said Sharpe. 'But I can remember the days when the commander-in-chief on the West India Station disposed of a squadron of ships of the line.'

'That was in time of war, sir,' explained Hornblower, recalling the verbal comments of the First Sea Lord in the interview when he had been offered this command. 'The House of Commons would sooner allow the Royal Navy to rot at its moorings than reimpose the income tax.'

'At any rate, Your Lordship has arrived,' said Sharpe. 'Your Lordship exchanged salutes with Fort St Philip?'

'Gun for gun, as your despatch informed me had been arranged.'

'Excellent!' said Sharpe.

It had been a strange little formality; all hands on board *Crab* had lined the rail, very properly, during the salute, and the officers had stood at attention on the quarterdeck, but 'all hands' amounted to very little with four men manning the saluting gun, and one at the signal halliards and one at the helm. It had poured with rain, too; Hornblower's glittering uniform had clung damply around him.

'Your Lordship made use of the services of a steam tug?'

'Yes, by George!' exclaimed Hornblower.

'A remarkable experience for Your Lordship, apparently?'

'Indeed, yes,' said Hornblower. 'I—'

He held himself back from giving utterance to all his thoughts on that subject; they would lead to too many exciting irrelevancies. But a steam tug had brought *Crab* against the hundred miles of current from the sea to New Orleans between dawn and dusk, arriving at the very minute the tug captain had predicted. And here was New Orleans, crowded not merely with ocean-going sailing ships, but also with a fleet of long, narrow steamers, manœuvring out into the stream and against piers with a facility (thanks to their two paddle-wheels) that even *Crab* with her handy fore-and-aft rig could not attempt to emulate. And with a thresh of those paddle-wheels they would go flying upstream with a rapidity almost unbelievable.

'Steam has laid open a continent, My Lord,' said Sharpe, echoing Hornblower's thoughts. 'A veritable empire. Thousands and thousands of miles of navigable waterways. The population of the Mississippi valley will be counted in millions within a few years.'

Hornblower remembered discussions at home, when he was a half-pay officer awaiting his promotion to flag rank, when the 'steam kettles' had been mentioned. Even the possibility of ocean-going ships propelled by steam had been suggested, and had been properly laughed to scorn – it would mean the ruin of good seamanship. Hornblower had not been quite so sure on either point, but he had been careful to keep his opinions to himself, having no desire to be regarded as a dangerous crank. He did not want to be drawn into any similar discussions now, not even with a mere civilian.

'What intelligence do you have for me, sir?' he asked.

'A considerable amount, My Lord.'

Mr Sharpe produced a fold of papers from his tail pocket.

'Here are the latest advices from New Granada – more recent I expect than anything you have had. The insurgents—'

Mr Sharpe entered into a rapid exposition of the military and political situation in Central America. The Spanish colonies were entering into the final stage of their struggle for independence.

'It cannot be long before His Majesty's Government recognises that independence,' said Sharpe. 'And our Minister in Washington informs me that the government of the United States meditates a similar recognition. It remains to be seen what the Holy Alliance will have to say on that score, My Lord.'

Europe under the rule of absolute monarchy would turn a jaundiced eye upon the establishment of a whole new series of republics, no doubt. But it hardly mattered what Europe had to say, as long as the Royal Navy – even the depleted peace-time navy – controlled the seas, and the two English-speaking governments continued in amity.

'Cuba shows small signs of restlessness,' went on Sharpe, 'and I have information of the issue of further letters of marque by the Spanish Government to vessels sailing from Havana—'

Letters of marque were one of the principal sources of Hornblower's troubles. They were being issued by insurgent and nationalist governments alike, to prey upon ships flying the old flags and the new, and the bearers of letters of marque turned pirates in the twinkling of an eye in the absence of legitimate prizes and efficient prize courts. Thirteen of Hornblower's fourteen small craft were scattered over the Caribbean keeping an eye on the activities of the privateers.

'I have prepared duplicates of my reports for Your Lordship's information,' concluded Sharpe. 'I have them here to give to Your Lordship, along with copies of the complaints of the master-mariners concerned.'

'Thank you, sir,' said Hornblower, while Gerard took the papers into his charge.

'Now for the slave trade, with Your Lordship's permission,' went on Sharpe, opening a fresh series of papers.

The slave trade was as acute a question as piracy, even more acute in some ways, because the Anti-Slavery Society in England commanded a great deal of powerful and vocal support in both Houses of Parliament, and would raise an even more violent to-do about a cargo of slaves run into Havana or Rio de Janeiro than a shipping company pestered by privateers.

'At this moment, My Lord,' said Sharpe, 'a raw hand newly brought from the Slave Coast is selling for eighty pounds in the Havana baracoons – and he costs no more than a pound in trade goods at Whydah. Those profits are tempting, My Lord.'

'Naturally,' said Hornblower.

'I have reason to believe that ships of both British and American registry are engaged in the traffic, My Lord.'

'So have I.'

The First Sea Lord had tapped ominously on the table in that interview when touching on this part of his instructions to Hornblower. Under the new law British subjects who engaged in the slave trade could be hanged, and the ships seized. But care would be necessary in dealing with ships flying American colours. If they refused to heave-to on the high seas for examination the utmost tact would have to be employed. To shoot away an American spar or to kill an American citizen would mean trouble. America had gone to war with England only nine years before over matters very similar.

'We want no trouble, My Lord,' said Sharpe. He had a pair of hard, intelligent, grey eyes deep-set in his puffy face.

'I am aware of that, sir.'

'And in this connection, My Lord, I must employ special emphasis in calling Your Lordship's attention to a vessel making ready for sea here in New Orleans.'

'Which ship is this?'

'She is visible from the deck, My Lord. In fact—' Sharpe struggled out of his chair and walked to the cabin window. – 'Yes, there she is. What do you make of her, My Lord?'

Hornblower looked out from beside Sharpe. He saw a beautiful ship of eight hundred tons or more. Her fine lines, the lofty rake of her masts, the wide spread of her yards, were all clear indications of speed, for which some sacrifice of cargo-carrying capacity had been made. She was flush-decked, with six painted gun-ports along each side. American shipbuilders had always evinced a tendency towards building fast ships, but this was an advanced example of the type.

'Are there guns behind those ports?' asked Hornblower.

'Twelve-pounders, My Lord.'

Even in these days of peace it was not unusual for merchant vessels to carry guns, whether for voyages in the West Indies or the East, but this was a heavier armament than usual.

'She was built as a privateer,' said Hornblower.

'Quite right, My Lord. She's the *Daring*; she was built during the war and made one voyage and took six prizes from us before the Treaty of Ghent. And now, My Lord?'

'She could be a slaver.'

'Your Lordship is right again, of course.'

That heavy armament would be desirable in a slaver anchoring up a West African river liable to a treacherous attack; she could easily have a slave deck with that flush build; her speed would minimise deaths among the slaves during the Middle Passage; her lack of capacity for bulk cargo would be unimportant in a slaver.

'*Is* she a slaver?' asked Hornblower.

'Apparently not, My Lord, despite her appearance. She is being chartered to carry a great many men, all the same.'

'I would like you to explain further, if you please, Mr Sharpe.'

'I can only tell Your Lordship the facts as disclosed to me. She is under charter to a French General, Count Cambronne.'

'Cambronne? Cambronne? The man who commanded the Imperial Guard at Waterloo?'

'That's the man, My Lord.'

'The man who said, "The Old Guard dies but does not surrender"?'

'Yes, My Lord, although report says he actually used a ruder expression. He was wounded and taken prisoner, but he did not die.'

'So I have heard. But what does he want with this ship?'

'It is all open and above board, apparently. After the war, Boney's Old Guard formed an organisation for mutual aid. In 1816 they decided to become colonists – Your Lordship must have heard something about the project?'

'Hardly anything.'

'They came out and seized an area of land on the coast of Texas, the province of Mexico adjacent to this State of Louisiana.'

'I have heard about it, but that is the extent of my knowledge.'

'It was easy enough to start, with Mexico in the throes of her revolt against Spain. There was no opposition to them, as you understand, My Lord. But it was not so easy to continue. I cannot imagine that soldiers of the Old Guard would ever make good agriculturists. And on that pestilential coast— It is a series of dreary lagoons, with hardly an inhabitant.'

'The scheme failed?'

'As your Lordship might expect. Half of them died of malaria and yellow fever, and half of the rest simply starved. Cambronne has come out from France to carry the survivors home, five hundred of them. The Government of the United States never liked the project, as Your Lordship can imagine, and now the insurgent government is strong enough to take exception to the presence on the shores of Mexico of a large body of trained soldiers, however peaceable their intentions. Your Lordship can see Cambronne's story could be perfectly true.'

'Yes.'

An eight-hundred-ton ship, equipped as a slaver, could pack five hundred soldiers on board and feed them during a long passage.

'Cambronne is stocking her largely with rice and water – slave rations, My Lord, but the best adapted to the purpose for that very reason.'

The slave trade had had long experience of how to keep alive a close-packed body of men.

'If Cambronne is going to take them back to France I should do nothing to hinder him,' said Hornblower. 'Rather on the contrary.'

'Exactly, My Lord.'

Sharpe's grey eyes met Hornblower's in an expressionless stare. The presence of five hundred trained soldiers afloat in the Gulf of Mexico was very much the concern of the British Admiral commanding in chief, when the shores of the Gulf and of the Caribbean were in as much of a turmoil as at present. Bolivar and the other Spanish-American insurgents would pay a high price for their services in the present war. Or someone might be meditating the conquest of Haiti, or a piratical descent upon Havana. Any sort of filibustering expedition was possible. The actual Bourbon Government in France might be looking for a pie in which to put a finger, for that matter, a chance to snap up a colony and confront the English-speaking powers with a *fait accompli*.

'I'll keep my eye on them until they are safely out of the way,' said Hornblower.

'I have called Your Lordship's attention officially to the matter,' said Sharpe.

It would be one more drain upon Hornblower's limited resources for the policing of the Caribbean; he already was wondering which of his few craft he could detach to observe the Gulf Coast.

'And now, My Lord,' said Sharpe, 'it is my duty to discuss the details of Your Lordship's stay here in New Orleans. I have arranged a programme of official calls for Your Lordship. Does Your Lordship speak French?'

'Yes,' said Hornblower, fighting down the urge to say, 'My Lordship does.'

'That is excellent, because French is commonly spoken among good society here. Your Lordship will, of course, be calling upon the naval authorities here, and upon the Governor. There is an evening reception planned for Your Lordship. My carriage is, of course, at Your Lordship's disposition.'

'That is extremely kind of you, sir.'

'No kindness at all, My Lord. It is a great pleasure to me to assist in making Your Lordship's visit to New Orleans as enjoyable as possible.

I have here a list of the prominent people Your Lordship will meet, along with brief notes regarding them. Perhaps it might be as well if I explain it to Your Lordship's flag-lieutenant?'

'Certainly,' said Hornblower; he was able now to relax his attention a little; Gerard was a good flag-lieutenant and had supported his commander-in-chief very satisfactorily during the ten months that Hornblower had held command. He supplied some of the social flair that Hornblower was too indifferent to acquire. The business was rapidly settled.

'Very well, then, My Lord,' said Sharpe. 'Now I can take my leave. I will have the pleasure of seeing Your Lordship again at the Governor's house.'

'I am deeply obliged to you, sir.'

This city of New Orleans was an enchanting place. Hornblower was bubbling internally with excitement at the prospect of exploring it. Nor was he the only one, as appeared as soon as Sharpe had taken his leave, when Lieutenant Harcourt, captain of the *Crab*, intercepted Hornblower on the quarterdeck.

'Pardon, My Lord,' he said, saluting. 'Are there any orders for me?'

There could be no doubt about what Harcourt had in mind. Forward of the mainmast most of the crew of *Crab* were congregated together looking eagerly aft – in a tiny ship like this everyone was aware of everyone else's business, and discipline ran on lines different from those in a big ship.

'Can you trust your men to be steady on shore, Mr Harcourt?' asked Hornblower.

'Yes, My Lord.'

Hornblower looked forward again. The hands looked remarkably smart – they had been labouring on making new clothes for themselves all the way from Kingston, from the moment when it was announced that *Crab* would have the astonishing distinction of flying the Admiral's flag. They were wearing neat blue frock-jumpers and white ducks and shady straw hats; Hornblower saw their self-conscious poses as he glanced towards them – they knew perfectly well what was being discussed. These were peace-time sailors, voluntarily enlisted: Hornblower had had twenty years of war-time service with pressed crews who could never be trusted not to desert, and even now he had consciously to adjust his mind to the change.

'If you could give me notice of when you intend to sail, sir – I mean My Lord,' said Harcourt.

'Until dawn tomorrow in any case,' said Hornblower coming to a sudden decision; his day was full until then.

'Aye, aye, My Lord.'

Would the grogshops of New Orleans waterfront be any different from the grogshops of Kingston or Port of Spain?

'Now perhaps I can have my breakfast, Mr Gerard,' said Hornblower. 'Unless you have any objection?'

'Aye aye, My Lord,' answered Gerard, carefully ignoring the sarcasm. He had long learned that his Admiral objected to nothing in the world as much as having to be active before breakfast.

It was after breakfast that a coloured man, trotting barefooted along the pier, came bearing on his head a basket of fruit which he handed in at the gangway at the moment when Hornblower was about to start off on his official round of calls.

'There's a note with it, My Lord,' said Gerard. 'Shall I open it?'

'Yes.'

'It is from Mr Sharpe,' reported Gerard, after breaking the seal, and then some seconds later, 'I think you had better read this yourself, My Lord.'

Hornblower took the thing impatiently.

My Lord (read the note),

I have imposed upon myself the pleasure of sending some fruit to Your Lordship.

It is my duty to inform Your Lordship that I have just received information that the freight which Count Cambronne brought out here from France, and which has been lying in bond in charge of the United States Customs Services, will shortly be transferred by lighter through the agency of a bonded carrier to the *Daring*. As Your Lordship will, of course, understand, this is an indication that the *Daring* will be sailing soon. My information is that the amount of bonded freight is very considerable, and I am endeavouring to discover in what it consists. Perhaps Your Lordship might, from Your Lordship's coign of vantage, find an opportunity of observing the nature of this freight.

I am, with great respect,
Your Lordship's humble and obedient servant,
CLOUDESLEY SHARPE,
H.B.M.'s Consul-General at New Orleans.

Now what could Cambronne have possibly brought from France in in large amount that could be legitimately needed for the purpose he had avowed when he chartered the *Daring*? Not personal effects, certainly. Not food or liquor – he could pick those up cheaply in New Orleans. Then what? Warm-weather clothing would be possible explanation. Those Guardsmen might well need it when returning to France from the Gulf of Mexico. It was possible. But a French General, with five hundred men of the Imperial Guard at his disposal, would bear the closest watching when the Caribbean was in such a turmoil. It would be a great help to know what kind of freight he was shipping.

'Mr Harcourt?'

'Sir – My Lord!'

'I would like your company in the cabin for a moment, if you please.'

The young lieutenant stood at attention in the cabin a little apprehensively waiting to hear what his Admiral had to say.

'This isn't a reprimand, Mr Harcourt,' said Hornblower testily. 'Not even an admonition.'

'Thank you, My Lord,' said Harcourt, relaxing.

Hornblower took him to the cabin window and pointed out through it, just as Sharpe had done previously.

'That's the *Daring*,' he said. 'An ex-privateer, now under charter to a French General.'

Harcourt looked his astonishment.

'That is the case,' went on Hornblower. 'And today she will be taking on some cargo out of bond. It will be brought round to her out of bond by lighter.'

'Yes, My Lord.'

'I want to know as much about that cargo as possible.'

'Yes, My Lord.'

'Naturally, I do not want the world to know that I am interested. I want nobody to know unnecessarily.'

'Yes, My Lord. I could use a telescope from here and see a good deal with luck.'

'Very true. You can take note of whether it is bales or boxes or bags. How many there are of each. From the tackle employed you can guess at the weights. You can do all that.'

'Aye aye, My Lord.'

'Make careful note of all you see.'

'Aye aye, My Lord.'

Hornblower fixed his eyes on his youthful flag-captain's face, trying to estimate his discretion. He remembered so well the emphatic words of the First Sea Lord regarding the necessity for the utmost tenderness regarding American susceptibilities. Hornblower decided the young man could be trusted.

'Now, Mr Harcourt,' he said, 'pay special attention to what I have to say. The more I know about that cargo the better. But don't go at it like a bull at a gate. Should an opportunity present itself for finding out what it is, you must seize upon it. I can't imagine what that opportunity may be, but opportunities come to those who are ready for them.'

Long, long ago, Barbara had said to him that good fortune is the portion of those who merit it.

'I understand, My Lord.'

'If the slightest hint of this gets out – if the Americans or the French get to know what you are doing – you will be sorry you were ever born, Mr Harcourt.'

'Yes, My Lord.'

'I've no use for a dashing officer in this connection, Mr Harcourt. I want someone with ingenuity, someone with cunning. You are sure you understand?'

'Yes, My Lord.'

Hornblower at last took his eyes from Harcourt's face. He himself had been a dashing young officer once. Now he had far more sympathy than ever before with the older men who had entrusted him with enterprises. A senior officer had perforce to trust his juniors, while still carrying the ultimate responsibility. If Harcourt should blunder, if he should be guilty of some indiscretion leading to a diplomatic protest, it would certainly be true that he might wish he had never been born – Hornblower would see to that. But Hornblower would be wishing he himself had never been born, too. But there was no useful purpose to be served in pointing that out.

'That is all, then, Mr Harcourt.'

'Aye aye, sir.'

'Come on, Mr Gerard. We're late already.'

The upholstery of Mr Sharpe's carriage was of green satin, and the carriage was admirably sprung, so that although it lurched and swayed over the uneven street surfaces, it did not jolt or jerk. Yet after five minutes of lurching and swaying – the carriage had been standing for some time in the hot May sun – Hornblower felt himself turning as green as the upholstery. The Rue Royale, the Place d'Armes, the Cathedral, received hardly a glance from him. He welcomed the halts despite the fact that each halt meant a formal meeting with strangers, the kind of meeting he disliked most heartily. He stood and gulped in the humid air during the blessed moments between descending from the carriage and entering in under the ornate porticoes that stood to welcome him. It had never occurred to him before that an Admiral's full-dress uniform might with advantage be made of something thinner than broadcloth, and he had worn his broad red ribbon and his glittering star far too often by now to feel the slightest pleasure in displaying it.

At the Naval Headquarters he drank an excellent Madeira; the General gave him a heavy Marsala; at the Governor's mansion he was given a tall drink which had been iced (presumably with ice sent down during the winter from New England and preserved in an ice-house until nearly at mid-summer it was more precious than gold) extraordinarily to the point where actual frost was visible on the tumbler. The delicious cold contents of that tumbler disappeared rapidly, and the tumbler was as rapidly refilled. He checked himself abruptly when he found himself talking a little too loudly and dogmatically regarding some point of trivial importance. He was glad to catch Gerard's eye and withdraw as gracefully as he could; he was also glad that Gerard seemed perfectly cool and sober and had charge of the card-case, dropping the necessary number of cards into the silver trays that the coloured butlers held out to receive them. By the time he reached Sharpe's house he was glad to see a friendly face – friendly even though it was only that morning that he had first set eyes on it.

'It is an hour before the guests are due to arrive, My Lord,' said Sharpe. 'Would Your Lordship care for a short rest?'

'I would indeed,' said Hornblower.

Mr Sharpe's house had a contrivance which merited much attention. It was a douche bath – Hornblower only knew the French name for it. It was in a corner of the bathroom, floored and walled with the most excellent teak; from the ceiling hung an apparatus of perforated zinc, and from this hung a bronze chain. When Hornblower stood under this apparatus and pulled the chain a deluge of delicious cold water came streaming down on him from some unseen reservoir above. It was as refreshing as ever it had been to stand under the wash-deck pump on the deck of a ship at sea, with the additional advantage of employing fresh water – and in his present condition, after his experiences of the day, it was doubly refreshing. Hornblower stood under the raining water for a long time, reviving with every second. He made a mental note to install a similar contrivance at Smallbridge House if ever he found himself at home again.

A coloured valet in livery stood by with towels to save him from the reheating exertion of drying himself, and while he was being dabbed a knock at the door heralded Gerard's entrance.

'I sent to the ship for a fresh shirt for you, My Lord,' he said.

Gerard was really displaying intelligence; Hornblower put on the fresh shirt with gratitude, but it was with distaste that he tightened his stock and pulled on his heavy uniform coat again. He hung the red ribbon over his shoulder, adjusted his star, and was ready to face the next situation. The darkness of evening was descending, but it had not brought much relief from the heat; on the contrary, the drawing-room of Mr Sharpe's house was brightly lit with wax candles that made it feel like an oven. Sharpe was awaiting him, wearing a black coat; his ruffled shirt made his bulky form appear larger than ever. Mrs Sharpe, sweeping in in turquoise blue, was of much the same size; she curtseyed deeply in response to Hornblower's bow when Sharpe presented him, and made him welcome to the house in a French whose soft tang rang pleasantly on Hornblower's ears.

'A little refreshment, My Lord?' asked Sharpe.

'Not at present, thank you, sir,' said Hornblower hastily.

'We are expecting twenty-eight guests besides Your Lordship and Mr Gerard,' said Sharpe. 'Some of them Your Lordship already met during Your Lordship's official calls today. In addition there are—'

Hornblower did his best to keep the list of names in his mind with mental labels attached. Gerard, who came in and found himself a secluded chair, listened intently.

'And there will be Cambronne, of course,' said Sharpe.

'Indeed?'

'I could hardly give a dinner party of this magnitude without inviting the most distinguished foreign visitor, after Your Lordship, present in this city.'

'Of course not,' agreed Hornblower.

Yet six years of peace had hardly stilled the prejudices established during twenty years of war, there was something a little unnatural about the prospect of meeting a French General on friendly terms, especially the late commander-in-chief of Bonaparte's Imperial Guard, and the meeting might be a little strained because Bonaparte was under lock and key in St Helena and complaining bitterly about it.

'The French Consul-General will accompany him,' said Sharpe. 'And there will be the Dutch Consul-General, the Swedish—'

The list seemed interminable; there was only just time to complete it before the first of the guests was announced. Substantial citizens and their substantial wives; the naval and military officers whom he had already met, and their ladies; the diplomatic officers; soon even that vast drawing room was crowded, men bowing and women curtseying. Hornblower straightened up from a bow to find Sharpe at his elbow again.

'I have the honour of making two distinguished figures acquainted with each other,' he said, in French.

'Son Excellence Rear-Admiral Milord Hornblower, Chevalier de l'Ordre Militaire du Bain. Son Excellence le Lieutenant-General le Comte de Cambronne, Grand Cordon de la Legion d'Honneur.'

Hornblower could not help being impressed, even at this moment, at the neat way in which Sharpe had evaded the thorny question of whom to introduce to whom, a French General and count and an English Admiral and peer. Cambronne was an immensely tall bean-pole of a man. Across one lean cheek and the beaky nose ran a purple scar – perhaps the wound he had received at Waterloo; perhaps a wound received at Austerlitz or Jena or any other of the battles in which the French Army had overthrown nations. He was wearing a blue uniform covered with gold lace, girt about with the watered red silk ribbon of the Legion of Honour, a vast plaque of gold on his left breast.

'Enchanted to make your acquaintance, sir,' said Hornblower in his best French.

'No more enchanted than I am to make yours, milord,' replied Cambronne. He had a cold, greeny-grey eye with a twinkle in it; a grey cat's-whisker moustache adorned his upper lip.

'The Baroness de Vautour,' said Sharpe. 'The Baron de Vautour, His Most Christian Majesty's Consul-General.'

Hornblower bowed and said again that he was enchanted. His Most Christian Majesty was Louis XVIII of France, using the papal title conferred on his house centuries earlier.

'The Count is being mischievous,' said Vautour. He indicated Cambronne's star. 'He is wearing the Grand Eagle, given him during the last régime. Officially the Grand Cordon has been substituted, as our host very properly said.'

Vautour called attention to his own star, a more modest affair. Cambronne's displayed an immense eagle of gold, the badge of the now defunct French Empire.

'I won this on the field of battle,' said Cambronne.

'Don Alphonso de Versage,' said Sharpe. 'His Most Catholic Majesty's Consul-General.'

This was the representative of Spain, then. A word or two with him regarding this pending cession of Florida might be informative, but Hornblower had hardly time to exchange formal courtesies before another presentation was being made. It was some time before Hornblower had a breathing space, and could look round the pretty scene in the candlelight, with the uniforms and the broadcloth coats, the bare arms and shoulders of the women in their bright gowns and flashing jewellery, and the two Sharpes moving unobtrusively through the throng marshalling their guests in order of precedence. The entrance of the Governor and his lady was the signal for the announcement of dinner.

The dining-room was as vast as the drawing-room; the table with covers for thirty-two stood comfortably in it with ample room all round for the numerous footmen. The candlelight was more subdued here, but it glittered impressively on the silver which crowded the long table. Hornblower, seated between the Governor's lady and Mrs Sharpe, reminded himself that he must be alert and careful regarding his table manners; it was the more necessary to be alert because he had to speak French on one side of him and English on the other. He looked dubiously at the six different wine glasses that stood at each place – the sherry was already being poured into the first of the glasses. He could see Cambronne seated between two pretty girls and obviously making himself pleasant to both of them. He did not look as if he had a care in the world; if he were meditating a filibustering expedition it did not weigh very heavily on his mind.

A steaming plate of turtle soup, thick with gobbets of green fat. This was to be a dinner served in the Continental fashion which had come in after Waterloo, with no hodge-podge of dishes set out on the table for the guests to help themselves. He spooned cautiously at the hot soup, and applied himself to making small talk with his dinner partners. Dish succeeded dish, and soon he had to face in the hot room the delicate question of etiquette as to whether it was more ungentlemanly to mop the sweat from his face or to leave it there, flowing and visible; his discomfort decided him in the end to mop, furtively. Now Sharpe was catching his eye, and he had to rise to his feet, striving to make his stupefied brain work while the buzz of conversation died down. He raised his glass.

'The President of the United States,' he said; he had been about to continue, idiotically, 'Long may he reign.' He checked himself with a jerk and went on, 'Long may the great nation of which he is President enjoy prosperity and the international amity of which this gathering is symbolic.'

The toast was drunk with acclaim, with nothing said about the fact that over half the continent Spaniards and Spanish-Americans were busy killing each other. He sat down and mopped again. Now Cambronne was on his feet.

'His Britannic Majesty George the Fourth, King of Great Britain and Ireland.'

The toast was drunk and now it was Hornblower's turn again, as evidenced by Sharpe's glance. He stood up, glass in hand, and began the long list.

'His Most Christian Majesty. His Most Catholic Majesty. His Most Faithful Majesty.' That disposed of France and Spain and Portugal. 'His Majesty the King of the Netherlands.'

For the life of him he could not remember who came next. But Gerard caught his despairing eye and gave a significant jerk of his thumb.

'His Majesty the King of Sweden,' gulped Hornblower. 'His Majesty the King of Prussia.'

A reassuring nod from Gerard told him that he had now included all nations represented, and he plucked the rest of his speech out of the whirlpool of his mind.

'Long may Their Majesties reign, in increasing honour and glory.'

Well, that was over, and he could sit down again. But now the Governor was on his feet, speaking in rhetorical phrases, and it broke in upon Hornblower's dulled intelligence that his own health was the next to be drunk. He tried to listen. He was aware of keen glances shot at him from around the table when the Governor alluded to the defence of this city of New Orleans from the 'misguided hordes' who had assailed it in vain – the allusion was perhaps inevitable even though it was over six years since the battle – and he tried to force a smile. At long last the Governor reached his end.

'His Lordship Admiral Hornblower, and I couple with his name a toast to the British Navy.'

Hornblower climbed back upon his feet as the approving murmur of the company died down.

'Thank you for this unexpected honour,' he said, and gulped as he sought for further words. 'And to have my name coupled with that of the great navy in which it has been my privilege to serve so long is an additional honour for which to thank you.'

The ladies were all rising, now that he had sat down, and he stood again while they withdrew. The highly trained footmen swept the table clear of its accessories in a trice, and the men gathered to one end of the table as the decanter was put into circulation. The glasses were filled as Sharpe brought one of the merchants present into the conversation with a question about the cotton crop. It was safe ground from which to make brief and cautious sorties upon the much more debatable ground of world conditions. But only a few minutes later the butler came in and murmured something to Sharpe, who turned to convey the news he brought to the French Consul-General. Vautour rose to his feet with an expression of dismay.

'Perhaps you will accept my excuses, sir,' he said. 'I much regret the necessity.'

'No more than I regret it, Baron,' said Sharpe. 'I trust it is only a slight indisposition.'

'I trust so,' said Vautour.

'The Baroness finds herself indisposed,' explained Sharpe to the company. 'I am sure you gentlemen will all join me in hoping, as I said, that the indisposition is slight, and regretting that it involves the loss to us of the Baron's charming company.'

There was a sympathetic murmur, and Vautour turned to Cambronne.

'Shall I send back the carriage for you, Count?' he asked.

Cambronne pulled at his cat's-whisker moustache.

'Perhaps it might be better if I came with you,' he said. 'Much as I regret leaving this delightful assembly.'

The two Frenchmen took their leave, after polite farewells.

'It is a great pleasure having made your acquaintance, milord,' said Cambronne, bowing to Hornblower. The stiffness of his bow was mitigated by the twinkle in his eye.

'It has been a profound experience to meet so distinguished a soldier of the late Empire,' replied Hornblower.

The Frenchmen were escorted out of the room by Sharpe, voluble in his regrets.

'Your glasses need refilling, gentlemen,' said Sharpe on his return.

There was nothing Hornblower disliked more than drinking large glasses of port in a hot and humid room, even though he now found himself free to discuss the Florida question with the Spanish Consul-General. He was glad when Sharpe made the move to rejoin the ladies. Somewhere within earshot of the drawing-room a string orchestra was playing, but luckily in a subdued manner, so that Hornblower was spared much of the irritation that he usually suffered when he was compelled to listen to music with his tone-deaf ear. He found himself sitting next to one of the pretty young women beside whom Cambronne had been sitting at dinner. In reply to her questions he was forced to admit that on this, his first day, he had seen almost nothing of the city of New Orleans, but the admission led to a discussion of other places he had visited. Two cups of coffee, poured for him by a footman passing round the drawing-room, cleared his head a little; the young woman was attentive and listened well, and nodded sympathetically when the conversation revealed that Hornblower had left behind, at the call of duty, a wife and a ten-year-old son in England.

Gradually the night wore on, and at last the Governor and his lady rose to their feet and the party was over. There were the last few weary minutes of awkward conversation as the carriages were announced one by one, and then Sharpe returned to the drawing-room after escorting the last of the guests to the door.

'A successful evening, I fancy. I trust Your Lordship agrees with me,' he said, and turned to his wife. 'But I must ask you, my dear, to remember to reprimand Grover about the soufflé.'

The entry of the butler with another murmured message prevented Mrs Sharpe's reply.

'Your Lordship's pardon for a moment,' said Sharpe. He wore an expression of dismay and hastened out of the room, leaving Hornblower and Gerard to begin polite words of thanks to his hostess for his pleasant evening.

'Cambronne's stolen a march on us!' exclaimed Sharpe, returning with a rapid waddle. '*Daring* left her mooring three hours ago! Cambronne must have gone on board her the moment he left here.'

He swung round on his wife.

'Was the Baroness really ill?' he demanded of her.

'She seemed decidedly faint,' replied Mrs Sharpe.

'It must have been all a plant,' said Sharpe. 'She was acting. Cambronne put the Vautours up to it because he wanted a chance to get clear away.'

'What do you think he means to do?' asked Hornblower.

'God knows. But I expect he was disconcerted by the arrival of a King's ship here. His leaving in this fashion means he's up to no good. San Domingo – Cartagena – where'll he take that Imperial Guard of his?'

'I'll get after him in any case,' said Hornblower, rising to his feet.

'You'll find it hard to overtake him,' said Sharpe – the fact that he said 'you' and not 'Your Lordship' was a proof of his agitation. 'He has taken two tugs – the *Lightning* and the *Star* – and with the new lighthouses on the river a galloping horse wouldn't overtake him before he reaches the Pass. He'll be clear out to sea by daylight. I don't know if we can find a tug for you tonight in any case, My Lord.'

'I'll start after him, all the same,' said Hornblower.

'I've ordered the carriage round, My Lord,' said Sharpe. 'Forgive us, my dear, if we leave without ceremony.'

Mrs Sharpe received the hasty bows of the three men; the butler was waiting with their hats; the carriage stood at the door, and they scrambled in.

'Cambronne's bonded freight went on board at nightfall,' said Sharpe. 'My man is meeting me at your ship with his report.'

'That may help us make up our minds,' said Hornblower.

The carriage lurched in along the pitch dark streets.

'May I make a suggestion, My Lord?' asked Gerard.

'Yes. What is it?'

'Whatever scheme Cambronne has in mind, My Lord, Vautour is party to it. And he is a servant of the French Government.'

'You're right. The Bourbons want a finger in every pie,' agreed Sharpe, thoughtfully. 'They take every opportunity to assert themselves. Anyone would think it was them that we beat at Waterloo, and not Boney.'

The sound of the horses' hoofs changed suddenly as the carriage reached the pier. They stopped, and Sharpe had the door open before the footman could leap down from the box, but as the three men scrambled out he stood beside the door hat in hand, his dark face illuminated by the carriage lamps.

'Wait!' snapped Sharpe.

They almost ran along the pier to where the glimmer of a lamp revealed the gangway; the two hands of the anchor watch stood at attention in the darkness as they hastened on board.

'Mr Harcourt!' shouted Hornblower as soon as his foot touched the deck; this was no time to stand on ceremony. There was a light in the companion and Harcourt was there.

'Here, My Lord.'

Hornblower pushed his way into the after cabin; a lighted lantern dangled from the deck beam, and Gerard brought in another one.

'What's your report, Mr Harcourt?'

'The *Daring* sailed at five bells in the first watch, My Lord,' said Harcourt. 'She had two tugs with her.'

'I know. What else?'

'The lighter with the freight came alongside her early in the second dog-watch. Just after dark, My Lord.'

A short, dark man came unobtrusively into the cabin as he spoke, and remained in the background.

'Well?'

'This gentleman whom Mr Sharpe sent kept watch as well as me on what they took on board, My Lord.'

'What was it?'

'I kept count as they swayed it up, My Lord. They had lights in the mizzen stay.'

'Well?'

Harcourt had a piece of paper in his hand, and he proceeded to read from it.

'There were twenty-five wooden cases, My Lord.' Harcourt went on just in time to forestall an exasperated exclamation from Hornblower. 'I recognised those cases, My Lord. They are the usual ones in which muskets are shipped, twenty-four stand of arms in each case.'

'Six hundred muskets and bayonets,' put in Gerard, calculating rapidly.

'I guessed as much,' said Sharpe.

'What else?' demanded Hornblower.

'There were twelve large bales, My Lord. Oblong ones, and twenty other bales, long, narrow ones.'

'Couldn't you guess—'

'Would you hear the report of the hand I sent, My Lord?'

'Very well.'

'Come down here, Jones,' yelled Harcourt up the companion, and then turned back to Hornblower. 'Jones is a good swimmer, My Lord. I sent him and another hand off in the quarterboat, and Jones swam to the lighter. Tell His Lordship what you found, Jones.'

Jones was a skinny, stunted young man, who came in blinking at the lights, ill at ease in this distinguished company. When he opened his mouth he spoke with the accent of Seven Dials.

'Uniforms, they was, in them big bales, sir.'

'How do you know?'

'I swum to the side of the lighter, sir. I could reach over an' feel 'em, sir.'

'Did anyone see you?' This was from Sharpe.

'No, sir. No one didn't see me at all, sir. They was all busy swayin' up the cases. Uniforms, they was, in the bales, like I said, sir. What I could feel through the sacking was buttons, sir. Not flat buttons, sir, like yours, sir. Round buttons, like bullets, sir, rows of 'em, on each coat. An' I thought I could feel hembroidery, too, gold lace, p'raps, sir. Uniforms, they was, sir, I'm sure of it.'

The dark man came forward at this moment; in his hands was a limp something that looked like a drowned black cat. Jones pointed to the object before he went on.

'I couldn't guess for the life of me what was in the other bales, sir, the long ones. So I outs with my knife—'

'You're sure no one saw you?'

'Certain sure, sir. I outs with my knife an' cuts the stitching at the end. They'll think it come apart in the handlin', sir. An' I takes the end of one out an' I swims with it back to the quarterboat, sir.'

The dark man held it forward for inspection, and Hornblower took it gingerly, a black, soggy, wet mass of hair, but his fingers encountered metal as he turned it in his hands.

'Heagles, sir,' said Jones.

There was a brass chain and a big brass badge – the same displayed eagle as he had seen that evening on Cambronne's chest. What he held in his hands was a bearskin uniform cap, soaked with its recent immersion, and adorned with the brass finery.

'Is that what the Imperial Guard wore, My Lord?' suggested Gerard.

'Yes,' said Hornblower.

He had seen prints for sale often enough purporting to illustrate the last stand of the Guard at Waterloo. In London now the Guards sported bearskin caps not unlike this that he held in his hand; they had been awarded to the Guards in recognition of their overthrow of the Imperial Guard at the crisis of the battle.

'Then we know all we need to know,' said Sharpe.

'I must try and catch him,' said Hornblower. 'Call all hands, Mr Harcourt.'

'Aye aye, My Lord.'

After the automatic reply Harcourt opened his mouth again to speak, but he could make no sound come from it.

'I remember,' said Hornblower, his cup of unhappiness filling to the brim. 'I said I would not need the hands before morning.'

'Yes, My Lord. But they'll not be far. I'll send along the waterfront and find 'em. I'll have 'em back here in an hour.'

'Thank you, Mr Harcourt. Do your best. Mr Sharpe, we shall need to be towed as far as the Pass. Will you send and order a steam tug for us?'

Sharpe looked over at the dark man who had brought in the bearskin cap.

'Doubt if there'll be one before noon,' said the dark man. '*Daring* took two – and I know now why she did. The *President Madison*'s laid up. *Toueur*'s gone up to Baton Rouge with flat boats. *Ecrevisse* – the one that brought this ship up – went down again in the afternoon. I think *Temeraire*'s on her way up. We might be able to get her to turn round as soon as she arrives. And that's all there are.'

'Noon,' said Hornblower. 'Thirteen hours' start. *Daring*'ll be at sea before we leave here.'

'And she's one of the fastest ships built,' said Sharpe. 'She logged fifteen knots when she was being chased by *Tenedos* during the war.'

'What's the Mexican port where she'll take the soldiers on board?'

'It's only a village on a lagoon, Corpus Christi, My Lord. Five hundred miles and a fair wind.'

Hornblower could picture the *Daring*, with her beautiful lines and enormous spread of canvas, booming along before the trade wind. The little *Crab* in whose cabin he stood was not intended for fast ocean runs. She had been built and rigged small and handy, to work in and out of obscure inlets, doing the police work of the West Indian archipelago. On the run to Corpus Christi *Daring* would certainly gain several hours, a day or more, perhaps, to add to the twelve hours' lead she already enjoyed. It would not take long to march or to ferry five hundred disciplined men on board, and then she would sail again. Where? Hornblower's weary brain baulked at the contemplation of the immensely complex political situation in the lands within easy run of Corpus Christi. If he could guess, he might be able to anticipate *Daring*'s arrival at the danger point; if he merely pursued her to Corpus Christi he would almost certainly arrive there to find her already gone, soldiers and all, having vanished out into the trackless sea on whatever errand of mischief she meditated.

'*Daring*'s an American ship, My Lord,' said Sharpe, to add to his troubles.

That was an important point, a very important point. *Daring* had an ostensibly legal errand, and she flew the Stars and Stripes. He could think of no excuse for taking her into port for examination. His instructions had been very strict regarding his treatment of the American flag. No more than nine years ago America had gone boldly to war against the greatest maritime power in the world on account of the Royal Navy's attitude towards the American mercantile marine.

'She's armed, and she'll be full of men, My Lord,' said Gerard.

That was another important point, and a very positive point at that. With her twelve-pounders and five hundred disciplined soldiers – and her large American crew as well – she could laugh at anything *Crab* could threaten with her six-pounders and her crew of sixteen. *Daring* would be within her rights to refuse to obey any signals from *Crab*, and *Crab* could do nothing to compel obedience. Shoot away a spar? Not so easy with a six-pounder, and even if no one were to be killed by accident there would be a terrible diplomatic storm if he were to fire on the Stars and Stripes. Could he shadow her, so at least to be on hand when her real purpose was revealed? No; impossible. Anywhere out at sea *Daring* had only to spread her wings to a fair wind to leave *Crab* below the horizon in an afternoon, and then *Daring* could resume her true course unpursued.

Sweating in the stifling night, Hornblower felt like a lassoed wild animal. At every moment some fresh coil was being wound about him to render him more helpless. He was tempted, like a wild animal, to lose all self control, to lapse into mad panic, to fling away all his strength in an explosion of rage. He had sometimes seen, during his long professional career, senior officers giving vent to explosions of that sort. But it would not help. He looked round at the circle of faces in the lamplight; the faces wore the sober expressions of men who were witnessing a failure, men who were aware that they were in the presence of an Admiral who had made a woeful hash of the first important business he had encountered. That in itself could drive him insane with fury.

Pride came to help him. He would not sink to human weaknesses in the sight of these men.

'I shall sail in any case,' he said, coldly, 'as soon as I have a crew and a steam tug.'

'May I ask what Your Lordship intends to do?' asked Sharpe.

Hornblower had to think quickly to make a reasonable answer to this question; he had no idea. All he knew was that he was not going to give up without a struggle; no crisis was ever alleviated by wasting time.

'I shall employ what time I have here in the composition of orders for my squadron,' he said. 'My flag-lieutenant will write them at my dictation, and I shall ask you, Mr Sharpe, to undertake the distribution of them by all the means you find available.'

'Very good, My Lord.'

Hornblower remembered at that moment something he should have done already. It was not too late; this part of his duty he must still carry out. And it would at least disguise the anguish he felt.

'Mr Harcourt,' he said. 'I have to commend you greatly on the excellent way in which you executed my orders. You carried out the task of observing *Daring* in most exemplary fashion. You can be sure I shall call the attention of Their Lordships to your behaviour.'

'Thank you, My Lord.'

'And this man Jones,' went on Hornblower. 'No seaman could have acted with more intelligence. You made a good selection, Mr Harcourt, and Jones justified it. I have it in mind to reward him. I can give him an acting rating and confirm it as soon as possible.'

'Thank you, My Lord. He has been rated before and disrated.'

'Drink? Is that why he was denied shore leave?'

'I'm afraid so, My Lord.'

'Then what do you recommend?'

Harcourt was at a loss.

'You could say to his face what you've already said to me, My Lord. You could shake his hand—'

Hornblower laughed.

'And be known through the Navy as the meanest Admiral who ever flew a flag? No. A golden guinea at least. Two guineas. I'll give them to him myself, and I shall request you to give him three days' leave as soon as we see Kingston again. Let him have his debauch, if that is the only way in which we can reward him. I have to consider the feelings of the whole squadron.'

'Aye aye, My Lord.'

'Now, Mr Gerard, I'll begin the writing of those orders.'

It was indeed noon before *Crab* cast off and was taken in tow by the tug *Temeraire*; it was significant of Hornblower's state of mind that he never gave a thought to the implication of that glorious name. The interval before sailing, all the long, stifling morning, was taken up by the dictation of orders, to be dispersed to every ship of his squadron. An infinity of copies was necessary. Sharpe would send them under seal by every British ship leaving New Orleans for the West Indies, in the hope that should one of them encounter a King's ship his orders would be passed on without the delay of being sent to Kingston and then transmitted through official channels. Every ship of the West India squadron was to keep a sharp look-out for the American ship *Daring*. Every ship was to enquire her business, and was to ascertain, if possible, whether *Daring* had troops on board; but (Hornblower sweated more feverishly than ever as he worded this) captains of H.M.'s vessels were reminded of that passage in the Commander-in-Chief's original instructions regarding behaviour towards the American flag. If troops were not on board an effort was to be made to ascertain where they had been landed; if they were, *Daring* was to be kept in sight until they should be landed. Captains were to exercise a wide discretion regarding any interference with *Daring*'s operations.

Seeing that these orders would not leave New Orleans until tomorrow, and would travel by slow merchant ship, it was hardly likely that they would reach any ship of the squadron before *Daring* had done whatever she planned to do. Yet it was necessary to take every possible precaution.

Hornblower signed twenty copies of his orders with a sweating hand, saw them sealed, and handed them over to Sharpe. They shook hands before Sharpe went down the gangway.

'Cambronne will head for Port au Prince or Havana, in my opinion, My Lord,' said Sharpe.

The two places were not more than a thousand miles apart.

'Might it not be Cartagena or La Guaira?' asked Hornblower with elaborate irony. Those places were about a thousand miles apart as well, and more than a thousand miles from Havana.

'It might well be,' said Sharpe, the irony quite wasted on him. Yet it could not be said that he was unsympathetic regarding Hornblower's difficulties, for he went on – 'The very best of good fortune, My Lord, in any case. I am certain Your Lordship will command success.'

Crab cast off, and *Temeraire* had her in tow, smoke and sparks belching from her chimneys, much to Harcourt's indignation. He was afraid not only of fire but of stains on his spotless deck; he had the hands at work pumping up water from overside continuously soaking deck and rigging.

'Breakfast, My Lord?' said Gerard at Hornblower's elbow.

Breakfast? It was one o'clock in the afternoon. He had not been to bed. He had drunk far too much last night, and he had had a busy morning, an anxious morning, and he was as desperately anxious at this moment. His first reaction was to say no; then he remembered how he had complained yesterday (only yesterday? it seemed more like a week ago) about his delayed breakfast. He would not allow his agitation to be so obvious.

'Of course. It could have been served more promptly, Mr Gerard,' he said, hoping he was displaying the irascibility of a man who had not broken his fast.

'Aye aye, My Lord,' said Gerard. He had been Hornblower's flag-lieutenant for several months now, and knew nearly as much about Hornblower's moods as a wife might have done. He knew, too, of Hornblower's kindly interior. He had received his appointment as the son of an old friend, at a moment when admirals' sons and dukes' sons had yearned to serve as flag-lieutenant to the fabulous Hornblower.

Hornblower forced himself to eat his fruit and his boiled eggs, to drink his coffee despite the heat. He whiled away a considerable time before he came on deck again, and during that period he had actually contrived to forget his problems – at least nearly to forget them. But they returned in full force as soon as he came on deck again. So harassing were they that he could feel no interest in this still unusual method of navigating a river, no interest in the low banks that were going by so fast alongside. This hurried departure from New Orleans was only a gesture of despair, after all. He could not hope to catch the *Daring*. She would bring off whatever coup she had in mind almost under his very nose and leave him the laughing-stock of the world – of his world, at least. This would be the last command he would ever hold. Hornblower looked back over the years of half pay he had endured since Waterloo. They had been dignified and happy years, one would think, with a seat in the Lords and a position of influence in the County, a loving wife and a growing son, but he had not been living the right life, even so. The five years after Waterloo, until at last the course of nature brought his promotion to flag rank, had been fretful years; he had only realised it when he knew the intense joy of his appointment to the West Indies. Now all the years to come until he went down into the grave would be as dreary as those five; more dreary, because they would be unrelieved by the hope of future employment at sea.

Here he was, pitying himself, he said to himself bitterly, when what he should be doing was working out the problems set him. What was it Cambronne had in mind? If he could head him off, arrive triumphantly at the place where Cambronne intended to strike his blow, he could retrieve his reputation. He might be able with great good fortune to intervene decisively. But there was turmoil everywhere through Spanish America, and through the West Indies as well, save for the British colonies. One place was as likely as another; in any case it would be extremely doubtful if he would have any excuse to interfere – Cambronne probably held a commission from Bolivar or some other leader; but on the other hand the precautions Cambronne had taken seemed to imply that he would at least prefer that the Royal Navy would not have a chance to intervene. Intervene? With a crew of sixteen not counting supernumeraries, and with nothing larger than a six-pounder? Rubbish. He was a fool. But he must think, think, think.

'It will be sunset before we sight St Philip, My Lord,' reported Harcourt, saluting.

'Very well, Mr Harcourt.'

There would be no salutes fired, then. He would make his departure from the United States with his tail between his legs, so to speak. There could hardly fail to be comment about the briefness of his visit. Sharpe might do his best to explain why he had left so hurriedly, but any explanation would be unsatisfactory. In every way this command for which he had yearned was turning out to be a ridiculous fiasco.

Even this visit, to which he had looked forward so eagerly, was a disappointment. He had seen almost nothing of New Orleans, of America or of the Americans. He could take no interest in this vast Mississippi. His problems deprived him of interest in his surroundings and his surroundings distracted him from a proper attention to his problems. This fantastic method of progression, for instance – *Crab* was going through the water at a good five knots, and there was the current as well. Quite a breeze was blowing past him in consequence; it was extraordinary to be going ahead with the wind dead foul, without a heel or a pitch, with the standing rigging uttering a faint note and yet not a creak from the running rigging.

'Your dinner is served, My Lord,' said Gerard, appearing on deck again.

Darkness was closing in round the *Crab* as Hornblower went below, but the cabin was hot and stuffy.

'Scotch broth, My Lord,' said Giles, putting a steaming plate before him.

Hornblower dipped his spoon perfunctorily into the plate, tried to swallow a few mouthfuls, and laid his spoon down again. Giles poured him a glass of wine; he wanted neither wine nor soup, yet he must not display human weaknesses. He forced himself to take a little more of the soup, enough to preserve appearances.

'Chicken Marengo, My Lord,' said Giles, putting another plate before him.

Appearances were more easily preserved with chicken; Hornblower haggled the joints apart, ate a couple of mouthfuls, and laid down his knife and fork. They would report to him from the deck if the miracle had happened, if *Daring*'s two steam tugs had broken down, or if *Daring* had run aground, and they were passing her triumphantly. Absurd hope. He was a fool.

Giles cleared the table, reset it with cheese dish and cheese plate, and poured a glass of port. A sliver of cheese, a sip of port, and dinner might be considered over. Giles set out the silver spirit lamp, the silver coffee pot, the porcelain cup – Barbara's last present to him. Somehow there was comfort in coffee despite his misery; the only comfort in a black world.

On deck again it was quite dark. On the starboard bow gleamed a light, moving steadily aft to the starboard beam; that must be one of the lighthouses installed by the Americans to make the navigation of the Mississippi as convenient by night as by day. It was one more proof of the importance of this developing commerce – the fact that as many as six steam tugs were being constantly employed was a further proof.

'If you please, My Lord,' said Harcourt in the darkness beside him. 'We are approaching the Pass. What orders, My Lord?'

What could he do? He could only play a losing game out to the bitter end. He could only follow *Daring*, far, far astern of her, in the hope of a miracle, a fortunate accident. The odds were a hundred to one that by the time he reached Corpus Christi the bird would be flown, completely vanished. Yet perhaps the Mexican authorities, if there were any, or local gossip, if he could pick up any, might afford him some indication of the next destination of the Imperial Guard.

'As soon as we are at sea, set a course for Corpus Christi, if you please, Mr Harcourt.'

'Aye aye, My Lord. Corpus Christi.'

'Study your Sailing Directions for the Gulf of Mexico, Mr Harcourt, for the pass into the lagoon there.'

'Aye aye, My Lord.'

That was done, then the decision was taken. Yet he stayed up on deck, trying to wrestle with the problem in all its vague and maddening complexity.

He felt rain on his face and soon it was falling in torrents, roaring on the deck, soaking his best uniform. His cocked hat weighed on his head like lead with the accumulation of water in the brim. He was about to take shelter below when his mind began to follow an old train of thought, and he stayed. Gerard loomed up in the darkness with his sou'wester and oilskins, but he paid no attention to him. Was it possible that all this was a false alarm? That Cambronne had nothing else in mind than to take back the Guard to France? No, of course not. He would not have taken six hundred muskets on board in that case, nor bales of uniforms, and there would have been no need for a hurried and clandestine departure.

'If you please, My Lord,' said Gerard, standing insistently by with his oilskins.

Hornblower remembered how, before he left England, Barbara had taken Gerard to one side and had talked to him long and earnestly. No doubt she had been telling him of the need to see he did not get wet and that he had his meals regularly.

'Too late now, Mr Gerard,' he said, with a grin. 'I'm soaked through.'

'Then please, My Lord, go below and shift your clothes.'

There was genuine anxiety in Gerard's voice, a real concern. The rain was roaring on Gerard's oilskins in the darkness like the nitre-crusher of a powder-mill.

'Oh, very well,' said Hornblower.

He made his way down the little companion, Gerard following him.

'Giles!' called Gerard sharply; Hornblower's servant appeared at once. 'Put out dry clothes for His Lordship.'

Giles began to bustle round the little cabin, kneeling on the deck to fish a fresh shirt out of the chest. Half a gallon of water cascaded down beside him as Hornblower took off his hat.

'See that His Lordship's things are properly dried,' ordered Gerard.

'Aye aye, sir,' said Giles, with sufficient restrained patience in his tone to make Gerard aware that it was an unnecessary order. Hornblower knew that these men were both fond of him. So far their affection had survived his failure – for how long?

'Very well,' he said in momentary irritation. 'I can look after myself now.'

He stood alone in the cabin, stooping under the deck beams. Unbuttoning his soaking uniform coat he realised he was still wearing his ribbon and star; the ribbon, as he passed it over his head, was soaking wet too. Ribbon and star mocked at his failure, just at the very moment when he was sneering at himself for hoping again that *Daring* might have gone aground somewhere during her passage down the river.

A tap at the door brought Gerard back into the cabin.

'I said I could look after myself,' snapped Hornblower.

'Message from Mr Harcourt, My Lord,' said Gerard unabashed. 'The tug will be casting off soon. The wind is fair, a strong breeze, east by north.'

'Very well.'

A strong breeze, a fair wind, would be all in *Daring*'s favour. *Crab* might have stood a chance of overhauling her in fluky, contrary airs. Fate had done everything possible to load the dice against them.

Giles had taken the opportunity to slip back into the cabin. He took the wet coat from Hornblower's hand.

'Didn't I tell you to get out?' blared Hornblower, cruelly.

'Aye aye, My Lord,' replied Giles imperturbably. 'What about this – this cap, My Lord?'

He had picked up the bearskin cap of the Imperial Guard which was still lying in the locker.

'Oh, take it away!' roared Hornblower.

He had kicked off his shoes and was beginning to peel off his stockings when the thought struck him; he remained stooping to consider it.

A bearskin cap – bales and bales of bearskin caps. Why? Muskets and bayonets he could understand. Uniforms, too, perhaps. But who in their sane senses would outfit a regiment for service in tropical America with bearskin caps? He straightened up slowly, and stood still again, thinking deeply. Even uniform coats with buttons and embroidery would be out of place among the ragged ranks of Bolivar's hordes; bearskin caps would be quite absurd.

'Giles!' he roared, and when Giles appeared round the door. 'Bring that cap back to me!'

He took it into his hands again; within him surged the feeling that he held in his hands the clue to the mystery. There was the heavy chain of lacquered brass, the brazen Imperial eagle. Cambronne was a fighting soldier of twenty years' experience in the field; he would never expect men wearing things like this to wage war in the pestilential swamps of Central America or the stifling canebrakes of the West Indies. Then—? The Imperial Guard in their uniforms and bearskins, already historic, would ‘be associated in everyone's mind with the Bonapartist tradition, even now making itself felt as a political force. A Bonapartist movement? In Mexico? Impossible. In France, then?

Within his wet clothes Hornblower felt a sudden surge of warmth as his blood ran hot with the knowledge that he had guessed the solution. St Helena! Bonaparte was there, a prisoner, an exile in one of the loneliest islands in the world. Five hundred disciplined troops arriving by surprise out of a ship flying American colours would set him free. And then? There were few ships in the world faster than the *Daring*. Sailing for France she would arrive there before any warning could reach the civilised world. Bonaparte would land with his Guard – oh, the purpose of the uniforms and bearskins was quite plain. Everyone would remember the glories of the Empire. The French Army would flock to his standard as it had done once before when he returned from Elba. The Bourbons had already outworn their welcome – Sharpe had remarked how they were acting as international busybodies in the hope of dazzling the people with a successful foreign policy. Bonaparte would march again to Paris without opposition. Then the world would be in a turmoil once more. Europe would experience again the bloody cycle of defeat and victory.

After Elba a campaign of a hundred days had been needed to overthrow Bonaparte at Waterloo, but a hundred thousand men had died during those hundred days, millions and millions of money had been expended. This time it might not even be as easy as that. Bonaparte might find allies in the disturbed state of Europe. There might be twenty more years of war, leaving Europe in ruins. Hornblower had fought through twenty years of war; he felt physically sick at the thought of their repetition. The prospect was so monstrous that he went back through the deductions he had been making, but he could not avoid reaching the same conclusion.

Cambronne was a Bonapartist; no man who had been Commander-in-Chief of the Imperial Guard could be anything else. It was even indicated by a trifle – he had worn the Bonapartist Grand Eagle of the Legion of Honour instead of the Bourbon Grand Cordon which had been substituted for it. He had done that with Vautour's knowledge and agreement. Vautour was a servant of the Bourbons, but he must be a traitorous one; the whole business of chartering the *Daring* and sending her fatal freight on board could only have been carried out with the connivance of the French authorities – presumably France was riddled with a fresh Bonapartist conspiracy. The Baroness's behaviour was further proof.

Central America and the West Indies might be in a turmoil, but there was no particular strategic point there (as he well knew after so much pondering about it) inviting an invasion by the Imperial Guard in uniforms and bearskins. It must be St Helena, and then France. He could have no doubt about it now. Now the lives of millions, the peace of the whole world, depended on the decisions he had to make at this moment.

There was a rush of feet on the deck just above his head. He heard ropes slapping down upon it, orders being given, loud creakings. The cabin suddenly leaned over sideways with the setting of sail, catching him completely unaware, so that he staggered and dropped the bearskin cap, which lay unnoticed at his feet. *Crab* rose to an even keel again. The deck under his feet felt suddenly lively, as if the breath of life had been breathed into it. They were at sea; they were heading for Corpus Christi.

With the wind east by north *Crab* would be running wing-and-wing, possibly. Now he had to think fast, with every second of value. He could not afford to run to leeward in this fashion if he were going to change his plans.

And he knew he was going to change them. He had yearned so desperately for a chance to guess whither *Daring* would head after calling at Corpus Christi. Now he could intervene. Now he had a chance to preserve the peace of the world. With his eyes, unseeing, focused upon an infinite distance, he stood in the swaying cabin calling up into his mental sight the charts of the Gulf of Mexico and the Caribbean. The North-east Trades blew across them, not quite as reliably at this time of year as during the winter, but constantly enough to be a calculable factor. A ship bound for the South Atlantic – for St Helena – from Corpus Christi would be bound to take the Yucatan Channel. Then – especially if her business were such as not to invite attention – she would head for the shoulder of South America, down the centre of the Caribbean, with scores of miles of open sea on either beam. But she would have to pass through the chain of the Antilles before breaking through into the Atlantic.

There were a hundred passages available, but only one obvious one, only one route that would be considered for a moment by a captain bound for St Helena and with the trade winds to contend with. He would round Galera Point, the northernmost extremity of Trinidad. He would give it as wide a berth as possible, but he could not give it a very wide berth because to the northward of Galera Point lay the island of Tobago, and the Tobago Channel between the two was no more than – Hornblower could not be sure exactly – certainly no more than fifty miles wide. In favourable conditions a single ship could patrol that channel and make certain that nothing passed through unsighted. It was a typical example of maritime strategy on a tiny scale. Sea power made its influence felt all over the wide oceans, but it was in the narrow seas, at the focal points, that the decisive moments occurred. The Yucatan Channel would not be nearly as suitable as the Tobago Channel, for the former was more than a hundred miles wide. *Crab* would get there first; that could be taken for granted seeing that *Daring* would have two sides of a triangle to cover, calling at Corpus Christi, and with a long beat to windward as a result. It would be best to employ the advantage so gained to hasten to the Tobago Channel. There would be just time to anticipate *Daring* there – just time – and there was a substantial chance that on the way he might meet some ship of his squadron, to take her along with him. A frigate, now. That would give him all the force he needed. He made his resolve at that moment, conscious as he did so of his quickened heartbeat.

'Giles!' shouted Hornblower.

Giles reappeared, and within the wide discretion of a spoiled servant displayed shocked disapproval at the sight of him still in his wet shirt and ducks.

'My compliments to Mr Harcourt, and I would be glad to see him here as quickly as is convenient to him.'

That was very quickly, naturally, when an Admiral needed the presence of a lieutenant.

'Mr Harcourt, I have decided on a change of plan. There is no time to be lost. Kindly set a course for Cape San Antonio.'

'Cape San Antonio. Aye aye, sir.'

Harcourt was a good officer. There was neither surprise nor doubt in his voice as he heard the surprising order.

'When we are on the new course I will explain what I intend to do, if you will have the goodness to report to me with the charts, Mr Harcourt. Bring Mr Gerard with you.'

'Aye aye, sir.'

Now he could take off his wet shirt and trousers, and dab himself dry with a towel. Somehow the little cabin did not seem so oppressively hot; perhaps because they were out at sea, perhaps because he had reached a decision. He was putting on his trousers at the moment when Harcourt had the helm put down. *Crab* came round like a top, with lusty arms hauling in on the sheets. She lay far over to starboard, with the wind abeam, and Hornblower, one leg in his trousers, after a frantic hop, trying to preserve his balance. fell on his nose across his cot with his legs in the air. He struggled to his feet again; *Crab* still heeled over to starboard, farther and then less, as each roller of the beam sea passed under her, each roll taking Hornblower by surprise as he tried to put his other leg into his trousers so that he sat down twice, abruptly, on his cot before he managed it. It was as well that Harcourt and Gerard re-entered the cabin only after he had succeeded. They listened soberly while Hornblower told them of his deductions regarding *Daring*'s plans and of his intention to intercept her at the Tobago Channel; Harcourt took his dividers and measured off the distances, and nodded when he had finished.

'We can gain four days on her to San Antonio, My Lord,' he said. 'That means we'll be three days ahead of her there.'

Three days should be just enough start for *Crab* in the long, long race down the length of the Caribbean.

'Could we call at Kingston on our way, My Lord?' asked Gerard.

It was tempting to consider it, but Hornblower shook his head. It would be no use calling at headquarters, telling the news, possibly picking up reinforcements, if *Daring* slipped past them as they were doing so.

'It would take too long to work in,' he said. 'Even if we had the sea breeze. And there would be delay while we were there. We've nothing to spare as it is.'

'I suppose not, My Lord,' agreed Gerard, grudgingly. He was playing the part of the staff officer, whose duty it was to be critical of any suggested plan. 'Then what do we do when we meet her?'

Hornblower met Gerard's eyes with a steady glance; Gerard was asking the question that had been already asked and left unanswered.

'I am forming plans to meet that situation,' said Hornblower, and there was a rasping tone in his voice which forbade Gerard to press the matter.

'There's not more than twenty miles of navigable water in the Tobago Channel, My Lord,' said Harcourt, still busy with his dividers.

'Then she can hardly pass us unobserved even by night,' said Hornblower. 'I think, gentleman, that we are acting on the best possible plan. Perhaps the only possible plan.'

'Yes, My Lord,' said Harcourt; his imagination was hard at work. 'If Boney once gets loose again—'

He could not go on. He could not face that appalling possibility.

'We have to see to it that he does not, gentlemen. And now that we have done all that we can it would be sensible if we took some rest. I don't think any one of us has had any sleep for a considerable time.'

That was true. Now that he had made up his mind upon a course of action, now that he was committed to it, for good or ill, Hornblower felt his eyelids drooping and sleep overcoming him. He lay down on his cot after his officers had left him. With the wind on the port beam and the cot against the bulkhead to starboard he could relax completely with no fear of rolling out. He closed his eyes. Already he had begun to form the answer to the question Gerard had asked. The answer was a hideous one, something horrible to contemplate. But it seemed to be inevitable. He had his duty to do, and now he could be sure that he was doing it to the best of his ability. With his conscience clear, with a reassuring certainty that he was using the best of his judgment, the inevitability of the rest of the future reinforced his need for sleep. He slept until dawn; he even dozed for a few minutes after that, before he began to think clearly enough again in the daylight for that horrible thought to begin to nag at at him again.

That was how the *Crab* began her historic race to the Tobago Channel, over a distance nearly as great as the Atlantic is wide, with the brave trade wind laying her over as she thrashed along. All hands on board knew that she was engaged in a race, for in a little ship like *Crab* nothing could be kept secret; and all hands entered into the spirit of the race with the enthusiasm to be expected of them. Sympathetic eyes were turned towards the lonely figure of the Admiral standing braced on the tiny quarterdeck with the wind singing round him. Everyone knew the chances he was taking; everyone thought that he deserved to win, and no one could guess at his real torment over the certainty that was crystallising in his mind that this was the end of his career, whether he should win the race or lose it.

No one on board begrudged the constant labour involved in getting every yard of speed out of *Crab*, the continual hauling in and letting out of the sheets as the sails were trimmed to the least variation of the wind, the lightening and urgent shortening of canvas at the last possible moment as squalls came hurtling down upon them, the instant resetting as the squalls passed on their way. All hands constituted themselves as unofficial lookouts; there were really no need for the Admiral to have offered a golden guinea to the man who should first sight *Daring* – there was always the chance of an encounter even before reaching the Tobago Channel. Nobody minded wet shirts and wet beds as the spray burst over *Crab*'s bows in dazzling rainbows and found its way below through the deck as the over-driven schooner worked her seams open in the heavy swell. The hourly casting of the log, the daily calculation of the ship's run, were eagerly anticipated by men who usually displayed all the fatalistic indifference towards these matters of the hardened sailor.

'I am shortening the water allowance, My Lord,' said Harcourt to Hornblower the first morning out.

'To how much?' Hornblower asked the question trying to appear if as he were really interested in the answer, so that his misery over something else should not be apparent.

'To half a gallon, My Lord.'

Two quarts of fresh water a day per man – that would be hardship for men labouring hard in the tropics.

'You are quite right, Mr Harcourt,' said Hornblower.

Every possible precaution must be taken. It was impossible to predict how long the voyage would last, nor how long they would have to remain on patrol without refilling their water casks; it would be absurd if they were driven prematurely into port as a result of thoughtless extravagance.

'I'll instruct Giles,' went on Hornblower, 'to draw the same ration for me.'

Harcourt blinked a little at that; his small experience with Admirals led him to think they led a life of maximum luxury. He had not thought sufficiently far into the problem to realise that if Giles had a free hand as regards drinking water for his Admiral, Giles, and perhaps all Giles's friends, would also have all the drinking water they needed. And there was no smile on Hornblower's face as he spoke; Hornblower wore the same bleak and friendless expression that he had displayed towards everyone since reaching his decision when they went to sea.

They sighted Cape San Antonio one afternoon, and knew they were through the Yucatan Channel; not only did this give them a fresh

departure, but they knew that from now on it would not be extremely
unlikely for them to sight *Daring* at any moment; they were pursuing
much the same course as she would be taking, from this point onwards.
Two nights later they passed Grand Cayman; they did not sight it but
they heard the roar of the surf on one of the outlying reefs. That was a
proof of how closely Harcourt was cutting his corners; Hornblower felt
that he would have given Grand Cayman a wider berth than that – it
was a moment when he chafed more than usual at the convention which
prohibited an Admiral from interfering in the management of his
flagship. The following night they picked up soundings on the Pedro Bank,
and knew that Jamaica and Kingston were a scant hundred miles to
windward of them. From this new departure Harcourt could set a fresh
course, direct for the Tobago Channel, but he could not hold it. The
trade wind took it into its head to veer round south of east, as was not
surprising with midsummer approaching, and it blew dead foul. Harcourt laid *Crab* on the starboard tack – never voluntarily would any
captain worth his salt yield a yard to the southward in the Caribbean –
and clawed his way as close to the wind as *Crab* would lie.

'I see you've taken in the tops'ls, Mr Harcourt,' remarked Hornblower, venturing on ticklish ground.

'Yes, My Lord.' In response to his Admiral's continued enquiring
glance Harcourt condescended to explain further. 'A beamy schooner
like this isn't intended to sail on her side, My Lord. We make less
leeway under moderate sail like this, My Lord, as long as we're closehauled with a strong breeze.'

'You know your own ship best, of course, Mr Harcourt,' said Hornblower, grudgingly.

It was hard to believe that *Crab* was making better progress without
her magnificent square topsails spread to the breeze. He could be sure
that *Daring* would have every stitch of canvas spread – perhaps a single
reef. *Crab* thrashed on her way, once or twice shipping it green over her
starboard bow; those were the moments when it was necessary for every
man to grab and hold on. At dawn next morning there was land right
ahead, a blue line on the horizon – the mountains of Haiti. Harcourt
held on until noon, raising them farther and farther out of the water, and
then he went about. Hornblower approved – in an hour or two the land
breeze might set in and there was Beata Point to weather. It was maddening that on this tack they would actually be losing a little ground, for
it was perfectly possible that *Daring*, wherever she was, might have the
wind a point or two more in her favour and could be able to hold her
course direct. And it was quite remarkable to see the foremast hands
raising wetted fingers to test the wind, and studying the windward
horizon, and criticising the way the quartermaster at the tiller struggled to
gain every yard to windward that he could.

For a day and a half the wind blew foul; in the middle of the second night Hornblower, lying sleepless in his cot, was roused by the call for all hands. He sat up and reaching for his dressing-gown while feet came running above his head. *Crab* was leaping madly.

'All hands shorten sail!'

'Three reefs in the mains'll!' Harcourt's voice was pealing out as Hornblower reached the deck.

The wind blew the tails of Hornblower's dressing-gown and nightshirt up round him as he stood out of the way by the taffrail; darkness was roaring all round him. A midsummer squall had come hurtling at them in the night, but someone had had a weather eye lifting and had been prepared for it. Out of the southward had come the squall.

'Let her pay off!' shouted Harcourt. 'Hands to the sheets!'

Crab came round in a welter of confused water, plunged and then steadied. Now she was flying along in the darkness, belying her unlovely name. She was gaining precious distance to the northward; an invaluable squall this was, as long as it permitted them to hold this course. The roaring night was hurrying by; Hornblower's dressing-gown was whipping about his legs. It was impossible not to feel exhilarated to stand thus, compelling the elements to work in their favour, cheating the wind that thought to take them by surprise.

'Well done, Mr Harcourt,' shouted Hornblower into the wind as Harcourt came and stood beside him in the darkness.

'Thank you, sir – My Lord. Two hours of this is what we need.'

Fate granted them an hour and a half at any rate, before the squall died away and the trade wind pigheadedly resumed its former direction of east by south. But next morning at breakfast Giles was able to report good news.

'Wind's backing to the nor'rard, My Lord,' he said – Giles was as interested as everyone else in the vessel's progress.

'Excellent,' said Hornblower; it was only some seconds later that the dull pain grew up again inside him. That wind would bear him more swiftly to his fate.

As the day wore on the trade wind displayed some of its midsummer freakishness. It died away, died away more and more, until it blew only in fitful puffs, so that there were intervals when *Crab* drifted idly over the glassy blue sea, turning her head to all points of the compass in turn, while the vertical sun blazed down upon a deck in whose seams the pitch melted. Flying fish left fleeting dark tracks upon the enamel surface of the sea. No one cared; every eye was scanning the horizon for the first hint of the next cat's-paw of wind creeping towards them. Perhaps, not too far away in this moody Caribbean, *Daring* was holding her course with all sail set and drawing. The day ended and the night went by, and still the trade wind did not blow; only occasionally would a puff send *Crab* ghosting along momentarily towards the Tobago Channel. The sun blazed down, and men limited to two quarts of water a day were thirsty, thirsty all the time.

They had seen very few sail, and the ones they saw were of no use in furthering Hornblower's plans. An island schooner bound to Belize. A Dutchman homeward bound from Curaçao, no one with whom Hornblower could entrust a letter, and no ship of his own squadron – that was something almost beyond the bounds of possibility. Hornblower could only wait, as the days went by, in grim, bleak patience. At last the freakish wind blew again, from one point north of east, and they were able to hold their course, with topsails set again, heading steadily for the Antilles, reeling off as much as six knots hour after hour. Now as they approached the islands they saw more sails, but they were only inter-island sloops trading between the Leeward Islands and Trinidad. A square rigger seen on the horizon roused momentary excitement, but she was not the *Daring*. She flew the red and gold of Spain – a Spanish frigate heading for the Venezuelan coast, presumably to deal with the insurgents. The voyage was nearly completed; Hornblower heard the cry of land from the mast-head look-out, and it was only a moment before Gerard came into the cabin.

'Grenada in sight, My Lord.'

'Very well.'

Now they were entering the waters where they could really expect to meet *Daring*; now the direction of the wind was of more importance than ever. It was blowing from the north-east, now, and that was helpful. It extinguished the very faint possibility that *Daring* might pass to the northward of Tobago instead of through the Tobago Channel.

'*Daring*'s bound to make the same landfall, My Lord,' said Gerard, 'and by daylight if she can.'

'We can hope for it, at least,' said Hornblower.

If *Daring* had been as long out of sight of land as had *Crab*, in the fluky winds and unpredictable currents of the Caribbean, her captain would certainly take all precautions in his approach.

'I think, Mr Harcourt,' said Hornblower, 'that we can safely hold our course for Point Galera.'

'Aye aye, My Lord.'

Now was the worst period of waiting, of wondering whether the whole voyage might not prove to be a fool's errand, patrolling, beating up to within sight of Trinidad and then going about and reaching past Tobago again towards Grenada. Waiting was bad; if the voyage should not turn out to be a fool's errand it meant something that Hornblower, and Hornblower alone, knew to be worse. Gerard raised the question again.

'How do you propose to stop him, My Lord?'

'There may be means,' answered Hornblower, trying to keep the harshness out of his voice that would betray his anxiety.

It was on a blue and gold, blazing day, with *Crab* ghosting along before only the faintest breeze, that the mast-head lookout hailed the deck with the news of the sighting.

'Sail ho! Dead to loo'ard, sir!'

A sail might be anything, but at long intervals, as *Crab* crept closer, the successive reports made it more and more likely that the strange sail was *Daring*. Three masts – even that first supplementary report made it reasonably sure, for not many big ships plied out into the South Atlantic from the Caribbean. All sail set, even skysails, and stu'ns'ls to the royals. That did not mean quite so much.

'She looks like an American, sir!'

The skysails had already hinted strongly in the same direction. Then Harcourt went up to the mainmast head with his own glass, and came down again with his eyes shining with excitement.

'That's *Daring*, My Lord. I'm sure of it.'

Ten miles apart they lay, on the brilliant blue of the sea with the brilliant blue of the sky above them, and on the far horizon a smudge of land. *Crab* had won her race by twenty-five hours. *Daring* was 'boxing the compass,' swinging idly in all directions under her pyramids of sails in the absence of all wind; *Crab* carried her way for a while longer, and then she, too, fell motionless under the blazing sun. All eyes turned on the Admiral standing stiffly with his hands locked behind him gazing at the distant white rectangles that indicated where lay his fate. The schooner's big mainsail flapped idly, flapped again, and then the boom began to swing over.

'Hands to the sheets!' yelled Harcourt.

The air was so light that they could not even feel it on their sweating faces, but it sufficed to push the booms out, and a moment later the helmsman could feel the rudder take hold just enough to give him control. With *Crab*'s bowsprit pointed straight at *Daring* the breath of wind was coming in over the starboard quarter, almost dead astern, almost dead foul for *Daring* if ever it should reach her, but she was still becalmed. The breath of wind increased until they could feel it, until they could hear under the bows the music of the schooner's progress through the water, and then it died away abruptly, leaving *Crab* to wallow on the swell. Then it breathed again, over the port quarter this time, and then it drew farther aft, so that the topsails were braced square and the foresail could be hauled over to the port side and *Crab* ran wing-and-wing for ten blessed minutes until the wind dropped again to a dead, flaming calm. Then they could see *Daring* catch a wind, see her trim her sails, but only momentarily, only long enough to reveal her intentions before she lay once more helpless. Despite her vast sail area her greater dead weight made her less susceptible to these very faint airs.

'Thank God for that,' said Gerard, glass to his eye, as he watched her swing idly again, 'I think she aims to pass us beyond cannon-shot, My Lord.'

'I shouldn't be surprised at that,' agreed Hornblower.

Another breath, another slight closing of the gap, another dead calm.

'Mr Harcourt, perhaps it would be best if you let the men have their dinners now.'

'Aye aye, My Lord.'

Salt beef and pease pudding under a noonday sun in the tropics – who could have any appetite for that, especially with the excitement of watching for a wind? And in the middle of dinner hands were sent again to the sheets and braces to take advantage of another breath of wind.

'At what time will you have your dinner, My Lord?' asked Giles.

'Not now,' was all the answer Hornblower would give him, glass to eye.

'He's hoisted his colours, My Lord,' pointed out Gerard. 'American colours.'

The Stars and Stripes, regarding which he had been expressly ordered to be particularly tender. But he could be nothing else in any case, seeing that *Daring* mounted twelve-pounders and was full of men.

Now both vessels had a wind, but *Crab* was creeping bravely along at a full two knots, and *Daring*, trying to head to the southward closehauled, was hardly moving; now she was not moving at all, turning aimlessly in a breeze too faint to give her steerage way.

'I can see very few people on her deck, My Lord,' said Harcourt; the eye with which he had been staring through his glass was watering with the glare of sun and sea.

'She'd keep 'em below out of sight,' said Gerard.

That was so likely as to be certain. Whatever *Daring*, and Cambronne, thought of *Crab*'s intentions, it would be safest to conceal the fact that she had five hundred men on board while heading for the South Atlantic.

And between her and that South Atlantic lay *Crab*, the frailest barrier imaginable. Let *Daring* once pass through the channel out into the open sea and nothing could be done to stop her. No ship could hope to overtake her. She would reach St Helena to strike her blow there, and no possible warning could be given. It was now or never, and it was Hornblower's fault that matters had reached such a pass. He had been utterly fooled in New Orleans. He had allowed Cambronne to steal a march on him. Now he had to make any sacrifice that circumstances demanded of him, any sacrifice whatever, to redeem the peace of the world. *Crab* could do nothing to stop *Daring*. It could only be done by his own personal exertions.

'Mr Harcourt,' said Hornblower, in his harsh, expressionless mono-
tone. 'I'll have the quarterboat cleared away ready to lower, if you
please. Have a full boat's crew told off, to double bank the oars.'

'Aye aye, My Lord.'

'Who'll go in her, My Lord?' asked Gerard.

'I will,' said Hornblower.

The mainsail flapped, the boom came creaking inboard, swung out
again, swung in. The breeze was dying away again. For a few minutes
more *Crab* held her course, and then the bowsprit began to turn away
from *Daring*.

'Can't keep her on her course, sir,' reported the quartermaster.

Hornblower swept his gaze round the horizon in the blazing afternoon.
There was no sign of a further breeze. The decisive moment had come,
and he snapped his telescope shut.

'I'll take that boat now, Mr Harcourt.'

'Let me come too, My Lord,' said Gerard, a note of protest in his
voice.

'No,' said Hornblower.

In case a breeze should get up during the next half-hour, he wanted
no useless weight in the boat while crossing the two-mile gap.

'Put your backs into it,' said Hornblower to the boat's crew as they
shoved off. The oarblades dipped in the blue, blue water, shining gold
against the blue. The boat rounded *Crab*'s stern, with anxious eyes
looking down on them; Hornblower brought the tiller over and pointed
straight for *Daring*. They soared up a gentle swell, and down again, up
again and down again; with each rise and fall *Crab* was perceptibly
smaller and *Daring* perceptibly larger, lovely in the afternoon light,
during what Hornblower told himself were the last hours of his professional life. They drew nearer and nearer to *Daring*, until at last a hail
came borne by the heated air.

'Boat ahoy!'

'Coming aboard!' hailed Hornblower back again. He stood up in the
stern-sheets so that his gold-laced Admiral's uniform was in plain sight.

'Keep off!' hailed the voice, but Hornblower held his course.

There could be no international incident made out of this, an un-
armed boat's crew taking an Admiral alone on board a becalmed ship. He
directed the boat towards the mizzen chains.

'Keep off!' hailed the voice, an American voice.

Hornblower swung the boat in.

'In oars!' he ordered.

With the way she carried the boat surged towards the ship; Hornblower timed his movements to the best of his ability, knowing his own
clumsiness. He leaped for the chains, got one shoe full of water, but held
on and dragged himself up.

'Lie off and wait for me!' he ordered the boat's crew, and then turned to swing himself over on to the deck of the ship.

The tall, thin man with a cigar in his mouth must be the American captain; the burly fellow beside him one of the mates. The guns were cast off, although not run out, and the American seamen were standing round them ready to open fire.

'Did you hear me say keep off, mister?' asked the captain.

'I must apologise for this intrusion, sir,' said Hornblower. 'I am Rear-Admiral Lord Hornblower of His Britannic Majesty's service, and I have the most urgent business with Count Cambronne.'

For a moment on the sunlit deck they stood and looked at each other, and then Hornblower saw Cambronne approaching.

'Ah, Count,' said Hornblower, and then made himself speak French. 'It is a pleasure to meet Monsieur le Comte again.'

He took off his cocked hat and held it over his breast and doubled himself in a bow which he knew to be ungainly.

'And to what do I owe this pleasure, milord?' asked Cambronne. He was standing very stiff and straight, his cat's-whisker moustache bristling out on either side.

'I have come to bring you the very worst of news, I regret to say,' said Hornblower. Through many sleepless nights he had rehearsed these speeches to himself. Now he was forcing himself to make them naturally. 'And I have come also to do you a service, Count.'

'What do you wish to say, milord?'

'Bad news.'

'Well?'

'It is with the deepest regret, Count, that I have to inform you of the death of your Emperor.'

'No!'

'The Emperor Napoleon died at St Helena last month. I offer you my sympathy, Count.'

Hornblower told the lie with every effort to appear like a man speaking the truth.

'It cannot be true!'

'I assure you that it is, Count.'

A muscle in the Count's cheek twitched restlessly beside the purple scar. His hard, slightly protruding eyes bored into Hornblower's like gimlets.

'I received the news two days back in Port of Spain,' said Hornblower. 'In consequence I cancelled the arrangements I had made for the arrest of this ship.'

Cambronne could not guess that *Crab* had not made as quick a passage as he indicated.

'I do not believe you,' said Cambronne, nevertheless. It was just the sort of tale that might be told to halt *Daring* in her passage.

'Sir!' said Hornblower, haughtily. He drew himself up even stiffer, acting as well as he could the part of the man of honour whose word was being impugned. The pose was almost successful.

'You must understand the importance of what you are saying. milord,' said Cambronne, with the faintest hint of apology in his voice, But then he said the fatal dreaded words that Hornblower had been expecting. 'Milord, do you give me your word of honour as a gentleman that what you say is true?'

'My word of honour as a gentleman,' said Hornblower.

He had anticipated this moment in misery for days and days. He was ready for it. He compelled himself to make his answer in the manner of a man of honour. He made himself say it steadily and sincerely, as if it did not break his heart to say it. He had been sure that Cambronne would ask him for his word of honour.

It was the last sacrifice he could make. In twenty years of war he had freely risked his life for his country. He had endured danger, anxiety, hardship. He had never until now been asked to give his honour. This was the further price he had to pay. It was through his own fault that the peace of the world was in peril. It was fitting that he should pay the price. And the honour of one man was a small price to pay for the peace of the world, to save his country from the renewal of the deadly perils she had so narrowly survived for twenty years. In those happy years of the past, returning to his country after an arduous campaign, he had looked about him and he had breathed English air and he had told himself with fatuous patriotism that England was worth fighting for, was worth dying for. England was worth a man's honour, too. Oh, it was true. But it was heartrending, it was far, far worse than death that it should be his honour that had to be sacrificed.

A little group of officers had appeared on deck and were standing grouped on either side of Cambronne listening to every word; to one side stood the American captain and his mate. Facing them, alone, his gaudy uniform flashing in the sun, stood Hornblower, waiting. The officer on Cambronne's right spoke next. He was some kind of adjutant or staff officer, clearly, of the breed that Hornblower hated. Of course, he had to repeat the question, to turn the iron in the wound.

'Your word of honour, milord?'

'My word of honour,' repeated Hornblower, still steadily, still like a man of honour.

No one could disbelieve the word of honour of a British Admiral, of a man who had held His Majesty's commission for more than twenty years. He went on now with the arguments he had rehearsed.

'This exploit of yours can be forgotten now, Count,' he said. 'With the Emperor's death all hope of reconstituting the Empire is at an end. No one need know of what you had intended. You, and these gentlemen, and the Imperial Guard below decks, can remain uncompromised with the régime that rules France. You can carry them all home as you had said you would do, and on the way you can drop your warlike stores quietly overboard. It is for this reason that I have visited you like this, alone. My country, your country, do not desire any new incident to imperil the amity of the world. No one need know; this incident can remain a secret between us.'

Cambronne heard what he said, and listened to it, but the first news he had heard was of such moving importance that he could speak of nothing else.

'The Emperor is dead!' he said.

'I have already assured you of my sympathy, Count,' said Hornblower 'I offer it to these gentlemen as well. My very deepest sympathy.'

The American captain broke into the murmurs of Cambronne's staff.

'There's a cat's-paw of wind coming towards us,' he said. 'We'll be under way again in five minutes. Are you coming with us, mister, or are you going over the side?'

'Wait,' said Cambronne; he seemingly had some English. He turned to his staff, and they plunged into debate. When they all spoke at once Hornblower's French was inadequate to follow the conversation in detail. But he could see they were all convinced. He might have been pleased, if there had been any pleasure left in the world for him. Someone walked across the deck and shouted down the hatchway, and next moment the Imperial Guard began to pour up on deck. The Old Guard, Bonaparte's Old Guard; they were all in full uniform, apparently in readiness for battle if *Crab* had been foolish enough to risk one. There were five hundred of them in their plumes and bearskins, muskets in hand. A shouted order formed them up on deck, line behind line, gaunt whiskered men who had marched into every capital in Europe save London alone. They carried their muskets and stood at rigid attention; only a few of them did not look straight to their front, but darted curious glances at the British Admiral. The tears were running down Cambronne's scarred cheeks as he turned and spoke to them. He told them the news in broken sentences, for he could hardly speak for sorrow. They growled like beasts as he spoke. They were thinking of their Emperor dying in his island prison under the harsh treatment of his English jailers; the looks that were turned upon Hornblower now showed hatred instead of curiosity, but Cambronne caught their attention again as he went on to speak of the future. He spoke of France and peace.

'The Emperor is dead!' he said again, as if he were saying that the world had come to an end.

The ranks were ragged now; emotion had broken down even the iron discipline of the Old Guard. Cambronne drew his sword, raising the hilt to his lips in the beautiful gesture of the salute; the steel flashed in the light of the sinking sun.

'I drew this sword for the Emperor,' said Cambronne. 'I shall never draw it again.'

He took the blade in both hands close to the hilt, and put it across his lifted knee. With a convulsive effort of his lean, powerful body he snapped the blade across, and, turning, he flung the fragments into the sea. The sound that came from the Old Guard was like a long-drawn moan. One man took his musket by the muzzle, swung the butt over his head, and brought it crashing down on the deck, breaking the weapon at the small of the butt. Others followed his example. The muskets rained overside.

The American captain was regarding the scene apparently unmoved, as if nothing more would ever surprise him, but the unlit cigar in his mouth was now much shorter, and he must have chewed off the end. He approached Hornblower obviously to ask the explanation of the scene but the French adjutant interposed.

'France,' said the adjutant. 'We go to France.'

'France?' repeated the captain. 'Not—?'

He did not say the words 'St Helena,' but they were implicit in his expression.

'France,' repeated the adjutant, heavily.

Cambronne came towards them, stiffer and straighter than ever as he mastered his emotion.

'I will intrude no further on your sorrow, Count,' said Hornblower. 'Remember always you have the sympathy of an Englishman.'

Cambronne would remember those words later, when he found he had been tricked by a dishonourable Englishman, but they had to be said at this moment, all the same.

'I will remember,' said Cambronne. He was forcing himself to observe the necessary formalities. 'I must thank you, milord, for your courtesy and consideration.'

'I have done my duty towards the world,' said Hornblower.

He would not hold out his hand; Cambronne later would feel contaminated if he touched him. He came stiffly to attention and raised his hand instead in salute.

'Good-bye, Count,' he said. 'I hope we shall meet again in happier circumstances.'

'Good-bye, milord,' said Cambronne, heavily.

Hornblower climbed into the mizzen chains and the boat pulled in to him, and he fell, rather than climbed, into the stern-sheets.

'Give way,' he said. No one could feel as utterly exhausted as he felt. No one could feel as utterly unhappy.

They were waiting for him eagerly on board *Crab*, Harcourt and

Gerard and the others. He still had to preserve an unmoved countenance as he went on board. He still had duties to do.

'You can let *Daring* go past, Mr Harcourt,' he said. 'It is all arranged.'

'Arranged, My Lord?' This was from Gerard.

'Cambronne has given up the attempt. They are going quietly to France.'

'France? To France? My Lord—?'

'You heard what I said.'

They looked across the strip of sea, purple now in the dying day; *Daring* was bracing round her yards to catch the faint breeze that was blowing.

'Your orders are to let them pass, My Lord?' persisted Gerard.

'Yes, damn you,' said Hornblower, and instantly regretted the flash of rage and bad language. He turned to the other. 'Mr Harcourt, we can now proceed into Port of Spain. I presume that even if the wind is fair you will prefer not to risk the Dragon's Mouth by night. You have my permission to wait until daylight.'

'Aye aye, My Lord.'

Even then they would not leave him in peace as he turned to go below.

'Dinner, My Lord?' asked Gerard. 'I'll give orders for it at once.'

Hopeless to snarl back that he wanted no dinner; the discussion that would have ensued would have been worse than going through the form of eating dinner. Even so it meant that on entering his cabin he could not do as he wanted and fall on his cot with his face in his hands and abandon himself to his misery. He had to sit up stiff and square while Giles laid and served and cleared away, while the tropical sunset flamed in the sky and black night swooped down upon the little ship on the purple sea. Only then, after Giles's last 'Good night, My Lord,' could he think again, and work back through all the horror of his thoughts.

He had ceased to be a gentlemen. He was disgraced. Everything was at an end. He would have to resign his command – he would have to resign his commission. How would he ever face Barbara? When little Richard grew up and could understand what had happened how would he ever be able to meet his eyes? And Barbara's aristocratic family would sneer knowingly to each other. And never again would he walk a quarter-deck, and never again step on board with his hand to his hat and the bosun's calls shrilling in salute. Never again; his professional life was at an end – everything was at an end. He had made the sacrifice deliberately and coldbloodedly, but that did not make it any less horrible.

His thoughts moved into the other half of the circle. He could have done nothing else. If he had turned aside to Kingston or Port of Spain *Daring* would have slipped past him, as her time of arrival off Tobago

proved, and any additional strength he might have brought with him –
if any, as was not likely – would have been useless. If he had stayed at
Kingston and sent a despatch to London? If he had done that he might
at least have covered himself with the authorities. But it would have
been unavailing. How much time would elapse between the arrival of his
letter in London and the arrival of *Daring* on the coast of France with
Bonaparte on board? Two weeks? Very likely less than that. The clerks
at the Admiralty would have treated his despatch at first as coming from
a madman. There would be delay in its reaching the First Lord's hands,
delay in its being laid before the Cabinet, delay while action was being
debated, delay while the French ambassador was informed, delay while
joint action was being agreed upon.

And what action, if any – if the Cabinet did not dismiss his letter as
that of an unbalanced alarmist? The peace-time navy of England could
never have been got to sea in time and in sufficient numbers to cover the
whole coast of France so as to make it impossible for *Daring* to land her
deadly cargo. And the mere inevitable leakage of the news that Bonaparte was at sea and expected to land would throw France into immediate
revolution – no doubt about that, and Italy was in a turmoil too. By
writing to London he would have covered himself, as he had already
decided, from the censure of the Government. But it was not the measure
of a man's duty to avoid blame. He had a positive duty to do, and he had
done it, in the only way possible. Nothing else would have stopped
Cambronne. Nothing else. He had seen where his duty lay. He had seen
what the price would be, and now he was paying it. He had bought the
peace of the world at the price of his own honour. He had ceased to be a
gentleman – his thoughts completed the other half of the circle.

His mind plunged on, struggling desperately, like a man in utter
darkness waist deep in a slough. It would not be long before the world
knew of his dishonour. Cambronne would talk, and so would the other
Frenchmen. The world would hear soon of a British Admiral giving his
plighted word in the certain knowledge that he was telling a lie. Before
then he would have left the Service, resigned his command and his
commission. That must be done at once; his contaminated flag must
fly no longer; he must give no further orders to gentlemen. In Port of
Spain there was the Governor of Trinidad. Tomorrow he would tell him
that the West India squadron no longer had a Commander-in-Chief.
The Governor could take all the necessary official action, in circularising
the squadron and informing the Government – just as if yellow fever or
apoplexy had taken off the Commander-in-Chief. In this way anarchy
would be reduced to a minimum, and a change of command arranged as
simply as possible; that was the last service he could perform for his
country, the very last. The Governor would think he was mad, of course
– he might be in a straitjacket tomorrow unless he confessed his shame.

And then the Governor would pity him; the first of the pity, the first of the contempt, he would have to face for the rest of his life. Barbara – Richard – the lost soul plunged on through the stinking slough, through the dark night.

At the end of that dark night a knock at the door brought in Gerard. The message he was bearing died on his lips as he looked at Hornblower's face, white under the tan, and at his hollow eyes.

'Are you quite well, My Lord?' he asked, anxiously.

'Quite well. What is it?'

'Mr Harcourt's respects, My Lord, and we are off the Dragon's Mouth. The wind is fair at nor'-nor'-east and we can make the passage as soon as day breaks, in half an hour, My Lord. We'll drop anchor in Port of Spain by two bells in the forenoon watch, My Lord.'

'Thank you, Mr Gerard.' The words came slowly and coldly as he forced himself to utter them. 'My compliments to Mr Harcourt and that will do very well.'

'Aye aye, My Lord. This will be the first appearance of your flag in Port of Spain, and a salute will be fired.'

'Very well.'

'The Governor, by virtue of his appointment, takes precedence of you, My Lord. Your Lordship must therefore pay the first call. Shall I make a signal to that effect?'

'Thank you, Mr Gerard. I would be obliged if you would.'

The horror still had to be gone through and endured. He had to make himself spick and span; he could not appear on deck unshaven and dirty and untidy. He had to shave and endure Giles's conversation.

'Fresh water, My Lord,' said Giles, bringing in a steaming can. 'Cap'n's given permission, seeing that we'll be watering today.'

There might once have been sheer sensuous pleasure in shaving in fresh water, but now there was none. There might have been pleasure in standing on deck watching *Crab* make the passage of the Dragon's Mouth, in looking about him at new lands, in entering a new port, but now there was none. There might have been pleasure once in fresh linen, even in a crisp new neckcloth, even in his ribbon and star and gold-hilted sword. There might have been pleasure in hearing the thirteen guns of his salute fired and answered, but there was none now – there was only the agony of knowing that never again would a salute be fired for him, never again would the whole ship stand at attention for him as he went over the side. He had to hold himself stiff and straight so as not to droop like a weakling in his misery. He even had to blink hard to keep the tears from overflowing down his cheeks as if he were a sentimental Frenchman. The blazing blue sky overhead might have been black for all he knew.

The Governor was a ponderous Major-General, with a red ribbon and a star, too. He went rigidly through the formalities of the reception, and then unbent as soon as they were alone together.

'Delighted to have this visit from you, My Lord,' he said. 'Please sit down. I think you will find that chair comfortable. I have some sherry which I think you will find tolerable. May I pour Your Lordship a glass?'

He did not wait for an answer, but busied himself with the decanter and glasses.

'By the way, My Lord, have you heard the news? Boney's dead.'

Hornblower had not sat down. He had intended to refuse the sherry; the Governor would not care to drink with a man who had lost his honour. Now he sat down with a jerk, and automatically took the glass offered him. The sound he made in reply to the Governor's news was only a croak.

'Yes,' went on the Governor. 'He died three weeks back in St Helena. They've buried him there, and that's the last of him. Well – are you quite well, My Lord?'

'Quite well, thank you,' said Hornblower.

The cool twilit room was swimming round him. As he came back to sanity he thought of St Elizabeth of Hungary. She, disobeying her husband's commands, had been carrying food to the poor – an apron full of bread – when her husband saw her.

'What have you in your apron?' he demanded.

'Roses,' lied St Elizabeth.

'Show me,' said her husband.

St Elizabeth showed him – and her apron was full of roses.

Life could begin anew, thought Hornblower.

THE STAR OF THE SOUTH

Here where the trade winds blew at their freshest, just within the tropics, in the wide unbroken Atlantic, was, as Hornblower decided at that moment, the finest stretch of water for a yachting excursion to be found anywhere on the globe. This was nothing more than a yachting excursion, to his mind. Only recently he had emerged from a profound spiritual experience during which the peace of the whole world had depended on his judgment; by comparison it seemed now as if the responsibilities of being Commander-in-Chief on the West Indian Station were mere nothings. He stood on the quarterdeck of His Britannic Majesty's frigate *Clorinda*, balancing easily as she reached to windward under moderate sail, and allowed the morning sunshine to stream down on him and the trade wind to blow round his ears. With the pitch and the roll as *Clorinda* shouldered against the sea the shadows of the weather rigging swooped back and forth over the deck; when she took a roll to windward, towards the nearly level morning sun, the shadows of the ratlines of the mizzen shrouds flicked across his eyes in rapid succession, hypnotically adding to his feeling of well-being. To be a Commander-in-Chief, with nothing more to worry about than the suppression of the slave trade, the hunting down of piracy, and the policing of the Caribbean, was an experience more pleasant than any Emperor, or even any poet, could ever know. The bare-legged seamen washing down the decks were laughing and joking; the level sun was calling up dazzling rainbows in the spray flung up by the weather bow; and he could have breakfast at any moment that he wanted it – standing here on the quarterdeck he was finding additional pleasure in anticipation and wantonly postponing that moment.

The appearance of Captain Sir Thomas Fell on the quarterdeck took something away from the feeling of well-being. Sir Thomas was a gloomy, lantern-jawed individual who would feel it his bounden duty to come and be polite to his Admiral, and who would never have the sensitivity to be aware when his presence was undesired.

'Good morning, My Lord,' said the captain, touching his hat.

'Good morning, Sir Thomas,' replied Hornblower, returning the salute.

'A fine fresh morning, My Lord.'

'Yes, indeed.'

Sir Thomas was looking over his ship with a captain's eye, along the decks, up aloft, and then turning aft to observe where, right astern, a smudgy line on the horizon marked the position of the hills of Puerto Rico. Hornblower suddenly realised that he wanted his breakfast more than anything on earth; and simultaneously he realised that he now could not gratify that desire as instantaneously as a Commander-in-Chief should be able to. There were limitations of politeness that constrained even a Commander-in-Chief – or that constrained him at least. He could not turn away and go below without exchanging a few more sentences with Fell.

'Maybe we'll catch something today, My Lord,' said Fell; instinctively with the words the eyes of both men turned aloft to where a look-out sat perched up at the dizzy height of the main topgallant masthead.

'Let's hope we do,' said Hornblower, and, because he had never succeeded in liking Fell, and because the last thing he wanted to do was to enter into a technical discussion before breakfast, he blundered on so as to conceal these feelings. 'It's likely enough.'

'The Spaniards will want to run every cargo they can before the convention's signed,' said Fell.

'So we decided,' agreed Hornblower. Re-hashing old decisions before breakfast was not to his taste, but it was typical of Fell to do that.

'And this is the landfall they'd make,' went on Fell, remorselessly, glancing astern again at Puerto Rico on the horizon.

'Yes,' said Hornblower. Another minute or two of this pointless conversation and he would be free to escape below.

Fell took the speaking-trumpet and directed it upwards.

'Mast-head, there! Keep a good look-out or I'll know the reason why!'

'Aye aye, sir!' came the reply.

'Head money, My Lord,' said Fell, in apologetic explanation.

'We all find it useful,' answered Hornblower, politely.

Head money was paid by the British Government for slaves freed on the high seas, to the Royal Naval ships concerned in the capture of the slaves, and divided among the ship's company like any other prize money. It was a small fund compared with the gigantic sums acquired during the great wars, but at five pounds a head a big capture could bring in a substantial sum to the ship making the capture. And of that substantial sum one-quarter went to the captain. On the other hand, one-eighth went to the Admiral commanding, wherever he happened to be. Hornblower, with twenty ships at sea under his command, was entitled to one-eighth of all their head money. It was a system of division which explained how during the great wars the Admirals commanding the Channel Fleet or in the Mediterranean became millionaires, like Lord Keith.

'No one could find it more useful than I, My Lord,' said Fell.

'Maybe,' said Hornblower.

Hornblower knew vaguely that Fell was in difficulties about money. He had had many years of half pay since Waterloo, and even now as captain of a fifth-rate his pay and allowances were less than twenty pounds a month – lucky though he was, in peace-time, to have command even of a fifth-rate. He had had experience himself of being a poor captain, of wearing cotton stockings instead of silk, and brass epaulettes instead of gold. But he had no desire whatever to discuss the Tables of Personal Pay before breakfast.

'Lady Fell, My Lord,' went on Fell, persistently, 'has a position to maintain in the world.'

She was an extravagant woman, so Hornblower had heard.

'Let's hope we have some luck today, then,' said Hornblower, still thinking about breakfast.

It was a melodramatic coincidence that at that very moment a hail came down from the mast-head.

'Sail ho! Sail right to wind'ard!'

'Perhaps that's what we're waiting for, Sir Thomas,' said Hornblower.

'As likely as not, My Lord. Mast-head, there! How's the sail heading? Mr Sefton, bring the ship to the wind.'

Hornblower backed away to the weather-rail. He felt he could never grow used to his situation as Admiral, and having to stand by and be no more than an interested spectator while the ship he was in was being handled at decisive moments. It was quite painful to be a spectator, but it would be more painful still to go below and remain in ignorance of what was going on – and much more painful than to postpone breakfast again.

'Deck, there! She's a two-master. Heading straight down for us. All sail to the royals. Captain, sir, she's a schooner! A big schooner, sir. Still running down for us.'

Young Gerard, the flag-lieutenant, had come running on deck at the first hail from the mast-head, to his place beside his Admiral.

'A tops'l schooner,' he said. 'A big one. She could be what we're looking for, My Lord.'

'Plenty of other things she could be,' said Hornblower, doing his best to conceal his absurd excitement.

Gerard had his telescope pointing to windward.

'There she is! Coming down fast, right enough. Look at the rake of those masts! Look at the cut of those tops'ls! My Lord, she's no island schooner.'

It would not be a very remarkable coincidence if she should be a slaver; he had brought *Clorinda* here to the windward of San Juan in the full expectation that slave cargoes would be hurrying here. Spain was meditating joining in the suppression of the slave trade, and every slaver would be tempted to run cargoes and take advantage of enhanced prices before the prohibition should take effect. The main slave market for the Spanish colonies was at Havana, a thousand miles to leeward, but it could be looked upon as certain that Spanish slavers, making their passage from the Slave Coast, would touch first at Puerto Rico to refill with water if not to dispose of part of their cargo. It had only been logical to station *Clorinda* to intercept them.

Hornblower took the telescope and trained it on the fast-nearing schooner. He saw what Gerard had spoken about. Hull up now, he could see how heavily sparred she was, and how built for speed. With those fine lines it would only pay for her to carry highly perishable cargo – human cargo. As he looked he saw the rectangle of her square sails narrow vertically; the small distance between her masts widened greatly. She was wheeling away from the waiting *Clorinda* – a final proof, if any was needed, that she was what she appeared to be. Laying herself on the starboard tack, she proceeded to keep at a safe distance, and to increase that distance as fast as possible.

'Mr Sefton!' shouted Fell. 'Fill the main tops'l! After her, on the starboard tack! Set the royals!'

In an orderly and disciplined rush some of the hands hurried to the braces while others scurried aloft to set more sail. It was only a matter of moments before *Clorinda*, as closehauled as she would lie, was thrashing to windward in pursuit. With everything braced up sharp, and carrying every inch of sail that the brisk trade wind would allow, she lay steeply over, plunging through the sea, each wave in turn bursting on her weather bow with the spray flying aft in sheets, and the taut weather-rigging shrieking in the wind. It was a remarkable transition from the quiet that had reigned not so long ago.

'Hoist the colours,' ordered Fell. 'Let's see what she says she is.'

Through the telescope Hornblower watched the schooner hoist her colours in reply – the red and yellow of Spain.

'You see, My Lord?' asked Fell.

'Pardon, Cap'n,' interposed Sefton, the officer of the watch, 'I know who she is. I saw her twice last commission. She's the *Estrella*.'

'The *Australia*?' exclaimed Fell, mishearing Sefton's Spanish pronunciation.

'The *Estrella*, sir. The *Estrella del Sur* – the Star of the South, sir.'

'I know about her, then,' said Hornblower. 'Her captain's Gomez – runs four hundred slaves every passage, if he doesn't lose too many.'

'Four hundred!' repeated Fell.

Hornblower saw a momentary calculating look pass over Fell's face. Five pounds a head meant two thousand pounds; a quarter of that was five hundred pounds. Two years' pay at one swoop. Fell darted glances aloft and overside.

'Keep your luff, there!' he shouted at the helmsman. 'Mr Sefton! Hands to the bowlines there, for'rard.'

'She's weathering on us,' said Gerard, the glass to his eye.

It was really only to be expected that a well-designed schooner would work to windward more efficiently than even the best of square-rigged frigates.

'She's fore-reaching on us, too,' said Hornblower, gauging the distances and angles. She was not only lying closer to the wind but travelling faster through the water. Very little faster, it was true – a knot or perhaps two knots – but enough to render her safe from *Clorinda*'s pursuit.

'I'll have her yet!' said Fell. 'Mr Sefton! Call all hands! Run out the guns on the weather side. Mr James! Find Mr Noakes. Tell him to start the water. Hands to the pumps, Mr Sefton! Pump her dry.'

Hands came pouring up through the hatchways. With the gun-ports opened the guns' crew flung their weight on the gun tackles, inch by inch dragging the guns on the weather side up the steep slope presented by the heeling deck. The rumble of the wooden wheels over the seams of the planking made a stirring sound; it had been the preliminary of many a desperate fight in the old days. Now the guns were merely being run out in order to keep the ship on a slightly more even keel, giving her a better grip on the water and minimising leeway. Hornblower watched the pumps being manned; the hands threw their weight on the handles with a will, the rapid clank-clank proving how hard they were at work, pumping overside the twenty tons of drinking water which might be thought of as the life-blood of a cruising ship. But the slight reduction of draught that would result might, combined with the running out of the weather guns, add a few yards to her speed.

The call for all hands had brought Mr Erasmus Spendlove on deck, Hornblower's secretary. He looked round him at the organised confusion on deck with that air of Olympian superiority which always delighted Hornblower. Spendlove cultivated a pose of unruffled calm that exasperated some and amused others. Yet he was a most efficient secretary, and Hornblower had never once regretted acting on the recommendation of Lord Exmouth and appointing him to his position.

'You see the vulgar herd all hard at work, Mr Spendlove,' said Hornblower.

'Truly they appear to be, My Lord.' He looked to windward at the *Estrella*. 'I trust their labours will not be in vain.'

Fell came bustling by, still looking up at the rigging and overside at the *Estrella*.

'Mr Sefton! Call the carpenter. I'll have the wedges of the main-mast knocked loose. More play there may give us more speed.'

Hornblower caught a change of expression on Spendlove's face, and their eyes met. Spendlove was a profound student of the theory of ship design, and Hornblower was a man with a lifetime of experience, and the glance they exchanged, brief as it was, was enough for each to know that the other thought the new plan unwise. Hornblower watched the main shrouds on the weather side taking the additional strain. It was as well that *Clorinda* was newly refitted.

'Can't say we're doing any better, My Lord,' said Gerard from behind his telescope.

The *Estrella* was perceptibly farther ahead and more to windward. If she wished, she would run *Clorinda* practically out of sight by noon. Hornblower observed an odd expression on Spendlove's face. He was testing the air with his nose, sniffing curiously at the wind as it blew past him. It occurred to Hornblower that once or twice he had been aware, without drawing any conclusions from the phenomenon, that the clean trade wind had momentarily been tainted with a hint of a horrible stench. He himself tried the air again, and caught another musky whiff. He knew what it was – twenty years ago he had smelt the same stench when a Spanish galley crowded with galley slaves had passed to windward. The trade wind, blowing straight from the *Estrella* to the *Clorinda*, was bearing with it the reek from the crowded slave ship, tainting the air over the clean blue sea far to leeward of her.

'We can be sure she's carrying a full cargo,' he said.

Fell was still endeavouring to improve *Clorinda*'s sailing qualities.

'Mr Sefton! Set the hands to work carrying shot up to wind'ard.'

'She's altering course!' Half a dozen voices made the announcement at the same moment.

'Belay that order, Mr Sefton!'

Fell's telescope, like all the others, was trained on the *Estrella*. She had put her helm up a little, and was boldly turning to cross *Clorinda*'s bows.

'Damned insolence!' exclaimed Fell.

Everyone watched anxiously as the two ships proceeded headlong on converging courses.

'She'll pass us out of range,' decided Gerard; the certainty became more apparent with every second of delay.

'Hands to the braces!' roared Fell. 'Quartermaster! Starboard your helm! Handsomely! Handsomely! Steady as you go!'

'Two points off the wind,' said Hornblower. 'We stand more chance now.'

Clorinda's bows were now pointed to intercept the *Estrella* at a far-distant point, several miles ahead. Moreover, lying a little off the wind as both ships now were, it seemed probable that *Estrella*'s fore-and-aft rig and fine lines might not convey so great an advantage.

'Take a bearing, Gerard,' ordered Hornblower.

Gerard went to the binnacle and read the bearing carefully.

'My impression,' said Spendlove, gazing over the blue, blue water, 'is that she's still fore-reaching on us.'

'If that's the case,' said Hornblower, 'then all we can hope for is that she carries something away.'

'We can at least hope for it, My Lord,' said Spendlove. The glance he directed upwards was indicative of his fear that it would be the *Clorinda* whose gear would give way. *Clorinda* now had wind and sea very nearly abeam. She was lying over very steeply under every inch of canvas she could carry, and lifting unwillingly to the seas which came rolling in upon her, swirling in through her open gun-ports. Hornblower realised that he had not a dry stitch of clothing on him, and probably no one else on board had, either.

'My Lord,' said Gerard, 'you've had no breakfast as yet.'

Hornblower tried to conceal the discomfiture he felt at this reminder. He had forgotten all about breakfast, despite the cheerful anticipation with which he had once been looking forward to it.

'Quite right, Mr Gerard,' he said, jocular, but only clumsily so, thanks to being taken by surprise. 'And what of it?'

'It's my duty to remind you, My Lord,' said Gerard. 'Her Lady-ship—'

'Her Ladyship told you to see that I took my meals regularly,' replied Hornblower. 'I am aware of that. But Her Ladyship, owing to her inexperience, made no allowance for encounters with fast-sailing slavers just at meal-times.'

'But can't I persuade you, My Lord?'

The thought of breakfast, now that it had been reimplanted in his mind, was more attractive than ever. But it was hard to go below with a pursuit being so hotly conducted.

'Take that bearing again before I decide,' he temporised.

Gerard walked to the binnacle again.

'Bearing's opening steadily, My Lord,' he reported. 'She must be drawing ahead fast.'

'Clearly so,' said Spendlove, telescope trained out towards the *Estrella*. 'And it looks – it looks as if she's hauling in on her sheets. Maybe—'

Hornblower had whipped his telescope to his eye on the instant.

'She's gibing over!' he pronounced. 'See how she comes round, by George!'

Estrella must have a bold captain and a well-trained crew. They had hauled in on her sheets and had stood ready at her topsail braces. Then, with the helm hard over, she had spun round on her heel. Her whole beautiful profile was now presented to Hornblower's telescope. She was headed to cross *Clorinda*'s bows from starboard to port, and not too far ahead, either.

'Damned insolence!' said Hornblower, but full of admiration for the daring and skill displayed.

Fell was standing close by, staring at the impertinent schooner. He was rigid, even though the wind was flapping his coat-tails round him. For a few seconds it seemed as if the two vessels were heading towards a common point, where they must meet. But the impression soon passed. Even without taking a compass bearing it became apparent that *Estrella* must pass comfortably ahead of the frigate.

'Run the guns in!' bellowed Fell. 'Stand by to wear ship! Clear away the bow chasers, there!'

It might be just possible that the schooner would pass within range of the bow chasers, but to take a shot at her, at long range and on that heaving sea, would be a chancy business. Should they score a hit, it might as likely take effect in the hull, among the wretched slaves, as on the spars or rigging. Hornblower was prepared to restrain Fell from firing.

The guns were run in, and after another minute's examination of the situation Fell ordered the helm to be put a-starboard and the ship laid right before the wind. Hornblower through his telescope could see the schooner lying right over with the wind abeam, so far over that she, as she heaved, presented a streak of copper to his view, pinkish against the blue of the sea. Clearly she was drawing across the frigate's bows, as Fell tacitly acknowledged when he ordered a further turn of two points to port. Thanks to her two knots superiority in speed, and thanks also to her superior handiness and weatherliness, the *Estrella* was literally making a circle round the *Clorinda*.

'She's built for speed, My Lord,' said Spendlove from behind his telescope.

So was *Clorinda*, but with a difference. *Clorinda* was a fighting ship, built to carry seventy tons of artillery; with forty tons of powder and shot in her magazines. It was no shame to her that she should be out-sailed and outmanoeuvred by such a vessel as the *Estrella*.

'I fancy she'll make for San Juan, Sir Thomas,' said Hornblower.

Fell's face bore an expression of helpless fury as he turned to his Admiral; it was with an obvious effort that he restrained himself from pouring out his rage, presumably in a torrent of blasphemy.

'It's – it's—' he spluttered.

'It's enough to madden a saint,' said Hornblower.

Clorinda had been ideally stationed, twenty miles to windward of San Juan; *Estrella* had run practically into her arms, so to speak, and had yet dodged neatly round her and had won for herself a clear run to the port.

'I'll see him damned, My Lord!' said Fell. 'Quartermaster!'

There was now the long run ahead to San Juan, one point off the wind, in what was practically a race with an even start. Fell laid a course for San Juan; it was obvious that *Estrella*, comfortably out of range on the starboard beam, was heading for the same point. Both ships had the wind practically abeam; this long run would be a final test of the sailing qualities of the two ships, as though they were a couple of yachts completing a triangular course in a race in the Solent. Hornblower reminded himself that earlier this morning he had compared the present voyage with a yachting excursion. But the expression in Fell's face showed that his flag-captain by no means looked on it in the same light. Fell was in the deadliest earnest, and not from any philanthropic feelings about slavery, either. It was the head money he wanted.

'About that breakfast, My Lord?' said Gerard.

An officer was touching his hat to Fell with the request that it might be considered noon.

'Make it so,' said Fell. The welcome cry of 'Up spirits' rang through the ship.

'Breakfast, My Lord?' asked Gerard again.

'Let's wait and see how we do on this course,' said Hornblower. He saw something of dismay in Gerard's face and laughed. 'It's a question of your breakfast, I fancy, as well as mine. You've had nothing this morning?'

'No, My Lord.'

'I starve my young men, I see,' said Hornblower, looking from Gerard to Spendlove; but the latter's expression was peculiarly unchanging, and Hornblower remembered all he knew about him. 'I'll wager a guinea that Spendlove hasn't spent the morning fasting.'

The suggestion was answered by a wide grin.

'I am no sailor, My Lord,' said Spendlove. 'But I have learned one thing while I have been at sea, and that is to snatch at any meal that makes its appearance. Fairy gold vanishes no faster than the opportunity of eating food at sea.'

'So, while your Admiral has been starving, you have been walking this deck with a full belly? Shame on you.'

'I feel that shame as deeply as the situation merits, My Lord.'

Spendlove obviously had all the tact that an Admiral's secretary needed to have.

'Hands to the main-brace,' bellowed Fell.

Clorinda was hurtling along over the blue sea with the wind abeam; it was her best point of sailing, and Fell was doing all he could to get the very best out of her. Hornblower looked over at *Estrella*.

'I fancy we're falling behind,' he said.

'I think so, too, My Lord,' said Gerard after a glance in the same direction. He walked over and took a bearing, and Fell glared at him with irritation before turning to Hornblower.

'I hope you will agree, My Lord,' he said, 'that *Clorinda* has done all a ship can do?'

'Certainly, Sir Thomas,' said Hornblower. Fell really meant to say that no fault could be found with his handling of the ship; and Hornblower, while convinced that he himself could have handled her better, had no doubt that in any case *Estrella* would have evaded capture.

'That schooner sails like a witch,' said Fell. 'Look at her now, My Lord.'

Estrella's lovely lines and magnificent sail plan were obvious even at this distance.

'She's a beautiful vessel,' agreed Hornblower.

'She's headreaching on us for sure,' announced Gerard from the binnacle. 'And I think she's weathering on us, too.'

'And there goes five hundred pounds,' said Fell, bitterly. Assuredly he was in need of money. 'Quartermaster! Bear up a point. Hands to the braces!'

He brought *Clorinda* a little closer to the wind and studied her behaviour before turning back to Hornblower.

'I'll not give up the chase until I'm compelled, My Lord,' he said.

'Quite right,' agreed Hornblower.

There was something of resignation, something of despair, in Fell's expression. It was not only the thought of the lost money that troubled him, Hornblower realised. The report that Fell had tried to capture the *Estrella*, and had failed, almost ludicrously, would reach their Lordships of the Admiralty, of course. Even if Hornblower's own report minimised the failure it would still be a failure. That meant that Fell would never be employed again after his present two years' appointment had expired. For every captain with a command in the Royal Navy now there were twenty at least hungry for commands. The slightest lapse would be seized upon as reason for ending a man's career; it could not be otherwise. Fell was now looking forward apprehensively to spending the rest of his life on half pay. And Lady Fell was an expensive and ambitious woman. No wonder that Fell's usually red cheeks had a grey tinge.

The slight alteration of course Fell had ordered was really a final admission of defeat. *Clorinda* was retaining her windward position only at the cost of seeing *Estrella* draw more rapidly ahead.

'But I fear she'll beat us easily into San Juan,' went on Fell with admirable stoicism. Right ahead the purple smear on the horizon that marked the hills of Puerto Rico was growing loftier and more defined. 'What orders have you for me in that case, My Lord?'

'What water have you left on board?' asked Hornblower in return.

'Five tons, My Lord. Say six days at short allowance.'

'Six days,' repeated Hornblower, mostly to himself. It was a tiresome complication. The nearest British territory was a hundred miles to windward.

'I had to try the effect of lightening the ship, My Lord,' said Fell, self-exculpatory.

'I know, I know.' Hornblower always felt testy when someone tried to excuse himself. 'Well, we'll follow *Estrella* in if we don't catch her first.'

'It will be an official visit, My Lord?' asked Gerard quickly.

'It can hardly be anything else with my flag flying,' said Hornblower. He took no pleasure in official visits. 'We may as well kill two birds with one stone. It's time I called on the Spanish authorities, and we can fill up with water at the same time.'

'Aye aye, My Lord.'

A visit of ceremony in a foreign port meant many calls on the activity of his staff – but not as many as on him, he told himself with irritation.

'I'll have my breakfast before anything else comes to postpone it,' he said. The perfect good humour of the morning had quite evaporated now. He would be in a bad temper now if he allowed himself to indulge in the weaknesses of humanity.

When he came on deck again the failure to intercept *Estrella* was painfully obvious. The schooner was a full three miles ahead, and had weathered upon *Clorinda* until the latter lay almost in her wake. The coast of Puerto Rico was very well defined now. *Estrella* was entering into territorial waters and was perfectly safe. All hands were hard at work in every part of the ship bringing everything into that condition of perfection – really no more perfect than invariably prevailed – which a British ship must display when entering a foreign port and submitting herself to the jealous inspection of strangers. The deck had been brought to a whiteness quite dazzling in the tropical sun; the metal-work was equally dazzling – painful when the eye received a direct reflection; gleaming cutlasses and pikes were ranged in decorative patterns on the bulkhead aft; white cotton lines were being rove everywhere, with elaborate Turk's heads.

'Very good, Sir Thomas,' said Hornblower approvingly.

'Authority in San Juan is represented by a Captain-General, My Lord,' said Spendlove.

'Yes. I shall have to call upon him,' agreed Hornblower. 'Sir Thomas, I shall be obliged if you will accompany me.'

'Aye aye, My Lord.'

'Ribbons and stars, I fear, Sir Thomas.'

'Aye aye, My Lord.'

Fell had received his knighthood of the Bath after a desperate frigate action back in 1813. It had been a tribute to his courage if not to his professional abilities.

'Schooner's taking a pilot on board!' hailed the mast-head look-out.

'Very well!'

'Our turn shortly,' said Hornblower. 'Time to array ourselves for our hosts. They will be grateful, I hope, that our arrival will take place after the hour of the siesta.'

It was also the hour when the sea breeze was beginning to blow. The pilot they took on – a big, handsome quadroon – took the ship in without a moment's difficulty, although, naturally, Fell stood beside him consumed with anxiety. Hornblower, free from any such responsibility, was able to go forward to the gangway and examine the approaches to the city; it was a time of peace, but Spain had been an enemy before and might perhaps be an enemy again, and at least nothing would be lost if he knew as much as possible about the defences first-hand. It did not take very long to perceive why San Juan had never been attacked, not to speak of captured, by the numerous enemies of Spain during the long life of the city. It was ringed by a lofty wall, of stout masonry, with ditches and bastions, moats and drawbridges. On the lofty bluff overlooking the entrance, Morro Castle covered the approaches with artillery; there was another fortress – which must be San Cristobal – and battery succeeded battery along the waterfront, with heavy guns visible in the embrasures. Nothing less than a formal siege, with powerful army and a battering train, could make any impression on San Juan as long as it was defended by an adequate garrison.

The sea breeze brought them up the entrance passage; there was the usual momentary anxiety about whether the Spaniards were prepared to salute his flag, but the anxiety was speedily allayed as the guns in the Morro began to bang out their reply. Hornblower held himself stiffly to attention as the ship glided in, the forecastle saluting carronade firing at admirably regular intervals. The hands took in the canvas with a rapidity that did them credit – Hornblower was watching unobtrusively from under the brim of his cocked hat – and then *Clorinda* rounded-to and the anchor cable rumbled through the hawse-hole. A deeply sun-burned officer in a fine uniform came up the side and announced himself, in passable English, as the port medical officer, and received Fell's declaration that *Clorinda* had experienced no infectious disease during the past twenty-one days.

Now that they were in the harbour, where the sea breeze circulated with difficulty, and the ship was stationary, they were aware of the crushing heat; Hornblower felt instantly the sweat trickling down inside his shirt under his heavy uniform coat, and he turned his head uncomfortably from side to side, feeling the constriction of his starched neckcloth. A brief gesture from Gerard beside him pointed out what he had already observed – the *Estrella del Sur* in her gleaming white paint lying at the pier close beside them. It seemed as if the reek of her still reached his nostrils from her open hatchways. A file of soldiers, in blue coats with white cross-belts, was drawn up on the pier, standing some-what negligently under command of a sergeant. From within the hold of the schooner came a most lamentable noise – prolonged and doleful wailings. As they watched they saw a string of naked Negroes come climbing with difficulty up through the hatchway. They could hardly walk – in fact some of them could not walk at all, but fell to their hands and knees and crawled in that fashion over the deck and on to the pier.

'They're landing their cargo,' said Gerard.

'Some of it at least,' replied Hornblower. In nearly a year of study he had learned much about the slave trade. The demand for slaves here in Puerto Rico was small compared with that at Havana. During the Middle Passage the slaves he saw had been confined on the slave decks, packed tight 'spoon fashion', lying on their sides with their knees bent up into the bend of the knees of the next man. It was only to be expected that the captain of the *Estrella* would take this opportunity of giving his perish-able cargo a thorough airing.

A hail from overside distracted them. A boat with the Spanish flag at the bow was approaching; sitting in the stern-sheets was an officer in a brilliant gold-laced uniform that reflected back the setting sun.

'Here comes Authority,' said Hornblower.

The side was manned and the officer came aboard to the trilling of the pipes of the bosun's mates, very correctly raising his hand in salute. Hornblower walked over to join Fell in receiving him. He spoke in Spanish, and Hornblower was aware that Fell had none of that language.

'Major Mendez-Castillo,' the officer announced himself. 'First and Principal Aide-de-Camp to His Excellency the Captain-General of Puerto Rico.'

He was tall and slender, with a thin moustache that might have been put on with grease paint; he looked cautiously, without committing himself, at the two officers in their red ribbons and stars, and glittering epaulettes, who were receiving him.

'Welcome, Major,' said Hornblower. 'I am Rear-Admiral Lord Hornblower, Commander-in-Chief of His Britannic Majesty's ships and vessels in West Indian waters. May I present Captain Sir Thomas Fell, commanding His Britannic Majesty's ship *Clorinda*.'

Mendez-Castillo bowed to each of them, his relief at knowing which was which was faintly apparent.

'Welcome to Puerto Rico, Your Excellency,' he said. 'We had, of course, heard that the famous Lord Hornblower was now Commander-in-Chief here, and we had long hoped for the honour of a visit from him.'

'Many thanks,' said Hornblower.

'And welcome to you and to your ship, Captain,' added Mendez-Castillo hastily, nervous in case it should be too apparent that he had been so engrossed in his meeting with the fabulous Hornblower that he had paid insufficient attention to a mere captain. Fell bowed awkwardly in reply – interpretation was unnecessary.

'I am instructed by His Excellency,' went on Mendez-Castillo, 'to enquire if there is any way in which His Excellency can be of service to Your Excellency on the notable occasion of this visit?'

In Spanish, the phrasing of the pompous sentence was even more difficult than in English. And as Mendez-Castillo spoke his glance wavered momentarily towards the *Estrella*; obviously all the details of the *Clorinda*'s attempted interception were already known – much of the unavailing pursuit must have been visible from the Morro. Something in the Major's attitude conveyed the impression that the subject of the *Estrella* was not open to discussion.

'We intend to make only a brief stay, Major. Captain Fell is anxious to renew the water supply of his ship,' said Hornblower, and Mendez-Castillo's expression softened at once.

'Of course,' he said, hastily. 'Nothing could be easier. I will give instructions to the Captain of the Port to afford Captain Fell every facility.'

'You are too kind, Major,' said Hornblower. Bows were exchanged again, Fell joining in although unaware of what had been said.

'His Excellency has also instructed me,' said Mendez-Castillo, 'that he hopes for the honour of a visit from Your Excellency.'

'I had hoped that His Excellency would be kind enough to invite me.'

'His Excellency will be charmed to hear it. Perhaps Your Excellency would be kind enough to visit His Excellency this evening. His Excellency would be charmed to receive Your Excellency at eight o'clock, along with the members of Your Excellency's staff, at La Fortaleza, the Palace of Santa Catalina.'

'His Excellency is too good. We shall be delighted, naturally.'

'I shall inform His Excellency. Perhaps Your Excellency would find it convenient if I were to come on board at that time to escort Your Excellency and Your Excellency's party?'

'We shall be most grateful, Major.'

The Major took his leave after a final reference to the Captain of the Port and the watering of the ship. Hornblower explained briefly to Fell.

'Aye aye, My Lord.'

Here came another visitor, up the port side of the ship, a squat, heavily built man in dazzling white linen, wearing a broad-brimmed hat which he took off with scrupulous politeness as he reached the quarter-deck. Hornblower watched him address himself to the midshipman of the watch, and saw the latter hesitate and look round him while trying to make up his mind as to whether he should grant the request.

'Very well, midshipman,' said Hornblower. 'What does the gentleman want?'

He could guess very easily what the gentleman wanted. This might be an opportunity of making contact with the shore other than through official channels – something always desirable, and peculiarly so at this moment. The visitor came forward; a pair of bright, quizzical blue eyes studied Hornblower closely as he did so.

'My Lord?' he said. He at least could recognise an Admiral's uniform when he saw it.

'Yes. I am Admiral Lord Hornblower.'

'I fear to trouble you with my business, My Lord.' He spoke English like an Englishman, like a Tynesider, perhaps, but obviously as if he had not spoken it for years.

'What is it?'

'I came on board to address myself to your steward, My Lord, and to the president of the wardroom mess, and to the purser. The principal ship chandler of the port. Beef cattle, My Lord, chickens, eggs, fresh bread, fruits, vegetables.'

'What is your name?'

'Eduardo Stuart – Edward Stuart, My Lord. Second mate of the brig *Columbine*, out of London. Captured back in 1806, My Lord, and brought in here as a prisoner. I made friends here, and when the Dons changed sides in 1808 I set up as ship chandler, and here I've been ever since.'

Hornblower studied the speaker as keenly as the speaker was studying him. He could guess at much of what was left unsaid. He could guess at a fortunate marriage, and probably at a change of religion – unless Stuart had been born a Catholic, as was possible enough.

'And I am at your service, My Lord,' went on Stuart, meeting his gaze without flinching.

'In a moment I'll let you speak to the purser,' said Hornblower. 'But tell me first, what impression has our arrival made here?'

Stuart's face crinkled into a grin.

'The whole town was out watching your chase of the *Estrella del Sur*, My Lord.'

'I guessed as much.'

'They all rejoiced when they saw her escape you. And then when they saw you coming in they manned the batteries.'

'Indeed?'

The Royal Navy's reputation for prompt action, both daring and high-handed, must still be very much alive, if there could be even a momentary fear that a single frigate would attempt to snatch a prize from out of the shelter of a port as well guarded as San Juan.

'In ten minutes your name was being spoken in all the streets, My Lord.'

Hornblower's keen glance reassured him that he was not being paid an idle compliment.

'And what is the *Estrella* going to do now?'

'She has only come in to land a few sickly slaves and renew with water, My Lord. It's a poor market for slaves here. She sails for Havana at once, as soon as she can be sure of your movements, My Lord.'

'At once?'

'She'll sail with the land breeze at dawn tomorrow, My Lord, unless you are lying outside the port.'

'I don't expect I shall be,' said Hornblower.

'Then she'll sail without a doubt, My Lord. She'll want to get her cargo landed and sold in Havana before Spain signs the Convention.'

'I understand,' said Hornblower.

Now what was this? Here were the old symptoms, as recognisable as ever, the quickened heart-beat, the feeling of warmth under the skin, the general restlessness. There was something just below the horizon of his mind, some stirring of an idea. And within a second the idea was up over the horizon, vague at present, like a hazy landfall, but as certain and as reassuring as any landfall. And beyond, still over the horizon, were other ideas, only to be guessed at. He could not help glancing over at the *Estrella*, sizing up the tactical situation, seeking further inspiration there, testing what he already had in mind.

It was all he could do to thank Stuart politely for his information, without betraying the excitement he felt, and without terminating the interview with suspicious abruptness. A word to Fell made certain that Stuart would receive the business of supplying the *Clorinda*, and Hornblower waved away Stuart's thanks. Hornblower turned away with as great an appearance of nonchalance as he could manage.

There was plenty of bustle over there by the *Estrella*, just as there was round the *Clorinda*, with preparations being made for filling the water casks. It was hard to think in the heat and the noise. It was hard to face the cluttered deck. And darkness was approaching, and then would come eight o'clock, when he would be making his call upon the Captain-General, and obviously everything must be thought out before that. And there were complications. Successive ideas were arising, one out of another, like Chinese boxes, and each one in turn had to be examined for flaws. The sun was down into the hills, leaving a flaming sky behind, when he came to his final resolution.

'Spendlove!' he snapped; excitement made him curt. 'Come below with me.'

Down in the big stern cabin it was oppressively hot. The red sky was reflected in the water of the harbour, shining up through the stern windows; the magnificent effect was dissipated with the lighting of the lamps. Hornblower threw himself into his chair; Spendlove stood looking at him keenly, as Hornblower was well aware. Spendlove could be in no doubt that his temperamental Commander-in-Chief had much on his mind. Yet even Spendlove was surprised at the scheme that was sketched out to him, and at the orders he received. He even ventured to protest.

'My Lord—' he said.

'Carry out your orders, Mr Spendlove. Not another word.'

'Aye aye, My Lord.'

Spendlove left the cabin, with Hornblower sitting there alone, waiting. The minutes passed slowly – precious minutes; there were few to spare – before the knock came on the door that he expected. It was Fell, entering with every appearance of nervousness.

'My Lord, have you a few minutes to spare?'

'Always a pleasure to receive you, Sir Thomas.'

'But this is unusual, I fear, My Lord. I have a suggestion to make – an unusual suggestion.'

'Suggestions are always welcome too, Sir Thomas. Please sit down and tell me. We have an hour at least before we go ashore. I am most interested.'

Fell sat bolt upright in his chair, his hands clutching the arms. He swallowed twice. It gave Hornblower no pleasure to see a man who had faced steel and lead and imminent death apprehensive before him; it made him uncomfortable.

'My Lord—' began Fell, and swallowed again.

'You have all my attention, Sir Thomas,' said Hornblower, gently.

'It has occurred to me,' said Fell, growing more fluent with each word until at last he spoke in a rush, 'that we still might have a chance at the *Estrella*.'

'Really, Sir Thomas? Nothing could give me greater pleasure, if it were possible. I would like to hear what you suggest.'

'Well, My Lord. She'll sail tomorrow. Most likely at dawn, with the land breeze. Tonight we might – we might fix some kind of drogue to her bottom. Perhaps to her rudder. She's no more than a knot or two faster than we are. We could follow her out and catch her at sea—'

'This is brilliant, Sir Thomas. Really ingenious – but nothing more than could be expected of a seaman of your reputation, let me add.'

'You are too kind, My Lord.' There was a struggle only too perceptible in Fell's expression, and he hesitated before he went on at last – 'It was your secretary, Spendlove, who put the idea in my mind, My Lord.'

'Spendlove? I can hardly believe it.'

'He was too timid to make the suggestion to you, My Lord, and so he came to me with it.'

'I'm sure he did no more than set the wheels of your thought turning, Sir Thomas. In any case, since you have assumed the responsibility the credit must be yours, of course, if credit is to be awarded. Let us hope there will be a great deal.'

'Thank you, My Lord.'

'Now about this drogue. What do you suggest, Sir Thomas?'

'It need be no more than a large sea anchor. A bolt of No. 1 canvas, sewn into a funnel, one end larger than the other.'

'It would have to be reinforced even so. Not even No. 1 canvas could stand the strain with *Estrella* going at twelve knots.'

'Yes, My Lord, I was sure of that. Bolt-ropes sewn in in plenty. That would be easy enough, of course. We have a spare bob-stay chain on board. That could be sewn round the mouth of the drogue—'

'And could be attached to the *Estrella* to take the main strain.'

'Yes, My Lord. That was what I thought.'

'It would serve to keep the drogue under water out of sight as well.'

'Yes, My Lord.'

Fell found Hornblower's quickness in grasping the technical points vastly encouraging. His nervousness was now replaced by enthusiasm.

'And where would you propose to attach this drogue, Sir Thomas?'

'I was thinking – Spendlove suggested, My Lord – that it might be passed over one of the lower pintles of the rudder.'

'It would be likely to tear the rudder clean away when exerting its full force.'

'That would serve our purpose equally well, My Lord.'

'Of course, I understand.'

Fell walked across the cabin to where the great cabin window stood open wide.

'You can't see her from here as we lie now, My Lord,' he said. 'But you can hear her.'

'And smell her,' said Hornblower, standing beside him.

'Yes, My Lord. They're hosing her out at present. But you can hear her, as I said.'

Over the water came very plainly to them, along with the miasma of her stench, the continued wailing of the wretched slaves; Hornblower fancied he could even hear the clanking of the leg irons.

'Sir Thomas,' said Hornblower, 'I think it would be very desirable if you would put a boat overside to row guard round the ship tonight.'

'Row guard, My Lord?' Fell was not very quick in the uptake. In the peace-time Navy it was unnecessary to take elaborate precautions against desertion.

'Oh, yes, most certainly. Half these men would be overside swimming for the shore as soon as night falls. Surely you understand that, Sir Thomas. We must restrain their passion to desert from this brutal service. And in any case a guard-boat will prevent the sale of liquor through the gun-ports.'

'Er – yes, I suppose so, My Lord.' But Fell clearly had not grasped the implications of the suggestion, and Hornblower had to elaborate.

'Let us set a boat-rowing guard now, before nightfall. I can explain to the authorities why it is necessary. Then when the time comes—'

'We'll have a boat ready in the water!' Enlightenment had broken in on Fell at last.

'Attracting no attention,' supplemented Hornblower.

'Of course!'

The red sunset showed Fell's face lit up with animation.

'It would be best if you gave that order soon, Sir Thomas. But meanwhile there's little time to spare. We must have this drogue in the making before we go ashore.'

'Shall I give the orders, My Lord?'

'Spendlove has figures at his fingertips. He can work out the measurements. Would you be kind enough to send for him, Sir Thomas?'

The cabin was soon crowded with people as the work was put in hand. Spendlove came first; after him Gerard was sent for, and then Sefton, the first-lieutenant. Next came the sail-maker, the armourer, the carpenter, and the boatswain. The sail-maker was an elderly Swede who had been forced into the British navy twenty years ago in some conscienceless action of the press gang, and who had remained in the service ever since. His wrinkled face broke into a grin, like a shattered window, as the beauties of the scheme dawned upon him when he was told about it. He just managed to restrain himself from slapping his thigh with glee when he remembered he was in the august presence of his Admiral and his captain. Spendlove was busy sketching out with pencil and paper a drawing of the drogue, with Gerard looking over his shoulder.

'Perhaps even I might make a contribution to this scheme,' said Hornblower, and everyone turned to look at him; he met Spendlove's eye with a glassy stare that forbade Spendlove to breathe a word to the effect that the whole scheme was his original idea.

'Yes, My Lord?' said Fell.

'A length of spun yarn,' said Hornblower, 'made fast to the tail of the drogue and led for'rard and the other end secured to the chain. Just a single strand, to keep it tail end forward while *Estrella* gets under way. Then when she sets all sail and the strain comes—'

'The yarn will part!' said Spendlove. 'You're right, My Lord. Then the drogue will take the water—'

'And she'll be ours, let's hope,' concluded Hornblower.

'Excellent, My Lord,' said Fell.

Was there perhaps a mild condescension, a tiny hint of patronage, in what he said? Hornblower felt that there was, and was momentarily nettled at it. Already Fell was quite convinced that the whole scheme was his own – despite his handsome earlier admission that Spendlove had contributed – and he was generously allowing Hornblower to add a trifling suggestion. Hornblower allayed his irritation with cynical amusement at the weaknesses of human nature.

'In this stimulating atmosphere of ideas,' he said, modestly, 'one can hardly help but be infected.'

'Y-yes, My Lord,' said Gerard, eyeing him curiously. Gerard was too sharp altogether, and knew him too well. He had caught the echo of mock-modesty in Hornblower's tone, and was on the verge of guessing the truth.

'No need for you to put your oar in, Mr Gerard,' snapped Hornblower. 'Do I have to recall you to your duty? Where's my dinner, Mr Gerard?

Do I always have to starve while I'm under your care? What will Lady Barbara say when she hears you allow me to go hungry?'

'I beg pardon, My Lord,' spluttered Gerard, entirely taken aback. 'I'd quite forgotten – you've been so busy, My Lord—'

His embarrassment was intense; he turned this way and that in the crowded cabin as if looking about him for the missing dinner.

'No time now, Mr Gerard,' said Hornblower. Until the need for distracting Gerard's attention had arisen he had been equally forgetful of the need for dinner. 'Let's hope His Excellency will offer us some small collation.'

'I really must beg your pardon, My Lord,' said Fell, equally embarrassed.

'Oh, no matter, Sir Thomas,' said Hornblower, waving the apologies aside testily. 'You and I are in the same condition. Let me see that drawing, Mr Spendlove.'

He was continually being led into playing the part of a peppery old gentleman, when he knew himself to be nothing of the sort. He was able to mellow again as they went once more through the details of the construction of the drogue, and he gave his approval.

'I believe, Sir Thomas,' he said, 'that you have decided to entrust the work to Mr Sefton during our absence ashore?'

Fell bowed his agreement.

'Mr Spendlove will remain under your orders, Mr Sefton. Mr Gerard will accompany Sir Thomas and me. I don't know what you have decided, Sir Thomas, but I would suggest that you bring a lieutenant and a midshipman with you to His Excellency's reception.'

'Aye aye, My Lord.'

'Mr Sefton, I am sure I can trust you to have this work completed by the time of our return, early in the middle watch, I fancy?'

'Yes, My Lord.'

So there it was all settled, except for the dreary interval of waiting. This was just like war-time, standing by with a crisis looming in the near future.

'Dinner, My Lord?' suggested Gerard, eagerly.

He wanted no dinner. He was weary now that all was settled and the tension easing.

'I'll call for Giles if I want some,' he said, looking round the crowded cabin. He wanted to dismiss the horde of people, and sought words to do so politely.

'Then I'll attend to my other duties, My Lord,' said Fell, suddenly and surprisingly tactful.

'Very well, Sir Thomas, thank you.'

The cabin emptied itself rapidly; Hornblower was able by a mere look to put an end to Gerard's tendency to linger. Then he could sink back into his chair and relax, sturdily ignoring Giles when he came in with another lighted lamp for the darkening cabin. The ship was full of the sound of the business of watering, sheaves squealing in blocks, pumps clanking, hoarse orders; the noise was sufficiently distracting to prevent his thoughts maintaining any regular course. He was in half a doze when a knock on the door preceded the arrival of a midshipman.

'Cap'n's respects, My Lord, and the shore boat is approaching.'

'My compliments to the captain, and I'll be on deck at once.'

The shore boat was bright with a lantern hanging over the stern-sheets in the midst of the darkness of the harbour. It lit up Mendez-Castillo's resplendent uniform. Down the side they went, midshipman, lieutenants, captain, Admiral, in the reversed order of naval precedence, and powerful strokes of the oars carried them over the black water towards the city, where a few lights gleamed. They passed close by the *Estrella*; there was a light hanging in her rigging, but apparently she had completed her watering, for there was no activity about her.

Nevertheless, there came a continuous faint wailing from up her open hatchways. Perhaps the slaves there were mourning the departure of those of them who had been taken from them; perhaps they were voicing their apprehension at what the future held in store for them. It occurred to Hornblower that these unfortunate people, snatched from their homes, packed into a ship whose like they had never seen before, guarded by white men (and white faces must be as extraordinary to them as emerald green ones would be to a European) could have no idea at all of what lay in store for them, any more than he himself would have if he were to be abducted to another planet.

'His Excellency,' said Mendez-Castillo behind him, 'has had pleasure in deciding to receive Your Excellency with full ceremonial.'

'That is most kind of His Excellency,' replied Hornblower, recalling himself to his present duties with an effort, and expressing himself in Spanish with even more effort.

The tiller was put over and the boat turned abruptly round a corner, revealing a brightly lit jetty, with a massive gateway beyond. The boat ran alongside and half a dozen uniformed figures stood to attention as the party climbed on shore.

'This way, Your Excellency,' murmured Mendez-Castillo.

They passed through the gateway into a courtyard lit by scores of lanterns, which shone on ranks of soldiers drawn up in two treble lines. As Hornblower emerged into the courtyard a shouted order brought the muskets to the present, and at the same moment a band burst into music. Hornblower's tone-deaf ear heard the jerky braying, and he halted at attention with his hand to the brim of his cocked hat, his fellow officers beside him, until the deafening noise – echoed and multiplied by the surrounding walls – came to an end.

'A fine military appearance, Major,' said Hornblower, looking down the rigid lines of white cross-belts.

'Your Excellency is too kind. Would Your Excellency please proceed to the door in front?'

An imposing flight of steps, lined on either side with more uniforms; beyond that an open doorway and a vast room. A prolonged whispered conference between Mendez-Castillo and an official beside the door, and then their names blared out in resounding Spanish – Hornblower had long given up hope of ever hearing his name pronounced intelligibly by a foreign tongue.

The central figure in the room rose from his chair – which was almost a throne – to receive the British Commander-in-Chief standing. He was a much younger man than Hornblower had expected, in his thirties, dark complexioned, with a thin, mobile face and a humorous expression at odds with his arrogant hooked nose. His uniform gleamed with gold lace, with the Order of the Golden Fleece on his breast.

Mendez-Castillo made the presentations; the Englishmen bowed deeply to the representative of His Most Catholic Majesty and each received a polite inclination in return. Mendez-Castillo ventured so far as to murmur their host's titles – probably a breach of etiquette, thought Hornblower, for it should be assumed that visitors were fully aware of them.

'His Excellency the Marques de Ayora, Captain-General of His Most Catholic Majesty's dominion of Puerto Rico.'

Ayora smiled in welcome.

'I know you speak Spanish, Your Excellency,' he said. 'I have already had the pleasure of hearing you do so.'

'Indeed, Your Excellency?'

'I was a major of migueletes under Claros at the time of the attack on Rosas. I had the honour of serving beside Your Excellency – I remember Your Excellency well. Your Excellency would naturally not remember me.'

It would have been too flagrant to pretend he did, and Hornblower was for once at a loss for a word, and could only bow again.

'Your Excellency,' went on Ayora, 'has changed very little since that day, if I may venture to say so. It is eleven years ago.'

'Your Excellency is too kind.' That was one of the most useful phrases in polite language.

Ayora had a word for Fell – a compliment on the appearance of his ship – and a supplementary smile for the junior officers. Then, as if it were a moment for which he had been waiting, Mendez-Castillo turned to them.

'Perhaps you gentlemen would care to be presented to the ladies of the company?' he said; his glance passed over Hornblower and Fell and took in only the lieutenants and the midshipmen. Hornblower translated, and saw them depart a little nervously under Mendez-Castillo's escort.

Ayora, etiquette and Spanish training notwithstanding, wasted no time in coming to the point the moment he found himself alone with Hornblower and Fell.

'I watched your pursuit of the *Estrella del Sur* today through my telescope,' he said, and Hornblower once more found himself at a loss for a word; a bow and a smile also seemed out of place in this connection. He could only look blank.

'It is an anomalous situation,' said Ayora. 'Under the preliminary convention between our governments the British Navy has the right to capture on the high seas Spanish ships laden with slaves. But once within Spanish territorial waters those ships are safe. When the new convention for the suppression of the slave trade is signed then those ships will be forfeit to His Most Catholic Majesty's government, but until that time it is my duty to give them every protection in my power.'

'Your Excellency is perfectly correct, of course,' said Hornblower. Fell was looking perfectly blank, not understanding a word of what was said, but Hornblower felt that the effort of translating was beyond him.

'And I fully intend to carry out my duty,' said Ayora, firmly.

'Naturally,' said Hornblower.

'So perhaps it would be best to come to a clear understanding regarding future events.'

'There is nothing I would like better, Your Excellency.'

'It is clearly understood, then, that I will tolerate no interference with the *Estrella del Sur* while she is in waters under my jurisdiction?'

'Of course I understand that, Your Excellency,' said Hornblower.

'The *Estrella* wishes to sail at the first light of morning tomorrow.'

'That is what I expected, Your Excellency.'

'And for the sake of the amity between our governments it would be best if your ship were to remain in this harbour until after she sails.'

Ayora's eyes met Hornblower's in a steady stare. His face was perfectly expressionless; there was no hint of a threat in that glance. But a threat was implied, the ultimate hint of superior strength was there. At Ayora's command a hundred thirty-two-pounders could sweep the waters of the harbour. Hornblower was reminded of the Roman who agreed with his Emperor because it was ill arguing with the master of thirty legions. He adopted the same pose as far as his acting ability allowed. He smiled the smile of a good loser.

'We have had our chance and lost it, Your Excellency,' he said. 'We can hardly complain.'

If Ayora felt any relief at his acquiescence it showed no more plainly than his previous hint of force.

'Your Excellency is most understanding,' he said.

'Naturally we are desirous of taking advantage of the land breeze to leave tomorrow morning,' said Hornblower, deferentially. 'Now that we have refilled with water – for the opportunity of doing so I have to thank Your Excellency – we would not like to trespass too far upon Your Excellency's hospitality.'

Hornblower did his best to maintain an appearance of innocence under Ayora's searching stare.

'Perhaps we might hear what Captain Gomez has to say,' said Ayora, turning aside to summon someone close at hand. He was a young man, strikingly handsome, dressed in plain but elegant blue clothes with a silver-hilted sword at his side.

'May I present,' said Ayora, 'Don Miguel Gomez y Gonzalez, Captain of the *Estrella del Sur?*'

Bows were exchanged.

'May I felicitate you on the sailing qualities of your ship, Captain?' said Hornblower.

'Many thanks, señor.'

'*Clorinda* is a fast frigate, but your ship is superior at all points of sailing.' Hornblower was not too sure about how to render that technical expression into Spanish, but apparently he contrived to make himself understood.

'Many thanks again, señor.'

'And I could even venture' – Hornblower spread his hands deprecatingly – 'to congratulate her captain on the brilliance with which he managed her.'

Captain Gomez bowed, and Hornblower suddenly checked himself. These high-flown Spanish compliments were all very well, but they could be overdone. He did not want to give the impression of a man too anxious to please. But he was reassured by a glance at the expression on Gomez's face. He was actually simpering; that was the only word for it. Hornblower mentally classified him as a young man of great ability and well pleased with himself. Another compliment would not be one too many.

'I shall suggest to my government,' he went on, 'that they request permission to take off the lines of the *Star of the South*, and study the plan of her sails, in order to build a similar vessel. She would be ideal for the work of the Navy in these waters. But, of course, it would be hard to find a suitable captain.'

Gomez bowed once more. It was hard not to be self-satisfied when complimented by a seaman with the legendary reputation of Hornblower.

'His Excellency,' put in Ayora, 'is desirous of leaving the harbour tomorrow morning.'

'So we understood,' said Gomez.

Even Ayora looked a trifle disconcerted at the admission. Hornblower could see it plainly. Stuart, so helpful with his information, had not hesitated to help both sides, as Hornblower had expected he would. He had gone straight to the Spanish authorities with the intelligence Hornblower had supplied him with. But Hornblower had no desire to allow a jarring note to creep into the present conversation.

'You can understand, Captain,' he said, 'that I would be glad to leave on the same tide and with the same land breeze that takes you out. After our experiences today I fear you need be under no apprehension.'

'None at all,' said Gomez. There was something of condescension in his smile. That agreement was all that Hornblower wanted. He was at pains to conceal his relief.

'It will be my duty to pursue you if you are still in sight when I leave,' he said, apologetically; by his glance he made it clear that the remark was addressed to the Captain-General as well as to Gomez, but it was Gomez who answered.

'I have no fear,' he said.

'In that case, Your Excellency,' said Hornblower, clinching the matter, 'I can inform Your Excellency officially that His Majesty's Ship in which my flag is being flown will leave harbour tomorrow morning as early as suits Captain Gomez's convenience.'

'That is understood,' agreed Ayora. 'I regret greatly that Your Excellency's visit should be so brief.'

'In the life of a sailor,' said Hornblower, 'duty seems invariably to interfere with inclination. But at least during this brief visit I have had the pleasure of making the acquaintance of Your Excellency, and of Captain Gomez.'

'There are numerous other gentlemen here also desirous of making Your Excellency's acquaintance,' said Ayora. 'May I be permitted to present them to Your Excellency?'

The real business of the evening had been transacted, and now it was only necessary to go through the other formalities. The rest of the reception was as dreary as Hornblower had expected and feared; the Puerto Rican magnates who were led up in turn to meet him were as dull. At midnight Hornblower caught the eye of Gerard and gathered his flock together. Ayora noted the gesture and gave, in courteous terms, the leave to depart which, as His Catholic Majesty's representative, he had to give unless his guests were to be guilty of discourtesy.

'Your Excellency has doubtless need to rest in readiness for your early start tomorrow,' he said. 'I will not attempt to detain Your Excellency in consequence, much as Your Excellency's presence here has been appreciated.'

The good-byes were said, and Mendez-Castillo undertook to escort the party back to the *Clorinda*. It was something of a shock to Hornblower to find that the band and the guard of honour were still in the courtyard to offer the official compliments on his departure. He stood at the salute while the band played some jerky tune or other; then they went down into the waiting boat.

The harbour was pitch dark as they rowed out into it, the few lights visible doing almost nothing to alleviate the blackness. They rounded the corner and passed astern of the *Estrella* again. There was a single lantern hanging in her main rigging, and she was quiet by now – no; in the still night, at one moment, Hornblower heard the faint rattle of leg-irons as some one of the slaves in her hold indicated that he was still awake and restless. That was good. Farther along, a quiet challenge came over the inky water, issuing from a nucleus of darkness even more solid than the darkness surrounding it.

'Flag,' answered the midshipman. '*Clorinda*.'

The two brief words were all that were needed to inform the guard-boat that an Admiral and a captain were approaching.

'You see, Major,' said Hornblower, 'that Captain Fell deemed it necessary to row guard round the ship during the night.'

'I understood that to be the case, Your Excellency,' answered Mendez-Castillo.

'Our seamen will go to great lengths to indulge themselves in the pleasures of the shore.'

'Naturally, Your Excellency,' said Mendez-Castillo.

The boat ran alongside the *Clorinda*; standing awkwardly in the stern-sheets Hornblower said his last good-byes, and uttered his last words of thanks, to the representative of his host before going up the side. From the entry port he watched the boat shove off again and disappear into the darkness.

'Now,' he said, 'we can make better use of our time.'

On the maindeck, just visible in the light from the lantern hanging from the main-stay, was a Thing; that was the only way to describe it, something of canvas and cordage, with a length of chain attached to it. Sefton was standing beside it.

'I see you've finished it, Mr Sefton.'

'Yes, My Lord. A full hour ago. The sail-maker and his mates worked admirably.'

Hornblower turned to Fell.

'I fancy, Sir Thomas,' he said, 'that you have in mind the necessary orders to give. Perhaps you would be kind enough to tell me about them before you issue them?'

'Aye aye, My Lord.'

That eternal Navy answer was the only one Fell could make in the circumstances, even if Fell had not yet given full thought to the next problems. Down in the cabin alone with his Admiral, Fell's unreadiness was a little apparent.

'I suppose,' prompted Hornblower, 'that you will tell off the necessary personnel for the expedition. Which officer can you trust fully to exercise discretion?'

Little by little the details were settled. Powerful swimmers who could work under water; an armourer's mate who could be relied upon to put the final shackle in the chain in the darkness; the boat's crew was decided upon, summoned, and instructed in all the details of the plan. When the guard-boat came in for the relief of its crew there was another crew standing by all ready, who went down overside rapidly and quietly although encumbered with the Thing and the necessary gear.

It pushed off again into the darkness, and Hornblower stood on the quarterdeck to watch it go. There might be an international incident arising out of this, or he might be made to appear a fool in the eyes of the world, which would be just as bad. He strained his ears for any sounds in the darkness which would tell him how the work was progressing, but he could hear nothing. The land breeze had just begun to blow, gently, but strongly enough to swing *Clorinda* to her anchor; it would carry any sounds away from him, he realised – but it would also serve to obscure any suspicious noises if anyone in the *Estrella* was awake enough to hear them. She had a full counter, with, as was only to be expected, plenty of rake. A swimmer who reached her stern unobserved would be able to work at her rudder unobserved, certainly.

'My Lord,' said Gerard's voice quietly beside him. 'Would not this be a suitable time to rest?'

'You are quite right, Mr Gerard. A most suitable time,' answered Hornblower, continuing to lean against the rail.

'Well, then, My Lord—?'

'I have agreed with you, Mr Gerard. Surely you can be content with that?'

But Gerard's voice went on, remorseless as the voice of conscience.

'There is cold beef laid out in the cabin, My Lord. Fresh bread and a bottle of Bordeaux.'

That was a different story. Hornblower suddenly realised how hungry he was; during the past thirty hours he had eaten one meagre meal, because the cold collation he had expected at the reception had failed to materialise. And he could still pretend to be superior to the weaknesses of the flesh.

'You would have made an excellent wet-nurse, Mr Gerard,' he said, 'if nature had treated you more generously. But I suppose my life will be unbearable until I yield to your importunity.'

On the way to the companion they passed Fell; he was striding up and down the quarterdeck in the darkness, and they could hear his hard breathing. It pleased Hornblower to know that even these muscular heroes could feel anxiety. It might be polite, even kind, to invite Fell to join them at this cold supper, but Hornblower dismissed the idea. He had had as much of Fell's company already as he could bear.

Down below, Spendlove was waiting in the lighted cabin.

'The vultures are gathered together,' said Hornblower. It was amusing to see Spendlove was pale and tense too. 'I hope you gentlemen will join me.'

The younger men were silent as they ate. Hornblower put his nose to his glass of wine and sipped thoughtfully.

'Six months in the tropics had done this Bordeaux no good,' he commented; it was inevitable that as host, and Admiral, and older man, his opinion should be received with deference. Spendlove broke the next silence.

'That length of spun yarn, My Lord,' he said. 'The breaking strain—'

'Mr Spendlove,' said Hornblower. 'All the discussion in the world won't change it now. We shall know in good time. Meanwhile, let's not spoil our dinner with technical discussions.'

'Your pardon, My Lord,' said Spendlove, abashed. Was it by mere coincidence or through telepathy that Hornblower had been thinking at that very moment about the breaking strain of that length of spun yarn in the drogue; but he would not dream of admitting that he had been thinking about it. The dinner continued.

'Well,' said Hornblower, raising his glass, 'we can admit the existence of mundane affairs long enough to allow of a toast. Here's to head money.'

As they drank they heard unmistakable sounds on deck and overside. The guard-boat had returned from its mission. Spendlove and Gerard exchanged glances, and poised themselves ready to stand up. Hornblower forced himself to lean back and shake his head sadly, his glass still in his hand.

'Too bad about this Bordeaux, gentlemen,' he said.

Then came the knock on the door and the expected message.

'Cap'n's respects, My Lord, and the boat has returned.'

'My compliments to the captain, and I'll be glad to see him and the lieutenant here as soon as is convenient.'

One glance at Fell as he entered the cabin was sufficient to indicate that the expedition had been successful, so far, at least.

'All well, My Lord,' he said, his florid face suffused with excitement.

'Excellent.' The lieutenant was a grizzled veteran older than Hornblower; and Hornblower could not help but think to himself that had he not enjoyed great good fortune on several occasions he would be only a lieutenant, too. 'Will you sit down, gentlemen? A glass of wine? Mr Gerard, order fresh glasses, if you please. Sir Thomas, would you mind if I hear Mr Field's story from his own lips?'

Field had no fluency of speech. His story had to be drawn from him by questions. Everything had gone well. Two strong swimmers, their faces blackened, had slipped overside from the guard-boat and had swum unseen to the *Estrella*. Working with their knives, they had been able to prise off the copper from the second rudder-brace below the waterline. With an auger they had made a space large enough to pass a line through. The most ticklish part of the work had been approaching near enough in the guard-boat and putting the drogue overside after it had been attached to the line, but Field reported that no hail had come from the *Estrella*. The chain had followed the line and had been securely shackled. Now the drogue hung at *Estrella*'s stern, safely out of sight below the surface, ready to exert its full force on her rudder when – and if – the spun yarn which held the drogue reversed should part.

'Excellent,' said Hornblower again, when Field's last halting sentence was uttered. 'You've done very well, Mr Field, thank you.'

'Thank you, My Lord.'

When Field had left, Hornblower could address himself to Fell.

'Your plan has worked out admirably, Sir Thomas. Now it only remains to catch the *Estrella*. I would strongly recommend you to make all preparations for getting under way at daylight. The sooner we leave after the *Estrella* has sailed the better, don't you think?'

'Aye aye, My Lord.'

The ship's bell overhead anticipated the next question Hornblower was about to ask.

'Three hours to daylight,' he said. 'I'll say good night to you gentlemen, then.'

It had been a busy day, of ceaseless activity, mental if not physical, since dawn. After a long, hot evening it seemed to Hornblower that his feet had swollen to twice their ordinary size and that his gold-buckled shoes had made no allowance for this expansion – he could hardly pry them off. He took off ribbon and star and gold-laced coat, and reluctantly reminded himself that he would have to put them on again for his ceremonial departure in three hours' time. He sponged himself down with water from his wash-basin, and sank down sighing with relief on his cot in the night cabin.

He woke automatically when the watch was called; the cabin was still quite dark and he was at a loss, for a couple of seconds, about why there should be this feeling of urgency within him. Then he remembered, and was wide awake at once, shouting to the sentry at the door to pass the word for Giles. He shaved by lamplight in feverish haste, and then, once more in the hated full-dress uniform, he sped up the ladder to the quarterdeck. It was still pitch dark; no, perhaps there was the slightest glimmering of daylight. Perhaps the sky was the smallest trifle brighter over the Morro. Perhaps. The quarterdeck was crowded with shadowy figures, more even than would be found there with the ship's company at stations for getting under way. At sight of them he nearly turned back, having no wish to reveal that he shared the same weaknesses as the rest of them, but Fell had caught sight of him.

'Good morning, My Lord.'

'Morning, Sir Thomas.'

'Land breeze blowing full, My Lord.'

No doubt about that; Hornblower could feel it breathing round him, delightful after the sweltering stuffiness of the cabin. In these mid-summer tropics it would be of short duration; it would be cut off short as soon as the sun, lifting over the horizon, should get to work in its brassy strength upon the land.

'*Estrella*'s making ready for sea, My Lord.'

There was no doubt about that either; the sounds of it made their way over the water through the twilight.

'I don't have to ask if you are ready, Sir Thomas.'

'All ready, My Lord. Hands standing by at the capstan.'

'Very well.'

Undoubtedly it was lighter already; the figures on the quarterdeck – now much more clearly defined – had all moved over to the starboard side, lining the rail. Half a dozen telescopes were being extended and pointed towards the *Estrella*.

'Sir Thomas, put an end to that, if you please. Send that crowd below.'

'They're anxious to see—'

'I know what they want to see. Send them below immediately.'

'Aye aye, My Lord.'

Everyone, of course, was desperately anxious to see if anything was visible at the *Estrella*'s waterline aft, which might reveal what had been done at night. But there could be no surer way of calling the attention of the *Estrella*'s captain to something suspicious under his stern than by pointing telescopes at it.

'Officer of the watch!'

'My Lord?'

'See to it that no one points a telescope for one moment towards the *Estrella*.'

'Aye aye, My Lord.'

'When there's enough light to see clearly, you can sweep round the harbour as you might be expected to do. Not more than five seconds for the *Estrella*, but make sure you see all there is to see.'

'Aye aye, My Lord.'

The eastern sky was now displaying faint greens and yellows, against which the Morro silhouetted itself magnificently though faintly, but in its shadow all was still dark. Even before breakfast it was a romantic moment. It occurred to Hornblower that the presence of an Admiral in full dress on the quarterdeck so early might itself be a suspicious circumstance.

'I'm going below, Sir Thomas. Please keep me informed.'

'Aye aye, My Lord.'

In the day cabin Gerard and Spendlove sprang to their feet as he entered; presumably they had been among those driven below by Fell's order.

'Mr Spendlove, I am profiting by your admirable example of yesterday. I shall make sure of my breakfast while I may. Would you please order breakfast, Mr Gerard? I presume you gentlemen will favour me with your company.'

He threw himself negligently into a chair and watched the preparations. Half-way through them a knock at the door brought in Fell himself.

'*Estrella*'s clearly in sight now, My Lord. And there's nothing visible under her stern.'

'Thank you, Sir Thomas.'

A cup of coffee was welcome at this time in the morning. Hornblower did not have to pretend eagerness to drink it. Daylight was creeping in through the cabin windows, making the lamplight garish and unnecessary. Another knock brought in a midshipman.

'Cap'n's respects, My Lord, and *Estrella*'s casting off.'

'Very well.'

Soon she would be under way, and their device would be put to the test. Hornblower made himself bite and masticate another mouthful of toast.

'Can't you young men sit still for even a moment?' he snapped. 'Pour me some more coffee, Gerard.'

'*Estrella*'s warping out into the channel, My Lord,' reported the midshipman again.

'Very well,' said Hornblower, sipping fastidiously at his coffee, and hoping that no one could guess how much his pulse rate had accelerated. The minutes dragged by.

'*Estrella*'s preparing to make sail, My Lord.'

'Very well.' Hornblower put down his coffee cup, slowly, and as slowly as he could manage it rose from his chair, the eyes of the two young men never leaving him.

'I think,' he said, dragging out his words, 'we might now go on deck.'

Pacing as slowly as when he had been a mourner at Nelson's funeral, he walked out past the sentry and up the ladder; behind him the young men had to curb their impatience. It was dazzling bright on deck; the sun was just over the Morro. In the centre of the fairway at less than a cable's length distance lay the *Estrella*, gleaming in her white paint. As

Hornblower's eyes rested on her her jib extended itself upwards, to catch the wind and swing her round. Next moment her mainsail took the wind, and she steadied herself, gathering way; in a few seconds she was moving forward past the *Clorinda*. This was the moment. Fell was standing staring at her and muttering to himself; he was blaspheming in his excitement. *Estrella* dipped her colours; on her deck Hornblower was able to recognise the figure of Gomez, standing directing the handling of the schooner. Gomez caught sight of him at the same moment, and bowed, holding his hat across his chest, and Hornblower returned the compliment.

'She's not making two knots through the water,' said Hornblower.

'Thank God for that,' said Fell.

Estrella glided on towards the entrance, preparatory to making the dog-legged turn out to sea; Gomez was handling her beautifully under her very easy sail.

'Shall I follow her now, My Lord?'

'I think it's time, Sir Thomas.'

'Hands to the capstan, there! Headsail sheets, Mr Field!'

Even at two knots there would be some strain on that length of spun yarn. It must not part – it must not – before *Estrella* was well out to sea. Lusty arms and sturdy backs were heaving *Clorinda*'s cable short.

'Clear away the saluting carronade, there!'

Estrella had made the turn; the last of her mainsail was vanishing round the corner. Fell was giving his orders to get *Clorinda* under way steadily and clearly, despite his excitement. Hornblower was watching him narrowly; this was not a bad test of how he would behave in action, of how he would take his ship down into the smoke and fury of a battle.

'Main tops'l braces!'

Fell was bringing the big frigate round in as neat a fashion as Gomez had handled *Estrella*. *Clorinda* steadied herself and gathered way, moving down the channel.

'Man the rail!'

Whatever was going on round the corner, whatever was happening to the *Estrella* out of sight, the compliments must be paid. Nine-tenths of *Clorinda*'s crew on deck could be spared for the purpose; with the ship creeping forward before the land breeze the other one-tenth sufficed to keep her under control. Hornblower drew himself up and faced the Spanish flag flying over the Morro, his hand to his hat brim, Fell beside him, the other officers in rank behind, while the salute banged out and was returned, the flags dipping respectfully.

'Carry on!'

They were approaching the turn. It was possible that at any moment one of those grinning cannons up there would pitch a warning shot at them – a shot warning them that a hundred other guns were ready to pound them into a wreck; that would be if the drogue had begun to take obvious effect on the *Estrella*.

'Main tops'l braces!' came Fell's order again.

Already the big Atlantic rollers were making their effect felt; Hornblower could feel *Clorinda*'s bows lift momentarily to a dying surge.

'Hard a-starboard!' *Clorinda* turned steadily. 'Meet her! Steady as you go.'

She had hardly settled on her new course when *Estrella* came in sight again a mile farther out to sea, her bows pointed in almost the opposite direction; she was still under very easy canvas, thank God, steadying herself for the final turn from the channel out into the ocean. *Clorinda*'s main topsail shivered briefly as the Morro height intercepted the land breeze, but drew again instantly. *Estrella* was turning again now. She was hardly within cannon shot of the Morro.

'Port!' came Fell's order. 'Steady!'

The land breeze was right aft now, but dying away, partly with their increased distance from land and partly with the growing heat of the sun.

'Set the mains'l.'

Fell was quite right; there was need to hasten, lest the ship be delayed in the belt of doldrums between the land breeze and the trade wind. The enormous sail area of the main course carried *Clorinda* forward boldly, and once more the sound of the ship's way through the water became audible. *Estrella* was clear of the channel now; Hornblower, watching anxiously, saw her set foresail and staysails and jibs, all her fore and aft canvas in fact. She was holding her course northward, closehauled, directly away from the land; she must have caught the trade wind and was making northing, very sensibly, because she would have to weather Haiti before next morning on her course to the Old Bahama Channel and Havana. They were far enough from the Morro now, and from *Estrella*, to incur no suspicion by staring through telescopes at her. Hornblower looked long and carefully. He could detect nothing unusual about her appearance. It suddenly occurred to him that perhaps Gomez had detected the drogue under his stern and had removed it. He might even now be exploding with laughter, along with his officers, looking back at the British frigate hopefully following them.

'Port!' came Fell's order again, and *Clorinda* took the final turn.

'Leading marks in line, sir!' reported the master, looking aft at the land with his telescope to his eye.

'Very well. Steady as you go.'

Now the waves they were encountering were true Atlantic rollers, heaving up *Clorinda*'s starboard bow, and passing aft as the bows dipped to heave up the port quarter. *Estrella* right ahead was still closehauled on a northerly course under fore-and-aft canvas.

'She'll be making six knots,' estimated Gerard, standing with Spendlove a yard from Hornblower.

'That spun yarn should hold at six knots,' said Spendlove, meditatively.

'No bottom with this line!' reported the leadsman in the chains.

'All hands make sail!'

The order was being piped through the ship. Topgallants and royals were being spread; it was not long before *Clorinda* had every stitch of canvas set.

Yet the land breeze was dying fast. *Clorinda* was hardly making steerage way. Once, twice, the sails flapped like thunder, but she still held her course, creeping forward over the blue and white sea, with the sun blazing down upon her from a blue sky with hardly a fleck of cloud.

'Can't keep her on her course, sir,' reported the quartermaster.

Clorinda was yawing sluggishly as the rollers came at her. Far ahead the *Estrella* was almost hull down. Now came a breath of a different air, the tiniest breath; Hornblower felt it, nearly imperceptible, on his sweating face long before *Clorinda* made response. It was a different air indeed, not the heated air of the land breeze, but the fresher air of the trade wind, clean with its passage over three thousand miles of ocean. The sails flapped and shivered; *Clorinda* swung more meaningly.

'Here it comes!' exclaimed Fell. 'Full and by!'

A stronger puff came, so that the rudder could bite. A lull, another puff, another lull, another puff, yet each puff was stronger yet. The next puff did not die away. It endured, heeling *Clorinda* over. A roller burst against her starboard bow in a dazzling rainbow. Now they had caught the trade wind; now they could thrust their way northwards close-hauled in the trail of the *Estrella*. With the clean, fresh wind blowing, and the sensation of successful striving with it, a new animation came over the ship. There were smiles to be seen.

'She hasn't set her tops'ls yet, My Lord,' said Gerard, his telescope still to his eye.

'I doubt if she will while she makes her northing,' replied Hornblower.

'On a wind she can weather and headreach on us,' said Spendlove. 'Just as she did yesterday.'

Yesterday? Was it only yesterday? It could have been a month ago, so much had happened since yesterday's chase.

'Do you think that drogue ought to have any effect?' asked Fell, approaching them.

'None, sir, practically speaking,' answered Spendlove. 'Not while that spun yarn keeps it tail forward.'

Fell had one huge hand clasped in the other, grinding his knuckles into his palm.

'For me,' said Hornblower, and every eye turned to him, 'I am going to say farewell to gold lace. A cooler coat and a looser neckcloth.'

Let Fell display worry and nervousness; he himself was going below as if he had no interest whatever in the outcome of the affair. Down in the hot cabin it was a relief to throw off his full-dress uniform – ten pounds of broadcloth and gold – and to have Giles get out a clean shirt and white duck trousers.

'I'll take my bath,' said Hornblower, meditatively.

He knew perfectly well that Fell thought it undignified and dangerous to discipline that an Admiral should disport himself under the wash-deck pump, hosed down by grinning seamen, and he neither agreed nor cared. No miserable sponging down could take the place of his bath. The seamen pumped vigorously, and Hornblower pranced with middle-aged abandon under the stinging impact of the water. Now the clean shirt and trousers were doubly delightful; he felt a new man as he came on deck again, and his unconcern was not all pretence when Fell nervously approached him.

'She's running clean away from us again, My Lord,' he said.

'We know she can, Sir Thomas. We can only wait until she puts her helm up and sets her tops'ls.'

'As long as we can keep her in sight—' said Fell.

Clorinda was lying right over, fighting her way to the northward.

'I can see that we're doing all we can, Sir Thomas,' said Hornblower soothingly.

The morning was wearing on. 'Up spirits!' was piped, and Fell agreed with the sailing master that it was noon, and the hands were sent to dinner. Now it was only when *Clorinda* lifted to a wave that a telescope, trained over the starboard bow from the quarterdeck, could detect the gleam of *Estrella*'s sails over the horizon. She still had no topsails set; Gomez was acting on the knowledge that closehauled his schooner behaved better without her square sails – unless he was merely playing with his pursuers. The hills of Puerto Rico had sunk out of sight below the horizon far, far astern. And the roast beef at dinner, roast fresh beef, had been most disappointing, tough and stringy and without any taste whatever.

'Stuart said he'd send me the best sirloin the island could produce, My Lord,' said Gerard, in answer to Hornblower's expostulations.

'I wish I had him here,' said Hornblower. 'I'd make him eat it, every bit, without salt. Sir Thomas, please accept my apologies.'

'Er – yes, My Lord,' said Fell, who had been invited to his Admiral's table and who had been recalled from his own private thoughts by Hornblower's apologies. 'That drogue—'

Having said those words – that special word, rather – he was unable to say more. He looked across the table at Hornblower. His lantern-jawed face – the brick-red cheeks always looked odd in that conformation – showed his anxiety, which was accentuated by the look in his eyes.

'If we don't know all about it today,' said Hornblower, 'we'll hear all about it at some later date.'

It was the truth, even though it was not the kindest thing to say.

'We'll be the laughing-stock of the Islands,' said Fell.

No one in the world could look more miserable than he did at that moment. Hornblower himself was inclined to give up hope, but the sight of that despair roused his contrary nature.

'There's all the difference in the world between six knots, which she's making now closehauled, and twelve knots, which she'll make when she puts up her helm,' he said. 'Mr Spendlove here will tell you that the water resistance is a function of the square of the speed. Isn't that so, Mr Spendlove?'

'Perhaps a function of the cube or even one of the higher powers, My Lord.'

'So we can still hope, Sir Thomas. That spun yarn will have eight times the pull upon it when she alters course.'

'It'll be chafing now, as well, My Lord,' added Spendlove.

'If they didn't see the thing last night and cast it off,' said Fell, still gloomy.

When they reached the deck again the sun was inclining towards the west.

'Mast-head, there!' hailed Fell. 'Is the chase still in sight?'

'Yes, sir. Hull down from here, sir, but plain in sight. Two points or thereabouts on the weather bow.'

'She's made all the northing she needs,' grumbled Fell. 'Why doesn't she alter course?'

There was nothing to do except wait, to try and extract some pleasure from the clean wind and the blue and white sea; but the pleasure was only faint now, the sea did not seem so blue. Nothing to do except wait, with the minutes dragging like hours. Then it happened.

'Deck, there! Chase is altering course to port. She's running right before the wind.'

'Very well.'

Fell looked round at all the faces of the crowd on the quarterdeck. His own was as tense as anyone else's.

'Mr Sefton, alter course four points to port.'

He was going to play the game out to the bitter end, even though yesterday's experience, closely parallel to the present, had shown that *Clorinda* stood no chance in normal circumstances of intercepting.

'Deck, there! She's settin' her tops'ls. T'garns'ls, too, sir!'

'Very well.'

'We'll soon know now,' said Spendlove. 'With the drogue in action she *must* lose speed. She *must*.'

'Deck, there! Cap'n, sir!' The look-out's voice had risen to a scream of excitement. 'She's flown up into the wind! She's all aback! Fore topmast's gone, sir!'

'So have her rudder pintles,' said Hornblower, grimly.

Fell was leaping on the deck, actually dancing with joy, his face radiant. But he recollected himself with all speed.

'Come two points to starboard,' he ordered. 'Mr James, get aloft with you and tell me how she bears.'

'She's taking in her mains'l!' shouted the look-out.

'Trying to get before the wind again,' commented Gerard.

'Cap'n, sir!' This was James's voice from the mast-head. 'You're heading a point to loo'ard of her.'

'Very well.'

'She's coming before the wind – no, she's all aback again sir!'

The Thing still had her by the tail, then; her struggles would be as unavailing as those of a deer in the claws of a lion.

'Steer small, you—' said Fell, using a horrible word to the helmsman.

Everyone was excited, everyone seemed to be obsessed with the fear that *Estrella* would clear away the wreck and make her escape after all.

'With her rudder gone she'll never be able to hold a course,' said Hornblower. 'And she's lost her fore-topmast, too.'

Another wait, but of a very different nature now. *Clorinda*, thrashing along, seemed to have caught the excitement and to have put on a spurt as she hurled herself at her quarry, racing forward to triumph.

'There she is!' said Gerard, telescope trained forward. 'All aback still.'

As the next wave lifted *Clorinda* they all caught sight of her; they were approaching her fast. A sorry, pitiful sight she looked, her fore-topmast broken off clean at the cap, her sails shivering in the wind.

'Clear away the bow chaser,' ordered Fell. 'Fire a shot across her bow.'

The shot was fired. Something rose to the schooner's main peak, and broke out into the red and gold of Spain. It hung there for a moment and then came slowly down again.

'Congratulations on the success of your plans, Sir Thomas,' said Hornblower.

'Thank you, My Lord,' answered Fell. He was beaming with pleasure. 'I could have done nothing without Your Lordship's acceptance of my suggestions.'

'That is very good of you, Sir Thomas,' said Hornblower, turning back to look at the prize.

The *Estrella* was a pitiful sight, the more pitiful as they approached her, and could see more clearly the raffle of wreckage dangling forward, and the rudder torn loose aft. The sudden tug of the drogue when it took effect, using enormous force and leverage, had broken or pulled straight the stout bronze pintles on which the rudder had hung suspended. The drogue itself, weighted by its chain, still hung out of sight below the dangling rudder. Gomez, brought triumphantly aboard, had still no idea of the cause of the disaster, and had not guessed at the reason for the loss of his rudder. He had been young and handsome and dignified in the face of undeserved misfortune when he arrived on *Clorinda*'s deck. There was no pleasure in observing the change in him when he was told the truth. No pleasure at all. The sight even took away the feeling of pleasure over a professional triumph, to see him wilting under the eyes of his captors. But still, more than three hundred slaves had been set free.

Hornblower was dictating his despatch to Their Lordships, and Spendlove, who numbered this newfangled shorthand among his surprising accomplishments, was slashing down the letter at a speed that made light of Hornblower's stumbling sentences – Hornblower had not yet acquired the art of dictation.

'In conclusion,' said Hornblower, 'it gives me particular pleasure to call Their Lordships' attention to the ingenuity and activity of Captain Sir Thomas Fell, which made this exemplary capture possible.'

Spendlove looked up from his pad and stared at him. Spendlove knew the truth; but the unblinking stare which answered him defied him to utter a word.

'Add the usual official ending,' said Hornblower.

It was not for him to explain his motives to his secretary. Nor could he have explained them if he had tried. He liked Fell no better now than before.

'Now a letter to my agent,' said Hornblower.

'Aye aye, My Lord,' said Spendlove, turning a page.

Hornblower began to assemble in his mind the sentences composing this next letter. He wanted to say that because the capture was due to Sir Thomas's suggestions he did not wish to apply for his share of head money for himself. It was his desire that the share of the Flag should be allocated to Sir Thomas.

'No,' said Hornblower. 'Belay that. I won't write after all.'

'Aye aye, My Lord,' said Spendlove.

It was possible to pass on to another man distinction and honour, but one could not pass on money. There was something obvious, something suspicious, about that. Sir Thomas might guess, and Sir Thomas's feelings might be hurt, and he would not risk it. But he wished he liked Sir Thomas better, all the same.

THE BEWILDERED PIRATES

Oh, the dames of France are fo-ond a-and free
And Flemish li-ips a-are willing.

That was young Spendlove singing lustily only two rooms away from Hornblower's at Admiralty House, and he might as well be in the same room, as all the windows were open to let in the Jamaican sea breeze.

And sweet the maids of I-Ita-aly—

That was Gerard joining in.

'My compliments to Mr Gerard and Mr Spendlove,' growled Hornblower to Giles, who was helping him dress, 'and that caterwauling is to stop. Repeat that to make sure you have the words right.'

'His Lordship's compliments, gentlemen, and that caterwauling is to stop,' repeated Giles, dutifully.

'Very well, run and say it.'

Giles ran, and Hornblower was gratified to hear the noise cease abruptly. The fact that those two young men were singing – and still more the fact that they had forgotten he was within earshot – was proof that they were feeling lighthearted, as might be expected, seeing they were dressing for a ball. Yet it was no excuse, for they knew well enough that their tone-deaf Commander-in-Chief detested music, and they should also have realised that he would be more testy than usual, on account of that very ball, because it meant that he would be forced to spend a long evening listening to those dreary sounds, cloying and irritating at the same moment. There would certainly be a table or two of whist – Mr Hough would be aware of his principal guest's tastes – but it was too much to hope for that all sound of music would be excluded from the card-room. The prospect of a ball was by no means as exhilarating to Hornblower as to his flag-lieutenant and to his secretary.

Hornblower tied his white neckcloth and painfully adjusted it to geometrical symmetry, and Giles helped him into his black dress-coat. Hornblower regarded the result in the mirror, by the light of the candles round its frame. At least tolerable, he said to himself. The growing peace-time convention whereby naval and military men appeared in civilian clothes had a good deal to recommend it; so had the other increasing fad for men to wear black dress-coats. Barbara had helped him select this one, and had supervised its fitting by the tailor. The cut was excellent, Hornblower decided, turning back and forth before the mirror, and black and white suited him. 'Only gentlemen can wear black and white,' Barbara had said, and that was very gratifying.

Giles handed him his tall hat and he studied the additional effect. Then he took up his white gloves, remembered to remove his hat again, and stepped out through the door which Giles opened for him and entered the corridor where Gerard and Spendlove, in their best uniforms, were waiting for him.

'I must apologise on behalf of Spendlove and myself for the singing, My Lord,' said Gerard.

The softening effect of the black dress-coat was evident when Hornblower refrained from a rasping reprimand.

'What would Miss Lucy say, Spendlove, if she heard you singing about the dames of France?' he asked.

Spendlove's answering grin was very attractive.

'I must ask Your Lordship's further indulgence not to tell her about it,' he said.

'I'll make that conditional upon your further good behaviour,' said Hornblower.

The open carriage was waiting outside the front door of Admiralty House; four seamen stood by with lanterns to add to the light thrown by the lamps on the porch. Hornblower climbed in and seated himself. Etiquette was different here on land; Hornblower missed the shrilling of the pipes that he felt should accompany this ceremonial, as it would if it were a boat he was entering, and in a carriage the senior officer entered first, so that after he was seated Spendlove and Gerard had to run round and enter by the other door. Gerard sat beside him and Spendlove sat opposite, his back to the horses. As the door shut the carriage moved forward, between the lanterns at the gate, and out to the pitch-dark Jamaican night. Hornblower breathed the warm, tropical air and grudgingly admitted to himself that after all it was no great hardship to attend a ball.

'Perhaps you have a rich marriage in mind, Spendlove?' he asked. 'I understand Miss Lucy will inherit it all. But I advise you to make certain before committing yourself that there are no nephews on the father's side.'

'A rich marriage might be desirable, My Lord,' replied Spendlove's voice out of the darkness, 'but I must remind you that in affairs of the heart I have been handicapped from birth – or at least from my baptism.'

'From your baptism?' repeated Hornblower, puzzled.

'Yes, My Lord. You remember my name, perhaps?'

'Erasmus,' said Hornblower.

'Exactly, My Lord. It is not adapted to endearments. Could any woman fall in love with an Erasmus? Could any woman bring herself to breathe the words "Razzy, darling"?'

'I fancy it could happen,' said Hornblower.

'May I live long enough to hear it,' said Spendlove.

It was remarkably agreeable to be driving thus through the Jamaican night behind two good horses and with two pleasant young men;

especially, as he told himself smugly, because he had done work satisfactory enough to justify relaxation. His command was in good order, the policing of the Caribbean was proceeding satisfactorily, and smuggling and piracy were being reduced to small proportions. Tonight he had no responsibilities. He was in no danger at all, not any. Danger was far away over the horizons both of time and space. He could lean back relaxed, against the leather cushions of the carriage, taking only moderate care not to crease his black dress-coat or crumple the careful pleats of his shirt.

Naturally, his reception at the Houghs' house was somewhat overpowering. There was a good deal of 'My Lord' and 'His Lordship'. Hough was a substantial planter, a man of considerable wealth, with enough of dislike for English winters not to be the usual West Indian absentee landlord. Yet for all his wealth he was greatly impressed by the fact that he was entertaining, in one and the same person, a Peer and an Admiral and a Commander-in-Chief – and someone whose influence might at any moment be of great importance to him. The warmth of his greeting, and of Mrs Hough's, was so great that it even overflowed round Gerard and Spendlove as well. Perhaps the Houghs felt that if they wished to be sure of standing well with the Commander-in-Chief it might be as well to cultivate good relations with his flag-lieutenant and secretary, too.

Lucy Hough was a pretty enough girl of some seventeen or eighteen years of age whom Hornblower had already met on a few occasions. Hornblower told himself he could feel no interest in a child straight from the schoolroom – almost straight from the nursery – however pretty. He smiled at her and she dropped her eyes, looked up at him again, and once more looked away. It was interesting that she was not nearly so timid when she met the glances and acknowledged the bows of the young men who were far more likely to be of interest to her.

'Your Lordship does not dance, I understand?' said Hough.

'It is painful to be reminded of what I am missing in the presence of so much beauty,' replied Hornblower with another smile at Mrs Hough and at Lucy.

'Perhaps a rubber of whist, then, My Lord?' suggested Hough.

'The Goddess of Chance instead of the Muse of Music,' said Hornblower – he always tried to talk about music as if it meant something to him – 'I will woo the one instead of the other.'

'From what I know about Your Lordship's skill at whist,' said Hough, 'I would say that as regards Your Lordship the Goddess of Chance has but small need for wooing.'

The ball had been in progress, apparently, for some time before Hornblower's arrival. There were two score young people on the floor of the great room, a dozen dowagers on chairs round the wall, an orchestra in the corner. Hough led the way to another room; Hornblower dismissed his two young men with a nod, and settled down to whist with Hough and a couple of formidable old ladies. The closing of the heavy door shut out, luckily, nearly all the exasperating din of the orchestra; the old ladies played a sound game, and a pleasant hour enough went by. It was terminated by the entrance of Mrs Hough.

'It is time for the Polonaise before supper,' she announced. 'I really must beg you to leave your cards and come and witness it.'

'Would Your Lordship—?' asked Hough apologetically.

'Mrs Hough's wish is my command,' said Hornblower.

The ballroom was, of course, stifling hot. Faces were flushed and shiny, but there was no lack of energy apparent as the double line formed up for the Polonaise while the orchestra grated out its mysterious noises to encourage the young people. Spendlove was leading Lucy by the hand and they were exchanging happy glances. Hornblower, from the weary age of forty-six, could look with condescension at these young men and women in their immature teens and twenties, tolerant of their youth and enthusiasm. The noises the orchestra made became more jerky and confusing, but the young people could find some sense in them. They capered round the room, skirts swaying and coat-tails flapping, everyone smiling and lighthearted; the double lines became rings, melted into lines again, turned and re-formed, until in the end with a final hideous crash from the orchestra the women sank low in curtsies and the men bent themselves double before them – a pretty sight once the music had ceased. There was a burst of laughter and applause before the lines broke up. The women, with sidelong looks at each other, gathered into groups which edged out of the room. They were retiring to repair the damages sustained in the heat of action.

Hornblower met Lucy's eyes again, and once more she looked away and then back at him. Shy? Eager? It was hard to tell with these mere children; but it was not the sort of glance she had bestowed on Spendlove.

'Ten minutes at least before the supper march, My Lord,' said Hough. 'Your Lordship will be kind enough to take in Mrs Hough?'

'Delighted, of course,' replied Hornblower.

Spendlove approached. He was mopping his face with his handkerchief.

'I would enjoy a breath of cooler air, My Lord,' he said. 'Perhaps—'

'I'll come with you,' said Hornblower, not sorry to have an excuse to be rid of Hough's ponderous company.

They stepped out into the dark garden; so bright had been the candles in the ballroom that they had to tread cautiously at first.

'I trust you are enjoying yourself,' said Hornblower.

'Very much indeed, thank you, My Lord.'

'And your suit is making progress?'

'Of that I am not so sure, My Lord.'

'You have my best wishes in any case.'

'Thank you, My Lord.'

Hornblower's eyes were more accustomed now to the darkness. He could see the stars now when he looked up. Sirius was visible, resuming once more his eternal chase of Orion across the night sky. The air was warm and still with the cessation of the sea breeze.

Then it happened. Hornblower heard a movement behind him, a rustling of foliage, but before he could pay attention to it hands gripped his arms, a hand came over his mouth. He began to struggle. A sharp, burning pain under his right shoulder-blade made him jump.

'Quiet,' said a voice, a thick, heavy voice. 'Or this.'

He felt the pain again. It was a knife point in his back, and he held himself still. The unseen hands began to hustle him away; there were at least three men round him. His nose told him they were sweating – with excitement, perhaps.

'Spendlove?' he said.

'Quiet,' said the voice again.

He was being hustled down the long garden. A momentary sharp cry, instantly stifled, presumably came from Spendlove behind him. Hornblower had difficulty in preserving his balance as he was hurried along, but the arms that held him sustained him; when he stumbled he could feel the pressure of the knife point against his back sharpen into pain as it pierced his clothes. At the far end of the garden they emerged into a narrow path where a darkness loomed up in the night. Hornblower bumped into something that snorted and moved – a mule, apparently.

'Get on,' said the voice beside him.

Hornblower hesitated, and felt the knife against his ribs.

'Get on,' said the voice; someone else was wheeling the mule round again for him to mount.

There were neither stirrups nor saddle. Hornblower put his hands on the withers and hauled himself up astride the mule. He could find no reins, although he heard the chink of a bit. He buried his fingers in the scanty mane. All round him he could hear a bustle as the other mules were mounted. His own mule started with something of a jerk that made him cling wildly to the mane. Someone had mounted the mule ahead and was riding forward with a leading rein attached to his mule. There seemed to be four mules altogether, and some eight men. The mules began to trot, and Hornblower felt himself tossed about precariously on the slippery back of the mule, but there was a man running on each side of him helping to keep him on his perch. A second or two later they slowed down again as the leading mule turned a difficult corner.

'Who are you?' demanded Hornblower, with the first breath that the motion had not shaken out of his body.

The man by his right knee waved something at him, something bright enough to shine in the starlight. It was a cutlass – the machete of the West Indies.

'Quiet,' he said, 'or I cut off your leg.'

The next moment the mule broke into a trot again, and Hornblower could have said no more even if he were inclined to do so. Mules and men hurried along a path between great fields of cane, with Hornblower bounding about on the mule's back. He tried to look up at the stars to see which way they were going, but it was difficult, and they altered course repeatedly, winding about over the countryside. They left the cane behind, and seemed to emerge into open savannah. Then there were trees; then they slowed down for a sharp ascent, broke into a trot again down the other side – the men on foot running tirelessly beside the mules – and climbed again, the mules slipping and plunging on what appeared to be an insecure surface. Twice Hornblower nearly fell off, to be heaved back again by the man beside him. Soon he was atrociously saddle-sore – if the word could be considered appropriate when he was riding bareback – and the ridge of the mule's spine caused him agony. He was drenched with sweat, his mouth was parched, and he was desperately weary. He grew stupefied with misery, despite the pain he suffered. More than once they splashed across small streams roaring down from the mountains; again they made their way through a belt of trees. Several times they seemed to be threading narrow passes.

Hornblower had no idea how long they had been travelling when they found themselves beside a small river, seemingly placid as it reflected the stars. On the far side faint in the darkness towered a lofty cliff. Here the party halted, and the man beside him tugged at his knee in an obvious invitation to dismount. Hornblower slid down the mule's side – he had to lean against the animal for a moment when his legs refused to hold him up. When he was able to stand upright and look about him he saw a white face among the dark ones that surrounded him. He could just make out Spendlove, his knees sagging and his head lolling as he stood supported on either side.

'Spendlove!' he said.

There was an agonising moment of waiting before the drooping figure said, 'My Lord?' The voice was thick and unnatural.

'Spendlove! Are you wounded?'

'I'm – well – My Lord.'

Someone pushed Hornblower in the back.

'Come. Swim,' said a voice.

'Spendlove!'

Several hands turned Hornblower away and thrust him stumbling down to the water's edge. It was hopeless to resist; Hornblower could only guess that Spendlove had been stunned by a blow and was only now recovering, his unconscious body having been carried so far by mule.

'Swim,' said the voice, and a hand pressed him forward to the water.

'No!' croaked Hornblower.

The water seemed immeasurably wide and dark. Even while Hornblower struggled at the water's edge he had a horrible realisation of the indignity he was undergoing, as a Commander-in-Chief, acting like a child in the hands of these people. Somebody led a mule slowly down into the water beside him.

'Hold his tail,' said the voice, and there was the knife in his back again.

He took hold of the mule's tail and despairingly let himself flop into the water, spreadeagled. For a moment the mule floundered and then struck out; the water, as it closed round Hornblower, seemed hardly colder than the warm air. It was no more than a moment, it seemed, before the mule was plunging up the other bank, and Hornblower found the bottom under his feet and waded out after him, the water streaming from his clothes, the rest of the gang and the animals splashing after him. The hand was back on his shoulder, turning him to one side and urging him along. He heard an odd creaking in front of him and a swaying object struck him on the chest. His hands felt smooth bamboo and some sort of creeper, liana, knotted to it – it was a makeshift rope ladder dangling in front of him.

'Up!' said the voice. 'Up!'

He could not – he would not – and there was the knife point at his back again. He stretched his arms up and grasped a rung, feeling desperately with his feet for another.

'Up!'

He began the climb, with the ladder writhing under his feet in the animal fashion rope ladders always display. It was horrible in the darkness, feeling with his feet for each elusive rung in turn, clutching desperately with his hands. His sodden shoes tended to slip on the smooth bamboo. Nor did his hands feel secure on the creeper. Someone else was climbing close after him, and the ladder twined about unpredictably. He knew himself to be swaying pendulum-fashion in the darkness. Up he went, one rung at a time, his hands gripping so convulsively that it was only by a conscious effort that he was able to make each one unclasp in turn and seek a fresh hold. Then the gyrations and swinging grew less. His upward-stretching hand touched earth, or rock. The next moment was not easy; he was unsure of his handhold and he hesitated. He knew himself to be a prodigious height up in the air. Just below him on the ladder he heard a sharp command issued by the man following him, and then a hand above him grasped his wrist and pulled. His feet found the next rung, and there he was, lying gasping on his belly on solid earth. The hand dragged at him again and he crawled on all fours forward to make room for the man behind him. He was almost sobbing; there was no trace left now of the haughty and self-satisfied human who had admired himself in the mirror not so many hours ago.

Other people trod past him.

'My Lord! My Lord!'

That was Spendlove asking for him.

'Spendlove!' he answered, sitting up.

'Are you all right, My Lord?' asked Spendlove, stooping over him.

Was it sense of humour or sense of the ridiculous, was it natural pride or force of habit, which made him take a grip on himself?

'As right as I might expect to be, thank you, after these rather remarkable experiences,' he said. 'But you – what happened to you?'

'They hit me on the head,' replied Spendlove, simply.

'Don't stand there. Sit down,' said Hornblower, and Spendlove collapsed beside him.

'Do you know where we are, My Lord?' he asked.

'Somewhere at the top of a cliff, as far as I can estimate,' said Hornblower.

'But where, My Lord?'

'Somewhere in His Majesty's loyal colony of Jamaica. More than that I can't say.'

'It will be dawn soon, I suppose,' said Spendlove, weakly.

'Soon enough.'

Nobody about them was paying them any attention. There was a great deal of chatter going on, in marked contrast with the silence – the almost disciplined silence – which had been preserved during their dash across country. The chatter mingled with the sound of a small waterfall, which he realised he had been hearing ever since his climb. The conversations were in a thick English which Hornblower could hardly understand, but he could be sure that their captors were expressing exultation. He could hear women's voices, too, while figures paced about, too excited to sit down despite the fatigues of the night.

'I doubt if we're at the top of the cliff, My Lord, if you'll pardon me,' said Spendlove.

He pointed upwards. The sky was growing pale, and the stars were fading; vertically over their heads they could see the cliff above them, overhanging them. Looking up, Hornblower could see foliage silhouetted against the sky.

'Strange,' he said. 'We must be on some sort of shelf.'

On his right hand the sky was showing a hint of light, of the palest pink, even while on his left it was still dark.

'Facing north-nor'west,' said Spendlove.

The light increased perceptibly; when Hornblower looked to the east again the pink had turned to orange, and there was a hint of green. They seemed immeasurably high up; almost at their feet, it seemed, as they sat, the shelf ended abruptly, and far down below them the shadowy world was taking form, concealed at the moment by a light mist. Hornblower was suddenly conscious of his wet clothes, and shivered.

'That might be the sea,' said Spendlove, pointing.

The sea it was, blue and lovely in the far distance; a broad belt of land, some miles across, extended between the cliff on which they were perched and the edge of the sea; the mist still obscured it. Hornblower rose to his feet, took a step forward, leaning over a low, crude parapet of piled rock; he shrank back before nerving himself to look again. Under his feet there was nothing. They were indeed on a shelf in the face of the cliff. About the height of a frigate's main-yard, sixty feet or so; vertically below them he could see the small stream he had crossed holding the mule's tail; the rope ladder still hung down from where he stood to the water's edge; when, with an effort of will, he forced himself to lean out and look over he could see the mules standing dispiritedly below him in the narrow area between the river and the foot of the cliff; the overhang must be considerable. They were on a shelf in a cliff, undercut through the ages by the river below when in spate. Nothing could reach them from above, and nothing from below if the ladder were to be drawn up. The shelf was perhaps ten yards wide at its widest, and perhaps a hundred yards long. At one end the waterfall he had heard tumbled down the cliff face in a groove it had cut for itself; it splashed against a cluster of gleaming rocks and then leaped out again. The sight of it told him how thirsty he was, and he walked along to it. It was a giddy thing to do, to stand there with the cliff face at one elbow and a vertical drop under the other, with the spray bursting round him, but he could fill his cupped hands with water and drink, and drink again, before splashing his face and head refreshingly. He drew back to find Spendlove waiting for him to finish. Matted in Spendlove's thick hair and behind his left ear and down his neck was a black clot of blood. Spendlove knelt to drink and to wash, and rose again touching his scalp cautiously.

'They spared me nothing,' he said.

His uniform was spattered with blood, too. At his waist dangled an empty scabbard; his sword was missing, and as they turned back from the waterfall they could see it – it was in the hand of one of their captors, who was standing waiting for them. He was short and square and heavily built, not entirely Negro, possibly as much as half white. He wore a dirty white shirt and loose, ragged blue trousers, with dilapidated buckled shoes on his splay feet.

'Now, Lord,' he said.

He spoke with the Island intonation, with a thickening of the vowels and a slurring of the consonants.

'What do you want?' demanded Hornblower, putting all the rasp into his voice that he could manage.

'Write us a letter,' said the man with the sword.

'A letter? To whom?'

'To the Governor.'

'Asking him to come and hang you?' asked Hornblower.

The man shook his big head.

'No. I want a paper, a paper with a seal on it. A pardon. For us all. With a seal on it.'

'Who are you?'

'Ned Johnson.' The name meant nothing to Hornblower, nor, as a glance showed, did it mean anything to the omniscient Spendlove.

'I sailed with Harkness,' said Johnson.

'Ah!'

That meant something to both the British officers. Harkness was one of the last of the petty pirates. Hardly more than a week ago his sloop, *Blossom*, had been cut off by the *Clorinda* off Savannalamar, and her escape to leeward intercepted. Under long-range fire from the frigate she had despairingly run herself aground at the mouth of the Sweet River, and her crew had escaped into the marshes and mangrove swamps of that section of coast, all except her captain, whose body had been found on her deck almost cut in two by a round shot from *Clorinda*. This was her crew, left leaderless – unless Johnson could be called their leader – and to hunt them down the Governor had called out two battalions of troops as soon as *Clorinda* beat back to Kingston with the news. It was to cut off their escape by sea that the Governor, at Hornblower's suggestion, had posted guards at every fishing beach in the whole big island – otherwise the cycle they had already probably followed would be renewed, with the theft of a fishing boat, the capture of a larger craft, and so on until they were a pest again.

'There's no pardon for pirates,' said Hornblower.

'Yes,' said Johnson. 'Write us a letter, and the Governor will give us one.'

He turned aside and from the foot of the cliff at the back of the shelf he picked up something. It was a leather-bound book – the second volume of *Waverley*, Hornblower saw when it was put in his hands – and Johnson produced a stub of pencil and gave him that as well.

'Write to the Governor,' he said; he opened the book at the beginning and indicated the fly-leaf as the place to write on.

'What do you think I should write?' asked Hornblower.

'Ask him for a pardon for us. With his seal on it.'

Apparently Johnson must have heard somewhere, in talk with fellow pirates, of 'a pardon under the Great Seal', and the memory had lingered.

'The Governor would never do that.'

'Then I send him your ears. Then I send him your nose,' said Johnson.

That was a horrible thing to hear. Hornblower glanced at Spendlove, who had turned white at the words.

'You, the Admiral,' continued Johnson. 'You, the Lord. The Governor will do that.'

'I doubt if he would,' said Hornblower.

He conjured up in his mind the picture of fussy old General Sir Augustus Hooper, and tried to imagine the reaction produced by Johnson's demand. His Excellency would come near to bursting a blood vessel at the thought of granting pardons to two dozen pirates. The home government, when it heard the news, would be intensely annoyed, and without doubt most of the annoyance would be directed at the man whose idiocy in allowing himself to be kidnapped had put everyone in this absurd position. That suggested a question.

'How did you come to be in the garden?' he asked.

'We was waiting for you to go home, but you came out first.'

If they had been intending—

'Stand back!' yelled Johnson.

He leaped backwards with astonishing agility for his bulk, bracing himself, knees bent, body tense, on guard with the sword. Hornblower looked round in astonishment, in time to see Spendlove relax; he had been poising himself for a spring. With that sword in his hand and its point against Johnson's throat, the position would have been reversed. Some of the others came running up at the cry; one of them had a staff in his hand – a headless pike stave apparently – and thrust it cruelly into Spendlove's face. Spendlove staggered back, and the staff was whirled up to strike him down. Hornblower leaped in front of him.

'No!' he yelled, and they all stood looking at each other, the drama of the situation ebbing away. Then one of the men came sidling towards Hornblower, cutlass in hand.

'Cut off his ear?' he asked over his shoulder to Johnson.

'No. Not yet. Sit down, you two.' When they hesitated Johnson's voice rose to a roar. 'Sit down!'

Under the menace of the cutlass there was nothing to do but sit down, and they were helpless.

'You write that letter?' asked Johnson.

'Wait a little,' said Hornblower wearily; he could think of nothing else to say in that situation. He was playing for time, hopelessly, like a child at bedtime confronted by stern guardians.

'Let's have some breakfast,' said Spendlove.

At the far end of the shelf a small fire had been lighted, its smoke clinging in the still dawn in a thin thread to the sloping overhang of the cliff. An iron pot hung from a chain attached to a tripod over the fire, and two women were crouching over it attending to it. Packed against the back wall of the shelf were chests and kegs and barrels. Muskets were ranged in a rack. It occurred to Hornblower that he was in the situation common in popular romances; he was in the pirates' lair. Perhaps those chests contained untold treasures of pearls and gold. Pirates, like any other seafarers, needed a land base, and these pirates had established one here instead of on some lonely cay. His brig *Clement* had cleaned out one of those last year.

'You write that letter, Lord,' said Johnson. He poked at Hornblower's breast with the sword, and the point pierced the thin shirt-front to prick him over the breastbone.

'What is it you want?' asked Hornblower.

'A pardon. With a seal.'

Hornblower studied the swarthy features in front of him. The jig was up for piracy in the Caribbean, he knew. American ships-of-war in the north, French ships-of-war working from the Lesser Antilles, and his own busy squadron based on Jamaica had made the business both unprofitable and dangerous. And this particular band of pirates, the remains of the Harkness gang, were in a more precarious position than any, with the loss of their ship, and with their escape to sea cut off by his precautions. It had been a bold plan, and well executed, to save their necks by kidnapping him. Presumably the plan had been made and executed by this rather stupid-seeming fellow, almost bewildered in appearance, before him. Appearances might be deceitful, or else the desperate need of the situation had stimulated that dull mind into unusual activity.

'You hear me?' said Johnson, offering another prick with the sword, and breaking in upon Hornblower's train of thought.

'Say you will, My Lord,' muttered Spendlove close to Hornblower's ear. 'Gain time.'

Johnson turned on him, sword pointed at his face.

'Shut that mouth,' he said. Another idea occurred to him, and he glanced round at Hornblower. 'You write. Or I prick his eye.'

'I'll write,' said Hornblower.

Now he sat with the volume of *Waverley* open at the fly-leaf, and the stub of pencil in his hand, while Johnson withdrew for a couple of paces, presumably to allow free play for inspiration. What was he to write? 'Dear Sir Augustus'? 'Your Excellency'? That was better. 'I am held to ransom here along with Spendlove by the survivors of the Harkness gang. Perhaps the bearer of this will explain the conditions. They demand a free pardon in exchange for—' Hornblower held the pencil poised over the paper debating the next words. 'Our lives'? He shook his head to himself and wrote 'our freedom'. He wanted no melodrama. 'Your Excellency will, of course, be a better judge of the situation than I am. Your ob'd't servant.' Hornblower hesitated again, and then he dashed off the 'Hornblower' of his signature.

'There you are,' he said, holding out the volume to Johnson, who took it and look at it curiously, and turned back to the group of a dozen or so of his followers who had been squatting on the ground behind him silently watching the proceedings.

They peered at the writing over Johnson's shoulder; others came to look as well, and they fell into a chattering debate.

'Not one of them can read, My Lord,' commented Spendlove.

'So it appears.'

The pirates were looking from the writing over to their prisoners and back again; the argument grew more intense. Johnson seemed to be expostulating, or exhorting, and some of the men he addressed drew back shaking their heads.

'It's a question of who shall carry that note to Kingston,' said Hornblower. 'Who shall beard the lion.'

'That fellow has no command over his men,' commented Spendlove. 'Harkness would have shot a couple of them by now.'

Johnson returned to them, pointing a dark, stubby finger at the writing.

'What you say here?' he asked.

Hornblower read the note aloud; it did not matter whether he spoke the truth or not, seeing they had no way of knowing. Johnson stared at him, studying his face; Johnson's own face betrayed more of the bewilderment Hornblower had noticed before. The pirate was facing a situation too complex for him; he was trying to carry out a plan which he had not thought out in all its details beforehand. No one of the pirates was willing to venture into the grip of justice bearing a message of unknown content. Nor, for that matter, would the pirates trust one of their number to go off on such a mission; he might well desert, throwing away the precious message, to try and make his escape on his own. The poor, ragged, shiftless devils and their slatternly women were in a quandary, with no master mind to find a way out for them. Hornblower could have laughed at their predicament, and almost did, until he thought of what this unstable mob could do in a fit of passion to the prisoners in their power. The debate went on furiously, with a solution apparently no nearer.

'Do you think we could get to the ladder, My Lord?' asked Spendlove, and then answered his own question. 'No. They'd catch us before we could get away. A pity.'

'We can bear the possibility in mind,' said Hornblower.

One of the women cooking over the fire called out at this moment in a loud, raucous voice, interrupting the debate. Food was being ladled out into wooden bowls. A young mulatto woman, hardly more than a child, in a ragged gown that had once been magnificent, brought a bowl over to them – one bowl, no spoon or fork. They stared at each other, unable to keep from smiling. Then Spendlove produced a penknife from his breeches pocket, and tendered it to his superior after opening it.

'Perhaps it may serve, My Lord,' he said, apologetically, adding, after a glance at the contents of the bowl, 'not such a good meal as the supper we missed at the Houghs', My Lord.'

Boiled yams and a trifle of boiled salt pork, the former presumably stolen from some slave garden and the latter from one of the hogsheads stored here on the cliff. They ate with difficulty, Hornblower insisting on their using the penknife turn about, juggling with the hot food for which both of them discovered a raging appetite. The pirates and the women were mostly squatting on their heels as they ate. After their first mouthfuls they were beginning to argue again over the use to be made of their prisoners.

Hornblower looked out again from the shelf at the view extended before them.

'That must be the Cockpit Country,' he said.

'No doubt of it, My Lord.'

The Cockpit Country was territory unknown to any white man, an independent republic in the north-west of Jamaica. At the conquest of the island from the Spaniards, a century and a half earlier, the British had found this area already populated by runaway slaves and the survivors of the Indian population. Several attempts to subdue the area had failed disastrously – yellow fever and the appalling difficulty of the country allying themselves with the desperate valour of the defenders – and a treaty had finally been concluded granting independence to the Cockpit Country on the sole condition that the inhabitants should not harbour runaway slaves in future. That treaty had already endured fifty years and seemed likely to endure far longer. The pirates' lair was on the edge of this area, with the mountains at the back of it.

'And that's Montego Bay, My Lord,' said Spendlove, pointing.

Hornblower had visited the place in *Clorinda* last year – a lonely roadstead providing fair anchorage, and shelter for a few fishing boats. He gazed over to the distant blue water with longing. He tried to think of ways of escape, of some method of coming to honourable terms with the pirates, but a night entirely without sleep made his brain sluggish, and now that he had eaten it was more sluggish still. He caught himself nodding and pulled himself up with a jerk. Now that he was in his middle forties the loss of a night's sleep was a serious matter, especially when the night had been filled with violent and unaccustomed exertion.

Spendlove had seen him nod.

'I think you could sleep, My Lord,' he said, gently.

'Perhaps I could.'

He let his body sink to the hard ground. He was pillowless and uncomfortable.

'Here, My Lord,' said Spendlove.

Two hands on his shoulders eased him round, and now he was pillowed on Spendlove's thigh. The world whirled round him for a moment. There was the whisper of a breeze; the loud debate of the pirates and their women was monotonous in pitch; the waterfall was splashing and gurgling; then he was asleep.

He awoke some time later, with Spendlove touching his shoulder.

'My Lord, My Lord.'

He lifted his head, a little surprised to find where it had been resting; it took him several seconds to recall where he was and how he had come there. Johnson and one or two other pirates were standing before him; in the background one of the women was looking on, in an attitude that conveyed the impression that she had contributed to the conclusion that had evidently been reached.

'We send you to the Governor, Lord,' said Johnson.

Hornblower blinked up at him; although the sun had moved round behind the cliff the sky above was dazzling.

'*You*,' said Johnson. '*You* go. We keep *him*.'

Johnson indicated Spendlove by a gesture.

'What do you mean?' asked Hornblower.

'*You* go to the Governor and get our pardon,' said Johnson. 'You can ask him, and he will give it. *He* stays here. We can cut off his nose, we can dig out his eyes.'

'Good God Almighty,' said Hornblower.

Johnson, or his advisers – perhaps that woman over there – were people of considerable insight after all. They had some conception of honour, of gentlemanly obligations. They had perceived something of the relationship between Hornblower and Spendlove – they may have been guided by the sight of Hornblower sleeping with his head pillowed on Spendlove's thigh. They knew that Hornblower could never abandon Spendlove to the mercy of his captors, that he would do everything possible to obtain his freedom. Even perhaps – Hornblower's imagination surged in a great wave over the barrier of his sleepiness – even perhaps to the extent of coming back to share Spendlove's captivity and fate in the event of not being able to obtain the necessary pardons.

'We send you, Lord,' said Johnson.

The woman in the background said something in a loud voice.

'We send you now,' said Johnson. 'Get up.'

Hornblower rose slowly; he would have taken his time in any case in an effort to preserve what dignity was left to him, but he could not have risen swiftly if he had wanted to. His joints were stiff – he could almost hear them crack as he moved. His body ached horribly.

'These two men take you,' said Johnson.

Spendlove had risen to his feet too.

'Are you all right, My Lord?' he asked, anxiously.

'Only stiff and rheumaticky,' replied Hornblower. 'But what about you?'

'Oh, I'm all right, My Lord. Please don't give another thought to me, My Lord.'

That was a very straight glance that Spendlove gave him, a glance that tried to convey a message.

'Not another thought, My Lord,' repeated Spendlove.

He was trying to tell his chief that he should be abandoned, that nothing should be done to ransom him, that he was willing to suffer whatever tortures might be inflicted on him so long as his chief came well out of the business.

'I'll be thinking about you all the time,' said Hornblower, giving back glance for glance.

'Hurry,' said Johnson.

The rope ladder still dangled down from the lip of the shelf. It was a tricky business to lower himself with his creaking joints over the edge and to find foothold on the slippery bamboo rungs. The ladder swung away under the thrust of his feet as if it was a live thing determined to cast him down; he clung with frantic hands, back downwards, forcing himself, against his instincts, to straighten up and allow the ladder to swing back again. Gingerly his feet found foothold again, and he continued his descent. Just as he grew accustomed to the motion of the ladder his rhythm was disturbed by the first of his escort lowering himself upon the ladder above him; he had to cling and wait again before he resumed his downward progress. His feet had hardly gratefully touched ground than first one and then the other of his escorts dropped beside him.

'Good-bye, My Lord. Good luck!'

That was Spendlove calling from above. Hornblower, standing on the very edge of the river, his face towards the cliff; had to bend far backwards to see Spendlove's head over the parapet and his waving hand, sixty feet above. He waved back as his escorts led the mules to the water's edge.

Once more it was necessary to swim the river. It was no more than thirty feet across; he could have swum it last night without assistance had he been sure about that in the darkness. Now he let himself flop into the water, clothes and all – alas for that beautiful black dress-coat – and, turning on his back, kicked out with his legs. But his clothes were already wet and were a ponderous burden to him, and he knew a moment of worry before his already weary limbs carried him to the rocky bank. He crawled out, the water streaming from his clothes, unwilling to move even while the mules came plunging up out of the water beside him. Spendlove up above, still leaning over the parapet, waved to him again.

Now it was a question of mounting a mule again. His wet clothes weighed upon him like lead. He had to struggle up – the animal's wet hide was slippery – and as soon as he settled himself astride he realised that he was horribly saddlesore from the night before, and the raw surfaces caused him agony. He had to brace himself to endure it; it was dreadfully painful as his mount plunged about making his way over the irregular surface. From the river they made an abrupt ascent into the mountains. They were retracing the path they had taken the night before; hardly a path, hardly a track. They picked their way up a steep gully, down the other side, up again. They splashed across little torrents, and wound their way among trees. Hornblower was numb both in body and in mind by now; his mule was weary and by no means as sure of foot as a mule should be; stumbling more than once so that only by frantic efforts could he retain his seat. The sun was sinking towards the west as they jolted on, downhill at last. Passage through a final belt of trees brought them into open country upon which the sun blazed in tropical glory. This was savannah country, hardly rocky at all; there were cattle to be seen in the distance, and, beyond, a great sea of green – the vast sugar-cane fields of Jamaica stretching as far as the eye could see. Half a mile farther they reached a well-defined track, and there his escorts checked their mounts.

'Now you can go on,' said one of them, pointing along the path winding towards the distant cane.

It was a second or two before Hornblower's stupefied brain could grasp the fact that they were turning him loose.

'That way?' he asked, unnecessarily.

'Yes,' said his escort.

The two men turned their mules; Hornblower had to struggle with his, who disliked the separation. One of the escorts struck the brute on the rump, sending him down the path in a jerky trot acutely painful to Hornblower as he sought to retain his seat. Soon the mule eased to a leg-weary walk, and Hornblower was content to sit idly as it crawled along down the path; the sun was now clouded over and it was not long before, heralded by a brisk wind, a blinding rain began to fall, blotting out the landscape and slowing the mule even more on the slippery surface. Hornblower sat exhausted on the sharp spine of the animal; so heavy was the rain that he found it difficult to breathe as it poured upon his face.

Gradually the roaring rain ceased; the sky, while it remained overcast above him, opened to the west and admitted a gleam of the setting sun, so that the landscape on his left was made glorious with a rainbow which Hornblower hardly noted. Here was the first cane-field; the track he was following became here a rough and narrow roadway through the cane, deeply rutted by cartwheels. The mule plodded on, eternally, through the cane. Now the road crossed another, and the mule pulled up at the crossroads. Before Hornblower could rouse himself to urge the mule onwards he heard a shout to his right. Far down the road he saw a group of horsemen illuminated against the sunset. With an urgent drumming of hoofs they came galloping towards him, and reined up at his side – a white man followed by two coloured men.

'It's Lord Hornblower, isn't it?' asked the white man – a young fellow; Hornblower noticed dully that, although mounted, he was still in full-dress clothes with his ruffled neckcloth all awry and bedraggled.

'Yes,' said Hornblower.

'Thank God you're safe, sir,' said the young man. 'Are you hurt? Are you wounded, My Lord?'

'No,' said Hornblower, swaying with fatigue on the back of the mule.

The young man turned to one of his coloured companions and issued rapid orders, and the coloured man wheeled his horse round and went galloping full pelt down the road.

'The whole island has been turned out to seek for you, My Lord,' said the young man. 'What happened to you? We have searched for you all day.'

It would never do for an Admiral, a Commander-in-Chief, to betray unmanly weakness. Hornblower made himself stiffen his spine.

'I was kidnapped by pirates,' he said. He tried to speak nonchalantly, as if that was something that could happen to anyone any day, but it was difficult. His voice was only a hoarse croak. 'I must go at once to the Governor. Where is His Excellency?'

'He must be at Government House, I fancy,' said the young man. 'No more than thirty miles away.'

Thirty miles! Hornblower felt as if he could not ride another thirty yards.

'Very well,' he said, stiffly. 'I must go there.'

'The Hough house is only two miles down the road here, My Lord,' said the young man. 'Your carriage is still there, I believe. I have already sent a messenger.'

'We'll go there first, then,' said Hornblower, as indifferently as he could manage.

A word from the white man brought the other coloured man from his horse, and Hornblower slid ungracefully from the mule. It was an enormous effort to get his foot up into the stirrup; the coloured man had to help him heave his right leg over. He had hardly gathered the reins in his hands – he had not yet discovered which was which – when the white man put his horse into a trot and Hornblower's mount followed him. It was torture to bump about in the saddle.

'My name is Colston,' said the white man, checking his horse so that Hornblower came up alongside him. 'I had the honour of being presented to Your Lordship at the ball last night.'

'Of course,' said Hornblower. 'Tell me what happened there.'

'You were missed, My Lord, after the supper march had been kept waiting for you to head it with Mrs Hough. You and your secretary, Mr – Mr—'

'Spendlove,' said Hornblower.

'Yes, My Lord. At first it was thought that some urgent business was demanding your attention. It was not for an hour or two, I suppose, that your flag-lieutenant and Mr Hough could agree that you had been spirited away. There was great distress among the company, My Lord.'

'Yes?'

'Then the alarm was given. All the gentlemen present rode out in search for you. The militia was called out at dawn. The whole country-side is being patrolled. I expect the Highland regiment is in full march for here at this moment.'

'Indeed?' said Hornblower. A thousand infantrymen were making a forced march of thirty miles on his account; a thousand horsemen were scouring the island.

Hoofbeats sounded in front of them. Two horsemen approached in the gathering darkness; Hornblower could just recognise Hough and the messenger.

'Thank God, My Lord,' said Hough. 'What happened?'

Hornblower was tempted to answer, 'Mr Colston will tell you,' but he made himself make a more sensible reply. Hough uttered the expected platitudes.

'I must go on to the Governor at once,' said Hornblower. 'There is Spendlove to think of.'

'Spendlove, My Lord? Oh, yes, of course, your secretary.'

'He is still in the hands of the pirates,' said Hornblower.

'Indeed, My Lord?' replied Hough.

No one seemed to have a care about Spendlove, except Lucy Hough, presumably.

Here was the house and the courtyard; lights were gleaming in every window.

'Please come in, My Lord,' said Hough. 'Your Lordship must be in need of refreshment.'

He had eaten yams and salt pork some time that morning; he felt no hunger now.

'I must go on to Government House,' he said. 'I can waste no time.'

'If Your Lordship insists—'

'Yes,' said Hornblower.

'I will go and have the horses put to, then, My Lord.'

Hornblower found himself alone in the brightly lit sitting-room. He felt that if he threw himself into one of the vast chairs there he would never get up again.

'My Lord! My Lord!'

It was Lucy Hough fluttering into the room, her skirts flying with her haste. He would have to tell her about Spendlove.

'Oh, you're safe! You're safe!'

What was this? The girl had flung herself on her knees before him. She had one of his hands in both hers, and was kissing it frantically. He drew back, he tried to snatch his hand away, but she clung on to it, and followed him on her knees, still kissing it.

'Miss Lucy!'

'I care for nothing as long as you're safe!' she said, looking up at him and still clasping his hand; tears were streaming down her cheeks. 'I've been through torment today. You're not hurt? Tell me! Speak to me!'

This was horrible. She was pressing her lips, her cheek, against his hand again.

'Miss Lucy! Please! Compose yourself!'

How could a girl of seventeen act like this towards a man of forty-five? Was she not enamoured of Spendlove? But perhaps that was the person she was thinking about.

'I will see that Mr Spendlove is safe,' he said.

'Mr Spendlove? I hope he's safe. But it's you – you – you—'

'Miss Lucy! You must not say these things! Stand up, please, I beg you!'

Somehow he got her to her feet.

'I couldn't bear it!' she said. 'I've loved you since the moment I saw you!'

'There, there!' said Hornblower, as soothingly as he knew how.

'The carriage will be ready in two minutes, My Lord,' said Hough's voice from the door. 'A glass of wine and a bite before you start?'

Hough came in with a smile.

'Thank you, sir,' said Hornblower, struggling with embarrassment.

'This child has been in a rare way since this morning,' said Hough, indulgently. 'These young people— She was the only person in the island, I fancy, who gave a thought to the secretary as well as to the Commander-in-Chief.'

'Er – yes. These young people,' said Hornblower.

The butler entered with a tray at that moment.

'Pour His Lordship a glass of wine, Lucy, my dear,' said Hough, and then to Hornblower, 'Mrs Hough has been considerably prostrated, but she will be down in a moment.'

'Please do not discommode her, I beg of you,' said Hornblower. His hand was shaking as he reached for the glass. Hough took up carving knife and fork and set about carving the cold chicken.

'Excuse me, please,' said Lucy.

She turned and ran from the room as quickly as she had entered it, sobbing wildly.

'I had no idea the attachment was so strong,' said Hough.

'Nor had I,' said Hornblower. He had gulped down the whole glass of wine in his agitation. He addressed himself to the cold chicken with all the calm he could muster.

'The carriage is at the door, sir,' announced the butler.

'I'll take these with me,' said Hornblower, a slice of bread in one hand and a chicken wing in the other. 'Would it be troubling you too much to ask you to send a messenger ahead of me to warn His Excellency of my coming?'

'That has already been done, My Lord,' answered Hough. 'And I have sent out messengers to inform the patrols that you are safe.'

Hornblower sank into the cushioned ease of the carriage. The incident with Lucy had at least had the effect of temporarily driving all thought of fatigue from his mind. Now he could lean back and relax; it was five minutes before he remembered the bread and chicken in his hands and set himself wearily to eat them. The long drive was not particularly restful, for there were continual interruptions. Patrols who had not heard that he was safe stopped the carriage. Ten miles down the road they encountered the Highland battalion encamped at the roadside and the colonel insisted on coming and paying his respects to the naval Commander-in-Chief and congratulating him. Farther on a galloping horse reined up beside the carriage; it was Gerard. The light of the carriage lamp revealed that he had ridden his horse into a lather. Hornblower had to listen to him say 'Thank God, you are safe, My Lord' – everyone used those same words – and explain to him what had happened. Gerard abandoned his horse at the first opportunity and got into the carriage beside Hornblower. He was full of self-reproach at having allowed this to happen to his Chief – Hornblower rather resented the implication that he was incapable of looking after himself even though the event seemed to prove it – and at not having rescued him.

'We tried to use the bloodhounds they track runaway slaves with, My Lord, but they were of no use.'

'Naturally, since I was on mule-back,' said Hornblower. 'In any case, the scent must have been several hours old. Now forget the past and let me think about the future.'

'We'll have those pirates dangling on ropes before two days are up, My Lord.'

'Indeed? And what about Spendlove?'

'Oh – er. Yes, of course, My Lord.'

Spendlove was very much of an afterthought with everyone, even with Gerard, who was his friend. But to Gerard must be given the credit at least for appreciating Hornblower's difficulty the moment it was pointed out to him.

'We can't let anything happen to him, of course, My Lord.'

'And how do we prevent it? Do we grant those pardons – do we persuade His Excellency to grant them?'

'Well, My Lord—'

'There's nothing I would not do to set Spendlove free,' said Hornblower. 'Do you understand that? Nothing!'

Hornblower caught himself setting his jaw in grim determination; his ineradicable tendency to self-analysis revealed him to himself. He was cynically surprised at his own flow of emotion. Ferocity and tenderness intermingled; let those pirates touch one hair of Spendlove's head and – but how was he to prevent it? How to free Spendlove from men who knew that their lives, their actual lives and not merely their fortunes, depended on keeping him prisoner? How could he ever live with himself if anything were to happen to Spendlove? If the worst came to the worst he would have to go back to the pirates and yield himself up to them, as that Roman – Regulus – returned to death at the hands of the Carthaginians; and the worst seemed likely to come to the worst.

'Government House, My Lord,' said Gerard, breaking in upon this train of nightmare thoughts.

Sentries at the gates, sentries at the door. A brightly lit entrance-hall, where aides-de-camp looked at him curiously, curse them. So did Gerard. He was ushered through into an inner room, where after only a moment another door opened to admit His Excellency, and the escorting aide-de-camp discreetly retired. His Excellency was an angry man, angry as a man can only be who had been badly scared.

'Now, what is all this, My Lord?'

There was none of the usual deference displayed towards the man who had attained a peerage, the man of legendary fame. Hooper was a full General, far above a mere Rear-Admiral; moreover, as Governor he was absolute ruler throughout this island. His red face and bulging blue eyes – as well as the rage he was displaying – seemed to confirm the rumour that he was a grandson of the royal blood. Hornblower explained briefly and quietly what had happened; his fatigue – if not his common sense – prevented an angry reply.

'Do you realise the cost of all this, My Lord?' blared Hooper. 'Every white man who can sit a horse is out. My last reserve – the Highlanders – are bivouacked at the roadside. What that will mean in malaria and yellow fever I do not dare guess. For two weeks every man of the garrison except for them has been out guarding fishing boats and watching beaches at your request. The sick-lists are enormous. And now this!'

'My instructions, and I believe Your Excellency's as well, laid the greatest stress on the suppression of piracy, sir.'

'I don't need any whipper-snapper jumped up Rear-Admiral to interpret my instructions,' roared Hooper. 'What sort of bargain did you make with these pirates of yours?'

There it was. It was not an easy thing to explain to a man in this mood.

'I made no actual bargain, Your Excellency.'

'Hard to believe you had that much sense.'

'But my honour is pledged.'

'Your honour pledged? To whom? The pirates?'

'No, Your Excellency. To my secretary, Spendlove.'

'What was the pledge?'

'He was retained as a hostage when I was set free.'

'What did you promise him?'

What? He had said something about thinking about him.

'I made no verbal promise, Your Excellency. But one was implied, undoubtedly.'

'What was implied?'

'That I should set him free.'

'And how did you think you could do that?'

Nothing for it but to take the bull by the horns.

'I was released in order that I might solicit from Your Excellency pardons under seal for the pirates.'

'Pardons! Par—' Hooper could not even finish the word a second time. He could only gobble like a turkey for several seconds before with a gulp he was able to continue. 'Are you insane, My Lord?'

'That was why I was released. And that is why Spendlove is still retained.'

'Then this Spendlove must take his chance.'

'Your Excellency!'

'Do you think I could grant pardons to a gang of pirates? What d'ye mean? So that they can live like lords on their booty? Rolling in coaches round the island? A fine way that would be of suppressing piracy! D'ye want the whole West Indies in a turmoil? Have you lost your senses?'

The effect of this speech was in no way modified by the fact that Hornblower had guessed long before that Hooper would argue exactly along this line.

'I fully see the difficulty of the situation, Your Excellency.'

'I'm glad you do. You know the hiding-place of these pirates?'

'Yes, Your Excellency. It is a very secure place.'

'No matter. It can be reduced, of course. A few hangings will quiet this island down again.'

What in the world was there that he could do or could say? The sentence he framed in his mind was patently absurd to him even before he uttered it.

'I shall have to go back there before you take any steps, Your Excellency.'

'Go back there?' Hooper's eyes almost came out of their sockets as the implications of what Hornblower was saying dawned upon him. 'What new foolery do you have in mind?'

'I must go back and join Spendlove if Your Excellency does not see fit to grant the pardons.'

'Rubbish! I can grant no pardons. I cannot. I will not.'

'Then I have no alternative, Your Excellency.'

'Rubbish, I said. Rubbish! You made no promise. You said yourself that you gave no pledge.'

'I am the judge of that, Your Excellency.'

'You're in no condition to judge anything at present, if ever you were. Can you imagine for one moment I'll let you tie my hands like this?'

'No one regrets the necessity more than I do, My Lord.'

'Necessity? Are you dictating to me? I'll have you know that I'm your superior officer as well as Governor of this island. One more word and you'll be under arrest, My Lord. Let's hear no more of this nonsense.'

'Your Excellency—'

'Not one more word, I said. This Spendlove is one of the King's servants. He must run the risks of his position, even though he is only a secretary.'

'But—'

'I order you to keep silence, My Lord. You have fair warning. Tomorrow when you're rested we can plan to smoke out this wasps' nest.'

Hornblower himself checked the protest that still rose to his lips. Hooper meant what he said when he threatened arrest. The massive discipline that permeated the armed forces of the Crown had Hornblower in its grip as surely as if he were the least seaman. To disobey an order was hopeless from the start. The irresistible force of his own conscience might be driving him forward, but here he was up against the immovable barrier of discipline. Tomorrow? Tomorrow was another day.

'Very well, Your Excellency.'

'A night's rest will do you all the good in the world, My Lord. Perhaps it would be best if you slept here. I will give the necessary orders. If you instruct your flag-lieutenant as to the fresh clothes you will need I will send to Admiralty House for them to be ready for you in the morning.'

Clothes? Hornblower looked down at himself. He had forgotten entirely that he was wearing his black full-dress. One glance was enough to tell him that never again could he wear that suit. Now he could guess about the rest of his appearance. He knew that his haggard cheeks must be sprouting a bristly beard, his neckcloth in wild disorder. No wonder that people had looked at him curiously in the anteroom.

'Your Excellency is very kind,' he said.

There was no harm in being formally polite in the face of the temporarily inevitable. There had been that in Hooper's tone which told him that the invitation might as well have been an order, that he was as much a prisoner in Government House as if Hooper had actually carried out his threat of putting him under arrest. It was best to yield gracefully since he had to yield for the moment at least. Tomorrow was another day.

'Allow me to conduct you to your room, My Lord,' said Hooper.

The mirror in the bedroom confirmed his worst fears regarding his appearance. The bed, with its enormous mosquito net, was wide and inviting. His aching joints clamoured that he should allow himself to fall across that bed and repose himself; his weary brain demanded that he should sink into oblivion, forget his troubles in sleep as a drunkard might forget them in liquor. It was a relaxation to soap himself in a tepid bath, despite the smarting protests of the raw places on his body. And yet, bathed and relaxed, with one of His Excellency's nightshirts flapping round his knees, he could not give way to his weaknesses. His innermost ego refused to recognise them. He found himself hobbling barefooted about the room. He had no quarterdeck to pace; the candle-heated tropical air of the bedroom was not as conducive to inspiration as was a fresh sea breeze; mosquitoes buzzed about him, stinging his neck and his bare legs and distracting him. It was one of those dreadful nights; sometimes he relaxed so far as to sit on a chair, but within a few seconds a new train of thought brought him to his feet again, to limp up and down.

It was maddening that he could not keep his thoughts concentrated on the problem of Spendlove. He felt a contempt for himself that he should find his mind deserting his devoted secretary; there was a rival train of thought which was frequently successful in holding his attention. He knew, before the night was over, just how he would deal with the pirates' lair if his hands were free; he even knew satisfaction in recapitulating his plans, only to find the satisfaction replaced by sick despair at the thought of Spendlove in the pirates' hands. There were moments when his stomach turned over as he remembered Johnson's threat to dig out Spendlove's eyes.

Weariness took him by surprise in the end; he had sat down and rested his head on his hand, and then awakened with a start as he fell forward in his chair. The awakening was not complete enough; unconscious of what he was doing he settled himself back in his chair and slept in that fashion, the vast comfortable bed untenanted, until a knocking at his door roused him to blink about him wondering where he was before bracing himself to make it seem as if it were the most ordinary thing in the world to sleep in a chair when a bed was available.

It was Giles who came in, bearing clean linen and a uniform and razors; the business of shaving and of dressing carefully served to steady him and kept him from thinking too furiously about the problem he would have to solve in the next few minutes.

'His Excellency would be glad if His Lordship would take breakfast with him.'

That was a message conveyed through the door to Giles; the invitation must be accepted, of course, as it was the equivalent of a royal command. Hooper, apparently, was partial to a steak for breakfast; a silver dish of steak and onions was brought in almost as soon as Hornblower had uttered his formal good morning. Hooper looked at Hornblower oddly when he answered the butler's enquiry with a request for papaya and a boiled egg – that was a bad start, for it confirmed Hooper in his opinions of Hornblower's eccentricity that he should have these outlandish Frenchified notions about breakfast. Years of living on shore had not yet dulled the appetite for fresh eggs in their shells which Hornblower had acquired during decades at sea. Hooper daubed mustard on his steak and set about it with appetite.

'Did you sleep well?'

'Well enough, thank you, Your Excellency.'

Hooper's abandonment of the formal 'My Lord' was a not too subtle indication that he was willing to forget last night's discussion and to act magnanimously as if Hornblower was a normal person with only a temporary lapse on his record.

'We'll leave business until we've eaten.'

'As you wish, Your Excellency.'

But not even a Governor can be sure of his future. There was a bustle at the door, and a whole group of people came hurrying in, not merely the butler but two aides-de-camp and Gerard and – and – who was that? Pale and ragged and weary, almost unable to stand on tottering legs.

'Spendlove!' said Hornblower, his spoon clattering to the floor as he rose and hurried to him.

Hornblower clasped his hand, grinning with delight. Perhaps there had never been a moment in his life which had held so much sheer pleasure for him.

'Spendlove!' He could only repeat the name at first.

'Is this the return of the prodigal?' asked Hooper from the table.

Hornblower remembered his manners.

'Your Excellency,' he said, 'may I take it upon myself to present my secretary, Mr Erasmus Spendlove?'

'Glad to see you, young man. Take a seat at the table. Bring Mr Spendlove some food! He looks as if a glass of wine would not come amiss. Bring the decanter and a glass.'

'You're not wounded?' asked Hornblower. 'You're not hurt?'

'No, My Lord,' said Spendlove, extending his legs cautiously under the table. 'It is only that seventy miles on horseback have stiffened my unaccustomed limbs.'

'Seventy miles?' asked Hooper. 'From where?'

'Montego Bay, Your Excellency.'

'Then you must have escaped in the night?'

'At nightfall, Your Excellency.'

'But what did you do, man?' demanded Hornblower. 'How did you get away?'

'I jumped, My Lord. Into the water.'

'Into the water?'

'Yes, My Lord. There was eight feet of water in the river at the foot of the cliff; enough to break my fall from any height.'

'So there was. But – but – in the dark?'

'That was easy, My Lord. I looked over the parapet during the day. I did when I said good-bye to Your Lordship. I marked the spot and I measured the distance with my eye.'

'And then?'

'And then I jumped when it was fully dark, and raining hard.'

'What were the pirates doing?' asked Hooper.

'They were taking shelter, Your Excellency. They were paying no attention to me, thinking I was safe enough there, with the ladder pulled up.'

'And so—?'

'So I took a run, Your Excellency, and jumped the parapet, as I said, and came down feet first into the water.'

'Unhurt?'

'Unhurt, Your Excellency.'

Hornblower's vivid imagination conjured up everything about the feat, the half-dozen strides through the dark and the roaring rain, the leap, the endless fall. He felt the hair at the back of his neck lifting.

'A most commendable deed,' commented Hooper.

'Nothing for a desperate man, Your Excellency.'

'Perhaps not. And then? After you were in the water? Were you pursued?'

'As far as I can tell, Your Excellency, I was not. Perhaps it was some time before they noticed my absence. Even then they would have to let down the ladder and climb down it. I heard nothing as I made off.'

'Which way did you go?' asked Hornblower.

'I kept to the river, My Lord, making my way downstream. It reaches the sea at Montego Bay, as we decided, if you remember, My Lord, when we were making our first observations.'

'Was it an easy journey?' asked Hornblower. Something was stirring in his mind, demanding his attention despite the strong emotions he was experiencing.

'Not easy in the dark, My Lord. There were rapids in places, and the boulders were slippery. I fancy the main pass is narrow, although I could not see it.'

'And at Montego Bay?' asked Hooper.

'There was the guard over the fishing boats, a half-company of the West Indian Regiment, Your Excellency. I had their officer awakened, and he found me a horse, and I took the road through Cambridge and Ipswich.'

'You got yourself remounts on the way?'

'I claimed I was on a mission of the greatest importance, Your Excellency.'

'You made good time, even then.'

'The patrol at Mandeville told me His Lordship was on his way to Your Excellency, and so I rode straight to Government House.'

'Very sensible.'

To the picture in Hornblower's mind of the leap in the darkness were now added others, of a nightmare journey down the river, falling over slippery boulders, tumbling into unexpected pools, struggling along invisible banks; then the endless, weary ride.

'I shall represent your conduct to the Lords Commissioners, Mr Spendlove,' he said, formally.

'I must thank Your Lordship.'

'And I shall represent it to the Secretary of State,' added Hooper.

'Your Excellency is too kind.'

To Hornblower it was not the least of Spendlove's achievements (guessed at from a glance at his plate) that Spendlove had contrived somehow to gulp down a whole plateful of steak and onions while making his report. The man must have learned to dispense with chewing.

'Enough of compliments,' said Hooper, mopping up his gravy with a piece of bread. 'Now we have to destroy these pirates. This lair of theirs – you say it is strong?'

Hornblower let Spendlove answer.

'Impregnable to direct assault, Your Excellency.'

'M'm. D'ye think they'll make a stand there?'

For the past several minutes Hornblower had been debating this point with himself. Those leaderless men, dazed now by the complete failure of their scheme – what would they do?'

'They could scatter all over the island, Your Excellency,' said Spendlove.

'So they could. Then I'll have to hunt them down. Patrols on every road, movable columns in the mountains. And the sick-list is high already.'

Troops exposed to the weather and the night air for long in the West Indies died like flies, and it might well take weeks to run the outlaws down.

'Maybe they'll scatter,' said Hornblower, and then he committed himself, 'but in my opinion, Your Excellency, they will not.'

Hooper look at him sharply.

'You think not?'

'I think not, Your Excellency.'

That gang had been despairing as well as desperate when he had been among them. There was something childlike about them, leaderless as they were. On the cliff they had shelter, food – they had a home, if the expression could be tolerated. They would not readily leave it.

'And you say this place is impregnable? It would mean a long siege?'

'I might reduce them quickly with a naval force, Your Excellency, if Your Excellency would give me leave to try.'

'Your Lordship is welcome to try anything that will save lives.'

Hooper was looking at him curiously.

'Then I'll make my arrangements,' said Hornblower.

'You'll go round to Montego Bay by sea?'

'Yes.'

Hornblower restrained himself from saying 'of course'. Soldiers always found it hard to realise the convenience of the sea for rapid and secret movements.

'I'll maintain my patrols in case they bolt while you smoke out the nest,' said Hooper.

'I think Your Excellency would be taking a wise precaution in doing so. I trust my plan will not take long in execution. With Your Excellency's leave—'

Hornblower rose from the table.

'You're going now?'

'Every hour is of importance, Your Excellency.'

Hooper was looking at him more inquisitively than ever.

'The Navy displays its notorious reserve,' he said, 'Oh, very well then. Order His Lordship's carriage. You have my leave to try, My Lord. Report to me by courier.'

There they were, in the warm morning air, sitting, the three of them, Hornblower, Spendlove, and Gerard, in the carriage.

'The dockyard,' ordered Hornblower briefly. He turned to Spendlove. 'From the dockyard you will go on board *Clorinda* and convey my order to Captain Fell to make ready for sea. I shall be hoisting my flag within an hour. Then it is my order to you that you get yourself some rest.'

'Aye aye, My Lord.'

At the dockyard the Captain-Superintendent did his best not to appear surprised at an unheralded visit from his Admiral who by the last news had been kidnapped.

'I want a boat mortar, Holmes,' said Hornblower, brushing aside the expressions of pleased surprise.

'A boat mortar, My Lord? Y-yes, My Lord. There's one in store, I know.'

'It's to go on board *Clorinda* at once. Now, there are shells for it?'

'Yes, My Lord. Uncharged, of course.'

'I'll have *Clorinda*'s gunner charge 'em while we're under way. Twenty pounds apiece, I believe. Send two hundred, with the fuses.'

'Aye aye, My Lord.'

'And I want a punt. Two punts. I've seen your hands using 'em for caulking and breaming. Twenty-foot, are they?'

'Twenty-two foot, My Lord,' answered Holmes; he was glad that he could answer this question while his Admiral had not insisted on an answer regarding so obscure a matter as the weight of boat-mortar shells.

'I'll have two, as I said. Send them round to be hove on deck.'

'Aye aye, My Lord.'

Captain Sir Thomas Fell had his best uniform on to greet his Admiral.

'I received your order, My Lord,' he said, as the twittering of the pipes died away in a last wail.

'Very well, Sir Thomas. I want to be under way the moment the stores I have ordered are on board. You can warp your ship out. We are going to Montego Bay to deal with pirates.'

'Aye aye, My Lord.'

Fell did his best not to look askance at the two filthy punts that he was expected to heave on to his spotless deck – they were only the floating stages used in the dockyard for work on ship's sides – and the two tons of greasy mortar shells for which he had to find space were no better. He was not too pleased when he was ordered to tell off the greater part of his ship's company – two hundred and forty men – and all his marine detachment for a landing party. The hands were naturally delighted with the prospect of a change of routine and the possibility of action. The fact that the gunner was weighing out gunpowder and putting two pounds apiece in the shells, a glimpse of the armourer going round with the Admiral on an inspection of the boarding-pikes, the sight of the boat mortar, squat and ugly, crouching on its bed at the break of the forecastle, all excited them. It was a pleasure to thrash along to the westward, under every stitch of canvas, leaving Portland Point abeam, rounding Negril Point at sunset, catching some fortunate puffs of the sea breeze which enabled them to cheat the trade wind, ghosting along in the tropical darkness with the lead at work in the chains, and anchoring with the dawn among the shoals of Montego Bay, the green mountains of Jamaica all fiery with the rising sun.

Hornblower was on deck to see it; he had been awake since midnight, having slept since sunset – two almost sleepless nights had disordered his habits – and he was already pacing the quarterdeck as the excited men were formed up in the waist. He kept a sharp eye on the preparations. That boat mortar weighed no more than four hundred pounds, a mere trifle for the yard-arm tackle to lower down into the punt alongside. The musketmen were put through an inspection of their equipment; it was puzzling to the crew that there were pikemen, axemen, and even malletmen and crowbarmen as well. As the sun climbed higher and blazed down hotter the men began to file down into the boats.

'Gig's alongside, My Lord,' said Gerard.

'Very well.'

On shore Hornblower returned the salute of the astonished subaltern commanding the detachment of the West Indian Regiment on guard over the boats – he had turned out his men apparently expecting nothing less than a French invasion – and dismissed him. Then he ran a final glance over the rigid lines of the marine detachment, scarlet tunics and white cross-belts and all. They would not be nearly as tidy by the end of the day.

'You can make a start, captain,' he said. 'Keep me informed, Mr Spendlove, if you please.'

'Aye aye, My Lord.'

With Spendlove as guide the marines marched forward; they were the advanced guard to secure the main body from surprise. It was time to give orders to *Clorinda*'s first-lieutenant.

'Now, Mr Sefton, we can move.'

The little river had a little bar at its mouth, but the two punts carrying the mortar and the ammunition had been floated in round it. For a

mile there was even a track beside the water, and progress was rapid
as they dragged the punts along, while the vegetation closed in round
them. The shade was gratifying when they first entered into it, but they
found it breathless, damp, stifling, as they progressed farther in. Mosquitoes stung with venomous determination. Men slipped and fell on
the treacherous mud-banks, splashing prodigiously. Then they reached
the first stretch of shallows, where the river came bubbling down a
long perceptible slope between steep banks under the light filtering in
through the trees.

At least they had saved a mile and more by water carriage even this
far. Hornblower studied the grounded punts, the soil and the trees.
This was what he had been thinking about; it was worth making the
experiment before putting the men to the toil of carrying the mortar up
by brute force.

'We'll try a dam here, Mr Sefton, if you please.'

'Aye aye, My Lord, Axemen! Pikemen! Malletmen!'

The men were still in high spirits; it called for exertion on the part
of the petty officers to restrain their exuberance. A line of pikes driven
head downward where the soil was soft enough to receive them formed
the first framework of the dam. Axemen felled small trees with a childish
delight in destruction. Crowbarmen levered at stumps and rocks. A small
avalanche came tumbling down into the river bed. The water swirled
about the trash; already there was sufficient obstruction to hold it.
Hornblower saw the level rise before his very eyes.

'More rocks here!' roared Sefton.

'Keep your eye on those punts, Mr Sefton,' said Hornblower – the
clumsy craft were already afloat again.

Felled trees and rocks extended, heightened, and strengthened the
dam. There was water spouting through the interstices, but not as
much as was being held back.

'Get the punts upstream,' ordered Hornblower.

Four hundred willing hands had achieved much; the water was
banked up sufficient to float the punts two-thirds of the way up the
shallows.

'Another dam, I think, Mr Sefton, if you please.'

Already they had learned much about the construction of temporary
dams. The stream bed was choked in a twinkling, it seemed. Splashing
knee-deep in water the men dragged the punts higher still. They
grounded momentarily, but a final heave ran them over the last of the
shallows into a reach where they floated with ease.

'Excellent, Mr Sefton.'

That was a clear gain of a quarter of a mile before the next shallows.

As they were preparing to work on the next dam the flat report of a
musket-shot came echoing back to them in the heated air, followed by

half a dozen more; it was several minutes before they heard the explanation, brought back by a breathless messenger.

'Captain Seymour reports, sir. We was fired on by someone up there, sir. Saw 'im in the trees, sir, but 'e got away.'

'Very well.'

So the pirates had posted a look-out downstream. Now they knew that a force was advancing against them. Only time would show what they would do next; meanwhile the punts were afloat again and it was time to push on. The river curved back and forth, washing at the foot of vertical banks, preserving, for a time, miraculously, enough depth of water to float the punts at the expense of occasionally dragging them up slight rapids. Now it began to seem to Hornblower as if he had spent days on this labour, in the blinding patches of sunlight and the dark stretches of shade, with the river swirling round his knees, and his feet slipping on the rocks. At the next dam he was tempted to sit and allow the sweat to stream down him. He had hardly done so when another messenger arrived from the advanced guard.

'Captain Seymour reporting, sir. 'E says to say the pirates 'ave gorn to ground, sir. They're in a cave, sir, right up in the cliff.'

'How far ahead of here?'

'Oh, not so very fur, sir.'

Hornblower could have expected no better answer, he realised.

'They was shooting at us, sir,' supplemented the messenger.

That defined the distance better, for they had heard no firing for a long time; the pirates' lair must be farther than the sound could carry.

'Very well. Mr Sefton, carry on, if you please. I'm going ahead. Come along, Gerard.'

He set himself to climb and scramble along the river bank. On his left hand as he progressed he noticed the bank was growing steeper and loftier. Now it was really a cliff. Another stretch of rapids at a corner, and then he opened up a fresh vista. There it was, just as he remembered it, the lofty, overhanging cliff with the waterfall tumbling down it to join the river at its foot, and the long horizontal seam halfway up the cliff; open grassland with a few trees on his right, and even the little group of mules on the narrow stretch of grass between the cliff and the river. Red-coated marines were strung out over the grassland, in a wide semi-circle whose centre was the cave.

Hornblower forgot his sweating fatigue and strode hastily forward to where he could see Seymour standing among his men gazing up at the cliff, Spendlove at his side. They came to meet him and saluted.

'There they are, My Lord,' said Seymour. 'They took a few shots at us when we arrived.'

'Thank you, captain. How do you like the look of the place now, Spendlove?'

'As much as before, My Lord, but no more.'

'Spendlove's Leap,' said Hornblower.

He was pressing forward along the river bank towards the cave, staring upwards.

'Have a care, My Lord,' said Spendlove, urgently.

A moment after he had spoken something whistled sharply just above Hornblower's head; a puff of smoke appeared over the parapet of the cave, and a sharp ringing report came echoing from the cliff face. Then, made tiny by the distance, doll-like figures appeared over the parapet, waving their arms in defiance, and the yells they were uttering came faintly to their ears.

'Someone has a rifle up there, My Lord,' said Seymour.

'Indeed? Perhaps then it would be best to withdraw out of range before he can reload.'

The incident had made little impression on Hornblower until that moment. Now he suddenly realised that the almost legendary career of the great Lord Hornblower might have been terminated then and there, that his future biographer might have had to deplore the ironic chance which, after so many pitched battles, brought him death at the hands of an obscure criminal in an unknown corner of a West Indian island. He turned and walked away, the others at his side. He found he was holding his neck rigid, his muscles tense; it had been a long time since his life was last in danger. He strove to appear natural.

'Sefton will be up with the mortar before long,' he said, after casting about in his mind for something natural to say; and he hoped it did not sound as unnatural to the others as it did to him.

'Yes, My Lord.'

'Where shall we site it?' He swung round and looked about him, measuring ranges with his eye. 'It had better be out of range of that rifle.'

His interest in what he was doing immediately erased the memory of his danger. Another puff of smoke from the parapet; another echoing report.

'Did anyone hear that bullet? No? Then we can assume we're out of rifle shot here.'

'If you please, My Lord,' asked Spendlove. 'What range can you expect with a boat mortar?'

'The encyclopedic Spendlove displaying ignorance! Seven hundred yards with a one-pound charge of powder, and a time of flight of fifteen seconds. But here we have to burst the shell sixty feet above the firing-point. A nice problem in ballistics.' Hornblower spoke with perfect indifference, confident that no one knew that at one o'clock that morning he had been studying those figures in the manual. 'Those trees there will be useful when we come to sway the mortar up. And there's level ground within twenty feet of them. Excellent.'

'Here they come, My Lord.'

The first of the main body appeared round the distant corner of the cliff, hurrying along the river bank. As they took in the situation they broke into a yell and a run, leaping and scrambling over the broken ground; Hornblower was reminded of hounds rushing up clamouring at sight of their quarry at bay.

'Silence, there!' he roared. 'You midshipman, there, can't you keep your men under control? Mark their names for punishment, and I'll mention yours to Mr Sefton.'

Abashed, the seamen formed up quietly. Here came the punts, gliding like fate along the silent pool, towed by working parties scrambling along the bank.

'Orders, My Lord?' asked Sefton.

Hornblower glanced finally round the terrain before issuing them. The sun was long past its zenith as eager men clambered up the trees to fix the tackles; soon the mortar hung dangling from a stout limb while the mortar bed was hoisted out and settled in a smooth spot, the gunner fussing over it with a spirit level to make sure it was horizontal. Then, with violent manual labour, the mortar was swung over and finally heaved up into position, and the gunner drove the keys through the eyebolts.

'Shall I open fire, My Lord?' asked Sefton.

Hornblower looked over at the distant seam in the face of the cliff across the river. The pirates there would be watching them. Had they recognised this squat object, inconsiderable in size, undistinguished in shape, which meant death to them? They might well not know what it was; they were probably peering over the parapet trying to make out what it was that had occupied the attention of so considerable a body of men.

'What's your elevation, gunner?'

'Sixty degrees, sir – My Lord.'

'Try a shot with a fifteen-second fuse.'

The gunner went carefully through the process of loading, measuring the powder charge and wadding it down into the chamber, clearing the touch-hole with the priming iron and then filling it with fine-grain powder from the horn. He took his bradawl and drove it carefully into the wooden stem of the fuse at the selected point – these were very new-fangled fuses, graduated with ink lines to mark the time of burning – and screwed it into the shell. He lowered the shell down upon the wad.

'Linstocks,' he said.

Someone had been chipping away with flint and steel to catch a spark upon the slow match. He transferred the glow to a second linstock which he handed to the gunner. The gunner, stooping, checked the pointing of the weapon.

'Fuse!' he said. His assistant touched his linstock down, and the fuse spluttered. Then the gunner thrust his glowing match upon the touch-hole. A roar and a billow of powder smoke.

Standing far back from the mortar Hornblower already had his face turned to the sky to track the shell in its flight. Against that light blue there was nothing to be seen – no, there at the height of the trajectory there was a brief black streak, instantly invisible again. A further wait; an inevitable thought that the fuse had failed, and then a distant explosion and a fountain of smoke, down at the base of the cliff somewhat to the right of the cave. There was a groan from the watching seamen.

'Silence, there!' bellowed Sefton.

'Try again, gunner,' said Hornblower.

The mortar was trained round a trifle on its bed. Its bore was sponged out and when the charge had been put in the gunner took a gill measure from his pocket and added a measure of powder to the charge. He pierced the fuse again, lowered the shell into the bore, gave his final order, and fired. A wait; and then a bold puff of smoke hung in the air, seemingly right in line with the seam in the cliff. The wretched people there were watching their fate creeping up on them.

'Fuse a little short,' said Hornblower.

'Range short, I fancy, My Lord,' said the gunner.

At the next shot there was a cloud of dust and a small avalanche from the cliff face high above the seam, and instantly afterwards the burst of the shell on the ground at the near edge of the river where it had fallen.

'Better,' said Hornblower. He had seen the principles of ranging with a mortar – a huge thirteen-inch one – at the siege of Riga nearly twenty years before.

Two more shots, both wasted – the shells exploded at the top of their trajectory, high, high up. Apparently those new-fangled fuses were not quite reliable. Fountains spouted momentarily from the river surface as fragments rained into it. But the pirates must by now be fully aware of what the mortar implied.

'Give me that telescope, Gerard.'

He trained the instrument on the seam in the face of the cliff. He could see every detail now, the rough stone parapet, the waterfall at one end, but he could see no sign of the garrison. They were at the back of the cave or crouching behind the parapet.

'Fire another shot.'

Fifteen long seconds after the report. Then he saw fragments flying from under the overhang.

'Good shot!' he called, still watching. The shell must have fallen right into the cave. But as he uttered the words a dark figure appeared at the parapet, the arms swinging together. He saw the tiny black disc of the shell against the background of rock curving downwards and then a burst of smoke. Someone had seized the hot shell in his two hands and slung it over the parapet in the nick of time. A desperate deed.

'Pitch another shell there with a second's less fuse and it will be all over,' he said, and then – 'Wait.'

Surely those helpless people must surrender, and not stay to be massacred. What must he do to persuade them? He knew perfectly well.

'Send a white flag forward, My Lord?' asked Spendlove, voicing his thoughts.

'I was thinking about it,' said Hornblower.

It would be a dangerous mission. If the pirates were determined not to surrender they would not respect a flag of truce, and would fire on the bearer of it. There were a score of muskets and at least one rifle up there. Hornblower wanted neither to order someone forward nor to ask for a volunteer.

'I'll do it, My Lord,' said Spendlove. 'They know me.'

This was the price he had to pay, thought Hornblower, for his lofty position, for being an Admiral. He had to order his friends to their death. Yet on the other hand—

'Very well,' said Hornblower.

'Let's have your shirt and your pike, my man,' said Spendlove.

A white shirt tied by the sleeves to a pikestaff made a fair white flag. As Spendlove went forward with it, through the cordon of red-coated marines, Hornblower was tempted to call him back. It was only unconditional surrender that could be offered, after all. He went as far as to open his mouth, but closed it again without saying the words he had in mind. Spendlove walked towards the river bank, stopping every few seconds to wave the flag. Through the telescope Hornblower could see nothing up in the cave. Then he saw a flash of metal, and a line of heads and shoulders over the parapet. A dozen muskets were taking aim at Spendlove. But Spendlove saw them too, and halted, with a wave of his flag. There were long seconds of tension, and then Spendlove turned his back upon the muskets and began to retrace his steps. As he did so there was a puff of smoke from the parapet; the rifleman had fired as soon as he had seen there was no chance of luring Spendlove within musket shot. Spendlove came walking back, trailing the pike and the shirt.

'He missed me, My Lord,' he said.

'Thank God,' said Hornblower. 'Gunner, fire.'

The wind may have shifted a little, or the powder was not consistent. The shell burst in the air just below the level of the cave – so that the fuse must have been efficient – but some considerable distance from the cliff.

'Fire again,' said Hornblower.

There it was. A burst of smoke, a fountain of fragments, right in the cave. Horrible to think of what was happening there.

'Fire again.'

Another burst right in the cave.

'Fire again – No! Wait.'

Figures were appearing on the parapet – there had been some survivors, then, from those two bursts. Two figures – tiny dolls in the field of the telescope – seemed to hang in the air as they leaped. The telescope followed them down. One struck water in a fountain of spray. The other fell on the rocky shore, broken and horrible. He raised the telescope again. There was the ladder being thrown over from the parapet. There was a figure – and another figure – climbing down. Hornblower shut the telescope with a snap.

'Captain Seymour! Send a party forward to secure the prisoners.'

He did not have to see the horrors of the cave, the mutilated dead and the screaming wounded. He could see them in his mind's eye when Seymour made his report of what he found when he ascended the ladder. It was done, finished. The wounded could be bandaged and carried down to the beach on litters to the death that awaited them, the unwounded driven along with them with their wrists bound. A courier could be sent off to the Governor to say that the pirate horde had been wiped out, so that the patrols could be called in and the militia sent home. He did not have to set eyes on the wretched people he had conquered. The excitement of the hunt was over. He had set himself a task to do, a problem to solve, just as he might work out a longitude from lunar observations, and he had achieved success. But the measure of that success could be expressed in hangings, in dead and in wounded, in that shattered, broken-backed figure lying on the rocks, and he had undertaken the task merely on a point of pride, to re-establish his self-esteem after the indignity of being kidnapped. It was no comfort to argue with himself – as he did – that what he had done would otherwise have been done by others, at great cost in disease and in economic disturbance. That only made him sneer at himself as a hair-splitting casuist. There were few occasions when Hornblower could do what was right in Hornblower's eyes.

Yet there was some cynical pleasure to be derived from his lofty rank, to be able to leave all this after curt orders to Sefton and Seymour to bring the landing party back to the shore with the least delay and the shortest exposure to the night air, to go back on board and eat a comfortable dinner – even if it meant Fell's rather boring company – and to sleep in a comfortable bed. And it was pleasant to find that Fell had already dined, so that he could eat his dinner merely in the company of his flag-lieutenant and his secretary. Nevertheless, there was one more unexpected crumpled petal in his roseleaf bed, and he discovered it, contrariwise, as a result of what he intended to be a kindly action.

'I shall have to add a further line to my remarks about you to Their Lordships, Spendlove,' he said. 'It was a brave deed to go forward with that flag of truce.'

'Thank you, My Lord,' said Spendlove, who bent his gaze down on the tablecloth and drummed with his fingers before continuing, eyes still lowered in unusual nervousness. 'Then perhaps Your Lordship will not be averse to putting in a word for me in another quarter?'

'Of course I will,' replied Hornblower in all innocence. 'Where?'

'Thank you, My Lord. It was with this in mind that I did the little you have been kind enough to approve of. I would be deeply grateful if Your Lordship would go to the trouble of speaking well of me to Miss Lucy.'

Lucy! Hornblower had forgotten all about the girl. He quite failed to conceal his surprise, which was clearly apparent to Spendlove when he lifted his glance from the tablecloth.

'We jested about a wealthy marriage, My Lord,' said Spendlove. The elaborate care with which he was choosing his words proved how deep were his emotions. 'I would not care if Miss Lucy had not a penny. My Lord, my affections are deeply engaged.'

'She is a very charming young woman,' said Hornblower, temporising desperately.

'My Lord, I love her,' burst out Spendlove, casting aside all restraint. 'I love her dearly. At the ball I tried to interest her in myself, and I failed.'

'I'm sorry to hear that,' said Hornblower.

'I could not but be aware of her admiration for you, My Lord. She spoke of Your Lordship repeatedly. I realised even then that one word from you would carry more weight than a long speech from me. If you would say that word, My Lord—'

'I'm sure you over-estimate my influence,' said Hornblower, choosing his words as carefully as Spendlove had done, but, he hoped, not as obviously. 'But of course I will do all I can.'

'There is no need for me to reiterate my gratitude, My Lord,' said Spendlove.

This pleading creature, this poor love-lorn fellow, was the Spendlove whose cool daring had risked a leap in the darkness down a sixty-foot precipice. Hornblower remembered Lucy's lips on his hands, remembered how she had followed him on her knees across the floor. The less he had to do with any of this the better, he decided. But the passion of a child hardly out of the schoolroom for a man of mature years was likely to be fleeting, transient, and the memory of her lost dignity would later be as painful to her as it was to him. She would find need to assert herself, to show him that he was not the only man in the world – and how could she demonstrate that more plainly than by marrying someone else? To use a vulgar phrase, there was quite a chance that Spendlove might catch her on the rebound.

'If good wishes can help,' he said, 'you have all mine, Spendlove.'

Even an Admiral had to choose his words with care. Two days later he was announcing his immediate departure to the Governor.

'I'm taking my squadron to sea in the morning, Your Excellency,' he said.

'Aren't you going to stay for the hangings?' asked Hooper in surprise.

'I fear not,' answered Hornblower, and added an unnecessary explanation. 'Hangings don't agree with me, Your Excellency.'

It was not merely an unnecessary explanation; it was a foolish one, as he knew as soon as he saw the open astonishment in Hooper's face. Hooper could hardly have been more surprised at hearing that hangings did not agree with Hornblower than he would have been if he had heard that Hornblower did not agree with hangings – and that was very nearly as correct.

THE GUNS OF CARABOBO

She was exactly like a British ship of war; naturally, perhaps, since she had been one most of her life until she was sold out of the service. Now, as she came up into the harbour, she could pass without question for a man-o'-war brig except that she flew the Royal Yacht Squadron burgee instead of a commission pendant. Hornblower put down the telescope through which he had been watching, curiously, her progress into Kingston harbour, and referred again to Barbara's letter, two months old now, which had arrived a fortnight ago.

My dearest husband (wrote Barbara. She sometimes misused her superlatives; that 'dearest', strictly, implied that she had at least three husbands, even though it also implied that Hornblower rated highest of the three).

You are shortly going to have a visitor, a Mr Charles Ramsbottom, a millionaire, who has purchased an old ship of the Navy to use as a yacht, which he has named the 'Bride of Abydos', *and in which he proposes to visit the West Indies. He has only lately made his appearance in society, having inherited his father's fortune – Bradford wool and army clothing contracts! Yet despite this obscure origin he has succeeded in entering into society, perhaps because he is very young, very charming, unmarried, mildly eccentric, and, as I said, a millionaire. I have met him frequently of late, in very good houses, and I recommend him to you, dearest, if for no other reason than that he has won some small portion of my heart by a delightful mixture of deference and interest which I might have found irresistible were I not married to the most irresistible man in the world. He has, indeed, won golden opinions in society, both on the Government side and with the Opposition, and he might become an important factor in politics should he decide to enter into them. I have no doubt that he will bring you introductions from personages even more influential than your loving wife. . . .*

Hornblower had to read the letter through to the end, although it contained no further reference to Mr Charles Ramsbottom, but he returned again to the opening paragraph. It was the first time he had ever seen this new word 'millionaire', which occurred twice. He disliked it on sight. It was inconceivable that a man should have a million pounds, and presumably not in broad estates but in factories and in stocks and shares, probably with a huge holding in Consols and an immense balance at the bank as well. The existence of millionaires, whether in society or not, was something as distasteful as the word itself now called into existence. And this one had been charming to Barbara – he was not too sure if that really constituted a recommendation. He picked up the telescope again and watched the brig come to anchor. The rapidity with which she took in sail showed that she carried a large crew. Hornblower, as a Commander-in-Chief of a squadron and accountable to the niggardly Lords of the Admiralty for every penny expended, knew perfectly well what this sort of thing cost. This Mr Ramsbottom, to indulge himself in his naval toy, was expending enough money to maintain a thousand families in bread and beer and bacon.

The brig rounded-to and anchored very neatly indeed; if she had been a vessel included in his command he would have grunted with grudging satisfaction. As it was he grunted with a mixture of envy and derision and turned away to await the inevitable call in the seclusion of Admiralty House.

When it came he fingered the visiting card with its plain 'Mr Charles Ramsbottom' and found some small satisfaction in deciding that he had at last come across a name more unlovely than his own. But the owner of the name, when he was ushered in, made a better impression. In his very early twenties, he was small and slight and – for what it was worth – strikingly handsome, with black hair and eyes and what could only be described as 'chiselled features' deeply tanned after weeks at sea; not at all what might be expected of a Bradford wool manufacturer, while his dark-green coat and formal white breeches were in quiet good taste.

Admiral Hornblower

'My wife wrote to me about you, Mr Ramsbottom,' said Hornblower.

'That was very kind of Lady Hornblower. But of course she is kindness personified. May I present my letters of introduction from Lord Liverpool and Bishop Wilberforce, My Lord?'

Barbara was perfectly right, then, in predicting that Ramsbottom would win favour with both political parties – here were letters from the Prime Minister himself and a prominent member of the Opposition. Hornblower glanced through them, and was conscious of an undernote of cordiality despite their formal wording.

'Excellent, Mr Ramsbottom,' said Hornblower. He tried to adopt the tone which he presumed would be adopted by a man who had just read a letter of introduction from the Prime Minister. 'Is there any way in which I can be of service to you?'

'None that I am aware of at present, My Lord. I must complete with water and stores, naturally, but my purser is a capable man. I intend to continue my voyage through these charming islands.'

'Of course,' said Hornblower, soothingly. He could not imagine why anyone should voluntarily spend any time in these waters where piracy was still smouldering, nor why anyone should wish to visit countries where malaria and yellow fever were endemic, and where civil war, revolution and massacre claimed even heavier toll.

'You find the *Bride of Abydos* a comfortable ship?' asked Hornblower.

Those eighteen-gun brigs of the Royal Navy were notoriously unpleasant craft, crowded and crank.

'Comfortable enough, My Lord, thank you,' answered Ramsbottom. 'I lightened her by changing the armament; she mounts only twelve guns now – two long sixes and ten carronades, twenty-four-pounders instead of thirty-two-pounders.'

'So you could still deal with a pirate?'

'Oh, yes indeed, My Lord. And with the reduction in weight on deck – a full ten tons – and modifications in her sail plan I have made a seaworthy craft of her, I believe and hope.'

'I'm sure you have, Mr Ramsbottom,' said Hornblower. It was likely enough; the brigs-of-war were naturally crammed with guns and warlike stores to the limit of stability and human endurance, so that a moderate reduction in dead weight might bring profound results in comfort and handiness.

'It would give me the greatest pleasure,' went on Mr Ramsbottom, 'if I could induce Your Lordship to visit me on board. It would indeed be an honour, and would gratify my crew. Perhaps I could even persuade Your Lordship to dine on board?'

'We can discuss that after you have dined with me, Mr Ramsbottom,' replied Hornblower, remembering his manners and his obligation to invite to dinner any bearer of a reasonable introduction.

'You are most kind, My Lord,' said Mr Ramsbottom. 'I must, of course, present my introductions to His Excellency at the earliest opportunity.'

There was something quite winning about Mr Ramsbottom's smile as he said this, an awareness and a tolerance of the rules of social etiquette. A visitor to Jamaica would normally be bound to pay his respects first to the Governor, but Ramsbottom was no ordinary visitor; as captain of a ship his first call was due to the Naval authorities, to Hornblower, in fact. A trivial point, as his smile implied, but, etiquette being etiquette, trivial points demanded strict attention.

By the time Ramsbottom took his leave he had made a very good impression on the reluctant Hornblower. He had talked sensibly about ships and the sea, he was easy and natural in his manner, and not in the least like Lord Byron, who was probably more responsible than anyone else for the growing fad for yachting among the wealthy. Hornblower was even prepared to forgive him for having 'won some small portion' of Barbara's heart. And in the course of his several days' stay in Jamaica Hornblower really came to like the young man, especially after having lost two pounds to him in a desperate tussle at whist and then winning ten pounds back in another tussle where admittedly Ramsbottom encountered a run of bad luck. Jamaican society gave Ramsbottom a warm welcome; even the Governor looked on him with approval, and the Governor's wife, Lady Hooper, was loud in her praises of his excellent manners and considerate ways.

'I wouldn't have expected it of a Bradford manufacturer's son,' said Hooper, grudgingly.

'Are you dining on board the *Bride of Abydos*, sir?' asked Hornblower.

'I am going there to dinner,' answered Hooper, who enjoyed food, 'but seeing that it is only a yacht I have little hope of dining.'

Hornblower arrived on board early, at Ramsbottom's suggestion, so as to have time to inspect the vessel. He was received in Navy fashion with sideboys attending the side and a long flourish on boatswain's pipes as he stepped on board. He looked keenly about him even while he shook Ramsbottom's hand. He could not have said he was not in a King's ship, as his eye took in the gleaming white deck, the ropes coiled in perfect symmetry, the gleaming trophy of pikes and cutlasses against the bulkhead, the brass winking in the sunshine, the disciplined orderly crew in blue jumpers and white trousers.

'May I present my officers, My Lord?' asked Ramsbottom.

They were two half-pay lieutenants, hardbitten men; as Hornblower shook their hands he told himself that if it had not been for a dozen strokes of luck he himself might still be a lieutenant, perhaps eking out his half-pay by serving in a rich man's yacht. As Ramsbottom led him forward he recognised one of the hands standing at attention by a gun.

'You were with me in the *Renown*, out here in 1800,' he said.

'Yes, sir, My Lord, so I was, sir.' The man grinned with uneasy pleasure as he shyly took Hornblower's outstretched hand. 'And Charlie Kemp, sir, My Lord, over there, sir, 'e was with you in the Baltic. And Bill Cummings, up on the fo'c'sle, 'e was foretopman in the *Lydia* round the Horn with you sir, My Lord.'

'Glad to see you again,' said Hornblower. That was true, but he was equally glad that he had not been under the necessity of remembering names. He moved on.

'You seem to have a Navy crew, Mr Ramsbottom,' he remarked.

'Yes, My Lord. They are nearly all man-o'wars men.'

In these years of peace and depression it would be easy enough to recruit a crew, thought Hornblower. Ramsbottom might be considered to be doing a public service in providing easy employment for these men who had deserved well of their country. Listening to the sharp orders given as the crew was put through its paces Hornblower could not suppress a smile. It was a harmless enough fad, he supposed, for Ramsbottom to indulge himself in playing at commanding a ship of war.

'You have a most efficient ship and a well-trained crew, Mr Ramsbottom,' he said.

'It is a pleasure to hear Your Lordship say so.'

'You have seen no service yourself?'

'None, My Lord.'

There was a certain degree of surprise still to be found in the fact that in this year of 1821 there were to be found grown men, even heads of families, who nevertheless had been too young to see service in the wars that had devastated the world for a whole generation. It made Hornblower feel like a centenarian.

'Here come further guests, My Lord, if you will pardon me.'

Two planters – Hough and Doggart – and then the Chief Justice of the island. So the arrival of the Governor would make a dinner party of six, three officials and three men in private life. They gathered under the awning, which, stretched across the main boom, shaded the quarter-deck, and watched the reception of His Excellency.

'Do you think the dinner will come up to the ceremonial?' asked Doggart.

'Ramsbottom's purser bought two tons of ice yesterday,' said Hough.

'At sixpence a pound that bids fair,' commented Doggart.

Jamaica was the centre of a small trade in ice, brought down from New England in fast schooners. Cut and stored away in deep places during the winter, it was hurried to the Caribbean insulated in a packing of sawdust. At the height of summer it commanded fantastic prices.

Hornblower was interested; he was more interested still in the sight of a seaman down in the waist steadily turning a crank. It did not seem a very hard labour, although unremitting. He could not for the life of him think of what function that crank could play in the life of the ship. The guests made their bows to His Excellency, and at his suggestion seated themselves in the comfortable chairs. A steward appeared at once passing round glasses of sherry.

'Excellent, by George!' exclaimed the Governor after his first cautious sip. 'None of your Olorosos, none of your sweet sticky dark sherries.'

The Governor by virtue of his reputed royal blood as well as in consequence of his position could make remarks that well might appear rude in another man. But the sherry was indeed delightful; pale, dry, infinitely delicate in flavour and bouquet, cool but not chilled. A new sound struck on Hornblower's ear, and he turned and looked forward. At the foot of the mainmast a small orchestra had struck up, of various stringed instruments whose names he had never bothered to learn except for the fiddle. If it were not for the intrusion of this horrible music there could be nothing more delightful than to sit under an awning on the deck of a well-found ship with the sea breeze just beginning to come in, drinking this excellent sherry. The Governor made a small gesture which brought a fresh glass promptly to him.

'Ah!' said the Governor. 'You keep a good orchestra, Mr Ramsbottom.'

It was well known that the royal family inherited a taste for music.

'I must thank Your Excellency,' said Ramsbottom, and the glasses went round again before he turned an ear to the murmured words of the steward. 'Your Excellency, My Lord, gentlemen, dinner is served.'

They filed down the companion; apparently every bulkhead had been taken down in the after part of the ship to make a cabin spacious though low. The carronades on either side struck a subdued warlike note in a scene of luxury, for there were flowers everywhere; the dining-table stood in the centre concealed under a glittering linen cloth. Wind scoops at the scuttles helped to deflect the trade wind into the cabin, which, under the double shade of the awning and the deck, was pleasantly cool, but Hornblower's eye at once caught sight of a couple of strange objects, like small wheels, set in two scuttles and ceaselessly whirling round. Then he knew why the seaman was turning that crank in the waist; he was driving these two wheels, which by some ingenious mechanism propelled currents of air from outside into the cabin, acting like windmill vanes but in the opposite sense.

Seated at the table in accordance with the courteous indication of their host, the guests awaited the serving of the dinner. The first course made its appearance – two ample dishes set in dishes even more ample filled with cracked ice. The inner dishes held a grey granular substance.

'Caviare!' exclaimed His Excellency, helping himself liberally after his first astonished stare.

'I hope it is to your taste, sir,' said Ramsbottom. 'And I hope you will accompany it with some of the vodka here. It is the same as is served at the Russian Imperial table.'

Conversation regarding caviare and vodka occupied the attention of all during the first course. The last time Hornblower had tasted the combination was during the defence of Riga in 1812; the experience enabled him to add his quota to the conversation. The next course made its appearance.

'You gentlemen are accustomed to this dish,' said Ramsbottom, 'but I need not apologise for it. It is, I believe, one of the delicacies of the Islands.'

It was flying fish.

'Certainly no need to apologise when it is served like this,' commented His Excellency. 'Your *chef de cuisine* must be a man of genius.'

The sauce that came with it had the merest hint of mustard.

''Ock or Champagne, My Lord?' murmured a voice in Hornblower's ear. Hornblower had already heard the Governor answer the same question with 'I'll try the hock first'. The champagne was dry and insidiously delicate, an ideal companion for the food. The great eaters of antiquity, Nero or Vitellius or Lucullus, had never known what it was like to partake of champagne and flying fish.

'You'll be living differently from this soon, Hornblower,' said His Excellency.

'No doubt about that, sir.'

Ramsbottom, between them, looked a polite inquiry.

'Your Lordship's going to sea?'

'Next week,' replied Hornblower. 'I take my squadron to sea for exercises before the coming of the hurricane season.'

'Of course that would be necessary to maintain efficiency,' agreed Ramsbottom. 'The exercises will last for long?'

'A couple of weeks or more,' said Hornblower. 'I have to keep my men accustomed to hard tack and salt pork and water from the cask.'

'And yourself too,' chuckled the Governor.

'Myself too,' agreed Hornblower ruefully.

'And you take your whole squadron, My Lord?' asked Ramsbottom.

'All I can. I work 'em hard and try to make no exceptions.'

'A good rule, I should think,' said Ramsbottom.

The soup that followed the flying fish was a fiery mulligatawny, well adapted to West Indian palates.

'Good!' was the Governor's brief comment after his first spoonful. The champagne went round again and conversation became livelier and livelier, and Ramsbottom deftly kept it going.

'What news from the mainland, sir?' he asked the Governor. 'This fellow Bolivar – is he making any progress?'

'He fights on,' answered the Governor. 'But Spain hurries out reinforcements whenever her own troubles permit. The government at Caracas is looking for the arrival of more at this moment, I believe. Then they may be able to conquer the plains and drive him out again. You know he was a refugee here in this very island a few years ago?'

'Indeed, sir?'

All the guests at the table were interested in the desperate civil war that was being fought on the mainland. Massacre and murder, blind heroism and devoted self-sacrifice, loyalty to the King and thirst for independence – all these were to be found in Venezuela; war and pestilence were laying waste the fertile plains and depopulating the crowded cities.

'How will the Spaniards stand now that Maracaibo has revolted, Hornblower?' asked the Governor.

'It's not a serious loss, sir. As long as they have the use of La Guaira their sea communications remain open – the roads are so bad that Caracas has always made use of La Guaira to preserve contact with the outside world; it's only an open roadstead but it provides good anchorage.'

'Has Maracaibo revolted, Your Excellency?' asked Ramsbottom mildly.

'The news came this morning. A feather in Bolivar's cap after his recent defeats. His army must have been growing disheartened.'

'His army, sir?' This was the Chief Justice speaking. 'Half his men are British infantry.'

Hornblower knew that to be true. British veterans formed the backbone of Bolivar's army. The llaneros – the men of the Venezuelan plains – supplied him with a brilliant cavalry, but not with the material for permanent conquest.

'Even British infantry could grow disheartened in a hopeless cause,' said the Governor, solemnly. 'The Spaniards control most of the coast – ask the Admiral here.'

'That's so,' agreed Hornblower. 'They've made it hard for Bolivar's privateers.'

'I hope you're not going to venture into that turmoil, Mr Ramsbottom,' said the Governor.

'They'll make short work of you if you do,' added the Chief Justice. 'The Dons will tolerate no interference. They'll snatch you up and you'll languish in a Spanish prison for years before we can extricate you from King Ferdinand's clutches. Unless jail fever carries you off first. Or they hang you as a pirate.'

'I have certainly no intention of venturing near the mainland,' said

Ramsbottom. 'At least not while this war continues. It is a pity, because Venezuela was my mother's country, and it would give me pleasure to visit it.'

'Your mother's country, Mr Ramsbottom?' asked the Governor.

'Yes, sir. My mother was a Venezuelan lady. There I would be Carlos Ramsbottom y Santona.'

'Most interesting,' remarked the Governor.

And more grotesque than Horatio Hornblower. It was significant of the world-wide interest of British commerce that a Bradford woollen manufacturer should have a Venezuelan mother. At any rate it accounted for Ramsbottom's dark almost swarthy, good looks.

'I can very well wait until peace is settled one way or the other,' said Ramsbottom off-handedly. 'There will be other voyages to make. Meanwhile, sir, let me call your attention to this dish here.'

The main course had now arrived on the table, roast chickens and a leg of pork as well as the dish that Ramsbottom indicated. What lay in it was concealed by poached eggs covering the surface.

'A made dish?' asked the Governor, doubtfully. His tone indicated that at this stage of the dinner he looked rather for a substantial roast.

'Please try it, sir,' said Ramsbottom coaxingly.

The Governor helped himself and tasted cautiously.

'Pleasant enough,' he decided. 'What is it?'

'A ragoût of preserved beef,' answered Ramsbottom. 'Can I persuade you gentlemen to try it? My Lord?'

At least it was something new; it was like nothing Hornblower had ever tasted before – certainly not in the least like the beef preserved in brine which he had eaten for twenty years.

'Extremely good,' said Hornblower. 'How is it preserved?'

Ramsbottom made a gesture to the waiting steward, who laid a square box, apparently of iron, upon the table. It weighed heavy in Hornblower's hand.

'Glass serves equally well,' explained Ramsbottom, 'but it is not as convenient on shipboard.'

The steward was now at work upon the iron box with a stout knife. He cut it open and prized back the top and offered it for inspection.

'A tinned box,' went on Ramsbottom, 'sealed at a high temperature. I venture to suggest that this new method will make a noticeable difference to the food supply on shipboard. This beef can be eaten cold on removal from the box, or it can be hashed as you have it here.'

'And the poached egg?' asked the Governor.

'That was the inspiration of my cook, sir.'

Discussion of this new invention – and of the excellent Burgundy served with this course – distracted attention from the troubles of Venezuela, and even from Ramsbottom's Venezuelan mother. Conversation became general, and somewhat disjointed, as the wine flowed. Hornblower had drunk as much as he desired, and, with his habitual dislike of excess, contrived to avoid drinking more. It was noticeable that Ramsbottom remained sober as well, cool and quiet-voiced, while the other faces grew redder and redder, and the cabin echoed to the roaring toasts and the bursts of inconsequential song. Hornblower guessed that his host was now finding the evening as tedious as he himself found it. He was glad when at last His Excellency rose, supporting himself by the table, to take his leave.

'A damned good dinner,' he said. 'And you're a damned good host, Ramsbottom. Wish there were more like you.'

Hornblower shook hands.

'It was very good of you to come, My Lord,' said Ramsbottom. 'I regret that I must take this opportunity to say goodbye to Your Lordship.'

'You are sailing soon?'

'In a couple of days, I expect, My Lord. I trust you will find your squadron exercises satisfactory.'

'Thank you very much. Where will you head for now?'

'I shall beat back through the Windward channel, My Lord. Perhaps I shall see something of the Bahamas.'

'Be careful of your navigation there. I must wish you good luck and a pleasant voyage. I shall write to my wife and tell her of your visit.'

'Please give Lady Hornblower my best wishes and respects, My Lord.'

Ramsbottom's good manners persisted to the end; he remembered to send round his cards '*Pour prendre congé*' before he left, and mothers of unmarried daughters much regretted his leaving. Hornblower saw the *Bride of Abydos* in the early dawn reaching to the eastward to round Morant Point with the land breeze, and then forgot about her in the bustle of taking his squadron to sea for exercises.

It never failed to raise a wry smile on his face when he looked about him at 'His Majesty's ships and vessels in the West Indies' under his command. In war-time he would have had a powerful fleet; now he had three small frigates and a motley collection of brigs and schooners. But they would serve his purpose; in his scheme the frigates became three-deckers and the brigs seventy-fours and the schooners frigates. He had a van, a centre, and a rear; he cruised in formation ready to meet the enemy, with rasping reprimands soaring up his signal halliards when any ship failed to keep station; he cleared for action and he turned by divisions into fighting line ahead; he tacked to double on the imaginary enemy's line. In pitch darkness he would burn blue lights with the signal 'Enemy in sight', so that a score of captains and a thousand seamen came tumbling from their beds to deal with the non-existent foe.

Without warning he would hang out a signal putting the most junior lieutenants in command of their respective ships, and then he would plunge into intricate manoeuvres calculated to turn the anxious substantive captains, looking helplessly on, grey with anxiety – but those junior lieutenants might some day be commanding ships of the line in a battle on which the destiny of England might depend, and it was necessary to steel their nerves and accustom them to handle ships in dangerous situations. In the middle of sail drill he would signal 'Flagship on fire. All boats away.' He called for landing parties to storm nonexistent batteries on some harmless, uninhabited cay, and he inspected those landing parties once they were on shore, to the last flint in the last pistol, with a rigid disregard for excuses that made men grind their teeth in exasperation. He set his captains to plan and execute cutting-out expeditions, and he commented mordantly on the arrangements for defence and the methods of attack. He paired off his ships to fight single-ship duels, sighting each other on the horizon and approaching ready to fire the vital opening broadside; he took advantage of calms to set his men towing and sweeping in desperate attempts to overtake the ship ahead. He worked his crews until they were ready to drop, and then he devised further tasks for them to prove to them that they still had one more effort left in them, so that it was doubtful whether 'Old Horny' was mentioned more often with curses or with admiration.

It was a toughened squadron that Hornblower led back to Kingston; but while *Clorinda* was still working up into the harbour a shore boat came pulling out to her, with on board an aide-de-camp of the Governor's with a note for Hornblower.

'Sir Thomas, would you have the kindness to call away my barge?' asked Hornblower.

There was much apparent need for haste, for the note from Government House said, briefly:

My Lord,

It is necessary that Your Lordship should attend here at the earliest possible moment to offer an explanation regarding the situation in Venezuela. Your Lordship is therefore requested and required to report to me immediately.

Augustus Hooper, Governor.

Hornblower naturally had no idea of what had happened in Venezuela for the last two weeks and more. He made no guess while the carriage took him up to Government House at its best pace, and in any case if he had tried he would never have succeeded in coming near to the truth.

'What is all this, Hornblower?' were the Governor's opening words to him. 'What authority have you for blockading the Venezuelan coast? Why was I not informed?'

'I've done nothing of the sort,' replied Hornblower, indignantly.

'But – Damn it, man, I've the proof here. I've Dutchmen and Spaniards and half the nations of the earth here all protesting about it.'

'I assure you, sir, I have taken no action on the Venezuelan coast. I have not been within five hundred miles of it.'

'Then what does this mean?' shouted the Governor. 'Look here at this!'

He held some papers up with one hand and slapped wildly at them with the other, so that Hornblower had some difficulty in taking them from him. Hornblower was bewildered already; he was more bewildered still as he read. One paper was an official dispatch in French, from the Dutch Governor of Curaçao; the other was larger and clearer, and he read it first. It was a big sheet of paper with bold writing.

Whereas – it began – notice has been received by the Lords Commissioners for executing the office of the Lord High Admiral from the Right Honourable Viscount Castlereagh, one of His Britannic Majesty's Principal Secretaries of State, concerning the need to establish a Blockade of the Coast of His Most Catholic Majesty's Dominion of Venezuela, and of the Islands pertaining to the Dominion of His Majesty the King of the Netherlands, namely and to wit Curaçao, Aruba, and Bonaire.

Therefore I, Horatio Lord Hornblower, Knight Grand Cross of the Most Honourable Order of the Bath, Rear-Admiral of the White Squadron, Commanding His Britannic Majesty's ships and vessels in West Indian Waters,

Hereby Proclaim that

The Coast of the Continent of South America from Cartagena to the Dragon's Mouth and

The Dutch Islands aforesaid of Curaçao, Aruba, and Bonaire

Are now in a state of blockade, and that

Any vessel of whatever description, whether carrying materials of war or not, found attempting to enter any port harbour or roadstead within the Territory so defined, or

Hovering with the intent to enter any such port harbour or roadstead

Will be boarded and sent in for adjudication under His Britannic Majesty's High Court of Admiralty and

Will be condemned and seized without compensation to owners, freight owners, charterers, captain, or crew.

Given under my hand this First Day of June 1821,

Hornblower, Rear-Admiral

Having read this document Hornblower was able to spare a second glance at the other. It was a vigorous protest from the Dutch Governor at Curaçao demanding explanations, apologies, the immediate with-drawal of the blockade, and exemplary compensation. Hornblower stared at Hooper in astonishment.

'This is in legal form,' he said, indicating the proclamation, 'but I never signed it. This is not my signature.'

'Then—?' spluttered Hooper. 'I thought you might be acting under secret orders from London.'

'Of course not, sir.' Hornblower stared at Hooper for another long second before the explanation came to him. 'Ramsbottom!'

'What do you mean?'

'He's been posing as me, or as one of my officers at least. Is the Dutch officer who brought this available?'

'He's waiting in the next room. There's a Spaniard there, too, sent over in a fishing boat by Morillo from La Guaira.'

'Can we have them in, sir?'

The Dutchman and the Spaniard were men full of indignation, which was not abated in the least by their presentation to the Admiral res-ponsible, in their minds, for this trouble. The Dutchman spoke fluent English, and it was to him that Hornblower first addressed himself.

'How was this proclamation delivered?' he asked.

'By one of your ships. By one of your officers.'

'What ship?'

'The brig-of-war *Desperate*.'

'I have no such ship. There's none in the Navy List. Who brought it?'

'The captain.'

'Who was he? What was he like?'

'He was an officer. A Commander, with epaulettes.'

'In uniform?'

'In full uniform.'

'Young? Old?'

'Very young.'

'Small? Slender? Handsome?'

'Yes.'

Hornblower exchanged a glance with Hooper.

'And this brig, the *Desperate*. About a hundred and seventy tons, bowsprit steved nearly level, mainmast stepped rather far aft?'

'Yes.'

'That settles it, sir,' said Hornblower to Hooper, and, to the Dutch-man, 'you've been fooled, I'm sorry to say. This man was an imposter. This proclamation is a forgery.'

The Dutchman stamped with annoyance. He was unable to find words to express himself in a foreign tongue for some moments. Finally from his splutterings emerged a name, which he repeated until it was under-standable.

'The *Helmond*! The *Helmond*!'

'What is the *Helmond*, sir?' asked Hornblower.

'One of our ships. Your ship – this *Desperate* – captured her.'

'A valuable ship?'

'She has on board the guns for the Spanish Army. Two batteries of field artillery, guns, limbers, ammunition, everything.'

'Piracy!' exclaimed Hooper.

'It sounds like it,' said Hornblower.

The Spanish officer had been standing by impatiently, apparently only half understanding the English conversation. Hornblower turned to him, and, after desperately trying to recapture his half-forgotten Spanish, entered upon a limping explanation. The Spaniard replied volubly, so volubly that more than once Hornblower had to ask him to speak more slowly. Ramsbottom had come sailing into La Guaira and had brought his precious proclamation with him. At the merest hint that the British Navy was instituting a blockade no ship had dared to stir on the South American coast, except for the *Helmond*. She had been badly needed. Bolivar was marching on Caracas; a battle was imminent on which depended the entire Spanish control of Venezuela. Morillo and the Spanish army were in need of artillery. Now not only were they left destitute, but with this news it could be taken as certain that those guns, those two batteries of field artillery, were in Bolivar's hands. The Spanish officer wrung his hands in despair.

Hornblower translated briefly for the Governor's benefit, and Hooper shook his head in sympathy.

'Bolivar has those guns. No doubt about it. Gentlemen, I much regret this occurrence. But I must impress upon you that His Majesty's Government assumes no responsibility for it. If your chiefs took no steps to detect this impostor—'

That touched off a new explosion. The British Government should make sure that no impostor wore its uniform or posed as an officer in its service. It called for all Hooper's elephantine tact to quiet down the angry officers.

'If you will permit me to consult with the Admiral, gentlemen, we may reach some satisfactory conclusion.'

Alone with the Governor again Hornblower struggled with a smile; he had never outgrown his tendency to laugh during a crisis. There was something amusing in the thought that a cocked hat and a pair of epaulettes should change the course of a war; it was a tribute to the power of the Navy that a single tiny ship should exert such enormous pressure.

'Ramsbottom and his Venezuelan mother!' said Hooper. 'It's not merely piracy, it's high treason. We shall have to hang him.'

'M'm,' said Hornblower. 'He probably holds a privateering commission from Bolivar.'

'But masquerading as a British officer? Forging official documents?'

'That was a ruse of war. An American officer deceived the Portuguese authorities in Brazil in much the same way in 1812.'

'I've heard some things about you, too,' added Hooper with a grin.

'No doubt, sir. In war a belligerent who believes what he's told is a fool.'

'But we're not belligerents.'

'No, sir. And we've suffered no loss. The Dutch and the Spaniards have only themselves to blame.'

'But Ramsbottom's a subject of His Majesty.'

'Quite true, sir. But if he holds Bolivar's commission he can do things as an officer of the revolutionary forces which he could not do as a private person.'

'D'ye mean to suggest we ought to allow him to continue this blockade of his? Nonsense, man.'

'Of course not, sir. I'll arrest him, and I'll send his ship in for adjudication, at the first opportunity. But a friendly Power has asked you, sir, the representative of His Majesty, if you have instituted a blockade. You must do everything in your power to demonstrate the truth.'

'Now for once you're talking like a sensible man. We must send word at once to Curaçao and Caracas. That will be your immediate duty. You'd better go in person.'

'Yes, sir. I'll sail with the land breeze. Have you any further instructions for me, sir?'

'None whatever. What goes on on the high seas is your affair, not mine. You're answerable to the Cabinet through the Admiralty. I don't envy you, frankly.'

'No doubt I'll survive, sir. I'll sail for La Guaira, and send another vessel to Curaçao. Perhaps if Your Excellency were to write official replies to the enquiries addressed to you they would be ready by the time I sail?'

'I'll draft 'em now.' The Governor could not repress one further outburst. 'This Ramsbottom – and his corned beef and caviare!'

'He used a sprat to catch a mackerel, Your Excellency,' said Hornblower.

So it came about that the crew of H.M.S. *Clorinda* did not spend that night in the debauchery of Kingston as they had expected. Instead they worked until dawn completing with stores and water, so hard that they had no breath to spare to curse the Admiral who did these things to them. In the very first light of morning they warped their ship out with the aid of the faint puffs of the land breeze; and *Clorinda*, her

Admiral's flag flying at the mizzen, headed closehauled to the south-eastward on her thousand-mile voyage to La Guaira. She had on board Brigadier-General Don Manuel Ruiz, Morillo's representative, to whom Hornblower had offered a passage back to his headquarters. The man was in a fever to return and put an end to Ramsbottom's blockade; it was clear that the royal forces in Venezuela were hard pressed. He had no thought for anything else during that voyage. The lovely sunset meant to him merely that another day had gone by without his reaching his destination. The gallant way in which *Clorinda* held her course, closehauled, shouldering the long rollers aside in showers of spray, held no fascination for him, for she was not flying before the wind at her best speed. At noon each day, when the ship's position was pricked off on the chart, he would look long and despairingly, estimating by eye the further distance to be traversed. He had not had sufficient experience at sea to acquire the knack of resigning himself to the influence of forces beyond human control. When the wind drew southerly and foul, as it did for two days consecutively, he was clearly on the verge of accusing Hornblower of being in league with his enemies, and made no attempt to understand Hornblower's soothing explanation that on the starboard tack on which *Clorinda* was compelled to lie they were making easting which might be invaluable in possible later eventualities. He resented the caution of Captain Fell which led to *Clorinda*'s shortening sail as they entered the dangerous proximity of Grand Cay, and at dawn next day he was climbing the foremast shrouds as high as he dared, looking out for the first sight of the mountains of Venezuela – and even then he did not recognise as land the blue streak which he saw.

A shore boat came out to them before ever they dropped anchor, and there was an urgent conference on *Clorinda*'s quarterdeck between Ruiz and the officer it brought out.

'My General is in Carabobo,' said Ruiz to Hornblower. 'A battle is going to be fought. Bolivar is marching on Puerto Cabello, and my General has taken the army to meet him.'

'What is Ramsbottom and his ship?'

Ruiz looked to the arrival for the information.

'Near Puerto Cabello.'

That was, of course, the likeliest place, a hundred miles or less to the westward, a roadstead where supplies might possibly be landed, and an ideal situation for intercepting all communications between Curaçao and La Guaira.

'Then I shall head for Puerto Cabello,' said Hornblower. 'You can accompany me if you wish, Don Manuel. The wind is fair and I'll land you there quicker than a horse would carry you.'

Ruiz hesitated for a moment; he knew all about horses and he was suspicious about ships. But the advantage was so obvious that he accepted.

'Very well, then,' said Hornblower. 'Sir Thomas, we'll hoist that anchor again, if you would be so kind. Set a course for Puerto Cabello.'

Now *Clorinda* had the lusty trade wind on her quarter, her best point of sailing; she had her studding sails out and every possible stitch of canvas out, and she flew along. A horse at full gallop might go faster, but no horse could do as *Clorinda* was doing and maintain full speed for hour after hour, nor could any horse ever attain full speed on the mountain tracks of the Maritime Andes. Naturally, no amount of speed could satisfy Ruiz. With telescope to his eye he watched the distant coast go by until his weary eye was almost blind, and then he paced about the quarterdeck, trickles of sweat running down his forehead and cheeks as the sun, climbing to its noontide height, blazed vertically down on him. He turned a suspicious eye on Hornblower when the crew of *Clorinda* poured aloft to take in sail.

'We are going in to shore now, General,' explained Hornblower soothingly.

The leadsmen were in the chains as *Clorinda* headed in towards the roadstead. In the middle of their chant Ruiz suddenly turned to Hornblower and stood rigid, listening to another, more distant, sound.

'Cannons!' he said.

Hornblower strained his ears. The faintest, almost inperceptible noise, and then silence, save for the sound of the ship through the water and the bustle of preparing to come to an anchor.

'Order the "still" for a moment, if you please, Sir Thomas.'

Now the leadsmen ceased their chant, and every man in *Clorinda* stood silent, even though the wind still played through the rigging and the sea chattered alongside. A very distant, flat detonation. Another. Two more.

'Thank you, Sir Thomas. You may carry on now.'

'Cannons!' repeated Ruiz, glaring at Hornblower. 'They are fighting the battle.'

Somewhere on the outskirts of Puerto Cabello Royalists and Republicans were locked in combat. And those guns that they had heard? They might well be those that the *Helmond* had carried, now in the hands of the insurgents and firing upon their legal owners. The fact that artillery was being employed indicated a pitched battle, no petty skirmish. Over there the fate of Venezuela was being decided. Ruiz was pounding his fist into his open palm.

'Sir Thomas, kindly have a boat ready to land the General without delay.'

As the gig pulled away from *Clorinda*'s side Hornblower looked up at the sun, called up before his mind's eye the chart of the Venezuelan coast, and reached a further decision. As always in the Service, a long, dull interval had heralded a period of activity. As the gig came skimming back again he was ready with his next order.

'Will you be so good as to make sail again, Sir Thomas? We can continue to search to the westward for Ramsbottom while daylight lasts.'

It was desirable to obtain the earliest possible news of the result of the battle, but it was also, or more, desirable to lay hands on Ramsbottom as quickly as might be. They had not sighted him between La Guaira and Puerto Cabello; he could not be much farther along the coast. The sun was descending now, dazzling the look-outs as they peered towards it while *Clorinda* continued her course along the shores of the province of Carabobo. Not so far ahead the land trended abruptly northward to San Juan Point – a lee shore. It was curious that Ramsbottom should have gone even this far to leeward; unless he had put up his helm and headed clear away, guessing that his period of grace was at an end.

'Deck, there!' The look-out at the fore-topgallant masthead was hailing. 'There's summat on the port bow, just in sight. Right in the eye of the sun. But it may be a ship, sir. A ship's masts an' yards, sir, with no sail set.'

It would be incredible that Ramsbottom had anchored here on this dangerous lee shore. But incredible things have to be done in war. *Clorinda* had long ago taken in her studding sails. Now after a sharp order from Fell, and five minutes' activity on the part of her crew, she was gliding along under topsails and headsails alone. The sun sank into a bank of cloud, suffusing it with scarlet.

'Deck, there! Two ships, sir. At anchor. One of 'em's a brig, sir.'

A brig! Ramsbottom almost for certain. Now with the sun behind the cloud it was possible to train a telescope in the direction indicated. There they were, sharp and clear against the sunset, silhouetted in black against the scarlet cloud, the masts and yards of a ship and a brig at anchor. Sir Thomas was looking to Hornblower for orders.

'Approach as close as you consider advisable, if you please, Sir Thomas. And have a boarding party ready to take possession.'

'An armed boarding party, My Lord?'

'As you please. He'll never dare to oppose us by force.'

The guns of the brig were not run out, there were no boarding nettings rigged. In any case the little brig stood no chance in an unsheltered anchorage against a frigate.

'I'll anchor if I may, My Lord.'

'Certainly.'

That was the *Bride of Abydos*, without a doubt. No mistaking her at all. And the other one? Most likely the *Helmond*. With the revolt of Maracaibo this part of the coast had fallen into the power of the insurgents. The batteries of field artillery that she had carried could be rafted ashore here – there was a beach in that little cove where it would be possible – and delivered to the insurgent army gathering for its march on Puerto Cabello. Ramsbottom, his task completed, would presumably be prepared to brazen it out, pleading – as Hornblower had already guessed – some privateering commission from Bolivar.

'I'll go with the boarding party, Sir Thomas.'

Fell shot a questioning glance. Admirals had no business boarding strange craft from small boats, not only when bullets might fly, but when one of the infinite variety of accidents possible in small boats might lead to an elderly and not so active senior officer being dropped overside and never coming up again, with endless trouble later for the captain. Hornblower could follow Fell's train of thought, but he was not going to wait quiescent on *Clorinda*'s quarterdeck until a report came back from the *Bride of Abydos* – not when a word would give him the power of finding out several minutes earlier.

'I'll get your sword and pistols, My Lord,' said Gerard.

'Nonsense!' said Hornblower. 'Look there!'

He had kept his telescope trained on the anchored ships, and had detected a significant activity around them. Boats were pulling hastily away from both of them and heading for the shore. Ramsbottom seemed to be absconding.

'Come along!' said Hornblower.

He ran to the ship's side and leaped for the boat's falls; sliding down, clumsily, cost him some of the skin from his soft palms.

'Cast off! Pull!' he ordered as Gerard tumbled in beside him. 'Pull!'

The boat swung away from the ship's side, soared giddily up a swell and down again, the men throwing their weight on the oars. But the boat that was leaving the *Bride of Abydos* was not being handled in the man-o'-war fashion one would have expected of Ramsbottom. The oars were being plied without any co-ordination; the boat swung round on the swell, and then as somebody caught a crab swung round again. In next to no time Hornblower found himself alongside the struggling craft. The men at the oars were not the spruce seamen he had seen on board the *Bride of Abydos*. They were swarthy men clothed in rags. Nor was that Ramsbottom in the stern-sheets. Instead, it was someone with a heavy black moustache wearing some vestiges of a blue and silver uniform. The reddening sunset glared down upon him.

'Who are you?' demanded Hornblower, and then repeated the question in Spanish.

The boat had ceased its struggles and was lying on its oars, rising and falling on the swell.

'Lieutenant Perez of the First Regiment of Infantry of the Army of Greater Colombia.'

Greater Colombia. That was what Bolivar called the republic he was trying to establish by his rebellion against Spain.

'Where is Mr Ramsbottom?'

'The Admiral has been on shore for the last week.'

'The Admiral?'

'Don Carlos Ramsbottom y Santona, Admiral of the Navy of Greater Colombia.' An Admiral; no less.

'What were you doing on board that ship?'

'I was taking care of her until Your Excellency came.'

'Is there nobody on board, then?'

'Nobody.'

The boats soared up a swell and sank down again. It was a sickly thing to do, not conducive to logical thought. He had been prepared to arrest Ramsbottom, but it would be another matter to arrest a lieutenant of infantry, in territorial waters.

'What is the crew of the ship?'

'On shore with the Admiral. With the army.'

Fighting for Bolivar, presumably. And presumably as artillerymen serving the stolen guns.

'Very well. You may go.'

It was sufficient to make sure of the *Bride of Abydos*; there was no purpose in laying hands on men of Bolivar's army who had only been obeying the orders of their superiors.

'Lay me alongside the brig.'

In the fading light the deck of the *Bride of Abydos* was not in too great disorder. The departing crew had apparently left everything shipshape, and the caretaking party of South American soldiers had not disturbed anything – although below deck it would probably be a different story. But what would have happened if a gale had blown up in this perilous anchorage on a lee shore would not bear thinking about. Presumably Ramsbottom had not cared what happened to his little ship once he had brought off his coup.

'Ahoy! Ahoy!'

Someone was hailing through a speaking trumpet from the other ship. Hornblower took the speaking trumpet from its becket by the wheel and hailed back.

'I am Admiral Lord Hornblower of His Britannic Majesty's Service. I am coming aboard.'

It was almost dark when he mounted to the deck of the *Helmond*, to be welcomed by the light of a couple of lanterns. The captain who greeted him was a thick-set man speaking excellent English with a marked accent, Dutch, presumably.

'You have not arrived too soon, sir,' was his uncompromising beginning, not the way to address any officer of the Royal Navy, certainly not an Admiral and a Peer.

'I'll thank you to be civil,' snapped Hornblower, his temper frayed.

Two angry men faced each other in the wavering light, and then the Dutchman realized that it would be better to restrain his ill-temper in dealing with someone who, after all, had the power on this lonely coast to enforce any orders he might issue.

'Please come below, sir,' he said. 'Perhaps a glass of Schnapps—?'

It was a comfortable, well-furnished cabin in which Hornblower was offered a seat and a glass.

'I was glad when I saw your topsails, sir,' said the Dutch captain. 'For ten days I have been through misery. My ship – my cargo – this shore—'

The disjointed words conveyed the anxieties of finding himself in the hands of the insurgents, and of being compelled to anchor off a lee shore with an armed guard on board.

'What happened?' asked Hornblower.

'That damned little brig fired a shot across my bows with Bonaire still in sight. They boarded me when I hove-to. Put an armed party on board. I thought she was one of yours, a ship-of-war. They brought me here and anchored, and the army came out to us. That was when I knew she was not a ship-of-war, not British.'

'Then they took your cargo?'

'They did. Twelve nine-pounder field guns, with limbers and caissons and horse harness. One ammunition waggon. One repair cart with tools. Two thousand rounds of ammunition. One ton of gunpowder in kegs. Everything.' The Dutchman was obviously quoting verbatim from his bill of lading.

'How did they get it ashore?'

'On rafts. Those Britishers worked like madmen. And there were seamen among them.'

It was a handsome admission, hardly grudging. Presumably keg-pontoons had been employed; Hornblower told himself that he would have tackled the problem of getting the cargo on to the beach in that way, at least. Presumably a good deal of unskilled labour had been provided on shore by the insurgent forces, but that hardly detracted from the achievement.

'And then every single man went off with the guns?' asked Hornblower.

'Every man. Not too many for twelve guns.'

Not too many. The *Bride of Abydos* carried a crew of some seventy-five men – hardly sufficient, in fact, to man two batteries in action.

'And they left a Venezuelan guard on board?'

'Yes. You saw them go when you came. They kept me here, at anchor on a lee shore.'

That, of course, was to prevent the Dutchman spreading the news of the fraud that had been practised.

'Those – those brigands knew nothing about ships.' The Dutchman was continuing his tale of tribulation. 'The *Desperate* started dragging her anchor once. I had to send my own men—'

'You were lucky they didn't burn your ship,' said Hornblower. 'Luckier still they didn't plunder it. You're lucky not to be in prison on shore.'

'That may be so, but—'

'As it is, sir,' said Hornblower, rising, 'you are free. You can use the land breeze to make an offing. Tomorrow night you can anchor in Willemstadt.'

'But my cargo, sir? I have been detained. I have been in danger. My country's flag—?'

'Your owners can take action as they please. I understand that Ramsbottom is a wealthy man. He can be sued for damages.'

'But – but—' The Dutchman could find no words that would express adequately his feelings regarding both his recent treatment and Hornblower's scant sympathy.

'Your Government can address protests, of course. To the Government of Greater Colombia, or to King Ferdinand.' Hornblower kept his face expressionless as he made the ridiculous suggestion. 'I must congratulate you, sir, on your escape from very serious dangers. I trust you will have a prosperous voyage home.'

He had freed the *Helmond*, and he had laid hands on the *Bride of Abydos*. That much he had accomplished so far, said Hornblower to himself as the boat took him back to *Clorinda*. The Government at home could squabble over the legal details, if they cared to go to the trouble. What the Cabinet and the Admiralty would think about his actions he could not imagine; he was conscious of a slight chill of apprehension when his mind dwelt upon that side of the situation. But an Admiral could not show apprehension to anyone, certainly not to a captain as stupid as Sir Thomas Fell.

'I'll be obliged, Sir Thomas,' he said, when he regained *Clorinda*'s deck, 'if you will send a prize crew on board the brig. Would you please be good enough to instruct the officer whom you put in command to keep company with us? We shall sail for Puerto Cabello again as soon as it is convenient to you.'

Fell might be stupid, but he was a capable seaman. Hornblower could leave to him the anxious business of making his way back along the coast at night; the land breeze, fluky and unpredictable though it might be, afforded an opportunity which must not be missed of regaining the precious miles that had been squandered to leeward. Hornblower could go down into his stifling cabin and compose himself to sleep. It had been a busy day, and he was physically weary. He lay on his cot with the sweat trickling irritatingly over his ribs, trying to persuade his mind to cease from debating the situation. The British public was turning a kindly eye on the struggle for liberty that was being waged in every corner of the world. British volunteers were playing their part – Richard Church had been leading the Greek rebellion against the Turks for years now; Cochrane was at this very moment fighting in the Pacific for South American independence. For that matter, as he knew, thousands of British soldiers were serving in the ranks of Bolivar's army just over there on the mainland. Private fortunes in England had been lavished in the cause of liberty, just as Ramsbottom had been lavishing his.

But none of this was any indication as to how the British Cabinet would react; national policy might well be at odds with national opinion. And the Lords of the Admiralty could be counted upon to be as unpredictable as ever. And that was equally true of His Majesty King George IV; Hornblower suspected that the First Gentleman of Europe had long ago forsaken his half-hearted liberalism. The near future might hold a severe reprimand for His Majesty's Commander-in-Chief in the West Indies; it might even hold disavowal and recall.

Hornblower's mind had now attained the comforting certainty that the future was uncertain, and that nothing he could do during the next few hours could change it. With that, he might well have gone to sleep; he was, in fact, on the point of dozing off when he brushed what he thought was a trickle of sweat from his bare ribs. It was not sweat. A flurry against his fingers told him it was a cockroach crawling over his skin, and he started up in disgust. The Caribbean was notorious for its cockroaches, but he had never grown to tolerate them. He walked across in the darkness and opened the door to the after cabin, admitting light from the lamp that swung there, and this revealed a dozen of the disgusting creatures scuttling about.

'My Lord?' It was the faithful Gerard hurrying out of bed as soon as he heard his Admiral stirring.

'Go back to bed,' said Hornblower.

He put on the silk nightshirt with the elaborate smocking down the front which had been laid out for him, and went on deck. The moon had risen now, and *Clorinda* was creeping steadily along with the land breeze now blowing fresh abeam. Cockroaches had driven away all thought of his troubles; he could lean against the rail and contemplate the beauties of the beautiful night with placidity. It fell calm at dawn, but half an hour later a fortunate slant of wind enabled *Clorinda*, and the *Bride of Abydos* a mile astern, to hold their course for Puerto Cabello; the town on its peninsula was already in sight through the telescope and *Clorinda* approached rapidly. There were fishing boats setting out from the town, small craft which were using oars to enable them to get to seaward despite the unfavourable wind. Something about them appeared strange in the telescope, and as *Clorinda* drew up to them it became apparent that they were crowded with people, ridiculously overloaded. But they plied their oars unceasingly, and boldly rounded the peninsula into the open sea, turning eastward towards La Guaira.

'I think General Morillo has lost his battle,' said Hornblower.

'Indeed, My Lord?' said Fell, deferentially.

'And I think there are plenty of people in Puerto Cabello who have no desire to be found there when El Liberador comes marching in,' added Hornblower.

He had heard that the war of independence was being waged with Spanish ferocity, that even Bolivar's reputation had been clouded by executions and massacres. Here was a proof of it. But those crowded boats were also a proof that Puerto Cabello was expected to fall to Bolivar. He had won his battle of Carabobo; a victory in the open field so close to Caracas meant the certain collapse of the royal cause. Carabobo would be the Yorktown of the South American war of independence; no doubt about that. Presumably Ramsbottom would consider the loss of the *Bride of Abydos* as a small thing compared with the freeing of a continent.

It was necessary that all this should be confirmed without doubt, however. The Cabinet would be anxious for early and first-hand information regarding the situation in Venezuela.

'Sir Thomas,' said Hornblower, 'I shall go ashore.'

'You'll have an armed guard, My Lord?'

'As you will,' said Hornblower. A dozen seamen with muskets would hardly save him from the clutches of a conquering army, but agreement saved him from argument and reproachful looks.

By the time Hornblower set foot on the pier in the blinding sunlight the little harbour was deserted. Not a fishing boat was left, nor was there a human being in sight. He pressed on, his guard tramping behind him and Gerard at his side. The long, winding street was not quite deserted; there were a few women, a few old men, a few children to be seen, peering out of the houses. Then away to his right he heard a brief rattle of musketry, the reports sounding flat in the heavy, damp air. Now here came a ghastly column of sick and wounded, half-naked, hobbling along the road; some fell down to struggle to their feet again, and some, under Hornblower's very eyes, fell, not to rise again, and of these some managed to roll to the side of the road while others lay still while their staggering comrades stumbled over them. Wounded, half-naked, barefooted, crazy with fever or bending double with abdominal pains, they came reeling along the road, while behind them the rattle of musketry came nearer and nearer. At the heels of the last of the wounded came the first of the rearguard, soldiers whose rags were faintly reminiscent of the blue and white of the Spanish royal army.

Hornblower made a mental note that the royal forces still could provide a disciplined rearguard, and so were not in total rout, but the rearguard was woefully small, a couple of hundred men, perhaps; they were not keeping good order, but they were fighting a steady fight, biting open their cartridges, ramming home their charges, spitting their bullets into their musket barrels, and waiting in ones and twos behind cover to get a fair shot at their pursuers. A dozen officers, their drawn swords flashing in the sun, were among them. The mounted officer-in-command caught sight of Hornblower and his party and reined round his horse in astonishment.

'Who are you?' he shouted.

'English,' replied Hornblower.

But before another word could be exchanged the firing in the rear increased in intensity; not only that, but suddenly from out of a side lane level with the rearguard appeared a dozen horsemen, lancers, their spear-points reflecting the sun, and the rearguard broke in disorder, running wildly down the road to escape being cut off. Hornblower saw a lance-point enter between the shoulders of a running man, saw him fall on his face, sliding over the surface of the road for a yard before the lance-point tore its way out again, leaving him struggling like a broken-backed animal. Over him swept the skirmishers of the insurgent advanced guard, a swarm of men of every shade of colour, running, loading, and firing. There was a moment when the air was full of bullets.

'My Lord—' expostulated Gerard.

'That's all right. It's all over now,' said Hornblower.

The fight had swept past them up the road; no one had paid them any attention save for the single question of the mounted Spanish officer. The small column of infantry marching in regular order behind the skirmishers saw them, however, saw the glittering gold, the epaulettes and the cocked hats. Again a mounted officer wheeled towards them with the same question, to receive the same answer from Hornblower.

'Ingleses?' repeated the officer. 'English? Why – you're a British Admiral!'

'Commanding the British Squadron in West Indian waters,' said Hornblower.

'A pleasure to see you, sir. William Jones, late Captain, Twenty-Third Foot, now Major commanding a battalion in the Army of Greater Colombia.'

'Delighted to make your acquaintance, Major.'

'Pardon me, but I must attend to my duties,' said Jones, wheeling his horse again.

'Hooray for England!' yelled someone in the marching ranks, and he was answered by a thin cheer; half of these ragged scarecrows must have been British, mingled indiscriminately with Negroes and South

Americans. The cavalry followed them, regiment after regiment, a flood of men and horses filling the road like a river brimming its banks. Lancers and light horse, sore-backed horses and lame horses; most of the men had coiled ropes at their saddle bows, and they were all ragged and drooping in their saddles with fatigue; from the appearance of both men and beasts they had marched far and fought hard, and now they were pressing on to the limit of their strength after their defeated foe. A thousand men had passed, estimated Hornblower, judging the column as well as he could, when a new sound came to his ears through the monotonous trampling of the horses' hoofs. A thumping and a jingling, loud and irregular. Here came the guns, dragged along by weary horses; at the heads of the horses walked men, ragged and bearded – they were wearing the remains of blue jumpers and white trousers. It was the crew of the *Bride of Abydos*. One of them lifted his weary head and recognised the party at the roadside.

'Good old Horny!' he shouted; his voice was thin with fatigue and sounded like an old man's.

In the mounted officer riding alongside Hornblower recognised one of Ramsbottom's lieutenants; he sat his plodding horse like a sailor, and raised his arm in a weary salute. One gun clattered by, and another followed it. The guns of Carabobo, which had won the independence of a continent.

Hornblower realised that he had not yet seen Ramsbottom, whom he would have expected to be at the head of the artillery column, but as the realisation came to him he saw something now beside the second gun. It was a horse litter, extemporised from two poles and some sheets of canvas. It was slung from two horses, one fore and one aft; the bight of canvas between the poles was shaded by an awning spread above it, and lying in the trough was a man, a smallish man, black-bearded, lying feebly against pillows behind his back. A seaman walked at the head of each horse, and with the plodding step of the animals the litter lurched and rolled, and the black-bearded man lurched and rolled at the same time. Yet he was able to take note of the group by the roadside, and he made an effort to sit up, and he called an order to the seamen leading the horses which caused them to turn out of the road and stop by Hornblower.

'Good morning, My Lord,' he said; he spoke shrilly, like someone hysterical.

Hornblower had to look twice and more to recognise him. The black beard, the feverish eyes, the shocking dead pallor upon which the tan looked like some unnatural coating, all made identification difficult.

'Ramsbottom!' exclaimed Hornblower.

'The very same but a little different,' said Ramsbottom, with a cackling laugh.

'Are you wounded?' asked Hornblower; at the moment the words passed his lips he perceived that Ramsbottom's left arm was concealed in a roll of rags – Hornblower had been looking so intently at the face that the arm had escaped his notice until then.

'I have made my sacrifice in the cause of liberty,' said Ramsbottom, with the same laugh – it might have been a laugh of derision or a laugh of mere hysteria.

'What happened?'

'My left hand lies on the field of Carabobo,' cackled Ramsbottom. 'I doubt if it has received Christian burial.'

'Good God!'

'Do you see my guns? My beautiful guns. They tore the Dons apart at Carabobo.'

'But you – what treatment have you received?'

'Field surgery, of course. Boiling pitch for the stump. Have you ever felt boiling pitch, My Lord?'

'My frigate is anchored in the roadstead. The surgeon is on board—'

'No – oh no. I must go on with my guns. I must clear El Liberador's path to Caracas.'

The same laugh. It was not derision – it was something the opposite. A man on the edge of delirium keeping a desperate hold on his sanity so as not to be diverted from his aim. Nor was it a case of a man laughing lest he weep. He was laughing lest he should indulge in heroics.

'Oh, you can't—'

'Sir! Sir! My Lord!'

Hornblower swung round. Here was a midshipman from the frigate touching his hat, agitated by the urgency of his message.

'What is it?'

'Message from the cap'n, My Lord. Ships-of-war in sight in the offing. A Spanish frigate an' what looks like a Dutch frigate, My Lord. Bearing down on us.'

Desperate news indeed. He must have his flag flying in *Clorinda* to meet these strangers, but it was a maddening moment in which to be told about it. He turned back to Ramsbottom and back again to the midshipman, his customary quickness of thought not as apparent as usual.

'Very well,' he rasped. 'Tell the captain I'm coming immediately.'

'Aye aye, My Lord.' He turned again to Ramsbottom.

'I must go,' he said. 'I must—'

'My Lord,' said Ramsbottom. Some of his feverish vitality had left him. He was leaning back again on his pillows, and it took him a second or two to gather his strength to speak again, and when he did the words lagged as he uttered them. 'Did you capture the *Bride*, My Lord?'

'Yes.' He must end this; he must get back to his ship.

'My bonny *Bride*. My Lord, there's another keg of caviare in the after lazarette. Please enjoy it, My Lord.'

The cackling laugh again. Ramsbottom was still laughing as he lay back with his eyes closed, not hearing the hurried 'good-bye' which Hornblower uttered as he turned away. It seemed to Hornblower as if that laugh followed him while he hastened to the pier and down into the boat.

'Shove off! Put your backs into it!'

There lay *Clorinda* at anchor, with the *Bride of Abydos* close to her. And there, undoubtedly, were the topsails of two frigates heading in towards them. He scrambled up the ship's side with hardly a moment to spare for the compliments with which he was received. He was too busy taking in the tactical situation, the trend of the shore, the position of the *Bride of Abydos*, the approach of the strangers.

'Hoist my flag,' he ordered, curtly, and then, recovering his poise, with the customary elaborate politeness, 'Sir Thomas, I'd be obliged if you'd get springs on the cable, out of the after ports on both sides.'

'Springs, My Lord? Aye aye, My Lord.'

Cables passed through the after ports to the anchor cable; by hauling in on one or the other with the capstan he could turn the ship to bring her guns to bear in any direction. It was only one of the many exercises Hornblower had put his crews through during the recent manoeuvres. It called for heavy, closely co-ordinated labour on the part of the hands. Orders were bellowed; warrant and petty officers ran at the heads of their different parties to rouse out the cables and drag them aft.

'Sir Thomas, please order the brig to kedge closer in. I want her inshore of us.'

'Aye aye, My Lord.'

Now it became apparent that there was some time in hand. The approaching frigates, hull up now when a glass was trained on them from the quarterdeck, were shortening sail, and then, even while Hornblower held them in the field of his telescope, he saw their main-topsails suddenly broaden as they were swung round. They were heaving-to, and a moment later he saw a boat lowered from the Dutch frigate and pull to the Spanish one. That would mean a consultation, presumably. Thanks to the difference of language they could hardly be expected to agree on a course of action by signal nor even by speaking trumpet.

'The Spaniard's wearing a commodore's broad pendant, Sir Thomas. Will you please be ready to salute it as soon as he salutes my flag?'

'Aye aye, My Lord.'

The consultation took some little time, the second half of one sandglass and the beginning of the next. A monstrous creaking down below, and a clanking of the capstan, told that the springs were being tested. *Clorinda* swung a trifle to starboard, and then a trifle to port.

'Springs are tested and ready, My Lord.'

'Thank you, Sir Thomas. Now will you be good enough to send the hands to quarters and clear for action?'

'Clear for action? Aye aye, My Lord.'

It was a detestable nuisance to take this precaution. It meant that his bedding and books and personal equipment down below would be swept away in a horrible muddle that might take days to straighten. But on the other hand, if those frigates came down determined to fight, his reputation would never survive being unready for them. It would be chaos to try to clear away the guns and bring up cartridges while actually under fire; the battle – if there were to be a battle – would be lost before it was begun. And there was something of the old thrill about these preparations; the pealing of the whistles, the hoarse cries of the petty officers, the orderly rush of the men to the guns, the tramp of the marines to the quarterdeck and the sharp order of their officer as they dressed into a rigid line.

'Ship cleared for action, My Lord.'

'Thank you, Sir Thomas. Stand by, if you please.'

There would have been just time even if the strangers had come instantly down and gone into action without parley. By a rapid use of his springs he would rake the first-comer thoroughly enough to have made her captain wish he had never been born. Now he must wait, and the ship's company, standing by their guns, must wait with him, the matches smouldering in their tubs, the fire parties standing by with their buckets, the powder boys, cartridge carriers in hand, waiting to start their race from powder magazine to guns and back again.

'Here they come, My Lord!'

Those topsails were narrowing again; those masts were coming into line. Now the frigates' bows were pointed straight at *Clorinda* as they came towards her. Hornblower held them steady in his telescope; no guns were run out, he could see, but it was impossible to tell if they were cleared for action. Nearer and nearer; now they were almost within extreme random cannon shot. At that moment where was a puff of smoke from the Spaniard's starboard bow, and for the life of him Hornblower could not check a gulp of excitement. The breeze blew the puff away, and then the puff was replaced by another; as the second appeared, the heavy thud of the first discharge came to Hornblower's ears. There was a momentary temptation to plunge into the luxury of mental arithmetic, involving the speed of sound conveyed over water, and the five seconds' interval between saluting guns, and the distance between the ships, but it had to be foregone.

'You may return the salute to the broad pendant, Sir Thomas.'

'Aye aye, My Lord.'

Thirteen guns for a Rear-Admiral's flag; eleven for a Commodore;

twenty-four guns, one hundred and twenty seconds, exactly two minutes; those ships, approaching at four miles in the hour would be a cable's length closer at the end of the salutes, within distant gunshot.

'Sir Thomas, I would be glad if you would take several turns upon the starboard spring.'

'Aye aye, My Lord.'

The violent creaking made itself heard again, and *Clorinda* turned herself to present her broadside towards the newcomers. No harm whatever in letting them know that a hot reception was awaiting them if they intended mischief; it might save much trouble later.

'They're taking in sail, My Lord!'

So he could see for himself, but there was nothing to be gained by saying so. The two ships obviously had heavy crews, judging by the rapidity with which sail was got in. Now round they went, up into the wind. Hornblower believed he could hear the roar of the cables as they anchored. It seemed like a decisive moment, and Hornblower was about to mark it by shutting up his telescope with a snap when he saw a boat lowering from the Spaniard.

'I fancy we'll be having a visitor shortly,' said Hornblower.

The boat seemed to fly over the glittering water; the men at the oars were pulling like madmen – presumably the eternal desire of the men of one navy to show another navy what they could do.

'Boat ahoy!' hailed the officer of the watch.

The Spanish officer in the sternsheets, conspicuous by his epaulettes, hailed back; Hornblower could not be sure of what he said, but the letter that was waved at the same time told the story.

'Receive him on board, if you please, Sir Thomas.'

The Spanish lieutenant looked sharply round him as he came over the ship's side; no harm in his seeing the men at quarters and the preparations made. He picked out Hornblower at once, and with a salute and a bow presented his letter.

Su excellencia el Almirante Sir Hornblower, said the superscription.

Hornblower broke the seal; he could read the Spanish of the letter easily enough.

> *The Brigadier, Don Luiz Argote, would be honoured if His Excellency Sir Hornblower would accord him the opportunity of an interview. The Brigadier would be delighted if he could visit His Excellency's ship and would be equally delighted if His Excellency would visit His Most Catholic Majesty's ship.*

In Spanish naval usage, Hornblower knew, 'Brigadier' was equivalent to 'Commodore'.

'I'll write a reply,' said Hornblower. 'Sir Thomas, please make this gentleman welcome. Come with me, Gerard.'

Down below, with the ship cleared for action, it was a nuisance to hunt up writing paper and ink; it was even more of a nuisance to have to compose a letter in Spanish, for in writing misspellings and bad grammar would be far more evident than in speech. Luckily the Brigadier's letter itself supplied most of the spelling and the tricky conditional form.

Rear Admiral Lord Hornblower would be delighted to receive the Brigadier Don Luiz Argote in his flagship whenever the Brigadier wishes.

Sealing wax and seal and candle had to be discovered; it would never do to appear careless about these formalities.

'Very well,' said Hornblower, giving grudging approval of the second impression after the failure of the first attempt. 'Take a boat to the *Bride of Abydos* as quick as lightning and see if there's any of that sherry left which Ramsbottom served at his dinner party.'

The Brigadier, when he came up *Clorinda*'s side, to be received with the appropriate compliments, was followed by another figure in cocked hat and epaulettes. Hornblower bowed and saluted and introduced himself.

'I took the liberty of asking Captain Van der Maesen, of the Royal Netherlands Navy, to accompany me,' said the Brigadier.

'It is with much pleasure that I welcome Captain Van der Maesen on board,' said Hornblower. 'Perhaps you gentlemen will accompany me below. I regret very much that we will not be very comfortable, but, as you see, I have been exercising my crew in their duties.'

A screen had been hurriedly run across the after part of the frigate, and the table and chairs replaced. The Brigadier sipped with increasing and astonished appreciation at the glass of wine offered him. Inevitably several minutes passed in desultory conversation – Spanish was the one language the three had in common – before the Brigadier began to discuss business.

'You have a beautiful ship here, milord,' he said. 'I regret much to find you in company with a pirate.'

'You mean the *Bride of Abydos*, señor?'

'Naturally, milord.'

Hornblower saw a trap opening before him.

'You call her a pirate, señor?'

'What do you call her, milord?'

'I am waiting to hear your opinion, señor.' It was important not to commit himself.

'Her actions call for explanation, milord. She has captured and plundered a Dutch ship. That can be interpreted as an act of piracy. On the other hand it might be said she is operating under a so-called commission issued by the rebels in Venezuela. In the one case Captain Van der Maesen will seize her as a pirate. On the other, if she is a privateer, I will seize her as an enemy of my country.'

'In neither case, señor, has a court of law determined her status. In the meanwhile, gentlemen, she is in my possession.'

Hats were in the ring now. Hornblower met the eyes of the others with the least expression he could manage. Of one thing he was certain, that whatever might be eventually decided regarding the *Bride of Abydos* neither the British Government nor the British public would approve of his tamely allowing her to be taken out of his hands.

'Milord, I have assured Captain Van der Maesen of my support in any action he may decide to take, and he has given me the same assurance.'

The Dutch captain confirmed this with a nod and a half-intelligible sentence. Two to one, in other words; odds that *Clorinda* could not hope to face.

'Then I hope, gentlemen, I hope very sincerely indeed, that you decide upon approving of my course of action.'

It was the politest way of defying them that he could think of.

'I find it very hard to believe, milord, that you extend the protection of His Britannic Majesty's Navy to pirates, or to privateers in a war in which His Majesty is neutral.'

'You may have noticed, señor, that the *Bride of Abydos* is flying His Britannic Majesty's flag. Of course, you understand that as a naval officer I cannot permit that flag to be hauled down.'

There it was, the ultimate defiance. Ten minutes from now and the guns might be firing. Ten minutes from now and this deck might be littered with dead and wounded. He might be dead himself. The Spaniard looked at the Dutchman and back to Hornblower.

'We would much regret taking strong action, milord.'

'I am delighted to hear that, señor. That confirms me in my decision. We can part the best of friends.'

'But—'

The Brigadier had not intended his last sentence to be interpreted as a sign of yielding. He had been uttering, he thought, a further threat. Hornblower's interpretation of it left him speechless for a moment.

'I am overjoyed to find that we are in agreement, gentlemen. Perhaps we can drink the healths of our sovereigns in another glass of this wine, señor – and may I take this opportunity of acknowledging the debt the rest of the world owes to your country for such an exquisite production?'

By taking their withdrawal for granted he was giving them a chance of withdrawing gracefully. The bitter moment of admitting that they had been outfaced had come and gone before they had realised it. Once more the Spaniard and the Dutchman exchanged unavailing glances, and Hornblower seized the opportunity to pour more wine.

'To His Most Catholic Majesty, señor. To His Majesty the King of the Netherlands.'

He held his glass high. They could not refuse that toast, even though the Brigadier's mouth still opened and shut as he struggled to find words for his emotions. Common politeness forced the Brigadier to complete the toast, as Hornblower waited, glass in hand.

'To His Britannic Majesty.'

They drank together.

'This has been a delightful visit, gentlemen,' said Hornblower. 'Another glass? No? It cannot be that you are leaving so soon? But I expect you have many duties calling for your attention.'

As the side boys, white-gloved, formed up at the entry port, and the bosun's mates pealed upon their whistles, and the ship's company, still at their guns, stood to attention, in compliment to the departing visitors, Hornblower could spare a moment to glance round. Those side boys and bosun's mates and guns' crews might be facing imminent death at this moment if that interview had taken a more stormy course. He deserved their gratitude, but of course he would never receive it. Shaking hands with the Brigadier he made the final clarification of the situation.

'A prosperous voyage, señor. I hope I shall have the pleasure of meeting you again. I shall be sailing for Kingston as soon as the land breeze serves.'

One of Barbara's regular letters, received months later, helped to round off the incident.

My dearest husband, (wrote Barbara as usual, and, as usual Hornblower read those words with a smile. There were several sheets to the letter, and the first sheet contained much of interest to Hornblower, but it was not until the second sheet that Barbara began her usual society and professional gossip.)

Last night the Lord Chancellor was my left-hand partner at dinner, and he had much to say about the 'Bride of Abydos', and in consequence, to my great pleasure, much to say about my dear husband. The Spanish and Dutch governments, through their ambassador and minister, have naturally lodged protests with the Foreign Secretary, who has only been able to acknowledge receipt of the notes and to promise a further reply when the legal aspects of the case are made clear. And, in all the history of Admiralty law, said the Lord Chancellor, there never was a case as complicated as this one. The insurers plead negligence on the part of the assured (I hope that I have these technical terms right, my very dearest) because the captain of the 'Helmond' took no steps to verify the bona fides of the 'Bride of Abydos', and they further plead negligence on the part of the Dutch government because the capture took place within Dutch territorial waters off Bonaire, and the Dutchmen deny hotly both that they were negligent and that the capture was really within their territorial waters. Further, the actual plundering and detention took place in Spanish territorial waters. And there seem to be untold complications arising from the fact that you found the 'Bride of Abydos' abandoned by her crew – did you know, dearest, that it seems a matter of great legal importance as to whether her anchor was actually touching bottom or not? In any case, there has been no legal action in any court so far because no one seems to be able to decide which court has jurisdiction in the matter (I hope, dearest, you will give your wife all credit for listening attentively and taking note of these difficult expressions). Taking one thing with another, and allowing four months on the average for each necessary round trip to the West Indies to take evidence on commission, and taking into account demurrers and rebuttals and sur-rebuttals, the Lord Chancellor thinks that it will be thirty-seven years before any case reaches the House of Lords, and he went on to say, cackling into his soup, that our interest in the case will be greatly diminished by then.

This is by no means all the news, dearest. There is something further which would greatly distress me if it were not for the fact that I know my husband the Admiral will be delighted. Taking tea today with Lady Exmouth (I know how your dear eyes open wide with horror at women being in possession of such secrets) I heard that Their Lordships take a most favourable view of your attitude towards the Spanish and Dutch naval authorities – dearest, I am so delighted, even though I could never doubt it. It has already been decided to extend your command for the extra year, and my pleasure in knowing how pleased you will be at this compliment almost – quite – allays my sorrow at the thought of our further separation. Dearest, there is no woman who could love you – there is no woman on earth who could love any man as much as I love you, the truest, the bravest, the boldest, the cleverest – I must not write like this because there is still further news to add.

This is that the Government has always, apparently, looked with favour at the attempt of the Spanish colonies to attain their independence, and with the greatest disfavour upon the decision of the Spanish government to attempt their reconquest with troops sent out from Europe. There have been hints that the other Powers, uneasy at the movement towards liberty, have been meditating giving military assistance to Spain in Spanish America. The victory at Carabobo, where poor Mr Ramsbottom and his guns played such a part, has made this intervention more unlikely. It is a great State secret, so great that over the teacups it is mentioned only in whispers, that the British Government meditates making a declaration that it will not permit military intervention in Spanish America. And it appears that our Government is in accord with the Americans over this, for it is believed that President Monroe is planning to

issue a declaration regarding a similar doctrine, and discussions regarding
it are taking place. So that my dearest husband finds himself at the centre
of world affairs, as he has always been at the centre of his wife's fondest
affections.

THE HURRICANE

Hornblower came walking into his office at Admiralty House at half-
past five o'clock in the morning exactly. Now that the summer was come
there was just enough daylight at that time to transact business and it
was a fairly cool moment as well. Gerard and Spendlove, his flag-
lieutenant and secretary, were waiting for him there – it would have
gone hard with them if they had not been – and they pulled themselves
erect, without any clicking of heels (for in three years they had found
that their chief discountenanced the practice) and they said 'Good
morning, My Lord,' 'Good morning, My Lord' as if they were the two
barrels of a shotgun.

'Morning,' said Hornblower. He had not had his breakfast coffee
yet; otherwise he would have put 'good' in front of 'morning'.

He sat down at his desk, and Spendlove came to hover over his
shoulder with a sheaf of papers while Gerard made the dawn report.

'Weather conditions normal, My Lord. High water today at eleven-
thirty. No arrivals during the night, and nothing in sight this morning
from the signal station. No news of the packet, My Lord, and no news
of *Triton.*'

'A negative report if ever there was one,' said Hornblower. The
negatives in the last two phrases balanced each other; H.M.S. *Triton* was
bringing out his successor to relieve him of his command at the end of
his three years' appointment, and Hornblower was not happy over the
prospect of ceasing to be Commander-in-Chief in the West Indies;
but the West India packet was bringing out his wife, whom he had not
seen during all this time, and to whose arrival he was eagerly looking
forward. She was coming out so as to make the return voyage to England
with him.

'The packet's due any day, My Lord,' said Gerard, soothingly.

'Your business is to tell me things I don't know, Mr Gerard,' snapped
Hornblower. It annoyed him to be soothed like a child, and it annoyed
him still more that his personal staff should think him human enough
to be anxious to see his wife. He looked over his shoulder at his secretary.
'What do you have there, Spendlove?'

Spendlove made a hasty rearrangement of the papers in his hand.

Hornblower's morning coffee was due at any moment, and Spendlove had something he did not want to show his chief until it had come and was half drunk at least.

'Here are the dockyard returns to the thirty-first ultimo, My Lord,' he said.

'Can't you say "to the end of last month?" ' demanded Hornblower, taking them from him.

'Aye aye, My Lord,' said Spendlove, passionately hoping the coffee would come soon.

'Anything in these?' asked Hornblower, glancing over them.

'Nothing for your special attention, My Lord.'

'Then why trouble me with them? Next?'

'The warrants for the new gunner in *Clorinda*, My Lord, and for the dockyard cooper.'

'Your coffee, My Lord,' said Gerard at this moment, the relief in his voice perfectly apparent.

'Better late than never,' snapped Hornblower. 'And for God's sake don't fuss round me. I'll pour it for myself.'

Spendlove and Gerard were busily making room on his desk for the tray to be put down, and Spendlove hastily withdrew his hand from the coffee-pot handle.

'Too damned hot,' said Hornblower, taking a sip. 'It's always too damned hot.'

Last week the new system had been begun, whereby coffee was brought in to him after his arrival in his office, instead of awaiting him there, because he had complained then that it was always too cold, but neither Spendlove nor Gerard saw fit to remind him of this.

'I'll sign those warrants,' said Hornblower. 'Not that I think that cooper's worth his salt. His barrels open up into birdcages.'

Spendlove scattered sand from the caster over the wet ink of Hornblower's signatures, and put the warrants aside. Hornblower took another sip of coffee.

'Here's your refusal of the Crichtons' invitation, My Lord. In the third person, so your signature isn't necessary.'

If that had been said to him a little while before, Hornblower would have demanded why in that case he was being bothered with it, forgetful of his own standing order that nothing was to go out in his name without his seeing it. But even two sips of coffee had done their work.

'Very well,' he said, glancing over it, and taking up his cup again.

Spendlove watched the level of the liquid sink in the cup, and judged the moment to be more propitious now. He laid a letter on the desk.

'From Sir Thomas, My Lord.'

Hornblower uttered a small groan as he picked it up; Captain Sir

Thomas Fell of H.M.S. *Clorinda* was a fussy individual, and a communication from him usually meant trouble – unnecessary trouble, and therefore to be grudged. Not in this case, though. Hornblower read the official document and then craned over his shoulder at Spendlove.

'What's all this about?' he demanded.

'It's rather a curious case, I hear, My Lord,' answered Spendlove.

It was a 'circumstantial letter', a formal request from Captain Fell for a court martial to be held on Bandsman Hudnutt of the Royal Marines, for 'wilful and persistent disobedience to orders'. Such a charge if substantiated meant death, or else such a flogging that death would be preferable. Spendlove was perfectly well aware that his admiral detested hangings and floggings.

'The charges are preferred by the Drum-Major,' commented Hornblower to himself.

He knew the Drum-Major, Cobb, perfectly well, or at least as well as the peculiar circumstances permitted. As Admiral and Commander-in-Chief Hornblower had his own band, which was under the command of Cobb, holding warrant rank. Previous to all official occasions where music had to be provided Cobb reported to Hornblower for orders and instructions, and Hornblower would go through the farce of agreeing with the suggestions put forward. He had never publicly admitted that he could not tell one note from another; he could actually distinguish one tune from another by the jigginess or otherwise of the time. He was a little uneasy in case all this was more common knowledge than he hoped.

'What d'you mean by "a curious case", Spendlove?' he asked.

'I believe an artistic conscience is involved, My Lord,' replied Spendlove, cautiously. Hornblower was pouring, and tasting, his second cup of coffee; that might have a bearing on the breaking of Bandsman Hudnutt's neck, thought Spendlove. At the same time Hornblower was feeling the inevitable irritation resulting from having to listen to gossip. An Admiral in his splendid isolation never – or only rarely – knew as much about what was going on as his most junior subordinate.

'An artistic conscience?' he repeated. 'I'll see the Drum-Major this morning. Send for him now.'

'Aye aye, My Lord.'

He had received the one necessary clue, and need not demean himself by prying further unless the interview with Cobb should prove unfruitful.

'Now let's have that draft report until he comes.'

Drum-Major Cobb did not arrive for some time, and his resplendent uniform when he did arrive hinted that he had taken care about his appearance; tunic and pantaloons were freshly ironed, his buttons glittered, his sash was exactly draped, his sword-hilt shone like silver. He was an enormous man with an enormous moustache, and he made an enormous entrance into the room, striding over the resounding floor as if he were twice as heavy as he actually was, clashing his boot-heels together as he halted before the desk and swept his hand upward in the salute fashionable at the moment among the Royal Marines.

'Good morning, Mr Cobb,' said Hornblower, mildly; the 'Mr', like the sword, was an indication that Cobb was a gentleman by virtue of his warrant even though he had risen from the ranks.

'Good morning, My Lord.' There was as much flourish in the phrase as there had been in the salute.

'I want to hear about these charges against this bandsman – Hudnutt.'

'Well, My Lord—' A sideways glance from Cobb gave Hornblower a hint.

'Get out of here,' said Hornblower to his staff. 'Leave Mr Cobb alone with me.'

When the door was shut Hornblower was all good manners.

'Please sit down, Mr Cobb. Then you can tell me at your ease what really happened.'

'Thank you, My Lord.'

'Well, now?'

'That young 'Udnutt, My Lord, 'e's a fool if ever there was one. I'm sorry this 'as 'appened, My Lord, but 'e deserves all 'e's going to get.'

'Yes? He's a fool, you say?'

' 'E's a downright fool, My Lord. I'm not saying 'e isn't a good musician, 'cause 'e is. There ain't no one 'oo can play the cornet the way 'e does. That's the truth, My Lord. 'E's a boy wonder at it. The cornet's a newfangled instrument, My Lord. We ain't 'ad it in our bands for more'n a year. Blow it like a trumpet, you do, you 'ave to 'ave a lip for it, although it 'as keys as well, My Lord. An' 'e's a marvel at it, or 'e was, My Lord.'

That change to the past tense indicated that in Cobb's positive opinion Hudnutt, through death or disablement, would never play the cornet again.

'He's young?'

'Nineteen, My Lord.'

'And what did he do?'

'It was mutiny, My Lord, flat mutiny, although I've only charged him with disobedience to orders.'

Mutiny meant death by the Articles of War; disobedience to orders meant 'death or such less penalty—'

'How did it happen?'

'Well, My Lord, it was like this. We was rehearsing the new march that come out in the last packet. *Dondello*, it's called, My Lord. Just the cornet an' the drums. An' it sounded different, an' I had 'Udnutt play it again. I could 'ear what 'e was doin', My Lord. There's a lot of B flat accidentals in that march, an' 'e wasn't flatting them. I asked 'im what 'e meant by it, an' he said it sounded too sweet. That's what 'e said, My Lord. An' it's written on the music. *Dolce*, it says, and *dolce* means sweet, My Lord.'

'I know,' lied Hornblower.

'So I says, "You play that again and you flat those B's." An' 'e says, "I can't." An' I says, "You mean you won't?" An' then I says, "I'll give you one more chance" – although by rights I shouldn't 'ave, My Lord – an' I says, "This is an order, remember," 'an I gives 'em the beat an' they starts off and there was the B naturals. So I says, "You 'eard me give you an order?" an' 'e says, "yes." So there wasn't nothing I could do after that, My Lord. I calls the guard an' I 'ad 'im marched to the guard-'ouse. An' then I 'ad to prefer charges, My Lord.'

'This happened with the band present?'

'Yes, My Lord. The 'ole band, sixteen of 'em.'

Wilful disobedience to an order, before sixteen witnesses. It hardly mattered if there were six or sixteen or sixty; the point was that everyone in Hornblower's command knew by now that discipline had been defied, an order deliberately disobeyed. The man must die, or he must be flogged into a crippled wreck, lest other men defy orders. Hornblower knew he had his command well in hand, but he knew, too, of the turbulence that lay below the surface. And yet – if the order that had been disobeyed had been something different, if there had been a refusal to lay out along a yard, say, however perilous the conditions, Hornblower would not have given all this thought to the matter, despite his detestation of physical cruelty. That sort of order must be instantly obeyed. 'Artistic conscience,' Spendlove had said. Hornblower had no idea of any difference between B and B flat, but he could dimly understand that it might be important to some people. A man might be tempted to refuse to do something that offended his artistic sensibilities.

'I suppose the man was sober?' he demanded suddenly.

'As sober as you and me, My Lord.'

Another idea crossed Hornblower's mind.

'What's the chances of a misprint in the music?' he asked; he was struggling with things he did not understand.

'Well, My Lord, there *is* such things. But it's for me to say if there's a misprint or not. An' although he can read music I don't know if 'e can read print, My Lord, an' if 'e can I don't expect 'e can read Eyetalian, but there it says *dolce*, it says, on the official music, My Lord.'

In Cobb's eyes this aggravated the offence, if aggravation were possible. Not only had his order been disobeyed, but Hudnutt had not respected the written instructions sent by whoever was responsible in London for sending out music to marine bands. Cobb was a marine first and a musician second; Hudnutt might be a musician first and a marine second. But – Hornblower pulled himself up sharply – that made Hudnutt's condemnation all the more necessary. A marine had to be a marine, first, foremost, and all the time. If marines started to choose whether they could be marines or not, the Royal Regiment would cease to be a military body, and it was his duty to maintain it as a military body.

Hornblower studied Cobb's expression intently. The man was speaking the truth, at least as far as the truth was apparent to him. He was not wilfully distorting facts because of personal prejudice or as a result of some old feud. If his action, and his report on it, had been influenced by jealousy or natural cruelty, he was unaware of it. A court martial would be impressed by his reliability as a witness. And he remained unperturbed under Hornblower's steady stare.

'Thank you, Mr Cobb,' said Hornblower at last. 'I am glad to have had such a clear statement of the facts. That will be all for the present.'

'Thank you, My Lord,' answered Cobb, shooting his great bulk up out of the chair with an astonishing mixture of agility and military rigidity. His heels clashed as his hand swept up in the salute; he turned about with parade precision, and marched out of the room with resounding steps as precise as if timed by his own metronome.

Gerard and Spendlove came back into the room to find Hornblower staring at nothing, but Hornblower shook off his preoccupation instantly. It would never do for his subordinates to guess that he was moved by human feelings over a mere administrative matter.

'Draft an answer to Sir Thomas for my signature, if you please, Mr Spendlove. It can be a mere acknowledgement, but then add that there is no possibility of immediate action, because I cannot assemble the necessary number of captains at present with so many ships detached.'

Except in emergency a court where sentence of death might be passed could not be convened unless there were seven captains and commanders at least available as judges. That gave him time to consider what action he should take.

'This man's in the dockyard prison, I suppose,' went on Hornblower. 'Remind me to take a look at him on my way through the dockyard today.'

'Aye aye, My Lord,' said Gerard, careful to betray no surprise at an Admiral allotting time to visit a mutinous marine.

Yet it was not far out of Hornblower's way. When the time came he strolled slowly down through the beautiful garden of Admiralty House, and Evans, the disabled sailor who was head gardener, came in a jerky hurry to open the wicket gate in the fifteen-foot palisade that protected the dockyard from thieves, in this portion of its course dividing the Admiralty garden from the dockyard. Evans took off his hat and stood bobbing by the gate, his pigtail bobbing at his back, and his swarthy face split by a beaming smile.

'Thank you, Evans,' said Hornblower, passing through.

The prison stood isolated at the edge of the dockyard, a small cubical building of mahogany logs, set diagonally in a curious fashion, possibly – probably – more than one layer. It was roofed with palm thatch a yard or more thick, which might at least help to keep it cool under the glaring sun. Gerard had run on ahead from the gate – with Hornblower grinning at the thought of the healthful sweat the exercise would produce – to find the officer-in-charge and obtain the key to the prison, and Hornblower stood by while the padlock was unfastened and he could look into the darkness within. Hudnutt had risen to his feet at the sound of the key, and when he stepped forward into the light he was revealed as a painfully young man, his cheeks hardly showing a trace of his one-day's beard. He was naked except for a waistcloth, and the officer-in-charge clucked with annoyance.

'Get some clothes on and be decent,' he growled, but Hornblower checked him.

'No matter. I've very little time. I want this man to tell me why he is under charges. You others keep out of earshot.'

Hudnutt had been taken by surprise by this sudden visit, but he was a bewildered person in any case, obviously. He blinked big blue eyes in the sunlight and wriggled his gangling form with embarrassment.

'What happened? Tell me,' said Hornblower.

'Well, sir—'

Hornblower had to coax the story out of him, but bit by bit it confirmed all that Cobb had said.

'I couldn't play that music, sir, not for nothing.'

The blue eyes looked over Hornblower's head at infinity; perhaps at some vision invisible to the rest of the world.

'You were a fool to disobey an order.'

'Yes, sir. Mebbe so, sir.'

The broad Yorkshire which Hudnutt spoke sounded odd in this tropical setting.

'How did you come to enlist?'

'For the music, sir.'

It called for more questions to extract the story. A boy in a Yorkshire village, not infrequently hungry. A cavalry regiment billeted there, in the last years of war. The music of its band was like a miracle to this child, who had heard no music save that of wandering pipers in the ten years of his life. It made him conscious of – it did not create for it already existed – a frightful, overwhelming need. All the children of the village hung round the band (Hudnutt smiled disarmingly as he said this) but none so persistently as he. The trumpeters noticed him soon enough, laughed at his infantile comments about music, but laughed with sympathy as time went on; they let him try to blow their instruments, showed him how to cultivate a lip, and were impressed by the eventual result. The regiment returned after Waterloo, and for two more years the boy went on learning, even though those were the hungry years following the peace, when he should have been bird-scaring and stone-picking from dawn to dark.

And then the regiment was transferred and the hungry years went on, and the boy labourer began to handle the plough still yearning for music, while a trumpet cost more than a year's full wages for a man. Then an interlude of pure bliss – the disarming smile again – when he joined a wandering theatrical troupe, as odd-job boy and musician; that was how he came to be able to read music although he could not read the printed word. His belly was empty as often as before; a stable yard meant a luxurious bed to him; those months were months of flea-bitten nights and foot-sore days, and they ended in his being left behind sick. That happened in Portsmouth, and then it was inevitable that, hungry and weak, he should be picked up by a marine recruiting-sergeant marching through the streets with a band. His enlistment coincided with the introduction of the *cornet à pistons* into military music, and the next thing that happened to him was that he was shipped off to the West Indies to take his place in the Commander-in-Chief's band under the direction of Drum-Major Cobb.

'I see,' said Hornblower; and indeed he could dimly see.

Six months with a travelling theatrical troupe would be poor preparation for the discipline of the Royal Marines; that was obvious, but he could guess at the rest, at this sensitiveness about music which was the real cause of the trouble. He eyed the boy again, seeking for ideas regarding how to deal with this situation.

'My Lord! My Lord!' This was Gerard hastening up to him. 'The packet's signalled, My Lord. You can see the flag at the look-out station mast-head!'

The packet? Barbara would be on board. It was three years since he had seen her last, and for three weeks now he had been awaiting her from minute to minute.

'Call away my barge. I'm coming,' he said.

A wave of excitement swept away his concern regarding the Hudnutt affair. He was about to hurry after Gerard, and then hesitated. What could he say in two seconds to a man awaiting trial for his life? What could he say when he himself was bubbling with happiness, to this man caged like an animal, like an ox helplessly awaiting the butcher?

'Good-bye, Hudnutt.' That was all he could say, leaving him standing dumbly there – he could hear the clash of keys and padlock as he hastened after Gerard.

Eight oars bit into the blue water, but no speed that they could give the dancing barge could be fast enough to satisfy him. There was the brig, her sails trimmed to catch the first hesitant puffs of the sea breeze. There was a white dot at her side, a white figure – Barbara waving her handkerchief. The barge surged alongside and Hornblower swung himself up into the main chains, and there was Barbara in his arms; there were her lips against his, and then her grey eyes smiling at him, and then her lips against his again, and the afternoon sun blazing down on them both. Then they could stand at arm's length and look at each other, and Barbara could raise her hands and twitch his neckcloth straight, so that he could be sure they were really together, for Barbara's first gesture was always to straighten his neckcloth.

'You look well, my dear,' she said.

'So do you!'

Her cheeks were golden with sunburn after a month at sea; Barbara never strove after the fashionable creaminess that distinguished the lady of leisure from the milkmaid or the goose-girl. And they laughed in each other's faces out of sheer happiness before they kissed again and then eventually drew apart.

'Dear, this is Captain Knyvett, who has looked after me so kindly on the voyage.'

'Welcome aboard, My Lord.' Knyvett was short and stocky and grizzled. 'But I fancy you'll not be staying with us long today.'

'We'll both be your passengers when you sail again,' said Barbara.

'If my relief has come,' said Hornblower, adding to Barbara, '*Triton* hasn't arrived yet.'

' 'Twill be two full weeks before we're ready to sail again, My Lord,' said Knyvett. 'I trust we shall have the pleasure of your company and her Ladyship's.'

'I sincerely hope so,' said Hornblower. 'Meanwhile we'll leave you for now – I hope you'll dine at Admiralty House as soon as you have leisure. Can you get down into the barge, my dear?'

'Of course,' said Barbara.

'Gerard, you'll stay on board and look after Her Ladyship's baggage.'

'Aye aye, My Lord.'

'No time even to say how d'ye do to you, Mr Gerard,' said Barbara, as Hornblower led her away to the main chains.

Barbara had no hoops in her skirts; she knew enough about shipboard breezes to dispense with those. Hornblower dropped down into the stern-sheets of the barge, and a growl from the coxswain at the tiller turned the eyes of the boat's crew to seaward so that they would see nothing they should not see, while Knyvett and Gerard swung Barbara down into Hornblower's arms in a flurry of petticoats.

'Give way!'

The barge surged away from the ship's side, over the blue water, towards the Admiralty House pier, with Barbara and Hornblower hand-in-hand in the stern-sheets.

'Delightful, dear,' said Barbara, looking about her when she landed. 'A Commander-in-Chief's life is spent in pleasant places.'

Pleasant enough, thought Hornblower, except for yellow fever and pirates and international crises and temperamental marines awaiting trial, but this was not the time to mention such things. Evans, hobbling on his wooden leg, was at the pier to greet them, and Hornblower could see that he was Barbara's slave from the first moment that he was presented to her.

'You must take me round the gardens the first moment I'm free,' said Barbara.

'Yes, Your Ladyship. Of course, Your Ladyship.'

They walked slowly up to the house; here it was a delicate business to show Barbara round and to present the staff to her, for Admiralty House was run along lines laid down at the Admiralty; to alter a stick of furniture or to change the status of any of the naval ratings working there was something Barbara would not be able to do. She was only a tolerated visitor there, and barely tolerated at that. She would certainly itch to change the furniture about and to reorganise the staff, but she was doomed to frustration.

'It seems to be as well, darling,' said Barbara with a twinkle, 'that my stay here is to be short. How short?'

'Until Ransome arrives in *Triton*,' answered Hornblower. 'You should know that, dear, considering how much gossip you picked up from Lady Exmouth and the others.'

'Yes, but it's still confusing to me. When does your appointment end?'

'It ended yesterday, legally. But my command continues until I am legally relieved of it by Ransome when he comes. *Triton* has made a long passage.'

'And when Ransome comes?'

'He takes over from me, and, of course, moves into this house. His Excellency has invited us to be his guests at Government House until we sail for home, dear.'

'I see. And if Ransome is so late that we miss the packet?'

'Then we wait for the next. I hope not. It would be uncomfortable.'

'Is Government House as bad as that?'

'It's tolerable, dear. But I was thinking of Ransome. No new Commander-in-Chief wants to have his predecessor staying on.'

'Criticising all his actions, of course. Is that what you'd do, dear?'

'I wouldn't be human if I did not.'

'And I know so well you're human, dear,' said Barbara, putting out her hand to him. They were in the bedroom now, out of sight of servants and staff, and they could be human for a few precious moments until a thunderous knock at the door heralded the arrival of Gerard and the baggage, and on his heels came Spendlove with a note for Barbara.

'A note of welcome from Her Excellency, dear,' explained Barbara when she had read it. 'We are commanded to dinner *en famille*.'

'No more than I expected,' said Hornblower, and then, looking round to see that Spendlove had withdrawn, 'no more than I feared.'

Barbara smiled into his eyes conspiratorially.

'A time will come,' she said.

There was so much to talk about, so much news to be exchanged; the long, long letters that had passed between them during their three years' separation needed amplification and explanation, and in any case, Barbara had been five weeks at sea without news. Late on the second day, while they were dining alone together, a mention of Hudnutt came into the conversation. Hornblower explained the situation briefly.

'You're going to court-martial him?' asked Barbara.

'Likely enough, when I can convene a court.'

'And what will the verdict be?'

'Guilty, of course. There's no doubt about it.'

'I don't mean the verdict. I mean the sentence. What will that be?' Barbara was entitled to ask questions like this, and even to express an opinion regarding her husband's performance of his official duties, now that he had let slip a mention of the subject to her.

Hornblower quoted from the Articles of War which had regulated his official life for nearly thirty years.

'Every person so offending, being convicted thereof by the sentence of the court martial, shall suffer death, or such less punishment as from the nature and degree of the offence the court martial shall deem him to deserve.'

'You don't mean that, dear?' Barbara's grey eyes opened wide across the little table from him. 'Death? But you said "such less punishment". What could that be?'

'Flogging round the fleet. Five hundred lashes.'

'Five hundred lashes? For playing B natural instead of B flat?'

That was exactly what one might expect a woman to say.

'Dear, that's not the charge. The charge is wilful disobedience to orders.'

'But it's such a trifling matter.'

'Dear, disobedience to orders can never be a trifling matter.'

'Would you flog a man to death because he won't play a B flat? What a bloodthirsty way to balance the account!'

'There's no thought of balancing accounts, dear. Punishment is inflicted to deter other men from disobeying orders. It's not revenge.'

But woman-like Barbara clung to her position, however much her flank might be turned by cold logic.

'But if you hang him – or if you flog him, I expect – he'll never play another B natural again. What good does that do?'

'It's the good of the Service, dear—'

Hornblower, on his part, was holding a position which he knew to be not quite tenable, but Barbara's vehemence was causing him to grow heated in defence of his beloved Service.

'They'll hear about this in England,' said Barbara, and then a new thought struck her. 'He can appeal, of course – can he?'

'In home waters he could. But I am a Commander-in-Chief in a foreign station, and from my decision there is no appeal.'

It was a sobering speech. Barbara gazed across the table at this man, changed suddenly from her tender, loving, sensitive husband into a potentate who held the power of life and death. And she knew that she could not, she must not, exploit her privileged position as wife to influence his decision. Not because of the good of the Service, but for the sake of their married happiness.

'And the trial will be soon?' she asked; the change in her was apparent in her tone.

'The moment I can convene a court. Delay in matters of discipline defeats its own object. If a man were to mutiny on Monday he should be tried on Tuesday and hanged on Wednesday. But there are not enough captains available. *Triton*'s captain, when Ransome arrives, would give the necessary number, but then I shall be relieved of command and the matter will be out of my hands. But if *Flora* should come in before that – I detached her to the Gulf Coast – I shall be responsible.'

'I see, dear,' said Barbara, not taking her eyes from his face. Even before he spoke again she was aware that there was something which would modify the harshness of what he had said so far.

'Naturally, I have not made up my mind yet, dear,' he said. 'But there is a further possibility which I'm considering.'

'Yes?' She could hardly breathe the word.

'The confirmation of the finding and the sentence would be the last act of my command. That would present an excuse – a reason. I could commute the sentence as an act of clemency in recognition of the good behaviour of the squadron during the period I have commanded it.'

'I see, dear. And if Ransome arrives before *Flora*?'

'I can do nothing, except—'

'Except—?'

'I could suggest to Ransome that he might begin his command with an act of clemency.'

'And would he?'

'I know very little about Ransome, dear. I simply cannot say.'

Barbara opened her mouth to speak. She was going to say, 'Will he think a B flat more important than a man's life?' but she changed her speech in the nick of time. Instead she said the other thing that had also, and longer, been hovering on her lips.

'I love you, darling,' she said.

Again their eyes met across the table, and Hornblower felt his passion flooding to meet hers like a union of two rushing rivers. He knew perfectly well that all he had said about discipline and examples had been of no effect in changing Barbara's mind; a woman (even more than a man) convinced against her will was of the same opinion still. But Barbara had not said so; she had said something else – and something (as always) more appropriate to the occasion. And not by one single variation of tone, not by a hair's-breadth raising of an eyebrow, had she brought into the conversation the fact that he was tone deaf. A lesser woman would have used that as if it were a relevant argument in this matter. She knew of his tone deafness, and he knew she knew, and she knew that he knew; and so on *ad infinitum*, but there had never been any need for him to admit the defect or for her to admit her knowledge, and he loved her.

Next morning he had to tell himself that the Commander-in-Chief in the West Indies, even if he were awaiting his relief, still had duties to do; even if his wife had newly joined him. But it was delightful to have Barbara walk down with him through the Admiralty House gardens to see him on his way as far as the wicket gate in the lofty dockyard palisade. It was a little unfortunate that at the moment when Evans was unlocking the gate Hudnutt should appear on the other side of the palisade taking his exercise. He was marching up and down between a file of marines under command of a corporal, the guard in parade uniform with bayonets fixed, Hudnutt hatless, as a prisoner under charges had to be.

'Pris'ner an' escort – halt!' bellowed the corporal at sight of his Admiral. 'Escort, present – arms!'

Hornblower formally acknowledged the salute before turning to say good-bye to his wife.

'Escort, sl-o-o-ope arms!' bellowed the corporal, in marine fashion, as if the escort had been at the other side of the dockyard instead of two yards from him.

'Is that the bandsman – Hudnutt, dear?' asked Barbara.

'Yes,' said Hornblower.

'Pris'ner an' escort, by the right, quick – march!' bellowed the corporal, and the little group marched off. Barbara watched it go; she could look now that Hudnutt had his back to her and was unaware of it. Previously she had refrained from staring at the man who would soon be on trial for his life. The trim marine uniform could not conceal the gangling, undeveloped body; and the sun shone on the fair hair.

'He's nothing more than a boy,' said Barbara.

That could be another irrelevant fact if she wanted to argue with her husband regarding his duty. Seventeen or seventy, a man under orders must obey orders.

'He's not very old, dear,' agreed Hornblower.

Then he kissed the cheek that Barbara held up to him – he was not at all sure if an Admiral in uniform should kiss his wife good-bye in the presence of his staff, but Barbara had no doubts about it. He left her standing there by the gate chatting to Evans, looking round her at the lovely garden on the one side of the palisade and at the business-like dockyard through the palings.

The presence of his wife was delightful, even though it meant greatly increased activities for him. The next two or three days involved considerable entertaining; island society wished to make the most of the fleeting presence of an Admiral's wife, a peeress, and of the bluest of blood in her own right. To Hornblower, regretfully contemplating the immediate end of his period in command, it was a little like the aristocrats during the French Revolution dancing before the summons to the guillotine, but Barbara seemed to enjoy it all, perhaps because she had just endured five very dull weeks at sea and was facing the prospect of five more.

'You danced a good deal with young Bonner, dear,' he remarked to her when they were home again after the Governor's party.

'He's a very good dancer,' said Barbara.

'He's something of a villain, I believe,' countered Hornblower. 'There's never been anything proved, but much suspected – smuggling, slave running, and all the rest of it.'

'He's invited to Government House,' said Barbara.

'Nothing proved, as I said. But in my official capacity I've often been interested in the activities of those fishing boats of his. You may find you've been dancing with a jailbird one of these days, dear.'

'Jailbirds are more amusing than military secretaries,' smiled Barbara.

Barbara's activity was astonishing. Even after a night's gaiety she went riding during the day, and Hornblower was content that she should, as long as there were young men available eager to act as Lady Hornblower's escort, seeing that he had his duties to attend to and disliked horses in any case. It was even amusing to observe the transparent adoration which she received from everyone, from His Excellency, from the young men who rode with her, from Evans the gardener, from everyone she had anything to do with.

Barbara was out riding one morning, before the heat of the day, when a messenger was brought in to Hornblower at Admiralty House.

'Message from the cap'n, My Lord. *Triton*'s signalled. She's heading in with a fair wind.'

Hornblower stared for a moment; although this was a message that might have come at any time during the last month he was not ready for its full impact.

'Very well. My compliments to the captain, and I'll come down.'

So this was the end of his three years as Commander-in-Chief. Ransome would take over command, possibly today, but certainly tomorrow, and he himself would be on half pay and due to go home. A queer mixture of thoughts went through his mind as he made himself ready to meet Ransome; young Richard about to enter Eton; the thought of a freezing winter in Smallbridge; the auditing of his final accounts; it was not until he was on his way to his barge that he remembered that now he would be relieved of the necessity to come to a decision in the Hudnutt case.

Triton wore no Admiral's flag, for Ransome legally held no command until he had taken over; the salutes at the moment merely acknowledged *Triton*'s joining the West Indian command. Ransome was a burly man with the heavy, fashionable side-whiskers, more grey than black. He wore a small decoration of Companion of the Bath, insignificant compared with Hornblower's magnificent Grand Cross. Presumably if he survived this appointment without any great blunder he might hope for knighthood. He presented his captain, Coleman, with whom Hornblower was quite unacquainted, and then turned an attentive ear to Hornblower's explanation of the arrangements made so far and of future plans.

'I'll assume command tomorrow,' decided Ransome.

'That will allow time to arrange the full ceremonial,' agreed Hornblower. 'In that case, sir, would you care to spend tonight at Government House? I understand a command there awaits you if you think it convenient.'

'No need to move twice,' said Ransome. 'I'll spend tonight on board here.'

'Admiralty House will be ready for you tomorrow, of course, sir. Perhaps you might like to give us the honour of your company at dinner today? There might perhaps be information that I could give you regarding the situation here.'

Ransome shot a glance at Hornblower charged with a certain amount of suspicion; he did not wish to have any ready-made policies thrust upon him by his predecessor. Yet the suggestion was obviously sensible.

'It would be a great pleasure. I must thank you, My Lord.'

Hornblower took a tactful step to allay that suspicion.

'The packet in which my wife and I are taking passage to England is making ready for sea at present, sir. We sail in her, in a matter of a few days only.'

'Very well, My Lord,' said Ransome.

'Then, having repeated my welcome, sir, I shall take my leave. Shall we expect you at four o'clock? Or would some other time be convenient?'

'Four o'clock will suit me well,' said Ransome.

The king is dead, long live the king, thought Hornblower, on his way back. Tomorrow he would be supplanted, and would become a mere half-pay officer. The splendour and dignity of a Commander-in-Chief would be transferred from him to Ransome. And he found the thought a little irksome; he had found his polite pose of deference to Ransome more than a little irksome; and he really thought Ransome could have been more polite in return. He gave vent to a good deal of this feeling as he told Barbara about the interview, and he checked himself at sight of Barbara's amused twinkle and raised eyebrow.

'You are the sweetest simpleton, my very dearest,' said Barbara. 'Have you no idea at all of any possible explanation?'

'None, I'm afraid,' said Hornblower.

Barbara came up close to him and looked into his face.

'No wonder that I love you,' she said. 'Don't you understand that no man could find it easy to replace Hornblower? Your period of command has been overwhelmingly successful. You've set a standard Ransome will find it hard to live up to. One might say he's jealous, envious – and he showed it.'

'I can't really believe that,' said Hornblower.

'And I love you because you can't believe it,' said Barbara. 'I could tell you so in a hundred ways, if I did not have to go and put on my finest gown to win Admiral Ransome's heart.'

Ransome was a man of fine presence, bulk and sidewhiskers and all; Hornblower had not really appreciated the fact at their first meeting. His manner was somewhat more cordial in Barbara's presence, which might have been the effect of Barbara's personality, but might also have been, as Hornblower realised, the result of Ransome's knowing that Lady Hornblower was a person of much influence in political circles. Hornblower did his best to exploit Ransome's faint cordiality. He passed the wine, he let slip as casually as possible bits of useful information regarding West Indian conditions – casually, so that Ransome could not suspect him of trying to bring influence to bear on him regarding his future policy, and yet useful information that Ransome could snap up and treasure with a smile at Hornblower's carelessness. Yet all the same, dinner was not a tremendous success. There was still a certain tenseness.

And as dinner was approaching its end Hornblower was conscious of a glance darted at him by Barbara; it was only one glance, and of the most fleeting nature. Ransome could not have been conscious of it, but Hornblower understood. Barbara was jogging his memory regarding a matter that was important to her. He awaited a suitable turn in the conversation before mentioning the subject.

'Oh, yes,' he said, 'there's a court martial pending. A marine bandsman—'

He went on to tell Ransome the circumstances of the case, treating it lightly. He was aware, even if Ransome was not, of the closeness with which Barbara was studying Ransome's expression as the narrative continued.

' "Repeated and deliberate disobedience to a lawful order," ' Ransome was repeating to himself Hornblower's own words. 'It could have been mutiny.'

'So it could,' agreed Hornblower. 'But it's rather a curious case. I'm glad you have the decision to make regarding it, and not I.'

'It seems to me as if the evidence will be quite incontrovertible.'

'No doubt.' Hornblower made himself smile, telepathically conscious of the intensity of Barbara's interest. 'But the circumstances are a little unusual.'

The stony expression on Ransome's face was most discouraging. Hornblower knew the situation to be hopeless. He would have abandoned any further effort if Barbara had not been there, but as it was he went on, uselessly.

'If the trial had been held during the period of my command I might have – naturally I had not made up my mind – commuted the sentence to mark my appreciation of the good behaviour of the squadron.'

'Yes?' said Ransome; no monosyllable could have expressed greater disinterest, but Hornblower plunged on.

'It had occurred to me that you might find this a favourable opportunity to display clemency as your first official act.'

'That will be a matter for my own decision.'

'Of course,' agreed Hornblower.

'And I cannot imagine my taking any action of that sort, naturally. I cannot have the squadron believing that I shall be lenient as regards discipline. I cannot have my command unsettled at the start.'

'Of course,' said Hornblower again. He could see the uselessness of further argument, and he might as well be graceful about it. 'You are the best judge of all the circumstances, as well as the only judge.'

'Now I shall leave you gentlemen to your wine,' said Barbara, suddenly. Hornblower looked at her just in time to see her frozen expression melt into the smile he knew so well. 'I shall say good night to you, Admiral. I shall make every effort – as far as the rules of the Navy allow – to see that this house is in good condition for you to take over tomorrow, and I hope you will be comfortable in it.'

'Thank you,' said Ransome; the two men were on their feet now.

'Good night, dear,' said Barbara to Hornblower. The latter was aware that the smile she gave him was not quite real, and he knew her to be acutely upset.

She left them, and Hornblower passed the port, and settled down again to what proved to be a long evening. Ransome, having asserted himself, and having made it perfectly clear that he would remain uninfluenced by any suggestion Hornblower might put forward, was by no means averse to acquiring any information that might come his way. Nor to finishing the bottle of port and starting on another.

So that it was very late before he went to bed, and he used no light for fear of disturbing Barbara. He crept about the room as silently as he could. In the darkness the glances that he directed at the other bed (naval establishments made small allowance for wives, and that allowance did not include double beds) under its mosquito net revealed nothing to him, and he was glad. If Barbara had been awake they could hardly have avoided discussing the Hudnutt case.

Nor was there any time next morning, for the moment Hornblower was called he had to hurry into the dressing-room and array himself in his best uniform with his ribbon and star and hasten away to the ceremony of the change of command. As the officer to be relieved he was first upon the quarterdeck of the *Clorinda*, and stationed himself on the starboard side, his staff behind him. Captain Sir Thomas Fell had received him, and next busied himself with receiving the other captains as they came on board. The marine band – without Hudnutt – played selections on the poop; the pipes of the bosun's mates twittered unceasingly to welcome the continuous arrivals; the sun blazed down as if this were just some ordinary day. Then came a pause, intense in its drama. Then the band burst into a march again, there were ruffles of drums and flourishes of bugles as Ransome came up the side with his staff behind him, to take up his station on the port side. Fell came forward to Hornblower with his hand at his hat brim.

'Ship's company fallen in, My Lord.'

'Thank you, Sir Thomas.' Spendlove pressed a paper into Hornblower's hand; Hornblower stepped forward. 'Orders from the Lords Commissioners for the execution of the office of Lord High Admiral, to me, Horatio Lord Hornblower, Knight Grand Cross of the Most Honourable Order of the Bath, Rear-Admiral of the Red Squadron—'

He really had trouble in preventing his voice from trembling, forcing himself to read in a harsh and matter-of-fact tone. He folded the paper and gave his last order.

'Sir Thomas, please have the goodness to haul down my flag.'

'Aye aye, My Lord.'

The first of the thirteen saluting guns went off as the red ensign came slowly down from the mizzen peak. A long, long, descent; sixty seconds for thirteen guns, and when the flag completed its descent Hornblower was the poorer by forty-nine pounds three shillings and seven pence a month command pay. A moment later Ransome came forward, paper in hand, to read the orders of the Lords Commissioners to him, Henry Ransome, Companion of the Most Honourable Order of the Bath, Rear-Admiral of the Blue Squadron.

'Hoist my flag, Sir Thomas.'

'Aye aye, sir.'

Up to the mizzen peak rose the Blue Ensign; until it broke at the peak the ship was silent, but then it unfolded itself in the breeze and the salute roared out and the band played. When the last gun fired Ransome was legally Commander-in-Chief of His Majesty's ships and vessels in West Indian waters. More blaring from the band, and in the midst of it Hornblower stepped forward raising his hand in salute to the new Commander-in-Chief.

'Permission to leave the ship, sir?'

'Permission granted.'

Ruffles of drums, bugle calls, pipes, and he went down the ship's side. He might have been sentimental; he might have felt agony of regret, but there was instant distraction awaiting him.

'My Lord,' said Spendlove beside him in the stern-sheets.

'Well?'

'That prisoner – Hudnutt, the marine bandsman—'

'What about him?'

'He's escaped, My Lord. He broke prison during the night.'

That settled Hudnutt's fate beyond all doubt. Nothing could save him. He was as good as dead; or soon perhaps he would be worse than dead. No deserter, no escaped prisoner, ever succeeded in evading recapture in Jamaica. It was an island, and not too large an island. And there was a standing reward of ten pounds sterling for information resulting in the apprehension of a deserter, and in Jamaica, far more than in England, ten pounds was a fortune. A journeyman's wages for a year or more; more money than any slave could hope to see in a lifetime. No deserter stood a chance; his white face, to say nothing of his uniform, would call attention to him wherever he might be in the island, and the standing reward made it certain that he would be betrayed. Hudnutt was doomed to recapture. And he was doomed beyond that. There would be additional charges at his court martial. Prison breaking. Desertion. Damage to government property. Damage to his uniform. He would probably be hanged. The only other chance was that he would be flogged round the fleet to die for certain under the lash. Hudnutt was a dead man, and this was the end of his talent for music.

It was a sombre enough thought to occupy his mind all the way to the pier, and it kept him silent as he climbed into the Governor's carriage to be driven to Government House – he had no Commander-in-Chief's carriage now. He was still silent as they drove away.

But they had hardly gone a mile when they met a lively cavalcade clattering down on horseback towards them. First Hornblower saw Barbara – he would have picked her out in any crowd even if she had not been conspicuous on a white horse. His Excellency rode on one side of her and Lady Hooper on the other, chattering eagerly. Behind them came a mixed party, of aides-de-camp and civilians; at the rear rode the Assistant Provost-Marshal and two troopers of his guard.

'Ha, Hornblower!' called the Governor, reining up. 'Your ceremonial seems to have finished earlier than I expected.'

'Good morning, sir,' said Hornblower. 'Your servant, ma'am.'

Then he smiled at Barbara – he could always smile at the sight of her despite any depression. In her hunting veil the smile she gave him in return was hardly apparent.

'You can join us in our hunt. One of my aides-de-camp will give you his horse,' said Hooper, and then, peering into the carriage, 'No, perhaps not, in those silk stockings. You can follow us in the carriage, like a lady with certain expectations. Like the Queen of France, by Gad! Turn that carriage, coachman.'

'What are you hunting, sir?' asked Hornblower, a little bewildered.

'That deserter of yours. He might show us some sport,' answered Hooper.

They were hunting man, the biggest game of all – but Hudnutt, dreamy, scatterbrained Hudnutt, would be poor game. Two coloured servants rode in the party, each holding a leash of bloodhounds, tawny and black; grim, horrible creatures. He wanted to have nothing to do with this hunt, nothing whatever. He wanted to order the carriage to turn back again. This was a nightmare, and it was beyond his power to awaken himself from it. It was horrible to see Barbara taking part in it. At the dockyard gate, at the high palisade, the cortège halted.

'That's the prison,' said the Assistant Provost-Marshal, pointing. 'You can see the hole in the roof, sir.'

An area of thatch had been torn away. Probably that prison was not very strongly built; to escape from it meant that the fifteen-foot palisade had to be scaled next – and even then certain recapture somewhere in the island awaited the man to achieve that feat.

'Come on,' said the Assistant Provost-Marshal, and he and his guard and the men with the bloodhounds trotted into the dockyard to the prison and dismounted. They took the bloodhounds into the prison, where presumably the hounds smelt at the prisoner's bedding. Then they reappeared at the door, smelling at the ground below the hole in the roof. Instantly they caught the scent, throwing themselves against their leashes so that the coloured servants had a difficult task to remount, and then they came pelting across the dockyard again. They threw themselves against the palisade, leaping up at it, slavering with excitement.

'Bring 'em round to this side!' shouted the Governor, and then, turning to Hornblower, 'Your man's a marine, isn't he? Even a sailor would find it hard to scale that palisade.'

Hudnutt might have done it in some exalted mood, thought Hornblower – those dreamers were like madmen sometimes.

The bloodhounds were brought round through the dockyard gate again and led to the corresponding point on the outside of the palisade. They caught the scent again in a flash, throwing themselves against their leashes and galloping down the road.

'Gone away!' yelled the Governor, spurring his horse after them.

Hudnutt had climbed that fifteen-foot palisade, then. He must have been insane. The cavalcade had all gone on ahead; the coachman was urging the carriage horses along as fast as their dignity and the inequalities of the road would permit; the carriage lurched and leaped, throwing Hornblower against Gerard beside him and sometimes even against Spendlove opposite. Straight up the road they went, heading for the open country and the Blue Mountains beyond. The horsemen ahead reined back into a trot, and the coachman followed their example, so that the progress of the carriage became more sedate.

'A hot enough scent, My Lord,' said Gerard, peering forward at the bloodhounds still straining at their leashes.

'And yet this road must have been well travelled since he went along it,' said Spendlove.

'Ah!' said Gerard, still peering forward. 'They're leaving the road.'

As the carriage reached the corner they saw that the horsemen had turned up a broad lane through fields of cane; the coachman, nothing daunted, swung up into the lane after them, but after two more miles of rapid progress he pulled his horses to a halt.

'A check here, Hornblower,' said the Governor. 'This lane fords the Hope River here.'

The halted cavalcade was breathing the horses; Barbara waved her gloved hand to him.

'No scent the other side,' explained the Governor, and then, calling to the men with the bloodhounds. 'Cast upstream as well as down. And on both sides.'

The Assistant Provost-Marshal acknowledged the order with a salute.

'Your man knew we'd have bloodhounds after him,' said the Governor. 'He waded along the river. But he has to come out sooner or later, and we'll pick up the scent again there.'

Barbara guided her horse to the side of the carriage, and raised her veil to speak to him.

'Good morning, dear,' she said.

'Good morning,' said Hornblower.

It was hard to say more, when the events of the last hour or two, and all their implications, were allowed for. And Barbara was hardly flushed with the heat and the exercise. She looked drawn and tired; her smile was positively wan. It occurred to Hornblower that she was participating in this hunt as unwillingly as he was. And it seemed likely that she had allowed the move from Admiralty House to Government House this morning to trouble her; womanlike she would not have been able to allow the Navy to execute the task without her supervision even though the Navy had made similar moves by the hundred thousand. She had tried to order it all and was weary in consequence.

'Come and sit in the carriage, dear,' he said. 'Gerard will take your horse.'

'Mr Gerard is wearing silk stockings the same as you are, dear,' replied Barbara, smiling through her weariness, 'and I have too much respect for his dignity to set him on a side saddle in any case.'

'My groom will lead your horse, Lady Hornblower,' interposed the Governor. 'This hunt looks as if it's going to turn out badly.'

Hornblower scrambled down from the carriage to help Barbara from the side-saddle and up into the carriage. Gerard and Spendlove, who had followed him out, followed them back after a moment's hesitation and sat with their backs to the horses.

'We should have heard something from the bloodhounds by now,' said the Governor. The four bloodhounds had now cast up and down both banks for a considerable distance. 'Can he have climbed a tree?'

A man could be more resourceful than any fox, Hornblower knew. But it was an unexpected aspect of Hudnutt's character.

'Not a trace of scent, Your Excellency,' said the Assistant Provost-Marshal trotting up. 'Nothing at all.'

'Oh, well then, we'll go home again. A poor day's sport after all. We'll precede you, Lady Hornblower, with your permission.'

'We'll see you at the house, dear Lady Hornblower,' echoed Lady Hooper.

The carriage turned again and followed the horsemen down the lane.

'You've had a busy morning, I fear, my dear,' said Hornblower; with his staff sitting across the carriage from them he had to retain a certain formality of tone.

'Not busy at all,' answered Barbara, turning her head to meet his glance. 'A very pleasant morning, thank you, dear. And you – your ceremonial went off without a hitch, I hope?'

'Well enough, thank you. Ransome—' he changed what he was going to say abruptly. What he would say about Ransome to Barbara's private ear was not the same as what he would say in the hearing of his staff.

The carriage trotted on, and conversation proceeded only fitfully in the heat. It was long before they swung through the gates of Government House, with Hornblower acknowledging the salute of the sentry, and drew up at the door. Aides-de-camp and butlers and maids awaited them; but Barbara had already dealt with the move, and in the vast, cavernous bedroom and dressing-room allotted to principal guests Hornblower's things were already disposed along with hers.

'At last alone,' smiled Barbara. 'Now we can look forward to Smallbridge.'

Indeed that was so; this was the beginning of one of those periods of transition which Hornblower knew so well, as did every sailor, the strange days, or weeks, between one life and the next. He had ceased to be a Commander-in-Chief; now he had to endure existence until he would at least be master in his own house. The urgent need at the moment was for a bath; his shirt was sticking to his ribs under his heavy uniform coat. Perhaps never again, never in all his life, would he take a bath under a wash-deck pump somewhere out with the trade winds blowing upon him. On the other hand, he would not, at least while he was in Jamaica, have to wear a uniform again.

It was later in the day that Barbara made her request to him.

'Dear, would you please give me some money?'

'Of course,' said Hornblower.

He felt a delicacy about this which most men would laugh at. Barbara had brought a good deal of money to their marriage, which, of course, was now his property, and he felt an absurd guilt that she should have to ask him for money. That feeling of guilt was perfectly ridiculous, of course. Women were not supposed to dispose of money in any way, except small sums for housekeeping. They could not legally sign a cheque, they could enter into no business transaction at all, which was perfectly right and proper seeing how incapable women were. Except perhaps Barbara. It was the husband's business to keep all moneys under his own hand and dole out under his own supervision what was needed.

'How much would you like, dear?' he asked.

'Two hundred pounds,' said Barbara.

Two hundred pounds? Two hundred pounds! That was something entirely different. It was a fortune. What in the world would Barbara want two hundred pounds for here in Jamaica? There could not be one single gown or pair of gloves in the whole island that Barbara could possibly want to buy. A few souvenirs, perhaps. The most elaborate tortoiseshell toilet set in Jamaica would not cost five pounds. Two hundred pounds? There would be a few maids to whom she would have to give vails on leaving, but five shillings each, half a guinea at most, would settle those.

'Two hundred pounds?' he said it aloud this time.

'Yes, dear, if you please.'

'It will be my business to tip the butler and grooms, of course,' he said, still trying to find reasons why she should think she needed this stupendous sum.

'Yes, no doubt, dear,' said Barbara, patiently. 'But I need some money for other purposes.'

'But it's a lot of money.'

'I think we can afford it, though. Please, dear—'

'Of course, of course,' said Hornblower hastily. He could not bear it that Barbara should have to plead to him. All he had was hers. It was always a pleasure to him to anticipate her wants, to forestall any request so that it never need be uttered. He felt shame that Barbara, exquisite Barbara, should ever have to abase herself so low as to ask a favour of him, unworthy as he was.

'I'll write an order on Summers,' he said. 'He's Coutts's correspondent in Kingston.'

'Thank you, dear,' said Barbara.

Yet as he handed the order over he could not refrain from further speech.

'You'll be careful, dear, won't you?' he said. 'Two hundred pounds, whether in notes or gold—'

His misgivings ceased to be voiced, died away in incoherent mumblings. He had no wish to pry. He had no wish to exert over Barbara the sort of parental authority that both law and custom gave a husband over his wife. And then he thought of a possible explanation. Lady Hooper was a keen and clever card player. Presumably Barbara had lost heavily to her. Well, in that case he need not worry. Barbara was a good player, too, and level headed, and cool. She would win it back. In any case she was no gambler. Perhaps on the voyage home they would have a few hands of piquet – if Barbara had any fault at all it was a tendency to discard a little thoughtlessly when playing the younger hand, and he could give a little unobtrusive advice. And there was a smug pleasure, and a tender pleasure, in the thought of Barbara not caring to admit, to a husband who notoriously won, that she had lost at cards. The deep respect that he felt for her was accompanied (as the flavour of a beef steak may be accompanied by that of mustard) by the knowledge that she was still human. Hornblower knew that there can be no love without respect – and no love without a twinkle of amusement as well.

'You are the dearest man in the world,' said Barbara, and he realised that her eyes had been fixed on his face for the last several seconds.

'It is my greatest happiness to hear you say so,' he answered, with a sincerity that no one could doubt. And then a recollection of their position in this house, as mere guests, came to them both to modify the intensity of their feelings.

'And we shall be the most unpopular people in Jamaica if we keep Their Excellencies waiting for their dinner,' said Hornblower.

They were only guests, now, mere hangers-on, their presence only tolerated by people who had their official lives still to live; that was what Hornblower thought at dinner-time when the new Commander-in-Chief sat in the place of honour. He thought of the Byzantine General, blinded and disgraced, begging in the market-place, and he nearly said, 'Spare a penny for Belisarius' when the Governor turned to include him in the conversation.

'Your marine hasn't been apprehended yet,' said Hooper.

'Not my marine any longer, sir,' laughed Hornblower. 'Admiral Ransome's marine now.'

'I understand there's no doubt that he *will* be apprehended,' said Ransome.

'We've not lost a deserter yet during the time of my appointment here,' said Hooper.

'That's very reassuring,' was Ransome's comment.

Hornblower stole a glance at Barbara across the table. She was eating her dinner with apparent composure; he had feared lest this reminder should upset her, for he knew how strongly she felt about Hudnutt's fate. A woman was liable to think that the inevitable should not be inevitable in matters in which she was interested. Barbara's mastery of her feelings was something more to admire about her.

Lady Hooper changed the subject, and conversation became general and gay. Hornblower actually began to enjoy himself, with a light-headed feeling of irresponsibility. There were no cares on his shoulders; soon – the moment the packet was ready to sail – he would be on his way to England, and he would be pleasantly settled in Smallbridge while these people here went on dealing with unrewarding problems in tropical heat. Nothing here mattered to him any more. If Barbara were happy he had not a care in the world, and Barbara was seemingly happy, chattering away to her neighbours on either hand.

It was pleasant, too, that there was not to be any heavy drinking, for after dinner there was to be a reception in honour of the new Commander-in-Chief to which all the island society not eligible for dinner had been invited. He found himself looking at life with fresh eyes and actually approving of it.

After dinner, when the men and the ladies met again in the drawing-room and the first new guests were being announced, he was able to exchange a word or two with Barbara and to see that she was happy and not over-tired. Her smile was bright and her eyes sparkling. He had to turn away from her in the end to shake hands with Mr Hough, just arrived with his wife. Other guests were streaming in; a sudden influx of blue and gold and white marked the arrival of Coleman, *Triton*'s captain, and a couple of his lieutenants. Ransome himself was presenting Coleman to Barbara, and Hornblower could not help but hear the conversation close behind him.

'Captain Coleman is an old friend of mine,' said Barbara. 'You were Perfecto Coleman in those days, weren't you, captain?'

'And you were Lady Leighton, ma'am,' said Coleman.

A harmless enough remark, but enough to shatter Hornblower's frail happiness, to darken the brightly lit room, to set the babble of conversation in the room roaring in Hornblower's ears like a torrent, through the din of which Barbara's words pierced shrill like a whistle note.

'Captain Coleman was my first husband's flag-lieutenant,' said Barbara.

She had had a first husband; she had been Lady Leighton. Hornblower nearly always contrived to forget this. Rear-Admiral Sir Percy Leighton had died for his country, of wounds received in the battle of Rosas Bay, thirteen full years ago. But Barbara had been Leighton's wife, Leighton's widow. She had been Leighton's wife before she had been Hornblower's. Hornblower hardly ever thought about it, but when he did he still experienced a jealousy which he knew to be insane. Any reminder not only reawoke that jealousy, but brought back to him with agonising clarity the recollection of the despair, the envy, the black self-derision he had known in those days. He had been a desperately unhappy man then, and this made him the same desperately unhappy man now. He was no longer the successful sailor, terminating a brilliant period of command. He was the thwarted lover, despised even by his own despicable self. He knew again all the misery of limitless and yet unsatisfied desire, to blend with the jealousies of the moment.

Hough was awaiting a reply to some remark he had made. Hornblower forced himself to extemporise some casual sentence which may or may not have been relevant. Hough drifted away, and Hornblower found himself against his will looking over at Barbara. She had her ready smile for him, and he had to smile back, and he knew it to be a dreadful, lopsided, mirthless smile, like a grin on the face of a dead man. He saw a worried look come on her face; he knew how instantly she was conscious of his moods, and that made it worse than ever. She was the heartless woman who had spoken of her first husband – that jealousy of his was a mood she knew nothing of, was not susceptible to. He was a man who had stepped suddenly from firm ground into a morass of uncertainty that would engulf him.

Captain Knyvett had entered the room, bluff and grizzled, dressed in blue broadcloth with unpretentious brass buttons. As he approached

Hornblower could only with an effort remember him as the captain of the Jamaica packet.

'We sail a week from today, My Lord,' he said. 'The announcement for the mail will be made tomorrow.'

'Excellent,' said Hornblower.

'And I can see from all this,' went on Knyvett, with a gesture indicating Admiral Ransome's presence, 'that I shall have the pleasure of Your Lordship's company, and Her Ladyship's.'

'Yes, yes, quite so,' said Hornblower.

'You will be my only passengers,' said Knyvett.

'Excellent,' repeated Hornblower.

'I trust Your Lordship will find the *Pretty Jane* a well-found and comfortable ship.'

'I trust so,' said Hornblower.

'Her Ladyship, of course, is familiar with the deck-house that will be your accommodation. I shall ask her if she can suggest any addition that will add to your comfort, My Lord.'

'Very well.'

Knyvett drifted away after this cold reception, and it was only after he had gone that Hornblower realised that Knyvett must have received an impression of a top-lofty peer with hardly bare politeness for a mere packet-captain. He regretted it, and made a desperate effort to get himself under control again. A glance at Barbara revealed her chatting animatedly with young Bonner, the fishing-boat owner and general merchant with the shady reputation, against whom Hornblower had already warned her. That could have added to his misery if it were possible.

Again he made the effort to control himself. He knew the expression on his face to be frozen and blank, and he tried to make it more pleasing as he forced himself to stroll through the crowd.

'Can we tempt you, Lord Hornblower?' asked an old lady standing by the card-table in an alcove. She was a good whist player, Hornblower remembered.

'Why certainly, with pleasure,' he made himself say.

He had something to think about now; for the first few hands it was hard to concentrate, especially as the noise of an orchestra was added to the din of the party, but old habits reasserted themselves with the necessity to remember the distribution of fifty-two cards. By sheer willpower he achieved the transformation of himself into a thinking machine, playing coldly and correctly, and then, when the rubber appeared to be lost, he was carried away despite himself. The next hand afforded an opportunity for brilliance, for that injection into his so-far mechanical play of the human quality, the flexibility, the unpredictable cunning which marked the difference between a second-class player and a first-class one. By the fourth lead he had made a fair estimate of the hands. One particular lead might enable him to clear the board, to win every trick and the rubber; with orthodox play the hand would end with his making only twelve tricks and the rubber still in doubt. It was worth trying – but it was now or never. Without hesitation he led his queen of hearts to the ace that his partner was forced to play; he took the next trick and along with it control of the situation, cleared trumps, led out his established winners, saw with satisfaction his opponents discard first the knave and then the king of hearts, and he finally laid down the three of hearts to take the last trick amid the dismay of his opponents.

'Why, that's Grand Slam,' said the old lady who was his partner, quite astonished. 'I don't understand – I don't see how – we've won the rubber after all!'

It had been a neat piece of work; there was a perceptible glow of accomplishment within him. That was a hand that he would be able to play over in his mind in future while composing himself to sleep. When the card playing was finished and the guests beginning to leave he was able to meet Barbara's eye with a more natural expression, and Barbara with a relieved sigh was able to tell herself that her husband was coming out of his unpredictable mood.

It was as well that he was, for the next few days were bound to be difficult. There was almost nothing for him to do as the *Pretty Jane* made ready for sea. As a helpless spectator he had to stand by and watch Ransome taking over the command he had held for three years. The Spanish question was likely to be difficult with the French invasion of Spain to restore Ferdinand VII; there was the Mexican question as well as the Venezuela question; he could not help fretting over the possibility of Ransome mishandling them. On the other hand, there was the small comfort that Hudnutt had so far succeeded in evading capture; Hornblower honestly feared that if he should be apprehended and sentenced while they were still in the island Barbara might take action herself with personal appeals to Ransome or even to the Governor. Barbara actually seemed to have forgotten about the case, which was more than Hornblower had; he was still profoundly disturbed about it, and inclined to fret himself into a fever at his complete lack of power to exert any influence in the matter. It was hard to be philosophic about it, to tell himself that no individual, not even Hornblower, could hold back the working of the inexorable machine of the Articles for the Regulating and Better Government of His Majesty's Navies. And Hudnutt was a more capable person than he had ever imagined, seeing that he had been able to maintain himself free from capture for a week now – unless perhaps he was dead. That might be best for Hudnutt.

Captain Knyvett came in person with the news that the *Pretty Jane* was almost ready for sea.

'The last of the cargo's going on board now, My Lord,' he said. 'The logwood's all in and the coir is on the quay. If Your Lordship and Her Ladyship will come on board this evening we'll sail with the land breeze at dawn.'

'Thank you, captain. I am greatly obliged to you,' said Hornblower, trying not to be fulsome to make up for his coldness at the Governor's party.

Pretty Jane was a flush-decked brig, save that amidships she carried a small but substantial deck-house for her passengers. Barbara had inhabited it for five weeks on the outward voyage. Now they entered it together, with all the bustle of the ship's getting ready for sea going on round them.

'I used to look at that other bed, dear,' she said to Hornblower as they stood in the deck-house, 'and I used to tell myself that soon my husband would be sleeping there. It seemed too good to be possible, dear.'

A noise outside distracted them.

'This case, ma'am?' asked the Government House servant who was bringing their baggage on board under Gerard's supervision.

'That? Oh, I've asked the captain about that already. It's to go in the steerage.'

'Yes, ma'am.'

'Delicacies in tin boxes,' explained Barbara to Hornblower. 'I brought them all the way out for you to enjoy while going home, dear.'

'You are too good to me,' said Hornblower.

A case that size and weight would be a nuisance in the deck-house. In the steerage its contents would be readily accessible.

'What is coir?' asked Barbara, looking out to see one of the final bales going down the hatchway.

'The hairy husks of coconuts,' explained Hornblower.

'What in the world are we carrying those to England for?' asked Barbara.

'There are machines now which can weave it. They make cocomatting by the mile in England now.'

'And logwood?'

'They extract a dye from it. A bright red dye.'

'You are my unfailing source of information, dear,' said Barbara, 'as well as everything else in life for me.'

'Here's Their Excellencies coming, My Lord,' warned Gerard, arriving at the deck-house door.

That meant the final good-byes, in the dying evening. A painful, sad moment; much shaking of hands; kisses on each cheek for Barbara from Lady Hooper; the word 'good-bye' repeated over and over again, overwhelming in its finality. Good-bye to friends and to acquaintances, good-bye to Jamaica and to the command-in-chief. Good-bye to one life, with the next still to disclose itself. Good-bye to the last shadowy figure disappearing in the darkness of the quay, and then to turn again to Barbara standing beside him, permanent in these transitions.

In the first light of next morning Hornblower could hardly be blamed for being on deck, feeling oddly awkward with the necessity for keeping out of the way, watching while Knyvett warped the *Pretty Jane* away from the quay, to catch the land breeze and head out of the harbour. Luckily Knyvett was made of sturdy stuff, and was not in the least discomposed at having to handle his ship under the eye of an Admiral. The land breeze filled the sails; *Pretty Jane* gathered way. They dipped the flag to Fort Augusta, and then, with the helm hard over, came round to leave Drunken Cay and South Cay on their port side before beginning the long reach to the eastward. And Hornblower could relax and contemplate the new prospect of breakfasting with his wife on shipboard.

He surprised himself at the ease with which he accustomed himself to being a passenger. At first he was so anxious to give no indication of interference that he did not even dare to look into the binnacle to note their course. He was content to sit with Barbara in two hammock chairs in the shade of the deck-house – there were beckets to which the chairs could be hooked to prevent them sliding down the deck to leeward as *Pretty Jane* heeled over – and think about nothing in particular, watching the flying fish furrowing the surface, and the patches of yellow Sargasso weed drift by, gold against the blue, and an occasional turtle swimming manfully along far from land. He could watch Captain Knyvett and his mate take their noon sight and assure himself that he had no interest at all in the figures they were obtaining – and in truth he was really more interested in the punctuality of meal-times. He could crack an idle joke with Barbara to the effect that *Pretty Jane* had made this run so often she could be trusted to find her way home without supervision; and his mind was lazy enough to think that funny.

It was actually his first holiday after three years of strenuous work. During much of that time he had frequently been under severe strain, and during all of it he had been busy. He sank into idleness as a man might sink into a warm bath, with the difference that he had not expected to find this relaxation and ease in idleness, and (more important, perhaps) in the cessation of responsibility. Nothing mattered during those golden days. He was the person least concerned in all the ship, as *Pretty Jane* thrashed her way northward, in the burning question as to whether the wind would hold steady to enable her to weather Point Maysi, without having to go about, and he did not care when they did not succeed. He endured philosophically the long beat to windward back towards Haiti, and he smiled patronisingly at the petty jubilation on board when they succeeded on the next tack and passed through the Windward Channel so that they might almost consider themselves out

of the Caribbean. A persistent northward slant in the Trades kept them
from attempting the Caicos Passage, and they had to hold away to the
eastward for Silver Bank Passage. Caicos or Silver Bank – or for that
matter Turks Island or Mouchoir – he did not care. He did not care
whether he arrived home in August or September.

Yet his instincts were only dormant. That evening, when they were
truly in the Atlantic, he felt restless and disturbed for the first time since
leaving Jamaica. There was something heavy in the breathing of the
air, and something unusual about the swell that was rolling the *Pretty
Jane* so heavily. A gale before morning, he decided. A little unusual in
these latitudes at this time of year, but nothing really to worry about.
He did not trouble Barbara with his notions, but he woke several times
in the night to find the ship still rolling heavily. When the watch was
called he noted that all hands were kept on deck to shorten sail, and he
was tempted to go out to see what was happening. A clatter outside
awoke Barbara.

'What's that?' she asked, sleepily.

'Only the deadlights, dear,' he answered.

Someone had slammed the deadlights against the deck-house windows
and clamped them home – Knyvett must be expecting to ship some heavy
seas. Barbara went back to sleep, and Hornblower actually followed her
example, but in half an hour hé was awake again. The gale was unceasing,
and the ship was working considerably in the swell, so that everything
was groaning and creaking. He lay in the darkness to feel the ship
heaving and lying over under him, and he could both hear and actually
feel the vibration of the taut standing rigging transmitted to his bunk
via the deck. He would like to go out and have a look at the weather, but
he did not wish to disturb Barbara.

'Awake, dear?' said a small voice the other side of the deck-house.

'Yes,' he answered.

'It seems to be getting rough.'

'A little,' he said. 'There's nothing to worry about. Go to sleep again,
dear.'

Now he could not go out because Barbara was awake and would
know about it. He made himself lie still; it was pitch dark in the deck-
house with the deadlights in, and, perhaps because of the cessation of
ventilation, it was now overpoweringly hot despite the gale. *Pretty Jane*
was leaping about extravagantly, and every now and then lying over so
far that he feared lest Barbara should be rolled out of her bunk. Then he
was conscious of a change in the vessel's behaviour, of a difference in the
thunderous creaking that filled the darkness. Knyvett had hove the
Pretty Jane to; she was not lying over, but she was pitching fantastically,
indicating a really heavy sea outside. He wanted so much to go out and
see for himself. He had no idea even of what the time was – it was far too

dark to look at his watch. At the thought that it might be dawn he could restrain himself no longer.

'Awake, dear?' he asked.

'Yes,' said Barbara.

She did not add, 'how could anyone sleep in this din?' for Barbara lived up to the principle that no person of breeding should ever complain about things he was unable, or unwilling, to do anything to remedy.

'I shall go out on deck if you do not mind my leaving you, dear,' he said.

'Please go if you wish to, of course, dear,' answered Barbara, nor did she add that she wished she could go out too.

Hornblower groped for his trousers and his shoes, and felt his way to the door. Long experience warned him to brace himself as he unfastened it, but even he was a little surprised at the raging wind that awaited him; it was wild even though, with *Pretty Jane* hove-to, the door on the after side was in the lee of the deck-house. He stepped over the coaming and managed to slam the door. The wind was tremendous, but what was more surprising still was its warmth; it seemed to be of brick-kiln heat as it screamed round him. He balanced himself on the heaving deck in the hot, noisy darkness, and timed his rush to the wheel, and he was only just prepared for the extra violence of the wind when he emerged from the lee of the deck-house. Out of that lee, too, the air was full of flying spray which drenched him and modified his impression of the heat of the air – he was aware of all this by the time he reached the wheel. There were shadowy figures there in the darkness; a white shirt-sleeve waved to him to acknowledge his presence, indicating that Knyvett was there. Hornblower looked into the binnacle; it was really an effort to collect his faculties and make the correct deductions from what he could see of the swinging needle. The wind was blowing from well out to the west of north. Looking up in the darkness he could just make out that the brig was hove-to under the main-topmast staysail, of which only a corner was showing. Knyvett was shouting into his ear.

'Hurricane!'

'Likely enough,' shouted Hornblower in reply. 'Worse before it's better!'

A hurricane had no business to appear at this time of year, a good two months earlier than one should be expected, but that hot breath, the indications of yesterday evening, the direction of the wind at present, all seemed to prove that that was what they were experiencing. It remained to be seen whether they were right in the path of it or only on its fringe. *Pretty Jane* shuddered and lurched drunkenly as a mass of water came in over her bow, gleaming white, almost phosphorescent, as it raced aft at them; Hornblower hung on desperately as it surged past him waist deep – a nasty warning of what might be still to come. They were in very considerable danger. *Pretty Jane* might not endure the pounding she would have to undergo, and in any case, with the considerable leeway she was making they might be cast ashore, and utterly destroyed, on San Domingo or Puerto Rico or some intervening cay. The wind shrieked at them, and a combination of wind and wave laid *Pretty Jane* over, over until the deck was almost vertical, with Hornblower hanging on as his feet could gain no hold on the planking. A wave burst against her exposed bottom clean over her, cascading round them, and then she came slowly back again. No ship would be expected to endure that sort of thing for long. A muffled bang aloft, followed by a series of sharper sounds, attracted his attention to the topmast staysail just as it blew out from its gaskets and flew into ribbons which cracked like whips while they lasted. One thundering small fragment remained, whipping from the stay, just enough to keep *Pretty Jane*'s starboard bow to the sea.

Daylight was coming; there was a yellow tinge all about them, shut in by the low sky overhead. As Hornblower looked aloft he saw a hump, a bubble, appear on the main yard, and the bubble promptly burst into fragments. The wind was tearing the sail from its gaskets. The process was repeated along the yard, as the wind with fingers of steel pried into the solid roll of the sail to tear it loose, rip it open, split it into ribbons, and then tear off the ribbons to whirl them away to leeward. It was hard to believe that a wind could have such power.

It was hard to believe, too, that waves could be so high. A glance at them explained at once the fantastic motion of the ship. They were appalling in their immensity. The one approaching the starboard bow was not as high as a mountain – Hornblower had used the expression 'mountain high' himself, and now, trying to estimate the height, had to admit to himself that it was an exaggeration – but it was as high as a lofty church steeple. It was a colossal ridge of water moving, not with the speed of a race-horse, but with the speed of a hurrying man, straight upon them. *Pretty Jane* lifted her bow to it, lurching and then climbing, rising ever more steeply as she lay upon the towering slope. Up – up – up; she seemed to be almost vertical as she reached the crest, where it was as if the end of the world awaited her. At the crest the wind, temporarily blanketed by the wave, flung itself upon her with redoubled force. Over she lay, over and over, while at the same time her stern heaved itself up as the crest passed under her. Down – down – down; the deck almost vertical, bows down, and almost vertical on her beam, and as she wallowed down the slope minor waves awaited her to burst over her. With the water surging round him waist deep, chest deep, Hornblower felt his legs carried away from under him and he had to hang on with every ounce of his strength to save himself.

Here was the ship's carpenter trying to say something to the captain – it was impossible to speak intelligently in that wind, but he held up one hand with the fingers spread. Five feet of water in the hold, then. But the carpenter repeated the gesture. Then he tried again. Two spreadings of the fingers – ten feet of water, then. It could hardly be the case, but it was true – the heavy heavings of the *Pretty Jane* showed she was water-logged. Then Hornblower remembered the cargo with which she was laden. Logwood and coir; logwood floated only sluggishly, but coir was one of the most buoyant substances known. Coconuts falling into the sea (as they often did, thanks to the palm's penchant for growing at the water's edge) floated for weeks and months, carried about by the currents, so that the wide distribution of the coconut palm was readily accounted for. It was coir that was keeping *Pretty Jane* afloat even though she was full of water. It would keep her afloat for a long time – it would outlast the *Pretty Jane*, for that matter. She would work herself to frag-ments before the coir allowed her to sink.

So perhaps they had another hour or two of life before them. Perhaps. Another wave, cascading green over *Pretty Jane*'s upturned side, brought a grim warning that it might not be as long as that. And amid the rumble and the roar of the bursting wave, even as he hung on desperately, he was conscious of a succession of other sounds, harder and sharper, and of a jarring of the deck under his feet. The deck-house! It was lifting on its bolts under the impact of the water. It could not be expected to stand that battering long; it was bound to be swept away, soon. And – Hornblower's visual imagination was feverishly at work – before then its seams would be forced apart, it would fill with water. Barbara would be drowned inside it before the weight of water within tore the deck-house from its bolts, for the waves to hurl it overside with Barbara's drowned body inside. Clinging to the binnacle Hornblower went through some seconds of mental agony, the worst he had ever known in his life. There had been times and times before when he had faced death for himself, when he had weighed chances, when he had staked his own life, but now it was Barbara's life that he was staking.

To leave her in the deck-house meant her certain death soon. The alternative was to bring her out upon the wave-swept deck. Here, tied to the mast, she would live as long as she could endure the buffeting and the exposure, until the *Pretty Jane* broke up into fragments, possibly. For himself he had played out a losing game to the bitter end more than once; now he had to brace himself to do the same for Barbara. He made the decision. On Barbara's behalf he decided to struggle on as long as was possible. Forcing himself to think logically while the stupe-fying wind roared round him, he made his plans. He awaited a compara-tively calm moment, and then made the perilous brief journey to the foot of the mainmast. Now he worked with frantic rapidity. Two lengths of the main-topsail halliards; he had to keep his head clear to prevent his fumbling fingers from entangling them. Then two desperate journeys, first to the wheel, and then to the deck-house. He tore open the door and stumbled in over the coaming, the lines in his hands. There were two feet of water in the deck-house, surging about with the motion of the ship. Barbara was there; he saw her in the light from the door. She had wedged herself as well as she might in her bunk.

'Dearest!' he said. Within the deck-house it was just possible to be heard, despite the frantic din all round.

'I'm here, dear,' she replied.

Another wave burst over the *Pretty Jane* at that moment; water came pouring in through the gaping seams of the deck-house and he could feel the whole thing lift again on its bolts and he knew a moment of wild despair at the thought that he might already be too late, that the deck-house was going to be swept away at this moment with them in it. But it held – the surge of the water as *Pretty Jane* lay over the other way flung Hornblower against the other bulkhead.

'I must get you out of here, dear,' said Hornblower, trying to keep his voice steady. 'You'll be safer tied to the mainmast.'

'As you wish, of course, dear,' said Barbara, calmly.

'I'm going to put these lines round you,' said Hornblower.

Barbara had managed to dress herself in his absence; at any rate she had some sort of dress or petticoat on. Hornblower made fast the lines about her while the ship rolled and swayed under their feet; she held her arms up for him to do so. He knotted the lines round her waist, below her tender bosom.

'Listen carefully,' said Hornblower, and he told her, while they were still in the comparative calm of the deck-house, what he wanted her to do, how she had to watch her chance, rush to the wheel, and from there to the mainmast.

'I understand, dear,' said Barbara. 'Kiss me once more, my very dearest.'

He kissed her hurriedly, his lips against her dripping cheek. It was only the most perfunctory kiss. To Hornblower's subconscious mind Barbara in making her request was risking their lives for it – staking ten thousand future kisses against one immediate one. It was woman-like for her to do so, but odds of ten thousand to one had no appeal for Hornblower. And still she lingered.

'Dearest, I've always loved you,' she said; she was speaking hurriedly and yet with no proper regard for the value of time. 'I've loved no one but you in all my life. I had another husband once. I couldn't say this before because it would have been disloyal. But now – I've never loved anyone but you. Never. Only you, darling.'

'Yes, dear,' said Hornblower. He heard the words, but at that urgent moment he could not give them their rightful consideration. 'Stand here. Hold on to this. Hold on!'

It was only a lesser wave that swept by them.

'Wait for my signal!' bellowed Hornblower into Barbara's ear, and then he made the hurried dash to the binnacle. One group of men had bound themselves to the wheel.

There was a frantic moment as he looked about him. He waved, and then Barbara crossed the heaving deck as he took up on the line. He had just time to fling a bight round her and pull it tight and seize hold himself as the next crest burst over the ship. Over – over – over. Sluggishly the *Pretty Jane* wallowed up again. He had an idea that one man at least was missing from the group at the wheel, but there was no time to think about that, for there was the passage to the mainmast still to be accomplished.

At last that was done. There were four men there already, but he was able to make Barbara as secure as possible, and then himself. *Pretty Jane* lay over again, and again; it was at some time shortly after this that a fresh monstrous wave swept away the deck-house and half the ship's rail – Hornblower saw the wreckage go off to leeward, and noted the fact, dully. He had been right in taking Barbara away from there.

It may have been the loss of the deck-house that called his attention to the behaviour of the *Pretty Jane*. She was lying in the trough of the sea, not riding with her bows to the waves. The loss of the windage of the deck-house, right aft, perhaps made this more noticeable. She was rolling wildly and deeply in consequence, and was being swept by the waves more thoroughly. She could not be expected to survive this for long, nor could the miserable human beings on her deck – of whom Barbara was one and he was another. The *Pretty Jane* would rack herself to pieces before long. Something was needed to keep her bows to the sea. In the normal way a small area of canvas exposed right aft would bring this about, but no canvas would stand against that wind, as had been early demonstrated. In the present circumstances the pressure of the wind against the foremast and bowsprit with their standing rigging balanced that against the mainmast, keeping her lying broadside on to wind and wave. If canvas could not be exposed aft then the windage forward must be reduced instead. The foremast should be cut away. Then the pressure on the mainmast would bring her bows on to the sea, increasing her chances, while the loss of the mast would perhaps ease the roll as well. There was no doubt about it; the mast should be cut away instantly.

Aft there was Knyvett, bound to the wheel, no more than a few feet away; it was his decision as captain. As *Pretty Jane* wallowed to bring her deck horizontal for a moment, with water no more than knee deep over it, Hornblower waved to him. He pointed forward to the weather foremast shrouds; he gesticulated, he thought he conveyed his meaning clearly enough, but Knyvett showed no sign of understanding. He certainly made no move to act upon the suggestion. He merely gazed stupidly and then looked away. Hornblower felt a moment of fury; the next roll and submergence made up his mind for him. The discipline of the sea might be disregarded in the face of this indifference and incompetence.

But the other men beside him at the mainmast were as indifferent as Knyvett. He could not rouse them to join him in the effort. They had a momentary safety here at the mast, and they would not leave it; probably they could not understand what he had in mind. That outrageous wind was perfectly stupefying as it screamed round them, and the constant deluges of water, and the desperate need to struggle for a footing, gave them no chance to collect their thoughts.

An axe would perhaps be best to cut those shrouds, but there was no axe. The man beside him had a knife in a sheath at his belt. Hornblower put his hand on the hilt, and made himself think reasonably again. He tested the edge, found it sharp, and then unbuckled belt and all and rebuckled it about his own waist – the man offering no objection, merely gazing stupidly at him as he did so. Again there was need to plan, to think clearly, in the howling wind and the driving spray and the solid water that surged round him. He cut himself two lengths of line from the raffle about him, and made each of them fast round his chest with an end hanging free. Then he looked over to the foremast shrouds, planning again. There would be no time to think things out when the moment for action began. A length of the rail still survived its battering there – presumably the weather shrouds had acted as some sort of breakwater to it. He eyed and measured the distance. He eased the knots that held him to the mast. He spared a glance at Barbara, forcing himself to smile. She was standing there in her bonds; the hurricane was blowing her long hair, wet though it was, straight out horizontally from her head. He put another line about her to make her secure. There was nothing else he could do. This was Bedlam, this was insanity, this was a wet, shrieking hell, and yet a hell in which he had to keep his head clear.

He watched his moment. First he almost misjudged it, and had to draw back, swallowing hard in the tense excitement, before the next wave engulfed him. As it surged away he watched *Pretty Jane*'s motion again, set his teeth, and cast off his bonds and made the rush up the steep deck – wave and deck offering him a lee which saved him from being blown away by the wind. He reached the rail with five seconds to spare – five seconds in which to secure himself, to knot himself to the shrouds as the crest burst over him, in a torrent of water which first swept his legs from under him, and next tore his grip loose so that for a second or two only the lines held him before an eddy enabled him to re-establish his grip.

Pretty Jane wallowed clear again. It was awkward to fasten the lanyard of the sheath knife to his wrist, but he had to consume precious moments in doing so; otherwise all his efforts so far would be wasted in ridiculous failure. Now he was sawing desperately at the shroud; the soaked fibres seemed like iron, but he felt them part little by little, a few fibres at a time. He was glad he had made sure the knife was sharp. He had half-severed the rope before the next deluge burst over him. The moment his shoulders were clear of the water he continued to saw at the rope; he could feel, as he cut, a slight variation of tension as the ship rolled and the shroud faintly slackened. He wondered if, when the rope parted, it would fly dangerously, and he decided that as long as the other shrouds held the reaction would not be too violent.

So it proved; the shroud simply vanished under his knife – the wind caught its fifty-foot length and whirled it away out of his world, presumably blowing it out as a streamer from the mast-head. He set about the next, sawing away in the intervals of being submerged under the crashing waves. He cut and he hung on; he struggled for air in the driving spray, he choked and suffocated under the green water, but one shroud after another parted under his knife. The knife was losing its edge, and now he was faced with an additional problem; he had severed nearly every shroud – the aftermost ones – within reach and soon he would have to shift his position to reach the foremost ones. But he did not have to solve that problem after all. At the next roll and the next wave, actually while he was struggling under water, he was conscious of a series of shocks transmitted through the fabric of the ship through his clutching hands – four minor ones and then a violent one. As the wave fell away from him his swimming eyes could see what had happened. The four remaining shrouds had parted under the strain, one, two, three, four, and then the mast had snapped off; looking back over his shoulder he could see the stump standing eight feet above the deck.

The difference it made to the *Pretty Jane* was instantly apparent. The very next roll ended half-heartedly in a mere violent pitch, as the shrieking wind, acting upon her mainmast, pushed her stern round and brought her bows to the sea, while the loss of the leverage of the lofty foremast reduced the amplitude of the roll in any case. The sea that broke over Hornblower's head was almost negligible in violence and quantity. Hornblower could breathe, he could look about him. He observed something else; the foremast, still attached to the ship by the lee shrouds, was now dragging ahead of her as she made stern way through the water under the impulse of the wind. It was acting as a sea anchor, a very slight restraint upon the extravagance of her motions; moreover, as the point of attachment was on the port side, she was slightly turned so that she met the waves a trifle on her port bow, so that she was riding at the best possible angle, with a very slight roll and a long pitch. Waterlogged though she was, she still had a chance – and Hornblower on the starboard bow was comparatively sheltered and able to contemplate his handiwork with some sort of pride.

He looked across at the pitiful groups of people, clustering bound to the mainmast and the wheel and binnacle; Barbara was out of his sight in the group at the mainmast, hidden from him by the men there, and he was consumed with a sudden anxiety lest further mishap might have befallen her. He began to cast himself loose to return to her, and it was then, with the cessation of the all-consuming preoccupation regarding the ship, that a sudden recollection struck him, so forcibly that he actually paused with his fingers on the knots. Barbara had kissed him, in the lee of the vanished deck-house. And she had said – Hornblower remembered well what she had said; it had lain stored in his memory until this moment, awaiting his attention when there should be a lull in the need for violent action. She had not merely said that she loved him; she had said she had never loved anyone else. Hornblower, huddled on the deck of a waterlogged ship with a hurricane shrieking round him, was suddenly aware that an old hurt was healed, that he would never again feel that dull ache of jealousy of Barbara's first husband, never, as long as he lived.

That was enough to bring him back to the world of practical affairs. The remaining length of his life might well be measured in hours. He would more likely than not be dead by nightfall, or by tomorrow at latest. And so would Barbara. So would Barbara. The absurd tiny feeling of well-being that had sprung up within him was instantly destroyed and replaced by a frantic sorrow and a despair that was almost overwhelming. He had to exert all his will-power to make himself master of his drooping body again, and of his weary mind. He had to act and to think, as though he was not exhausted and as though he did not despair. The discovery that the sheath knife still dangled at his wrist awoke the self-contempt that invariably stimulated him; he untied the lanyard and secured the knife in its sheath before setting himself to study the motion of the *Pretty Jane*.

He cast himself loose and dashed for the mainmast. The tremendous wind might well have carried him clean after and overboard, but the upheaving of the stern checked his progress sufficiently for him to swing into the lee of the group at the mainmast and to clutch one of the lines there and hang on. The men there, hanging apathetic in their lashings, spared him hardly a glance and made no move to help him. Barbara, her wet hair streaming out sideways, had a smile and a hand for him, and he forced his way into the group beside her and bound himself next to her. He took her hand in his again, and was reassured by the return of the pressure he gave it. Then there was nothing to do except to remain alive.

Part of the process of remaining alive was not to think about being thirsty, as the day wore on and the yellow daylight was replaced by black night. It was hard not to do so, once he had realised how thirsty he was, and now he had a new torment when he thought that Barbara was suffering in that way, too. There was nothing he could do about that at all, nothing, except to stand in his bonds and endure along with her. With the coming of night, however, the wind lost its brick-kiln heat and blew almost chilly, so that Hornblower found himself shivering a little. He turned in his bonds and put his arms round Barbara, holding her to him to conserve her bodily warmth. It was during the night that he was troubled by the behaviour of the man next to him, who persisted in leaning against him, more and more heavily, so that repeatedly Hornblower had to take his arms from around Barbara and thrust him fiercely away. At the third or fourth of those thrusts he felt the man fall limply away from him and guessed he was dead. That made a little more room about the mast, and he could put Barbara squarely against it, where she could lean back with her shoulders supported. Hornblower could guess that she would find that a help, judging by the agonising cramp in his legs, and the utter weariness of every part of his body. There was a temptation, a terrible temptation, to give up, to let everything go, to let himself fall to the deck and die like the man beside him. But he would not; that was for the sake of the wife in his arms more than for himself; because of his love rather than because of his pride.

With the change in the temperature of the wind came a gradual moderation in its violence; Hornblower, during those black hours, would not allow himself to hope at first, but he became more and more convinced of it as the night wore on. At last there was no denying the fact. The wind was dying away – the hurricane was moving away from them, most likely. Some time during the night it was only a strong gale, and later on Hornblower, lifting his head, made himself admit that it was nothing more than a fresh breeze which would call for only a single reef – a topgallant breeze, in fact. The motion of the *Pretty Jane* continued to be violent, as was only to be expected; the sea would take much longer to die away than would the wind. She was still pitching and plunging wildly, heaving up and racing down, but she was not being swept by the waves to nearly such a great extent, even allowing for her improved behaviour, bows to sea. It was not great cataracts of water that came surging by them, dragging them against their bonds to lacerate their skin. The water ceased to be waist high; later on it only surged past their knees and the spray had ceased to drive past them.

With that Hornblower was able to notice something else. It was raining, raining in torrents. If he turned his face to the sky a few precious drops fell into his parched, open mouth.

'Rain!' he said into Barbara's ear.

He released himself from her arms – he did it actually roughly, so anxious was he not to waste a single second of this rainstorm. He took off his shirt – it tore into rags as he dragged it from the lines that encompassed him – and held it out in the invisible rain that lashed down on them in the darkness. He must not waste a second. The shirt was wet with sea water; he wrung it out, working over it feverishly, alternately with spreading it in the rain. He squeezed a fragment into his mouth; it was still salt. He tried again. He had never wished for anything so much as now, for the rainstorm to continue in this violence and for the sea spray not to be driving too thickly. The water he wrung from the fragment of shirt could be considered fresh now. He felt for Barbara's face with the sopping wet object, pressing it against her.

'Drink!' he croaked into her ear.

When she put up her hands to it he guessed from her movements that she understood, that she was sucking the precious liquid from the fabric. He wanted her to hurry, to drink all she could, while the rain persisted; his hands were shaking with desire. In the darkness she would not know that he was waiting so anxiously. She yielded the shirt back to him at last, and he spread it to the rain again, hardly able to endure the delay. Then he could press it to his mouth, head back, and gulp and swallow, half mad with pleasure. The difference it made to squeeze that water into his mouth was beyond measure.

He felt strength and hope returning – the strength came with the hope. Perhaps that shirt held five or six wineglassfuls of water; it was sufficient to make this vast difference. He spread the shirt again above his head, to soak it again in the torrential rain, and gave it to Barbara, and when she returned it to him in the darkness he repeated the process for himself. And when he had squeezed it almost dry he realised that while he was doing so the rain had ceased, and he felt a moment's regret. He should have saved that wet shirt as a reserve, but he ceased to chide himself. Most of the water in it would have drained out, and there was still enough spray in the air to have made the remainder undrinkable in a few minutes.

But now he could think better; he could soberly decide that the wind was moderating fast – the rainstorm itself was an indication that the hurricane had gone on its way, leaving in its wake the prodigious rains that were not unusual then. And there, over the starboard bow, was the faintest hint of pink in the sky, not the threatening yellow of the hurricane, but the dawn of a different day. He felt for the knots that held him bound, and by slow degrees he fumbled them undone. As the last one released him he staggered back with the heave of the ship, and sank back with a thump and a splash into a sitting position on the wet deck. That was a fantastic pleasure, to sit down, hip deep in the water still washing over the deck. Just to sit, and very slowly flex and straighten his knees, to feel life returning into his dead thighs; that was heaven, and it would be a seventh heaven to put his head down and allow sleep to overcome him.

That was something he must not do, all the same. Sleeplessness and physical fatigue were things that must be stoically ignored, as long as there was a chance that they would survive, and daylight increasing round them. He heaved himself up to his feet and walked back to the mast on legs that would hardly obey him. He released Barbara, and she at least could sit down, deck awash or not. He eased her until her back was to the mast and then passed a line around her again. She could sleep in that fashion; she was already so weary that she did not notice – or she gave no sign of it if she did – the doubled-up corpse that lay within a yard of her. He cut the corpse loose and dragged it with the heave of the ship out of the way, before attending to the other three there. They were already fumbling with the knots of their lashings, and as Hornblower began to cut the lines first one and then another opened their mouths and croaked at him.

'Water!' they said. 'Water!'

They were as helpless and as dependent as nestlings. It was apparent to Hornblower that not one of them had had the sense, during that roaring rainstorm in the dark, to soak his shirt; they could hardly have failed to have held up open mouths to the rain, but what they would catch then would be a trifle. He looked round the horizon. One or two distant squalls were visible there, but there was no predicting when or if they would pass over the *Pretty Jane*.

'You'll have to wait for that, my lads,' he said.

He made his way aft to the other group around the wheel and binnacle. There was a corpse here still hanging in its lashings – Knyvett. Hornblower took note of the fact, with the terse requiem that perhaps with death overpowering him there might be some excuse for his not attempting to cut away the foremast. Another corpse lay on the deck, among the feet of the six survivors here. Nine men had survived of the crew of sixteen, and apparently four had disappeared entirely, washed overboard during the night, or perhaps during the night before. Hornblower recognised the second mate and the steward; the group, even the second mate, were croaking for water just like the others, and to them Hornblower made the same grim reply.

'Get those dead men overboard,' he added.

He took stock of the situation. Looking over the side he could see that *Pretty Jane* had about three feet of freeboard remaining, as close as he could judge while she was pitching extravagantly in the still-turbulent sea. He was conscious now, as he walked about right aft, of dull thumpings under his feet corresponding to the heave and the roll. That meant floating objects battering on the underside of the deck as they were flung up against it by the water inside surging about. The wind was steady from the north-east – the trade wind had reasserted itself after the temporary interruption of the hurricane; the sky was still gloomy and overcast, but Hornblower could feel in his bones that the barometer must be rising rapidly. Somewhere down to leeward, fifty miles away, a hundred miles, two hundred perhaps, was the chain of the Antilles – he could not guess how far, or in what direction, *Pretty Jane* had drifted during the storm. There was still a chance for them, or there would be if he could solve the water problem.

He turned to the tottering crew.

'Get the hatches up,' he ordered. 'You, Mr Mate, where are the water casks stowed?'

'Amidships,' said the mate, running a dry tongue over his dry lips at the thought of water. 'Aft of the main hatchway.'

'Let's see,' said Hornblower.

Water casks constructed to keep fresh water in would also perhaps keep sea water out. But no cask was ever quite tight; every cask leaked to some extent, and only a small amount of water percolating in would make the contents unfit to drink. And casks that had been churned about for two nights and a day by the surging sea water below decks would probably be stove in, every one of them.

'It's only a faint hope,' said Hornblower, anxious to minimise the almost certain disappointment ahead of them; he looked round again to see what chance there was of a rain-squall coming.

When they looked down the open hatchway they could appreciate the difficulties. The hatchway was jammed with a couple of bales of coir; as they watched them they could see them move uneasily with the motion of the ship. The water that had invaded the ship had floated up the cargo – *Pretty Jane* was actually supported by the upward pressure of the cargo on the underside of the deck. It was a miracle that she had not broken her back. And there was not a chance of going down there. It would be certain death to venture amid those surging bales. There was a general groan of disappointment from the group round the hatchway.

But another possibility was present in Hornblower's mind, and he turned upon the steward.

'There were green coconuts for the use of the cabin,' he said. 'Were there any left?'

'Yes, sir. Four or five dozen.' The man could hardly speak, with thirst, or weakness, or excitement.

'In the lazarette?'

'Yes, sir.'

'In a sack?'

'Yes, sir.'

'Come along,' said Hornblower.

Coconuts floated as lightly as coir, and were more watertight than any cask.

They pried up the after-hatch cover, and looked down at the heaving water below. There was no cargo there; the bulkhead had stood the strain. The distance down to the surface corresponded to the three-foot freeboard remaining to *Pretty Jane*. There were things to be seen there – almost at once a wooden piggin came floating into sight, and the surface was nearly covered with fragments. Then something else floated into view – a coconut. Apparently the sack had not been fastened – Hornblower had hoped he might find a whole sackful floating there. He leaned far down and scooped it up. As he rose to his feet again with the thing in his hand there was a simultaneous wordless croak from the whole group; a dozen hands stretched out for it, and Hornblower realised that he must maintain order.

'Stand back!' he said, and when the men still advanced on him he pulled out his sheath knife.

'Stand back! I'll kill the first man to lay a hand on me!' he said. He knew himself to be snarling like a wild beast, his teeth bared with the intensity of his feeling, and he knew that he would stand no chance in fight, one against nine.

'Come now, lads,' he said. 'We'll have to make these last. We'll ration 'em out. Fair divs all round. See how many more you can find.'

The force of his personality asserted itself; so did what remained of the common sense of the crew, and they drew back. Soon three men were kneeling round the hatchway, with the others leaning precariously over them to look over their shoulders.

'There's one!' croaked a voice.

An arm went down and a coconut was scooped up.

'Give it here,' said Hornblower, and he was obeyed without question; another was already visible, and another after that. They began to pile up at Hornblower's feet, a dozen, fifteen, twenty, twenty-three of the precious things, before they ceased to appear further.

'With luck we'll find some more later,' said Hornblower. He looked round the group, and over at Barbara huddled at the foot of the main-mast. 'Eleven of us. Half a one each for today. Another half each tomorrow. And I'll go without for today.'

No one questioned his decision – partly, perhaps, because they were all too anxious to wet their lips. The first coconut was chopped open at the end, with desperate care lest a drop be spilt, and the first man took a drink. There was no chance at all of his drinking more than his half, with everyone grouped round him, and the man destined for the other half snatching it from his lips at every sip to see how far down the surface had sunk. The men forced to wait were wild with eagerness, but they had to wait all the same. Hornblower could not trust them to make a division without fighting or waste unless he was supervising. After the last man had drunk he took the remaining half over to Barbara.

'Drink this, dear,' he said, as at the touch of his hand she blinked awake from her heavy doze.

She drank eagerly before she took the nut from her lips.

'You've had some, dear?' she asked.

'Yes, dear, I've had mine,' said Hornblower steadily.

When he returned to the group they were scraping the thin jelly out from inside the nuts.

'Don't damage these shells, lads,' he said. 'We'll need 'em when we get a rain-squall. And we'll put those nuts under Her Ladyship's guard. We can trust her.'

They obeyed him again.

'We got two more up while you was away, sir,' volunteered one of the men.

Hornblower peered down the hatchway at the litter-covered water. Another idea came up into his mind, and he turned to the steward again.

'Her ladyship sent a chest of food on board,' he said. 'Food in tin boxes. It was put aft here somewhere. Do you know where?'

'It was right aft, sir. Under the tiller ropes.'

'M'm,' said Hornblower.

As he thought about it a sudden motion of the ship tossed the water below up in a fountain through the hatchway. But it ought to be possible to reach that chest, break it open, and bring up its contents. A strong man, able to stay submerged for long periods, could do it, if he did not mind being flung about by the send of the water below.

'We'd have something better to eat than coconut jelly if we got those boxes up,' he said.

'I'll have a go, sir,' said a young seaman, and Hornblower was inexpressibly relieved. He did not want to go down there himself.

'Good lad,' he said. 'Put a line round yourself before you go down. Then we can haul you out if we have to.'

They were setting about their preparations when Hornblower checked them.

'Wait. Look for'rard!' he said.

There was a rain-squall a mile away. They could see it, a vast pillar of water to windward streaming down from the sky, well defined; the cloud was lower whence it fell, and the surface of the sea which received it was a different grey from the rest. It was moving down towards them – no, not quite. The centre was heading for a point some distance on their beam, as everyone could see after a moment's study. There was an explosion of blasphemy from the grouped hands as they watched.

'We'll get the tail of it, by God!' said the mate.

'Make the most of it when it comes,' said Hornblower.

For three long minutes they watched it approach. A cable's length away it seemed to stand still, even though they could feel the freshening breeze around them. Hornblower had run to Barbara's side.

'Rain,' he said.

Barbara turned her face to the mast, and bent down and fumbled under her skirt. A moment's struggle brought down a petticoat, and she stepped out of it and did her best to wring the salt damp out of it as they waited. Then came a few drops, and then the full deluge. Precious rain; ten shirts and a petticoat were extended to it, wrung out, re-extended, wrung out again, until the wringings tasted fresh. Everyone could drink, madly, with the rain roaring about them. After two minutes of it Hornblower was shouting to the crew to fill the empty coconut shells, and a few men had sense and public spirit enough to wring their shirts into them before returning to the ecstasy of drinking again – no one wanted to waste a single second of this precious rain. But it passed as quickly as it came; they could see the squall going away over the quarter, as far out of their reach as if it were raining in the Sahara Desert. But the young hands of the crew were laughing and joking now; there was an end to their care and their apathy. There was not one man on board except Hornblower who spared a thought for the possibility, the probability, that this might be the only rain-squall to touch the ship for the next week. There was urgent need for action, even though every joint and muscle in his body ached, even though his mind was clouded with weariness. He made himself think; he made himself rally his strength. He cut short the silly laughter, and turned on the man who had volunteered to venture down into the steerage.

'Put two men to tend your line. The steward had better be one of 'em,' he said. 'Mr Mate, come for'rard with me. We want to get sail on this ship as soon as may be.'

That was the beginning of a voyage which was destined to become legendary, just as did the hurricane which had just passed – it was called Hornblower's Hurricane, singled out not only because Hornblower was involved in it but also because its unexpected arrival caused widespread damage. Hornblower never thought that the voyage itself was particularly notable, even though it was made in a waterlogged hulk precariously balanced upon bales of coir. It was only a matter of getting the hulk before the wind; a spare jib-boom (the only spare spar surviving the storm) made a jury mast when fished to the stump of the foremast, and the sacking from coir bales provided sails. Spread on the jury foremast these enabled them to get the *Pretty Jane* before the trade wind, to creep along at a mile an hour while they set to work on extemporising after-sails that doubled her speed.

There were no navigating instruments – even the compass had been dashed from its gimbals during the storm – and on the first two days they had no idea where they were, except that somewhere to leeward lay the chain of the Antilles, but the third day proved fine and clear, and dawn had hardly broken before a hand at the mainmast-head saw the faintest, tiniest dark streak on the horizon far ahead. It was land; it might be the high mountains of San Domingo far off, or the low mountains of Puerto Rico somewhat nearer; there was no knowing at present, and even when the sun had set they were still ignorant – and they were thirsty, with small appetite for the meagre ration of corned beef that Hornblower doled out to them from the recovered stores.

And despite fatigue they could sleep that night on their coir mattresses on the deck that an occasional small wave still swept. Next morning the land was nearer still, a low profile that seemed to indicate it might be Puerto Rico, and it was in the afternoon that they saw the fishing boat. It headed for them, puzzled at the strange vessel bearing down on them, and it was not long before it was alongside, the mulatto fishermen staring at the group of strange figures waving to them. Hornblower had to urge his dazed mind, stupid with lack of sleep and fatigue and hunger, to remember his Spanish as he hailed them. They had a breaker of water on board, and they had a jar of cold garbanzos as well; there was a can of corned beef to add to the feast. Barbara caught, even though she spoke no Spanish, two words of the excited conversation that went on.

'Puerto Rico?' she asked.

'Yes, dear,' said Hornblower. 'Not very surprising – and much more convenient for us than San Domingo. I wish I could remember the name of the Captain-General there – I had dealings with him in the affair of the *Estrella del Sur*. He was a marquis. The Marques de – de – Dearest, why don't you lie down and close your eyes? You're worn out.'

He was shocked anew at her pallor and look of distress.

'I'm well enough, thank you, dear,' replied Barbara, even though the strained tone of her voice denied her words. It was one more proof of her indomitable spirit.

It was when they were discussing what to do next that the second mate showed the first sign of any spirit. They could all desert the water-logged hulk and sail into Puerto Rico in the fishing boat, but he stoutly refused to do so. He knew the law about salvage, and there might be some value still in the poor hull, and certainly in its cargo. He would work the *Pretty Jane* in tomorrow himself, and he insisted on staying on board with the hands.

Hornblower faced a decision of a sort he had never yet encountered in a varied career. To leave the ship now savoured of desertion, but there was Barbara to think of. And his first reaction, that he would not dream of deserting his men, was promptly ended by his reminding himself that they were not 'his men' at all.

'You're only a passenger, My Lord,' said the mate – it was odd how 'My Lord' seemed to come naturally again now that they were in touch with civilisation.

'That's so,' agreed Hornblower. Nor could he possibly condemn Barbara to another night on the deck of this waterlogged hulk.

So they came sailing into San Juan de Puerto Rico, two years after Hornblower had last visited the place in very different circumstances. Not unnaturally their arrival set the whole place in an uproar. Messengers sped to the Fortaleza, and it was only a few minutes later that a figure appeared on the quay which Hornblower's swimming eyes contrived to recognise, tall and thin, with a thin moustache.

'Mendez-Castillo,' he said, saving Hornblower any further trouble about remembering his name. 'It grieves me greatly to see Your Excellencies in such distress, even while I have much pleasure in welcoming Your Excellency again to Puerto Rico.'

Some sort of formalities had to be observed, even in these conditions.

'Barbara, my dear, allow me to present Señor – Major – Mendez-Castillo, aide-de-camp to His Excellency the Captain-General.' Then he continued in Spanish. 'My wife, la Baronesa Hornblower.'

Mendez-Castillo bowed deeply, his eyes still busy estimating the extent of the weakness of the new arrivals. Then he reached the very important decision.

'If Your Excellencies are agreeable, I would suggest that your formal welcome by His Excellency should be postponed until Your Excellencies are better prepared for it.'

'We are agreeable,' said Hornblower. In his exasperation he was about to burst out violently regarding Barbara's need for rest and care, but Mendez-Castillo, now that the point of etiquette was settled, was all consideration.

'Then if Your Excellencies will give yourselves the trouble of stepping down into my boat I shall have the pleasure of escorting you to make your informal entrance into the Palace of Santa Catalina. Their Excellencies will receive you, but formal etiquette need not be observed, and Your Excellencies will be able to recover from the dreadful experiences I fear Your Excellencies have undergone. Would Your Excellencies be so kind as to come this way?'

'One moment, first, if you please, señor. The men out there in the ship. They need food and water. They may need help.'

'I will give an order for the port authorities to send out to them what they need.'

'Thank you.'

So they went down into the boat for the brief trip across the harbour; despite his mortal fatigue Hornblower was able to note that every fishing boat and coasting craft there was hurriedly getting to sea, presumably to

Admiral Hornblower

examine the chances of salvaging or plundering the *Pretty Jane*; the second mate had been perfectly right in refusing to leave her. But he did not care, now. He put his arm about Barbara as she drooped beside him. Then up through the water-gate of the Palace, with attentive servants awaiting them. Here were His Excellency and a dark, beautiful woman, his wife: she took Barbara under her protection instantly. Here were cool, dark rooms, and more servants scurrying about in obedience to the orders His Excellency volleyed out. Valets and maids and body servants.

'This is Manuel, my principal valet, Your Excellency. Any orders Your Excellency may give him will be obeyed as if they came from me. My physician has been sent for and will be here at any moment. So now my wife and I will withdraw and leave Your Excellencies to rest, assuring Your Excellencies that our sincerest hope is for your rapid recovery.'

The crowd thinned away. For one more moment Hornblower had to keep his faculties alert, for the doctor came bustling in, to feel pulses and to look at tongues. He produced a case of lancets and was making preparations to draw blood from Barbara and it was only with difficulty that Hornblower stopped him, and with further difficulty prevented him from substituting leeches for venesection. He could not believe that bleeding would hasten the cure of the lacerations Barbara bore on her body. He thanked the doctor and saw him out of the room again with a sigh of relief and mental reservations regarding the medicines he promised to send in. The maids were waiting to relieve Barbara of the few rags she wore.

'Do you think you will sleep, darling? Is there anything more I can ask for?'

'I shall sleep, dearest.' Then the smile on Barbara's weary face was replaced by something more like a grin, perfectly unladylike. 'And as nobody else but us here can speak English I am free to tell you that I love you, dearest. I love you, I love you, more than any words that I know can tell you.'

Servants or no servants, he kissed her then before he left her to go into the adjoining room where the valets awaited him. His body was criss-crossed with angry welts still raw where, during the storm, the force of the waves had flung him against the ropes that held him to the mast. They were horribly painful as he was sponged with warm water. He knew that Barbara's sweet, tender body must be marked in the same fashion. But Barbara was safe; she would soon be well, and she had said that she loved him. – And – and she had said more than that. What she had told him in that deck-house had drawn out all the pain from a mental wound far, far, deeper than the physical hurts he now bore. He was a happy man as he lay down in the silk nightshirt with the elaborate heraldic embroidery which the valet had ready for him. His sleep was at first deep and untroubled, but conscience awoke him before dawn, and he went out on to the balcony in the first light, to see the *Pretty Jane* creeping into the harbour, escorted by a dozen small craft. It irked him that he was not on board, until he thought again of the wife sleeping in the next room.

There were happy hours still to come. That balcony was deep and shaded, looking out over harbour and sea, and there he sat in his dressing-gown an hour later, rocking idly in his chair, with Barbara opposite him, drinking sweet chocolate and eating sweet rolls.

'It is good to be alive,' said Hornblower; there was a potency, an inner meaning, about those words now – it was no hackneyed turn of speech.

'It is good to be with you,' said Barbara.

'*Pretty Jane* came in this morning safely,' said Hornblower.

'I peeped out at her through my window,' said Barbara.

Mendez-Castillo was announced, presumably having been warned that His Excellency's guests were awake and breakfasting. He made enquiries on behalf of His Excellency, to receive every assurance of a rapid recovery, and he announced that news of the recent events would be despatched at once to Jamaica.

'Most kind of His Excellency,' said Hornblower. 'Now, as regards the crew of the *Pretty Jane*. Are they being looked after?'

'They have been received into the military hospital. The port authorities have stationed a guard on board the vessel.'

'That is very well indeed,' said Hornblower, telling himself that now he need feel no more responsibility.

The morning could be an idle one now, only broken by a visit from the doctor, to be dismissed, after a new feeling of pulses and looking at tongues, with grateful thanks for his untasted medicines. There was dinner at two o'clock, a vast meal served ceremoniously but only sampled. A siesta, and then supper eaten with more appetite, and a peaceful night.

Next morning was busier, for there was now the question of clothes to be dealt with. Dressmakers were sent in to Barbara by Her Excellency, so that Hornblower found all the mental exercise he needed in acting as interpreter over matters demanding a vocabulary he did not possess, and shirt-makers and tailors sent in to him by His Excellency. The tailor was somewhat disappointed on being told that Hornblower did not wish him to make a complete uniform for a British Rear-Admiral, gold lace and all. As a half-pay officer, with no appointment, Hornblower did not need anything of the sort.

After the tailor came a deputation, the mate and two members of the crew of *Pretty Jane*.

'We've come to enquire after Your Lordship's health, and Her Ladyship's,' said the mate.

'Thank you. You can see Her Ladyship and I are quite recovered,' said Hornblower. 'And you? Are you being well looked after?'

'Very well, thank you.'

'You're master of the *Pretty Jane* now,' commented Hornblower.

'Yes, My Lord.'

It was a strange first command for a man to have.

'What are you going to do with her?'

'I'm having her hauled out today, My Lord. Maybe she can be patched up. But she'll have lost all her copper.'

'Very likely.'

'I expect I'll have to sell her for what she'll fetch, hull and cargo,' said the mate, with a note of bitterness in his voice – that was to be expected in a man who had received his first command only to face losing it instantly.

'I hope you're lucky,' said Hornblower.

'Thank you, My Lord.' There was a moment's hesitation before the next words came. 'And I have to thank Your Lordship for all you did.'

'The little I did I did for my own sake and Her Ladyship's,' said Hornblower.

He could smile as he said it; already, in these blissful surroundings, the memory of the howl of the hurricane and the crash of the waves sweeping *Pretty Jane*'s deck was losing its painful acuteness. And the two seamen could grin back at him. Here in a viceregal palace it was hard to remember how he had stood, with bared teeth and drawn knife, disputing with them possession of a single green coconut. It was pleasant that the interview could end with smiles and goodwill, so that Hornblower could lapse back into delightful idleness with Barbara beside him.

Seamstresses and tailors must have worked hard and long, for next day some of the results of their efforts were ready to be tried on.

'My Spanish grandee!' said Barbara, eyeing her husband dressed in coat and breeches of Puerto Rican cut.

'My lovely señora,' answered Hornblower with a bow. Barbara was wearing comb and mantilla.

'The señoras of Puerto Rico wear no stays, fortunately,' said Barbara. 'I could bear nothing of the sort at present.'

That was one of the few allusions Barbara made regarding the lacerations and bruises that she bore all over her body. She was of a Spartan breed, trained in a school which scorned to admit physical weakness. Even in making her mock-formal curtsey to him as she spoke she was careful to betray none of the pain the movement cost her; Hornblower could hardly guess at it.

'What am I to tell Mendez-Castillo today when he comes to make his enquiries?' asked Hornblower.

'I think, dear, that now we can safely be received by Their Excellencies,' said Barbara.

Here in little Puerto Rico was to be found all the magnificence and ceremonial of the court of Spain. The Captain-General was the representative of a king in whose veins ran the blood of Bourbons and Habsburgs, of Ferdinand and Isabella, and his person had to be surrounded by the same ritual and etiquette, lest the mystic sanctity of his master should be called into question. Even Hornblower did not come to realise, until he began to discuss the arrangements with Mendez-Castillo, the enormous condescension, the extreme strain put upon palace etiquette, involved in the back-stairs visit Their Excellencies had paid to the battered castaways who had claimed their hospitality. Now that was all to be forgotten in their formal reception.

There was amusement to be found in Mendez-Castillo's apologetic and nervous mentioning of the fact that Hornblower could not expect the same formalities as had welcomed him on his last visit. Then he had been a visiting Commander-in-Chief; now he was only a half-pay officer, a distinguished visitor (Mendez-Castillo hastened to add) but an unofficial one. It dawned upon him that Mendez-Castillo expected him to flare out and be offended at being told that this time he would be received only by flourishes and not by a full band, by the salutes of the sentries instead of by the turning out of the whole guard. He was able to confirm his reputation for tact by declaring quite truthfully – his candour was mistaken for the most diplomatic concealment of his own feelings – that he did not care in the least.

So it turned out. Barbara and Hornblower were smuggled unobtrusively out of the postern gate of the Palace and escorted into a boat, to be rowed round to the massive watergate where Hornblower had made his previous entrance. There with slow and solemn step they passed in through the gate, Barbara on Hornblower's left arm. On either hand the sentries presented arms and Hornblower acknowledged the salute by taking off his hat. As they came into the courtyard beyond they were welcomed by the flourishes that Mendez-Castillo had promised. Even Hornblower's tone-deaf ear could assure him that there was no stinting of those flourishes. Long drawn out, continued until Hornblower wondered how the trumpeter's breath could last so long; and he could guess from the variation between squeakiness and dullness that the trumpeter was displaying a considerable virtuosity. Two more sentries stood at the foot of the steps beyond, presenting arms; the trumpeter stood at the top of the steps over to one side, and he put his instrument to his lips for a further series of fanfares as Hornblower removed his hat again and he and Barbara began the climb. Tremendous, those flourishes were; even though Hornblower was bracing himself to make his ceremonial entrance into the great hall he could not help but dart a glance at the trumpeter. One glance called for a second glance. Pigtailed and powdered; dressed in a glittering uniform; what was there about that figure to demand his attention? He felt Barbara on his arm stiffen and miss her step. The trumpeter took his instrument from his lips. It was – it was Hudnutt. Hornblower almost dropped his hat with surprise.

But they were over the threshold of the great door, and he must walk steadily forward with Barbara if he were not to ruin all the precious ceremonial. A voice bellowed their names. Ahead of them at the end of an avenue of halberdiers were two chairs of state backed by a semicircle of uniforms and court gowns, with Their Excellencies sitting awaiting them. On Hornblower's last visit the Captain-General had risen and taken seven steps forward to meet him, but that had been when he was a Commander-in-Chief; now he and Barbara were only private persons and Their Excellencies remained sitting, as he and Barbara went through the moves they had been instructed to make. He bowed to His Excellency, having already been presented to him; he waited while Barbara was presented and made her two curtsies; he bowed again as he was presented to Her Excellency; then they drew a little to one side to await Their Excellencies' words.

'A great pleasure to welcome Lord Hornblower again,' said His Excellency.

'An equally great pleasure to make the acquaintance of Lady Hornblower,' said Her Excellency.

Hornblower went through the form of consulting with Barbara as to how he should reply.

'My wife and I are deeply appreciative of the great honour done us by our reception,' said Hornblower.

'You are our welcome guests,' said His Excellency, with a finality in his tone that indicated the end of the conversation. Hornblower bowed again, twice, and Barbara went down in two more curtsies, and then they withdrew diagonally so as to allow Their Excellencies no glimpse of their backs. Mendez-Castillo was on hand to present them to other guests, but Hornblower had first to pour out to Barbara his astonishment at the recent encounter.

'Did you see the trumpeter, dear?' he asked.

'Yes,' answered Barbara, in an expressionless tone. 'It was Hudnutt.'

'Amazing,' went on Hornblower. 'Extraordinary. I'd never have believed he was capable of it. He broke out of prison and he climbed that fence and he got himself out of Jamaica over to Puerto Rico – Quite remarkable.'

'Yes,' said Barbara.

Hornblower turned to Mendez-Castillo. 'Your – your trompetero,' he said; he was guessing at the Spanish word for 'trumpeter', and he put his hand up before his mouth in a gesture that indicated what he was trying to say.

'You thought he was good?' asked Mendez-Castillo.

'Superb,' said Hornblower. 'Who is he?'

'The best of the musicians in His Excellency's orchestra,' answered Mendez-Castillo.

Hornblower looked keenly at him, but Mendez-Castillo preserved a diplomatic lack of expression.

'A fellow countryman of yours, sir?' persisted Hornblower.

Mendez-Castillo spread his hands and elevated his shoulders.

'Why should I concern myself about him, My Lord?' he countered. 'In any case, art knows no frontiers.'

'No,' said Hornblower. 'I suppose not. Frontiers are elastic in these days. For instance, señor, I cannot remember if a convention exists between your government and mine regarding the mutual return of deserters.'

'A strange coincidence!' said Mendez-Castillo. 'I was investigating that very question a few days ago – quite idly, I assure you, My Lord. And I found that no such convention exists. There have been many occasions when, as a matter of goodwill, deserters have been handed back. But most lamentably, My Lord, His Excellency has altered his views in that respect since a certain ship – the *Estrella del Sur*, whose name you may possibly recall, My Lord – was seized as a slaver outside this very harbour in circumstances that His Excellency found peculiarly irritating.'

There was no hostility; nor was there any hint of glee in Mendez-Castillo's expression as he made this speech. He might as well have been discussing the weather.

'I appreciate His Excellency's kindness and hospitality even more now,' said Hornblower. He hoped he was giving no indication that he was a man who had just been hoist by his own petard.

'I will convey that information to His Excellency,' said Mendez-Castillo. 'Meanwhile there are many guests who are anxious to make Your Lordship's acquaintance and that of Her Ladyship.'

Later in the evening it was Mendez-Castillo who came to Hornblower with a message from Her Excellency, to the effect that the Marquesa quite understood that Barbara might be tired, not having fully recovered yet from her recent experiences, and suggesting that if Her Ladyship and His Lordship chose to retire informally Their Excellencies would understand; and it was Mendez-Castillo who guided them to the far end of the room and through an unobtrusive door to where a back stairs led to their suite. The maid allotted to attend to Barbara was waiting up.

'Ask the maid to go, please,' said Barbara. 'I can look after myself.'

Her tone was still flat and expressionless, and Hornblower looked at
her anxiously in fear lest her fatigue should be too much for her. But he
did what she asked.

'Can I help in any way, dear?' he asked as the maid withdrew.

'You can stay and talk to me, if you will,' answered Barbara.

'With pleasure, of course,' said Hornblower. There was something
strange about this situation. He tried to think of some topic to relieve the
tension. 'I still can hardly believe it about Hudnutt—'

'It is about Hudnutt that I wanted to speak,' said Barbara. There was
something positively harsh about her voice. She was standing more
stiffly and more rigidly than usual – no back could ever be straighter –
and she was meeting Hornblower's eyes with a kind of fixed stare like a
soldier at attention awaiting sentence of death.

'Whatever is the matter, dearest?'

'You are going to hate me,' said Barbara.

'Never! Never!'

'You don't know what it is I'm going to tell you.'

'Nothing you could tell me—'

'Don't say that yet! Wait until you hear. I set Hudnutt free. It was I
who arranged for his escape.'

The words came like sudden forked lightning. Or it was as if in a dead
calm the main-topsail yard had fallen without warning from its slings
on to the deck.

'Dearest,' said Hornblower, unbelievingly, 'you're tired. Why don't
you—'

'Do you think I'm delirious?' asked Barbara. Her voice was still
unlike anything Hornblower had ever heard; so was the brief, bitter
laugh that accompanied her words. 'I could be. This is the end of all
my happiness.'

'Dearest—' said Hornblower.

'Oh—' said Barbara. There was a sudden overwhelming tenderness
in that single sound, and her rigid attitude relaxed, but instantly she
stiffened again and snatched back the hands she had held out to him.
'Please listen. I've told you now. I set Hudnutt free – I set him free!'

There could be no doubting that she meant what she said, truth or
not. And Hornblower, standing unable to move, staring at her, gradually
reached the realisation that it was true after all. The realisation seeped
through the weak places in his unbelief, and as he thought of each piece
of evidence it was as if he were marking off a new height in a rising
tide.

'That last night at Admiralty House!' he said.

'Yes.'

'You took him out through the wicket gate into the gardens!'

'Yes.'

'Then Evans helped you. He had the key.'

'Yes.'

'And that fellow in Kingston – Bonner – must have helped you, too.'

'You said he was something of a villain. He was ready for adventure at least.'

'But – but the scent the bloodhounds followed?'

'Someone dragged Hudnutt's shirt along the ground on a rope.'

'But – but even so—?' She did not need to tell him; as he said those words he made the next deduction. 'That two hundred pounds!'

'The money I asked you for,' said Barbara, sparing herself nothing. A ten-pound reward would not avail if someone were willing to spend two hundred pounds to help a prisoner escape.

Hornblower knew all about it now. His wife had flouted the law. She had set at naught the authority of the Navy. She had – the rising tide reached suddenly up to a new level.

'It's a felony!' he said. 'You could be transported for life – you could be sent to Botany Bay!'

'Do I care?' exclaimed Barbara. 'Botany Bay! Does that matter now that you know? Now that you'll never love me?'

'Dearest!' Those last words were so fantastically untrue that he had nothing else to say in reply. His mind was hard at work thinking about the effect of all this on Barbara. 'That fellow Bonner – he could blackmail you.'

'He's as guilty as I am,' said Barbara. The unnatural harshness of her voice reached its climax there, and a sudden softness came back into her voice with her next words, an overwhelming tenderness, which she could not help as she smiled her old quizzical smile at this husband of hers. 'You're only thinking about me!'

'Of course,' said Hornblower, surprised.

'But you must think about yourself. I've deceived you. I've cheated you. I took advantage of your kindness, of your generosity – oh!'

The smile changed to tears. It was horrible to see Barbara's face distort itself. She was still standing like a soldier at attention. She would not allow her hands to cover her face; she stood with the tears streaming down and her features working, sparing herself nothing of her shame. He would have taken her into his arms at that moment except that he was still immobilised by astonishment, and Barbara's last words had set a fresh torrent of thought pouring through his mind to hold him paralysed. If any of this were to come out the consequences would be without limit. Half the world would believe that Hornblower, the legendary Hornblower, had connived at the escape and desertion of a petty criminal. Nobody would believe the truth – but if the truth did find credence half the world would laugh at Hornblower being outwitted by his wife. There was a horrible gaping chasm opening right beside him. But there was already this other chasm – this awful distress that Barbara was suffering.

'I was going to tell you,' said Barbara, still erect, blinded by her tears so that she could see nothing. 'When we reached home I was going to tell you. That's what I thought before the hurricane. And there in the deck-house I was going to tell you, after – after I told you the other. But there wasn't time – you had to leave me. I had to tell you I loved you, first. I told you that, and I.should have told you this instead. I should have.'

She was advancing no excuse for herself; she would not plead; she would face the consequences of her act. And there in the deck-house she had told him she loved him, that she had never loved any other man. The last realisation came upon him. Now he could shake off the astonishment, the bewilderment, that had held him helpless up to that moment. Nothing counted in the world except Barbara. Now he could move. Two steps forward and she was in his arms. Her tears wetted his lips.

'My love! My darling!' he said, for, unbelieving and blinded she had not responded.

And then she knew, in the darkness that surrounded her, and her arms went about him, and there was no such happiness in all the world. There had never been such perfection of harmony. Hornblower found himself smiling. He could laugh out loud out of sheer happiness. That was an old weakness of his, to laugh – to giggle – in moments of crisis. He could laugh now, if he allowed himself – he could laugh at the whole ridiculous incident; he could laugh and laugh. But his judgment told him that laughter might be misunderstood at this moment. He could not help smiling, though, smiling as he kissed.